American Jewish Fiction

A Century of Stories

EDITED BY GERALD SHAPIRO

University of Nebraska Press : Lincoln & London

The Norman and Bernice Harris Center
for Judaic Studies and the Research Council
of the University of Nebraska–Lincoln are
gratefully acknowledged for financial support in assistance of this volume.

Acknowledgments for the use of previously
published material appear on pages 443–45,
which constitute an extension of the copyright page.

LIBRARY OF CONGRESS CATALOGING
in Publication Data
American Jewish fiction: a century of stories /
edited by Gerald Shapiro.   p.   cm.
ISBN 0-8032-4264-6 (alkaline paper). – ISBN
0-8032-9252-X (pbk: alkaline paper)
1. American fiction – Jewish authors. 2. Jews,
American – Social life and customs – Fiction.
I. Shapiro, Gerald, 1950–.
PS647.J4A49   1998   813′.50808924–dc21
98-14410   CIP

Contents

Group Portrait vii

Abraham Cahan	*A Ghetto Wedding,* 1
Anzia Yezierska	*How I Found America,* 15
Isaac Bashevis Singer	*A Wedding in Brownsville,* 38
Tillie Olsen	*Tell Me a Riddle,* 51
Delmore Schwartz	*In Dreams Begin Responsibilities,* 86
Bernard Malamud	*The Lady of the Lake,* 94
Saul Bellow	*A Silver Dish,* 115
Grace Paley	*Goodbye and Good Luck,* 142
Norma Rosen	*What Must I Say to You?,* 152
Wallace Markfield	*The Decline of Sholem Waldman,* 163
Cynthia Ozick	*Envy; or, Yiddish in America,* 174
E. M. Broner	*Ghost Stories,* 223
Stanley Elkin	*Among the Witnesses,* 230
Bruce Jay Friedman	*When You're Excused, You're Excused,* 251
Philip Roth	*On the Air,* 262
Francine Prose	*Electricity,* 300
Steve Stern	*The Tale of a Kite,* 320
Melvin Jules Bukiet	*The Library of Moloch,* 335
Lev Raphael	*History (with Dreams),* 346
Michelle Herman	*Auslander,* 360
Robin Hemley	*The 19th Jew,* 388
Helen Schulman	*The Revisionist,* 410
Allegra Goodman	*Sarah,* 424

Acknowledgments, 443

Group Portrait

When the great Rabbi Israel Baal Shem-Tov saw misfortune threatening the Jews it was his custom to go into a certain part of the forest to meditate. There he would light a fire, say a special prayer, and the miracle would be accomplished and the misfortune averted.

Later, when his disciple, the celebrated Magid of Mezritch, had occasion, for the same reason, to intercede with heaven, he would go to the same place in the forest and say: "Master of the Universe, listen! I do not know how to light the fire, but I am still able to say the prayer." And again the miracle would be accomplished.

Still later, Rabbi Moshe-Leib of Sasov, in order to save his people once more, would go into the forest and say: "I do not know how to light the fire, I do not know the prayer, but I know the place and this must be sufficient." It was sufficient and the miracle was accomplished.

Then it fell to Rabbi Israel of Rizhyn to overcome misfortune. Sitting in his armchair, his head in his hands, he spoke to God: "I am unable to light the fire and I do not know the prayer; I cannot even find the place in the forest. All I can do is tell the story, and this must be sufficient." And it was sufficient.

God made man because he loves stories.

ELIE WIESEL, The Gates of the Forest

I rving Howe, in the 1977 essay that introduced his landmark anthology, *Jewish-American Fiction,* said that the party was over — that with the demise of the immigrant culture, the shared experience of tenement squalor, and the tumult of city streets that spawned the great flowering of Jewish-American literature in the first half of this century, Jewish-American fiction as a distinct "regional" literature was dead, or had, in any event, "moved past its high point." "Insofar as [American Jewish fiction] draws heavily from the immigrant experience, it must suffer a depletion of resources, a thinning-out of materials and memories," he wrote. "Other than in books and sentiment, there just isn't enough left of that experience."

So here I sit, twenty years later, writing another introductory es-say for a new anthology of stories by American Jewish writers — an anthology that covers a century of literature, including not just the period surveyed in Howe's wonderful book but also a couple of sto-ries that pre-date the bulk of his selections, plus a number of writers who have come to prominence in the past twenty years. Maybe Howe was right about the death of Jewish-American fiction, but the good news is that the current crop of writers — among them, Allegra Goodman, Steve Stern, Melvin Bukiet, and Michelle Herman — ap-parently missed the obituary notice. They are among the best of a host of young (or youngish) Jewish writers publishing fiction in con-temporary America. The fact is, as we reach the end of this century, new, relatively unknown, but very promising Jewish-American fic-tion writers seem to be everywhere; and though I'm tempted to is-sue a Howe-like proclamation of my own (*This is it — the last word — the final anthology! The store is closing! Everything's got to go! No more Jewish-American fiction!*), as far as I can see, there's no end in sight.

If you buy Howe's basic premise — that Jewish-American fiction arose from and was tied to a specific place, a particular time, a temporary state of affairs — then a casual glance at history books, even a nodding acquaintance with demographics, will tell you that by now the whole enterprise must be as stale as a sixty-year-old loaf of pumpernickel. You don't have to go back to New York's Lower East Side to realize that the immigrant Jewish culture of the urban American ghetto has largely vanished. Save the airfare and just take it from me: it's all gone. It doesn't matter that Russ & Daughters, purveyors of fine smoked fish, still survives on Houston Street be-tween Orchard and Allen, and the Second Avenue Kosher Delica-tessen is thriving a few blocks to the north. The world of Eastern European Jewish immigrants (depicted in remarkably unsentimen-tal detail in the stories of Abraham Cahan and Anzia Yezierska in-cluded in this volume) is dead — and a trip to the old neighborhood for a nice piece of sturgeon or a chopped liver sandwich drenched in *schmaltz* won't bring it back.

Gone, too, for that matter, is the reckless Depression-era Chi-cago immigrant bluster at the heart of Saul Bellow's "A Silver Dish." The rich, enchanted world of the Yiddish theater portrayed in Grace Paley's "Goodbye and Good Luck" is just a memory — as is Yiddish itself, for the most part. (Hershel Edelshtein, the grieving Yiddishist of Cynthia Ozick's "Envy; or, Yiddish in America," might gain some perverse pleasure from the knowledge that, thirty years after he appeared in that marvelous story, Yiddish is in fashion again; it's now being taught at a handful of colleges around the country, to a new generation of acculturated Jews who've never heard it spoken, except in the form of occasional curses. But still, this miniature academic revival of Yiddish only serves as a reminder that the vibrant world it once described is gone.) The Catskills resorts of Stanley Elkin's "Among the Witnesses" still advertise in the Sunday *New York Times* Travel section—but the clientele has changed dramatically. And although the attitudes and assumptions of Henry Freeman (né Levin) in Bernard Malamud's "The Lady of the Lake" might seem on the surface more modern—rootless, determinedly existential—beneath that contemporary veneer they, too, proceed from a world-view rooted in the culture of the "old neighborhood," a world-view that sprang from a uniquely bittersweet blend of deprivation, isolation, and exultation.

So how are we to explain Allegra Goodman and Robin Hemley, Lev Raphael, Melvin Bukiet and Steve Stern and Francine Prose, Michelle Herman and E. M. Broner, Helen Schulman and so many more, alive and well, scribbling away at their fiction, blissfully ignorant of the fact that Irving Howe pronounced their literature dead (or moribund) twenty years ago, when some of them were in middle school? If we buy Howe's argument, it's tempting to think of them as the literary equivalent of a flock of chickens with their heads cut off, running for their lives around the barnyard, pumping blood like crazy, making a mess, the only ones on the scene not to hear the news of their recent demise.

But of course I don't buy Howe's argument—and neither would he, I'd like to think, if he were alive and able to survey the current scene. Because it's become clear to me that the authors I've listed above (as well as the many others I haven't been able to include in this volume) are working at their craft—not only writing as Jews, but writing directly *about* their Jewishness—not *despite* the disappearance of what Howe identified as the world, the literary "region," of Jewish-American fiction, but *because* of this disappearance. Jews have always (since the destruction of the Second Temple in 70 A.D., at any rate) written as a way of reinventing themselves, reidentifying themselves, coming to grips all over again with the problem of being a Jew in *galut*—the Diaspora. Just as Abraham Cahan, Anzia Yezierska, and other Jewish-American writers in the early years of this century wrote to explore their sense of abandonment and alienation as newly arrived immigrants in a strange land, subsequent generations, first Delmore Schwartz, Tillie Olsen, Bernard Malamud, Grace Paley, and Saul Bellow, then their younger colleagues Philip Roth, Norma Rosen, Cynthia Ozick, Wallace Markfield, and Bruce Jay Friedman, wrote to redefine themselves as children of the inner city who were able to move beyond the neighborhoods of their youth. Now, contemporary Jewish-American writers continue the ongoing process—a very *Jewish* process, by the way—of using stories to explore the same age-old questions: What does it mean to be a Jew? What obligations come with membership in this small (and always, always shrinking) club—a club not of survivors, but of remnants?

My purpose in compiling this anthology was not to discount the brilliant work of Howe's *Jewish-American Stories* but rather to extend it—to display between two covers, in a cohesive context, a rich sampling from the ongoing conversation between generations of Jewish-American fiction writers over the past century. That's what literature is, after all, at its essence—an enduring conversation. In the case of Jewish-American writers, it seems to me that the conversation has been primarily concerned with two intertwined moral issues: the thorny question of Jewish identity and its attendant obligations, and the tug-of-war between skepticism and belief (made particularly poignant for Jews in the lingering aftermath of the Holocaust). These might be seen as the concerns of a culture at its leisure, with time on its hands to ponder imponderable questions—and yet I think the same questions, the same issues, can be found in stories like Sholom Aleichem's "On Account of a Hat" or Isaac Bashevis Singer's "Gimpel the Fool"—classic Yiddish stories that arose from and describe an earlier, much more desperate time in Jewish history. They are, in fact, issues that have been at the heart of Jewish stories since the very beginning—since Abraham's tortured journey up Mount Moriah to offer his son Isaac as a sacrifice to God.

In Francine Prose's "Electricity," a secularized Jewish daughter in contemporary New York frets over her father's "conversion" to a form of ecstatic Hasidism; and if we're listening carefully to Prose's story, we can hear ironic echoes of Sholom Aleichem's "Hodel" and "Chava," written in the waning years of the nineteenth century—as well as any number of other "Where Did We Go Wrong?" stories in which parents lament their children's turn from the old ways. Steve Stern's "The Tale of a Kite" takes another deliciously comic spin on this same merry-go-round, in a story set in Stern's

Yoknapatawpha, The Pinch—the Jewish ghetto in Memphis he has brought to life in many distinguished stories, novels, and novellas in recent years. "The Tale of a Kite," in its magical whimsy, openly and affectionately recalls the stories of Isaac Bashevis Singer and Bernard Malamud; indeed, it's hard to imagine Stern's work *without* Singer and Malamud (and also Cynthia Ozick and Grace Paley) as his literary ancestors. (I have an image of a parade of Jewish writers, noisy, ranting, swaggering, full of *chutzpah*; Steve Stern's a young boy in the bleachers, shielding his eyes from the bright sunshine, munching on popcorn, then suddenly two members of the parade motion to him—it's Singer and Malamud, they put down their clarinets and wave at him: *Come on down!* they're saying. *Don't just sit there watching! You can do it! Join the parade!*) Similarly, in Melvin Bukiet's "The Library of Moloch," Dr. Arthur Ricardo, head of the scholarly project of the story's title, is a direct literary descendent of Dr. Tree and his "Repressed Animation" study in Cynthia Ozick's "Rosa," and Leslie Shakespere of the Concordance Institute in Lore Segal's "The Reverse Bug"—all of them engaged in the dubious work of quantifying, cataloging, and dehumanizing the Holocaust. In Michelle Herman's "Auslander" the title character, a young woman with a gift for languages, ponders her obligations as a Jew and as a translator, taking over the role of Hannah in Ozick's "Envy; or, Yiddish in America" and investing it with new moral authority.

Over and over again in these stories, you'll see the same themes explored: the overwhelming weight of familial obligations and the contortions one generation must go through in order to live up to the expectations of another (in E. M. Broner's "Ghost Stories," Lev Raphael's "History [With Dreams]," Allegra Goodman's "Sarah," and Saul Bellow's "A Silver Dish"); and the inescapable obligation—both an affliction and a deliverance—of Jewish identity (in Bruce Jay Friedman's "When You're Excused, You're Excused," Bernard Malamud's "The Lady of the Lake," Anzia Yezierska's "How I Found America," and Norma Rosen's "What Must I Say to You?"). Many of the stories in this volume are comic in tone: Grace Paley's "Goodbye and Good Luck," for example—a monologue in the manner of Sholom Aleichem's stories; Stanley Elkin's "Among the Witnesses," Allegra Goodman's "Sarah," Bruce Jay Friedman's "When You're Excused, You're Excused," Robin Hemley's "The 19th Jew" (a satiric look at the entire subject of Jewish-American fiction, featuring Isaac Bashevis Singer himself in a walk-on part); and perhaps most notably Philip Roth's antic, outrageously funny

"On the Air," surely one of the most manic literary convulsions of the last thirty years—the fictional equivalent of a Lenny Bruce stand-up routine. Even the most serious stories in this anthology have moments of grim humor (I'm primarily thinking of Ozick's "Envy; or, Yiddish in America"). But despite the humor, the satire, the irony, even the occasional slapstick, the subject of the stories I've selected is always deeply serious.

There is a very wide range of religious belief—and range of responses to Jewish identity—in these stories: from Nathan and Goldy, the young couple in Abraham Cahan's "A Ghetto Wedding," for whom Orthodox Judaism is simply a given, a part of the basic fabric of the world, to Eva, Tillie Olsen's dying heroine in "Tell Me a Riddle," whose Jewish identity is subsumed—and to a large extent canceled out—by her identity as a Socialist; and from Anzia Yezierska's nameless narrator, a woman locked in the prison of her Jewishness and aching to break out into the freedom of America, to Robin Hemley's Edith Margareten, a renowned Jewish writer and intellectual, a "professional Jew" of sorts, enjoying the fruits of her ethnic identity yet obviously bereft of anything resembling true faith. Sholem Waldman, the desperate protagonist of Wallace Mark-field's "The Decline of Sholem Waldman," makes his living as a professional mourner, one of the last of a dying breed of cemetery-loiterers, curiously joyless yet still a Hasid down to his earlocks and fringed undergarments, adrift in a new world but very much a rem-nant of the old. On the other hand, Hershelder, the hapless pro-tagonist of Helen Schulman's "The Revisionist," is quintessentially American. Like Norma Rosen's narrator in "What Must I Say to You?" (a woman raised without Jewish tradition, now married to a Holocaust survivor whose faith has been strengthened, rather than diminished, by his ordeal), Hershelder considers himself blessed: "he was lucky; his ancestors were not." He is affluent, edu-cated, married to a *shiksa* (a non-Jew); in short, he's everything Sholem Waldman isn't—can't be, in fact. Yet Schulman's story isn't so far removed from Markfield's; their protagonists share a certain homeless quality: they're unanchored, *farblondjet*—lost and con-fused—each in his own way, admittedly, but still *farblondjet*. Like Dr. Margolin in Isaac Bashevis Singer's "A Wedding in Brownsville," Milton Lippman, the radio talent agent in Philip Roth's "On the Air," Woody Selbst in Saul Bellow's "A Silver Dish," or Richard Preminger in Stanley Elkin's "Among the Witnesses," Sholem Wald-man and Hershelder are on a meandering moral journey; and it's the meandering that matters—the journey *itself*, hapless and confusing (like the Children of Israel's loopy forty-year trek through the desert)—rather than the destination.

Sholom Aleichem wrote "On Account of a Hat," a masterpiece of absurdist humor and one of his best-known stories, over a century ago. Its central character is an absentminded *schlemiel* named Sholem Shachnah—or "Sholem Shachnah Rattlebrain," as he's called by his neighbors in Kasrilevke, his hometown in the Pale of Settlement. The story describes Shachnah's desperate efforts to get home from a miserable business trip in time for Passover. In a fit of unwarranted confidence, he cables his wife from Zolodievka, a distant train station: "Arriving home Passover without fail." As he waits for his train, exhausted and edgy, he falls asleep on a bench next to a non-Jew, an official of some kind, wearing a uniform and an official-looking cap with a red band. Awakened by the station porter just in time to catch his train, Sholem Shachnah realizes in a panic that his hat has fallen off, and in his haste he grabs the wrong hat—the official's hat—and claps it on his head. Suddenly, to his amazement, he's being ushered to a first-class car on the train instead of the crowded, fetid third-class compartment he's used to. Everyone on the platform makes way for him: "Right this way, Your Excellency," and so on. What's going on? Is he dreaming? Finally he catches a glimpse of himself in the mirror, and he's shocked. All he sees is the hat on his head—his own identity is obliterated. In a moment of transcendent rattle-brained lunacy, Sholem Shachnah realizes what has happened. "Twenty times I tell him to wake me and I even give him a tip, and what does he do, that dumb ox, may he catch cholera in his face, but wake the official instead! And me he leaves asleep on the bench!" So he hustles back to the train station bench to wake himself up—and thereby misses the train home to Kasrilevke for Passover.

A hundred years later, the absurd humor of Sholem Aleichem's story remains, but the bitter, painful reality behind the story's comedy has faded. It's difficult for us now to grasp the fact that in the Pale of Settlement, our great-grandparents really did ride in third-class and live their lives as noncitizens, unwelcome guests of the state, in constant dread, fearful of anyone, anyone at all, in a uniform. Outside the study-house, away from *shul*, a Jew's sense of identity was a tenuous, fragile thing, trembling on the verge of disintegration at any moment.

Not only is it hard to remember all of this, it's also very tempting to forget it—who, after all, would want to linger on such a thought? And for that matter, why should we? Jews have become the most successful immigrant group in the history of this country. In fact, Jews aren't even thought of as an "ethnic" group in our society anymore—they've moved so far into the power structure of contemporary mainstream America that in many ways they've become an indistinguishable part of it. But this is an accident of history and geography (remember Hershelder's understanding: "He was lucky; his ancestors were not"). It's also useful to note that the current climate of success and acceptance that Jews enjoy in America echoes earlier situations in Spain, in Poland, and, in the last years of the nineteenth century and the first three decades of the twentieth, in Germany itself. In other words, everything is temporary—which makes it all the more important to read contemporary American Jewish fiction in the context of generations that have come before it.

Hence the purpose of this anthology: to put together what is in effect a group portrait—a celebratory photo session, men and women squeezed shoulder to shoulder, some sitting, some standing, a few peeking into the frame from a dark corner. Had there been room, I would have included stories by still other writers, to form a portrait of an even larger group. But the stories I've chosen work well, I think, to represent the full scope of twentieth-century American Jewish fiction. Their value comes both from the questions they ask and from the variety of answers they offer.

What has it meant, and what does it mean now, to be identified (to ourselves and to others) as a Jew in America? What obligations (to our ourselves, to our parents and children, to our community) come with the territory? How is it possible, as we reach the end of this most terrible of centuries, to sustain our belief—and in any event, a belief in *what*? These questions are as relevant—indeed, as essential—to the youngest writers in this anthology as they were to earlier generations. *In every generation the story must be told,* the Passover Haggadah tells us, the point being that if we're to understand fully the story of the deliverance of the Children of Israel, we must believe that we were the ones who came out of slavery in Egypt— we ourselves, not some nameless, forgotten ancestors. American Jewish writers at the end of the twentieth century continue the process of exploring these old questions through the telling of stories, because these are still questions that seem to matter, and because stories, though they exist in the world of the imagination, somehow keep us rooted in the real world, connected to the past, that for-gotten forest so far away, which might otherwise be inaccessible to us now.

The move from Castle Garden and Ellis Island to Rivington Street and then to the suburbs, from steerage to the working class to the middle class and beyond, did not constitute an end to the journey of American Jews. We're still *en route* — like Sholem Shach-nah, rattlebrained and a little desperate, embarked on an endless and perilous journey home. That journey is the one true unchang-ing fact of our lives. The fiction of American Jews is, as it has always been, a series of stories told along the way to wherever it is we're headed — stories told around a fire. Their fundamental value lies in their power to remind us of who we were and where we've been, and in the process, to give us the courage and the purpose to keep pushing forward to whatever lies in wait for us ahead.

American Jewish Fiction

A Ghetto Wedding

ABRAHAM CAHAN

Abraham Cahan (1860–1951): *The son of a Hebrew school teacher and grandson of a Rabbi, Abraham Cahan broke with traditional Judaism as a young man in Eastern Europe and turned to socialism instead, a faith he carried with him for the rest of his life. As a result of the wave of repression that followed the assassination of Czar Alexander II in 1881, he fled to America, arriving in New York in 1882. Cahan quickly learned English and became a journalist, a labor organizer, an English teacher at the Young Men's Hebrew Association, and a fiction writer. For fifty years he was senior editor of the* Jewish Daily Forward, *a Yiddish newspaper published in New York. Among his duties as editor of the* Forward *was handling the advice column—A* Bintel Brief—*a predecessor of Dear Abby and Ann Landers. In this column Cahan dispensed common-sense advice as well as a steady stream of prolabor opinions, turning the column into an influential voice for labor reform and enlightened social policy. His books include the novels* Yekl: A Tale of the New York Ghetto *and* The White Terror and the Red: A novel of Revolutionary Russia, *and* The Imported Bridegroom and Other Stories. *His masterpiece, and one of the most important works of early Jewish-American fiction, is* The Rise of David Levinsky, *a novel tracing the progress of its title character from his lowly beginnings in an Eastern European* shtetl *to great economic success in America.*

Had you chanced to be in Grand Street on that starry February night, it would scarcely have occurred to you that the Ghetto was groaning under the culmination of a long season of enforced idleness and distress. The air was exhilaratingly crisp, and the glare of the cafés and millinery shops flooded it with contentment and kindly good will. The sidewalks were alive with shoppers and promenaders, and lined with peddlers.

Yet the dazzling, deafening chaos had many a tale of woe to tell. The greater part of the surging crowd was out on an errand of self-torture. Straying forlornly by inexorable window displays, men and women would pause here and there to indulge in a hypothetical selection, to feast a hungry eye upon the object of an imaginary purchase, only forthwith to pay for the momentary joy with all the pangs of awakening to an empty purse.

Many of the peddlers, too, bore piteous testimony to the calamity which was then preying upon the quarter. Some of them performed their task of yelling and gesticulating with the desperation of imminent ruin; others implored the passers-by for custom with the abject effect of begging alms; while in still others this feverish urgency was disguised by an air of martyrdom or of shamefaced unwontedness, as if peddling were beneath the dignity of their habitual occupations, and they had been driven to it by sheer famine — by the hopeless dearth of employment at their own trades.

One of these was a thick-set fellow of twenty-five or twenty-six, with honest, clever blue eyes. It might be due to the genial, inviting quality of his face that the Passover dishes whose praises he was sounding had greater attraction for some of the women with an "effectual demand" than those of his competitors. Still, his comparative success had not as yet reconciled him to his new calling. He was constantly gazing about for a possible passer-by of his acquaintance, and when one came in sight he would seek refuge from identification in closer communion with the crockery on his pushcart.

"Buy nice dishes for the holidays! Cheap and strong! Buy dishes for Passover!" When business was brisk, he sang with a bashful relish; when the interval between a customer and her successor was growing too long, his singsong would acquire a mournful ring that was suggestive of the psalm-chanting at an orthodox Jewish funeral.

He was a cap-blocker, and in the busy season his earnings ranged from ten to fifteen dollars a week. But he had not worked full time for over two years, and during the last three months he had not been able to procure a single day's employment.

Goldy, his sweetheart, too, who was employed in making knee breeches, had hardly work enough to pay her humble board and rent. Nathan, after much hesitation, was ultimately compelled to take to peddling; and the longed-for day of their wedding was put off from month to month.

They had become engaged nearly two years before; the wedding ceremony having been originally fixed for a date some three months later. Their joint savings then amounted to one hundred and twenty dollars — a sum quite adequate, in Nathan's judgment, for a modest, quiet celebration and the humble beginnings of a household establishment. Goldy, however, summarily and indignantly overruled him.

"One does not marry every day," she argued, "and when I have at last lived to stand under the bridal canopy with my predestined one, I will not do so like a beggar maid. Give me a respectable wedding, or none at all, Nathan, do you hear?"

It is to be noted that a "respectable wedding" was not merely a casual expression with Goldy. Like its antithesis, a "slipshod wedding," it played in her vocabulary the part of something like a well-established scientific term, with a meaning as clearly defined as that of "centrifugal force" or "geometrical progression." Now, a slipshod wedding was anything short of a gown of white satin and slippers to match; two carriages to bring the bride and the bridegroom to the ceremony, and one to take them to their bridal apartments; a wedding bard and a band of at least five musicians; a spacious ballroom crowded with dancers, and a feast of a hundred and fifty covers. As to furniture, she refused to consider any which did not include a pier-glass and a Brussels carpet.

Nathan contended that the items upon which she insisted would cost a sum far beyond their joint accumulations. This she met by the declaration that he had all along been bent upon making her the target of universal ridicule, and that she would rather descend into an untimely grave than be married in a slipshod manner. Here she burst out crying; and whether her tears referred to the untimely grave or to the slipshod wedding, they certainly seemed to strengthen the cogency of her argument; for Nathan at once proceeded to signify his surrender by a kiss, and when ignominiously repulsed he protested his determination to earn the necessary money to bring things to the standard which she held up so uncompromisingly.

Hard times set in. Nathan and Goldy pinched and scrimped; but all their heroic economies were powerless to keep their capital from dribbling down to less than one hundred dollars. The wedding was postponed again and again. Finally the curse of utter idleness fell upon Nathan's careworn head. Their savings dwindled apace. In dismay they beheld the foundation of their happiness melt gradually away. Both were tired of boarding. Both longed for the bliss and economy of married life.

They grew more impatient and restless every day, and Goldy made concession after concession. First the wedding supper was sacrificed; then the pier-mirror and the bard were stricken from the program; and these were eventually succeeded by the hired hall and the Brussels carpet.

After Nathan went into peddling, a few days before we first find him hawking chinaware on Grand Street, matters began to look brighter, and the spirits of our betrothed couple rose. Their capital, which had sunk to forty dollars, was increasing again, and Goldy advised waiting long enough for it to reach the sum necessary for a slipshod wedding and establishment.

It was nearly ten o'clock. Nathan was absently drawling his "Buy nice dishes for the holidays!" His mind was engrossed with the question of making peddling his permanent occupation.

Presently he was startled by a merry soprano mocking him: "Buy nice di-i-shes! Mind that you don't fall asleep murmuring like this. A big lot you can make!"

Nathan turned a smile of affectionate surprise upon a compact little figure, small to drollness, but sweet in the amusing grace of its diminutive outlines—an epitome of exquisite femininity. Her tiny face was as comically lovely as her form: her applelike cheeks were firm as marble, and her inadequate nose protruded between them like the result of a hasty tweak; a pair of large, round black eyes and a thick-lipped little mouth inundating it all with passion and rest-less, good-natured shrewdness.

"Goldy! What brings you here?" Nathan demanded, with a fond look which instantly gave way to an air of discomfort. "You know I hate you to see me peddling."

"Are you really angry? Bite the feather bed, then. Where is the disgrace? As if you were the only peddler in America! I wish you were. Wouldn't you make heaps of money then! But you had better hear what does bring me here. Nathan, darling-dearest little heart, dearest little crown that you are, guess what a plan I have hit upon!" she exploded all at once. "Well, if you hear me out, and you don't say that Goldy has the head of a cabinet minister, then—well, then you will be a big hog, and nothing else."

And without giving him time to put in as much as an interjection, she rattled on, puffing for breath and smacking her lips for ecstasy. Was it not stupid of them to be racking their brains about the wed-ding while there was such a plain way of having both a "respect-able" celebration and fine furniture—Brussels carpet, pier-glass, and all—with the money they now had on hand?

"Come, out with it, then," he said morosely.

But his disguised curiosity only whetted her appetite for torment-ing him, and she declared her determination not to disclose her great scheme before they had reached her lodgings.

"You have been yelling long enough today, anyhow," she said, with abrupt sympathy. "Do you suppose it does not go to my very heart to think of the way you stand out in the cold screaming your-self hoarse?"

Half an hour later, when they were alone in Mrs. Volpiansky's parlor, which was also Goldy's bedroom, she set about emptying his pockets of the gross results of the day's business, and counting the money. This she did with a preoccupied, matter-of-fact air, Nathan submitting to the operation with fond and amused willingness; and the sum being satisfactory, she went on to unfold her plan.

"You see," she began, almost in a whisper, and with the mien of a care-worn, experience-laden old matron, "in a week or two we shall have about seventy-five dollars, shan't we? Well, what is seventy-five dollars ? Nothing! We could just have the plainest furniture, and no wedding worth speaking of. Now, if we have no wedding, we shall get no presents, shall we?"

Nathan shook his head thoughtfully.

"Well, why shouldn't we be up to snuff and do this way? Let us spend all our money on a grand, respectable wedding, and send out a big lot of invitations, and then — well, won't uncle Leiser send us a carpet or a parlor set? And aunt Beile, and cousin Shapiro, and Charley, and Meyerke, and Wolfke, and Bennie, and Sore-Gitke — won't each present something or other, as is the custom among re-spectable people? May God give us a lump of good luck as big as the wedding present each of them is sure to send us! Why, did not Beilke get a fine carpet from uncle when she got married? And am I not a nearer relative than she?"

She paused to search his face for a sign of approval, and, fondly smoothing a tuft of his dark hair into place, she went on to enumer-ate the friends to be invited and the gifts to be expected from them.

"So you see," she pursued, "we will have both a respectable wed-ding that we shan't have to be ashamed of in after years and the nicest things we could get if we spent two hundred dollars. What do you say?"

"What *shall I* say?" he returned dubiously.

The project appeared reasonable enough, but the investment struck him as rather hazardous. He pleaded for caution, for delay;

but as he had no tangible argument to produce, while she stood her ground with the firmness of conviction, her victory was an easy one.

"It will all come right, depend upon it," she said coaxingly. "You just leave everything to me. Don't be uneasy, Nathan," she added. "You and I are orphans, and you know the Uppermost does not forsake a bride and bridegroom who have nobody to take care of them. If my father were alive, it would be different," she concluded, with a disconsolate gesture.

There was a pathetic pause. Tears glistened in Goldy's eyes.

"May your father rest in a bright paradise," Nathan said feelingly. "But what is the use of crying? Can you bring him back to life? I will be a father to you."

"If God be pleased," she assented. "Would that mamma, at least — may she be healthy a hundred and twenty years — would that she, at least, were here to attend our wedding! Poor mother! it will break her heart to think that she has not been foreordained by the Uppermost to lead me under the canopy."

There was another desolate pause, but it was presently broken by Goldy, who exclaimed with unexpected buoyancy, "By the way, Nathan, guess what I did! I am afraid you will call me braggart and make fun of me, but I don't care," she pursued, with a playful pout, as she produced a strip of carpet from her pocketbook. "I went into a furniture store, and they gave me a sample three times as big as this. I explained in my letter to mother that this is the kind of stuff that will cover my floor when I am married. Then I enclosed the sample in the letter, and sent it all to Russia."

Nathan clapped his hands and burst out laughing. "But how do you know that is just the kind of carpet you will get for your wedding present?" he demanded, amazed as much as amused.

"How do I know? As if it mattered what sort of carpet! I can just see mamma going the rounds of the neighbors, and showing off the 'costly tablecloth' her daughter will trample upon. Won't she be happy!"

Over a hundred invitations, printed in as luxurious a black and gold as ever came out of an Essex Street hand press, were sent out for an early date in April. Goldy and Nathan paid a month's rent in advance for three rooms on the second floor of a Cherry Street tenement house. Goldy regarded the rent as unusually low, and the apartments as the finest on the East Side.

"Oh, haven't I got lovely rooms!" she would ejaculate, beaming with the consciousness of the pronoun. Or, "You ought to see my rooms! How much do you pay for yours?" Or again, "I have made up my mind to have my parlor in the rear room. It is as light as the front one, anyhow, and I want that for a kitchen, you know. What do you say?" For hours together she would go on talking nothing but rooms, rent, and furniture; every married couple who had recently moved into new quarters, or were about to do so, seemed bound to her by the ties of a common cause; in her imagination, humanity was divided into those who were interested in the question of rooms, rent and furniture and those who were not — the former, of whom she was one, constituting the superior category; and whenever her eye fell upon a bill announcing rooms to let, she would experience something akin to the feeling with which an artist, in passing, views some accessory of his art.

It is customary to send the bulkier wedding presents to a young couple's apartments a few days before they become man and wife, the closer relatives and friends of the betrothed usually settling among themselves what piece of furniture each is to contribute. Accordingly, Goldy gave up her work a week in advance of the day set for the great event, in order that she might be on hand to receive the things when they arrived.

She went to the empty little rooms, with her lunch, early in the morning, and kept anxious watch till after nightfall, when Nathan came to take her home.

A day passed, another, and a third, but no expressman called out her name. She sat waiting and listening for the rough voice, but in vain.

"Oh, it is too early, anyhow. I am a fool to be expecting anything so soon at all," she tried to console herself. And she waited another hour, and still another; but no wedding gift made its appearance.

"Well, there is plenty of time, after all; wedding presents do come a day or two before the ceremony," she argued; and again she waited, and again strained her ears, and again her heart rose in her throat.

The vacuity of the rooms, freshly cleaned, scrubbed, and smelling of whitewash, began to frighten her. Her overwrought mind was filled with sounds which her over-strained ears did not hear. Yet there she sat on the window sill, listening and listening for an expressman's voice.

"Hush, hush-sh, hush-sh-sh!" whispered the walls; the corners muttered awful threats; her heart was ever and anon contracted with fear; she often thought herself on the brink of insanity; yet she stayed on, waiting, waiting, waiting.

At the slightest noise in the hall she would spring to her feet, her heart beating wildly, only presently to sink in her bosom at finding it to be some neighbor or a peddler; and so frequent were these violent throbbings that Goldy grew to imagine herself a prey to heart disease. Nevertheless the fifth day came, and she was again at her post, waiting, waiting, waiting for her wedding gifts. And what is more, when Nathan came from business, and his countenance fell as he surveyed the undisturbed emptiness of the rooms, she set a merry face against his rueful inquiries, and took to bantering him as a woman quick to lose heart, and to painting their prospects in roseate hues, until she argued herself, if not him, into a more cheerful view of the situation.

On the sixth day an expressman did pull up in front of the Cherry Street tenement house, but he had only a cheap huge rocking chair for Goldy and Nathan; and as it proved to be the gift of a family who had been set down for nothing less than a carpet or a parlor set, the joy and hope which its advent had called forth turned to dire disappointment and despair. For nearly an hour Goldy sat mournfully rocking and striving to picture how delightful it would have been if all her anticipations had come true.

Presently there arrived a flimsy plush-covered little corner table. It could not have cost more than a dollar. Yet it was the gift of a near friend, who had been relied upon for a pier-glass or a bedroom set. A little later a cheap alarm clock and an icebox were brought in. That was all.

Occasionally Goldy went to the door to take in the entire effect; but the more she tried to view the parlor as half finished, the more cruelly did the few lonely and mismated things emphasize the remaining emptiness of the apartments: whereupon she would sink into her rocker and sit motionless, with a drooping head, and then desperately fall to swaying to and fro, as though bent upon swinging herself out of her woebegone, wretched self.

Still, when Nathan came, there was a triumphant twinkle in her eye, as she said, pointing to the gifts, "Well, mister, who was right? It is not very bad for a start, is it? You know most people do send their wedding presents after the ceremony—why, of course!" she added, in a sort of confidential way. "Well, we have invited a big crowd, and all people of no mean sort, thank God; and who ever heard of a lady or a gentleman attending a respectable wedding and having a grand wedding supper, and then cheating the bride and the bridegroom out of their present?"

The evening was well advanced; yet there were only a score of people in a hall that was used to hundreds.

Everybody felt ill at ease, and ever and anon looked about for the possible arrival of more guests. At ten o'clock the dancing preliminary to the ceremony had not yet ceased, although the few waltzers looked as if they were scared by the ringing echoes of their own footsteps amid the austere solemnity of the surrounding void and the depressing sheen of the dim expanse of floor.

The two fiddles, the cornet, and the clarinet were shrieking as though for pain, and the malicious superabundance of gaslight was fiendishly sneering at their tortures. Weddings and entertainments being scarce in the Ghetto, its musicians caught the contagion of misery: hence the greedy, desperate gusto with which the band plied their instruments.

At last it became evident that the assemblage was not destined to be larger than it was, and that it was no use delaying the ceremony. It was, in fact, an open secret among those present that by far the greater number of the invited friends were kept away by lack of employment: some having their presentable clothes in the pawn shop; others avoiding the expense of a wedding present, or simply being too cruelly borne down by their cares to have a mind for the excitement of a wedding; indeed, some even thought it wrong of Nathan to have the celebration during such a period of hard times, when everybody was out of work.

It was a little after ten when the bard — a tall, gaunt man, with a grizzly beard and a melancholy face — donned his skullcap, and, advancing toward the dancers, called out in a synagogue intonation, "Come, ladies, let us veil the bride!"

An odd dozen of daughters of Israel followed him and the musicians into a little side room where Goldy was seated between her two brideswomen (the wives of two men who were to attend upon the groom). According to the orthodox custom she had fasted the whole day, and as a result of this and of her gnawing grief, added to the awe-inspiring scene she had been awaiting, she was pale as death; the effect being heightened by the wreath and white gown she wore. As the procession came filing in, she sat blinking her round dark eyes in dismay, as if the bard were an executioner come to lead her to the scaffold.

The song or address to the bride usually partakes of the qualities of prayer and harangue, and includes a melancholy meditation upon life and death; lamenting the deceased members of the young woman's family, bemoaning her own woes, and exhorting her to discharge her sacred duties as a wife, mother, and servant of God. Composed in verse and declaimed in a solemn, plaintive recitative, often broken by the band's mournful refrain, it is sure to fulfill its mission of eliciting tears even when hearts are brimful of glee. Imagine, then, the funereal effect which it produced at Goldy's wedding ceremony.

The bard, half starved himself, sang the anguish of his own heart; the violins wept, the clarinet moaned, the cornet and the doublebass groaned, each reciting the sad tale of its povertystricken master. He began:

> Silence, good women, give heed to my verses!
> Tonight, bride, thou dost stand before the Uppermost.
> Pray to him to bless thy union,
> To let thee and thy mate live a hundred and twenty peaceful
> years,
> To give you your daily bread,
> To keep hunger from your door.

Several women, including Goldy, burst into tears, the others sadly lowering their gaze. The band sounded a wailing chord, and the whole audience broke into loud, heartrending weeping.

The bard went on sternly:

> Wail bride, wail!
> This is a time of tears.
> Think of thy past days:
> Alas! they are gone to return nevermore.

Heedless of the convulsive sobbing with which the room resounded, he continued to declaim, and at last, his eye flashing fire and his voice tremulous with emotion, he sang out in a dismal, uncanny high key:

> And thy good mother beyond the seas,
> And thy father in his grave
> Near where thy cradle was rocked,
> Weep, bride, weep!
> Though his soul is better off
> Than we are here underneath
> In dearth and cares and ceaseless pangs,
> Weep, sweet bride, weep!

Then, in the general outburst that followed the extemporaneous verse, there was a cry — "The bride is fainting! Water! quick!"

"Murderer that you are!" flamed out an elderly matron, with an air of admiration for the bard's talent as much as of wrath for the far-fetched results it achieved.

Goldy was brought to, and the rest of the ceremony passed without accident. She submitted to everything as in a dream. When the bridegroom, escorted by two attendants, each carrying a candelabrum holding lighted candles, came to place the veil over her face, she stared about as though she failed to realize the situation or to recognize Nathan. When, keeping time to the plaintive strains of a time-honored tune, she was led, blindfolded, into the large hall and stationed beside the bridegroom under the red canopy, and then marched around him seven times, she obeyed instructions and moved about with the passivity of a hypnotic. After the Seven Blessings had been recited, when the cantor, gently lifting the end of her veil, presented the wineglass to her lips, she tasted its contents with the air of an invalid taking medicine. Then she felt the ring slip down her finger, and heard Nathan say, "Be thou dedicated to me by this ring, according to the laws of Moses and Israel."

Whereupon she said to herself, "Now I am a married woman!" But somehow, at this moment the words were meaningless sounds to her. She knew she was married, but could not realize what it implied. As Nathan crushed the wineglass underfoot, and the band struck up a cheerful melody, and the gathering shouted, "Good luck! Good luck!" and clapped their hands, while the older women broke into a wild hop, Goldy felt the relief of having gone through a great ordeal. But still she was not distinctly aware of any change in her position.

Not until fifteen minutes later, when she found herself in the basement, at the head of one of three long tables, did the realization of her new self strike her consciousness full in the face, as it were.

The dining room was nearly as large as the dancing hall on the floor above. It was as brightly illuminated, and the three tables, which ran almost its entire length, were set for a hundred and fifty guests. Yet there were barely twenty to occupy them. The effect was still more depressing than in the dancing room. The vacant benches and the untouched covers still more agonizingly exaggerated the emptiness of the room, in which the sorry handful of a company lost themselves.

Goldy looked at the rows of plates, spoons, forks, knives, and they weighed her down with the cold dazzle of their solemn, pompous array.

"I am not the Goldy I used to be," she said to herself. "I am a married woman, like mamma, or auntie, or Mrs. Volpiansky. And we have spent every cent we had on this grand wedding, and now we are left without money for furniture, and there are no guests to send us any, and the supper will be thrown out, and everything is lost, and I am to blame for it all!"

The glittering plates seemed to hold whispered converse and to exchange winks and grins at her expense. She transferred her glance to the company, and it appeared as if they were vainly forcing themselves to partake of the food — as though they, too, were looked out of countenance by that ruthless sparkle of the unused plates.

Nervous silence hung over the room, and the reluctant jingle of the score of knives and forks made it more awkward, more enervating, every second. Even the bard had not the heart to break the stillness by the merry rhymes he had composed for the occasion.

Goldy was overpowered. She thought she was on the verge of another fainting spell, and, shutting her eyes and setting her teeth, she tried to imagine herself dead. Nathan, who was by her side, noticed it. He took her hand under the table, and, pressing it gently, whispered, "Don't take it to heart. There is a God in heaven."

She could not make out his words, but she felt their meaning. As she was about to utter some phrase of endearment, her heart swelled in her throat, and a piteous, dovelike, tearful look was all the response she could make.

By-and-by, however, when the foaming lager was served, tongues were loosened, and the bard, although distressed by the meager collection in store for him, but stirred by an ardent desire to relieve the insupportable wretchedness of the evening, outdid himself in offhand acrostics and witticisms. Needless to say that his efforts were thankfully rewarded with unstinted laughter; and as the room rang with merriment, the gleaming rows of undisturbed plates also seemed to join in the general hubbub of mirth, and to be laughing a hearty, kindly laugh.

Presently, amid a fresh outbreak of deafening hilarity, Goldy bent close to Nathan's ear and exclaimed with sobbing vehemence, "My husband! My husband! My husband!"

"My wife!" he returned in her ear.

"Do you know what you are to me now?" she resumed. "A husband! And I am your wife! Do you know what it means — *do* you, *do* you, Nathan?" she insisted, with frantic emphasis.

"I do, my little sparrow; only don't worry over the wedding presents."

It was after midnight, and even the Ghetto was immersed in repose. Goldy and Nathan were silently wending their way to the three empty little rooms where they were destined to have their first joint home. They wore the wedding attire which they had rented for the evening: he a swallowtail coat and high hat, and she a white satin gown and slippers, her head uncovered — the wreath and veil done up in a newspaper, in Nathan's hand.

They had gone to the wedding in carriages, which had attracted large crowds both at the point of departure, and in front of the hall; and of course they had expected to make their way to their new home in a similar "respectable" manner. Toward the close of the last dance, after supper, they found, however, that some small change was all they possessed in the world.

The last strains of music were dying away. The guests, in their hats and bonnets, were taking leave. Everybody seemed in a hurry to get away to his own world, and to abandon the young couple to their fate.

Nathan would have borrowed a dollar or two of some friend. "Let us go home as behooves a bride and bridegroom," he said. "There is a God in heaven: he will not forsake us."

But Goldy would not hear of betraying the full measure of their poverty to their friends. "No! no!" she retorted testily. "I am not going to let you pay a dollar and a half for a few blocks' drive, like a Fifth Avenue nobleman. We can walk," she pursued, with the grim determination of one bent upon self-chastisement. "A poor woman who dares spend every cent on a wedding must be ready to walk after the wedding."

When they found themselves alone in the deserted street, they were so overcome by a sense of loneliness, of a kind of portentous, haunting emptiness, that they could not speak. So on they trudged in dismal silence; she leaning upon his arm, and he tenderly pressing her to his side.

Their way lay through the gloomiest and roughest part of the Seventh Ward. The neighborhood frightened her, and she clung closer to her escort. At one corner they passed some men in front of a liquor saloon.

"Look at dem! Look at dem! A sheeny feller an' his bride, I'll betch ye!" shouted a husky voice. "Jes' comin' from de weddin'.."

"She ain't no bigger 'n a peanut, is she?" The simile was greeted with a horse-laugh.

"Look a here, young feller, what's de madder wid carryin' dat lady of yourn in your vest pocket?"

When Nathan and Goldy were a block away, something like a potato or a carrot struck her in the back. At the same time the gang of loafers on the corner broke into boisterous merriment. Nathan tried to face about, but she restrained him.

"Don't! They might kill you!" she whispered, and relapsed into silence.

He made another attempt to disengage himself, as if for a desperate attack upon her assailants, but she nestled close to his side and held him fast, her every fiber tingling with the consciousness of the shelter she had in him.

"Don't mind them, Nathan," she said.

And as they proceeded on their dreary way through a somber, impoverished street, with here and there a rustling tree — a melancholy witness of its better days — they felt a stream of happiness uniting them, as it coursed through the veins of both, and they were filled with a blissful sense of oneness the like of which they had never tasted before. So happy were they that the gang behind them, and the bare rooms toward which they were directing their steps, and the miserable failure of the wedding, all suddenly appeared too insignificant to engage their attention — paltry matters alien to their new life, remote from the enchanted world in which they now dwelt.

The very notion of a relentless void abruptly turned to a beatific sense of their own seclusion, of there being only themselves in the universe, to live and to delight in each other.

"Don't mind them, Nathan darling," she repeated mechanically, conscious of nothing but the tremor of happiness in her voice.

"I should give it to them!" he responded, gathering her still closer to him. "I should show them how to touch my Goldy, my pearl, my birdie!"

They dived into the denser gloom of a sidestreet.

A gentle breeze ran past and ahead of them, proclaiming the bride and the bridegroom. An old tree whispered overhead its tender felicitations.

How I Found America

ANZIA YEZIERSKA

Anzia Yezierska (1885?–1970): *Like her contemporary Abraham Cahan, Anzia Yezierska wrote about the struggles and moral conflicts of her protagonists as they strove to become Americanized and "liberated." She portrayed the way in which the customs of the Old World — respect for tradition, adherence to the restrictions and rituals of Orthodoxy — can be undermined and overturned by the experience of living in America. Yezierska's special contribution to Jewish-American fiction is that she wrote about the immigrant experience from the standpoint of a woman. Born in Plinsk, a village on the Russian-Polish border, Yezierska came to the United States with her family at the age of fifteen. She worked in sweatshops on the Lower East Side while attending night school to learn English. Soon she began to write — in English — and found early success in publishing her stories in women's magazines. In the 1920s Yezierska's fiction was immensely popular, and she became a celebrity. Samuel Goldwyn bought the movie rights to her first collection of stories,* Hungry Hearts, *and she was quickly labeled "Queen of the Ghetto" and "The Immigrant Cinderella" by the media. But she was unhappy in the artificial world of Hollywood and soon returned to New York.*

Yezierska's other books include Salome of the Tenements, Arrogant Beggar, Bread Givers, All I Could Never Be, *and* Red Ribbon on a White Horse, *all novels, and* Children of Loneliness, *a collection of stories. Although her celebrity faded in the 1930s and she never regained the wide audience she'd enjoyed at the beginning of her career, she continued to write, and after her death new editions of her work began to appear in print. Much of her writing is once again available, and her position as a seminal figure in the story of twentieth-century Jewish-American fiction is now once again very secure.*

PART 1

Every breath I drew was a breath of fear, every shadow a stifling shock, every footfall struck on my heart like the heavy boot of the Cossack.

On a low stool in the middle of the only room in our mud hut sat my father — his red beard falling over the Book of Isaiah open before him. On the tile stove, on the benches that were our beds, even on the earthen floor, sat the neighbors' children, learning from him the ancient poetry of the Hebrew race.

As he chanted, the children repeated:

"The voice of him that crieth in the wilderness,
Prepare ye the way of the Lord.
Make straight in the desert a highway for our God

"Every valley shall be exalted,
And every mountain and hill shall be made low,
And the crooked shall be made straight,
And the rough places plain.

"And the glory of the Lord shall be revealed,
And all flesh shall see it together."

Undisturbed by the swaying and chanting of teacher and pupils, old Kakah, our speckled hen, with her brood of chicks, strutted and pecked at the potato-peelings which fell from my mother's lap, as she prepared our noon meal.

I stood at the window watching the road, lest the Cossack come upon us unawares to enforce the ukaz of the Czar, which would tear the bread from our mouths: "No Chadir [Hebrew school] shall be held in a room used for cooking and sleeping."

With one eye I watched ravenously my mother cutting chunks of black bread. At last the potatoes were ready. She poured them out of the iron pot into a wooden bowl and placed them in the center of the table.

Instantly the swaying and chanting ceased, the children rushed forward. The fear of the Cossacks was swept away from my heart by the fear that the children would get my potato.

The sentry deserted his post. With a shout of joy I seized my portion and bit a huge mouthful of mealy delight.

At that moment the door was driven open by the blow of an iron heel. The Cossack's whip swished through the air. Screaming, we scattered.

The children ran out — our livelihood gone with them.

"Oi weh," wailed my mother, clutching her breast, "is there a God over us — and sees all this?"

With grief-glazed eyes my father muttered a broken prayer as the Cossack thundered the ukaz: "A thousand rubles fine or a year in prison if you are ever found again teaching children where you're eating and sleeping."

"Gottuniu!" pleaded my mother, "would you tear the last skin from our bones? Where else can we be eating and sleeping? Or should we keep chadir in the middle of the road? Have we houses with separate rooms like the Czar?"

Ignoring my mother's entreaties the Cossack strode out of the hut. My father sank into a chair, his head bowed in the silent grief of the helpless.

"God from the world" — my mother wrung her hands — "is there no end to our troubles? When will the earth cover me and my woes?"

I watched the Cossack disappear down the road. All at once I saw the whole village running toward us. I dragged my mother to the window to see the approaching crowd.

"Gewalt! What more is falling over our heads?" she cried in alarm.

Masheh Mindel, the water-carrier's wife, headed a wild procession. The baker, the butcher, the shoemaker, the tailor, the goatherd, the workers of the fields, with their wives and children, pressed toward us through a cloud of dust.

Masheh Mindel, almost fainting, fell in front of the doorway. "A letter from America!" she gasped.

"A letter from America!" echoed the crowd, as they snatched the letter from her and thrust it into my father's hands.

"Read! Read!" they shouted tumultuously.

My father looked through the letter, his lips uttering no sound. In breathless suspense the crowd gazed at him. Their eyes shone with wonder and reverence for the only man in the village who could read.

Masheh Mindel crouched at his feet, her neck stretched toward him to catch each precious word of the letter.

"To my worthy wife, Masheh Mindel, and to my loving son, Susha Feifel, and to my precious darling daughter, the apple of my eye, the pride of my life, Tzipkeleh!

"Long years and good luck on you! May the blessings from heaven fall over your beloved heads and save you from all harm!

"First I come to tell you that I am well and in good health. May I hear the same from you.

"Secondly, I am telling you that my sun is beginning to shine in America. I am becoming a person — a business man.

"I have for myself a stand in the most crowded part of America, where people are as thick as flies and every day is like market-day by a fair. My business is from bananas and apples. The day begins with my pushcart full of fruit, and the day never ends before I count up at least $2.00 profit — that means four rubles. Stand before your eyes . . . I . . . Gedalyeh Mindel, four rubles a day, twenty-four rubles a week!"

"Gedalyeh Mindel, the water-carrier, twenty-four rubles a week . . ." The words leaped like fire in the air.

We gazed at his wife, Masheh Mindel — a dried-out bone of a woman.

"Masheh Mindel, with a husband in America — Masheh Mindel, the wife of a man earning twenty-four rubles a week!"

We looked at her with new reverence. Already she was a being from another world. The dead, sunken eyes became alive with light. The worry for bread that had tightened the skin of her cheek-bones was gone. The sudden surge of happiness filled out her features, flushing her face as with wine.

The two starved children clinging to her skirts, dazed with excitement, only dimly realized their good fortune by the envious glances of the others.

"Thirdly, I come to tell you," the letter went on, "white bread and meat I eat every day just like the millionaires.

"Fourthly, I have to tell you that I am no more Gedalyeh Mindel — *Mister* Mindel they call me in America.

"Fifthly, Masheh Mindel and my dear children, in America there are no mud huts where cows and chickens and people live all together. I have for myself a separate room with a closed door, and before any one can come to me, I can give a say, 'Come in,' or 'Stay out,' like a king in a palace.

"Lastly, my darling family and people of the Village of Sukovoly, there is no Czar in America."

My father paused; the hush was stifling. No Czar — no Czar in America! Even the little babies repeated the chant: "No Czar in America!"

"In America they ask everybody who should be the President, and I, Gedalyeh Mindel, when I take out my Citizens papers, will have as much to say who shall be the next President in America, as Mr. Rockefeller the greatest millionaire.

"Fifty rubles I am sending you for your ship-ticket to America. And may all Jews who suffer in Goluth from ukazes and pogroms live yet to lift up their heads like me, Gedalyeh Mindel, in America."

Fifty rubles! A ship-ticket to America! That so much good luck should fall on one head! A savage envy bit me. Gloomy darts from narrowed eyes stabbed Masheh Mindel.

Why should not we too have a chance to get away from this dark land? Has not every heart the same hunger for America? The same longing to live and laugh and breathe like a free human being? America is for all. Why should only Masheh Mindel and her children have a chance to the new world?

Murmuring and gesticulating the crowd dispersed.

Each one knew every one else's thought: How to get to America. What could they pawn? From where could they borrow for a ship-ticket?

Silently we followed my father back into the hut from which the Cossack had driven us a while before.

We children looked from mother to father and from father to mother.

"Gottuniu! The Czar himself is pushing us to America by this last ukaz." My mother's face lighted up the hut like a lamp.

"Meshugeneh Yidini!" admonished my father. "Always your head in the air. What—where—America? With what money? Can dead people lift themselves up to dance?"

"Dance?" The samovar and the brass pots rang and reëchoed with my mother's laughter. "I could dance myself over the waves of the ocean to America."

In amazed delight at my mother's joy we children rippled and chuckled with her.

My father paced the room—his face dark with dread for the morrow.

"Empty hands—empty pockets—yet it dreams itself in you America."

"Who is poor who has hopes on America?" flaunted my mother.

"Sell my red quilted petticoat that grandmother left for my dowry," I urged in excitement.

"Sell the feather beds, sell the samovar," chorused the children.

"Sure we can sell everything—the goat and all the winter things," added my mother; "it must be always summer in America."

I flung my arms around my brother and he seized Bessie by the curls, and we danced about the room crazy with joy.

"Beggars!" laughed my mother, "why are you so happy with yourselves? How will you go to America without a shirt on your back—without shoes on your feet?"

But we ran out into the road, shouting and singing: "We'll sell everything we got—we'll go to America."

"White bread and meat we'll eat every day—in America! In America!"

That very evening we fetched Berel Zalman, the usurer, and showed him all our treasures, piled up in the middle of the hut.

"Look, all these fine feather beds, Berel Zalman." urged my mother; "this grand fur coat came from Nijny itself. My grandfather bought it at the fair."

I held up my red quilted petticoat, the supreme sacrifice of my ten-year-old life.

Even my father shyly pushed forward the samovar. "It can hold enough tea for the whole village."

"Only a hundred rubles for them all," pleaded my mother; "only enough to lift us to America. Only one hundred little rubles."

"A hundred rubles? Pfui!" sniffed the pawnbroker. "Forty is overpaid. Not even thirty is it worth."

But coaxing and cajoling my mother got a hundred rubles out of him.

Steerage—dirty bundles—foul odors—seasick humanity—but I saw and heard nothing of the foulness and ugliness around me. I floated in showers of sunshine; visions upon visions of the new world opened before me.

From lips to lips flowed the golden legend of the golden country:

"In America you can say what you feel—you can voice your thoughts in the open streets without fear of a Cossack."

"In America is a home for everybody. The land is your land. Not like in Russia where you feel yourself a stranger in the village where you were born and raised—the village in which your father and grandfather lie buried."

"Everybody is with everybody alike, in America. Christians and Jews are brothers together."

"An end to the worry for bread. An end to the fear of the bosses over you. Everybody can do what he wants with his life in America."

"There are no high or low in America. Even the President holds hands with Gedalyeh Mindel."

"Plenty for all. Learning flows free like milk and honey."

"Learning flows free."

The words painted pictures in my mind. I saw before me free schools, free colleges, free libraries, where I could learn and learn and keep on learning.

In our village was a school, but only for Christian children. In the schools of America I'd lift up my head and laugh and dance — a child with other children. Like a bird in the air, from sky to sky, from star to star, I'd soar and soar.

"Land! Land!" came the joyous shout.

"America! We're in America!" cried my mother, almost smothering us in her rapture.

All crowded and pushed on deck. They strained and stretched to get the first glimpse of the "golden country," lifting their children on their shoulders that they might see beyond them.

Men fell on their knees to pray. Women hugged their babies and wept. Children danced. Strangers embraced and kissed like old friends. Old men and women had in their eyes a look of young people in love.

Age-old visions sang themselves in me — songs of freedom of an oppressed people.

America! — America!

PART 2

Between buildings that loomed like mountains, we struggled with our bundles, spreading around us the smell of the steerage. Up Broadway, under the bridge, and through the swarming streets of the ghetto, we followed Gedalyeh Mindel.

I looked about the narrow streets of squeezed-in stores and houses, ragged clothes, dirty bedding oozing out of the windows, ash-cans and garbage-cans cluttering the side-walks. A vague sadness pressed down my heart — the first doubt of America.

"Where are the green fields and open spaces in America?" cried my heart. "Where is the golden country of my dreams?"

A loneliness for the fragrant silence of the woods that lay beyond our mud hut welled up in my heart, a longing for the soft, responsive earth of our village streets. All about me was the hardness of brick and stone, the stinking smells of crowded poverty.

"Here's your house with separate rooms like in a palace."
Gedalyeh Mindel flung open the door of a dingy, airless flat.

"Oi weh!" my mother cried in dismay. "Where's the sunshine in America?"

She went to the window and looked out at the blank wall of the next house. "Gottuniu! Like in a grave so dark . . ."

"It ain't so dark, it's only a little shady." Gedalyeh Mindel lighted the gas. "Look only" — he pointed with pride to the dim gaslight. "No candles, no kerosene lamps in America, you turn on a screw and put to it a match and you got it light like with sunshine."

Again the shadow fell over me, again the doubt of America!

In America were rooms without sunlight, rooms to sleep in, to eat in, to cook in, but without sunshine. And Gedalyeh Mindel was happy. Could I be satisfied with just a place to sleep and eat in, and a door to shut people out — to take the place of sunlight? Or would I always need the sunlight to be happy?

And where was there a place in America for me to play? I looked out into the alley below and saw pale-faced children scrambling in the gutter. "Where is America?" cried my heart.

My eyes were shutting themselves with sleep. Blindly, I felt for the buttons on my dress, and buttoning I sank back in sleep again — the deadweight sleep of utter exhaustion.

"Heart of mine!" my mother's voice moaned above me. "Father is already gone an hour. You know how they'll squeeze from you a nickel for every minute you're late. Quick only!"

I seized my bread and herring and tumbled down the stairs and out into the street. I ate running, blindly pressing through the hurrying throngs of workers — my haste and fear choking each mouthful.

I felt a strangling in my throat as I neared the sweatshop prison; all my nerves screwed together into iron hardness to endure the day's torture.

For an instant I hesitated as I faced the grated window of the old dilapidated building — dirt and decay cried out from every crumbling brick.

In the maw of the shop, raging around me the roar and the clatter, the clatter and the roar, the merciless grind of the pounding machines. Half maddened, half deadened, I struggled to think, to feel, to remember — what am I — who am I — why was I here?

I struggled in vain — bewildered and lost in a whirlpool of noise.

"America — America — where was America?" it cried in my heart.

The factory whistle — the slowing-down of the machines — the shout of release hailing the noon hour.

I woke as from a tense nightmare — a weary waking to pain.

In the dark chaos of my brain reason began to dawn. In my stifled heart feelings began to pulse. The wound of my wasted life began to throb and ache. My childhood choked with drudgery — must my youth too die — unlived?

The odor of herring and garlic — the ravenous munching of food — laughter and loud, vulgar jokes. Was it only I who was so wretched? I looked at those around me. Were they happy or only insensible to their slavery? How could they laugh and joke? Why were they not torn with rebellion against this galling grind — the crushing, deadening movements of the body, where only hands live and hearts and brains must die?

A touch on my shoulder. I looked up. It was Yetta Solomon from the machine next to mine.

"Here's your tea."

I stared at her, half hearing.

"Ain't you going to eat nothing?"

"Oi weh! Yetta! I can't stand it!" The cry broke from me. "I didn't come to America to turn into a machine. I came to America to make from myself a person. Does America want only my hands — only the strength of my body — not my heart — not my feelings — my thoughts?"

"Our heads ain't smart enough," said Yetta, practically. "We ain't been to school like the American-born."

"What for did I come to America but to go to school — to learn — to think — to make something beautiful from my life . . ."

"Sh-sh! Sh-sh! The boss — the boss!" came the warning whisper.

A sudden hush fell over the shop as the boss entered. He raised his hand.

Breathless silence.

The hard, red face with pig's eyes held us under its sickening spell. Again I saw the Cossack and heard him thunder the ukaz.

Prepared for disaster, the girls paled as they cast at each other sidelong, frightened glances.

"Hands," he addressed us, fingering the gold watch-chain that spread across his fat belly, "it's slack in the other trades and I can get plenty girls begging themselves to work for half what you're getting — only I ain't a skinner. I always give my hands a show to earn their bread. From now on, I'll give you fifty cents a dozen shirts instead of seventy-five, but I'll give you night-work, so you need n't lose nothing." And he was gone.

The stillness of death filled the shop. Each one felt the heart of the other bleed with her own helplessness.

A sudden sound broke the silence. A woman sobbed chokingly. It was Balah Rifkin, a widow with three children.

"Oi weh!" She tore at her scrawny neck. "The blood-sucker — the thief! How will I give them to eat — my babies — my babies — my hungry little lambs!"

"Why do we let him choke us?"

"Twenty-five cents less on a dozen — how will we be able to live?"

"He tears the last skin from our bones!"

"Why did n't nobody speak up to him?"

"Tell him he couldn't crush us down to worse than we had in Russia?"

"Can we help ourselves? Our life lies in his hands."

Something in me forced me forward. Rage at the bitter greed tore me. Our desperate helplessness drove me to strength.

"I'll go to the boss!" I cried, my nerves quivering with fierce excitement. "I'll tell him Balah Rifkin has three hungry mouths to feed."

Pale, hungry faces thrust themselves toward me, thin, knotted hands reached out, starved bodies pressed close about me.

"Long years on you!" cried Balah Rifkin, drying her eyes with a corner of her shawl.

"Tell him about my old father and me, his only bread-giver," came from Bessie Sopolsky, a gaunt-faced girl with a hacking cough.

"And I got no father or mother and four of them younger than me hanging on my neck." Jennie Feist's beautiful young face was already scarred with the gray worries of age.

America, as the oppressed of all lands have dreamed America to be, and America *as it is*, flashed before me — a banner of fire! Behind me I felt masses pressing — thousands of immigrants — thousands upon thousands crushed by injustice, lifted me as on wings.

I entered the boss's office without a shadow of fear. I was not I — the wrongs of my people burned through me till I felt the very flesh of my body a living flame of rebellion.

I faced the boss.

"We can't stand it!" I cried. "Even as it is we're hungry. Fifty cents a dozen would starve us. Can you, a Jew, tear the bread from another Jew's mouth?"

"You, fresh mouth, you! Who are you to learn me my business?"

"Were n't you yourself once a machine slave — your life in the hands of your boss?"

"You — loaferin — money for nothing you want! The minute they begin to talk English they get flies in their nose. . . . A black year on you — trouble-maker! I'll have no smart heads in my shop! Such freshness! Out you get . . . out from my shop!"

Stunned and hopeless, the wings of my courage broken, I groped my way back to them — back to the eager, waiting faces — back to the crushed hearts aching with mine.

As I opened the door they read our defeat in my face.

"Girls!" I held out my hands. "He's fired me."

My voice died in the silence. Not a girl stirred. Their heads only bent closer over their machines.

"Here, you! Get yourself out of here!" The boss thundered at me. "Bessie Sopolsky and you, Balah Rifkin, take out her machine into the hall. . . . I want no big-mouthed Americanerins in my shop."

Bessie Sopolsky and Balah Rifkin, their eyes black with tragedy, carried out my machine.

Not a hand was held out to me, not a face met mine. I felt them shrink from me as I passed them on my way out.

In the street I found I was crying. The new hope that had flowed in me so strong bled out of my veins. A moment before, our togetherness had made me believe us so strong — and now I saw each alone — crushed — broken. What were they all but crawling worms, servile grubbers for bread?

I wept not so much because the girls had deserted me, but because I saw for the first time how mean, how vile, were the creatures with whom I had to work. How the fear for bread had dehumanized their last shred of humanity! I felt I had not been working among human beings, but in a jungle of savages who had to eat one another alive in order to survive.

And then, in the very bitterness of my resentment, the hardness broke in me. I saw the girls through their own eyes as if I were inside of them. What else could they have done? Was not an immediate crust of bread for Balah Rifkin's children more urgent than truth — more vital than honor?

Could it be that they ever had dreamed of America as I had

dreamed? Had their faith in America wholly died in them? Could my faith be killed as theirs had been?

Gasping from running, Yetta Solomon flung her arms around me.

"You golden heart! I sneaked myself out from the shop — only to tell you I'll come to see you to-night. I'd give the blood from under my nails for you — only I got to run back — I got to hold my job — my mother — "

I hardly saw or heard her — my senses stunned with my defeat. I walked on in a blind daze — feeling that any moment I would drop in the middle of the street from sheer exhaustion.

Every hope I had clung to — every human stay — every reality was torn from under me. I sank in bottomless blackness. I had only one wish left — to die.

Was it then only a dream — a mirage of the hungry-hearted people in the desert lands of oppression — this age-old faith in America — the beloved, the prayed-for "golden country"?

Had the starved villagers of Sukovoly lifted above their sorrows a mere rainbow vision that led them — where — where? To the stifling submission of the sweatshop or the desperation of the streets!

"O God! What is there beyond this hell?" my soul cried in me. "Why can't I make a quick end to myself?"

A thousand voices within me and about me answered:

"My faith is dead, but in my blood their faith still clamors and aches for fulfillment — *dead generations whose faith though beaten back still presses on — a resistless, deathless force!*

"In this America that crushes and kills me their spirit drives me on — to struggle — to suffer — but never to submit."

In my desperate darkness their lost lives loomed — a living flame of light. Again I saw the mob of dusty villagers crowding around my father as he read the letter from America — their eager faces thrust out — their eyes blazing with the same hope, the same age-old faith that drove me on —

A sudden crash against my back. Dizzy with pain I fell — then all was darkness and quiet.

I opened my eyes. A white-clad figure bent over me. Had I died? Was I in the heaven of the new world — in America?

My eyes closed again. A misty happiness filled my being.

"Learning flows free like milk and honey," it dreamed itself in me.

I was in my heaven in the schools of America—in open, sunny fields—a child with other children. Our lesson-books were singing birds and whispering trees—chanting brooks and beckoning skies. We breathed in learning and wisdom as naturally as flowers breathe in sunlight.

After our lessons were over, we all joined hands skipping about like a picture of dancing fairies I had once seen in a shop-window.

I was so full of the joy of togetherness—the great wonder of the new world; it pressed on my heart like sorrow. Slowly, I stole away from the other children into silent solitude, wrestling and praying to give out what surged in me into some form of beauty. And out of my struggle to shape my thoughts beautifully, a great song filled the world.

"Soon she's all right to come back to the shop—yes, nurse?" The voice of Yetta Solomon broke into my dreaming.

Wearily I opened my eyes. I saw I was still on earth.

Yetta's broad, generous face smiled anxiously at me. "Lucky yet the car that run you over did n't break your hands or your feet. So long you got yet good hands you'll soon be back by the machine."

"Machine?" I shuddered. "I can't go back to the shop again. I got so used to sunlight and quiet in the hospital I'll not be able to stand the hell again."

"Shah!—Shah!" soothed Yetta. "Why don't you learn yourself to take life like it is? What's got to be, got to be. In Russia, you could hope to run away from your troubles to America. But from America where can you go?"

"Yes," I sighed. "In the blackest days of Russia, there was always the hope from America. In Russia we had only a mud hut; not enough to eat and always the fear from the Cossack, but still we managed to look up to the sky, to dream, to think of the new world where we'll have a chance to be people, not slaves."

"What's the use to think so much? It only eats up the flesh from your bones. Better rest . . ."

"How can I rest when my choked-in thoughts tear me to pieces? I need school more than a starving man needs bread."

Yetta's eyes brooded over me. Suddenly a light broke. "I got an idea. There's a new school for greenhorns where they learn them anything they want . . ."

"What—where?" I raised myself quickly, hot with eagerness. "How do you know from it—tell me only—quick—since when—"

"The girl next door by my house—she used to work by cigars and now she learns there."

"What does she learn?"

"Don't get yourself so excited. Your eyes are jumping out from your head."

I fell back weakly: "Oi weh! Tell me!" I begged.

"All I know is that she likes what she learns better than rolling cigars. And it's called 'School for Immigrant Girls.'"

"Your time is up. Another visitor is waiting to come in," said the nurse.

As Yetta walked out, my mother, with the shawl over her head, rushed in and fell on my bed kissing me.

"Oi weh! Oi weh! Half my life is out from me from fright. How did all happen?"

"Don't worry yourself so. I'm nearly well already and will go back to work soon."

"Talk not work. Get only a little flesh on your bones. They say they send from the hospital people to the country. Maybe they'll send you."

"But how will you live without my wages?"

"Davy is already peddling with papers and Bessie is selling lollypops after school in the park. Yesterday she brought home already twenty-eight cents."

For all her efforts to be cheerful, I looked at her pinched face and wondered if she had eaten that day.

Released from the hospital, I started home. As I neared Allen Street, the terror of the dark rooms swept over me. "No—no—I can't yet go back to the darkness and the stinking smells," I said to myself. "So long they're getting along without my wages, let them think I went to the country and let me try out that school for immigrants that Yetta told me about."

So I went to the Immigrant School.

A tall, gracious woman received me, not an employee, but a benefactress.

The love that had rushed from my heart toward the Statue in the Bay, rushed out to Mrs. Olney. She seemed to me the living spirit of America. All that I had ever dreamed America to be shone to me out of the kindness of her brown eyes. She would save me from the sordidness that was crushing me I felt the moment I looked at her. Sympathy and understanding seemed to breathe from her serene presence.

I longed to open my heart to her, but I was so excited I didn't know where to begin.

"I'm crazy to learn!" I gasped breathlessly, and then the very pressure of the things I had to say choked me.

An encouraging smile warmed the fine features.

"What trade would you like to learn — sewing-machine operating?"

"Sewing-machine operating?" I cried. "Oi weh!" I shuddered. "Only the thought 'machine' kills me. Even when I only look on clothes, it weeps in me when I think how the seams from everything people wear is sweated in the shop."

"Well, then" — putting a kind hand on my shoulder — "how would you like to learn to cook? There's a great need for trained servants and you'd get good wages and a pleasant home."

"Me — a servant?" I flung back her hand. "Did I come to America to make from myself a cook?"

Mrs. Olney stood abashed a moment. "Well, my dear," she said deliberately, "what would you like to take up?"

"I got ideas how to make America better, only I don't know how to say it out. Ain't there a place I can learn?"

A startled woman stared at me. For a moment not a word came. Then she proceeded with the same kind smile. "It's nice of you to want to help America, but I think the best way would be for you to learn a trade. That's what this school is for, to help girls find themselves, and the best way to do is to learn something useful."

"Ain't thoughts useful? Does America want only the work from my body, my hands? Ain't it thoughts that turn over the world?"

"Ah! But we don't want to turn over the world." Her voice cooled.

"But there's got to be a change in America!" I cried. "Us immigrants want to be people — not 'hands' — not slaves of the belly! And it's the chance to think out thoughts that makes people."

"My child, thought requires leisure. The time will come for that. First you must learn to earn a good living."

"Did I come to America for a living?"

"What did you come for?"

"I came to give out all the fine things that was choked in me in Russia. I came to help America make the new world. . . . They said, in America I could open up my heart and fly free in the air — to sing — to dance — to live — to love. . . . Here I got all those grand things in me, and America won't let me give nothing."

"Perhaps you made a mistake in coming to this country. Your own land might appreciate you more." A quick glance took me in from head to foot. "I'm afraid that you have come to the wrong place. We only teach trades here."

She turned to her papers and spoke over her shoulder. "I think you will have to go elsewhere if you want to set the world on fire."

PART 3

Blind passion swayed me as I walked out of the Immigrant School, not knowing where I was going, not caring. One moment I was swept with the fury of indignation, the next moment bent under the burden of despair. But out of this surging conflict one thought — one truth gradually grew clearer and clearer to me: Without comprehension, the immigrant would forever remain shut out — a stranger in America. Until America can release the heart as well as train the hand of the immigrant, he would forever remain driven back upon himself, corroded by the very richness of the unused gifts within his soul.

I longed for a friend — a real American friend — some one different from Mrs. Olney, some one who would understand this vague, blind hunger for release that consumed me. But how, where could I find such a friend?

As I neared the house we lived in, I paused terror-stricken. On the sidewalk stood a jumbled pile of ragged house-furnishings that looked familiar — chairs, dishes, kitchen pans. Amidst bundles of bedding and broken furniture stood my mother. Oblivious of the curious crowd, she lit the Sabbath candles and prayed over them.

In a flash I understood it all. Because of the loss of my wages while I was in the hospital, we had been evicted for unpaid rent. It was Sabbath eve. My father was in the synagogue praying and my mother, defiant of disgrace, had gone on with the ceremony of the Sabbath.

All the romance of our race was in the light of those Sabbath candles. Homeless, abandoned by God and man, yet in the very desolation of the streets my mother's faith burned — a challenge to all America.

"Mammeh!" I cried, pushing through the crowd. Bessie and Dave darted forward. In a moment the four of us stood clinging to one another, amid the ruins of our broken home.

A neighbor invited us into her house for supper. No sooner had we sat down at the table than there was a knock at the door and a square-figured young woman entered, asking to see my mother.

"I am from the Social Betterment Society," she said. "I hear you've been dispossessed. What's the trouble here?"

"Oi weh! My bitter heart!" I yet see before me the anguish of my mother's face as she turned her head away from the charity lady.

My father's eyes sank to the floor. I could feel him shrink in upon himself like one condemned.

The bite of food turned to gall in my throat.

"How long have you been in America? Where were you born?" She questioned by rote, taking out pad and pencil.

The silence of the room was terrible. The woman who had invited us for supper slunk into the bedroom, unable to bear our shame.

"How long have you been in America?" repeated the charity lady.

Choked silence.

"Is there any one here who can speak?" She translated her question into Yiddish.

"A black year on Gedalyeh Mindel, the liar!" my mother burst out at last. "Why did we leave our home? We were among our own. We were people there. But what are we here? Nobodies — nobodies! Cats and dogs at home ain't thrown in the street. Such things could only happen in America — the land without a heart — the land without a God!"

"For goodness' sakes! Is there any one here intelligent enough to answer a straight question?" The charity lady turned with disgusted impatience from my mother to me. "Can you tell me how long you have been in this country? Where were you born?"

"None of your business!" I struck out blindly, not aware of what I was saying.

"Why so bold? We are only trying to help you and you are so resentful."

"To the Devil with your help! I'm sick no longer. I can take care of my mother — without your charity!"

The next day I went back to the shop — to the same long hours — to the same low wages — to the same pig-eyed, fat-bellied boss. But I was no longer the same. For the first time in my life I bent to the inevitable. I accepted my defeat. But something in me, stronger than I, rose triumphant even in my surrender.

"Yes, I must submit to the shop," I thought. "But the shop shall not crush me. Only my body I must sell into slavery — not my heart — not my soul.

"To any one who sees me from without, I am only a dirt-eating worm, a grub in the ground, but I know that above this dark earth-place in which I am sunk is the green grass — and beyond the green grass, the sun and sky. Alone, unaided, I must dig my way up to the light!"

Lunch-hour at the factory. My book of Shelley's poems before me and I was soon millions of miles beyond the raucous voices of the hungry eaters.

"Did you already hear the last news?" Yetta tore my book from me in her excitement.

"What news?" I scowled at her for waking me from my dreams.

"We're going to have electricity by the machines. And the fore-lady says that the new boss will give us ten cents more on a dozen waists!"

"God from the world! How did it happen — electricity — better pay?" I asked in amazement. For that was the first I had heard of improved conditions of work.

But little by little, step by step, the sanitation improved. Open windows, swept floors, clean wash-rooms, individual drinking-cups introduced a new era of factory hygiene. Our shop was caught up in the general movement for social betterment that stirred the country.

It was not all done in a day. Weary years of struggle passed before the workers emerged from the each-for-himself existence into an organized togetherness for mutual improvement.

At last, with the shortened hours of work, I had enough vitality left at the end of the day to join the night-school. Again my dream flamed. Again America beckoned. In the school there would be education — air, life for my cramped-in spirit. I would learn to form the thoughts that surged formless in me. I would find the teacher that would make me articulate.

Shelley was English literature.

So I joined the literature class. The course began with the "De Coverley Papers." Filled with insatiate thirst, I drank in every line with the feeling that any minute I would get to the fountain-heart of revelation.

Night after night I read with tireless devotion. But of what? The manners and customs of the eighteenth century, of people two hundred years dead.

One evening after a month's attendance, when the class had

dwindled from fifty to four and the teacher began scolding us who were left for those who were absent, my bitterness broke.

"Do you know why all the girls are dropping away from the class? It's because they have too much sense to waste themselves on the 'De Coverley Papers.' Us four girls are four fools. We could learn more in the streets. It's dirty and wrong, but it's life. What are the 'De Coverley Papers'? Dry dust fit for the ash can."

"Perhaps you had better tell the board of education your ideas of the standard classics," she scoffed, white with rage.

"Classics? If all the classics are as dead as the 'De Coverley Papers,' I'd rather read the ads in the papers. How can I learn from this old man that's dead two hundred years how to live my life?"

That was the first of many schools I had tried. And they were all the same. A dull course of study and the lifeless, tired teachers — no more interested in their pupils than in the wooden benches before them — chilled all my faith in the American schools.

More and more the all-consuming need for a friend possessed me. In the street, in the cars, in the subways, I was always seeking, ceaselessly seeking, for eyes, a face, the flash of a smile that would be light in my darkness.

I felt sometimes that I was only burning out my heart for a shadow, an echo, a wild dream. But I could n't help it. Nothing was real to me but my hope of finding a friend.

One day my sister Bessie came home much excited over her new high-school teacher. "Miss Latham makes it so interesting!" she exclaimed. "She stops in the middle of the lesson and tells us things. She ain't like a teacher. She's like a real person."

At supper next evening, Bessie related more wonder stories of her beloved teacher. "She's so different! She's friends with us. . . . To-day, when she gave us out our composition, Mamie Cohen asked from what book we should read up and she said, 'Just take it out of your heart and say it.'"

"Just take it out of your heart and say it." The simple words lingered in my mind, stirring a whirl of hidden thoughts and feelings. It seemed as if they had been said directly to me.

A few days later Bessie ran in from school, her cheeks flushed, her eyes dancing with excitement. "Give a look at the new poem teacher gave me to learn!" It was a quotation from Kipling:

"Then only the Master shall praise us,
And only the Master shall blame,

And no one shall work for money,
And no one shall work for fame;
But each for the joy of the working,
And each in his separate Star,
Shall draw the thing as he sees it
For the God of things as they are."

Only a few brief lines, but in their music the pulses of my being leaped into life. And so it was from day to day. Miss Latham's sayings kept turning themselves in my mind like a lingering melody that could not be shaken off. Something irresistible seemed to draw me to her. She beckoned to me almost as strongly as America had on the way over in the boat.

I wondered, "Should I go to see her and talk myself out from my heart to her?

"Meshugeneh! Where—what? How come you to her? What will you say for your reason?

"What's the difference what I'll say! I only want to give a look on her . . ."

And so I kept on restlessly debating. Should I follow my heart and go to her, or should I have a little sense?

Finally the desire to see her became so strong that I could no longer reason about it. I left the factory in the middle of the day to seek her out.

All the way to her school I prayed: "God—God! If I could only find one human soul that cared . . ."

I found her bending over her desk. Her hair was gray, but she did not look tired like the other teachers. She was correcting papers and was absorbed in her task. I watched her, not daring to interrupt. Presently she threw back her head and gave a little laugh.

Then she saw me. "Why, how do you do?" She rose. "Come and sit down."

I felt she was as glad to see me as though she had expected me.

"I feel you can help me," I groped toward her.

"I hope I can." She grasped my outstretched hands and led me to a chair which seemed to be waiting for me.

A strange gladness filled me.

"Bessie showed me the poem you told her to learn . . ." I paused bewildered.

"Yes?" Her friendly eyes urged me to speak.

"From what Bessie told me I felt I could talk myself out to you what's bothering me." I stopped again.

She leaned forward with an inviting interest. "Go on! Tell me all."

"I'm an immigrant many years already here, but I'm still seeking America. My dream America is more far from me than it was in the old country. Always something comes between the immigrant and the American," I went on blindly. "They see only his skin, his outside — not what's in his heart. They don't care if he has a heart. . . . I wanted to find some one that would look on me — myself . . . I thought you'd know yourself on a person first off."

Abashed at my boldness I lowered my eyes to the floor.

"Do go on . . . I want to hear."

With renewed courage I continued my confessional.

"Life is too big for me. I'm lost in this each-for-himself world. I feel shut out from everything that's going on. . . . I'm always fighting — fighting — with myself and everything around me. . . . I hate when I want to love and I make people hate me when I want to make them love me."

She gave me a quick nod. "I know — I know what you mean. Go on."

"I don't know what is with me the matter. I'm so choked. . . . Sundays and holidays when the other girls go out to enjoy themselves, I walk around by myself — thinking — thinking. . . . My thoughts tear in me and I can't tell them to no one! I want to do something with my life and I don't know what."

"I'm glad you came," she said. And after a pause, "You can help me."

"Help you?" I cried. It was the first time that an American suggested that I could help her.

"Yes, indeed! I have always wanted to know more of that mysterious vibrant life — the immigrant. You can help me know my girls."

The repression of centuries seemed to rush out of my heart. I told her everything — of the mud hut in Sukovoly where I was born, of the Czar's pogroms, of the constant fear of the Cossack, of Gedalyeh Mindel's letter and of our hopes in coming to America.

After I had talked myself out, I felt suddenly ashamed for having exposed so much, and I cried out to her: "Do you think like the others that I'm all wrapped up in self?"

For some minutes she studied me, and her serenity seemed to project itself into me. And then she said, as if she too were groping, "No — no — but too intense."

"I hate to be so all the time intense. But how can I help it? Everything always drives me back in myself. How can I get myself out into the free air?"

"Don't fight yourself." Her calm, gray eyes penetrated to the very soul in me. "You are burning up too much vitality. . . .

"You know some of us," she went on — "not many, unfortunately — have a sort of divine fire which if it does not find expression turns into smoke. This egoism and self-centeredness which troubles you is only the smoke of repression."

She put her hand over mine. "You have had no one to talk to — no one to share your thoughts."

I marveled at the simplicity with which she explained me to myself. I could n't speak. I just looked at her.

"But now," she said, gently, "you have some one. Come to me whenever you wish."

"I have a friend," it sang itself in me. "I have a friend."

"And you are a born American?" I asked. There was none of that sure, all-right look of the Americans about her.

"Yes, indeed! My mother, like so many mothers," — and her eyebrows lifted humorously whimsical, — "claims we're descendants of the Pilgrim fathers. And that one of our lineal ancestors came over in the Mayflower."

"For all your mother's pride in the Pilgrim fathers, you yourself are as plain from the heart as an immigrant."

"Were n't the Pilgrim fathers immigrants two hundred years ago?"

She took from her desk a book called "Our America," by Waldo Frank, and read to me: "We go forth all to seek America. And in the seeking we create her. In the quality of our search shall be the nature of the America that we create."

"Ach, friend! Your words are life to me! You make it light for my eyes!"

She opened her arms to me and breathlessly I felt myself drawn to her. Bonds seemed to burst. A suffusion of light filled my being. Great choirings lifted me in space.

I walked out unseeingly.

All the way home the words she read flamed before me: "We go forth all to seek America. And in the seeking we create her. In the quality of our search shall be the nature of the America that we create."

So all those lonely years of seeking and praying were not in vain! How glad I was that I had not stopped at the husk—a good job—a good living—but pressed on, through the barriers of materialism.

Through my inarticulate groping and reaching-out I had found the soul—the spirit—of America!

A Wedding in Brownsville

ISAAC BASHEVIS SINGER

Isaac Bashevis Singer (1904–1991): *Isaac Bashevis Singer is the only Yiddish writer ever to win the Nobel Prize in Literature. While he was by no means the only great Yiddish writer of his generation, his work, much of which is characterized by an arresting combination of sensuality and fable-like simplicity, has found an audience much wider than that enjoyed by any other author writing in Yiddish. The son and grandson of Hasidic rabbis, Isaac Bashevis Singer was born in the village of Leoncin, Poland, and raised in Warsaw. He was educated at Orthodox yeshivas and the Warsaw Rabbinical Seminary, but he turned his back on traditional Judaism as a young man. In 1935 he came to America, following in the footsteps of his older brother, Israel Joshua Singer (the author of* The Family Carnovsky *and* The Brothers Ashkenazi, *epic novels written and published in Yiddish). During his early years in America, while working to learn the craft of fiction, Isaac Bashevis Singer supported himself as a journalist, publishing his work in the* Jewish Daily Forward, *a New York Yiddish newspaper. In 1953 Saul Bellow's translation of Singer's story "Gimpel the Fool" appeared; it helped to gain a much wider audience for Singer's work. Over the last forty years of his life, many of Isaac Bashevis Singer's novels and collections of stories were published in English, all translated from the Yiddish by the author and a host of others. His novels include* The Family Moskat, Satan in Goray, The Magician of Lublin, The Slave, The Manor, The Estate, Shoshe, *and* The Penitent. *His stories were collected in* Gimpel the Fool, The Spinoza of Market Street, A Friend of Kafka, *and* A Crown of Feathers, *among other volumes. Most of these stories originally appeared in the* Daily Forward. *For many years he lived with his wife, Alma, on the Upper West Side of New York.*

T he wedding had been a burden to Dr. Solomon Margolin from the very beginning. True, it was to take place on a Sunday, but Gretl had been right when she said that was the only evening in the week they could spend together. It always turned out that way. His responsibilities to the community made him give away the evenings that belonged to her. The Zionists had appointed him to a committee; he was a board member of a Jewish scholastic society; he had become co-editor of an academic Jewish quarterly. And though he often referred to himself as an agnostic and even an atheist, nevertheless for years he had been dragging Gretl to seders at Abraham Mekheles', a *Landsman* from Sencimin. Dr. Margolin treated rabbis, refugees, and Jewish writers without charge, supplying them with medicines and, if necessary, a hospital bed. There had been a time when he had gone regularly to the meetings of the Senciminer Society, had accepted positions in their ranks, and had attended all the parties. Now Abraham Mekheles was marrying off his youngest daughter, Sylvia. The minute the invitation arrived, Gretl had announced her decision: she was not going to let herself be carted off to a wedding somewhere out in the wilds of Brownsville. If he, Solomon, wanted to go and gorge himself on all kinds of greasy food, coming home at three o'clock in the morning, that was his prerogative.

Dr. Margolin admitted to himself that his wife was right. When would he get a chance to sleep? He had to be at the hospital early Monday morning. Moreover he was on a strict fat-free diet. A wedding like this one would be a feast of poisons. Everything about such celebrations irritated him now: the Anglicized Yiddish, the Yiddishized English, the ear-splitting music and unruly dances. Jewish laws and customs were completely distorted; men who had no regard for Jewishness wore skullcaps; and the reverend rabbis and cantors aped the Christian ministers. Whenever he took Gretl to a wedding or Bar Mitzvah, he was ashamed. Even she, born a Christian, could see that American Judaism was a mess. At least this time he would be spared the trouble of making apologies to her.

Usually after breakfast on Sunday, he and his wife took a walk in Central Park, or, when the weather was mild, went to the Palisades. But today Solomon Margolin lingered in bed. During the years, he had stopped attending the functions of the Senciminer Society; meanwhile the town of Sencimin had been destroyed. His family there had been tortured, burned, gassed. Many Senciminers had survived, and, later, come to America from the camps, but most of them were younger people whom he, Solomon, had not known in the old country. Tonight everyone would be there: the Senciminers belonging to the bride's family and the Tereshpolers belonging to the groom's. He knew how they would pester him, reproach him for growing aloof, drop hints that he was a snob. They would address him familiarly, slap him on the back, drag him off to dance. Well, even so, he had to go to Sylvia's wedding. He had already sent out the present.

The day had dawned, grey and dreary as dusk. Overnight, a heavy snow had fallen. Solomon Margolin had hoped to make up for the sleep he was going to lose, but unfortunately he had waked even earlier than usual. Finally he got up. He shaved himself meticulously at the bathroom mirror and also trimmed the grey hair at his temples. Today of all days he looked his age: there were bags under his eyes, and his face was lined. Exhaustion showed in his features. His nose appeared longer and sharper than usual; there were deep folds at the sides of his mouth. After breakfast he stretched out on the living-room sofa. From there he could see Gretl, who was standing in the kitchen, ironing—blonde, faded, middle-aged. She had on a skimpy petticoat, and her calves were as muscular as a dancer's. Gretl had been a nurse in the Berlin hospital where he had been a member of the staff. Of her family, one brother, a Nazi, had died of typhus in a Russian prison camp. A second, who was a Communist, had been shot by the Nazis. Her aged father vegetated at the home of his other daughter in Hamburg, and Gretl sent him money regularly. She herself had become almost Jewish in New York. She had made friends with Jewish women, joined Hadassah, learned to cook Jewish dishes. Even her sigh was Jewish. And she lamented continually over the Nazi catastrophe. She had her plot waiting for her beside his in that part of the cemetery that the Senciminers had reserved for themselves.

Dr. Margolin yawned, reached for the cigarette that lay in an ashtray on the coffee table beside him, and began to think about himself. His career had gone well. Ostensibly he was a success. He had an office on West End Avenue and wealthy patients. His colleagues respected him, and he was an important figure in Jewish circles in New York. What more could a boy from Sencimin expect? A self-taught man, the son of a poor teacher of Talmud? In person he was tall, quite handsome, and he had always had a way with women. He still pursued them—more than was good for him at his age and with his high blood pressure. But secretly Solomon Margolin had always felt that he was a failure. As a child he had been acclaimed a prodigy, reciting long passages of the Bible and studying the Talmud and Commentaries on his own. When he was a boy of eleven, he had sent for a Responsum to the Rabbi of Tarnow who had referred to him in his reply as "great and illustrious." In his teens he had become a master in the *Guide of the Perplexed* and the *Kuzari*. He had taught himself algebra and geometry. At seventeen he had attempted a translation of Spinoza's *Ethics* from Latin into Hebrew, unaware that it had been done before. Everyone predicted he would turn out to be a genius. But he had squandered his talents, continually changing his field of study; and he had wasted years in learning languages, in wandering from country to country. Nor had he had any luck with his one great love, Raizel, the daughter of Melekh the watchmaker. Raizel had married someone else and later had been shot by the Nazis. All his life Solomon Margolin had been plagued by the eternal questions. He still lay awake at night trying to solve the mysteries of the universe. He suffered from hypochondria and the fear of death haunted even his dreams. Hitler's carnage and the extinction of his family had rooted out his last hope for better days, had destroyed all his faith in humanity. He had begun to despise the matrons who came to him with their petty ills while millions were devising horrible deaths for one another.

Gretl came in from the kitchen.

"What shirt are you going to put on?"

Solomon Margolin regarded her quietly. She had had her own share of troubles. She had suffered in silence for her two brothers, even for Hans, the Nazi. She had gone through a prolonged change of life. She was tortured by guilt feelings toward him, Solomon. She had become sexually frigid. Now her face was flushed and covered with beads of sweat. He earned more than enough to pay for a maid, yet Gretl insisted on doing all the housework herself, even the laundry. It had become a mania with her. Every day she scoured the oven. She was forever polishing the windows of their apartment on the sixteenth floor and without using a safety belt. All the other housewives in the building ordered their groceries delivered, but Gretl lugged the heavy bags from the supermarket herself. At night she sometimes said things that sounded slightly insane to him. She still suspected him of carrying on with every female patient he treated.

Now husband and wife sized each other up wryly, feeling the strangeness that comes of great familiarity. He was always amazed at how she had lost her looks. No one feature had altered, but something in her aspect had given way: her pride, her hopefulness, her curiosity. He blurted out:

"What shirt? It doesn't matter. A white shirt."

"You're not going to wear the tuxedo? Wait, I'll bring you a vitamin."

"I don't want a vitamin."

"But you yourself say they're good for you."

"Leave me alone."

"Well, it's your health, not mine."

And slowly she walked out of the room, hesitating as if she expected him to remember something and call her back.

Dr. Solomon Margolin took a last look in the mirror and left the house. He felt refreshed by the half-hour nap he had had after dinner. Despite his age, he still wanted to impress people with his appearance — even the Senciminers. He had his illusions. In Germany he had taken pride in the fact that he looked like a *Junker*, and in New York he was often aware that he could pass for an Anglo-Saxon. He was tall, slim, blond, blue-eyed. His hair was thinning, had turned somewhat grey, but he managed to disguise these signs of age. He stooped a little, but in company was quick to straighten up. Years ago in Germany he had worn a monocle and though in New York that would have been too pretentious, his glance still retained a European severity. He had his principles. He had never broken the Hippocratic Oath. With his patients he was honorable to an extreme, avoiding every kind of cant; and he had refused a number of dubious associations that smacked of careerism. Gretl claimed his sense of honor amounted to a mania. Dr. Margolin's car was in the garage — not a Cadillac like that of most of his colleagues — but he decided to go by taxi. He was unfamiliar with Brooklyn and the heavy snow made driving hazardous. He waved his hand and at once a taxi pulled over to the curb. He was afraid the driver might refuse to go as far as Brownsville, but he flicked the meter on without a word. Dr. Margolin peered through the frosted window into the wintry Sunday night but there was nothing to be seen. The New York streets sprawled out, wet, dirty, impenetrably dark. After awhile, Dr. Margolin leaned back, shut his eyes, and retreated into his own warmth. His destination was a wedding. Wasn't the world, like this taxi, plunging away somewhere into the unknown toward a cosmic destination? Maybe a cosmic Brownsville, a cosmic wedding? Yes. But why did God — or whatever anyone wanted to call Him — create a Hitler, a Stalin? Why did He need world wars? Why heart attacks, cancers? Dr. Margolin took out a cigarette and lit it mechanically. What had they been thinking of, those pious uncles of his, when they were digging their own graves? Was immortality possible? Was there such a thing as the soul? All the arguments for and against weren't worth a pinch of dust.

The taxi turned onto the bridge across the East River and for the first time Dr. Margolin was able to see the sky. It sagged low, heavy, red as glowing metal. Higher up, a violet glare suffused the vault of the heavens. Snow was sifting down gently, bringing a winter peace to the world, just as it had in the past — forty years ago, a thousand years ago, and perhaps a million years ago. Fiery pillars appeared to glow beneath the East River; on its surface, through black waves jagged as rocks, a tugboat was hauling a string of barges loaded with cars. A front window in the cab was open and icy gusts of wind blew in, smelling of gasoline and the sea. Suppose the weather never changed again? Who then would ever be able to imagine a summer day, a moonlit night, spring? But how much imagination — for what it's worth — does a man actually have? On Eastern Parkway the taxi was jolted and screeched suddenly to a stop. Some traffic accident, apparently. The siren on a police car shrieked. A wailing ambulance drew nearer. Dr. Margolin closed his eyes. Another victim. Someone makes a false turn of the wheel and all a man's plans in this world are reduced to nothing.

Some time later the taxi started moving again. Solomon Margolin was now driving through streets he had never seen before. It was New York, but it might just as well have been Chicago or Cleveland. They passed through an industrial district with factory buildings, warehouses of coal, lumber, scrap iron. Negroes, strangely black, stood about on the sidewalks, staring ahead, their great dark eyes full of a gloomy hopelessness. Occasionally the car would pass a tavern. The people at the bar seemed to have something unearthly about them, as if they were being punished here for sins committed in another incarnation. Just when Solomon Margolin was beginning to suspect that the driver, who had remained stubbornly silent the whole time, had gotten lost or else was deliberately taking him out of his way, the taxi entered a thickly populated neighborhood. They passed a synagogue, a funeral parlor, and there, ahead, was the wedding hall, all lit up, with its neon Jewish sign and Star of David. Dr. Margolin gave the driver a dollar tip and the man took it without uttering a word.

Dr. Margolin entered the outer lobby and immediately the comfortable intimacy of the Senciminers engulfed him. All the faces he saw were familiar, though he didn't recognize individuals. Leaving his hat and coat at the checkroom, he put on a skullcap and entered the hall. It was filled with people and music, with tables heaped with food, a bar stacked with bottles. The musicians were playing an Israeli march that was a hodgepodge of American jazz with Oriental flourishes. Men were dancing with men, women with women, men with women. He saw black skullcaps, white skullcaps, bare heads. Guests kept arriving, pushing their way through the crowd, some still in their hats and coats, munching hors d'oeuvres, drinking *schnapps*. The hall resounded with stamping, screaming, laughing, clapping. Flash bulbs went off blindingly as the photographers made their rounds. Seeming to come from nowhere, the bride appeared, briskly sweeping up her train, followed by a retinue of bridesmaids. Dr. Margolin knew everybody, and yet knew nobody. People spoke to him, laughed, winked, and waved, and he answered each one with a smile, a nod, a bow. Gradually he threw off all his worries, all his depression. He became half-drunk on the amalgam of odors: flowers, sauerkraut, garlic, perfume, mustard, and that nameless odor that only Senciminers emit. "Hello, Doctor!" "Hello, Schloime-Dovid, you don't recognize me, eh? Look, he forgot!" There were the encounters, the regrets, the reminiscences of long ago. "But after all, weren't we neighbors? You used to come to our house to borrow the Yiddish newspaper!" Someone had already kissed him: a badly shaven snout, a mouth reeking of whiskey and rotten teeth. One woman was so convulsed with laughter that she lost an earring. Margolin tried to pick it up, but it had already been trampled underfoot. "You don't recognize me, eh? Take a good look! It's Zissl, the son of Chaye Beyle!" "Why don't you eat something?" "Why don't you have something to drink? Come over here. Take a glass. What do you want? Whiskey? Brandy? Cognac? Scotch? With soda? With Coca Cola? Take some, it's good. Don't let it stand. So long as you're here, you might as well enjoy yourself." "My father? He was killed. They were all killed. I'm the only one left of the entire family." "Berish the son of Feivish? Starved to death in Russia — they sent him to Kazakhstan. His wife? In Israel. She married a Lithuanian." "Sorele? Shot. Together with her children." "Yentl? Here at the wedding. She was standing here just a moment ago. There she is, dancing with that tall fellow." "Abraham Zilberstein? They burned him in the synagogue with twenty others. A mound of charcoal was all that was left, coal and ash." "Yosele Budnik? He passed away years ago. You must mean

Yekele Budnik. He has a delicatessen store right here in Brownsville — married a widow whose husband made a fortune in real
estate."

"*Lechayim*, Doctor! *Lechayim*, Schloime-Dovid! It doesn't offend
you that I call you Schloime-Dovid? To me you're still the same
Schloime-Dovid, the little boy with the blond side-curls who recited
a whole tractate of the Talmud by heart. You remember, don't you?
It seems like only yesterday. Your father, may he rest in peace, was
beaming with pride . . ." "Your brother Chayim? Your Uncle Oyzer?
They killed everyone, everyone. They took a whole people and
wiped them out with German efficiency: *gleichgeschaltet!*" "Have you
seen the bride yet? Pretty as a picture, but too much make-up. Imagine, a grandchild of Reb Todros of Radzin! And her grandfather
used to wear two skullcaps, one in front and one in back." "Do you
see that young woman dancing in the yellow dress? It's Riva's sister — their father was Moishe the candlemaker. Riva herself? Where
all the others ended up: Auschwitz. How close we came ourselves!
All of us are really dead, if you want to call it that. We were exter-
minated, wiped out. Even the survivors carry death in their hearts.
But it's a wedding, we should be cheerful." "*Lechayim*, Schloime-
Dovid! I would like to congratulate you. Have you a son or daughter
to marry off? No? Well, it's better that way. What's the sense of having children if people are such murderers?"

It was already time for the ceremony, but someone still had not
come. Whether it was the rabbi, the cantor, or one of the in-laws
who was missing, nobody seemed able to find out. Abraham Mekheles, the bride's father, rushed around, scowled, waved his hand,
whispered in people's ears. He looked strange in his rented tuxedo.
The Tereshpol mother-in-law was wrangling with one of the photographers. The musicians never stopped playing for an instant.
The drum banged, the bass fiddle growled, the saxophone blared.
The dances became faster, more abandoned, and more and more
people were drawn in. The young men stamped with such force
that it seemed the dance floor would break under them. Small boys
romped around like goats, and little girls whirled about wildly together. Many of the men were already drunk. They shouted boasts,
howled with laughter, kissed strange women. There was so much
commotion that Solomon Margolin could no longer grasp what was
being said to him and simply nodded yes to everything. Some of the
guests had attached themselves to him, wouldn't move, and kept

pulling him in all directions, introducing him to more and more people from Sencimin and Tereshpol. A matron with a nose covered with warts pointed a finger at him, wiped her eyes, called him Schloimele. Solomon Margolin inquired who she was and somebody told him. Names were swallowed up in the tumult. He heard the same words over and over again: died, shot, burned. A man from Tereshpol tried to draw him aside and was shouted down by several Senciminers calling him an intruder who had no business there. A latecomer arrived, a horse and buggy driver from Sencimin who had become a millionaire in New York. His wife and children had perished, but already, he had a new wife. The woman, weighted with diamonds, paraded about in a low-cut gown that bared a back, covered with blotches, to the waist. Her voice was husky. "Where did she come from? Who was she?" "Certainly no saint. Her first husband was a swindler who amassed a fortune and then dropped dead. Of what? Cancer. Where? In the stomach. First you don't have anything to eat, then you don't have anything to eat it with. A man is always working for the second husband." "What is life anyway? A dance on the grave." "Yes, but as long as you're playing the game, you have to abide by the rules." "Dr. Margolin, why aren't you dancing? You're not among strangers. We're all from the same dust. Over there you weren't a doctor. You were only Schloime-Dovid, the son of the Talmud teacher. Before you know it, we'll all be lying side by side."

Margolin didn't recall drinking anything but he felt intoxicated all the same. The foggy hall was spinning like a carousel; the floor was rocking. Standing in a corner, he contemplated the dance. What different expressions the dancers wore. How many combinations and permutations of being, the Creator had brought together here. Every face told its own story. They were dancing together, these people, but each one had his own philosophy, his own approach. A man grabbed Margolin and for a while he danced in the frantic whirl. Then, tearing himself loose, he stood apart. Who was that woman? He found his eye caught by her familiar form. He knew her! She beckoned to him. He stood baffled. She looked neither young nor old. Where had he known her—that narrow face, those dark eyes, that girlish smile? Her hair was arranged in the old manner, with long braids wound like a wreath around her head. The grace of Sencimin adorned her—something he, Margolin, had long since forgotten. And those eyes, he was in love with those eyes and had been all his life. He half smiled at her and the woman smiled back. There were dimples in her cheeks. She too appeared surprised. Margolin, though he realized he had begun to blush like a boy, went up to her.

"I know you — but you're not from Sencimin?"

"Yes, from Sencimin."

He had heard that voice long ago. He had been in love with that voice.

"From Sencimin — who are you, then?"

Her lips trembled.

"You've forgotten me already?"

"It's a long time since I left Sencimin."

"You used to visit my father."

"Who was your father?"

"Melekh the watchmaker."

Dr. Margolin shivered.

"If I'm not out of my mind then I'm seeing things."

"Why do you say that?"

"Because Raizel is dead."

"I'm Raizel."

"You're Raizel? Here? Oh my God, if that's true — then anything is possible! When did you come to New York?"

"Some time ago."

"From where?"

"From over there."

"But everyone told me that you were all dead."

"My father, my mother, my brother Hershl . . ."

"But you were married!"

"I was."

"If that's true, then anything is possible!" repeated Dr. Margolin, still shaken by the incredible happening. Someone must have purposely deceived him. But why? He was aware there was a mistake somewhere but could not determine where.

"Why didn't you let me know? After all . . ."

He fell silent. She too was silent for a moment.

"I lost everything. But I still had some pride left."

"Come with me somewhere quieter — anywhere. This is the happiest day of my life!"

"But it's night . . ."

"Then the happiest night! Almost — as if the Messiah had come, as if the dead had come to life!"

"Where do you want to go? All right, let's go."

Margolin took her arm and felt at once the thrill, long forgotten, of youthful desire. He steered her away from the other guests, afraid that he might lose her in the crowd, or that someone would break in and spoil his happiness. Everything had returned on the instant: the embarrassment, the agitation, the joy. He wanted to take her away, to hide somewhere alone with her. Leaving the reception hall, they went upstairs to the chapel where the wedding ceremony was to take place. The door was standing open. Inside, on a raised platform stood the permanent wedding canopy. A bottle of wine and a silver goblet were placed in readiness for the ceremony. The chapel with its empty pews and only one glimmering light was full of shadows. The music, so blaring below, sounded soft and distant up here. Both of them hesitated at the threshold. Margolin pointed to the wedding canopy.

"We could have stood there."

"Yes."

"Tell me about yourself. Where are you now? What are you doing?"

"It is not easy to tell."

"Are you alone? Are you attached?"

"Attached? No."

"Would you never have let me hear from you?" he asked. She didn't answer.

Gazing at her, he knew his love had returned with full force. Already, he was trembling at the thought that they might soon have to part. The excitement and expectancy of youth filled him. He wanted to take her in his arms and kiss her, but at any moment someone might come in. He stood beside her, ashamed that he had married someone else, that he had not personally confirmed the reports of her death. "How could I have suppressed all this love? How could I have accepted the world without her? And what will happen now with Gretl? — I'll give her everything, my last cent." He looked round toward the stairway to see if any of the guests had started to come up. The thought came to him that by Jewish law he was not married, for he and Gretl had only a civil ceremony. He looked at Raizel.

"According to Jewish law, I'm a single man."

"Is that so?"

"According to Jewish law, I could lead you up there and marry you."

She seemed to be considering the import of his words.

"Yes, I realize . . ."

"According to Jewish law, I don't even need a ring. One can get married with a penny."

"Do you have a penny?"

He put his hand to his breast pocket, but his wallet was gone. He started searching in his other pockets. Have I been robbed? he wondered. But how? I was sitting in the taxi the whole time. Could someone have robbed me here at the wedding? He was not so much disturbed as surprised. He said falteringly:

"Strange, but I don't have any money."

"We'll get along without it."

"But how am I going to get home?"

"Why go home?" she said, countering with a question. She smiled with that familiar smile of hers that was so full of mystery. He took her by the wrist and gazed at her. Suddenly it occurred to him that this could not be his Raizel. She was too young. Probably it was her daughter who was playing along with him, mocking him. For God's sake, I'm completely confused! he thought. He stood bewildered, trying to untangle the years. He couldn't tell her age from her features. Her eyes were deep, dark, and melancholy. She also appeared confused, as if she, too, sensed some discrepancy. The whole thing is a mistake, Margolin told himself. But where exactly was the mistake? And what had happened to the wallet? Could he have left it in the taxi after paying the driver? He tried to remember how much cash he had had in it, but was unable to. "I must have had too much to drink. These people have made me drunk — dead drunk!" For a long time he stood silent, lost in some dreamless state, more profound than a narcotic trance. Suddenly he remembered the traffic collision he had witnessed on Eastern Parkway. An eerie suspicion came over him: Perhaps he had been more than a witness? Perhaps he himself had been the victim of that accident! He began to examine himself as though he were one of his own patients. He could find no trace of pulse or breathing. And he felt oddly deflated as if some physical dimension were missing. The sensation of weight, the muscular tension of his limbs, the hidden aches in his bones, all seemed to be gone. It can't be, it can't be, he murmured. Can one die without knowing it? And what will Gretl do? He blurted out:

"You're not the same Raizel."

"No? Then who am I?"

"Unless we're both dead."

"What do you mean?"

"They shot Raizel."

"Shot her? Who told you that?"

She seemed both frightened and confused. Silently she lowered her head like someone receiving the shock of bad news. Dr. Margolin continued to ponder. Apparently Raizel didn't realize her own condition. He had heard of such a stage—what was it called? Hovering in the World of Twilight. But death couldn't be that simple. This kind of survival would be less than oblivion.

He leaned over and whispered in her ear: "What's the difference? As long as we're together." "I've been waiting for that all these years."

"Where have you been?"

She didn't answer, and he didn't ask again. He looked around. The empty hall was full, all the seats taken. A ceremonious hush fell over the audience. The music played softly. The cantor intoned the benedictions. With measured steps, Abraham Mekheles led his daughter down the aisle.

Tell Me a Riddle

TILLIE OLSEN

Tillie Olsen (1913–): *Tillie Olsen was born Tillie Lerner in Omaha, Nebraska, the daughter of Russian immigrants who had fled Europe after the 1905 rebellion. Her father was state secretary of the Nebraska Socialist party, and Olsen inherited her parents' political commitment, becoming involved in labor organizing efforts in the Midwest at an early age. In the 1930s she moved to California, wrote her first fiction (including the beginning of her novel,* Yonnondio*), and continued her work in the labor movement. She married and began to raise a family, meanwhile supporting herself at a succession of low-paying jobs. In the late 1950s she won a fellowship to Stanford, which allowed her to resume her writing career. Over the next few years she completed the stories of her first published book,* Tell Me a Riddle*, the title story of which won an O. Henry Prize.* Tell Me a Riddle *appeared when Olsen was nearly fifty, to general critical acclaim. In the following years, Olsen received fellowships from the Radcliffe Foundation, the National Endowment for the Arts, and the MacDowell Colony and taught at Amherst, the University of Massachusetts—Boston, Stanford, and M.I.T. Her impact as a feminist—both as a writer and as an educator— has been significant. Her other books are* Yonnondio: From the Thirties, *a feminist working-class novel which Olsen originally began in the 1930s but did not finish for forty years, and* Silences, *a work of nonfiction about the tragic difficulties of writers who have been "silenced" by the hardships (political, economic, or gender-related) of their lives.*

1

For forty-seven years they had been married. How deep back the stubborn, gnarled roots of the quarrel reached, no one could say — but only now, when tending to the needs of others no longer shackled them together, the roots swelled up visible, split the earth between them, and the tearing shook even to the children, long since grown.

Why now, why now? wailed Hannah.

As if when we grew up weren't enough, said Paul.

Poor Ma. Poor Dad. It hurts so for both of them, said Vivi. They never had very much? at least in old age they should be happy.

Knock their heads together, insisted Sammy; tell 'em: you're too old for this kind of thing; no reason not to get along now.

Lennie wrote to Clara: They've lived over so much together; what could possibly tear them apart?

Something tangible enough.

Arthritic hands, and such work as he got, occasional. Poverty all his life, and there was little breath left for running. He could not, could not turn away from this desire: to have the troubling of responsibility, the fretting with money, over and done with; to be free, to be *care*free where success was not measured by accumulation, and there was use for the vitality still in him.

There was a way. They could sell the house, and with the money join his lodge's Haven, cooperative for the aged. Happy communal life, and was he not already an official; had he not helped organize it, raise funds, served as a trustee?

But she — would not consider it.

"What do we need all this for?" he would ask loudly, for her hearing aid was turned down and the vacuum was shrilling. "Five rooms" (pushing the sofa so she could get into the corner) "furniture" (smoothing down the rug) "floors and surfaces to make work. Tell me, why do we need it?" And he was glad he could ask in a scream.

"Because I'm use't."

"Because you're use't. This is a reason, Mrs. Word Miser? Used to can get unused!"

"Enough unused I have to get used to already. . . . Not enough words?" turning off the vacuum a moment to hear herself answer. "Because soon enough we'll need only a little closet, no windows, no furniture, nothing to make work, but for worms. Because now I want room. . . . Screech and blow like you're doing, you'll need that closet even sooner. . . . Ha, again!" for the vacuum bag wailed, puffed half up, hung stubbornly limp. "This time fix it so it stays; quick before the phone rings and you get too important-busy."

But while he struggled with the motor, it seethed in him. Why fix it? Why have to bother? And if it can't be fixed, have to wring the mind with how to pay the repair? At the Haven they come in with their own machines to clean your room or your cottage; you fish, or play cards, or make jokes in the sun, not with knotty fingers fight to mend vacuums.

Over the dishes, coaxingly: "For once in your life, to be free, to have everything done for you, like a queen."

"I never liked queens."

"No dishes, no garbage, no towel to sop, no worry what to buy, what to eat."

"And what else would I do with my empty hands? Better to eat at my own table when I want, and to cook and eat how I want."

"In the cottages they buy what you ask, and cook it how you like. *You* are the one who always used to say: better mankind born without mouths and stomachs than always to worry for money to buy, to shop, to fix, to cook, to wash, to clean."

"How cleverly you hid that you heard. I said it then because eighteen hours a day I ran. And you never scraped a carrot or knew a dish towel sops. Now—for you and me—who cares? A herring out of a jar is enough. But when *I* want, and nobody to bother." And she turned off her ear button, so she would not have to hear.

But as *he* had no peace, juggling and rejuggling the money to figure: how will I pay for this now?; prying out the storm windows (there they take care of this); jolting in the streetcar on errands (there I would not have to ride to take care of this or that); fending the patronizing relatives just back from Florida (at the Haven it matters what one is, not what one can afford), he gave *her* no peace.

"Look! In their bulletin. A reading circle. Twice a week it meets."

"Haumm," her answer of not listening.

"A reading circle. Chekhov they read that you like, and Peretz. Cultured people at the Haven that you would enjoy."

"Enjoy!" She tasted the word. "Now, when it pleases you, you find a reading circle for me. And forty years ago when the children were morsels and there was a Circle, did you stay home with them once so I could go? Even once? You trained me well. I do not need others to enjoy. Others!" Her voice trembled. "Because *you* want to be there with others. Already it makes me sick to think of you always around others. Clown, grimacer, floormat, yesman, entertainer, whatever they want of you."

And now it was he who turned on the television loud so he need not hear.

Old scar tissue ruptured and the wounds festered anew. Chekhov indeed. She thought without softness of that young wife, who in the deep night hours while she nursed the current baby, and perhaps held another in her lap, would try to stay awake for the only time there was to read. She would feel again the weather of the outside on his cheek when, coming late from a meeting, he would find her so, and stimulated and ardent, sniffing her skin, coax: "I'll put the baby to bed, and you—put the book away, don't read, don't read."

That had been the most beguiling of all the "don't read, put your book away" her life had been. Chekhov indeed!

"Money?" She shrugged him off. "Could we get poorer than once we were? And in America, who starves?"

But as still he pressed:

"Let me alone about money. Was there ever enough? Seven little ones—for every penny I had to ask—and sometimes, remember, there was nothing. But always *I* had to manage. Now *you* manage. Rub your nose in it good."

But from those years she had had to manage, old humiliations and terrors rose up, lived again, and forced her to relive them. The children's needings; that grocer's face or this merchant's wife she had had to beg credit from when credit was a disgrace; the scenery of the long blocks walked around when she could not pay; school coming, and the desperate going over the old to see what could yet be remade? the soups of meat bones begged "for-the-dog" one winter. . . .

Enough. Now they had no children. Let *him* wrack his head for how they would live. She would not exchange her solitude for any-thing. *Never again to be forced to move to the rhythms of others.*

For in this solitude she had won to a reconciled peace.

Tranquillity from having the empty house no longer an enemy, for it stayed clean—not as in the days when it was her family, the life in it, that had seemed the enemy: tracking, smudging, littering, dirtying, engaging her in endless defeating battle—and on whom her endless defeat had been spewed.

The few old books, memorized from rereading; the pictures to ponder (the magnifying glass superimposed on her heavy eye-glasses). Or if she wishes, when he is gone, the phonograph, that if she turns up very loud and strains, she can hear: the ordered sounds and the struggling.

Out in the garden, growing things to nurture. Birds to be kept out of the pear tree, and when the pears are heavy and ripe, the old fury of work, for all must be canned, nothing wasted.

And her one social duty (for she will not go to luncheons or meetings) the boxes of old clothes left with her, as with a life-practiced eye for finding what is still wearable within the worn (again the magnifying glass superimposed on the heavy glasses) she scans and sorts—this for rag or rummage, that for mending and cleaning, and this for sending away.

Being able at last to live within, and not move to the rhythms of others, as life had forced her to: denying; removing; isolating; taking the children one by one; then deafening, half-blinding—and at last, presenting her solitude.

And in it she had won to a reconciled peace.

Now he was violating it with his constant campaigning: *Sell the house and move to the Haven.* (You sit, you sit—there too you could sit like a stone.) He was making of her a battleground where old grievances torc. (Turn on your ear button—I am talking.) And stubbornly she resisted—so that from wheedling, reasoning, manipulation, it was bitterness he now started with.

And it came to where every happening lashed up a quarrel.

"I will sell the house anyway," he flung at her one night. "I am putting it up for sale. There will be a way to make you sign."

The television blared, as always it did on the evenings he stayed home, and as always it reached her only as noise. She did not know if the tumult was in her or outside. Snap! she turned the sound off. "Shadows," she whispered to him, pointing to the screen, "look, it is only shadows." And in a scream: "Did you say that you will sell the house? Look at me, not at that. I am no shadow. You cannot sell without me."

"Leave on the television. I am watching."

"Like Paulie, like Jenny, a four-year-old. Staring at shadows. *You cannot sell the house.*"

"I will. We are going to the Haven. There you would not hear the television when you do not want it. I could sit in the social room and watch. You could lock yourself up to smell your unpleasantness in a room by yourself—for who would want to come near you?"

"No, no selling." A whisper now.

"The television is shadows. Mrs. Enlightened! Mrs. Cultured! A world comes into your house—and it is shadows. People you would never meet in a thousand lifetimes. Wonders. When you were four years old, yes, like Paulie, like Jenny, did you know of Indian dances, alligators, how they use bamboo in Malaya? No, you scratched in your dirt with the chickens and thought Olshana was the world. Yes,

Mrs. Unpleasant, I will sell the house, for there better can we be rid of each other than here."

She did not know if the tumult was outside, or in her. Always a ravening inside, a pull to the bed, to lie down, to succumb.

"Have you thought maybe Ma should let a doctor have a look at her?" asked their son Paul after Sunday dinner, regarding his mother crumpled on the couch, instead of, as was her custom, busying herself in Nancy's kitchen.

"Why not the President too?"

"Seriously, Dad. This is the third Sunday she's lain down like that after dinner. Is she that way at home?"

"A regular love affair with the bed. Every time I start to talk to her."

Good protective reaction, observed Nancy to herself. The workings of hos-til-ity.

"Nancy could take her. I just don't like how she looks. Let's have Nancy arrange an appointment."

"You think she'll go?" regarding his wife gloomily. "All right, we have to have doctor bills, we have to have doctor bills." Loudly: "Something hurts you?"

She startled, looked to his lips. He repeated: "Mrs. Take It Easy, something hurts?"

"Nothing. . . . Only you."

"A woman of honey. That's why you're lying down?"

"Soon I'll get up to do the dishes, Nancy."

"Leave them, Mother, I like it better this way."

"Mrs. Take It Easy, Paul says you should start ballet. You should go to see a doctor and ask: how soon can you start ballet?"

"A doctor?" she begged. "Ballet?"

"We were talking, Ma," explained Paul, "you don't seem any too well. It would be a good idea for you to see a doctor for a checkup."

"I get up now to do the kitchen. Doctors are bills and foolishness, my son. I need no doctors."

"At the Haven," he could not resist pointing out, "a doctor is *not* bills. He lives beside you. You start to sneeze, he is there before you open up a Kleenex. You can be sick there for free, all you want."

"Diarrhea of the mouth, is there a doctor to make you dumb?"

"Ma. Promise me you'll go. Nancy will arrange it."

"It's all of a piece when you think of it," said Nancy, "the way she attacks my kitchen, scrubbing under every cup hook, doing the inside of the oven so I can't enjoy Sunday dinner, knowing that half-blind or not, she's going to find every speck of dirt. . . ."

"Don't, Nancy, I've told you — it's the only way she knows to be useful. What did the *doctor* say?"

"A real fatherly lecture. Sixty-nine is young these days. Go out, enjoy life, find interests. Get a new hearing aid, this one is antiquated. Old age is sickness only if one makes it so. Geriatrics, Inc."

"So there was nothing physical."

"Of course there was. How can you live to yourself like she does without there being? Evidence of a kidney disorder, and her blood count is low. He gave her a diet, and she's to come back for follow-up and lab work. . . . But he was clear enough: Number One prescription — start living like a human being. . . . When I think of your dad, who could really play the invalid with that arthritis of his, as active as a teenager, and twice as much fun. . . ."

"You didn't tell me the doctor says your sickness is in you, how you live." He pushed his advantage. "Life and enjoyments you need better than medicine. And this diet, how can you keep it? To weigh each morsel and scrape away each bit of fat, to make this soup, that pudding. There, at the Haven, they have a dietician, they would do it for you."

She is silent.

"You would feel better there, I know it," he says gently. "There there is life and enjoyments all around."

"What is the matter, Mr. Importantbusy, you have no card game or meeting you can go to?" — turning her face to the pillow.

For a while he cut his meetings and going out, fussed over her diet, tried to wheedle her into leaving the house, brought in visitors:

"I should come to a fashion tea. I should sit and look at pretty babies in clothes I cannot buy. This is pleasure?"

"Always you are better than everyone else. The doctor said you should go out. Mrs. Brem comes to you with goodness and you turn her away."

"Because *you* asked her to, she asked me."

"They won't come back. People you need, the doctor said. Your own cousins I asked; they were willing to come and make peace as if nothing had happened. . . ."

"No more crushers of people, pushers, hypocrites, around me. No more in my house. You go to them if you like."

"Kind he is to visit. And you, like ice."
"A babbler. All my life around babblers. Enough!"

"She's even worse, Dad? Then let her stew a while," advised Nancy. "You can't let it destroy you; it's a psychological thing, maybe too far gone for any of us to help."

So he let her stew. More and more she lay silent in bed, and sometimes did not even get up to make the meals. No longer was the tongue-lashing inevitable if he left the coffee cup where it did not belong, or forgot to take out the garbage or mislaid the broom. The birds grew bold that summer and for once pocked the pears, undisturbed.

A bellyful of bitterness and every day the same quarrel in a new way and a different old grievance the quarrel forced her to enter and relive. And the new torment: I am not really sick, the doctor said it, then why do I feel so sick?

One night she asked him: "You have a meeting tonight? Do not go. Stay . . . with me."

He had planned to watch "This Is Your Life," but half sick himself from the heavy heat, and sickening therefore the more after the brooks and woods of the Haven, with satisfaction he grated:

"Hah, Mrs. Live Alone And Like It wants company all of a sudden. It doesn't seem so good the time of solitary when she was a girl exile in Siberia. 'Do not go. Stay with me.' A new song for Mrs. Free As A Bird. Yes, I am going out, and while I am gone chew this aloneness good, and think how you keep us both from where if you want people, you do not need to be alone."

"Go, go. All your life you have gone without me."

After him she sobbed curses he had not heard in years, old-country curses from their childhood: Grow, oh shall you grow like an onion, with your head in the ground. Like the hide of a drum shall you be, beaten in life, beaten in death. Oh shall you be like a chandelier, to hang, and to burn. . . .

She was not in their bed when he came back. She lay on the cot on the sun porch. All week she did not speak or come near him; nor did he try to make peace or care for her.

He slept badly, so used to her next to him. After all the years, old harmonies and dependencies deep in their bodies; she curled to him, or he coiled to her, each warmed, warming, turning as the other turned, the nights a long embrace.

It was not the empty bed or the storm that woke him, but a faint singing. *She* was singing. Shaking off the drops of rain, the lightning riving her lifted face, he saw her so; the cot covers on the floor.

"This is a private concert?" he asked. "Come in, you are wet."

"I can breathe now," she answered; "my lungs are rich." Though indeed the sound was hardly a breath.

"Come in, come in." Loosing the bamboo shades. "Look how wet you are." Half helping, half carrying her, still faint-breathing her song.

A Russian love song of fifty years ago.

He had found a buyer, but before he told her, he called together those children who were close enough to come. Paul, of course, Sammy from New Jersey, Hannah from Connecticut, Vivi from Ohio.

With a kindling of energy for her beloved visitors, she arrayed the house, cooked and baked. She was not prepared for the solemn after-dinner conclave, they too probing in and tearing. Her frightened eyes watched from mouth to mouth as each spoke.

His stories were eloquent and funny of her refusal to go back to the doctor; of the scorned invitations; of her stubborn silence or the bile "like a Niagara"; of her contrariness: "If I clean it's no good how I cleaned; if I don't clean, I'm still a master who thinks he has a slave."

(Vinegar he poured on me all his life; I am well marinated; how can I be honey now?)

Deftly he marched in the rightness for moving to the Haven; their money from social security free for visiting the children, not sucked into daily needs and into the house; the activities in the Haven for him; but mostly the Haven for *her:* her health, her need of care, distraction, amusement, friends who shared her interests.

"This does offer an outlet for Dad," said Paul; "he's always been an active person. And economic peace of mind isn't to be sneezed at, either. I could use a little of that myself."

But when they asked: "And you, Ma, how do you feel about it?" could only whisper:

"For him it is good. It is not for me. I can no longer live between people."

"You lived all your life *for* people," Vivi cried.

"Not with." Suffering doubly for the unhappiness on her children's faces.

"You have to find some compromise," Sammy insisted. "Maybe sell the house and buy a trailer. After forty-seven years there's surely some way you can find to live in peace."

"There is no help, my children. Different things we need."

"Then live alone!" He could control himself no longer. "I have a buyer for the house. Half the money for you, half for me. Either alone or with me to the Haven. You think I can live any longer as we are doing now?"

"Ma doesn't have to make a decision this minute, however you feel, Dad," Paul said quickly, "and you wouldn't want her to. Let's let it lay a few months, and then talk some more."

"I think I can work it out to take Mother home with me for a while," Hannah said. "You both look terrible, but especially you, Mother. I'm going to ask Phil to have a look at you."

"Sure," cracked Sammy. "What's the use of a doctor husband if you can't get free service out of him once in a while for the family? And absence might make the heart . . . you know."

"There was something after all," Paul told Nancy in a colorless voice. "That was Hannah's Phil calling. Her gall bladder. . . . Surgery."

"Her *gall* bladder. If that isn't classic. 'Bitter as gall' — talk of psychosom — "

He stepped closer, put his hand over her mouth, and said in the same colorless, plodding voice. "We have to get Dad. They operated at once. The cancer was everywhere, surrounding the liver, everywhere. They did what they could . . . at best she has a year. Dad . . . we have to tell him."

2

Honest in his weakness when they told him, and that she was not to know. "I'm not an actor. She'll know right away by how I am. Oh that poor woman. I am old too, it will break me into pieces. Oh that poor woman. She will spit on me: 'So my sickness was how I live.' Oh Paulie, how she will be, that poor woman. Only she should not suffer. . . . I can't stand sickness, Paulie, I can't go with you."

But went. And play-acted.

"A grand opening and you did not even wait for me. . . . A good thing Hannah took you with her."

"Fashion teas I needed. They cut out what tore in me; just in my throat something hurts yet. . . . Look! so many flowers, like a funeral. Vivi called, did Hannah tell you? And Lennie from San Francisco, and Clara; and Sammy is coming." Her gnome's face pressed happily into the flowers.

It is impossible to predict in these cases, but once over the immediate effects of the operation, she should have several months of comparative well-being.

The money, where will come the money?

Travel with her, Dad. Don't take her home to the old associations. The other children will want to see her.

The money, where will I wring the money?

Whatever happens, she is not to know. No, you can't ask her to sign papers to sell the house; nothing to upset her. Borrow instead, then after. . . .

I had wanted to leave you each a few dollars to make life easier, as other fathers do. There will be nothing left now. (Failure! you and your "business is exploitation." Why didn't you make it when it could be made?—Is that what you're thinking of me, Sammy?)

Sure she's unreasonable, Dad—but you have to stay with her; if there's to be any happiness in what's left of her life, it depends on you.

Prop me up, children, think of me, too. Shuffled, chained with her, bitter woman. No Haven, and the little money going. . . . How happy she looks, poor creature.

The look of excitement. The straining to hear everything (the new hearing aid turned full). Why are you so happy, dying woman?

How the petals are, fold on fold, and the gladioli color. The autumn air.

Stranger grandsons, tall above the little gnome grandmother, the little spry grandfather. Paul in a frenzy of picture-taking before going.

She, wandering the great house. Feeling the books; laughing at the maple shoemaker's bench of a hundred years ago used as a table. The ear turned to music.

"Let us go home. See how good I walk now." "One step from the hospital," he answers, "and she wants to fly. Wait till Doctor Phil says."

"Look — the birds too are flying home. Very good Phil is and will not show it, but he is sick of sickness by the time he comes home."

"Mrs. Telepathy, to read minds," he answers; "read mine what it says: when the trunks of medicines become a suitcase, then we will go."

The grandboys, they do not know what to say to us. . . . Hannah, she runs around here, there, when is there time for herself?

Let us go home. Let us go home.

Musing; gentleness — *but for the incidents of the rabbi in the hospital, and of the candles of benediction.*

Of the rabbi in the hospital:

Now tell me what happened, Mother.

From the sleep I awoke, Hannah's Phil, and he stands there like a devil in a dream and calls me by name. I cannot hear. I think he prays. Go away, please, I tell him, I am not a believer. Still he stands, while my heart knocks with fright.

You scared *him*, Mother. He thought you were delirious.

Who sent him? Why did he come to me?

It is a custom. The men of God come to visit those of their religion they might help. The hospital makes up the list for them — race, religion — and you are on the Jewish list.

Not for rabbis. At once go and make them change. Tell them to write: Race, human; Religion, none.

And of the candles of benediction:

Look how you have upset yourself, Mrs. Excited Over Nothing. Pleasant memories you should leave.

Go in, go back to Hannah and the lights. Two weeks I saw candles and said nothing. But she asked me.

So what was so terrible? She forgets you never did, she asks you to light the Friday candles and say the benediction like Phil's mother when she visits. If the candles give her pleasure, why shouldn't she have the pleasure?

Not for pleasure she does it. For emptiness. Because his family does. Because all around her do.

That is not a good reason too? But you did not hear her. For heritage, she told you. For the boys, from the past they should have tradition.

Superstition! From our ancestors, savages, afraid of the dark, of themselves: mumbo words and magic lights to scare away ghosts.

She told you: how it started does not take away the goodness. For centuries, peace in the house it means.

Swindler! does she look back on the dark centuries? Candles bought instead of bread and stuck into a potato for a candlestick? Religion that stifled and said: in Paradise, woman, you will be the footstool of your husband, and in life — poor chosen Jew — ground under, despised, trembling in cellars. And cremated. And cremated.

This is religion's fault? You think you are still an orator of the 1905 revolution? Where are the pills for quieting? Which are they?

Heritage. How have we come from our savage past, how no longer to be savages — this to teach. To look back and learn what humanizes — this to teach. To smash all ghettos that divide us — not to go back, not to go back — this to teach. Learned books in the house, will humankind live or die, and she gives to her boys — superstition.

Hannah that is so good to you. Take your pill, Mrs. Excited For Nothing, swallow.

Heritage! But when did I have time to teach? Of Hannah I asked only hands to help.

Swallow.

Otherwise — musing; gentleness.

Not to travel. To go home.

The children want to see you. We have to show them you are as thorny a flower as ever.

Not to travel.

Vivi wants you should see her new baby. She sent the tickets — airplane tickets — a Mrs. Roosevelt she wants to make of you. To Vivi's we have to go.

A new baby. How many warm, seductive babies. She holds him stiffly, *away* from her, so that he wails. And a long shudder begins, and the sweat beads on her forehead.

"Hush, shush," croons the grandfather, lifting him back. "You should forgive your grand-mamma, little prince, she has never held a baby before, only seen them in glass cases. Hush, shush."

"You're tired, Ma," says Vivi. "The travel and the noisy dinner. I'll take you to lie down."

(A long travel from, to, what the feel of a baby evokes.)

In the airplane, cunningly designed to encase from motion (no wind, no feel of flight), she had sat severely and still, her face turned to the sky through which they cleaved and left no scar.

So this was how it looked, the determining, the crucial sky, and this was how man moved through it, remote above the dwindled earth, the concealed human life. Vulnerable life, that could scar.

There was a steerage ship of memory that shook across a great circular sea: clustered, ill human beings; and through the thick-stained air, tiny fretting waters in a window round like the airplane's — sun round, moon round. (The round thatched roofs of Olshana.) Eye round — like the smaller window that framed distance the solitary year of exile when only her eyes could travel and no voice spoke. And the polar winds hurled themselves across snows trackless and endless and white — like the clouds which had closed together below and hidden the earth.

Now they put the baby in her lap. Do not ask me, she would have liked to beg. Enough the worn face of Vivi, the remembered grandchildren. I cannot, cannot. . . .

Cannot what? Unnatural grandmother, not able to make herself embrace a baby.

She lay there in the bed of the two little girls, her new hearing aid turned full, listening to the sound of the children going to sleep, the baby's fretful crying and hushing, the clatter of dishes being washed and put away. They thought she slept. Still she rode on.

It was not that she had not loved her babies, her children. The love — the passion of tending — had risen with the need like a torrent; and like a torrent drowned and immolated all else. But when the need was done — oh the power that was lost in the painful damming back and drying up of what still surged, but had nowhere to go. Only the thin pulsing left that could not quiet, suffering over lives one felt, but could no longer hold nor help.

On that torrent she had borne them to their own lives, and the riverbed was desert long years now. Not there would she dwell, a memoried wraith. Surely that was not all, surely there was more. Still the springs, the springs were in her seeking. Somewhere an older power that beat for life. Somewhere coherence, transport, meaning. If they would but leave her in the air now stilled of clamor, in the reconciled solitude, to journey on.

And they put a baby in her lap. Immediacy to embrace, and the breath of *that* past: warm flesh like this that had claims and nuzzled away all else and with lovely mouths devoured; hot-living like an animal — intensely and now; the turning maze; the long drunkenness; the drowning into needing and being needed. Severely she looked back — and the shudder seized her again, and the sweat. Not that way. Not there, not now could she, not yet. . . .

And all that visit, she could not touch the baby.

"Daddy, is it the . . . sickness she's like that?" asked Vivi. "I was so glad to be having the baby — for her. I told Tim, it'll give her more happiness than anything, being around a baby again. And she hasn't played with him once."

He was not listening, "Aahh little seed of life, little charmer," he crooned, "Hollywood should see you. A heart of ice you would melt. Kick, kick. The future you'll have for a ball. In 2050 still kick. Kick for your grandaddy then."

Attentive with the older children; sat through their performances (command performance; we command you to be the audience); helped Ann sort autumn leaves to find the best for a school program; listened gravely to Richard tell about his rock collection, while her lips mutely formed the words to remember: *igneous, sedimentary, metamorphic;* looked for missing socks, books, and bus tickets; watched the children whoop after their grandfather who knew how to tickle, chuck, lift, toss, do tricks, tell secrets, make jokes, match riddle for riddle. (Tell me a riddle, Grammy. I know no riddles, child.) Scrubbed sills and woodwork and furniture in every room; folded the laundry; straightened drawers; emptied the heaped baskets waiting for ironing (while he or Vivi or Tim nagged: You're supposed to rest here, you've been sick) but to none tended or gave food — and could not touch the baby.

After a week she said: "Let us go home. Today call about the tickets."

"You have important business, Mrs. Inahurry? The President waits to consult with you?" He shouted, for the fear of the future raced in him. "The clothes are still warm from the suitcase, your children cannot show enough how glad they are to see you, and you want home. There is plenty of time for home. We cannot be with the children at home."

"Blind to around you as always: the little ones sleep four in a room because we take their bed. We are two more people in a house with a new baby, and no help."

"Vivi is happy so. The children should have their grandparents a while, she told to me. I should have my mommy and daddy. . . ."

"Babbler and blind. Do you look at her so tired? How she starts to talk and she cries? I am not strong enough yet to help. Let us go home."

(To reconciled solitude.)

For it seemed to her the crowded noisy house was listening to her, listening for her. She could feel it like a great ear pressed under her heart. And everything knocked: quick constant raps: let me in, let me in.

How was it that soft reaching tendrils also became blows that knocked?

C'mon, Grandma, I want to show you. . . .

Tell me a riddle, Grandma. *(I know no riddles.)*

Look, Grammy, he's so dumb he can't even find his hands. (Dody and the baby on a blanket over the fermenting autumn mould.)

I made them — for you. (Ann) (Flat paper dolls with aprons that lifted on scalloped skirts that lifted on flowered pants; hair of yarn and great ringed questioning eyes.)

Watch me, Grandma. (Richard snaking up the tree, hanging exultant, free, with one hand at the top. Below Dody hunching over in pretend-cooking.) *(Climb too, Dody, climb and look.)*

Be my nap bed, Grammy. (The "No!" too late.) Morty's abandoned heaviness, while his fingers ladder up and down her hearing-aid cord to his drowsy chant: eentsiebeentsiespider. *(Children trust.)*

It's to start off your own rock collection, Grandma. That's a trilobite fossil, 200 million years old (millions of years on a boy's mouth) and that one's obsidian, black glass.

Knocked and knocked.

Mother, I *told* you the teacher said we had to bring it back all filled out this morning. Didn't you even ask Daddy? Then tell *me* which plan and I'll check it: evacuate or stay in the city or wait for you to come and take me away. (Seeing the look of straining to hear.) It's for Disaster, Grandma. *(Children trust.)*

Vivi in the maze of the long, the lovely drunkenness. The old old noises: baby sounds; screaming of a mother flayed to exasperation; children quarreling; children playing; singing; laughter.

And Vivi's tears and memories, spilling so fast, half the words not understood.

She had started remembering out loud deliberately, so her mother would know the past was cherished, still lived in her.

Nursing the baby: My friends marvel, and I tell them, oh it's easy to be such a cow. I remember how beautiful my mother seemed nursing my brother, and the milk just flows. . . . Was that Davy? It must have been Davy. . . .

Lowering a hem: How did you ever . . . when I think how you made everything we wore . . . Tim, just think, seven kids and Mommy sewed everything . . . do I remember you sang while you sewed? That white dress with the red apples on the skirt you fixed over for me, was it Hannah's or Clara's before it was mine?

Washing sweaters: Ma, I'll never forget, one of those days so nice you washed clothes outside; one of the first spring days it must have been. The bubbles just danced while you scrubbed, and we chased after, and you stopped to show us how to blow our own bubbles with green onion stalks . . . you always. . . .

"Strong onion, to still make you cry after so many years," her father said, to turn the tears into laughter.

While Richard bent over his homework: Where is it now, do we still have it, the Book of the Martyrs? It always seemed so, well — exalted, when you'd put it on the round table and we'd all look at it together; there was even a halo from the lamp. The lamp with the beaded fringe you could move up and down; they're in style again, pulley lamps like that, but without the fringe. You know the book I'm talking about, Daddy, the Book of the Martyrs, the first picture was a bust of Spartacus . . . Socrates? I wish there was something like that for the children, Mommy, to give them what you. . . . (And the tears splashed again.)

(What I intended and did not? Stop it, daughter, stop it, leave that time. And he, the hypocrite, sitting there with tears in his eyes — it was nothing to you then, nothing.)

. . . The time you came to school and I almost died of shame because of your accent and because I knew you knew I was ashamed; how could I? . . . Sammy's harmonica and you danced to it once, yes you did, you and Davy squealing in your arms. . . . That time you bundled us up and walked us down to the railway station to stay the night 'cause it was heated and we didn't have any coal, that winter of the strike, you didn't think I remembered that, did you, Mommy? . . . How you'd call us out to see the sunsets. . . .

Day after day, the spilling memories. Worse now, questions, too.

Even the grandchildren: Grandma, in the olden days, when you were little. . . .

It was the afternoons that saved.

While they thought she napped, she would leave the mosaic on the wall (of children's drawings, maps, calendars, pictures, Ann's cardboard dolls with their great ringed questioning eyes) and hunch in the girls' closet on the low shelf where the shoes stood, and the girls' dresses covered.

For that while she would painfully sheathe against the listening house, the tendrils and noises that knocked, and Vivi's spilling memories. Sometimes it helped to braid and unbraid the sashes that dangled, or to trace the pattern on the hoop slips.

Today she had jacks and children under jet trails to forget. Last night, Ann and Dody silhouetted in the window against a sunset of flaming man-made clouds of jet trail, their jacks ball accenting the peaceful noise of dinner being made. Had she told them, yes she had told them of how they played jacks in her village though there was no ball, no jacks. Six stones, round and flat, toss them out, the seventh on the back of the hand, toss, catch and swoop up as many as possible, toss again. . . . Of stones (repeating Richard) there are three kinds: earth's fire jetting; rock of layered centuries; crucibled new out of the old (*igneous, sedimentary, metamorphic*). But there was that other — frozen to black glass, never to transform or hold the fossil memory . . . (let not my seed fall on stone). There was an ancient man who fought to heights a great rock that crashed back down eternally — eternal labor, freedom, labor . . . (stone will perish, but the word remain). And you, David, who with a stone slew, screaming: Lord, take my heart of stone and give me flesh.

Who was screaming? Why was she back in the common room of the prison, the sun motes dancing in the shafts of light, and the informer being brought in, a prisoner now, like themselves. And Lisa leaping, yes, Lisa, the gentle and tender, biting at the betrayer's jugular. Screaming and screaming.

No, it is the children screaming. Another of Paul and Sammy's terrible fights?

In Vivi's house. Severely: you are in Vivi's house.

Blows, screams, a call: "Grandma!" For her? Oh please not for her. Hide, hunch behind the dresses deeper. But a trembling little body hurls itself beside her — surprised, smothered laughter, arms surround her neck, tears rub dry on her cheek, and words too soft to understand whisper into her ear (Is this where you hide too, Grammy? It's my secret place, we have a secret now).

And the sweat beads, and the long shudder seizes.

It seemed the great ear pressed inside now, and the knocking. "We have to go home," she told him, "I grow ill here."

"It's your own fault, Mrs. Bodybusy, you do not rest, you do too much." He raged, but the fear was in his eyes. "It was a serious operation, they told you to take care. . . . All right, we will go to where you can rest."

But where? Not home to death, not yet. He had thought to Lennie's, to Clara's; beautiful visits with each of the children. She would have to rest first, be stronger. If they could but go to Florida—it glittered before him, the never-realized promise of Florida. California: of course. (The money, the money, dwindling!) Los Angeles first for sun and rest, then to Lennie's in San Francisco.

He told her the next day. "You saw what Nancy wrote: snow and wind back home, a terrible winter. And look at you—all bones and a swollen belly. I called Phil: he said: 'A prescription, Los Angeles sun and rest.'"

She watched the words on his lips. "You have sold the house," she cried, "that is why we do not go home. That is why you talk no more of the Haven, why there is money for travel. After the children you will drag me to the Haven."

"The Haven! Who thinks of the Haven any more? Tell her, Vivi, tell Mrs. Suspicious: a prescription, sun and rest, to make you healthy. . . . And how could I sell the house without *you*?"

At the place of farewells and greetings, of winds of coming and winds of going, they say their good-byes.

They look back at her with the eyes of others before them: Richard with her own blue blaze; Ann with the nordic eyes of Tim; Morty's dreaming brown of a great-grandmother he will never know; Dody with the laughing eyes of him who had been her springtide love (who stands beside her now); Vivi's, all tears.

The baby's eyes are closed in sleep.

Good-bye, my children.

3

It is to the back of the great city he brought her, to the dwelling places of the cast-off old. Bounded by two lines of amusement piers to the north and to the south, and between a long straight paving rimmed with black benches facing the sand — sands so wide the ocean is only a far fluting.

In the brief vacation season, some of the boarded stores fronting the sands open, and families, young people and children, may be seen. A little tasselled tram shuttles between the piers, and the lights of roller coasters prink and tweak over those who come to have sensation made in them.

The rest of the year it is abandoned to the old, all else boarded up and still; seemingly empty, except the occasional days and hours when the sun, like a tide, sucks them out of the low rooming houses, casts them onto the benches and sandy rim of the walk — and sweeps them into decaying enclosures once again.

A few newer apartments glint among the low bleached squares. It is in one of these Lennie's Jeannie has arranged their rooms. "Only a few miles north and south people pay hundreds of dollars a month for just this gorgeous air, Grandaddy, just this ocean closeness."

She had been ill on the plane, lay ill for days in the unfamiliar room. Several times the doctor came by — left medicine she would not take. Several times Jeannie drove in the twenty miles from work, still in her Visiting Nurse uniform, the lightness and brightness of her like a healing.

"Who can believe it is winter?" he asked one morning. "Beautiful it is outside like an ad. Come, Mrs. Invalid, come to taste it. You are well enough to sit in here, you are well enough to sit outside. The doctor said it too."

But the benches were encrusted with people, and the sands at the sidewalk's edge. Besides, she had seen the far ruffle of the sea: "there take me," and though she leaned against him, it was she who led.

Plodding and plodding, sitting often to rest, he grumbling. Patting the sand so warm. Once she scooped up a handful, cradling it close to her better eye; peered, and flung it back. And as they came almost to the brink and she could see the glistening wet, she sat down, pulled off her shoes and stockings, left him and began to run. "You'll catch cold," he screamed, but the sand in his shoes weighed him down — he who had always been the agile one and already the white spray creamed her feet.

He pulled her back, took a handkerchief to wipe off the wet and the sand. "Oh no," she said, "the sun will dry," seized the square and smoothed it flat, dropped on it a mound of sand, knotted the kerchief corners and tied it to a bag—"to look at with the strong glass" (for the first time in years explaining an action of hers)—and lay down with the little bag against her cheek, looking toward the shore that nurtured life as it first crawled toward consciousness the millions of years ago.

He took her one Sunday in the evil-smelling bus, past flat miles of blister houses, to the home of relatives. Oh what is this? she cried as the light began to smoke and the houses to dim and recede. Smog, he said, everyone knows but you. . . . Outside he kept his arms about her, but she walked with hands pushing the heavy air as if to open it, whispered: who has done this? sat down suddenly to vomit at the curb and for a long while refused to rise.

One's age as seen on the altered face of those known in youth. Is this they he has come to visit? This Max and Rose, smooth and pleasant, introducing them to polite children, disinterested grandchildren, "the whole family, once a month on Sundays. And why not? We have the room, the help, the food."

Talk of cars, of houses, of success: this son that, that daughter this. And *your* children? Hastily skimped over, the intermarriages, the obscure work—"my doctor son-in-law, Phil"—all he has to offer. She silent in a corner. (Car-sick like a baby, he explains.) Years since he has taken her to visit anyone but the children, and old apprehensions prickle: "no incidents," he silently begs, "no incidents." He itched to tell them. "A very sick woman," significantly, indicating her with his eyes, "a very sick woman." Their restricted faces did not react. "Have you thought maybe she'd do better at Palm Springs?" Rose asked. "Or at least a nicer section of the beach, nicer people, a pool." Not to have to say "money" he said instead: "would she have sand to look at through a magnifying glass?" and went on, detail after detail, the old habit betraying of parading the queerness of her for laughter.

After dinner—the others into the living room in men- or women-clusters, or into the den to watch TV—the four of them alone. She sat close to him, and did not speak. Jokes, stories, people they had known, beginning of reminiscence, Russia fifty-sixty years ago. Strange words across the Duncan Phyfe table: *hunger; secret meetings; human rights; spies; betrayals; prison; escape*—interrupted by one of the grandchildren: "Commercial's on; any Coke left? Gee, you're missing a real hair-raiser." And then a granddaughter (Max proudly: "look at her, an American queen") drove them home on her way back to U.C.L.A. No incident — except that there had been no incidents.

The first few mornings she had taken with her the magnifying glass, but he would sit only on the benches, so she rested at the foot, where slatted bench shadows fell, and unless she turned her hearing aid down, other voices invaded.

Now on the days when the sun shone and she felt well enough, he took her on the tram to where the benches ranged in oblongs, some with tables for checkers or cards. Again the blanket on the sand in the striped shadows, but she no longer brought the magnifying glass. He played cards, and she lay in the sun and looked towards the waters; or they walked — two blocks down to the scaling hotel, two blocks back — past chili-hamburger stands, open-doored bars, Next-to-New and perpetual rummage sale stores.

Once, out of the aimless walkers, slow and shuffling like themselves, someone ran unevenly towards them, embraced, kissed, wept: "dear friends, old friends." A friend of *hers*, not his: Mrs. Mays who had lived next door to them in Denver when the children were small.

Thirty years are compressed into a dozen sentences; and the present, not even in three. All is told: the children scattered; the husband dead; she lives in a room two blocks up from the sing hall — and points to the domed auditorium jutting before the pier. The leg? phlebitis; the heavy breathing? that, one does not ask. She, too, comes to the benches each day to sit. And tomorrow, tomorrow, are they going to the community sing? Of course he would have heard of it, everybody goes — the big doings they wait for all week. They have never been? She will come to them for dinner tomorrow and they will all go together.

So it is that she sits in the wind of the singing, among the thousand various faces of age.

She had turned off her hearing aid at once they came into the auditorium — as she would have wished to turn off sight.

One by one they streamed by and imprinted on her — and though the savage zest of their singing came voicelessly soft and distant, the faces still roared — the faces densened the air — chorded into

children-chants, mother-croons, singing of the chained love serenades, Beethoven storms, mad Lucia's scream drunken joy-songs, keens for the dead, work-singing

while from floor to balcony to dome a bare-footed sore-covered little girl threaded the sound-thronged tumult, danced her ecstasy of grimace to flutes that scratched at a cross-roads village wedding

Yes, faces became sound, and the sound became faces; and faces and sound became weight—pushed, pressed

"Air" — her hands claw his.

"Whenever I enjoy myself. . . ." Then he saw the gray sweat on her face. "Here. Up. Help me, Mrs. Mays," and they support her out to where she can gulp the air in sob after sob.

"A doctor, we should get for her a doctor."

"Tch, it's nothing," says Ellen Mays, "I get it all the time. You've missed the tram; come to my place. Fix your hearing aid, honey . . . close . . . tea. My view. See, she *wants* to come. Steady now, that's how." Adding mysteriously: "Remember your advice, easy to keep your head above water, empty things float. Float."

The singing a fading march for them, tall woman with a swollen leg, weaving little man, and the swollen thinness they help between.

The stench in the hall: mildew? decay? "We sit and rest then climb. My gorgeous view. We help each other and here we are."

The stench along into the slab of room. A washstand for a sink, a box with oilcloth tacked around for a cupboard, a three-burner gas plate. Artificial flowers, colorless with dust. Everywhere pictures foaming: wedding, baby, party, vacation, graduation, family pictures. From the narrow couch under a slit of window, sure enough the view: lurching rooftops and a scallop of ocean heaving, preening, twitching under the moon.

"While the water heats. Excuse me . . . down the hall." Ellen Mays has gone.

"You'll live?" he asks mechanically, sat down to feel his fright; tried to pull her alongside.

She pushed him away. "For air," she said; stood clinging to the dresser. Then, in a terrible voice:

After a lifetime of room. Of many rooms.

Shhh.

You remember how she lived. Eight children. And now one room like a coffin.

She pays rent!

Shrinking the life of her   into one room   like a coffin   Rooms and rooms like this   I lie on the quilt and hear them talk

Please, Mrs. Orator-without-Breath.

Once you went for coffee   I walked   I saw   A Balzac   a Chekhov to write it   Rummage Alone   On scraps

Better old here than in the old country!

On scraps   Yet they sang like   like   Wondrous!   *Humankind   one has to believe*   So strong   for what? To rot   not grow?

Your poor lungs beg you. They sob between each word.

Singing.   Unused   the life in them.   She   in this poor room with her   pictures   Max   You   The children   Everywhere unused the life   And who has meaning?   Century after century   still all in us   not   to grow?

Coffins, rummage, plants: sick woman. Oh lay down. We will get for you the doctor.

"And when will it end. Oh, *the end.*" *That* nightmare thought, and this time she writhed, crumpled against him, seized his hand (for a moment again the weight, the soft distant roaring of humanity) and on the strangled-for breath, begged: "Man . . . we'll destroy ourselves?"

And looking for answer—in the helpless pity and fear for her (for *her*) that distorted his face—she understood the last months, and knew that she was dying.

4

"Let us go home," she said after several days.

"You are in training for a cross-country run? That is why you do not even walk across the room? Here, like a prescription Phil said, till you are stronger from the operation. You want to break doctor's orders?"

She saw the fiction was necessary to him, was silent; then: "At home I will get better. If the doctor here says?"

"And winter? And the visits to Lennie and to Clara? All right," for he saw the tears in her eyes, "I will write Phil, and talk to the doctor."

Days passed. He reported nothing. Jeannie came and took her out for air, past the boarded concessions, the hooded and tented amusement rides, to the end of the pier. They watched the spent waves feeding the new, the gulls in the clouded sky; even up where they sat, the wind-blown sand stung.

She did not ask to go down the crooked steps to the sea.

Back in her bed, while he was gone to the store, she said: "Jeannie, this doctor, he is not one I can ask questions. Ask him for me, can I go home?"

Jeannie looked at her, said quickly: "Of course, poor Granny. You want your own things around you, don't you? I'll call him tonight. . . . Look, I've something to show you," and from her purse unwrapped a large cookie, intricately shaped like a little girl. "Look at the curls — can you hear me well, Granny? — and the darling eyelashes. I just came from a house where they were baking them."

"The dimples, there in the knees," she marveled, holding it to the better light, turning, studying, "like art. Each singly they cut, or a mold?"

"Singly," said Jeannie, "and if it is a child only the mother can make them. Oh Granny, it's the likeness of a real little girl who died yesterday — Rosita. She was three years old. *Pan del Muerto*, the Bread of the Dead. It was the custom in the part of Mexico they came from."

Still she turned and inspected. "Look, the hollow in the throat, the little cross necklace. . . . I think for the mother it is a good thing to be busy with such bread. You know the family?"

Jeannie nodded. "On my rounds. I nursed. . . . Oh Granny, it is like a party; they play songs she liked to dance to. The coffin is lined with pink velvet and she wears a white dress. There are candles. . . ."

"In the house?" Surprised, "They keep her in the house?"

"Yes," said Jeannie, "and it *is* against the health law. The father said it will be sad to bury her in this country; in Oaxaca they have a feast night with candles each year; everyone picnics on the graves of those they loved until dawn."

"Yes, Jeannie, the living must comfort themselves." And closed her eyes.

"You want to sleep, Granny?"

"Yes, tired from the pleasure of you. I may keep the Rosita? There stand it, on the dresser, where I can see; something of my own around me."

In the kitchenette, helping her grandfather unpack the groceries, Jeannie said in her light voice:

"I'm resigning my job, Grandaddy."

"Ah, the lucky young man. Which one is he?"

"Too late. You're spoken for." She made a pyramid of cans, unstacked, and built again.

"Something is wrong with the job?"

"With me. I can't be" — she searched for the word — "What they call professional enough. I let myself feel things. And tomorrow I have to report a family. . . ." The cans clicked again. "It's not that, either. I just don't know what I want to do, maybe go back to school, maybe go to art school. I thought if you went to San Francisco I'd come along and talk it over with Momma and Daddy. But I don't see how you can go. She wants to go home. She asked me to ask the doctor."

The doctor told her himself. "Next week you may travel, when you are a little stronger." But next week there was the fever of an infection, and by the time that was over, she could not leave the bed — a rented hospital bed that stood beside the double bed he slept in alone now.

Outwardly the days repeated themselves. Every other afternoon and evening he went out to his newfound cronies, to talk and play cards. Twice a week, Mrs. Mays came. And the rest of the time, Jeannie was there.

By the sickbed stood Jeannie's FM radio. Often into the room the shapes of music came. She would lie curled on her side, her knees drawn up, intense in listening (Jeannie sketched her so, coiled, convoluted like an ear), then thresh her hand out and abruptly snap the radio mute — still to lie in her attitude of listening, concealing tears.

Once Jeannie brought in a young Marine to visit, a friend from high-school days she had found wandering near the empty pier. Because Jeannie asked him to, gravely, without self-consciousness, he sat himself cross-legged on the floor and performed for them a dance of his native Samoa.

Long after they left, a tiny thrumming sound could be heard where, in her bed, she strove to repeat the beckon, flight, surrender of his hands, the fluttering footbeats, and his low plaintive calls.

Hannah and Phil sent flowers. To deepen her pleasure, he placed one in her hair. "Like a girl," he said, and brought the hand mirror so she could see. She looked at the pulsing red flower, the yellow skull face; a desolate, excited laugh shuddered from her, and she pushed the mirror away — but let the flower burn.

The week Lennie and Helen came, the fever returned. With it the excited laugh, and incessant words. She, who in her life had spoken but seldom and then only when necessary (never having learned the easy, social uses of words), now in dying, spoke incessantly.

In a half-whisper: "Like Lisa she is, your Jeannie. Have I told you of Lisa who taught me to read? Of the highborn she was, but noble in herself. I was sixteen; they beat me; my father beat me so I would not go to her. It was forbidden, she was a Tolstoyan. At night, past dogs that howled, terrible dogs, my son, in the snows of winter to the road, I to ride in her carriage like a lady, to books. To her, life was holy, knowledge was holy, and she taught me to read. They hung her. Everything that happens one must try to understand why. She killed one who betrayed many. Because of betrayal, betrayed all she lived and believed. In one minute she killed, before my eyes (there is so much blood in a human being, my son), in prison with me. All that happens, one must try to understand.

"The name?" Her lips would work. "The name that was their pole star; the doors of the death houses fixed to open on it; I read of it my year of penal servitude. Thuban!" very excited, "Thuban, in ancient Egypt the pole star. Can you see, look out to see it, Jeannie, if it swings around our pole star that seems to *us* not to move.

"Yes, Jeannie, at your age my mother and grandmother had already buried children . . . yes, Jeannie, it is more than oceans between Olshana and you . . . yes, Jeannie, they danced, and for all the bodies they had they might as well be chickens, and indeed, they scratched and flapped their arms and hopped.

"And Andrei Yefimitch, who for twenty years had never known of it and never wanted to know, said as if he wanted to cry: but why my dear friend this malicious laughter?" Telling to herself half-memorized phrases from her few books. "Pain I answer with tears and cries, baseness with indignation, meanness with repulsion . . . for life may be hated or wearied of, but never despised."

Delirious: "Tell me, my neighbor, Mrs. Mays, the pictures never lived, but what of the flowers? Tell them who ask: no rabbis, no ministers, no priests, no speeches, no ceremonies: ah, false — let the living comfort themselves. Tell Sammy's boy, he who flies, tell him to go to Stuttgart and see where Davy has no grave. And what? . . . And what? where millions have no graves — save air."

In delirium or not, wanting the radio on; not seeming to listen, the words still jetting, wanting the music on. Once, silencing it abruptly as of old, she began to cry, unconcealed tears this time. "You have pain, Granny?" Jeannie asked.

"The music," she said, "still it is there and we do not hear;

knocks, and our poor human ears too weak. What else, what else we do not hear?"

Once she knocked his hand aside as he gave her a pill, swept the bottles from her bedside table: "no pills, let me feel what I feel," and laughed as on his hands and knees he groped to pick them up.

Nighttimes her hand reached across the bed to hold his.

A constant retching began. Her breath was too faint for sustained speech now, but still the lips moved:

When no longer necessary   to injure others
Pick   pick pick   Blind chicken
As a human being   responsibility

"David!" imperious, "Basin!" and she would vomit, rinse her mouth, the wasted throat working to swallow, and begin the chant again.

She will be better off in the hospital now, the doctor said.

He sent the telegrams to the children, was packing her suitcase, when her hoarse voice startled. She had roused, was pulling herself to sitting.

"Where now?" she asked. "Where now do you drag me?"

"You do not even have to have a baby to go this time," he soothed, looking for the brush to pack. "Remember, after Davy you told me — worthy to have a baby for the pleasure of the ten-day rest in the hospital?"

"Where now? Not home yet?" Her voice mourned. "Where *is* my home?"

He rose to ease her back. "The doctor, the hospital," he started to explain, but deftly, like a snake, she had slithered out of bed and stood swaying, propped behind the night table.

"Coward," she hissed, "runner."

"You stand," he said senselessly.

"To take me there and run. Afraid of a little vomit."

He reached her as she fell. She struggled against him, half slipped from his arms, pulled herself up again.

"Weakling," she taunted, "to leave me there and run. Betrayer. All your life you have run."

He sobbed, telling Jeannie. "A Marilyn Monroe to run for her virtue. Fifty-nine pounds she weighs, the doctor said, and she beats at me like a Dempsey. Betrayer, she cries, and I running like a dog when she calls; day and night, running to her, her vomit, the bedpan. . . ."

"She needs you, Grandaddy," said Jeannie. "Isn't that what they call love? I'll see if she sleeps, and if she does, poor worn-out darling, we'll have a party, you and I: I brought us rum babas."

They did not move her. By her bed now stood the tall hooked pillar that held the solutions—blood and dextrose—to feed her veins. Jeannie moved down the hall to take over the sickroom, her face so radiant, her grandfather asked her once: "you are in love?" (Shameful the joy, the pure overwhelming joy from being with her grandmother; the peace, the serenity that breathed.)

"My darling escape," she answered incoherently, "my darling Granny"—as if that explained.

Now one by one the children came, those that were able. Hannah, Paul, Sammy. Too late to ask: and what did you learn with your living, Mother, and what do we need to know?

Clara, the eldest, clenched:

Pay me back, Mother, pay me back for all you took from me. Those others you crowded into your heart. The hands I needed to be for you, the heaviness, the responsibility.

Is this she? Noises the dying make, the crablike hands crawling over the covers. The ethereal singing.

She hears that music, that singing from childhood; forgotten sound— not heard since, since. . . . And the hardness breaks like a cry: Where did we lose each other, first mother, singing mother?

Annulled: the quarrels, the gibing, the harshness between; the fall into silence and the withdrawal.

I do not know you, Mother. Mother, I never knew you.

Lennie, suffering not alone for her who was dying, but for that in her which never lived (for that which in him might never come to live). From him too, unspoken words: *good-bye Mother who taught me to mother myself.*

Not Vivi, who must stay with her children; not Davy, but he is already here, having to die again with *her* this time, for the living take their dead with them when they die.

Light she grew, like a bird, and, like a bird, sound bubbled in her throat while the body fluttered in agony. Night and day, asleep or awake (though indeed there was no difference now) the songs and the phrases leaping.

And he, who had once dreaded a long dying (from fear of himself, from horror of the dwindling money) now desired her quick death profoundly, for *her* sake. He no longer went out, except when Jeannie forced him; no longer laughed, except when, in the bright kitchenette, Jeannie coaxed his laughter (and she, who seemed to hear nothing else, would laugh too, conspiratorial wisps of laughter).

Light, like a bird, the fluttering body, the little claw hands, the beaked shadow on her face; and the throat, bubbling, straining.

He tried not to listen, as he tried not to look on the face in which only the forehead remained familiar, but trapped with her the long night in that little room, the sounds worked themselves into his consciousness, with their punctuation of death swallows, whimpers, gurglings.

Even in reality (swallow) *life's lack of it*
Slaveships deathtrains clubs eeenough
The bell summon what enables

78,000 in one minute (whisper of a scream) *78,000 human beings we'll destroy ourselves?*

"Aah, Mrs. Miserable," he said, as if she could hear, "all your life working, and now in bed you lie, servants to tend, you do not even need to call to be tended, and still you work. Such hard work it is to die? Such hard work?"

The body threshed, her hand clung in his. A melody, ghost-thin, hovered on her lips, and like a guilty ghost, the vision of her bent in listening to it, silencing the record instantly he was near. Now, heedless of his presence, she floated the melody on and on.

"Hid it from me," he complained, "how many times you listened to remember it so?" And tried to think when she had first played it, or first begun to silence her few records when he came near — but could reconstruct nothing. There was only this room with its tall hooked pillar and its swarm of sounds.

No man one except through others
Strong with the not yet in the now
Dogma dead war dead one country

"It helps, Mrs. Philosopher, words from books? It helps?" And it seemed to him that for seventy years she had hidden a tape recorder, infinitely microscopic, within her, that it had coiled infinite mile on mile, trapping every song, every melody, every word read, heard, and spoken — and that maliciously she was playing back only what said nothing of him, of the children, of their intimate life together.

"Left us indeed, Mrs. Babbler," he reproached, "you who called others babbler and cunningly saved your words. A lifetime you tended and loved, and now not a word of us, for us. Left us indeed? Left me."

And he took out his solitaire deck, shuffled the cards loudly, slapped them down.

Lift high   banner of reason (tatter of an orator's voice) *justice   freedom   light*

Humankind   life worthy   capacities

Seeks (blur of shudder) *belong   human being*

"Words, words," he accused, "and what human beings did *you* seek around you, Mrs. Live Alone, and what humankind think worthy?"

Though even as he spoke, he remembered she had not always been isolated, had not always wanted to be alone (as he knew there had been a voice before this gossamer one; before the hoarse voice that broke from silence to lash, make incidents, shame him — a girl's voice of eloquence that spoke their holiest dreams). But again he could reconstruct, image, nothing of what had been before, or when, or how, it had changed.

Ace, queen, jack. The pillar shadow fell, so, in two tracks; in the mirror depths glistened a moonlike blob, the empty solution bottle. And it worked in him: *of reason and justice and freedom . . . Dogma dead:* he remembered the full quotation, laughed bitterly. "Hah, good you do not know what you say; good Victor Hugo died and did not see it, his twentieth century."

Deuce, ten, five. Dauntlessly she began a song of their youth of belief:

These things shall be, a loftier race
than e'er the world hath known shall rise
with flame of freedom in their souls
and light of knowledge in their eyes

King, four, jack "In the twentieth century, hah!"

They shall be gentle, brave and strong
to spill no drop of blood, but dare
all . . .
    on earth and fire and sea and air

"To spill no drop of blood, hah! So, cadaver, and you too, cadaver Hugo, 'in the twentieth century ignorance will be dead, dogma will be dead, war will be dead, and for all mankind one country — of fulfilment?' Hah!"

And every life (long strangling cough) *shall
be a song*

The cards fell from his fingers. Without warning, the bereavement and betrayal he had sheltered — compounded through the years — hidden even from himself — revealed itself,
uncoiled,
released,
sprung

and with it the monstrous shapes of what had actually happened in the century.

A ravening hunger or thirst seized him. He groped into the kitchenette, switched on all three lights, piled a tray — "you have finished your night snack, Mrs. Cadaver, now I will have mine." And he was shocked at the tears that splashed on the tray.

"Salt tears. For free. I forgot to shake on salt?"

Whispered: "Lost, how much I lost."

Escaped to the grandchildren whose childhoods were childish, who had never hungered, who lived unravaged by disease in warm houses of many rooms, had all the school for which they cared, could walk on any street, stood a head taller than their grandparents, towered above — beautiful skins, straight backs, clear straightforward eyes. "Yes, you in Olshana," he said to the town of sixty years ago, "they would seem nobility to you."

And was this not the dream then, come true in ways undreamed? he asked.

And are there no other children in the world? he answered, as if in her harsh voice.

And the flame of freedom, the light of knowledge?
And the drop, to spill no drop of blood?

And he thought that at six Jeannie would get up and it would be his turn to go to her room and sleep, that he could press the buzzer and she would come now; that in the afternoon Ellen Mays was coming, and this time they would play cards and he could marvel at how rouge can stand half an inch on the cheek; that in the evening the doctor would come, and he could beg him to be merciful, to stop the feeding solutions, to let her die.

To let her die, and with her their youth of belief out of which her bright, betrayed words foamed; stained words, that on her working lips came stainless.

Hours yet before Jeannie's turn. He could press the buzzer and wake her to come now; he could take a pill, and with it sleep; he could pour more brandy into his milk glass, though what he had poured was not yet touched.

Instead he went back, checked her pulse, gently tended with his knotty fingers as Jeannie had taught.

She was whimpering; her hand crawled across the covers for his. Compassionately he enfolded it, and with his free hand gathered up the cards again. Still was there thirst or hunger ravening in him.

That world of their youth — dark, ignorant, terrible with hate and disease — how was it that living in it, in the midst of corruption, filth, treachery, degradation, they had not mistrusted man nor themselves; had believed so beautifully, so . . . falsely?

"Aaah, children," he said out loud, "how we believed, how we belonged." And he yearned to package for each of the children, the grandchildren, for everyone, *that joyous certainty, that sense of mattering, of moving and being moved, of being one and indivisible with the great of the past, with all that freed, ennobled.* Package it, stand on corners, in front of stadiums and on crowded beaches, knock on doors, give it as a fabled gift.

"And why not in cereal boxes, in soap packages?" he mocked himself. "Aah. You have taken my senses, cadaver."

Words foamed, died unsounded. Her body writhed; she made kissing motions with her mouth. (Her lips moving as she read, poring over the Book of the Martyrs, the magnifying glass superimposed over the heavy eyeglasses.) *Still she believed?* "Eva!" he whispered. "Still you believed? You lived by it? These Things Shall Be?"

"One pound soup meat," she answered distinctly, "one soup bone."

"My ears heard you. Ellen Mays was witness: 'Humankind . . . one has to believe.'" Imploringly: "Eva!"

"Bread, day-old." She was mumbling. "Please, in a wooden box . . . for kindling. The thread, hah, the thread breaks. Cheap thread" — and a gurgling, enormously loud, began in her throat.

"I ask for stone; she gives me bread — day-old." He pulled his hand away, shouted: "Who wanted questions? Everything you have to wake?" Then dully, "Ah, let me help you turn, poor creature."

Words jumbled, cleared. In a voice of crowded terror:

"Paul, Sammy, don't fight.

"Hannah, have I ten hands?

"How can I give it, Clara, how can I give it if I don't have?"

"You lie," he said sturdily, "there was joy too." Bitterly: "Ah how cheap you speak of us at the last."

As if to rebuke him, as if her voice had no relationship with her flailing body, she sang clearly, beautifully, a school song the children had taught her when they were little; begged:

"Not look   my hair   where they cut. . . ."

(The crown of braids shorn.) And instantly he left the mute old woman poring over the Book of the Martyrs; went past the mother treading at the sewing machine, singing with the children; past the girl in her wrinkled prison dress, hiding her hair with scarred hands, lifting to him her awkward, shamed, imploring eyes of love; and took her in his arms, dear, personal, fleshed, in all the heavy passion he had loved to rouse from her.

"Eva!"

Her little claw hand beat the covers. How much, how much can a man stand? He took up the cards, put them down, circled the beds, walked to the dresser, opened, shut drawers, brushed his hair, moved his hand bit by bit over the mirror to see what of the reflection he could blot out with each move, and felt that at any moment he would die of what was unendurable. Went to press the buzzer to wake Jeannie, looked down, saw on Jeannie's sketch pad the hospital bed, with *her*; the double bed alongside, with him; the tall pillar feeding into her veins, and their hands, his and hers, clasped, feeding each other. And as if he had been instructed he went to his bed, lay down, holding the sketch (as if it could shield against the monstrous shapes of loss, of betrayal, of death) and with his free hand took hers back into his.

So Jeannie found them in the morning.

That last day the agony was perpetual. Time after time it lifted her almost off the bed, so they had to fight to hold her down. He could not endure and left the room; wept as if there never would be tears enough.

Jeannie came to comfort him. In her light voice she said: Grandaddy, Grandaddy don't cry. She is not there, she promised me. On the last day, she said she would go back to when she first heard music, a little girl on the road of the village where she was born. She promised me. It is a wedding and they dance, while the flutes so joyous and vibrant tremble in the air. Leave her there, Grandaddy, it is all right. She promised me. Come back, come back and help her poor body to die.

For my mother, my father,
and
Two of that generation
Seevya and Genya
Infinite, dauntless, incorruptible

Death deepens the wonder

In Dreams Begin Responsibilities

DELMORE SCHWARTZ

Delmore Schwartz (1913–1966): *Delmore Schwartz was born and raised in Brooklyn, the son of unhappy immigrant parents who divorced when he was a boy. Brilliant as a child, he was educated at the University of Wisconsin, New York University, and Harvard (which he left after failing to get a prestigious fellowship). Schwartz was only twenty-four when his first book,* In Dreams Begin Responsibilities, *a compilation of fiction, poetry, and verse drama, was published to great critical acclaim. (The title story had appeared in* The Partisan Review *several years earlier.) Although he spent years laboring at the craft of fiction and published two collections of stories in his lifetime (*The World Is a Wedding *and* Successful Love*), Schwartz's major critical reputation rests on his poetry, particularly the poems collected in* In Dreams Begin Responsibilities *and in a later volume,* Summer Knowledge: New and Selected Poems. *Other volumes of his poetry include* Shenandoah, *a verse play, and* Genesis: Book One, *an autobiographical poem. During the last thirty years of his life he enjoyed troubled but intense friendships with many of the greatest writers and intellectuals of his day—including Saul Bellow, whose novel* Humboldt's Gift *painted a fictionalized portrait of Schwartz. During this period, he taught at a series of prestigious institutions—Harvard, Kenyon College, Princeton, and Syracuse University—and won the Bollingen Prize for Poetry. But despite Schwartz's many gifts, his life was troubled and wracked by despair. His decline, fostered by a twenty-year battle with drug and alcohol abuse and an increasing tendency toward paranoia, eventually led to a fatal heart attack at the age of fifty-three.*

1

I think it is the year 1909. I feel as if I were in a motion picture theatre, the long arm of light crossing the darkness and spinning, my eyes fixed on the screen. This is a silent picture as if an old Biograph one, in which the actors are dressed in ridiculously old-fashioned clothes, and one flash succeeds another with sudden jumps. The actors too seem to jump about and walk too fast. The shots themselves are full of dots and rays, as if it were raining when the picture was photographed. The light is bad.

It is Sunday afternoon, June 12th, 1909, and my father is walking down the quiet streets of Brooklyn on his way to visit my mother. His clothes are newly pressed and his tie is too tight in his high collar. He jingles the coins in his pockets, thinking of the witty things he will say. I feel as if I had by now relaxed entirely in the soft darkness of the theatre; the organist peals out the obvious and approximate emotions on which the audience rocks unknowingly. I am anonymous, and I have forgotten myself. It is always so when one goes to the movies, it is, as they say, a drug.

My father walks from street to street of trees, lawns and houses, once in a while coming to an avenue on which a street-car skates and gnaws, slowly progressing. The conductor, who has a handle-bar mustache, helps a young lady wearing a hat like a bowl with feathers on to the car. She lifts her long skirts slightly as she mounts the steps. He leisurely makes change and rings his bell. It is obviously Sunday, for every one is wearing Sunday clothes, and the street-car's noises emphasize the quiet of the holiday. Is not Brooklyn the City of Churches? The shops are closed and their shades drawn, but for an occasional stationery store or drug-store with great green balls in the window.

My father has chosen to take this long walk because he likes to walk and think. He thinks about himself in the future and so arrives at the place he is to visit in a state of mild exaltation. He pays no attention to the houses he is passing in which the Sunday dinner is being eaten, nor to the many trees which patrol each street, now coming to their full leafage and the time when they will room the whole street in cool shadow. An occasional carriage passes, the horse's hooves falling like stones in the quiet afternoon, and once in a while an automobile, looking like an enormous upholstered sofa, puffs and passes.

My father thinks of my mother, of how nice it will be to introduce her to his family. But he is not yet sure that he wants to marry her, and once in a while he becomes panicky about the bond already established. He reassures himself by thinking of the big men he admires who are married: William Randolph Hearst, and William Howard Taft, who has just become President of the United States.

My father arrives at my mother's house. He has come too early and so is suddenly embarrassed. My aunt, my mother's sister, answers the loud bell with her napkin in her hand, for the family is still at dinner. As my father enters, my grandfather rises from the table and shakes hands with him. My mother has run upstairs to tidy herself. My grandmother asks my father if he has had dinner, and tells him that Rose will be downstairs soon. My grandfather opens the conversation by remarking on the mild June weather. My father sits uncomfortably near the table, holding his hat in his hand. My grandmother tells my aunt to take my father's hat. My uncle, twelve years old, runs into the house, his hair tousled. He shouts a greeting to my father, who has often given him a nickel, and then runs upstairs. It is evident that the respect in which my father is held in this household is tempered by a good deal of mirth. He is impressive, yet he is very awkward.

2

Finally my mother comes downstairs, all dressed up, and my father being engaged in conversation with my grandfather becomes uneasy, not knowing whether to greet my mother or continue the conversation. He gets up from the chair clumsily and says "hello" gruffly. My grandfather watches, examining their congruence, such as it is, with a critical eye, and meanwhile rubbing his bearded cheek roughly, as he always does when he reflects. He is worried; he is afraid that my father will not make a good husband for his oldest daughter. At this point something happens to the film, just as my father is saying something funny to my mother; I am awakened to myself and my unhappiness just as my interest was rising. The audience begins to clap impatiently. Then the trouble is cared for but the film has been returned to a portion just shown, and once more I see my grandfather rubbing his bearded cheek and pondering my father's character. It is difficult to get back into the picture once more and forget myself, but as my mother giggles at my father's words, the darkness drowns me.

My father and mother depart from the house, my father shaking hands with my mother once more, out of some unknown uneasiness. I stir uneasily also, slouched in the hard chair of the theatre. Where is the older uncle, my mother's older brother? He is studying in his bedroom upstairs, studying for his final examination at the College of the City of New York, having been dead of rapid pneumonia for the last twenty-one years. My mother and father walk down the same quiet streets once more. My mother is holding my father's arm and telling him of the novel which she has been reading; and my father utters judgments of the characters as the plot is made clear to him. This is a habit which he very much enjoys, for he feels the utmost superiority and confidence when he approves and condemns the behavior of other people. At times he feels moved to utter a brief "Ugh" — whenever the story becomes what he would call sugary. This tribute is paid to his manliness. My mother feels satisfied by the interest which she has awakened; she is showing my father how intelligent she is, and how interesting.

They reach the avenue, and the street-car leisurely arrives. They are going to Coney Island this afternoon, although my mother considers that such pleasures are inferior. She has made up her mind to indulge only in a walk on the boardwalk and a pleasant dinner, avoiding the riotous amusements as being beneath the dignity of so dignified a couple.

My father tells my mother how much money he has made in the past week, exaggerating an amount which need not have been exaggerated. But my father has always felt that actualities somehow fall short. Suddenly I begin to weep. The determined old lady who sits next to me in the theatre is annoyed and looks at me with an angry face, and being intimidated, I stop. I drag out my handkerchief and dry my face, licking the drop which has fallen near my lips. Meanwhile I have missed something, for here are my mother and father alighting at the last stop, Coney Island.

3

They walk toward the boardwalk, and my father commands my mother to inhale the pungent air from the sea. They both breathe in deeply, both of them laughing as they do so. They have in common a great interest in health, although my father is strong and husky, my mother frail. Their minds are full of theories of what is good to eat and not good to eat, and sometimes they engage in heated discussions of the subject, the whole matter ending in my father's announcement, made with a scornful bluster, that you have to die sooner or later anyway. On the boardwalk's flagpole, the American flag is pulsing in an intermittent wind from the sea.

My father and mother go to the rail of the boardwalk and look down on the beach where a good many bathers are casually walking about. A few are in the surf. A peanut whistle pierces the air with its pleasant and active whine, and my father goes to buy peanuts. My mother remains at the rail and stares at the ocean. The ocean seems merry to her; it pointedly sparkles and again and again the pony waves are released. She notices the children digging in the wet sand, and the bathing costumes of the girls who are her own age. My father returns with the peanuts. Overhead the sun's lightning strikes and strikes, but neither of them are at all aware of it. The boardwalk is full of people dressed in their Sunday clothes and idly strolling. The tide does not reach as far as the boardwalk, and the strollers would feel no danger if it did. My mother and father lean on the rail of the boardwalk and absently stare at the ocean. The ocean is becoming rough; the waves come in slowly, tugging strength from far back. The moment before they somersault, the moment when they arch their backs so beautifully, showing green and white veins amid the black, that moment is intolerable. They finally crack, dashing fiercely upon the sand, actually driving, full force downward, against the sand, bouncing upward and forward, and at last petering out into a small stream which races up the beach and then is recalled. My parents gaze absentmindedly at the ocean, scarcely interested in its harshness. The sun overhead does not disturb them. But I stare at the terrible sun which breaks up sight, and the fatal, merciless, passionate ocean, I forget my parents. I stare fascinated and finally, shocked by the indifference of my father and mother, I burst out weeping once more. The old lady next to me pats me on the shoulder and says "There, there, all of this is only a movie, young man, only a movie," but I look up once more at the terrifying sun and the terrifying ocean, and being unable to control my tears, I get up and go to the men's room, stumbling over the feet of the other people seated in my row.

4

When I return, feeling as if I had awakened in the morning sick for lack of sleep, several hours have apparently passed and my parents are riding on the merry-go-round. My father is on a black horse, my mother on a white one, and they seem to be making an eternal circuit for the single purpose of snatching the nickel rings which are attached to the arm of one of the posts. A hand-organ is playing; it is one with the ceaseless circling of the merry-go-round.

For a moment it seems that they will never get off the merry-go-round because it will never stop. I feel like one who looks down on the avenue from the fiftieth story of a building. But at length they do get off; even the music of the hand-organ has ceased for a moment. My father has acquired ten rings, my mother only two, although it was my mother who really wanted them.

They walk on along the boardwalk as the afternoon descends by imperceptible degrees into the incredible violet of dusk. Everything fades into a relaxed glow, even the ceaseless murmuring from the beach, and the revolutions of the merry-go-round. They look for a place to have dinner. My father suggests the best one on the board- walk and my mother demurs, in accordance with her principles.

However they do go to the best place, asking for a table near the window, so that they can look out on the boardwalk and the mobile ocean. My father feels omnipotent as he places a quarter in the waiter's hand as he asks for a table. The place is crowded and here too there is music, this time from a kind of string trio. My father orders dinner with a fine confidence.

As the dinner is eaten, my father tells of his plans for the future, and my mother shows with expressive face how interested she is, and how impressed. My father becomes exultant. He is lifted up by the waltz that is being played, and his own future begins to intoxi- cate him. My father tells my mother that he is going to expand his business, for there is a great deal of money to be made. He wants to settle down. After all, he is twenty-nine, he has lived by himself since he was thirteen, he is making more and more money, and he is envious of his married friends when he visits them in the cozy se- curity of their homes, surrounded, it seems, by the calm domestic pleasures, and by delightful children, and then, as the waltz reaches the moment when all the dancers swing madly, then, then with aw- ful daring, then he asks my mother to marry him, although awk- wardly enough and puzzled, even in his excitement, at how he had arrived at the proposal, and she, to make the whole business worse, begins to cry, and my father looks nervously about, not knowing at all what to do now, and my mother says: "It's all I've wanted from the moment I saw you," sobbing, and he finds all of this very diffi- cult, scarcely to his taste, scarcely as he had thought it would be, on his long walks over Brooklyn Bridge in the revery of a fine cigar, and it was then that I stood up in the theatre and shouted: "Don't do it. It's not too late to change your minds, both of you. Nothing good will come of it, only remorse, hatred, scandal, and two chil- dren whose characters are monstrous." The whole audience turned to look at me, annoyed, the usher came hurrying down the aisle flashing his searchlight, and the old lady next to me tugged me down into my seat, saying: "Be quiet. You'll be put out, and you paid thirty-five cents to come in." And so I shut my eyes because I could not bear to see what was happening. I sat there quietly.

5

But after awhile I begin to take brief glimpses, and at length I watch again with thirsty interest, like a child who wants to maintain his sulk although offered the bribe of candy. My parents are now having their picture taken in a photographer's booth along the boardwalk. The place is shadowed in the mauve light which is apparently necessary. The camera is set to the side on its tripod and looks like a Martian man. The photographer is instructing my parents in how to pose. My father has his arm over my mother's shoulder, and both of them smile emphatically. The photographer brings my mother a bouquet of flowers to hold in her hand but she holds it at the wrong angle. Then the photographer covers himself with the black cloth which drapes the camera and all that one sees of him is one protruding arm and his hand which clutches the rubber ball which he will squeeze when the picture is finally taken. But he is not satisfied with their appearance. He feels with certainty that somehow there is something wrong in their pose. Again and again he issues from his hidden place with new directions. Each suggestion merely makes matters worse. My father is becoming impatient. They try a seated pose. The photographer explains that he has pride, he is not interested in all of this for the money, he wants to make beautiful pictures. My father says: "Hurry up, will you? We haven't got all night." But the photographer only scurries about apologetically, and issues new directions.

The photographer charms me. I approve of him with all my heart, for I know just how he feels, and as he criticizes each revised pose according to some unknown idea of rightness, I become quite hopeful. But then my father says angrily: "Come on, you've had enough time, we're not going to wait any longer." And the photographer sighing unhappily, goes back under his black covering, holds out his hand, says: "One, two, three, Now!," and the picture is taken, with my father's smile turned to a grimace and my mother's bright and false. It takes a few minutes for the picture to be developed and as my parents sit in the curious light they become quite depressed.

6

They have passed a fortune-teller's booth, and my mother wishes to go in, but my father does not. They begin to argue about it. My mother becomes stubborn, my father once more impatient, and then they begin to quarrel, and what my father would like to do is walk off and leave my mother there, but he knows that that would never do. My mother refuses to budge. She is near to tears, but she feels an uncontrollable desire to hear what the palm-reader will say. My father consents angrily, and they both go into a booth which is in a way like the photographer's, since it is draped in black cloth and its light is shadowed. The place is too warm, and my father keeps saying this is all nonsense, pointing to this crystal ball on the table. The fortune-teller, a fat, short woman, garbed in what is supposed to be Oriental robes, comes into the room from the back and greets them, speaking with an accent. But suddenly my father feels that the whole thing is intolerable; he tugs at my mother's arm, but my mother refuses to budge. And then, in terrible anger, my father lets go of my mother's arm and strides out, leaving my mother stunned. She moves to go after my father, but the fortune-teller holds her arm tightly and begs her not to do so, and I in my seat am shocked more than can ever be said, for I feel as if I were walking a tight-rope a hundred feet over a circus-audience and suddenly the rope is showing signs of breaking, and I get up from my seat and begin to shout once more the first words I can think of to communicate my terrible fear and once more the usher comes hurrying down the aisle flashing his searchlight, and the old lady pleads with me, and the shocked audience has turned to stare at me, and I keep shouting: "What are they doing? Don't they know what they are doing? Why doesn't my mother go after my father? If she does not do that, what will she do? Doesn't my father know what he is doing?" — But the usher has seized my arm and is dragging me away, and as he does so, he says: "What are *you* doing? Don't you know you can't do whatever you want to do? Why should a young man like you, with your whole life before you, get hysterical like this? Why don't you *think* of what you're doing? You can't act like this even if other people aren't around! You will be sorry if you do not do what you should do, you can't carry on like this, it is not right, you will find that out soon enough, everything you do matters too much," and he said that dragging me through the lobby of the theatre into the cold light, and I woke up into the bleak winter morning of my twenty-first birthday, the windowsill shining with its lip of snow, and the morning already begun.

The Lady of the Lake

BERNARD MALAMUD

Bernard Malamud (1914–1986): *Born and raised in Brooklyn as the son of Russian immigrant parents, Bernard Malamud was educated at City College and Columbia. Although he wrote a number of highly respected novels, including* The Natural, The Assistant, A New Life, The Fixer *(which won the National Book Award and the Pulitzer Prize), Dubin's Lives, The Tenants, and* God's Grace, *Malamud is known primarily as a writer of exquisitely structured, deceptively simple short stories. These stories, collected in* The Magic Barrel *(which won a National Book Award),* Idiots First, Rembrandt's Hat, *and finally* The Stories of Bernard Malamud, *often combine realism with a fanciful, fablelike imaginative lilt. His best work manages to articulate the anxieties—even the language—of Eastern European Jewish life, in the context of American culture. Malamud once said that he saw Jews "as a symbol of the tragic experience of man existentially. I try to see the Jew as a universal man. Every man is a Jew though he may not know it. . . . Jewish drama . . . is a symbol of the fight for existence in the highest possible human terms. Jewish history is God's gift of drama." For the last twenty-five years of his life he and his wife and children divided their time between Vermont and New York City.*

H enry Levin, an ambitious, handsome thirty, who walked the floors in Macy's book department wearing a white flower in his lapel, having recently come into a small inheritance, quit, and went abroad seeking romance. In Paris, for no reason he was sure of, except that he was tired of the past—tired of the limitations it had imposed upon him; although he had signed the hotel register with his right name, Levin took to calling himself Henry R. Freeman. Freeman lived for a short while in a little hotel on a narrow gas lamp-lit street near the Luxembourg Gardens. In the beginning he liked the sense of foreignness of the city—of things different, anything likely to happen. He liked, he said to himself, the possible combinations. But not much did happen; he met no one he particularly cared for (he had sometimes in the past deceived himself about women, they had come to less than he had expected); and since the heat was hot and tourists underfoot, he felt he must flee. He boarded the Milan express, and after Dijon, developed a painful, palpitating anxiety. This grew so troublesome that he had serious visions of leaping off the train, but reason prevailed and he rode on. However, he did not get to Milan. Nearing Stresa, after a quick, astonished look at Lake Maggiore, Freeman, a nature lover from early childhood, pulled his suitcase off the rack and hurriedly left the train. He at once felt better.

An hour later he was established in a pensione in a villa not far from the line of assorted hotels fronting the Stresa shore. The padrona, a talkative woman, much interested in her guests, complained that June and July had been lost in unseasonable cold and wet. Many had cancelled; there were few Americans around. This didn't exactly disturb Freeman, who had had his full share of Coney Island. He lived in an airy, French-windowed room, including soft bed and spacious bath, and though personally the shower type, was glad of the change. He was very fond of the balcony at his window, where he loved to read, or study Italian, glancing up often to gaze at the water. The long blue lake, sometimes green, sometimes gold, went out of sight among distant mountains. He liked the red-roofed town of Pallanza on the opposite shore, and especially the four beautiful islands in the water, tiny but teeming with palazzi, tall trees, gardens, visible statuary. The sight of these islands aroused in Freeman a deep emotion; each a universe — how often do we come across one in a lifetime? — filled him with expectancy. Of what, he wasn't sure. Freeman still hoped for what he hadn't, what few got in the world and many dared not think of; to wit, love, adventure, freedom. Alas, the words by now sounded slightly comical. Yet there were times, when he was staring at the islands, if you pushed him a little he could almost cry. Ah, what names of beauty: Isola Bella, dei Pescatori, Madre, and del Dongo. Travel is truly broadening, he thought; who ever got emotional over Welfare Island?

But the islands, the two he visited, let him down. Freeman walked off the vaporetto at Isola Bella amid a crowd of late-season tourists in all languages, especially German, who were at once beset by many vendors of cheap trinkets. And he discovered there were guided tours only — strictly no unsupervised wandering — the pink palazzo full of old junk, surrounded by artificial formal gardens, including grottoes made of seashells, the stone statuary a tasteless laugh. And although Isola dei Pescatori had some honest atmosphere, old houses hugging crooked streets, thick nets drying in piles near fishermen's dories drawn up among trees; again there were tourists snapping all in pictures, and the whole town catering to them. Everybody had something to sell you could buy better in Macy's basement. Freeman returned to his pensione, disappointed. The islands, beautiful from afar, up close were so much stage scenery. He complained thus to the padrona and she urged him to visit Isola del Dongo. "More natural," she persuaded him. "You never saw such unusual gardens. And the palazzo is historical, full of the tombs of famous men of the region, including a cardinal who became a saint. Napoleon, the emperor, slept there. The French have always loved this island. Their writers have wept at its beauty."

However, Freeman showed little interest. "Gardens I've seen in my time." So, when restive, he wandered in the back streets of Stresa, watching the men playing at boccia, avoiding the laden store windows. Drifting by devious routes back to the lake, he sat at a bench in the small park, watching the lingering sunset over the dark mountains and thinking of a life of adventure. He watched alone, talked now and then to stray Italians — almost everybody spoke a good broken English — and lived too much on himself. On weekends, there was, however, a buzz of merriment in the streets. Excursionists from around Milan arrived in busloads. All day they hurried to their picnics; at night one of them pulled an accordion out of the bus and played sad Venetian or happy Neapolitan songs. Then the young Italians and their girls got up and danced in tight embrace in the public square; but not Freeman.

One evening at sunset, the calm waters so marvelously painted they drew him from inactivity, he hired a rowboat, and for want of anyplace more exciting to go, rowed toward the Isola del Dongo. He had no intention other than reaching it, then turning back, a round trip completed. Two-thirds of the way there, he began to row with growing uneasiness which soon became dread, because a stiff breeze had risen, driving the sucking waves against the side of the boat. It was a warm wind, but a wind was a wind and the water was wet. Freeman didn't row well — had learned late in his twenties, despite the nearness of Central Park — and he swam poorly, always swallowing water, never enough breath to get anywhere; clearly a landlubber from the word go. He strongly considered returning to Stresa — it was at least a half mile to the island, then a mile and a half in return — but chided himself for his timidity. He had, after all, hired the boat for an hour; so he kept rowing though he feared the risk. However, the waves were not too bad and he had discovered the trick of letting them hit the prow head-on. Although he handled his oars awkwardly, Freeman, to his surprise, made good time. The wind now helped rather than hindered; and daylight — reassuring — still lingered in the sky among streaks of red.

At last Freeman neared the island. Like Isola Bella, it rose in terraces through hedged gardens crowded with statuary, to a palazzo on top. But the padrona had told the truth — this island looked more interesting than the others, the vegetation lush, wilder, exotic birds flying around. By now the place was bathed in mist, and despite the thickening dark, Freeman recaptured the sense of awe and beauty he had felt upon first beholding the islands. At the same time he recalled a sad memory of unlived life, his own, of all that had slipped through his fingers. Amidst these thoughts he was startled by a movement in the garden by the water's edge. It had momentarily seemed as though a statue had come to life, but Freeman quickly realized a woman was standing this side of a low marble wall, watching the water. He could not, of course, make out her face, though he sensed she was young; only the skirt of her white dress moved in the breeze. He imagined someone waiting for her lover, and was tempted to speak to her, but then the wind blew up strongly and the waves rocked his rowboat. Freeman hastily turned the boat with one oar, and pulling hard, took off. The wind drenched him with spray, the rowboat bobbed among nasty waves, the going grew frighteningly rough. He had visions of drowning, the rowboat swamped, poor Freeman slowly sinking to the bottom, striving fruitlessly to reach the top. But as he rowed, his heart like a metal disk in his mouth, and still rowed on, gradually he overcame his fears; also the waves and wind. Although the lake was by now black, though the sky still dimly reflected white, turning from time to time to peer ahead, he guided himself by the flickering lights of the Stresa shore. It rained hard as he landed, but Freeman, as he beached the boat, considered his adventure an accomplishment and ate a hearty supper at an expensive restaurant.

The curtains billowing in his sunny room the next morning, awoke him. Freeman rose, shaved, bathed, and after breakfast got a haircut. Wearing his bathing trunks under slacks, he sneaked onto the Hotel Excelsior beach for a dip, short but refreshing. In the early afternoon he read his Italian lesson on the balcony, then snatched a snooze. At four-thirty — he felt he really hadn't made up his mind until then—Freeman boarded the vaporetto making its hourly tour of the islands. After touching at Isola Madre, the boat headed for the Isola del Dongo. As they were approaching the island, coming from the direction opposite that which Freeman had taken last night, he observed a lanky boy in bathing trunks sunning himself on a raft in the lake—nobody he recognized. When the vaporetto landed at the dock on the southern side of the island, to Freeman's surprise and deep regret, the area was crowded with the usual stalls piled high with tourist gewgaws. And though he had hoped otherwise, inspection of the island was strictly in the guide's footsteps, and *vietato* trying to go anywhere alone. You paid a hundred lire for a ticket, then trailed behind this unshaven, sad-looking clown, who stabbed a jaunty cane at the sky as he announced in three languages to the tourists who followed him: "Please not stray nor wander. The family del Dongo, one of the most illustrious of Italy, so requests. Only thus ees eet able to remain open thees magnificent 'eestorical palatz and supreme jardens for the inspection by the members of all nations."

They tailed the guide at a fast clip through the palace, through long halls hung with tapestries and elaborate mirrors, enormous rooms filled with antique furniture, old books, paintings, statuary—a lot of it in better taste than the stuff he had seen on the other island; and he visited where Napoleon had slept—a bed. Yet Freeman secretly touched the counterpane, though not quickly enough to escape the all-seeing eye of the Italian guide, who wrathfully raised his cane to the level of Freeman's heart and explosively shouted, "Basta!" This embarrassed Freeman and two British ladies carrying parasols. He felt bad until the group—about twenty—were led into the garden. Gazing from here, the highest point of the island, at the panorama of the golden-blue lake, Freeman gasped. And the luxuriant vegetation of the island was daring, voluptuous. They went among orange and lemon trees (he had never known that lemon was a perfume), magnolia, oleander—the guide called out the names. Everywhere were flowers in great profusion, huge camellias, rhododendron, jasmine, roses in innumerable colors and varieties, all bathed in intoxicating floral fragrance. Freeman's head swam; he felt dizzy, slightly off his rocker at this extraordinary assailment of his senses. At the same time, though it was an "underground" reaction, he experienced a painful, contracting remembrance—more like a warning—of personal poverty. This he had difficulty accounting for, because he usually held a decent opinion of himself. When the comical guide bounced forward, with his cane indicating cedars, eucalyptus, camphor and pepper trees, the former floorwalker, overcome by all he was for the first time seeing, at the same moment choked by almost breathless excitement, fell behind the group of tourists, and pretended to inspect the berries of a pepper tree. As the guide hurried forward, Freeman, although not positive he had planned it so, ducked behind the pepper tree, ran along a path beside a tall laurel shrub and down two flights of stairs; he hopped over a marble wall and went hastily through a small wood, expectant, seeking, he thought only God knew what.

He figured he was headed in the direction of the garden by the water where he had seen the girl in the white dress last night, but after several minutes of involved wandering, Freeman came upon a little beach, a pebbly strand, leading down stone steps into the lake. About a hundred feet away a raft was anchored, nobody on it. Exhausted by the excitement, a little moody, Freeman sat down under a tree, to rest. When he glanced up, a girl in a white bathing suit was coming up the steps out of the water. Freeman stared as she sloshed up the shore, her wet skin glistening in bright sunlight. She had seen him and quickly bent for a towel she had left on a blanket, draped it over her shoulders and modestly held the ends together over her high-arched breast. Her wet black hair fell upon her shoulders. She stared at Freeman. He rose, forming words of apology in his mind. A haze that had been before his eyes, evaporated. Freeman grew pale and the girl blushed.

Freeman was, of course, a New York City boy from away back. As the girl stood there unselfconsciously regarding him — it could not have been longer than thirty seconds — he was aware of his background and certain other disadvantages; but he also knew he wasn't a bad-looking guy, even, it could be said, quite on the handsome side. Though a pinprick bald at the back of his noggin — not more than a dime could adequately cover — his head of hair was alive, expressive; Freeman's gray eyes were clear, unenvious, nose well-molded, the mouth generous. He had well-proportioned arms and legs and his stomach lay respectfully flat. He was a bit short, but on him, he knew, it barely showed. One of his former girl friends had told him she sometimes thought of him as tall. This counterbalanced the occasions when he had thought of himself as short. Yet though he knew he made a good appearance, Freeman feared this moment, partly because of all he hungered for from life, and partly because of the uncountable obstacles existing between strangers, may the word forever perish.

She, apparently, had no fear of their meeting; as a matter of surprising fact, seemed to welcome it, immediately curious about him. She had, of course, the advantage of position — which included receiving, so to speak, the guest-intruder. And she had grace to lean on; herself also favored physically — mama, what a queenly high-assed form — itself the cause of grace. Her dark, sharp Italian face had that quality of beauty which holds the mark of history, the beauty of a people and civilization. The large brown eyes, under straight slender brows, were filled with sweet light; her lips were purely cut as if from red flowers; her nose was perhaps the one touch of imperfection that perfected the rest — a trifle long and thin. Despite the effect, a little of sculpture, her ovoid face, tapering to a small chin, was soft, suffused with the loveliness of youth. She was about twenty-three or -four. And when Freeman had, to a small degree, calmed down, he discovered in her eyes a hidden hunger, or memory thereof; perhaps it was sadness; and he felt he was, for this reason, if not unknown others, sincerely welcomed. Had he, Oh God, at last met his fate?

"Si é perduto?" the girl asked, smiling, still tightly holding her white towel. Freeman understood and answered in English. "No, I came on my own. On purpose you might say." He had in mind to ask her if she remembered having seen him before, namely in last night's rowboat, but didn't.

"Are you an American?" she inquired, her Italian accent pleasantly touched with an English one.

"That's right."

The girl studied him for a full minute, and then hesitantly asked, "Are you, perhaps, Jewish?"

Freeman suppressed a groan. Though secretly shocked by the question, it was not, in a way, unexpected. Yet he did not look Jewish, could pass as not — had. So without batting an eyelash, he said, no, he wasn't. And a moment later added, though he personally had nothing against them.

"It was just a thought. You Americans are so varied," she explained vaguely.

"I understand," he said, "but have no worry." Lifting his hat, he introduced himself: "Henry R. Freeman, traveling abroad."

"My name," she said, after an absent-minded pause, "is Isabella del Dongo."

Safe on first, thought Freeman. "I'm proud to know you." He bowed. She gave him her hand with a gentle smile. He was about to surprise it with a kiss when the comical guide appeared at a wall a few terraces above. He gazed at them in astonishment, then let out a yell and ran down the stairs, waving his cane like a rapier.

"Transgressor," he shouted at Freeman.

The girl said something to calm him, but the guide was too furious to listen. He grabbed Freeman's arm, yanking him toward the stairs. And though Freeman, in the interest of good manners, barely resisted, the guide whacked him across the seat of the pants; but the ex-floorwalker did not complain.

Though his departure from the island had been, to put it mildly, an embarrassment (the girl had vanished after her unsuccessful momentary intercession), Freeman dreamed of a triumphant return. The big thing so far was that she, a knockout, had taken to him; he had been favored by her. Just why, he couldn't exactly tell, but he could tell yes, had seen in her eyes. Yet wondering if yes why yes — an old habit — Freeman, among other reasons he had already thought of, namely the thus and therefore of man-woman attraction — laid it to the fact that he was different, had dared. He had, specifically, dared to duck the guide and be waiting for her at the edge of the lake when she came out of it. And she was different too, (which of course quickened her response to him). Not only in her looks and background, but of course different as regards past. (He had been reading with fascination about the del Dongos in all the local guide books.) Her past he could see boiling in her all the way back to the knights of old, and then some; his own history was something else again, but men were malleable, and he wasn't afraid of attempting to create certain daring combinations: Isabella and Henry Freeman. Hoping to meet someone like her was his main reason for having come abroad. And he had also felt he would be appreciated more by a European woman; his personality, that is. Yet, since their lives were *so* different, Freeman had moments of grave doubt, wondered what trials he was in for if he went after her, as he had every intention of doing: with her unknown family — other things of that sort. And he was in after-thought worried because she had asked him if he was Jewish. Why had the question popped out of her pretty mouth before they had even met? He had never before been asked anything like this by a girl, under let's call it similar circumstances. Just when they were looking each other over. He was puzzled because he absolutely did not look Jewish. But then he figured her question might have been a "test" of some kind, she making it a point, when a man attracted her, quickly to determine his "eligibility." Maybe she had once had some sort of unhappy experience with a Jew? Unlikely, but possible, they were now everywhere. Freeman finally explained it to himself as "one of those things," perhaps a queer thought that had for no good reason impulsively entered her mind. And because it was queer, his answer, without elaboration, was sufficient. With ancient history why bother? All these things — the odds against him, whetted his adventurous appetite.

He was in the grip of an almost unbearable excitement and must see her again soon, often, become her friend — not more than a beginning but where begin? He considered calling her on the telephone, if there was one in a palazzo where Napoleon had slept. But if the maid or somebody answered the phone first, he would have a ridiculous time identifying himself; so he settled for sending her a note. Freeman wrote a few lines on good stationery he had bought for the purpose, asking if he might have the pleasure of seeing her again under circumstances favorable to leisurely conversation. He suggested a carriage ride to one of the other lakes in the neighborhood, and signed his name not Levin, of course, but Freeman. Later he told the padrona that anything addressed to that name was meant for him. She was always to refer to him as Mr. Freeman. He gave no explanation, although the padrona raised interested brows; but after he had slipped her — for reasons of friendship — a thousand lire, her expression became serene. Having mailed the letter, he felt time descend on him like an intricate trap. How would he ever endure until she answered? That evening he impatiently hired a rowboat and headed for Isola del Dongo. The water was glassy smooth but when he arrived, the palazzo was dark, almost gloomy, not a single window lit; the whole island looked dead. He saw no one, though he imagined her presence. Freeman thought of tying up at a dock and searching around a bit, but it seemed like folly. Rowing back to Stresa, he was stopped by the lake patrol and compelled to show his passport. An officer advised him not to row on the lake after dark; he might have an accident. The next morning, wearing sunglasses, a light straw, recently purchased, and a seersucker suit, he boarded the vaporetto and soon landed on the island of his dreams, together with the usual group of tourists. But the fanatic guide at once spied Freeman, and waving his cane like a schoolmaster's rod, called on him to depart peacefully. Fearing a scene that the girl would surely hear of, Freeman left at once, greatly annoyed. The padrona, that night, in a confidential mood, warned him not to have anything to do with anybody on the Isola del Dongo. The family had a perfidious history and was known for its deceit and trickery.

On Sunday, at the low point of a depression after an afternoon nap, Freeman heard a knock on his door. A long-legged boy in short pants and a torn shirt handed him an envelope, the corner embossed with somebody's coat of arms. Breathlessly, Freeman tore it open and extracted a sheet of thin bluish paper with a few lines of spidery writing on it: "You may come this afternoon at six. Ernesto will accompany you. I. del D." It was already after five. Freeman was overwhelmed, giddy with pleasure.

"Tu sei Ernesto?" he asked the boy.

The boy, perhaps eleven or twelve, who had been watching Freeman with large curious eyes, shook his head. "No, Signore. Sono Giacobbe."

"Dov'è Ernesto?"

The boy pointed vaguely at the window, which Freeman took to mean that whoever he was was waiting at the lake front.

Freeman changed in the bathroom, emerging in a jiffy with his new straw hat on and the seersucker suit. "Let's go." He ran down the stairs, the boy running after him.

At the dock, to Freeman's startled surprise, "Ernesto" turned out to be the temperamental guide with the pestiferous cane, probably a major domo in the palazzo, long with the family. Now a guide in another context, he was obviously an unwilling one, to judge from his expression. Perhaps a few wise words had subdued him and though haughty still, he settled for a show of politeness. Freeman greeted him courteously. The guide sat not in the ritzy launch Freeman had expected to see, but at the stern of an oversize, weather-beaten rowboat, a cross between a fishing dory and small lifeboat. Preceded by the boy, Freeman climbed in over the unoccupied part of the rear seat, then, as Giacobbe took his place at the oars, hesitantly sat down next to Ernesto. One of the boatmen on the shore gave them a shove off and the boy began to row. The big boat seemed hard to maneuver, but Giacobbe, working deftly with a pair of long, heavy oars, managed with ease. He rowed quickly from the shore and toward the island where Isabella was waiting.

Freeman, though heartened to be off, contented, loving the wide airy world, wasn't comfortable sitting so snug with Ernesto, who smelled freshly of garlic. The talkative guide was a silent traveler. A dead cheroot hung from the corner of his mouth, and from time to time he absently poked his cane in the slats at the bottom of the boat; if there was no leak, Freeman thought, he would create one. He seemed tired, as if he had been carousing all night and had found no time to rest. Once he removed his black felt hat to mop his head with a handkerchief, and Freeman realized he was bald and looked surprisingly old.

Though tempted to say something pleasant to the old man — no hard feelings on this marvelous journey, Freeman had no idea where to begin. What would he reply to a grunt? After a time of prolonged silence, now a bit on edge, Freeman remarked, "Maybe I'd better row and give the boy a rest?"

"As you weesh." Ernesto shrugged.

Freeman traded places with the boy, then wished he hadn't. The oars were impossibly heavy; he rowed badly, allowing the left oar to sink deeper into the water than the right, thus twisting the boat off course. It was like pulling a hearse, and as he awkwardly splashed the oars around, he was embarrassedly aware of the boy and Ernesto, alike in their dark eyes and greedy beaks, a pair of odd birds, openly staring at him. He wished them far far away from the beautiful island and in exasperation pulled harder. By dint of determined effort, though his palms were painfully blistered, he began to row rhythmically, and the boat went along more smoothly. Freeman gazed up in triumph but they were no longer watching him, the boy trailing a straw in the water, the guide staring dreamily into the distance.

After a while, as if having studied Freeman and decided, when all was said and done, that he wasn't exactly a villain, Ernesto spoke in a not unfriendly tone.

"Everybody says how reech ees America?" he remarked.

"Rich enough," Freeman grunted.

"Also thees ees the same with you?" The guide spoke with a half-embarrassed smile around his drooping cheroot butt.

"I'm comfortable," Freeman replied, and in honesty added, "but I have to work for a living."

"For the young people ees a nice life, no? I mean there ees always what to eat, and for the woman een the house many remarkable machines?"

"Many," Freeman said. Nothing comes from nothing, he thought. He's been asked to ask questions. Freeman then gave the guide an earful on the American standard of living, and he meant living. This for whatever it was worth to such as the Italian aristocracy. He hoped for the best. You could never tell the needs and desires of others.

Ernesto, as if memorizing what he had just heard, watched Freeman row for a while.

"Are you in biziness?" he ultimately asked.

Freeman searched around and came up with, "Sort of in public relations."

Ernesto now threw away his butt. "Excuse me that I ask. How much does one earn in thees biziness in America?"

Calculating quickly, Freeman replied, "I personally average about a hundred dollars a week. That comes to about a quarter million lire every month."

Ernesto repeated the sum, holding onto his hat in the breeze. The boy's eyes had widened. Freeman hid a satisfied smile.

"And your father?" Here the guide paused, searching Freeman's face.

"What about him?" asked Freeman, tensing.

"What ees hees trade?"

"Was. He's dead — insurance."

Ernesto removed his respectful hat, letting the sunlight bathe his bald head. They said nothing more until they had reached the island, then Freeman, consolidating possible gain, asked him in a complimentary tone where he had learned his English.

"Everywhere," Ernesto replied, with a weary smile, and, Freeman, alert for each shift in prevailing wind, felt that if he hadn't made a bosom friend, he had at least softened an enemy; and that, on home grounds, was going good.

They landed and watched the boy tie up the boat; Freeman asked Ernesto where the signorina was. The guide, now looking bored by it all, pointed his cane at the top terraces, a sweeping gesture that seemed to take in the whole upper half of the luscious island. Freeman hoped the man would not insist on accompanying him and interfering with his meeting with the girl; but when he looked down from looking up without sighting Isabella, both Ernesto and Giacobbe had made themselves scarce. Leave it to the Italians at this sort of thing, Freeman thought.

Warning himself to be careful, tactful, he went quickly up the stairs. At each terrace he glanced around, then ran up to the next, his hat already in his hand. He found her, after wandering through profusions of flowers, where he had guessed she would be, alone in the garden behind the palazzo. She was sitting on an old stone bench near a little marble fountain, whose jets from the mouths of mocking elves sparkled in mellow sunlight.

Beholding her, the lovely face, sharply incised, yet soft in its femininity, the dark eyes pensive, her hair loosely knotted at the nape of her graceful neck, Freeman ached to his oar-blistered fingers. She was wearing a linen blouse of some soft shade of red that fell gently upon her breasts, and a long, slender black skirt; her tanned legs were without stockings; and on her narrow feet she wore sandals. As Freeman approached her, walking slowly to keep from loping, she brushed back a strand of hair, a gesture so beautiful it saddened him, because it was gone in the doing; and though Freeman, on this miraculous Sunday evening was aware of his indefatigable reality, he could not help thinking as he dwelt upon her lost gesture, that she might be as elusive as it, as evanescent; and so might this island be, and so, despite all the days he had lived through, good, bad and boring, that too often sneaked into his thoughts — so, indeed, might he today, tomorrow. He went toward her with a deep sense of the transitoriness of things, but this feeling was overwhelmed by one of pure joy when she rose to give him her hand.

"Welcome," Isabella said, blushing; she seemed happy, yet, in her manner, a little agitated to see him — perhaps one and the same thing — and he wanted then and there to embrace her but could not work up the nerve. Although he felt in her presence a fulfillment, as if they had already confessed love for one another, at the same time Freeman sensed an uneasiness in her which made him think, though he fought the idea, that they were far away from love; or at least were approaching it through opaque mystery. But that's what happened, Freeman, who had often been in love, told himself. Until you were lovers you were strangers.

In conversation he was at first formal. "I thank you for your kind note. I have been looking forward to seeing you."

She turned toward the palazzo. "My people are out. They have gone to a wedding on another island. May I show you something of the palace?"

He was at this news both pleased and disappointed. He did not at the moment feel like meeting her family. Yet if she had presented him, it would have been a good sign.

They walked for a while in the garden, then Isabella took Freeman's hand and led him through a heavy door into the large rococo palazzo.

"What would you care to see?"

Though he had superficially been through two floors of the building, wanting to be led by her, this close to him, Freeman replied, "Whatever you want me to."

She took him first to the chamber were Napoleon had slept. "It wasn't Napoleon himself, who slept here," Isabella explained. "He slept on Isola Bella. His brother Joseph may have been here, or perhaps Pauline, with one of her lovers. No one is sure."

"Oh ho, a trick," said Freeman.

"We often pretend," she remarked. "This is a poor country."

They entered the main picture gallery. Isabella pointed out the Titians, Tintorettos, Bellinis, making Freeman breathless; then at the door of the room she turned with an embarrassed smile and said that most of the paintings in the gallery were copies.

"Copies?" Freeman was shocked.

"Yes, although there are some fair originals from the Lombard school."

"All the Titians are copies?"

"All."

This slightly depressed him. "What about the statuary—also copies?"

"For the most part."

His face fell.

"Is something the matter?"

"Only that I couldn't tell the fake from the real."

"Oh, but many of the copies are exceedingly beautiful," Isabella said. "It would take an expert to tell they weren't originals."

"I guess I've got a lot to learn," Freeman said.

At this she squeezed his hand and he felt better.

But the tapestries, she remarked as they traversed the long hall hung with them, which darkened as the sun set, were genuine and valuable. They meant little to Freeman: long floor-to-ceiling, bluish-green fabrics of woodland scenes: stags, unicorns and tigers disporting themselves, though in one picture, the tiger killed the unicorn. Isabella hurried past this and led Freeman into a room he had not been in before, hung with tapestries of somber scenes from the *Inferno*. One before which they stopped, was of a writhing leper, spotted from head to foot with pustulating sores which he tore at with his nails but the itch went on forever.

"What did he do to deserve his fate?" Freeman inquired.

"He falsely said he could fly."

"For that you go to hell?"

She did not reply. The hall had become gloomily dark, so they left.

From the garden close by the beach where the raft was anchored, they watched the water turn all colors. Isabella had little to say about herself — she seemed to be quite often pensive — and Freeman, concerned with the complexities of the future, though his heart contained multitudes, found himself comparatively silent. When the night was complete, as the moon was rising, Isabella said she would be gone for a moment, and stepped behind a shrub. When she came forth, Freeman had this utterly amazing vision of her, naked, but before he could even focus his eyes on her flower-like behind, she was already in the water, swimming for the raft. After an anguished consideration of could he swim that far or would he drown, Freeman, eager to see her from up close (she was sitting on the raft, showing her breasts to the moon) shed his clothes behind the shrub where her delicate things lay, and walked down the stone steps into the warm water. He swam awkwardly, hating the picture he must make in her eyes, Apollo Belvedere slightly maimed; and still suffered visions of drowning in twelve feet of water. Or suppose she had to jump in to rescue him? However, nothing risked, nothing gained, so he splashed on and made the raft with breath to spare, his worries always greater than their cause.

But when he had pulled himself up on the raft, to his dismay, Isabella was no longer there. He caught a glimpse of her on the shore, darting behind the shrub. Nursing gloomy thoughts, Freeman rested a while, then, when he had sneezed twice and presupposed a nasty cold, jumped into the water and splashed his way back to the island. Isabella, already clothed, was waiting with a towel. She threw it to Freeman as he came up the steps, and withdrew while he dried himself and dressed. When he came forth in his seersucker, she offered salami, prosciutto, cheese, bread, and red wine, from a large platter delivered from the kitchen. Freeman, for a while angered at the runaround on the raft, relaxed with the wine and feeling of freshness after a bath. The mosquitoes behaved long enough for him to say he loved her. Isabella kissed him tenderly, then Ernesto and Giacobbe appeared and rowed him back to Stresa.

Monday morning Freeman didn't know what to do with himself. He awoke with restless memories, enormously potent, many satisfying, some burdensome; they ate him, he ate them. He felt he should somehow have made every minute with her better, hadn't begun to say half of what he had wanted — the kind of man he was, what they could get out of life together. And he regretted that he hadn't gotten quickly to the raft, still excited by what might have happened if he had reached it before she had left. But a memory was only a memory — you could forget, not change it. On the other hand, he was pleased, surprised by what he had accomplished: the evening alone with her, the trusting, intimate sight of her beautiful body, her kiss, the unspoken promise of love. His desire for her was so splendid it hurt. He wandered through the afternoon, dreaming of her, staring often at the glittering islands in the opaque lake. By nightfall he was exhausted and went to sleep oppressed by all he had lived through.

It was strange, he thought, as he lay in bed waiting to sleep, that of all his buzzing worries he was worried most about one. If Isabella loved him, as he now felt she did or would before very long; with the strength of this love they could conquer their problems as they arose. He anticipated a good handful, stirred up, in all probability, by her family; but life in the U.S.A. was considered by many Italians, including aristocrats (else why had Ernesto been sent to sniff out conditions there?) a fine thing for their marriageable daughters. Given this additional advantage, things would somehow get worked out, especially if Isabella, an independent girl, gazed a little eagerly at the star-spangled shore. Her family would give before flight in her eyes. No, the worry that troubled him most was the lie he had told her, that he wasn't a Jew. He could, of course, confess, say she knew Levin, not Freeman, man of adventure, but that might ruin all, since it was quite clear she wanted nothing to do with a Jew, or why, at first sight, had she asked so searching a question? Or he might admit nothing and let her, more or less, find out after she had lived a while in the States and seen it was no crime to be Jewish; that a man's past was, it could safely be said, expendable. Yet this treatment, if the surprise was upsetting, might cause recriminations later on. Another solution might be one he had thought of often: to change his name (he had considered Le Vin but preferred Free-man) and forget he had ever been born Jewish. There was no ques-tion of hurting family, or being embarrassed by them, he the only son of both parents dead. Cousins lived in Toledo, Ohio, where they would always live and never bother. And when he brought Is-abella to America they could skip N.Y.C. and go to live in a place like San Francisco, where nobody knew him and nobody "would know." To arrange such details and prepare other minor changes was why he figured on a trip or two home before they were married; he was prepared for that. As for the wedding itself, since he would have to marry her here to get her out of Italy, it would probably have to be in a church, but he would go along with that to hasten things. It was done everyday. Thus he decided, although it did not entirely satisfy him; not so much the denial of being Jewish — what had it brought him but headaches, inferiorities, unhappy memories? — as the lie to the beloved. At first sight love and a lie; it lay on his heart like a sore. Yet, if that was the way it had to be, it was the way.

He awoke the next morning, beset by a swarm of doubts concerning his plans and possibilities. When would he see Isabella again, let alone marry her? ("When?" he had whispered before getting into the boat, and she had vaguely promised, "Soon.") Soon was brutally endless. The mail brought nothing and Freeman grew dismayed.

Had he, he asked himself, been constructing a hopeless fantasy, wish seducing probability? Was he inventing a situation that didn't exist, namely, her feeling for him, the possibility of a future with her? He was desperately casting about for something to keep his mood from turning dark blue, when a knock sounded on his door. The padrona, he thought, because she often came up for one unimportant thing or another, but to his unspeakable joy it was Cupid in short pants — Giacobbe holding forth the familiar envelope. She would meet him, Isabella wrote, at two o'clock in the piazza where the electric tram took off for Mt. Mottarone, from whose summit one saw the beautiful panorama of lakes and mountains in the region. Would he share this with her?

Although he had quashed the morning's anxiety, Freeman was there at one P.M., smoking impatiently. His sun rose as she appeared, but as she came towards him he noticed she was not quite looking at him (in the distance he could see Giacobbe rowing away) her face neutral, inexpressive. He was at first concerned, but she had, after all, written the letter to him, so he wondered what hot nails she had had to walk on to get off the island. He must sometime during the day drop the word "elope" to see if she savored it. But whatever was bothering her, Isabella immediately shook off. She smiled as she greeted him; he hoped for her lips but got instead her polite fingers. These he kissed in broad daylight (let the spies tell papa) and she shyly withdrew her hand. She was wearing — it surprised him, though he gave her credit for resisting foolish pressures — exactly the same blouse and skirt she had worn on Sunday. They boarded the tram with a dozen tourists and sat alone on the open seat in front; as a reward for managing this she permitted Freeman to hold her hand. He sighed. The tram, drawn by an old electric locomotive moved slowly through the town and more slowly up the slope of the mountain. They rode for close to two hours, watching the lake fall as the mountains rose. Isabella, apart from pointing to something now and then, was again silent, withdrawn, but Freeman, allowing her her own rate at flowering, for the moment without plans, was practically contented. A long vote for an endless journey; but the tram at last came to a stop and they walked through a field thick with wildflowers, up the slope to the summit of the mountain. Though the tourists followed in a crowd, the mountain top was broad and they stood near its edge, to all intents and purposes alone. Below them, on the green undulating plains of Piedmont and Lombardy, seven lakes were scattered, each a mirror reflecting whose fate? And high in the distance rose a ring of astonishing snow-clad Alps. Ah, he murmured, and fell silent.

"We say here," Isabella said, " 'un pezzo di paradiso caduto dal cielo.' "

"You can say it again." Freeman was deeply moved by the sublimity of the distant Alps. She named the white peaks from Mt. Rosa to the Jungfrau. Gazing at them, he felt he had grown a head taller and was inspired to accomplish a feat men would wonder at.

"Isabella — " Freeman turned to ask her to marry him; but she was standing apart from him, her face pale.

Pointing to the snowy mountains, her hand moving in a gentle arc, she asked, "Don't those peaks — those seven — look like a Menorah?"

"Like a what?" Freeman politely inquired. He had a sudden frightening remembrance of her seeing him naked as he came out of the lake and felt constrained to tell her that circumcision was de rigueur in stateside hospitals; but he didn't dare. She may not have noticed.

"Like a seven-branched candelabrum holding white candles in the sky?" Isabella asked.

"Something like that."

"Or do you see the Virgin's crown adorned with jewels?"

"Maybe the crown," he faltered. "It all depends how you look at it."

They left the mountain and went down to the water. The tram ride was faster going down. At the lake front, as they were waiting for Giacobbe to come with the rowboat, Isabella, her eyes troubled, told Freeman she had a confession to make. He, still eager to propose, hoped she would finally say she loved him. Instead, she said, "My name is not del Dongo. It is Isabella della Seta. The del Dongos have not been on the island in years. We are the caretakers of the palace, my father, brother and I. We are poor people."

"Caretakers?" Freeman was astonished.

"Yes."

"Ernesto is your father?" His voice rose.

She nodded.

"Was it his idea for you to say you were somebody else?"

"No, mine. He did what I asked him to. He has wanted me to go to America, but under the right circumstances."

"So you had to pretend," he said bitterly. He was more greatly disturbed than he could account for, as if he had been expecting just this to happen.

She blushed and turned away. "I was not sure of the circumstances. I wanted you to stay until I knew you better."

"Why didn't you say so?"

"Perhaps I wasn't serious in the beginning. I said what I thought you wanted to hear. At the same time I wished you to stay. I thought you would be clearer to me after a while."

"Clearer how?"

"I don't really know." Her eyes searched his, then she dropped her glance.

"I'm not hiding anything," he said. He wanted to say more but warned himself not to.

"That's what I was afraid of."

Giacobbe had come with the boat and steadied it for his sister. They were alike as the proverbial peas—two dark Italian faces, the Middle Ages looking out of their eyes. Isabella got into the boat and Giacobbe pushed off with one oar. She waved from afar.

Freeman went back to his pensione in a turmoil, hurt where it hurts—in his dreams, thinking he should have noticed before how worn her blouse and skirt were, should have seen more than he had. It was this that irked. He called himself a damn fool for making up fairy tales—Freeman in love with the Italian aristocracy. He thought of taking off for Venice or Florence, but his heart ached for love of her, and he could not forget that he had originally come in the simple hope of finding a girl worth marrying. If the desire had developed complications, the fault was mostly his own. After an hour in his room, burdened by an overpowering loneliness, Freeman felt he must have her. She mustn't get away from him. So what if the countess had become a caretaker? She was a natural-born queen, whether by del Dongo or any other name. So she had lied to him, but so had he to her; they were quits on that score and his conscience was calm. He felt things would be easier all around now that the air had been cleared.

Freeman ran down to the dock; the sun had set and the boatmen were home, swallowing spaghetti. He was considering untying one of the rowboats and paying tomorrow, when he caught sight of someone sitting on a bench — Ernesto, in his hot winter hat, smoking a cheroot. He was resting his wrists on the handle of his cane, his chin on them.

"You weesh a boat?" the guide asked in a not unkindly tone.

"With all my heart. Did Isabella send you?"

"No."

He came because she was unhappy, Freeman guessed — maybe crying. There's a father for you, a real magician despite his appearance. He waves his stick and up pops Freeman for his little girl.

"Get een," said Ernesto.

"I'll row," said Freeman. He had almost added "father," but had caught himself. As if guessing the jest, Ernesto smiled, a little sadly. But he sat at the stern of the boat, enjoying the ride.

In the middle of the lake, seeing the mountains surrounding it lit in the last glow of daylight, Freeman thought of the "Menorah" in the Alps. Where had she got the word, he wondered, and decided anywhere, a book or picture. But wherever she had, he must settle this subject once and for all tonight.

When the boat touched the dock, the pale moon rose. Ernesto tied up, and handed Freeman a flashlight.

"Een the jarden," he said tiredly, pointing with his cane.

"Don't wait up." Freeman hastened to the garden at the lake's edge, where the roots of trees hung like hoary beards above the water; the flashlight didn't work, but the moon and his memory were enough. Isabella, God bless her, was standing at the low wall among the moonlit statuary: stags, tigers and unicorns, poets and painters, shepherds with pipes, and playful shepherdesses, gazing at the light shimmering on the water.

She was wearing white, the figure of a future bride; perhaps it was an altered wedding dress — he would not be surprised if a hand-me-down, the way they saved clothes in this poor country. He had pleasant thoughts of buying her some nifty outfits.

She was motionless, her back toward him — though he could picture her bosom breathing. When he said good evening, lifting his light straw, she turned to him with a sweet smile. He tenderly kissed her lips; this she let him do, softly returning the same.

"Goodbye," Isabella whispered.

"To whom goodbye?" Freeman affectionately mocked. "I have come to marry you."

She gazed at him with eyes moistly bright, then came the soft, inevitable thunder: "Are you a Jew?"

"Why should I lie?" he thought; she's mine for the asking. But then he trembled with the fear of at the last moment losing her, so Freeman answered, though his scalp prickled, "How many no's make never? Why do you persist with such foolish questions?"

"Because I hoped you were." Slowly she unbuttoned her bodice, arousing Freeman, though he was thoroughly confused as to her intent. When she revealed her breasts — he could have wept at their beauty (now recalling a former invitation to gaze at them, but he had arrived too late on the raft) — to his horror he discerned tattooed on the soft and tender flesh a bluish line of distorted numbers.

"Buchenwald," Isabella said, "when I was a little girl. The Fascists sent us there. The Nazis did it."

Freeman groaned, incensed at the cruelty, stunned by the desecration.

"I can't marry you. We are Jews. My past is meaningful to me. I treasure what I suffered for."

"Jews," he muttered, " —you? Oh, God, why did you keep this from me, too?"

"I did not wish to tell you something you would not welcome. I thought at one time it was possible you were — I hoped but was wrong."

"Isabella — " he cried brokenly. "Listen, I — I am — "

He groped for her breasts, to clutch, kiss or suckle them; but she had stepped among the statues, and when he vainly sought her in the veiled mist that had risen from the lake, still calling her name, Freeman embraced only moonlit stone.

A Silver Dish

SAUL BELLOW

Saul Bellow (1915–): *Saul Bellow is, and has been during much of the last half century, one of America's most widely read and admired literary novelists. Born in Lachine, Quebec, a suburb of Montreal, the youngest child of Russian immigrant parents, Bellow moved with his family to Humboldt Park, Chicago, when he was a boy. He was educated in the Chicago public schools, then at the University of Chicago, Northwestern University, and the University of Wisconsin. Bellow is primarily noted as a novelist* (The Victim, The Adventures of Augie March, Henderson the Rain King, Herzog, Mr. Sammler's Planet, *and* Humboldt's Gift *are among the most accomplished of his works), but he has also written for the stage* (The Last Analysis*) and has published two collections of stories (*Mosby's Memoirs *and* Him with His Foot in His Mouth*), several novellas (most notably* Seize the Day*), and collections of occasional essays and memoirs (among them* To Jerusalem and Back *and* It All Adds Up.*) Throughout his distinguished career, Bellow has received highly respectful critical attention and praise: several Guggenheim fellowships, three National Book Awards, a Pulitzer Prize, a grant from the Ford Foundation, and, in 1976, the Nobel Prize for Literature. In 1990 he received the National Book Foundation Medal for his distinguished contribution to American letters. He has taught at the University of Minnesota, Bard College, and most prominently at the University of Chicago, where for many years he was a part of the Committee on Social Thought. Retired from teaching but still writing and publishing, Bellow currently lives near Boston.*

What do you do about death — in this case, the death of an old father? If you're a modern person, sixty years of age, and a man who's been around, like Woody Selbst, what do you do? Take this matter of mourning, and take it against a contemporary background. How, against a contemporary background, do you mourn an octogenarian father, nearly blind, his heart enlarged, his lungs filling with fluid, who creeps, stumbles, gives off the odors, the moldiness or gassiness, of old men. I *mean*! As Woody put it, be realistic. Think what times these are. The papers daily give it to you — the Lufthansa pilot in Aden is described by the hostages on his knees, begging the Palestinian terrorists not to execute him, but they shoot him through the head. Later they themselves are killed. And still others shoot others, or shoot themselves. That's what you read in the press, see on the tube, mention at dinner. We know now what goes daily through the whole of the human community, like a global death-peristalsis.

Woody, a businessman in South Chicago, was not an ignorant person. He knew more such phrases than you would expect a tile contractor (offices, lobbies, lavatories) to know. The kind of knowledge he had was not the kind for which you get academic degrees. Although Woody had studied for two years in a seminary, preparing to be a minister. Two years of college during the Depression was more than most high-school graduates could afford. After that, in his own vital, picturesque, original way (Morris, his old man, was also, in his days of nature, vital and picturesque), Woody had read up on many subjects, subscribed to *Science* and other magazines that gave real information, and had taken night courses at De Paul and Northwestern in ecology, criminology, existentialism. Also he had traveled extensively in Japan, Mexico, and Africa, and there was an African experience that was especially relevant to mourning. It was this: on a launch near the Murchison Falls in Uganda, he had seen a buffalo calf seized by a crocodile from the bank of the White Nile. There were giraffes along the tropical river, and hippopotamuses, and baboons, and flamingos and other brilliant birds crossing the bright air in the heat of the morning, when the calf, stepping into the river to drink, was grabbed by the hoof and dragged down. The parent buffaloes couldn't figure it out. Under the water the calf still threshed, fought, churned the mud. Woody, the robust traveler, took this in as he sailed by, and to him it looked as if the parent cattle were asking each other dumbly what had happened. He chose to assume that there was pain in this, he read brute grief into it. On the White Nile, Woody had the impression that he had gone back to the pre-Adamite past, and he brought reflections on this impression home to South Chicago. He brought also a bundle of hashish from Kampala. In this he took a chance with the customs inspectors, banking perhaps on his broad build, frank face, high color. He didn't look like a wrongdoer, a bad guy; he looked like a good guy. But he liked taking chances. Risk was a wonderful stimulus. He threw down his trenchcoat on the customs counter. If the inspectors searched the pockets, he was prepared to say that the coat wasn't his. But he got away with it, and the Thanksgiving turkey was stuffed with hashish. This was much enjoyed. That was practically the last feast at which Pop, who also relished risk or defiance, was present. The hashish Woody had tried to raise in his backyard from the Africa seeds didn't take. But behind his warehouse, where the Lincoln Continental was parked, he kept a patch of marijuana. There was no harm at all in Woody, but he didn't like being entirely within the law. It was simply a question of self-respect.

After that Thanksgiving, Pop gradually sank as if he had a slow leak. This went on for some years. In and out of the hospital, he dwindled, his mind wandered, he couldn't even concentrate enough to complain, except in exceptional moments on the Sundays Woody regularly devoted to him. Morris, an amateur who once was taken seriously by Willie Hoppe, the great pro himself, couldn't execute the simplest billiard shots anymore. He could only conceive shots; he began to theorize about impossible three-cushion combinations. Halina, the Polish woman with whom Morris had lived for over forty years as man and wife, was too old herself now to run to the hospital. So Woody had to do it. There was Woody's mother, too—a Christian convert—needing care; she was over eighty and frequently hospitalized. Everybody had diabetes and pleurisy and arthritis and cataracts and cardiac pacemakers. And everybody had lived by the body, but the body was giving out.

There were Woody's two sisters as well, unmarried, in their fifties, very Christian, very straight, still living with Mama in an entirely Christian bungalow. Woody, who took full responsibility for them all, occasionally had to put one of the girls (they had become sick girls) in a mental institution. Nothing severe. The sisters were wonderful women, both of them gorgeous once, but neither of the poor things was playing with a full deck. And all the factions had to be kept separate—Mama, the Christian convert; the fundamentalist sisters; Pop, who read the Yiddish paper as long as he could still see print; Halina, a good Catholic. Woody, the seminary forty years behind him, described himself as an agnostic. Pop had no more religion than you could find in the Yiddish paper, but he made Woody promise to bury him among Jews, and that was where he lay now, in the Hawaiian shirt Woody had bought for him at the tilers' convention in Honolulu. Woody would allow no undertaker's assistant to dress him, but came to the parlor and buttoned the stiff into the shirt himself, and the old man went down looking like Ben-Gurion in a simple wooden coffin, sure to rot fast. That was how Woody wanted it all. At the graveside, he had taken off and folded his jacket, rolled up his sleeves on thick freckled biceps, waved back the little tractor standing by, and shoveled the dirt himself. His big face, broad at the bottom, narrowed upward like a Dutch house. And, his small good lower teeth taking hold of the upper lip in his exertion, he performed the final duty of a son. He was very fit, so it must have been emotion, not the shoveling, that made him redden so. After the funeral, he went home with Halina and her son, a decent Polack like his mother, and talented, too — Mitosh played the organ at hockey and basketball games in the Stadium, which took a smart man because it was a rabble-rousing kind of occupation — and they had some drinks and comforted the old girl. Halina was true blue, always one hundred percent for Morris.

Then for the rest of the week Woody was busy, had jobs to run, office responsibilities, family responsibilities. He lived alone; as did his wife; as did his mistress: everybody in a separate establishment. Since his wife, after fifteen years of separation, had not learned to take care of herself, Woody did her shopping on Fridays, filled her freezer. He had to take her this week to buy shoes. Also, Friday night he always spent with Helen — Helen was his wife de facto. Saturday he did his big weekly shopping. Saturday night he devoted to Mom and his sisters. So he was too busy to attend to his own feelings except, intermittently, to note to himself, "First Thursday in the grave." "First Friday, and fine weather." "First Saturday; he's got to be getting used to it." Under his breath he occasionally said, "Oh, Pop."

But it was Sunday that hit him, when the bells rang all over South Chicago — the Ukrainian, Roman Catholic, Greek, Russian, African Methodist churches, sounding off one after another. Woody had his offices in his warehouse, and there had built an apartment for himself, very spacious and convenient, in the top story. Because he left every Sunday morning at seven to spend the day with Pop, he had forgotten by how many churches Selbst Tile Company was surrounded. He was still in bed when he heard the bells, and all at once he knew how heartbroken he was. This sudden big heartache in a man of sixty, a practical, physical, healthy-minded, and experienced man, was deeply unpleasant. When he had an unpleasant condition, he believed in taking something for it. So he thought: What shall I take? There were plenty of remedies available. His cellar was stocked with cases of Scotch whisky, Polish vodka, Armagnac, Moselle, Burgundy. There were also freezers with steaks and with game and with Alaskan king crab. He bought with a broad hand — by the crate and by the dozen. But in the end, when he got out of bed, he took nothing but a cup of coffee. While the kettle was heating, he put on his Japanese judo-style suit and sat down to reflect.

Woody was moved when things were *honest*. Bearing beams were honest, undisguised concrete pillars inside high-rise apartments were honest. It was bad to cover up anything. He hated faking. Stone was honest. Metal was honest. These Sunday bells were very straight. They broke loose, they wagged and rocked, and the vibrations and the banging did something for him — cleansed his insides, purified his blood. A bell was a one-way throat, had only one thing to tell you and simply told it. He listened.

He had had some connections with bells and churches. He was after all something of a Christian. Born a Jew, he was a Jew facially, with a hint of Iroquois or Cherokee, but his mother had been converted more than fifty years ago by her brother-in-law, the Reverend Doctor Kovner. Kovner, a rabbinical student who had left the Hebrew Union College in Cincinnati to become a minister and establish a mission, had given Woody a partly Christian upbringing. Now, Pop was on the outs with these fundamentalists. He said that the Jews came to the mission to get coffee, bacon, canned pineapple, day-old bread, and dairy products. And if they had to listen to sermons, that was okay — this was the Depression and you couldn't be too particular — but he knew they sold the bacon.

The Gospels said it plainly: "Salvation is from the Jews."

Backing the Reverend Doctor were wealthy fundamentalists, mainly Swedes, eager to speed up the Second Coming by converting all Jews. The foremost of Kovner's backers was Mrs. Skoglund, who had inherited a large dairy business from her late husband. Woody was under her special protection.

Woody was fourteen years of age when Pop took off with Halina, who worked in his shop, leaving his difficult Christian wife and his converted son and his small daughters. He came to Woody in the backyard one spring day and said, "From now on you're the man of the house." Woody was practicing with a golf club, knocking off the heads of dandelions. Pop came into the yard in his good suit, which was too hot for the weather, and when he took off his fedora the skin of his head was marked with a deep ring and the sweat was sprinkled over his scalp — more drops than hairs. He said, "I'm going to move out." Pop was anxious, but he was set to go — determined. "It's no use. I can't live a life like this." Envisioning the life Pop simply *had* to live, his free life, Woody was able to picture him in the billiard parlor, under the El tracks in a crap game, or playing poker at Brown and Koppel's upstairs. "You're going to be the man of the house," said Pop. "It's okay. I put you all on welfare. I just got back from Wabansia Avenue, from the relief station." Hence the suit and the hat. "They're sending out a caseworker." Then he said, "You got to lend me money to buy gasoline — the caddie money you saved."

Understanding that Pop couldn't get away without his help, Woody turned over to him all he had earned at the Sunset Ridge Country Club in Winnetka. Pop felt that the valuable life lesson he was transmitting was worth far more than these dollars, and whenever he was conning his boy a sort of high-priest expression came down over his bent nose, his ruddy face. The children, who got their finest ideas at the movies, called him Richard Dix. Later, when the comic strip came out, they said he was Dick Tracy.

As Woody now saw it, under the tumbling bells, he had bankrolled his own desertion. Ha ha! He found this delightful; and especially Pop's attitude of "That'll teach you to trust your father." For this was a demonstration on behalf of real life and free instincts, against religion and hypocrisy. But mainly it was aimed against being a fool, the disgrace of foolishness. Pop had it in for the Reverend Doctor Kovner, not because he was an apostate (Pop couldn't have cared less), not because the mission was a racket (he admitted that the Reverend Doctor was personally honest), but because Doctor Kovner behaved foolishly, spoke like a fool, and acted like a fiddler. He tossed his hair like a Paganini (this was Woody's addition; Pop had never even heard of Paganini). Proof that he was not a spiritual leader was that he converted Jewish women by stealing their hearts. "He works up all those broads," said Pop. "He doesn't even know it himself, I swear he doesn't know how he gets them."

From the other side, Kovner often warned Woody, "Your father is a dangerous person. Of course, you love him; you should love him and forgive him, Voodrow, but you are old enough to understand he is leading a life of wice."

It was all petty stuff: Pop's sinning was on a boy level and therefore made a big impression on a boy. And on Mother. Are wives children, or what? Mother often said, "I hope you put that brute in your prayers. Look what he has done to us. But only pray for him, don't see him." But he saw him all the time. Woodrow was leading a double life, sacred and profane. He accepted Jesus Christ as his personal redeemer. Aunt Rebecca took advantage of this. She made him work. He had to work under Aunt Rebecca. He filled in for the janitor at the mission and settlement house. In winter, he had to feed the coal furnace, and on some nights he slept near the furnace room, on the pool table. He also picked the lock of the storeroom. He took canned pineapple and cut bacon from the flitch with his pocketknife. He crammed himself with uncooked bacon. He had a big frame to fill out.

Only now, sipping Melitta coffee, he asked himself: Had he been so hungry? No, he loved being reckless. He was fighting Aunt Rebecca Kovner when he took out his knife and got on a box to reach the bacon. She didn't know, she couldn't prove that Woody, such a frank, strong, positive boy, who looked you in the eye, so direct, was a thief also. But he was also a thief. Whenever she looked at him, he knew that she was seeing his father. In the curve of his nose, the movements of his eyes, the thickness of his body, in his healthy face, she saw that wicked savage Morris.

Morris, you see, had been a street boy in Liverpool — Woody's mother and her sister were British by birth. Morris's Polish family, on their way to America, abandoned him in Liverpool because he had an eye infection and they would all have been sent back from Ellis Island. They stopped awhile in England, but his eyes kept running and they ditched him. They slipped away, and he had to make out alone in Liverpool at the age of twelve. Mother came of better people. Pop, who slept in the cellar of her house, fell in love with her. At sixteen, scabbing during a seamen's strike, he shoveled his way across the Atlantic and jumped ship in Brooklyn. He became an American, and America never knew it. He voted without papers, he drove without a license, he paid no taxes, he cut every corner. Horses, cards, billiards, and women were his lifelong interests, in ascending order. Did he love anyone (he was so busy)? Yes, he loved Halina. He loved his son. To this day, Mother believed that he had loved her most and always wanted to come back. This gave her a chance to act the queen, with her plump wrists and faded Queen Victoria face. "The girls are instructed never to admit him," she said. The Empress of India speaking.

Bell-battered Woodrow's soul was whirling this Sunday morning, indoors and out, to the past, back to his upper corner of the warehouse, laid out with such originality — the bells coming and going, metal on naked metal, until the bell circle expanded over the whole of steel-making, oil-refining, power-producing mid-autumn South Chicago, and all its Croatians, Ukrainians, Greeks, Poles, and respectable blacks heading for their churches to hear Mass or to sing hymns.

Woody himself had been a good hymn singer. He still knew the hymns. He had testified, too. He was often sent by Aunt Rebecca to get up and tell a churchful of Scandihoovians that he, a Jewish lad, accepted Jesus Christ. For this she paid him fifty cents. She made the disbursement. She was the bookkeeper, fiscal chief, general manager of the mission. The Reverend Doctor didn't know a thing about the operation. What the Doctor supplied was the fervor. He was genuine, a wonderful preacher. And what about Woody himself. He also had fervor. He was drawn to the Reverend Doctor. The Reverend Doctor taught him to lift up his eyes, gave him his higher life. Apart from this higher life, the rest was Chicago — the ways of Chicago, which came so natural that nobody thought to question them. So, for instance, in 1933 (what ancient, ancient times!), at the Century of Progress World's Fair, when Woody was a coolie and pulled a rickshaw, wearing a peaked straw hat and trotting with powerful, thick legs, while the brawny red farmers — his boozing passengers — were laughing their heads off and pestered him for whores, he, although a freshman at the seminary, saw nothing wrong, when girls asked him to steer a little business their way, in making dates and accepting tips from both sides. He necked in Grant Park with a powerful girl who had to go home quickly to nurse her baby. Smelling of milk, she rode beside him on the streetcar to the West Side, squeezing his rickshaw puller's thigh and wetting her blouse. This was the Roosevelt Road car. Then, in the apartment where she lived with her mother, he couldn't remember that there were any husbands around. What he did remember was the strong milk odor. Without inconsistency, next morning he did New Testament Greek: The light shineth in darkness — *to fos en te skotia fainei* — and the darkness comprehended it not.

And all the while he trotted between the shafts on the fairgrounds he had one idea, nothing to do with these horny giants having a big time in the city: that the goal, the project, the purpose was (and he couldn't explain why he thought so; all evidence was against it) — God's idea was that this world should be a love world, that it should eventually recover and be entirely a world of love. He wouldn't have said this to a soul, for he could see himself how stupid it was — personal and stupid. Nevertheless there it was at the center of his feelings. And at the same time, Aunt Rebecca was right when she said to him, strictly private, close to his ear even, "You're a little crook, like your father."

There was some evidence for this, or what stood for evidence to an impatient person like Rebecca. Woody matured quickly — he had to — but how could you expect a boy of seventeen, he wondered, to interpret the viewpoint, the feelings, of a middle-aged woman, and one whose breast had been removed? Morris told him that this happened only to neglected women, and was a sign. Morris said that if titties were not fondled and kissed, they got cancer in protest. It was a cry of the flesh. And this had seemed true to Woody. When his imagination tried the theory on the Reverend Doctor, it worked out — he couldn't see the Reverend Doctor behaving in that way to Aunt Rebecca's breasts! Morris's theory kept Woody looking from bosoms to husbands and from husbands to bosoms. He still did that. It's an exceptionally smart man who isn't marked forever by the sexual theories he hears from his father, and Woody wasn't all that smart. He knew this himself. Personally, he had gone far out of his way to do right by women in this regard. What nature demanded. He and Pop were common, thick men, but there's nobody too gross to have ideas of delicacy.

The Reverend Doctor preached, Rebecca preached, rich Mrs. Skoglund preached from Evanston, Mother preached. Pop also was on a soapbox. Everyone was doing it. Up and down Division Street, under every lamp, almost, speakers were giving out: anarchists, Socialists, Stalinists, single-taxers, Zionists, Tolstoyans, vegetarians, and fundamentalist Christian preachers — you name it. A beef, a hope, a way of life or salvation, a protest. How was it that the accumulated gripes of all the ages took off so when transplanted to America?

And that fine Swedish immigrant Aase (Osie, they pronounced it), who had been the Skoglunds' cook and married the eldest son, to become his rich, religious widow — she supported the Reverend Doctor. In her time she must have been built like a chorus girl. And women seem to have lost the secret of putting up their hair in the high basketry fence of braid she wore. Aase took Woody under her special protection and paid his tuition at the seminary. And Pop said . . . But on this Sunday, at peace as soon as the bells stopped banging, this velvet autumn day when the grass was finest and thickest, silky green: before the first frost, and the blood in your lungs is redder than summer air can make it and smarts with oxygen, as if the iron in your system was hungry for it, and the chill was sticking it to you in every breath . . . Pop, six feet under, would never feel this blissful sting again. The last of the bells still had the bright air streaming with vibrations.

On weekends, the institutional vacancy of decades came back to the warehouse and crept under the door of Woody's apartment. It felt as empty on Sundays as churches were during the week. Before each business day, before the trucks and the crews got started, Woody jogged five miles in his Adidas suit. Not on this day still reserved for Pop, however. Although it was tempting to go out and run off the grief. Being alone hit Woody hard this morning. He thought: Me and the world; the world and me. Meaning that there always was some activity to interpose, an errand or a visit, a picture to paint (he was a creative amateur), a massage, a meal — a shield between himself and that troublesome solitude which used the world as its reservoir. But Pop! Last Tuesday, Woody had gotten into the hospital bed with Pop because he kept pulling out the intravenous needles. Nurses stuck them back, and then Woody astonished them all by climbing into bed to hold the struggling old guy in his arms. "Easy, Morris, Morris, go easy." But Pop still groped feebly for the pipes.

When the tolling stopped, Woody didn't notice that a great lake of quiet had come over his kingdom, the Selbst Tile warehouse. What he heard and saw was an old red Chicago streetcar, one of those trams the color of a stockyard steer. Cars of this type went out before Pearl Harbor — clumsy, big-bellied, with tough rattan seats and brass grips for the standing passengers. Those cars used to make four stops to the mile, and ran with a wallowing motion. They stank of carbolic or ozone and throbbed when the air compressors were being charged. The conductor had his knotted signal cord to pull, and the motorman beat the foot gong with his mad heel.

Woody recognized himself on the Western Avenue line and riding through a blizzard with his father, both in sheepskins and with hands and faces raw, the snow blowing in from the rear platform when the doors opened and getting into the longitudinal cleats of the floor. There wasn't warmth enough inside to melt it. And Western Avenue was the longest car line in the world, the boosters said, as if it was a thing to brag about. Twenty-three miles long, made by a draftsman with a T square, lined with factories, storage buildings, machine shops, used-car lots, trolley barns, gas stations, funeral parlors, six-flats, utility buildings, and junkyards, on and on from the prairies on the south to Evanston on the north. Woodrow and his father were going north to Evanston, to Howard Street, and then some, to see Mrs. Skoglund. At the end of the line they would still have about five blocks to hike. The purpose of the trip? To raise money for Pop. Pop had talked him into this. When they found out, Mother and Aunt Rebecca would be furious, and Woody was afraid, but he couldn't help it.

Morris had come and said, "Son, I'm in trouble. It's bad."

"What's bad, Pop?"

"Halina took money from her husband for me and has to put it back before old Bujak misses it. He could kill her."

"What did she do it for?"

"Son, you know how the bookies collect? They send a goon. They'll break my head open."

"Pop! You know I can't take you to Mrs. Skoglund."

"Why not? You're my kid, aren't you? The old broad wants to adopt you, doesn't she? Shouldn't I get something out of it for my trouble? What am I—outside? And what about Halina? She puts her life on the line, but my own kid says no."

"Oh, Bujak wouldn't hurt her."

"Woody, he'd beat her to death."

Bujak? Uniform in color with his dark-gray work clothes, short in the legs, his whole strength in his tool-and-die-maker's forearms and black fingers; and beat-looking—there was Bujak for you. But, according to Pop, there was big, big violence in Bujak, a regular boiling Bessemer inside his narrow chest. Woody could never see the violence in him. Bujak wanted no trouble. If anything, maybe he was afraid that Morris and Halina would gang up on him and kill him, screaming. But Pop was no desperado murderer. And Halina was a calm, serious woman. Bujak kept his savings in the cellar (banks were going out of business). The worst they did was to take some of his money, intending to put it back. As Woody saw him, Bujak was trying to be sensible. He accepted his sorrow. He set minimum requirements for Halina: cook the meals, clean the house, show respect. But at stealing Bujak might have drawn the line, for money was different, money was vital substance. If they stole his savings he might have had to take action, out of respect for the substance, for himself—self-respect. But you couldn't be sure that Pop hadn't invented the bookie, the goon, the theft—the whole thing. He was capable of it, and you'd be a fool not to suspect him. Morris knew that Mother and Aunt Rebecca had told Mrs. Skoglund how wicked he was. They had painted him for her in poster colors—purple for vice, black for his soul, red for Hell flames: a gambler, smoker, drinker, deserter, screwer of women, and atheist. So Pop was determined to reach her. It was risky for everybody. The Reverend Doctor's operating costs were met by Skoglund Dairies. The widow paid Woody's seminary tuition; she bought dresses for the little sisters.

Woody, now sixty, fleshy and big, like a figure for the victory of American materialism, sunk in his lounge chair, the leather of its armrests softer to his fingertips than a woman's skin, was puzzled and, in his depths, disturbed by certain blots within him, blots of light in his brain, a blot combining pain and amusement in his breast (how did *that* get there?). Intense thought puckered the skin between his eyes with a strain bordering on headache. Why had he let Pop have his way? Why did he agree to meet him that day, in the dim rear of the poolroom?

"But what will you tell Mrs. Skoglund?"

"The old broad? Don't worry, there's plenty to tell her, and it's all true. Ain't I trying to save my little laundry-and-cleaning shop? Isn't the bailiff coming for the fixtures next week?" And Pop rehearsed his pitch on the Western Avenue car. He counted on Woody's health and his freshness. Such a straightforward-looking body was perfect for a con.

Did they still have such winter storms in Chicago as they used to have? Now they somehow seemed less fierce. Blizzards used to come straight down from Ontario, from the Arctic, and drop five feet of snow in an afternoon. Then the rusty green platform cars, with revolving brushes at both ends, came out of the barns to sweep the tracks. Ten or twelve streetcars followed in slow processions, or waited, block after block.

There was a long delay at the gates of Riverview Park, all the amusements covered for the winter, boarded up—the dragon's-back high-rides, the Bobs, the Chute, the Tilt-a-Whirl, all the fun machinery put together by mechanics and electricians, men like Bujak the tool-and-die-maker, good with engines. The blizzard was having it all its own way behind the gates, and you couldn't see far inside; only a few bulbs burned behind the palings. When Woody wiped the vapor from the glass, the wire mesh of the window guards was stuffed solid at eye level with snow. Looking higher, you saw mostly the streaked wind horizontally driving from the north. In the seat ahead, two black coal heavers, both in leather Lindbergh flying helmets, sat with shovels between their legs, returning from a job. They smelled of sweat, burlap sacking, and coal. Mostly dull with black dust, they also sparkled here and there.

There weren't many riders. People weren't leaving the house. This was a day to sit legs stuck out beside the stove, mummified by both the outdoor and the indoor forces. Only a fellow with an angle, like Pop, would go and buck such weather. A storm like this was out of the compass, and you kept the human scale by having a scheme to raise fifty bucks. Fifty soldiers! Real money in 1933.

"That woman is crazy for you," said Pop.

"She's just a good woman, sweet to all of us."

"Who knows what she's got in mind. You're a husky kid. Not such a kid, either."

"She's a religious woman. She really has religion."

"Well, your mother isn't your only parent. She and Rebecca and Kovner aren't going to fill you up with their ideas. I know your mother wants to wipe me out of your life. Unless I take a hand, you won't even understand what life is. Because they don't know — those silly Christers."

"Yes, Pop."

"The girls I can't help. They're too young. I'm sorry about them, but I can't do anything. With you it's different."

He wanted me like himself, an American.

They were stalled in the storm, while the cattle-colored car waited to have the trolley reset in the crazy wind, which boomed, tingled, blasted. At Howard Street they would have to walk straight into it, due north.

"You'll do the talking at first," said Pop.

Woody had the makings of a salesman, a pitchman. He was aware of this when he got to his feet in church to testify before fifty or sixty people. Even though Aunt Rebecca made it worth his while, he moved his own heart when he spoke up about his faith. But occasionally, without notice, his heart went away as he spoke religion and he couldn't find it anywhere. In its absence, sincere behavior got him through. He had to rely for delivery on his face, his voice — on behavior. Then his eyes came closer and closer together. And in this approach of eye to eye he felt the strain of hypocrisy. The twisting of his face threatened to betray him. It took everything he had to keep looking honest. So, since he couldn't bear the cynicism of it, he fell back on mischievousness. Mischief was where Pop came in. Pop passed straight through all those divided fields, gap after gap, and arrived at his side, bent-nosed and broad-faced. In regard to Pop, you thought of neither sincerity nor insincerity. Pop was like the man in the song: he wanted what he wanted when he wanted it. Pop was physical; Pop was digestive, circulatory, sexual. If Pop got serious, he talked to you about washing under the arms or in the crotch or of drying between your toes or of cooking supper, of baked beans and fried onions, of draw poker or of a certain horse in the fifth race at Arlington. Pop was elemental. That was why he gave such relief from religion and paradoxes, and things like that. Now, Mother *thought* she was spiritual, but Woody knew that she was kidding herself. Oh, yes, in the British accent she never gave up she was always talking to God or about Him — please God, God willing, praise God. But she was a big substantial bread-and-butter down-to-earth woman, with down-to-earth duties like feeding the girls, protecting, refining, keeping pure the girls. And those two protected doves grew up so overweight, heavy in the hips and thighs, that their poor heads looked long and slim. And mad. Sweet but cuckoo — Paula cheerfully cuckoo, Joanna depressed and having episodes.

"I'll do my best by you, but you have to promise, Pop, not to get me in Dutch with Mrs. Skoglund."

"You worried because I speak bad English? Embarrassed? I have a mockie accent?"

"It's not that. Kovner has a heavy accent, and she doesn't mind."

"Who the hell are those freaks to look down on me? You're practically a man and your dad has a right to expect help from you. He's in a fix. And you bring him to her house because she's bighearted, and you haven't got anybody else to go to."

"I got you, Pop."

The two coal trimmers stood up at Devon Avenue. One of them wore a woman's coat. Men wore women's clothing in those years, and women men's, when there was no choice. The fur collar was spiky with the wet, and sprinkled with soot. Heavy, they dragged their shovels and got off at the front. The slow car ground on, very slow. It was after four when they reached the end of the line, and somewhere between gray and black, with snow spouting and whirling under the street lamps. In Howard Street, autos were stalled at all angles and abandoned. The sidewalks were blocked. Woody led the way into Evanston, and Pop followed him up the middle of the street in the furrows made earlier by trucks. For four blocks they bucked the wind and then Woody broke through the drifts to the snowbound mansion, where they both had to push the wrought-iron gate because of the drift behind it. Twenty rooms or more in this dignified house and nobody in them but Mrs. Skoglund and her servant Hjordis, also religious.

As Woody and Pop waited, brushing the slush from their sheep-skin collars and Pop wiping his big eyebrows with the ends of his scarf, sweating and freezing, the chains began to rattle and Hjordis uncovered the air holes of the glass storm door by turning a wooden bar. Woody called her "monk-faced." You no longer see women like that, who put no female touch on the face. She came plain, as God made her. She said, "Who is it and what do you want?"

"It's Woodrow Selbst. Hjordis? It's Woody."

"You're not expected."

"No, but we're here."

"What do you want?"

"We came to see Mrs. Skoglund."

"What for do you want to see her?"

"Just tell her we're here."

"I have to tell her what you came for, without calling up first."

"Why don't you say it's Woody with his father, and we wouldn't come in a snowstorm like this if it wasn't important."

The understandable caution of women who live alone. Respect-able old-time women, too. There was no such respectability now in those Evanston houses, with their big verandas and deep yards and with a servant like Hjordis, who carried at her belt keys to the pan-try and to every closet and every dresser drawer and every pad-locked bin in the cellar. And in High Episcopal Christian Science Women's Temperance Evanston, no tradespeople rang at the front door. Only invited guests. And here, after a ten-mile grind through the blizzard, came two tramps from the West Side. To this mansion where a Swedish immigrant lady, herself once a cook and now a philanthropic widow, dreamed, snowbound, while frozen lilac twigs clapped at her storm windows, of a new Jerusalem and a Second Coming and a Resurrection and a Last Judgment. To hasten the Second Coming, and all the rest, you had to reach the hearts of these scheming bums arriving in a snowstorm.

Sure, they let us in.

Then in the heat that swam suddenly up to their mufflered chins Pop and Woody felt the blizzard for what it was; their cheeks were frozen slabs. They stood beat, itching, trickling in the front hall that *was* a hall, with a carved newel post staircase and a big stained-glass window at the top. Picturing Jesus with the Samaritan woman. There was a kind of Gentile closeness to the air. Perhaps when he was with Pop, Woody made more Jewish observations than he would otherwise. Although Pop's most Jewish characteristic was that Yiddish was the only language he could read a paper in. Pop was with Polish Halina, and Mother was with Jesus Christ, and Woody ate uncooked bacon from the flitch. Still, now and then he had a Jewish impression.

Mrs. Skoglund was the cleanest of women — her fingernails, her white neck, her ears — and Pop's sexual hints to Woody all went wrong because she was so intensely clean, and made Woody think of a waterfall, large as she was, and grandly built. Her bust was big. Woody's imagination had investigated this. He thought she kept things tied down tight, very tight. But she lifted both arms once to raise a window and there it was, her bust, beside him, the whole unbindable thing. Her hair was like the raffia you had to soak before you could weave with it in a basket class — pale, pale. Pop, as he took his sheepskin off, was in sweaters, no jacket. His darting looks made him seem crooked. Hardest of all for these Selbsts with their bent noses and big, apparently straightforward faces was to look honest. All the signs of dishonesty played over them. Woody had often puzzled about it. Did it go back to the muscles, was it fundamentally a jaw problem — the projecting angles of the jaws? Or was it the angling that went on in the heart? The girls called Pop Dick Tracy, but Dick Tracy was a good guy. Whom could Pop convince? Here Woody caught a possibility as it flitted by. Precisely because of the way Pop looked, a sensitive person might feel remorse for condemning unfairly or judging unkindly. Just because of a face? Some must have bent over backward. Then he had them. Not Hjordis. She would have put Pop into the street then and there, storm or no storm. Hjordis was religious, but she was wised up, too. She hadn't come over in steerage and worked forty years in Chicago for nothing.

Mrs. Skoglund, Aase (Osie), led the visitors into the front room. This, the biggest room in the house, needed supplementary heating. Because of fifteen-foot ceilings and high windows, Hjordis had kept the parlor stove burning. It was one of those elegant parlor stoves that wore a nickel crown, or miter, and this miter, when you moved it aside, automatically raised the hinge of an iron stove lid.

That stove lid underneath the crown was all soot and rust, the same as any other stove lid. Into this hole you tipped the scuttle and the anthracite chestnut rattled down. It made a cake or dome of fire visible through the small isinglass frames. It was a pretty room, three-quarters paneled in wood. The stove was plugged into the flue of the marble fireplace, and there were parquet floors and Axminster carpets and cranberry-colored tufted Victorian upholstery, and a kind of Chinese étagère, inside a cabinet, lined with mirrors and containing silver pitchers, trophies won by Skoglund cows, fancy sugar tongs and cut-glass pitchers and goblets. There were Bibles and pictures of Jesus and the Holy Land and that faint Gentile odor, as if things had been rinsed in a weak vinegar solution.

"Mrs. Skoglund, I brought my dad to you. I don't think you ever met him," said Woody.

"Yes, Missus, that's me, Selbst."

Pop stood short but masterful in the sweaters, and his belly sticking out, not soft but hard. He was a man of the hard-bellied type. Nobody intimidated Pop. He never presented himself as a beggar. There wasn't a cringe in him anywhere. He let her see at once by the way he said "Missus" that he was independent and that he knew his way around. He communicated that he was able to handle himself with women. Handsome Mrs. Skoglund, carrying a basket woven out of her own hair, was in her fifties — eight, maybe ten years his senior.

"I asked my son to bring me because I know you do the kid a lot of good. It's natural you should know both of his parents."

"Mrs. Skoglund, my dad is in a tight corner and I don't know anybody else to ask for help."

This was all the preliminary Pop wanted. He took over and told the widow his story about the laundry-and-cleaning business and payments overdue, and explained about the fixtures and the attachment notice, and the bailiff's office and what they were going to do to him; and he said, "I'm a small man trying to make a living."

"You don't support your children," said Mrs. Skoglund.

"That's right," said Hjordis.

"I haven't got it. If I had it, wouldn't I give it? There's bread lines and soup lines all over town. Is it just me? What I have I divvy with. I give the kids. A bad father? You think my son would bring me if I was a bad father into your house? He loves his dad, he trusts his dad, he knows his dad is a good dad. Every time I start a little business going I get wiped out. This one is a good little business, if I could hold on to that little business. Three people work for me, I meet a payroll, and three people will be on the street, too, if I close down. Missus, I can sign a note and pay you in two months. I'm a common man, but I'm a hard worker and a fellow you can trust."

Woody was startled when Pop used the word "trust." It was as if from all four corners a Sousa band blew a blast to warn the entire world: "Crook! This is a crook!" But Mrs. Skoglund, on account of her religious preoccupations, was remote. She heard nothing. Although everybody in this part of the world, unless he was crazy, led a practical life, and you'd have nothing to say to anyone, your neighbors would have nothing to say to you, if communications were not of a practical sort, Mrs. Skoglund, with all her money, was unworldly — two-thirds out of this world.

"Give me a chance to show what's in me," said Pop, "and you'll see what I do for my kids."

So Mrs. Skoglund hesitated, and then she said she'd have to go upstairs, she'd have to go to her room and pray on it and ask for guidance — would they sit down and wait. There were two rocking chairs by the stove. Hjordis gave Pop a grim look (a dangerous person) and Woody a blaming one (he brought a dangerous stranger and disrupter to injure two kind Christian ladies). Then she went out with Mrs. Skoglund.

As soon as they left, Pop jumped up from the rocker and said in anger, "What's this with the praying? She has to ask God to lend me fifty bucks?"

Woody said, "It's not you, Pop, it's the way these religious people do."

"No," said Pop. "She'll come back and say that God wouldn't let her."

Woody didn't like that; he thought Pop was being gross and he said, "No, she's sincere. Pop, try to understand: she's emotional, nervous, and sincere, and tries to do right by everybody."

And Pop said, "That servant will talk her out of it. She's a toughie. It's all over her face that we're a couple of chiselers."

"What's the use of us arguing," said Woody. He drew the rocker closer to the stove. His shoes were wet through and would never dry. The blue flames fluttered like a school of fishes in the coal fire. But Pop went over to the Chinese-style cabinet or étagère and tried the handle, and then opened the blade of his penknife and in a second had forced the lock of the curved glass door. He took out a silver dish.

"Pop, what is this?" said Woody.

Pop, cool and level, knew exactly what this was. He relocked the étagère, crossed the carpet, listened. He stuffed the dish under his belt and pushed it down into his trousers. He put the side of his short thick finger to his mouth.

So Woody kept his voice down, but he was all shook up. He went to Pop and took him by the edge of his hand. As he looked into Pop's face, he felt his eyes growing smaller and smaller, as if something were contracting all the skin on his head. They call it hyperventilation when everything feels tight and light and close and dizzy. Hardly breathing, he said, "Put it back, Pop."

Pop said, "It's solid silver; it's worth dough."

"Pop, you said you wouldn't get me in Dutch."

"It's only insurance in case she comes back from praying and tells me no. If she says yes, I'll put it back."

"How?"

"It'll get back. If I don't put it back, you will."

"You picked the lock. I couldn't. I don't know how."

"There's nothing to it."

"We're going to put it back now. Give it here."

"Woody, it's under my fly, inside my underpants. Don't make such a noise about nothing."

"Pop, I can't believe this."

"For cry-ninety-nine, shut your mouth. If I didn't trust you I wouldn't have let you watch me do it. You don't understand a thing. What's with you?"

"Before they come down, Pop, will you dig that dish out of your long johns."

Pop turned stiff on him. He became absolutely military. He said, "Look, I order you!"

Before he knew it, Woody had jumped his father and begun to wrestle with him. It was outrageous to clutch your own father, to put a heel behind him, to force him to the wall. Pop was taken by surprise and said loudly, "You want Halina killed? Kill her! Go on, you be responsible." He began to resist, angry, and they turned about several times, when Woody, with a trick he had learned in a Western movie and used once on the playground, tripped him and they fell to the ground. Woody, who already outweighed the old man by twenty pounds, was on top. They landed on the floor beside the stove, which stood on a tray of decorated tin to protect the carpet. In this position, pressing Pop's hard belly, Woody recognized that to have wrestled him to the floor counted for nothing. It was impossible to thrust his hand under Pop's belt to recover the dish. And now Pop had turned furious, as a father has every right to be when his son is violent with him, and he freed his hand and hit Woody in the face. He hit him three or four times in mid-face. Then Woody dug his head into Pop's shoulder and held tight only to keep from being struck and began to say in his ear, "Jesus, Pop, for Christ sake remember where you are. Those women will be back!" But Pop brought up his short knee and fought and butted him with his chin and rattled Woody's teeth. Woody thought the old man was about to bite him. And because he was a seminarian, he thought: Like an unclean spirit. And held tight. Gradually Pop stopped threshing and struggling. His eyes stuck out and his mouth was open, sullen. Like a stout fish. Woody released him and gave him a hand up. He was then overcome with many many bad feelings of a sort he knew the old man never suffered. Never, never. Pop never had these groveling emotions. There was his whole superiority. Pop had no such feelings. He was like a horseman from Central Asia, a bandit from China. It was Mother, from Liverpool, who had the refinement, the English manners. It was the preaching Reverend Doctor in his black suit. You have refinements, and all they do is oppress you? The hell with that.

The long door opened and Mrs. Skoglund stepped in, saying, "Did I imagine, or did something shake the house?"

"I was lifting the scuttle to put coal on the fire and it fell out of my hand. I'm sorry I was so clumsy," said Woody.

Pop was too huffy to speak. With his eyes big and sore and the thin hair down over his forehead, you could see by the tightness of his belly how angrily he was fetching his breath, though his mouth was shut.

"I prayed," said Mrs. Skoglund.

"I hope it came out well," said Woody.

"Well, I don't do anything without guidance, but the answer was yes, and I feel right about it now. So if you'll wait, I'll go to my office and write a check. I asked Hjordis to bring you a cup of coffee. Coming in such a storm."

And Pop, consistently a terrible little man, as soon as she shut the door, said, "A check? Hell with a check. Get me the greenbacks."

"They don't keep money in the house. You can cash it in her

bank tomorrow. But if they miss that dish, Pop, they'll stop the check, and then where are you?"

As Pop was reaching below the belt, Hjordis brought in the tray. She was very sharp with him. She said, "Is this a place to adjust clothing, Mister? A men's washroom?"

"Well, which way is the toilet, then?" said Pop.

She had served the coffee in the seamiest mugs in the pantry, and she bumped down the tray and led Pop down the corridor, standing guard at the bathroom door so that he shouldn't wander about the house.

Mrs. Skoglund called Woody to her office and after she had given him the folded check said that they should pray together for Morris. So once more he was on his knees, under rows and rows of musty marbled-cardboard files, by the glass lamp by the edge of the desk, the shade with flounced edges, like the candy dish. Mrs. Skoglund, in her Scandinavian accent — an emotional contralto — raising her voice to Jesus-uh Christ-uh, as the wind lashed the trees, kicked the side of the house, and drove the snow seething on the windowpanes, to send light-uh, give guidance-uh, put a new heart-uh in Pop's bosom. Woody asked God only to make Pop put the dish back. He kept Mrs. Skoglund on her knees as long as possible. Then he thanked her, shining with candor (as much as he knew how), for her Christian generosity and he said, "I know that Hjordis has a cousin who works at the Evanston YMCA. Could she please phone him and try to get us a room tonight so that we don't have to fight the blizzard all the way back? We're almost as close to the Y as to the car line. Maybe the cars have even stopped running."

Suspicious Hjordis, coming when Mrs. Skoglund called to her, was burning now. First they barged in, made themselves at home, asked for money, had to have coffee, probably left gonorrhea on the toilet seat. Hjordis, Woody remembered, was a woman who wiped the doorknobs with rubbing alcohol after guests had left. Nevertheless, she telephoned the Y and got them a room with two cots for six bits.

Pop had plenty of time, therefore, to reopen the étagère, lined with reflecting glass or German silver (something exquisitely delicate and tricky), and as soon as the two Selbsts had said thank you and goodbye and were in midstreet again up to the knees in snow, Woody said, "Well, I covered for you. Is that thing back?"

"Of course it is," said Pop.

They fought their way to the small Y building, shut up in wire grille and resembling a police station — about the same dimensions. It was locked, but they made a racket on the grille, and a small black man let them in and shuffled them upstairs to a cement corridor with low doors. It was like the small-mammal house in Lincoln Park. He said there was nothing to eat, so they took off their wet pants, wrapped themselves tightly in the khaki army blankets, and passed out on their cots.

First thing in the morning, they went to the Evanston National Bank and got the fifty dollars. Not without difficulties. The teller went to call Mrs. Skoglund and was absent a long time from the wicket. "Where the hell has he gone?" said Pop.

But when the fellow came back, he said, "How do you want it?"

Pop said, "Singles." He told Woody, "Bujak stashes it in one-dollar bills."

But by now Woody no longer believed Halina had stolen the old man's money.

Then they went into the street, where the snow-removal crews were at work. The sun shone broad, broad, out of the morning blue, and all Chicago would be releasing itself from the temporary beauty of those vast drifts.

"You shouldn't have jumped me last night, Sonny."

"I know, Pop, but you promised you wouldn't get me in Dutch."

"Well, it's okay. We can forget it, seeing you stood by me."

Only, Pop had taken the silver dish. Of course he had, and in a few days Mrs. Skoglund and Hjordis knew it, and later in the week they were all waiting for Woody in Kovner's office at the settlement house. The group included the Reverend Doctor Crabbie, head of the seminary, and Woody, who had been flying along, level and smooth, was shot down in flames. He told them he was innocent. Even as he was falling, he warned that they were wronging him. He denied that he or Pop had touched Mrs. Skoglund's property. The missing object — he didn't even know what it was — had probably been misplaced, and they would be very sorry on the day it turned up. After the others were done with him, Dr. Crabbie said that until he was able to tell the truth he would be suspended from the seminary, where his work had been unsatisfactory anyway. Aunt Rebecca took him aside and said to him, "You are a little crook, like your father. The door is closed to you here."

To this Pop's comment was "So what, kid?"

"Pop, you shouldn't have done it."

"No? Well, I don't give a care, if you want to know. You can have the dish if you want to go back and square yourself with all those hypocrites."

"I didn't like doing Mrs. Skoglund in the eye, she was so kind to us."

"Kind?"

"Kind."

"Kind has a price tag."

Well, there was no winning such arguments with Pop. But they debated it in various moods and from various elevations and perspectives for forty years and more, as their intimacy changed, developed, matured.

"Why did you do it, Pop? For the money? What did you do with the fifty bucks?" Woody, decades later, asked him that.

"I settled with the bookie, and the rest I put in the business."

"You tried a few more horses."

"I maybe did. But it was a double, Woody. I didn't hurt myself, and at the same time did you a favor."

"It was for me?"

"It was too strange of a life. That life wasn't *you*, Woody. All those women . . . Kovner was no man, he was an in-between. Suppose they made you a minister? Some Christian minister! First of all, you wouldn't have been able to stand it, and second, they would throw you out sooner or later."

"Maybe so."

"And you wouldn't have converted the Jews, which was the main thing they wanted."

"And what a time to bother the Jews," Woody said. "At least *I* didn't bug them."

Pop had carried him back to his side of the line, blood of his blood, the same thick body walls, the same coarse grain. Not cut out for a spiritual life. Simply not up to it.

Pop was no worse than Woody, and Woody was no better than Pop. Pop wanted no relation to theory, and yet he was always pointing Woody toward a position — a jolly, hearty, natural, likable, unprincipled position. If Woody had a weakness, it was to be unselfish. This worked to Pop's advantage, but he criticized Woody for it, nevertheless. "You take too much on yourself," Pop was always saying. And it's true that Woody gave Pop his heart because Pop was so selfish. It's usually the selfish people who are loved the most. They do what you deny yourself, and you love them for it. You give them your heart.

Remembering the pawn ticket for the silver dish, Woody startled himself with a laugh so sudden that it made him cough. Pop said to him after his expulsion from the seminary and banishment from the settlement house, "You want in again? Here's the ticket. I hocked that thing. It wasn't so valuable as I thought."

"What did they give?"

"Twelve-fifty was all I could get. But if you want it you'll have to raise the dough yourself, because I haven't got it anymore."

"You must have been sweating in the bank when the teller went to call Mrs. Skoglund about the check."

"I was a little nervous," said Pop. "But I didn't think they could miss the thing so soon."

That theft was part of Pop's war with Mother. With Mother, and Aunt Rebecca, and the Reverend Doctor. Pop took his stand on realism. Mother represented the forces of religion and hypochondria. In four decades, the fighting never stopped. In the course of time, Mother and the girls turned into welfare personalities and lost their individual outlines. Ah, the poor things, they became dependents and cranks. In the meantime, Woody, the sinful man, was their dutiful and loving son and brother. He maintained the bungalow — this took in roofing, pointing, wiring, insulation, air-conditioning — and he paid for heat and light and food, and dressed them all out of Sears, Roebuck and Wieboldt's, and bought them a TV, which they watched as devoutly as they prayed. Paula took courses to learn skills like macramé-making and needlepoint, and sometimes got a little job as recreational worker in a nursing home. But she wasn't steady enough to keep it. Wicked Pop spent most of his life removing stains from people's clothing. He and Halina in the last years ran a Cleanomat in West Rogers Park — a so-so business resembling a laundromat — which gave him leisure for billiards, the horses, rummy and pinochle. Every morning he went behind the partition to check out the filters of the cleaning equipment. He found amusing things that had been thrown into the vats with the clothing — sometimes, when he got lucky, a locket chain or a brooch. And when he had fortified the cleaning fluid, pouring all that blue and pink stuff in from plastic jugs, he read the *Forward* over a second cup of coffee, and went out, leaving Halina in charge. When they needed help with the rent, Woody gave it.

After the new Disney World was opened in Florida, Woody treated all his dependents to a holiday. He sent them down in separate batches, of course. Halina enjoyed this more than anybody else. She couldn't stop talking about the address given by an Abraham Lincoln automaton. "Wonderful, how he stood up and moved his hands, and his mouth. So real! And how beautiful he talked." Of them all, Halina was the soundest, the most human, the most honest. Now that Pop was gone, Woody and Halina's son, Mitosh, the organist at the Stadium, took care of her needs over and above Social Security, splitting expenses. In Pop's opinion, insurance was a racket. He left Halina nothing but some out-of-date equipment.

Woody treated himself, too. Once a year, and sometimes oftener, he left his business to run itself, arranged with the trust department at the bank to take care of his gang, and went off. He did that in style, imaginatively, expensively. In Japan, he wasted little time on Tokyo. He spent three weeks in Kyoto and stayed at the Tawaraya Inn, dating from the seventeenth century or so. There he slept on the floor, the Japanese way, and bathed in scalding water. He saw the dirtiest strip show on earth, as well as the holy places and the temple gardens. He visited also Istanbul, Jerusalem, Delphi, and went to Burma and Uganda and Kenya on safari, on democratic terms with drivers, Bedouins, bazaar merchants. Open, lavish, familiar, fleshier and fleshier but (he jogged, he lifted weights) still muscular — in his naked person beginning to resemble a Renaissance courtier in full costume — becoming ruddier every year, an outdoor type with freckles on his back and spots across the flaming forehead and the honest nose. In Addis Ababa he took an Ethiopian beauty to his room from the street and washed her, getting into the shower with her to soap her with his broad, kindly hands. In Kenya he taught certain American obscenities to a black woman so that she could shout them out during the act. On the Nile, below Murchison Falls, those fever trees rose huge from the mud, and hippos on the sandbars belched at the passing launch, hostile. One of them danced on his spit of sand, springing from the ground and coming down heavy, on all fours. There, Woody saw the buffalo calf disappear, snatched by the crocodile.

Mother, soon to follow Pop, was being lightheaded these days. In company, she spoke of Woody as her boy — "What do you think of my Sonny?" — as though he was ten years old. She was silly with him, her behavior was frivolous, almost flirtatious. She just didn't seem to know the facts. And behind her all the others, like kids at the playground, were waiting their turn to go down the slide: one on each step, and moving toward the top.

Over Woody's residence and place of business there had gathered a pool of silence of the same perimeter as the church bells
while they were ringing, and he mourned under it, this melancholy
morning of sun and autumn. Doing a life survey, taking a deliberate
look at the gross side of his case—of the other side as well, what
there was of it. But if this heartache continued, he'd go out and run
it off. A three-mile jog—five, if necessary. And you'd think that this
jogging was an entirely physical activity, wouldn't you? But there was
something else in it. Because, when he was a seminarian, between
the shafts of his World's Fair rickshaw, he used to receive, pulling
along (capable and stable), his religious experiences while he trotted. Maybe it was all a single experience repeated. He felt truth
coming to him from the sun. He received a communication that
was also light and warmth. It made him very remote from his horny
Wisconsin passengers, those farmers whose whoops and whore cries
he could hardly hear when he was in one of his states. And again
out of the flaming of the sun would come to him a secret certainty
that the goal set for this earth was that it should be filled with
good, saturated with it. After everything preposterous, after dog
had eaten dog, after the crocodile death had pulled everyone into
his mud. It wouldn't conclude as Mrs. Skoglund, bribing him to
round up the Jews and hasten the Second Coming, imagined it, but
in another way. This was his clumsy intuition. It went no further.
Subsequently, he proceeded through life as life seemed to want him
to do it.

There remained one thing more this morning, which was ex-
plicitly physical, occurring first as a sensation in his arms and
against his breast and, from the pressure, passing into him and going into his breast.

It was like this: When he came into the hospital room and saw
Pop with the sides of his bed raised, like a crib, and Pop, so very
feeble, and writhing, and toothless, like a baby, and the dirt already
cast into his face, into the wrinkles—Pop wanted to pluck out the
intravenous needles and he was piping his weak death noise. The
gauze patches taped over the needles were soiled with dark blood.
Then Woody took off his shoes, lowered the side of the bed, and
climbed in and held him in his arms to soothe and still him. As if
he were Pop's father, he said to him, "Now, Pop. Pop." Then it was
like the wrestle in Mrs. Skoglund's parlor, when Pop turned angry
like an unclean spirit and Woody tried to appease him, and warn
him, saying, "Those women will be back!" Beside the coal stove,

when Pop hit Woody in the teeth with his head and then became sullen, like a stout fish. But this struggle in the hospital was weak — so weak! In his great pity, Woody held Pop, who was fluttering and shivering. From those people, Pop had told him, you'll never find out what life is, because they don't know what it is. Yes, Pop — well, what is it, Pop? Hard to comprehend that Pop, who was dug in for eighty-three years and had done all he could to stay, should now want nothing but to free himself. How could Woody allow the old man to pull the intravenous needles out? Willful Pop, he wanted what he wanted when he wanted it. But what he wanted at the very last Woody failed to follow, it was such a switch.

After a time, Pop's resistance ended. He subsided and subsided. He rested against his son, his small body curled there. Nurses came and looked. They disapproved, but Woody, who couldn't spare a hand to wave them out, motioned with his head toward the door. Pop, whom Woody thought he had stilled, only had found a better way to get around him. Loss of heat was the way he did it. His heat was leaving him. As can happen with small animals while you hold them in your hand, Woody presently felt him cooling. Then, as Woody did his best to restrain him, and thought he was succeeding, Pop divided himself. And when he was separated from his warmth, he slipped into death. And there was his elderly, large, muscular son, still holding and pressing him when there was nothing anymore to press. You could never pin down that self-willed man. When he was ready to make his move, he made it — always on his own terms. And always, always, something up his sleeve. That was how he was.

Goodbye and Good Luck

GRACE PALEY

Grace Paley (1922–): *Grace Paley was born in the Bronx and raised in Manhattan, the daughter of immigrants who had fled Russia as a result of their political activism. Although she attended Hunter College, New York University, and the New School for Social Research (where she studied with W. H. Auden), she earned no degrees. Paley married young and bore two children, then spent nearly twenty years as a typist and housewife before coming to prominence both as a political activist (she was one of the founders of the Greenwich Village Peace Center) and as a fiction writer. Her output has been relatively small—three collections of stories over the past forty years—but her writing has met with widespread critical acclaim, and her influence as a writer, political figure, and teacher has been significant. Her stories are often characterized by a delicate balance between deeply serious subject matter and a light, witty, deceptively simple tone. Her books are* The Little Disturbances of Man, Enormous Changes at the Last Minute, *and* Later the Same Day. *Recently all three collections were combined in one volume,* The Stories of Grace Paley. *Her work has received many honors, including fellowships from the Guggenheim Foundation and the National Endowment for the Arts. She is a member of the American Institute of Arts and Letters. Paley has taught, with great success, at Columbia, Syracuse University, and Sarah Lawrence and has lectured and read her work across the country, often in conjunction with political events. She is now retired and lives most of the year in Vermont.*

I was popular in certain circles, says Aunt Rose. I wasn't no thinner then, only more stationary in the flesh. In time to come, Lillie, don't be surprised—change is a fact of God. From this no one is excused. Only a person like your mama stands on one foot, she don't notice how big her behind is getting and sings in the canary's ear for thirty years. Who's listening? Papa's in the shop. You and Seymour, thinking about yourself. So she waits in a spotless kitchen for a kind word and thinks—poor Rosie. . . .

Poor Rosie! If there was more life in my little sister, she would know my heart is a regular college of feelings and there is such information between my corset and me that her whole married life is a kindergarten.

Nowadays you could find me any time in a hotel, uptown or downtown. Who needs an apartment to live like a maid with a dustrag in the hand, sneezing? I'm in very good with the bus boys, it's more interesting than home, all kinds of people, everybody with a reason. . . .

And my reason, Lillie, is a long time ago I said to the forelady, "Missus, if I can't sit by the window, I can't sit." "If you can't sit, girlie," she says politely, "go stand on the street corner." And that's how I got unemployed in novelty wear.

For my next job I answered an ad which read. "Refined young lady, medium salary, cultural organization." I went by trolley to the address, the Russian Art Theater of Second Avenue where they played only the best Yiddish plays. They needed a ticket seller, someone like me, who likes the public but is very sharp on crooks. The man who interviewed me was the manager, a certain type.

Immediately he said: "Rosie Lieber, you surely got a build on you!"

"It takes all kinds, Mr. Krimberg."

"Don't misunderstand me, little girl," he said. "I appreciate, I appreciate. A young lady lacking fore and aft, her blood is so busy warming her toes and the finger tips, it don't have time to circulate where it's most required."

Everybody likes kindness. I said to him: "Only don't be fresh, Mr. Krimberg, and we'll make a good bargain."

We did: Nine dollars a week, a glass of tea every night, a free ticket once a week for Mama, and I could go watch rehearsals any time I want.

My first nine dollars was in the grocer's hands ready to move on already, when Krimberg said to me, "Rosie, here's a great gentleman, a member of this remarkable theater, wants to meet you, impressed no doubt by your big brown eyes."

And who was it, Lillie? Listen to me, before my very eyes was Volodya Vlashkin, called by the people of those days the Valentino of Second Avenue. I took one look, and I said to myself: Where did a Jewish boy grow up so big? "Just outside Kiev," he told me.

How? "My mama nursed me till I was six. I was the only boy in the village to have such health."

"My goodness, Vlashkin, six years old! She must have had shredded wheat there, not breasts, poor woman."

"My mother was beautiful," he said. "She had eyes like stars."

He had such a way of expressing himself, it brought tears.

To Krimberg, Vlashkin said after this introduction: "Who is responsible for hiding this wonderful young person in a cage?"

"That is where the ticket seller sells."

"So, David, go in there and sell tickets for a half hour. I have something in mind in regards to the future of this girl and this company. Go, David, be a good boy. And you, Miss Lieber, please, I suggest Feinberg's for a glass of tea. The rehearsals are long. I enjoy a quiet interlude with a friendly person."

So he took me there, Feinberg's, then around the corner, a place so full of Hungarians, it was deafening. In the back room was a table of honor for him. On the tablecloth embroidered by the lady of the house was "Here Vlashkin Eats." We finished one glass of tea in quietness, out of thirst, when I finally made up my mind what to say.

"Mr. Vlashkin, I saw you a couple weeks ago, even before I started working here, in *The Sea Gull*. Believe me, if I was that girl, I wouldn't look even for a minute on the young bourgeois fellow. He could fall out of the play altogether. How Chekhov could put him in the same play as you, I can't understand."

"You liked me?" he asked, taking my hand and kindly patting it. "Well, well, young people still like me . . . so, and you like the theater too? Good. And you, Rose, you know you have such a nice hand, so warm to the touch, such a fine skin, tell me, why do you wear a scarf around your neck? You only hide your young, young throat. These are not olden times, my child, to live in shame."

"Who's ashamed?" I said, taking off the kerchief, but my hand right away went to the kerchief's place, because the truth is, it really was olden times, and I was still of a nature to melt with shame.

"Have some more tea, my dear."

"No, thank you, I am a samovar already."

"Dorfmann!" he hollered like a king. "Bring this child a seltzer with fresh ice!"

In weeks to follow I had the privilege to know him better and better as a person — also the opportunity to see him in his profession. The time was autumn; the theater full of coming and going. Rehearsing without end. After *The Sea Gull* flopped *The Salesman from Istanbul* played, a great success.

Here the ladies went crazy. On the opening night, in the middle of the first scene, one missus — a widow or her husband worked too long hours — began to clap and sing out, "Oi, oi, Vlashkin." Soon there was such a tumult, the actors had to stop acting. Vlashkin stepped forward. Only not Vlashkin to the eyes . . . a younger man with pitch-black hair, lively on restless feet, his mouth clever. A half a century later at the end of the play he came out again, a grey philosopher, a student of life from only reading books, his hands as smooth as silk. . . . I cried to think who I was — nothing — and such a man could look at me with interest.

Then I got a small raise, due to he kindly put in a good word for me, and also for fifty cents a night I was given the pleasure together with cousins, in-laws, and plain stage-struck kids to be part of a crowd scene and to see like he saw every single night the hundreds of pale faces waiting for his feelings to make them laugh or bend down their heads in sorrow.

The sad day came, I kissed my mama goodbye. Vlashkin helped me to get a reasonable room near the theater to be more free. Also my outstanding friend would have a place to recline away from the noise of the dressing rooms. She cried and she cried. "This is a different way of living, Mama," I said. "Besides, I am driven by love."

"You! You, a nothing, a rotten hole in a piece of cheese, are you telling me what is life?" she screamed.

Very insulted, I went away from her. But I am good-natured — you know fat people are like that — kind, and I thought to myself, poor Mama . . . it is true she got more of an idea of life than me. She married who she didn't like, a sick man, his spirit already swallowed up by God. He never washed. He had an unhappy smell. His teeth fell out, his hair disappeared, he got smaller, shriveled up little by little, till goodbye and good luck he was gone and only came to Mama's mind when she went to the mailbox under the stairs to get the electric bill. In memory of him and out of respect for mankind, I decided to live for love.

Don't laugh, you ignorant girl.

Do you think it was easy for me? I had to give Mama a little something. Ruthie was saving up together with your papa for linens, a couple knives and forks. In the morning I had to do piecework if I wanted to keep by myself. So I made flowers. Before lunch time every day a whole garden grew on my table.

This was my independence, Lillie dear, blooming, but it didn't have no roots and its face was paper.

Meanwhile Krimberg went after me too. No doubt observing the success of Vlashkin, he thought, "Aha, open sesame . . ." Others in the company similar. After me in those years were the following: Krimberg I mentioned. Carl Zimmer, played innocent young fellows with a wig. Charlie Peel, a Christian who fell in the soup by accident, a creator of beautiful sets. "Color is his middle name," says Vlashkin, always to the point.

I put this in to show you your fat old aunt was not crazy out of loneliness. In those noisy years I had friends among interesting people who admired me for reasons of youth and that I was a first-class listener.

The actresses — Raisele, Marya, Esther Leopold — were only interested in tomorrow. After them was the rich men, producers, the whole garment center; their past is a pincushion, future the eye of a needle.

Finally the day came, I no longer could keep my tact in my mouth. I said: "Vlashkin, I hear by carrier pigeon you have a wife, children, the whole combination."

"True, I don't tell stories. I make no pretense."

"That isn't the question. What is this lady like? It hurts me to ask, but tell me, Vlashkin . . . a man's life is something I don't clearly see."

"Little girl, I have told you a hundred times, this small room is the convent of my troubled spirit. Here I come to your innocent shelter to refresh myself in the midst of an agonized life."

"Ach, Vlashkin, serious, serious, who is this lady?"

"Rosie, she is a fine woman of the middle classes, a good mother to my children, three in number, girls all, a good cook, in her youth handsome, now no longer young. You see, could I be more frank? I entrust you, dear, with my soul."

It was some few months later at the New Year's ball of the Russian Artists Club, I met Mrs. Vlashkin, a woman with black hair in a low bun, straight and too proud. She sat at a small table speaking in a deep voice to whoever stopped a moment to converse. Her Yiddish was perfect, each word cut like a special jewel. I looked at her. She noticed me like she noticed everybody, cold like Christmas morning. Then she got tired. Vlashkin called a taxi and I never saw her again. Poor woman, she did not know I was on the same stage with her. The poison I was to her role, she did not know.

Later on that night in front of my door I said to Vlashkin, "No more. This isn't for me. I am sick from it all. I am no home breaker."

"Girlie," he said, "don't be foolish."

"No, no, goodbye, good luck," I said. "I am sincere."

So I went and stayed with Mama for a week's vacation and cleaned up all the closets and scrubbed the walls till the paint came off. She was very grateful, all the same her hard life made her say, "Now we see the end. If you live like a bum, you are finally a lunatic."

After a few days I came back to my life. When we met, me and Vlashkin, we said only hello and goodbye, and then for a few sad years, with the head we nodded as if to say, "Yes, yes, I know who you are."

Meanwhile in the field was a whole new strategy. Your mama and your grandmama brought around — boys. Your own father had a brother, you never even seen him. Ruben. A serious fellow, his idealism was his hat and his coat. "Rosie, I offer you a big new free happy unusual life." How? "With me, we will raise up the sands of Palestine to make a nation. That is the land of tomorrow for us Jews." "Ha-ha, Ruben, I'll go tomorrow then." "Rosie!" says Ruben. "We need strong women like you, mothers and farmers." "You don't fool me, Ruben, what you need is dray horses. But for that you need more money." "I don't like your attitude, Rose." "In that case, go and multiply. Goodbye."

Another fellow: Yonkel Gurstein, a regular sport, dressed to kill, with such an excitable nature. In those days — it looks to me like yesterday — the young girls wore undergarments like Battle Creek, Michigan. To him it was a matter of seconds. Where did he practice, a Jewish boy? Nowadays I suppose it is easier, Lillie? My goodness, I ain't asking you nothing — touchy, touchy. . . .

Well, by now you must know yourself, honey, whatever you do, life don't stop. It only sits a minute and dreams a dream.

While I was saying to all these silly youngsters "no, no, no," Vlashkin went to Europe and toured a few seasons . . . Moscow, Prague, London, even Berlin — already a pessimistic place. When he came back he wrote a book, you could get from the library even today, *The Jewish Actor Abroad*. If someday you're interested enough in my lonesome years, you could read it. You could absorb a flavor of the man from the book. No, no, I am not mentioned. After all, who am I?

When the book came out I stopped him in the street to say con-
gratulations. But I am not a liar, so I pointed out, too, the egotism
of many parts — even the critics said something along such lines.

"Talk is cheap," Vlashkin answered me. "But who are the critics?
Tell me, do they create? Not to mention," he continues, "there is a
line in Shakespeare in one of the plays from the great history of
England. It says, 'Self-loving is not so vile a sin, my liege, as self-
neglecting.' This idea also appears in modern times in the moralis-
tic followers of Freud. . . . Rosie, are you listening? You asked a question. By the way, you look very well. How come no wedding ring?"

I walked away from this conversation in tears. But this talking
in the street opened the happy road up for more discussions. In
regard to many things. . . . For instance, the management — very
narrow-minded — wouldn't give him any more certain young men's
parts. Fools. What youngest man knew enough about life to be as
young as him?

"Rosie, Rosie," he said to me one day, "I see by the clock on your
rosy, rosy face you must be thirty."

"The hands are slow, Vlashkin. On a week before Thursday I was
thirty-four."

"Is that so? Rosie, I worry about you. It has been on my mind to
talk to you. You are losing your time. Do you understand it? A
woman should not lose her time."

"Oi, Vlashkin, if you are my friend, what is time?"

For this he had no answer, only looked at me surprised. We went
instead, full of interest but not with our former speed, up to my new
place on 94th Street. The same pictures on the wall, all of Vlashkin,
only now everything painted red and black, which was stylish, and
new upholstery.

A few years ago there was a book by another member of that fine
company, an actress, the one that learned English very good and
went uptown — Marya Kavkaz, in which she says certain things regarding Vlashkin. Such as, he was her lover for eleven years, she's
not ashamed to write this down. Without respect for him, his wife
and children, or even others who also may have feelings in the
matter.

Now, Lillie, don't be surprised. This is called a fact of life. An
actor's soul must be like a diamond. The more faces it got the more
shining is his name. Honey, you will no doubt love and marry
one man and have a couple kids and be happy forever till you die
tired. More than that, a person like us don't have to know. But a

great artist like Volodya Vlashkin . . . in order to make a job on the stage, he's got to practice. I understand it now, to him life is like a rehearsal.

Myself, when I saw him in *The Father-in-Law* — an older man in love with a darling young girl, his son's wife, played by Raisele Maisel — I cried. What he said to this girl, how he whispered such sweetness, how all his hot feelings were on his face. . . . Lillie, all this experience he had with me. The very words were the same. You can imagine how proud I was.

So the story creeps to an end.

I noticed it first on my mother's face, the rotten handwriting of time, scribbled up and down her cheeks, across her forehead back and forth — a child could read — it said, old, old, old. But it troubled my heart most to see these realities scratched on Vlashkin's wonderful expression.

First the company fell apart. The theater ended. Esther Leopold died from being very aged. Krimberg had a heart attack. Marya went to Broadway. Also Raisele changed her name to Roslyn and was a big comical hit in the movies. Vlashkin himself, no place to go, retired. It said in the paper, "an actor without peer, he will write his memoirs and spend his last years in the bosom of his family among his thriving grandchildren, the apple of his wife's doting eye."

This is journalism.

We made for him a great dinner of honor. At this dinner I said to him, for the last time, I thought, "Goodbye, dear friend, topic of my life, now we part." And to myself I said further: Finished. This is your lonesome bed. A lady what they call fat and fifty. You made it personally. From this lonesome bed you will finally fall to a bed not so lonesome, only crowded with a million bones.

And now comes? Lillie, guess.

Last week, washing my underwear in the basin, I get a buzz on the phone. "Excuse me, is this the Rose Lieber formerly connected with the Russian Art Theater?"

"It is."

"Well, well, how do you do, Rose? This is Vlashkin."

"Vlashkin! Volodya Vlashkin?"

"In fact. How are you, Rose?"

"Living, Vlashkin, thank you."

"You are all right? Really, Rose? Your health is good? You are working?"

"My health, considering the weight it must carry, is first-class. I am back for some years now where I started, in novelty wear."

"Very interesting."

"Listen, Vlashkin, tell me the truth, what's on your mind?"

"My mind? Rosie, I am looking up an old friend, an old warm-hearted companion of more joyful days. My circumstances, by the way, are changed. I am retired, as you know. Also I am a free man."

"What? What do you mean?"

"Mrs. Vlashkin is divorcing me."

"What come over her? Did you start drinking or something from melancholy?"

"She is divorcing me for adultery."

"But, Vlashkin, you should excuse me, don't be insulted, but you got maybe seventeen, eighteen years on me, and even me, all this nonsense — this daydreams and nightmares — is mostly for the pleasure of conversation alone."

"I pointed all this out to her. My dear, I said, my time is past, my blood is as dry as my bones. The truth is, Rose, she isn't accustomed to have a man around all day, reading out loud from the papers the interesting events of our time, waiting for breakfast, waiting for lunch. So all day she gets madder and madder. By nighttime a furious old lady gives me my supper. She has information from the last fifty years to pepper my soup. Surely there was a Judas in that theater, saying every day, 'Vlashkin, Vlashkin, Vlashkin . . .' and while my heart was circulating with his smiles he was on the wire passing the dope to my wife."

"Such a foolish end, Volodya, to such a lively story. What is your plans?"

"First, could I ask you for dinner and the theater — uptown, of course? After this . . . we are old friends. I have money to burn. What your heart desires. Others are like grass, the north wind of time has cut out their heart. Of you, Rosie, I recreate only kindness. What a woman should be to a man, you were to me. Do you think, Rosie, a couple of old pals like us could have a few good times among the material things of this world?"

My answer, Lillie, in a minute was altogether. "Yes, yes, come up," I said. "Ask the room by the switchboard, let us talk."

So he came that night and every night in the week, we talked of his long life. Even at the end of time, a fascinating man. And like men are, too, till time's end, trying to get away in one piece.

"Listen, Rosie," he explains the other day. "I was married to my wife, do you realize, nearly half a century. What good was it? Look at the bitterness. The more I think of it, the more I think we would be fools to marry."

"Volodya Vlashkin," I told him straight, "when I was young I warmed your cold back many a night, no questions asked. You admit it, I didn't make no demands. I was softhearted. I didn't want to be called Rosie Lieber, a breaker up of homes. But now, Vlashkin, you are a free man. How could you ask me to go with you on trains to stay in strange hotels, among Americans, not your wife? Be ashamed."

So now, darling Lillie, tell this story to your mama from your young mouth. She don't listen to a word from me. She only screams, "I'll faint, I'll faint." Tell her after all I'll have a husband, which, as everybody knows, a woman should have at least one before the end of the story.

My goodness, I am already late. Give me a kiss. After all, I watched you grow from a plain seed. So give me a couple wishes on my wedding day. A long and happy life. Many years of love. Hug Mama, tell her from Aunt Rose, goodbye and good luck.

What Must I Say to You?

NORMA ROSEN

Norma Rosen (1925–): *Like many of her characters, Norma Rosen, born and raised in New York, grew up in a largely assimilated family. "No religion, no philosophy, no language, no literature, no culture," she has written of her upbringing. She studied modern dance with Martha Graham at Mt. Holyoke College. After graduating she taught English and dance at a private school and wrote articles for* Dance *magazine, then returned to school as a graduate student in English at Columbia. For several years she worked at a copyeditor at Harper and Row, writing in her spare time. Her marriage to Robert Rosen, who was born and raised in a traditional European Jewish household, sparked a renewal of her own interest in Judaism. Her books include novels,* Joy to Levine!, Touching Evil, At the Center, *and* John and Anzia: An American Romance; *a collection of stories,* Green: A Novella and Eight Stories; Biblical Women Unbound, *a volume of short fiction and nonfiction on Biblical themes; and* Accidents and Influence: Writing as a Woman and a Jew in America. *Rosen has received fellowships from the MacDowell Colony, The Eugene F. Saxon Fund, the Radcliffe Institute, and the New York State Creative Artists Public Service Fund. She has taught at Yale, the New School, the University of Pennsylvania, Herbert Lehman College, New York University, and the College of New Rochelle. She lives in New York with her husband.*

When I open the door for Mrs. Cooper at two in the afternoon, three days a week, that is the one time her voice fails us both. She smiles over my left shoulder and hurries out the words "Just fine," to get past me. She is looking for the baby, either in the bassinet in the living room or in the crib in the baby's room. When she finds her, she can talk more easily to me — through the baby. But at the doorway again, in the early evening, taking leave, Mrs. Cooper speaks up in her rightful voice, strong and slow: "I am saying good night." It seems to me that the "I am saying" form, once removed from herself, frees her of her shyness. As if she had already left and were standing in the hall, away from strangers, and were sending back the message "I am saying good night."

Maybe. I know little about Mrs. Cooper, and so read much into her ways. Despite the differences between us, each of us seems to read the other the same—tender creature, prone to suffer. Mrs. Cooper says to me, many times a day, "That is all right, that is all right," in a soothing tone. I say to her, "That's such a help, thank you, such a help." What can I guess, except what reflects myself, about someone so different from me? Mrs. Cooper is from Jamaica. She is round-faced and round-figured. She is my age, thirty, and about my height, five-five. But because she is twice my girth (not fat; if there is any unfavorable comparison to be drawn, it may as well be that I am, by her standard, meager) and because she has four children to my one, she seems older. She is very black; I am—as I remember the campus doctor at the women's college I attended saying—"surprisingly fair." Though, of course, not Anglo-Saxon. If you are not Anglo-Saxon, being fair counts only up to a point. I learned that at the women's college. I remember a conversation with a girl at college who had an ambiguous name—Green or Black or Brown. She said in the long run life was simpler if your name was Finkelstein. And I said it was better to be dark and done with it.

Mrs. Cooper had been coming to us, with her serious black bulk and her beautiful voice, for some months now, so that I can get on with my work, which is free-lance editorial. The name is light-hearted enough, but the lance is heavy and keeps me pinned to my desk. Mrs. Cooper's work, in her hands, seems delightful. Though she comes to relieve me of that same work, it is a little like watching Tom Sawyer paint a fence—so attractive one would gladly pay an apple to be allowed to lend a hand. Even the slippery bath, the howls as my daughter's sparse hairs are shampooed, become amusing mites on the giant surface of Mrs. Cooper's calm. They raise Mrs. Cooper's laugh. "Ooh, my! You can certainly sing!"

I sneak from my desk several times an afternoon to watch the work and to hear Mrs. Cooper speak. Her speech, with its trotty Jamaican rhythm, brings every syllable to life and pays exquisite attention to the final sounds of words. When she telephones home to instruct the oldest of her children in the care of the youngest, it is true that her syntax relaxes. I hear "Give she supper and put she to bed." Or "When I'm coming home I am going to wash the children them hair." But the tone of her voice is the same as when she speaks to me. It is warm, melodious. Always the diction is glorious—ready, with only a bit of memorizing, for Shakespeare. Or, if one could connect a woman's voice with the Old Testament, for that.

"God is not a God of confusion." Mrs. Cooper says that to me one day while the baby naps and she washes baby clothes in the double tub in the kitchen. I have come in to get an apple from the refrigerator. She refuses any fruit, and I stand and eat and watch the best work in the world: rhythmic rubbing-a-dubbing in a sudsy tub. With sturdy arms.

She says it again. "God is not a God of confusion, that is what my husband cousin say." A pause. "And that is what I see."

She washes; I suspend my apple.

"It is very noisy in these churches you have here." She has been in this country for three years—her husband came before, and later sent for her and the children, mildly surprising her mother, who had other daughters and daughters' kids similarly left but not reclaimed—and still she is bothered by noisy churches. Her family in Jamaica is Baptist. But when she goes to the Baptist church in Harlem, she is offended by the stamping and handclapping, by the shouted confessions and the tearful salvations. "They say wherever you go you are at home in your church. But we would never do that way at home."

She lifts her arms from the tub and pushes the suds down over her wrists and hands. "But I will find a church." The purity of her diction gives the words great strength. The tone and timbre would be fitting if she had said, "I will build a church."

Again she plunges her arms in suds. "Do you ever go," she asks me, "to that church? To that Baptist church?"

Now is the time for me to tell her that my husband and I are Jewish—and so, it occurs to me suddenly and absurdly, is our three-month-old daughter, Susan.

It is coming to Christmas. I have already mentioned to my husband that Mrs. Cooper, who has said how her children look forward to the tree, will wonder at our not having one for our child. "I don't feel like making any announcements," I tell my husband, "but I suppose I should. She'll wonder."

"You don't owe her an explanation." My husband doesn't know how close, on winter afternoons, a woman is drawn to another woman who works in her house. It would surprise him to hear that I have already mentioned to Mrs. Cooper certain intimate details of my life, and that she has revealed to me a heartache about her husband.

"But I think I'll tell her," I say. "Not even a spray of balsam. I'd rather have her think us Godless than heartless."

My husband suggests, "Tell her about Chanukah" — which with us is humor, because he knows I wouldn't know what to tell.

Cooper stands before my tub in the lighted kitchen. I lean in the doorway, watching her. The kitchen window is black. Outside, it is a freezing four o'clock. Inside, time is suspended, always when the baby sleeps. I smell the hot, soaped flannel, wrung out and heaped on the drainboard, waiting to be rinsed in three pure waters. "We don't attend church," I say. "We go — at least, my husband goes — to a synagogue. My husband and I are Jewish, Mrs. Cooper."

Mrs. Cooper looks into the tub. After a moment, she says, "That is all right." She fishes below a cream of suds, pulls up a garment, and unrolls a mitten sleeve. She wrings it and rubs it and plunges it down to soak. Loving work, as she performs it — mother's work. As I watch, my body seems to pass into her body.

I am glad that my reluctance to speak of synagogues at all has led me to speak while Mrs. Cooper is working. That is the right way. We never, I realize while she scrubs, still seeming to be listening, talk face to face. She is always looking somewhere else — at the washing or the baby's toy she is going to pick up. Being a shy person, I have drilled myself to stare people in the eyes when I speak. But Mrs. Cooper convinces me this is wrong. The face-to-face stare is for selling something, or for saying, "Look here, I don't like you and I never have liked you," or for answering, "Oh, no, Madam, we never accept for refund after eight days."

The time Mrs. Cooper told me her husband had stopped going to church altogether, she was holding Susan, and she uttered those exquisite and grieved tones — "He will not go with me, or alone, or at all any more" — straight into the baby's face, not mine.

Mrs. Cooper now pulls the stopper from the tub and the suds choke down. While she is waiting, she casts a sidelong look at me, which I sense rather than see, as I am examining my apple core. She likes to see the expression on my face after I have spoken, though not while I speak. She looks back at the sucking tub.

When Mrs. Cooper comes again on Friday, she tells me, as she measures formula into bottles, "My husband says we do not believe Christmas is Christ's birthday."

I, of course, do not look at her, except to snatch a glance out of the corner of my eye, while I fold diapers unnecessarily. Her expression is calm and bland, high round cheekbones shining, slightly slanted eyes narrowed to the measuring. "He was born, we believe, sometime in April." After a bit, she adds, "We believe there is one God for everyone."

Though my husband has told me over and over again that this is what Jews say, Mrs. Cooper's words move me as though I have never heard them before. I murmur something about my work, and escape to my desk and my lance again.

Mrs. Cooper has quoted her husband to me several times. I am curious about him, as I am sure she is about my husband. She and my husband have at least met once or twice in the doorway, but I have only seen a snapshot of her husband: a stocky man with a mustache, who is as black as she, with no smiles for photographers. Mrs. Cooper has added, in the winter afternoons, certain details important to my picture.

Her husband plays cricket on Staten Island on Sundays and goes on vacations in the summer without her or the children, sometimes with the cricketers. But to balance that, he brings her shrimp and rice when he returns at 1:00 A.M. from cricket-club meetings on Friday nights. His opinion of the bus strike in the city was that wages should go up but it was unfair to make bus riders suffer. About Elizabeth Taylor he thought it was all just nonsense; she was not even what he called pretty—more like skinny and ugly.

In most other respects, it seems to me, he is taking on the coloration of a zestful America-adopter. There are two kinds of immigrants, I observe. One kind loves everything about America, is happy to throw off the ways of the old country, and thereafter looks back largely with contempt. The other kind dislikes, compares, regrets, awakens to *Welt-* and *Ichschmerz* and feels the new life mainly as a loss of the old. Often, the two marry each other.

Mr. Cooper, though he still plays cricket, now enjoys baseball, the fights on television, his factory job and union card, and the bustle and opportunity of New York. I mention this last with irony. Mr. Cooper's job opportunities here are infinitely better than in Jamaica, where there aren't employers even to turn him down. He goes to school two nights a week for technical training. He became a citizen three years ago, destroying his wife's hopes of returning to Jamaica in their young years. But she dreams of going back when they are old. She would have servants there, she told me. "Because there aren't enough jobs, servants are cheap." Her husband, in her dream, would have a job, and so they would also have a car. And a quiet, gossipy life. She likes to move slowly, and this, as she herself points out, is very nice for my baby.

Christmas Week comes, and we give Mrs. Cooper presents for her children. And since Christmas Day falls on the last of her regular three days a week, we pay her for her holiday at the end of the second day. "Merry Christmas, Mrs. Cooper," I say. "Have a happy holiday."

Mrs. Cooper looks with interest at the baby in my arms, whom she had a moment before handed over to me. Suddenly she laughs and ducks her knees. Her fingers fly with unaccustomed haste to her cheek and she asks, "What must I say to you?"

"You can wish me the same," I say. "We have a holiday. My husband gets the day off, too."

I am glad that Mrs. Cooper has not grown reticent, since her embarrassment at Christmas, in speaking to me of holidays. Soon she is telling me how her children are looking forward to Easter. The oldest girl is preparing already for her part in a church play.

I fuss with the can of Enfamil, helping Mrs. Cooper this way when what I want is to help her another way. "Will your husband come to the play?" I ask casually.

"I am not sure," she says. After a while, "We haven't told him yet." Another little while. "Because it seems also he is against these plays." Then, with just enough of a pause to send those tones to my heart, she says, "I think he will not come."

Because the Judaeo-Christian tradition will have its little joke, Passover Week sometimes coincides with Easter Week, overlaying it like a reproach. It does the year Mrs. Cooper is with us. First, Good Friday, then in a few days is the first day of Passover.

"This year," my husband says, "because of Susie, to celebrate her first year with us, I want us to put a mezuzah outside our door before Passover."

"I'm not in favor." I manage to say it quietly.

"You don't understand enough about it," my husband says.

"I understand that much."

"Do you know what a mezuzah is? Do you know what's in it?" Taking my silence as an admission of ignorance, my husband produces a Bible. "Deuteronomy," he says. He reads:

Hear, O Israel: The Lord our God, the Lord is one Lord:
   And thou shalt love the Lord thy God with all thine heart, and
with all thy soul, and with all thy might.

And these words, which I command thee this day, shall be in thine heart:

And thou shalt teach them diligently unto thy children, and shalt talk of them when thou sittest in thine house, and when thou walkest by the way, and when thou liest down, and when thou risest up. . . .

All this and more is written on a parchment that is rolled up tight and fitted into the metal or wooden mezuzah, which is no more than two inches high and less than half an inch across and is mounted on a base for fastening to the doorframe. My husband finishes his reading:

And thou shalt write them upon the door-posts of thine house, and upon thy gates:

That your days may be multiplied, and the days of your children, in the land which the Lord sware unto your fathers to give them, as the days of heaven upon the earth.

The words might move me if I allowed them to, but I will not allow them to.

My husband closes the Bible and asks, "What did your family observe? What was Passover like?"

"My grandfather sat on a pillow, and I was the youngest, so I found the matzos and he gave me money."

"No questions? No answers?"

"Just one. I would ask my grandfather, 'Where is my prize?' And he would laugh and give me money."

"Is that all?" my husband asks.

"That was a very nice ceremony in itself," I say. "And I remember it with pleasure, and my grandfather with love!"

"But besides the food, besides the children's game. Didn't your grandparents observe anything?"

"I don't remember."

"You sat at their table for eighteen years!"

"Well, my grandmother lit Friday-night candles, and that was something I think she did all her life. But she did it by herself, in the breakfast room."

"Didn't they go to a synagogue?"

"My grandmother did. My grandfather did, too, but then I remember he stopped. He'd be home on holidays, not at the services."

"Your parents didn't tell you anything?"

"My parents were the next generation," I say. "And I'm the generation after that. We evolved," I say—and luckily that is also humor between my husband and me.

But my husband rubs his head. It's different now, and not so funny, because this year we have Susan.

My husband was born in Europe, of an Orthodox family. He is neither Orthodox nor Reform. He is his own council of rabbis, selecting as he goes. He has plenty to say about the influence of America on Jewishness, Orthodox or not. "The European Jew," my husband says, "didn't necessarily feel that if he rose in the social or economic scale he had to stop observing his Jewishness. There were even a number of wealthy and prominent German Jews who were strictly observant."

"I'm sure that helped them a lot!" This is as close as I come to speaking of the unspeakable. Somewhere in the monstrous testimony I have read about concentration camps and killings are buried the small, intense lives of my husband's family. But why is it I am more bitter than my husband about his own experiences? And why should my bitterness cut the wrong way? It is the word "German" that does it to me. My soul knots in hate. "German!" Even the softening, pathetic sound of "Jew" that follows it now doesn't help. All words fail. If I could grasp words, I would come on words that would jump so to life they would jump into my heart and kill me. All I can do is make a fantasy. Somewhere in New York I will meet a smiling German. In his pocket smile the best export accounts in the city— he is from the land of scissors and knives and ground glass. Because I am surprisingly fair, he will be oh, so surprised when I strike at him with all my might. "For the children! For the children!" My words come out shrieks. He protests it was his duty and, besides, he didn't know. I am all leaking, dissolving. How can a mist break stone? Once we exchange words it is hopeless; the words of the eyewitness consume everything, as in a fire:

> The children were covered with sores. . . .They screamed and wept all night in the empty rooms where they had been put. . . . Then the police would go up and the children, screaming with terror, would be carried kicking and struggling to the courtyard.

How is it my husband doesn't know that after this there can be no mezuzahs?

"It's too painful to quarrel," my husband says. He puts his

hands on my shoulders, his forehead against mine. "This is something I want very much. And you feel for me. I know you feel for me in this."

"Yes, I do, of course I do." I use Mrs. Cooper's trick, and even at that close range twist my head elsewhere. "Only that particular symbol—"

"No, with you it's all the symbols." My husband drops his hands from my shoulders. "You don't know enough about them to discard them."

I don't have the right to judge them—that is what I feel he means. Since I was not even scorched by the flames of their futility. As he was, and came out cursing less than I.

"But besides everything else"—I take hasty shelter in practicalness—"a mezuzah is ugly. I remember that ugly tin thing nailed to the door of my grandmother's room. If I spend three weeks picking out a light fixture for my foyer, why should I have something so ugly on my door?"

Then, as my husband answers, I see that this shabby attack has fixed my defeat, because he is immediately reasonable. "Now, that's something else. I won't argue aesthetics with you. The outer covering is of no importance. I'll find something attractive."

The next night my husband brings home a mezuzah made in the East. It is a narrow green rectangle, twice the normal size, inlaid with mosaic and outlined in brass. It does not look Jewish to me at all. It looks foreign—a strange bit of green enamel and brass.

"I don't like it," I say. "I'm sorry."

"But it's only the idea you don't like?" My husband smiles teasingly. "In looks, you at least relent?"

"It doesn't look bad," I admit.

"Well, that is the first step." I am happy to see the mezuzah disappear in his dresser drawer before we go in to our dinner.

When Mrs. Cooper comes next day, she asks, "What have you on your door?"

I step out to look, and at first have the impression that a praying mantis has somehow hatched out of season high on our doorway. Then I recognize it. "Oh, that's . . ." I say. "That's . . ." I find I cannot explain a mezuzah to someone who has never heard of one.

While Mrs. Cooper changes her clothes, I touch the mezuzah to see if it will fall off. But my husband has glued it firmly to the metal doorframe.

My husband's office works a three-quarter day on Good Friday. I ask Mrs. Cooper if she would like time off, but she says no, her husband will be home ahead of her to look after things. I have the impression she would rather be here.

My husband comes home early, bestowing strangeness on the rhythm of the house in lieu of celebration. I kiss him and put away his hat. "Well, that was a nasty thing to do." I say it lazily and with a smirk. The lazy tone is to show that I am not really involved, and the smirk that I intend to swallow it down like bad medicine. He will have his way, but I will have my say — that's all I mean. My say will be humorous, with just a little cut to it, as is proper between husband and wife. He will cut back a little, with a grin, and after Mrs. Cooper goes we will have our peaceful dinner. The conversation will meander, never actually picking sore points, but winding words about them, making pads and cushions, so that should they ever bleed, there, already softly wrapped around them, will be the bandages our words wove. Weave enough of these bandages and nothing will ever smash, I say. I always prepare in advance a last line, too, so that I will know where to stop. "When mezuzahs last in the doorway bloomed," I will say tonight. And then I expect us both to laugh.

But where has he been all day? The same office, the same thirty-minute subway ride to and from each way, the same lunch with the same cronies. . . . But he has traveled somewhere else in his head. "Doesn't anything mean anything to you?" he says, and walks by me to the bedroom.

I follow with a bandage, but it slips from my hand. "I know a lot of women who would have taken that right down!" It is something of a shout, to my surprise.

He says nothing.

"I left it up. All I wanted was my say."

He says nothing.

"I live here, too. That's my door also."

He says nothing.

"And I don't like it!"

I hear a loud smashing of glass. It brings both our heads up. My husband is the first to understand. "Mrs. Cooper broke a bottle." He puts his arms around me and says, "Let's not quarrel about a doorway. Let's not quarrel at all, but especially not about the entrance to our home."

I lower my face into his tie. What's a mezuzah? Let's have ten, I think, so long as nothing will smash.

Later, I reproach myself. I am in the living room, straightening piles of magazines, avoiding both kitchen and bedroom. A woman, I think, is the one creature who builds satisfaction of the pleasure she gets from giving in. What might the world be if women would continue the dialogue? But no, they must give in and be satisfied. Nevertheless, I don't intend to take back what I've given in on and thereby give up what I've gained.

I am aware of Mrs. Cooper, boiling formula in the kitchen, and of my baby, registering in sleep her parents' first quarrel since her birth. "What must I say to you?" I think of saying to my daughter — Mrs. Cooper's words come naturally to my mind.

I go to the kitchen doorway and look at Mrs. Cooper. Her face indicates deaf and dumb. She is finishing the bottles.

When Mrs. Cooper is dressed and ready to leave, she looks into the living room. "I am saying good night."

"I hope you and your family will have a happy Easter," I say, smiling for her.

I know in advance that Mrs. Cooper will ask, "What must I say to you?"

This time she asks it soberly, and this time my husband, who has heard, comes in to tell Mrs. Cooper the story of Passover. As always in the traditional version, there is little mention of Moses, the Jews having set down from the beginning not the tragedy of one but their intuition for the tragedy of many.

When my husband leaves us, Mrs. Cooper takes four wrapped candies from the candy bowl on the desk, holds them up to be sure I see her taking them, and puts them in her purse. "I do hope everything will be all right," she says.

"Oh, yes," I say, looking at the magazines. "It was such a help today. I got so much work done. Thank you."

I hear that she is motionless.

"I will not be like this all the days of my life." It is a cry from the heart, stunningly articulated. I lift my head from the magazines, and this time I do stare. Not be like what? A Jamaican without a servant? A wife who never vacations? An exile? A baby nurse? A woman who gives in? What Mrs. Cooper might not want to be flashes up in a lightning jumble. "I am going to find a church," she says, and strains her face away from mine.

I think of all the descriptions of God I have ever heard — that He is jealous, loving, vengeful, waiting, teaching, forgetful, permissive, broken-hearted, dead, asleep.

Mrs. Cooper and I wish each other a pleasant weekend.

The Decline of Sholem Waldman

WALLACE MARKFIELD

Wallace Markfield (1926–): *Born in Brooklyn and educated at Brooklyn College and New York University, Wallace Markfield, like so many other New York Jewish writers of his generation, wrote about a world saturated with "Jewishness," though not necessarily with Judaism itself. His work constitutes an informal digest of Brooklyn Jewish culture before the war—a kind of composite portrait of an era and a place. His output over the past forty years has been fairly modest: three darkly comic satiric novels—*To an Early Grave, Teitelbaum's Window, *and* You Could Live If They Let You—*plus a handful of skillfully rendered short stories (published in magazines such as* The Partisan Review, The Hudson Review, Commentary, *and* Midstream*) and a number of film reviews and occasional essays. Despite the brevity of his list of publications, his place among the ranks of Jewish-American writers is secure. Markfield has received fellowships from the Guggenheim Foundation and the National Council on the Arts. Although he has taught at San Francisco State University, Queens College, and Columbia, Markfield's career has been largely devoted to publicity and fund-raising work for a variety of Jewish agencies in the New York area. For many years he has lived with his family on the north shore of Long Island.*

In memory of Isaac Rosenfeld   Kommst du nur immer anzuklagen?
Ist auf der Erde ewig dir nichts recht?
FAUST

O f Sholem Waldman it was said that worms would not devour him nor dogs defile his grave. He had fought with every storekeeper on his street, and even the seltzer-man would no longer deliver to him. So was he hated, that for all his years—and he himself was certain only that he had passed seventy—nobody troubled to give him a hand when he lugged his bundles or offered to save him the five flights down with garbage. They cursed him as a troublemaker who could bring two walls together and claimed he had sent his wife to an early grave. For though she had suffered from a condition that slowly turned her blood to water, he had treated her like an Eskimo woman, forcing her to do her own windows and sheets, even sew her own house-dresses. As for his children, Sholem Waldman had hardened his heart against them. One son, a student of the finest cantors, had defied him and turned to butter and eggs. His eldest he would not speak to for reasons long forgotten. Only once had he relented, and they talked yet of how he had gone to a grandchild's bar-mitzvah bearing not even a bag of hopjes.

Years ago he had made a miserable living distributing Yeshivah money-boxes and selling honey-jars from Israel. But the market was dead and what was left the fund-raisers had taken over, with pledge cards and big dinners. Now he did far better hustling out on Sunday to the cemetery, a professional mourner. He could take in as much as twenty dollars for the day and during the weeks before the holi-days was good for nearly double. In comparison to his rivals, a dwarf-ish band of limpers and twitchers and runny-eyed, Sholem Wald-man stood out like a Cossack. Tall and lion-headed, his beard was clean and parted down the middle, his earlocks were still fiercely red and well-kept, and he took pains always to clip unseemly hair from nostrils. The strength of his voice was almost unnatural, and upon those who refused his services he would call down such ter-rible curses that the blood drained out of their faces. He would stand before the giant gates where the cars turned in, seek out the most prosperous and labor slowly along, all the while smiting his breast, praising the days and works of the dead, weeping hot tears for his own parents, for his bitter childhood, for the way God had short-changed him with wife and sons. When the car could go no further, he followed down the stony paths, thrusting off the self-styled cantors hanging about the monuments and vaults. His cus-tom at the grave was to stand silent till the first sob. Then he would quickly change his hat for a neat little *yarmalke* and give out with an *El moley rachamim* that unnerved even the ancient caretakers. He took pride in his work, and before he was done the family had got-ten full value for their money.

One such Sunday, when an icy drizzle sent vapors rising from his beard and not a half-dozen cars had been seen all afternoon, Sho-lem Waldman sought refuge in the office of Goldfarb, cemetery manager and member of his burial society. Ordinarily this would have been permitted, though Goldfarb despised him for his habit of mixing in and steaming-up people. But it so happened that a batch of lawyer letters on the conditions of two old plots had put him in bad temper. When he saw Sholem Waldman make himself at home in the swivel-chair, open his lunch-bag and eat heartily from an over-loaded sandwich his gall began to rise. "Hey," he said, "what do you think, this is a cafeteria? Who sent for you, who needs you here?" To which Sholem Waldman replied: "Go rot in the earth, I'm not in your way."

Goldfarb came over by the chair. He looked as if he would have a stroke in a minute. "All right, out. In your own house make dirt."

Without interrupting his meal Sholem Waldman said, "You should be stricken by each of the seven and seventy forms of ulcer and paralysis. When the Messiah comes and bids you follow, your legs should turn to clay. You should swell and burst, you should grow hair behind, horns in front and bleat like a goat. Finally," — as he rended a chicken-wing — "turn ritual slaughter for all good Jews. Become like a river and overflow."

"This minute out," Goldfarb shouted, "you rotten old bum, you old faker."

And he laid hands upon Sholem Waldman, pulling him by his vest and flailing him about the side of the head. But, no youngster himself, Goldfarb was beset by such kicks, such nasty pinches, that tears came to his eyes. "You want, I'll give you good," he gasped, and true to his word, dealt out buffets right and left. Sholem Waldman screeched and writhed like a wild creature and spit full into Goldfarb's face. "Apostate, Israel's enemy," he cried, voice harsher than a ram's horn. Holding fast to a desk, he called upon God to learn wherein he had sinned, he, a giver of alms, a mortifier of self, a keeper of fasts. Goldfarb sprang upon him now, pried loose his hands and bore him, wailing, to the steps. Then, how it happened he could not tell, Sholem Waldman took a tumble. His hat went sailing, his satin coat flapped between his legs, dragging him down, and all his forces failed him. With the last snatch of consciousness he gave up everything he had eaten, and more. He lay on the concrete walk like a dead one.

A flood of remorse swept over Goldfarb. He summoned a pair of husky young guards, who carried the groaning Sholem Waldman inside, and he massaged his temples and put pinches of strong stuff in his nostrils. "Live to be a hundred and twenty," he pleaded frantically. "God spare us both, you'll never be in my way again." He sent out for a lemon, squeezed the juice on Sholem Waldman's lips, but to no avail. He whispered into his ears fantastic promises of students he would recommend, weddings and catered affairs where Sholem Waldman would officiate, huge bake-shops that would pay him well only to oversee the making of matzoth. At which point Sholem Waldman revived, his earlocks and beard dirt-matted, his eyes glazed. "Finish me off," he said quietly. "Go, go, take a knife to me." "Live and be well," replied Goldfarb, much relieved. "God send your enemies such an end."

And though the roads were so iced and slippery that even taximen would not go beyond the subway stations, he was happy to drive him home. In the car, Sholem Waldman came to himself a little. He shook his fists, and if he had been able, he would have thrown himself at Goldfarb. "A *dybbuk* should enter you," he cried, "and by day and by night, year in and year out drive you from bed to bed, from house to house, from town to town. He should give you no peace, he should burn you and smite you, he should put snakes in your nostrils and frogs in your entrails."

In such fashion he continued, till they reached the house and the super, for a dollar, called out some candy-store boys and lugged him up the stairs. Waldman's kitchen filled with neighbors, who found in his fate a judgment from God, who whispered of the bundle he had socked away, of mysterious delicatessen stores and two-family houses in the Bronx. With great care, his garments were removed and he was put to bed. Mrs. Tannanbaum, a retired midwife, probed his bruises, hinted at cupping and the powers of pressed garlic. She called for steaming water, claiming that the vapors would flush his insides, drive the poisons from his pores. But that was all he needed, Sholem Waldman, and quivering and turning blue, he began to carry on over the mixing of his meat and dairy pots. Goldfarb could take it no longer. He himself ran down and put in a call to the doctor from the burial society, using all his guile, calling him 'Professor,' babbling benedictions over the phone.

Long after nightfall the doctor came, a small fat man with ponderous ways, muttering darkly that he had not been told of the flights, that the two dollars he got from the Society barely covered his gas. With pleasure, Goldfarb slipped him something extra. In better humor, the doctor began to laugh and wisecrack, saying "Pull the sheet up, you're exciting the *vyblach.*" It turned out, finally, to be nothing so terrible. "A little bit of a slipped disc," said the doctor. "Let him stay off his feet a few days and maybe sitz-bath, as hot as he can stand." In private, he let Goldfarb know that Sholem Waldman would have a hard time if he decided to make a case. Thus assured, Goldfarb left, settling first with the super's wife, who promised to shop and cook and do the light work.

All of the next week Sholem Waldman lay about groaning, though in no great pain. He complained of shortness of breath, of a heaviness in his head, of cold chills and palpitations and feebleness in his joints. Sometimes he would fall into a doze and waken in panic, crying aloud that demons were blowing into his ears and plucking patches of hair. Now and then he would rise, peering into every crack and crevice. He would follow the super's wife around, hiss at her and call her vile names over the way she left food-bits and pillow feathers to bring mice. He grumbled, too, that she gave him only the thinnest of soups and filched the chicken-fat for her family. And sometimes when she thought him immersed in prayer, she would come upon him counting the sheets and towels or sifting the bags she set aside for garbage. He begrudged her even a handful of salt to kosher his meat.

Once, as he had not for long years, Sholem Waldman dreamed of his mother. He was walking through his village again. He had the sense that some terrible thing had happened, that rivers were dried up, fields overgrown, the wind bearing smells of blood and grief. No one was in the market, the study house was closed, and he seemed all alone in the whole world. Through the streets he sought his mother, wandering from hut to hut, thinking he glimpsed her scouring a table with ashes or crushing almonds and raisins in a pestle. He feared she might not show herself, for he has been a stubborn and contrary child, a devil, and in the dream he tore at his flesh and cried "Good for you, good for you." At last, when he had lost his way and was ready to fall from his feet, she called his name and he ran toward her, trembling with love. In a desolate courtyard she stood, wearing kerchief and heavy earrings of gold, and Sholem Waldman was dazzled to find her tall and handsome, her face glowing like honey.

And Sholem Waldman lamented: "O Momma, Momma, what should I tell you and what should I say? It's so miserable, it's so hard and bitter. All for the snip of bread. Everything costs blood and strength. Believe me, if you could taste from my heart you would taste poison."

He had the impression then that his mother, for no reason at all, had become angry. She appeared to wrinkle, to shrink and bend over like a candle. "Feh," she cried, and without warning gave him a sharp crack across the face and fled swifter than a cat along the dark doorways.

Though the bed was wet from his tears, Sholem Waldman woke strangely refreshed, as if his mother had carried off that which hung over him. For the first time, he was almost cordial to the super's wife, making little jokes and even singing Hasidic songs while she ironed on the kitchen table. He told cock-and-bull stories of his flight over the frontier, how a pair of Polish nuns had hidden him in a convent cellar, how for three days and three nights he had refused their pig-dishes, filling himself with soup-greens and water. Taking his Torah, he read aloud lines, expounded to her, showing off over paradox and hidden allusion, even though by the scholars he was no scholar. She only looked at him as if he was crazy and said, "You're such a wise man, if your wisdom went into a cockroach it would stand on its hind legs and wag its tail."

More out of habit than anger, Sholem Waldman answered, "Your tongue should get enlarged and cleave to your gullet." In his mood, he could reflect only that tomorrow was Sunday, and with good weather he could more than make up the loss he had sustained from his misfortune. The thought occurred to him that he would need a cane, that he wouldn't have it easy when it came to following after the cars. But there was a merciful God in heaven, who gave back two drops of blood for every one he drew, and even the cheapest of the cheap could not bargain with a limper. With a tickle of nervous excitement, he laid out his cemetery shoes and had the super's wife press down again the fringes of his undervest.

Thus, after a night that brought not even a pretense toward sleep, Sholem Waldman rose while the last stars sparkled and caught his train long before the candy-store-man had taken his bundle of newspapers off the sidewalk. He was so early, as a matter of fact, that the cemetery gates were still shut and he had to look high and low for a place to sit. He came upon Tante Faygele, a brawny old woman who sold pretzels and pumpkin seeds; though they had often exchanged words she made room on her folding chair, saying, "There's still some decency in the world." For a good hour they squatted side by side, chewing seeds, comparing their wasted lives, their few pleasures. He told her of his dream and she said "It's a good sign, it means your luck is turning, that your mother is putting in a good word for you in heaven." "From your lips to God's ear," he replied. He rose now, for the gates were open and the first few cars were turning in. Tante Faygele gave him a bunch of pretzels for later on; they had her flavor to them, but he was nevertheless deeply moved.

In no time, Sholem Waldman's pockets were bulging with change and bills, and he began to assume a mild, fatherly air, refusing to talk price, smiling and sighing, murmuring "Who asks and who counts? Whatever you can, whatever won't grieve the dead." Over the grave a light seemed to shine through his face, his voice was fire and lightning, and droplets of sweat glowed in his beard; he made women carry on and young children hiccup in fright. Hobbling briskly from plot to plot, he bestowed blessings with a grand manner, shedding tears at the praises called after him: "One of a kind. . . . a *Zaddik* . . . a *gedillah* . . . he shouldn't know from a bad day." By mid-day, Sholem Waldman had run up a good thirty-eight dollars — nor had he bothered yet to count the change. Elated, he bought himself some pears from the Italian near the gate, though the man was a thief in his heart and no friend to Jews. With the pretzels from Tante Faygele, he was able to make a meal.

Afterwards, when he was on his way to the newer plots, he felt some slight pain in his back. Sure, he told himself, he had risen too soon, he had done too well; God was warning him against the spite of his enemies. Believing it would pass, he sat down on a bench, but found no relief. Every little movement brought extraordinary torture, as though his bones could no longer bear his body. He began to rock back and forth and if he had not been ashamed for people, would have flung himself upon the earth. A young couple passed, and the wife eyed him. "Mister," she said, "excuse me Mister, what's the matter, you don't feel all right?" "What then?" Sholem Waldman answered, triumphant. "Maybe I'm doing it for show?" With difficulty, he dragged himself to his feet and limped off, calling upon his mother for aid. Gradually, the pain let up.

He got himself a customer, then another. They started to hail him from right and left, and he had to beg them to show a little respect, not to hustle him. Nadelman, also a limper, gave him a hand, happy for the business. When suddenly, a new affliction. Whether from the cold or being too long on his feet, Sholem Waldman had to go all the way across the cemetery to pass his water. Emerging, he saw a fresh grave and hung about. But then, even before the first spadeful was flung, it came again. And three times more yet within the half-hour, back and forth, bringing anger and mockery from the old Negro who cleaned up the toilets. At last he took a taxi home, humiliating himself before he arrived. The super's wife, taking one look at him, shrieked and ran out of the house. Not knowing what else to do, she phoned Goldfarb from the candy-store, and he promised to come and bring the Society doctor as soon as he was able.

This time, though he made light of it all ("I should only have such a heart"), the doctor spoke of specialists and x-ray treatment and how even the best machine lasts just so long. "This should be your worst trouble," he said, meaning well. "Sure, worst trouble," Sholem Waldman mimicked. "What I have in my back you should have in your unmentionable."

Winking and motioning with his head, the doctor drew Goldfarb into the hall.

"The best thing, a home," he told him. "He pays a little, the Society pays a little. Otherwise you have him on your hands a couple of years yet."

Goldfarb smoked a cigarette and then went back. "You know," he told Sholem Waldman, "it's no wonder you get sick. One man alone in such an apartment. What do you need it for? This way, you go to a home, you have with whom to say a few words, where they would bring you and serve you. You'd be a hundred per cent better off."

Sholem Waldman gave him a look that could blacken a mirror and turned his face to the wall.

During the days that followed, Sholem Waldman went downhill. His face yellowed, his beard turned greyish, the tip of his nose was ugly with veins and old age overtook him all at once. A bad patient, he longed for spices and greasy foods and fought the super's wife when she came with his drops. He would not budge from his bed, and on the few occasions when a neighbor entered, made believe he was asleep. Late at night he would sometimes come awake, furious over old grievances, remembering how some colleague had diddled him out of a customer, how his father-in-law had promised him the sun and the moon for a dowry, the way his son, as a child, had set fire to the curtains.

Each day Goldfarb came, bringing him the paper, a jar of hard candies. With medicines and drops and injections and what the super's wife chiseled, the whole business was costing Goldfarb a nice few dollars. And he had his own troubles. To say the least. This he finally tried making clear to Sholem Waldman, explaining that in this life nobody gives you for nothing, that he who pays, rides, and that's how the world was ordered. You could no more change it than you could grow a new set of teeth. Fifteen, twenty minutes he gave Sholem Waldman a headful, then made his point. His brother-in-law, a big giver and a community leader of some standing was executive vice-president of a home by Central Park West, and would use influence. Whereupon Sholem Waldman wished him that all his years should become like days and that even then he should have a short life. Nor would he hear more.

But the very next day Goldfarb returned with colored pictures of the home, spreading them across the bed as Sholem Waldman sobbed and flailed his arms. "See," he said soothingly, "aren't you foolish? Here is not a *moshav zekeinim* where the city throws you around, but a modern, beautiful apartment house, with a canopy and inside a little *shul* like a diamond. As I understand it, even their own newspaper."

"O Momma, Momma," Sholem Waldman screamed, "you'll let this happen? You're not going to open up your grave and take me in?"

"Who talks of graves?" said Goldfarb. "Who? Here they'll treat you as though you were the Lubavitcher Rabbi, you'll have honey-cake by day and bird's milk at night."

Goldfarb said many more things, and in the end prevailed. He arranged for everything, selling the apartment lock, stock and barrel to the super's wife, who made believe she was doing him a favor, though she would have had to pay more for the crystal closet alone. The following week he took off a morning and came for Sholem Waldman in his car. When it was time to hand over the keys the old man made a racket that brought the house together. At the last minute he refused to budge, till Goldfarb ran up the flights and pried his *mezuzah* from the doorpost. A neighbor or two called a good-bye and wished him luck. But no tears were shed.

Soon enough, everybody at the home learned with whom they were dealing. The rabbi, an American type and always with a brief-bag, he would not trust, and spoke out against him, claiming he catered only to those with wealthy children. He accused the management of buying meats from the A & P and snooped around the kitchen, his nose in every pot. If he saw a man even sit with a woman he would bawl out such things that, old as they were, they blushed and sometimes wept with shame. Where he could, he made mischief.

Sometimes Friedman, who shared his room, would ask him in a nice way to come downstairs and start to learn an instrument or join the still-life people. "I mean it for your benefit," he would say. "What kind of person sits all day like a stone?"

Only one thing Sholem Waldman enjoyed. When his condition permitted, he would go to the social hall and watch television with the paralytics and half-wits who babbled and cackled at everything on the screen. Their heads would joggle, they would gasp, click tongues and call out all their sorrows. Then one, perhaps Yente Gersh, would grow suddenly frightened and point and screech: "Look, look. Look what he's doing to her."

And Chanah Malkeh would reply, "Mamele, why should you aggravate? Did she also care when your children lifted hands against you?"

"It's a terrible thing, nevertheless. A young girl like that. Though God spare us all, maybe she's better off."

"I like better with the horses."

"Shah, he's giving her good again."

"Blessed the hand that deals a blow to an evil woman."

And they would go on till Sholem Waldman beat his fists on the table and looked upon them with terrible eyes. Him they feared.

It turned out one day that Sholem Waldman missed a box of sucrets, which he took once in a while against heartburn. He rummaged through every one of Friedman's drawers and the pockets of his suits and when Friedman came in, cried, "They should stick in your throat and fester. You should pay it back in snips of flesh."

Now Friedman had never in his life said a loud word and was known to rise often in the middle of the night to help Sholem Waldman to the bathroom or fetch him water. But he could endure no more. "Everything, they call a man," he said. "I'll tell you something, a little story. Once a tortoise is standing by a river and a snake comes to him and says, 'Do me a favor, put me on your back and swim me across?' 'What, I'm crazy?' says the tortoise. 'You'll only sting me and I'll die.' 'Don't be foolish,' says the snake. 'If I should sting you, God forbid, the two of us'll get killed.' All right, the tortoise puts him on his back and they're in the middle of the water when all of a sudden the snake gives him a bite. They're both drowning and the tortoise says, 'Why, why did you do that?' And the snake answers, 'What can I do, it's my nature.' You understand, my friend? I make myself, I hope, clear."

And Sholem Waldman leaned over and put his face close to Friedman. "You'll tell me a story? I'll give you a story, too. You want to know something? You smell bad, it's impossible to be in the same room with you. You stink already from death and worms and the dirt of the grave."

Whereupon Friedman rose and said, "My friend, that's your own stink you smell, your own worms and your own grave." With dignity, he left the room.

For a long time Sholem Waldman sat, oppressed by the pain in his back, suddenly conscious, though he was the cleanest of men, of a disgusting smell from his person and his breath. Then he hobbled to the elevator and rode down to the social hall.

A few nervous giggles, and then waves of laughter stunned and flayed him. Thinking it was something from the screen, he was about to take his customary seat, when one and all they swivelled in their wheelchairs and pedalwagons and from every corner of the room chanted at him "STINK STINK STINK STINK."

Sholem Waldman gasped and his heart turned to ice. He considered seeking out Friedman, asking forgiveness, pleading not to be buried alive. He opened and closed his mouth, but nothing came out of it. "STINK STINK STINK STINK" they chanted again, some pinching noses or twisting mouths as though gagging for air. And returning to himself, Sholem Waldman did what he had to do, raging out at them and making commotion. In the end, he told himself, he was better off with his spite. Do him something.

Envy; or, Yiddish in America

CYNTHIA OZICK

Cynthia Ozick (1928–): *Cynthia Ozick was born in the Bronx, the daughter of immigrant parents. She was educated at New York University and Ohio State, where she completed a master's thesis on the work of Henry James. Her distinguished career has been divided between novels (*Trust, The Cannibal Galaxy, The Messiah of Stockholm, *and* The Puttermesser Papers*); volumes of short fiction (*The Pagan Rabbi and Other Stories, Bloodshed and Three Novellas, *and* Levitation: Five Fictions*); and critical essays, mostly on a range of literary topics, collected in* Art and Ardor, Metaphor and Memory, *and* Fame and Folly. *In recent years she completed a stage adaptation of her story "The Shawl," which was produced in New York. Over the past thirty years, her work has been greeted with almost universal acclaim. Three of her stories have won first prize in the annual O. Henry Awards. In addition, Ozick's writing has received the Edward Lewis Wallant Award for Jewish fiction, the National Book Award, the Distinguished Service in Jewish Letters Award from the Jewish Theological Seminary, the American Academy of the Arts Award for Literature, the Jewish Heritage Award, the Rea Award for the Short Story, and the American Academy of Arts and Letters Strauss Living Award. She lives in the suburbs of New York, with her husband.*

Edelshtein, an American for forty years, was a ravenous reader of novels by writers "of" — he said this with a snarl — "Jewish extraction." He found them puerile, vicious, pitiable, ignorant, contemptible, above all stupid. In judging them he dug for his deepest vituperation — they were, he said, "*Amerikanergeboren.*" Spawned in America, pogroms a rumor, *mamaloshen* a stranger, history a vacuum. Also many of them were still young, and had black eyes, black hair, and red beards. A few were blue-eyed, like the *cheder-yinglach* of his youth. Schoolboys. He was certain he did not envy them, but he read them like a sickness. They were reviewed and praised, and meanwhile they were considered Jews, and knew nothing. There was even a body of Gentile writers in reaction, beginning to show familiarly whetted teeth: the Jewish Intellectual Establishment was misrepresenting American letters, coloring it with an alien dye, taking it over, and so forth. Like Berlin and Vienna in the twenties. *Judenrein ist Kulturrein* was Edelshtein's opinion. Take away the Jews and where, O so-called Western Civilization, is your literary culture?

For Edelshtein Western Civilization was a sore point. He had never been to Berlin, Vienna, Paris, or even London. He had been to Kiev, though, but only once, as a young boy. His father, a *melamed*, had traveled there on a tutoring job and had taken him along. In Kiev they lived in the cellar of a house owned by rich Jews, the Kirilovs. They had been born Katz, but bribed an official in order to Russify their name. Every morning he and his father would go up a green staircase to the kitchen for a breakfast of coffee and stale bread and then into the schoolroom to teach *chumash* to Alexei Kirilov, a red-cheeked little boy. The younger Edelshtein would drill him while his father dozed. What had become of Alexei Kirilov? Edelshtein, a widower in New York, sixty-seven years old, a Yiddishist (so-called), a poet, could stare at anything at all—a subway car-card, a garbage can lid, a streetlight—and cause the return of Alexei Kirilov's face, his bright cheeks, his Ukraine-accented Yiddish, his shelves of mechanical toys from Germany—trucks, cranes, wheel-barrows, little colored autos with awnings overhead. Only Edelshtein's father was expected to call him Alexei—everyone else, including the young Edelshtein, said Avremeleh. Avremeleh had a knack of getting things by heart. He had a golden head. Today he was a citizen of the Soviet Union. Or was he finished, dead, in the ravine at Babi Yar? Edelshtein remembered every coveted screw of the German toys. With his father he left Kiev in the spring and returned to Minsk. The mud, frozen into peaks, was melting. The train carriage reeked of urine and dirt seeped through their shoelaces into their socks.

And the language was lost, murdered. The language—a museum. Of what other language can it be said that it died a sudden and definite death, in a given decade, on a given piece of soil? Where are the speakers of ancient Etruscan? Who was the last man to write a poem in Linear B? Attrition, assimilation. Death by mystery not gas. The last Etruscan walks around inside some Sicilian. Western Civilization, that pod of muck, lingers on and on. The Sick Man of Europe with his big globe-head, rotting, but at home in bed.

Yiddish, a littleness, a tiny light—oh little holy light!—dead, vanished. Perished. Sent into darkness.

This was Edelshtein's subject. On this subject he lectured for a living. He swallowed scraps. Synagogues, community centers, labor unions underpaid him to suck on the bones of the dead. Smoke. He traveled from borough to borough, suburb to suburb, mourning in English the death of Yiddish. Sometimes he tried to read one or two of his poems. At the first Yiddish word the painted old ladies of the Reform Temples would begin to titter from shame, as at a stand-up television comedian. Orthodox and Conservative men fell instantly asleep. So he reconsidered, and told jokes:

> Before the war there was held a great International Esperanto Convention. It met in Geneva. Esperanto scholars, doctors of letters, learned men, came from all over the world to deliver papers on the genesis, syntax, and functionalism of Esperanto. Some spoke of the social value of an international language, others of its beauty. Every nation on earth was represented among the lecturers. All the papers were given in Esperanto. Finally the meeting was concluded, and the tired great men wandered companionably along the corridors, where at last they began to converse casually among themselves in their international language: "*Nu, vos macht a yid?*"

> After the war a funeral cortège was moving slowly down a narrow street on the Lower East Side. The cars had left the parking lot behind the chapel in the Bronx and were on their way to the cemetery in Staten Island. Their route took them past the newspaper offices of the last Yiddish daily left in the city. There were two editors, one to run the papers off the press and the other to look out the window. The one looking out the window saw the funeral procession passing by and called to his colleague: "Hey Mottel, print one less!"

But both Edelshtein and his audiences found the jokes worthless. Old jokes. They were not the right kind. They wanted jokes about weddings—spiral staircases, doves flying out of cages, bashful medical students—and he gave them funerals. To speak of Yiddish was to preside over a funeral. He was a rabbi who had survived his whole congregation. Those for whom his tongue was no riddle were specters.

The new Temples scared Edelshtein. He was afraid to use the

word *shul* in these palaces—inside, vast mock-bronze Tablets, mobiles of oustretched hands rotating on a motor, gigantic dangling Tetragrammatons in transparent plastic like chandeliers, platforms, altars, daises, pulpits, aisles, pews, polished-oak bins for prayerbooks printed in English with made-up new prayers in them. Everything smelled of wet plaster. Everything was new. The refreshment tables were long and luminous—he saw glazed cakes, snowheaps of egg salad, herring, salmon, tuna, whitefish, gefilte fish, pools of sour cream, silver electric coffee urns, bowls of lemon-slices, pyramids of bread, waferlike teacups from the Black Forest, Indian-brass trays of hard cheeses, golden bottles set up in rows like ninepins, great sculptured butter-birds, Hansel-and-Gretel houses of cream cheese and fruitcake, bars, butlers, fat napery, carpeting deep as honey. He learned their term for their architecture: "soaring." In one place—a flat wall of beige brick in Westchester—he read Scripture riveted on in letters fashioned from 14-karat gold molds: "And thou shalt see My back; but My face shall not be seen." Later that night he spoke in Mount Vernon, and in the marble lobby afterward he heard an adolescent girl mimic his inflections. It amazed him: often he forgot he had an accent. In the train going back to Manhattan he slid into a miniature jogging doze—it was a little nest of sweetness there inside the flaps of his overcoat, and he dreamed he was in Kiev, with his father. He looked through the open schoolroom door at the smoking cheeks of Alexei Kirilov, eight years old. "Avremeleh," he called, "Avremeleh, *kum tsu mir, lebst ts' geshtorben?*" He heard himself yelling in English: Thou shalt see my asshole! A belch woke him to hot fear. He was afraid he might be, unknown to himself, all his life long, a secret pederast.

He had no children and only a few remote relations (a druggist cousin in White Plains, a cleaning store in-law hanging on somewhere among the blacks in Brownsville), so he loitered often in Baumzweig's apartment—dirty mirrors and rusting crystal, a hazard and invitation to cracks, an abandoned exhausted corridor. Lives had passed through it and were gone. Watching Baumzweig and his wife—gray-eyed, sluggish, with a plump Polish nose—it came to him that at this age, his own and theirs, it was the same having children or not having them. Baumzweig had two sons, one married and a professor at San Diego, the other at Stanford, not yet thirty, in love with his car. The San Diego son had a son. Sometimes it seemed that it must be in deference to his childlessness that Baumzweig and his wife pretended a detachment from their offspring. The grandson's photo—a fat-lipped child of three or so—was wedged between two wine glasses on top of the china closet. But then it became plain they could not imagine the lives of their children. Nor could the children imagine their lives. The parents were too helpless to explain, the sons were too impatient to explain. So they had given each other up to a common muteness. In that apartment Josh and Mickey had grown up answering in English the Yiddish of their parents. Mutes. Mutations. What right had these boys to spit out the Yiddish that had bred them, and only for the sake of Western Civilization? Edelshtein knew the titles of their Ph.D. theses: literary boys, one was on *Sir Gawain and the Green Knight*, the other was on the novels of Carson McCullers.

Baumzweig's lethargic wife was intelligent. She told Edelshtein he too had a child, also a son. "Yourself, yourself," she said. "You remember yourself when you were a little boy, and *that* little boy is the one you love, *him* you trust, *him* you bless, *him* you bring up in hope to a good manhood." She spoke a rich Yiddish, but high-pitched.

Baumzweig had a good job, a sinecure, a pension in disguise, with an office, a part-time secretary, a typewriter with Hebrew characters, ten-to-three hours. In 1910 a laxative manufacturer—a philanthropist—had founded an organization called the Yiddish-American Alliance for Letters and Social Progress. The original illustrious members were all dead—even the famous poet Yehoash was said to have paid dues for a month or so—but there was a trust providing for the group's continuation, and enough money to pay for a biannual periodical in Yiddish. Baumzweig was the editor of this, but of the Alliance nothing was left, only some crumbling brown snapshots of Jews in derbies. His salary check came from the laxative manufacturer's grandson—a Republican politician, an Episcopalian. The name of the celebrated product was LUKE-WARM: it was advertised as delightful to children when dissolved in lukewarm cocoa. The name of the obscure periodical was *Bitterer Yam*, Bitter Sea, but it had so few subscribers that Baumzweig's wife called it Invisible Ink. In it Baumzweig published much of his own poetry and a little of Edelshtein's. Baumzweig wrote mostly of Death, Edelshtein mostly of Love. They were both sentimentalists, but not about each other. They did not like each other, though they were close friends.

Sometimes they read aloud among the dust of empty bowls their newest poems, with an agreement beforehand not to criticize:

Paula should be the critic. Carrying coffee back and forth in cloudy glasses, Baumzweig's wife said: "Oh, very nice, very nice. But so sad. Gentlemen, life is not that sad." After this she would always kiss Edelshtein on the forehead, a lazy kiss, often leaving stuck on his eyebrow a crumb of Danish: very slightly she was a slattern.

Edelshtein's friendship with Baumzweig had a ferocious secret: it was moored entirely to their agreed hatred for the man they called *der chazer*. He was named Pig because of his extraordinarily white skin, like a tissue of pale ham, and also because in the last decade he had become unbelievably famous. When they did not call him Pig they called him *shed* — Devil. They also called him Yankee Doodle. His name was Yankel Ostrover, and he was a writer of stories.

They hated him for the amazing thing that had happened to him — his fame — but this they never referred to. Instead they discussed his style: his Yiddish was impure, his sentences lacked grace and sweep, his paragraph transitions were amateur, vile. Or else they raged against his subject matter which was insanely sexual, pornographic, paranoid, freakish — men who embraced men, women who caressed women, sodomists of every variety, boys copulating with hens, butchers who drank blood for strength behind the knife. All the stories were set in an imaginary Polish village, Zwrdl, and by now there was almost no American literary intellectual alive who had not learned to say Zwrdl when he meant lewd. Ostrover's wife was reputed to be a high-born Polish Gentile woman from the "real" Zwrdl, the daughter in fact of a minor princeling, who did not know a word of Yiddish and read her husband's fiction falteringly, in English translation — but both Edelshtein and Baumzweig had encountered her often enough over the years, at this meeting and that, and regarded her as no more impressive than a pot of stale fish. Her Yiddish had an unpleasant gargling Galician accent, her vocabulary was a thin soup — they joked that it was correct to say she spoke no Yiddish — and she mewed it like a peasant, comparing prices. She was a short square woman, a cube with low-slung udders and a flat backside. It was partly Ostrover's mockery, partly his self-advertising, that had converted her into a little princess. He would make her go into their bedroom to get a little whip he claimed she had used on her bay, Romeo, trotting over her father's lands in her girlhood. Baumzweig often said this same whip was applied to the earlobes of Ostrover's translators, unhappy pairs of collaborators he changed from month to month, never satisfied.

Ostrover's glory was exactly in this: that he required translators.

Though he wrote only in Yiddish, his fame was American, national, international. They considered him a "modern." Ostrover was free of the prison of Yiddish! Out, out—he had burst out, he was in the world of reality.

And how had he begun? The same as anybody, a columnist for one of the Yiddish dailies, a humorist, a cheap fast article-writer, a squeezer-out of real-life tales. Like anybody else, he saved up a few dollars, put a paper clip over his stories, and hired a Yiddish press to print up a hundred copies. A book. Twenty-five copies he gave to people he counted as relatives, another twenty-five he sent to enemies and rivals, the rest he kept under his bed in the original cartons. Like anybody else, his literary gods were Chekhov and Tolstoy, Peretz and Sholem Aleichem. From this, how did he come to *The New Yorker*, to *Playboy*, to big lecture fees, invitations to Yale and M.I.T. and Vassar, to the Midwest, to Buenos Aires, to a literary agent, to a publisher on Madison Avenue?

"He sleeps with the right translators," Paula said. Edelshtein gave out a whinny. He knew some of Ostrover's translators—a spinster hack in dresses below the knee, occasionally a certain half-mad and drunken lexicographer, college boys with a dictionary.

Thirty years ago, straight out of Poland via Tel Aviv, Ostrover crept into a toying affair with Mireleh, Edelshtein's wife. He had left Palestine during the 1939 Arab riots, not, he said, out of fear, out of integrity rather—it was a country which had turned its face against Yiddish. Yiddish was not honored in Tel Aviv or Jerusalem. In the Negev it was worthless. In the God-given State of Israel they had no use for the language of the bad little interval between Canaan and now. Yiddish was inhabited by the past, the new Jews did not want it. Mireleh liked to hear these anecdotes of how rotten it was in Israel for Yiddish and Yiddishists. In Israel the case was even lamer than in New York, thank God! There was after all a reason to live the life they lived: it was worse somewhere else. Mireleh was a tragedian. She carried herself according to her impression of how a barren woman should sit, squat, stand, eat and sleep, talked constantly of her six miscarriages, and was vindictive about Edelshtein's sperm-count. Ostrover would arrive in the rain, crunch down on the sofa, complain about transportation from the Bronx to the West Side, and begin to woo Mireleh. He took her out to supper, to his special café, to Second Avenue vaudeville, even home to his apartment near Crotona Park to meet his little princess Pesha. Edelshtein noticed with self-curiosity that he felt no jealousy whatever, but he thought himself obliged to throw a kitchen chair at Ostrover. Ostrover had very fine teeth, his own; the chair knocked off half a lateral incisor, and Edelshtein wept at the flaw. Immediately he led Ostrover to the dentist around the corner.

The two wives, Mireleh and Pesha, seemed to be falling in love: they had dates, they went to museums and movies together, they poked one another and laughed day and night, they shared little privacies, they carried pencil-box rulers in their purses and showed each other certain hilarious measurements, they even became pregnant in the same month. Pesha had her third daughter, Mireleh her seventh miscarriage. Edelshtein was griefstricken but elated. "*My* sperm-count?" he screamed. "*Your* belly! Go fix the machine before you blame the oil!" When the dentist's bill came for Ostrover's jacket crown, Edelshtein sent it to Ostrover. At this injustice Ostrover dismissed Mireleh and forbade Pesha to go anywhere with her ever again.

About Mireleh's affair with Ostrover Edelshtein wrote the following malediction:

> *You, why do you snuff out my sons, my daughters?*
> *Worse than Mother Eve, cursed to break waters*
> *For little ones to float out upon in their tiny barks of skin,*
> *you, merciless one, cannot even bear the fruit of sin.*

It was published to much gossip in *Bitterer Yam* in the spring of that year—one point at issue being whether "snuff out" was the right term in such a watery context. (Baumzweig, a less oblique stylist, had suggested "drown.") The late Zimmerman, Edelshtein's cruelest rival, wrote in a letter to Baumzweig (which Baumzweig read on the telephone to Edelshtein):

> Who is the merciless one, after all, the barren woman who makes the house peaceful with no infantile caterwauling, or the excessively fertile poet who bears the fruit of his sin—namely his untalented verses? He bears it, but who can bear it? In one breath he runs from seas to trees. Like his ancestors the amphibians, puffed up with arrogance. Hersheleh Frog! Why did God give Hersheleh Edelshtein an unfaithful wife? To punish him for writing trash.

Around the same time Ostrover wrote a story: two women loved each other so much they mourned because they could not give birth to one another's children. Both had husbands, one virile and hearty, the other impotent, with a withered organ, a *shlimazal*. They seized the idea of making a tool out of one of the husbands: they agreed to transfer their love for each other into the man, and bear the child of their love through him. So both women turned to the virile husband, and both women conceived. But the woman who had the withered husband could not bear her child: it withered in her womb. "As it is written," Ostrover concluded, "Paradise is only for those who have already been there."

A stupid fable! Three decades later — Mireleh dead of a cancerous uterus, Pesha encrusted with royal lies in *Time* magazine (which photographed the whip) — this piece of insignificant mystification, this *pollution*, included also in Ostrover's *Complete Tales* (Kimmel & Segal, 1968), was the subject of graduate dissertations in comparative literature, as if Ostrover were Thomas Mann, or even Albert Camus. When all that happened was that Pesha and Mireleh had gone to the movies together now and then — and such a long time ago! All the same, Ostrover was released from the dungeon of the dailies, from *Bitterer Yam* and even seedier nullities, he was free, the outside world knew his name. And why Ostrover? Why not somebody else? Was Ostrover more gifted than Komorsky? Did he think up better stories than Horowitz? Why does the world outside pick on an Ostrover instead of an Edelshtein or even a Baumzweig? What occult knack, what craft, what crooked convergence of planets drove translators to grovel before Ostrover's naked swollen sentences with their thin little threadbare pants always pulled down? Who had discovered that Ostrover was a "modern"? His Yiddish, however fevered on itself, bloated, was still Yiddish, it was still *mamaloshen*, it still squeaked up to God with a littleness, a familiarity, an elbow-poke, it was still pieced together out of *shtetl* rags, out of a baby *aleph*, a toddler *beys* — so why Ostrover? Why only Ostrover? Ostrover should be the only one? Everyone else sentenced to darkness, Ostrover alone saved? Ostrover the survivor? As if hidden in the Dutch attic like that child. *His* diary, so to speak, the only documentation of what was. Like Ringelblum of Warsaw. Ostrover was to be the only evidence that there was once a Yiddish tongue, a Yiddish literature? And all the others lost? Lost! Drowned. Snuffed out. Under the earth. As if never.

Edelshtein composed a letter to Ostrover's publishers:

Kimmel & Segal
244 Madison Avenue, New York City

My dear Mr. Kimmel, and very honored Mr. Segal:

I am writing to you in reference to one Y. Ostrover, whose works you are the company that places them before the public's eyes. Be kindly enough to forgive all flaws of English Expression. Undoubtedly, in the course of his business with you, you have received from Y. Ostrover, letters in English, even worse than this. (I HAVE NO TRANSLATOR!) We immigrants, no matter how long already Yankified, stay inside always green and never attain to actual native writing Smoothness. For one million green writers, one Nabokov, one Kosinski. I mention these to show my extreme familiarness with American Literature in all Contemporaneous avatars. In your language I read, let us say, wolfishly. I regard myself as a very Keen critic, esp. concerning so-called Amer.-Jewish writers. If you would give time I could willingly explain to you many clear opinions I have concerning these Jewish-Amer. boys and girls such as (not alphabetical) Roth Philip/ Rosen Norma/ Melammed Bernie/ Friedman B.J./ Paley Grace/ Bellow Saul/ Mailer Norman. Of the latter having just read several recent works including political I would like to remind him what F. Kafka, rest in peace, said to the German-speaking, already very comfortable, Jews of Prague, Czechoslovakia: "Jews of Prague! You know more Yiddish than you think!"

Perhaps, since doubtless you do not read the Jewish Press, you are not informed. Only this month all were taken by surprise! In that filthy propaganda *Sovietish Heymland* which in Russia they run to show that their prisoners the Jews are not prisoners—a poem! By a 20-year-old young Russian Jewish girl! Yiddish will yet live through our young. Though I doubt it as do other pessimists. However, this is not the point! I ask you—what does the following personages mean to you, you who are Sensitive men, Intelligent, and with closely-warmed Feelings! Lyessin, Reisen, Yehoash! H. Leivik himself! Itzik Manger, Chaim Grade, Aaron Zeitlin, Jacob Glatshtein, Eliezer Greenberg! Molodowsky and Korn, ladies, gifted! Dovid Ignatov, Morris Rosenfeld, Moishe Nadir, Moishe Leib Halpern, Reuven Eisland, Mani Leib, Zisha Landau! I ask you! Frug, Peretz, Vintchevski, Bovshover, Edelshtat! Velvl Zhbarzher, Avrom Goldfaden! A. Rosenblatt! Y.Y. Schwartz, Yoisef Rollnick! These are all our glorious Yiddish poets. And if I would add to them our beautiful recent Russian brother-poets that were killed by Stalin with his pockmarks, for instance Peretz Markish, would you know any name of theirs? No! THEY HAVE NO TRANSLATORS!

Esteemed Gentlemen, you publish only one Yiddish writer, not even a Poet, only a Story-writer. I humbly submit you give serious wrong Impressions. That we have produced nothing else. I again refer to your associate Y. Ostrover. I do not intend to take away from him any possible talent by this letter, but wish to WITH VIGOROUSNESS assure you that others also exist without notice being bothered over them! I myself am the author and also publisher of four tomes of poetry: *N'shomeh un Guf, Zingen un Freyen, A Velt ohn Vint, A Shtundeh mit Shney.* To wit, "Soul and Body," "Singing and Being Happy," "A World with No Wind," "An Hour of Snow," these are my Deep-Feeling titles.

Please inform me if you will be willing to provide me with a translator for these very worthwhile pieces of hidden writings, or, to use a Hebrew Expression, "Buried Light."

Yours very deeply respectful.

He received an answer in the same week.

Dear Mr. Edelstein:

Thank you for your interesting and informative letter. We regret that, unfortunately, we cannot furnish you with a translator. Though your poetry may well be of the quality you claim for it, practically speaking, reputation must precede translation.

Yours sincerely.

A lie! Liars!

Dear Kimmel, dear Segal,

Did YOU, Jews without tongues, ever hear of Ostrover before you found him translated everywhere? In Yiddish he didn't exist for you! For you Yiddish has no existence! A darkness inside a cloud! Who can see it, who can hear it? The world has no ears for the prisoner! You sign yourself "Yours." You're not mine and I'm not Yours!

Sincerely.

He then began to search in earnest for a translator. Expecting little, he wrote to the spinster hack.

Esteemed Edelshtein [she replied]:

To put it as plainly as I can — a plain woman should be as plain in her words — you do not know the world of practicality, of reality. Why should you? You're a poet, an idealist. When a big magazine pays Ostrover $500, how much do I get? Maybe $75. If he takes a rest for a month and doesn't write, what then? Since he's the only one they want to print he's the only one worth translating. Suppose I translated one of your nice little love songs? Would anyone buy it? Foolishness even to ask. And if they bought it, should I slave for the $5? You don't know what I go through with Ostrover anyhow. He sits me down in his dining room, his wife brings in a samovar of tea — did you ever hear anything as pretentious as this — and sits also, watching me. She has jealous eyes. She watches my ankles, which aren't bad. Then we begin. Ostrover reads aloud the first sentence the way he wrote it, in Yiddish. I write it down, in English. Right away it starts. Pesha reads what I put down and says, "That's no good, you don't catch his idiom." Idiom! She knows! Ostrover says, "The last word sticks in my throat. Can't you do better than that? A little more robustness." We look in the dictionary, the thesaurus, we scream out different words, trying, trying. Ostrover doesn't like any of them. Suppose the word is "big." We go through huge, vast, gigantic, enormous, gargantuan, monstrous, etc., etc., etc., and finally Ostrover says — by now it's five hours later, my tonsils hurt, I can hardly stand — "all right, so let it be 'big.' Simplicity above all." Day after day like this! And for $75 is it worth it? Then after this he fires me and gets himself a college boy! Or that imbecile who cracked up over the mathematics dictionary! Until he needs me. However I get a little glory out of it. Everyone says, "There goes Ostrover's translator." In actuality I'm his pig, his stool (I mean that in both senses, I assure you). You write that he has no talent. That's your opinion, maybe you're not wrong, but let me tell you he has a talent for pressure. The way among *them* they write careless novels, hoping they'll be transformed into beautiful movies and sometimes it happens — that's how it is with him. Never mind the quality of his Yiddish, what will it turn into when it becomes English? Transformation is all he cares for — and in English he's a cripple — like, please excuse me, yourself and everyone of your generation. But Ostrover has the sense to be a suitor. He keeps all his translators in a perpetual frenzy of envy for each other, but they're just rubble and offal to him, they aren't the object of his suit. What he woos is *them*. Them! You understand me, Edelshtein? He stands on backs of hacks to reach. I know you call me hack, and it's all right, by myself I'm what you think me, no imagination, so-so ability (I too once wanted to be a poet, but that's another life) — with Ostrover on my back I'm something else: I'm "Ostrover's translator." You think that's nothing? It's an entrance into *them*. I'm invited everywhere, I go to the same parties Ostrover goes to. Everyone looks at me and thinks I'm a bit freakish, but they say: "It's Ostrover's translator." A marriage. Pesha, that junk-heap, is less married to Ostrover than I am. Like a wife, I have the supposedly passive role. Supposedly: who knows what goes on in the bedroom? An unmarried person like myself becomes good at guessing at these matters. The same with translation. Who makes the language Ostrover is famous for? You ask: what has persuaded *them* that he's a "so-called modern"? — a sneer. Aha. *Who* has read James Joyce, Ostrover or I? I'm fifty-three years old. I wasn't born back of Hlusk for nothing, I didn't go to Vassar for nothing — do you understand me? I got caught in between, so I got squeezed. Between two organisms. A cultural hermaphrodite, neither one nor the other. I have a forked tongue. When I fight for five hours to make Ostrover say "big" instead of "gargantuan," when I take out all the nice homey commas he sprinkles like a fool, when I drink his wife's stupid tea and then go home with a watery belly — *then* he's being turned into a "modern," you see? I'm the one! No one recognizes this, of course, they think it's something inside the stories themselves, when actually it's the way I dress them up and paint over them. It's all cosmetics, I'm a cosmetician, a painter, the one they pay to do the same job on the corpse in the mortuary, among *them* . . . don't, though, bore me with your criticisms. I tell you his Yiddish doesn't matter. Nobody's Yiddish matters. Whatever's in Yiddish doesn't matter.

The rest of the letter — all women are long-winded, strong-minded — he did not read. He had already seen what she was after: a little bit of money, a little bit of esteem. A miniature megalomaniac: she fancied herself the *real* Ostrover. She believed she had fashioned herself a genius out of a rag. A rag turned into a sack, was that genius? She lived out there in the light, with *them:* naturally she wouldn't waste her time on an Edelshtein. In the bleakness. Dark where he was. An idealist! How had this good word worked itself up in society to become an insult? A darling word nevertheless. Idealist. The difference between him and Ostrover was this: Ostrover wanted to save only himself, Edelshtein wanted to save Yiddish.

Immediately he felt he lied.

With Baumzweig and Paula he went to the 92nd Street Y to hear Ostrover read. "Self-mortification," Paula said of this excursion. It was a snowy night. They had to shove their teeth into the wind, tears of suffering iced down their cheeks, the streets from the subway were Siberia. "Two Christian saints, self-flagellation," she muttered, "with chains of icicles they hit themselves." They paid for the tickets with numb fingers and sat down toward the front. Edelshtein felt paralyzed. His toes stung, prickled, then seemed diseased, gangrenous, furnace-like. The cocoon of his bed at home, the pen he kept on his night table, the first luminous line of his new poem lying there waiting to be born — *Oh that I might like a youth be struck with the blow of belief* — all at once he knew how to go on with it, what it was about and what he meant by it, the hall around him seemed preposterous, unnecessary, why was he here? Crowds, huddling, the whine of folding chairs lifted and dropped, the babble, Paula yawning next to him with squeezed and wrinkled eyelids, Baumzweig blowing his flat nose into a blue plaid handkerchief and exploding a great green flower of snot, why was he in such a place as this? What did such a place have in common with what he knew, what he felt?

Paula craned around her short neck inside a used-up skunk collar to read the frieze, mighty names, golden letters, Moses, Einstein, Maimonides, Heine. Heine. Maybe Heine knew what Edelshtein knew, a convert. But these, ushers in fine jackets, skinny boys carrying books (Ostrover's), wearing them nearly, costumed for blatant bookishness, blatant sexuality, in pants crotch-snug, penciling buttocks on air, mustachioed, some hairy to the collarbone, shins and calves menacing as hammers, and girls, tunics, knees, pants, boots, little hidden sweet tongues, black-eyed. Woolly smell of piles and piles of coats. For Ostrover! The hall was full, the ushers with raised tweed wrists directed all the rest into an unseen gallery nearby: a television screen there, on which the little gray ghost of Ostrover, palpable and otherwise white as a washed pig, would soon flutter. The Y. Why? Edelshtein lectured at Y's — Elmhurst, Eastchester, Rye, tiny platforms, lecterns too tall for him, catalogues of vexations, his sad recitations to old people. Ladies and Gentlemen, they have cut out my vocal cords, the only language I can freely and fluently address you in, my darling *mamaloshen*, surgery, dead, the operation was a success. Edelshtein's Y's were all old people's homes, convalescent factories, asylums. To himself he sang,

Why	*Farvos di Vy?*
the Y?	*Ich reyd*
Lectures	*ohn freyd*
to specters,	*un sheydim tantsen derbei,*

aha! specters, if my tongue has no riddle for you, Ladies and Gentlemen, you are specter, wraith, phantom, I have invented you, you are my imagining, there is no one here at all, an empty chamber, a vacant valve, abandoned, desolate. Everyone gone. *Pust vi dem kalten shul mein harts* (another first line left without companion-lines, fellows, followers), the cold study-house, spooks dance there. Ladies and Gentlemen, if you find my tongue a riddle, here is another riddle: How is a Jew like a giraffe? A Jew too has no vocal cords. God blighted Jew and giraffe, one in full, one by half. And no salve. Baumzweig hawked up again. Mucus the sheen of the sea. In God's Creation no thing without beauty however perverse. *Khrakeh khrakeh.* Baumzweig's roar the only noise in the hall. "Shah," Paula said, "*ot kumt der shed.*"

Gleaming, gleaming, Ostrover stood — high, far, the stage broad, brilliant, the lectern punctilious with microphone and water pitcher. A rod of powerful light bored into his eye sockets. He had a moth-mouth as thin and dim as a chalk line, a fence of white hair erect over his ears, a cool voice.

"A new story," he announced, and spittle flashed on his lip. "It isn't obscene, so I consider it a failure."

"Devil," Paula whispered, "washed white pig, Yankee Doodle."

"Shah," Baumzweig said, "*lomir heren.*"

Baumzweig wanted to hear the devil, the pig! Why should anyone want to hear him? Edelshtein, a little bit deaf, hung forward. Before him, his nose nearly in it, the hair of a young girl glistened — some of the stage light had become enmeshed in it. Young, young! Everyone young! Everyone for Ostrover young! A modern.

Cautiously, slyly, Edelshtein let out, as on a rope, little bony shiverings of attentiveness. Two rows in front of him he glimpsed the spinster hack, Chaim Vorovsky the drunken lexicographer whom too much mathematics had crazed, six unknown college boys.

Ostrover's story:

Satan appears to a bad poet. "I desire fame," says the poet, "but I cannot attain it, because I come from Zwrdl, and the only language I can write is Zwrdlish. Unfortunately no one is left in the world who can read Zwrdlish. That is my burden. Give me fame, and I will trade you my soul for it."

"Are you quite sure," says Satan, "that you have estimated the dimensions of your trouble entirely correctly?" "What do you mean?" says the poet. "Perhaps," says Satan, "the trouble lies in your talent. Zwrdl or no Zwrdl, it's very weak." "Not so!" says the poet, "and I'll prove it to you. Teach me French, and in no time I'll be famous." "All right," says Satan, "as soon as I say Glup you'll know French perfectly, better than de Gaulle. But I'll be generous with you. French is such an easy language, I'll take only a quarter of your soul for it."

And he said Glup. And in an instant there was the poet scribbling away in fluent French. But still no publisher in France wanted him and he remained obscure. Back came Satan: "So the French was no good, *mon vieux? Tant pis!*" "Feh," says the poet, "what do you expect from a people that kept colonies, they should know what's good in the poetry line? Teach me Italian, after all even the Pope dreams in Italian." "Another quarter of your soul," says Satan, ringing it up in his portable cash register. And Glup! There he was again, the poet, writing *terza rima* with such fluency and melancholy that the Pope would have been moved to holy tears of praise if only he had been able to see it in print — unfortunately every publisher in Italy sent the manuscript back with a plain rejection slip, no letter.

"What? Italian no good either?" exclaims Satan. "*Mamma mia,* why don't you believe me, little brother, it's not the language, it's you." It was the same with Swahili and Armenian, Glup! — failure, Glup! — failure, and by now, having rung up a quarter of it at a time, Satan owned the poet's entire soul, and took him back with him to the Place of Fire. "I suppose you'll burn me up," says the poet bitterly. "No, no," says Satan, "we don't go in for that sort of treatment for so silken a creature as a poet. Well? Did you bring everything? I told you to pack carefully! Not to leave behind a scrap!" "I brought my whole file," says the poet, and sure enough, there it was, strapped to his back, a big black metal cabinet. "Now empty it into the Fire," Satan orders. "My poems! Not all my poems? My whole life's output?" cries the poet in anguish. "That's right, do as I say," and the poet obeys, because, after all, he's in hell and Satan owns him. "Good," says Satan, "now come with me, I'll show you to your room."

A perfect room, perfectly appointed, not too cold, not too hot, just the right distance from the great Fire to be comfortable. A jewel of a desk, with a red leather top, a lovely swivel chair cushioned in scarlet, a scarlet Persian rug on the floor, nearby a red refrigerator stocked with cheese and pudding and pickles, a glass of reddish tea already steaming on a little red table. One window without a curtain. "That's your Inspiring View," says Satan, "look out and see." Nothing outside but the Fire cavorting splendidly, flecked with unearthly colors, turning itself and rolling up into unimaginable new forms. "It's beautiful," marvels the poet. "Exactly," says Satan. "It should inspire you to the composition of many new verses." "Yes, yes! May I begin, your Lordship?" "That's why I brought you here," says Satan. "Now sit down and write, since you can't help it anyhow. There is only one stipulation. The moment you finish a stanza you must throw it out of the window, like this." And to illustrate, he tossed out a fresh page.

Instantly a flaming wind picked it up and set it afire, drawing it into the great central conflagration. "Remember that you are in hell," Satan says sternly, "here you write only for oblivion." The poet begins to weep. "No difference, no difference! It was the same up there! O Zwrdl, I curse you that you nurtured me!" "And still he doesn't see the point!" says Satan, exasperated. "Glup glup glup glup glup glup glup! Now write." The poor poet began to scribble, one poem after another, and lo! suddenly he forgot every word of Zwrdlish he ever knew, faster and faster he wrote, he held on to the pen as if it alone kept his legs from flying off on their own, he wrote in Dutch and in English, in German and in Turkish, in Santali and in Sassak, in Lapp and in Kurdish, in Welsh and in Rhaeto-Romanic, in Niasese and in Nicodarese, in Galcha and in Ibanag, Ho and in Khmer, in Ro and in Volapük, in Jagatai and in Swedish, in Tulu and in Russian, in Irish and in Kalmuck! He wrote in every language but Zwrdlish, and every poem he wrote he had to throw out the window because it was trash anyhow, though he did not realize it. . . .

Edelshtein, spinning off into a furious and alien meditation, was not sure how the story ended. But it was brutal, and Satan was again in the ascendancy: he whipped down aspiration with one of Ostrover's sample aphorisms, dense and swollen as a phallus, but sterile all the same. The terrifying laughter, a sea-wave all around: it broke toward Edelshtein, meaning to lash him to bits. Laughter for Ostrover. Little jokes, little jokes, all they wanted was jokes! "Baumzweig," he said, pressing himself down across Paula's collar (under it her plump breasts), "he does it for spite, you see that?"

But Baumzweig was caught in the laughter. The edges of his mouth were beaten by it. He whirled in it like a bug. "Bastard!" he said.

"Bastard," Edelshtein said reflectively.

"He means you," Baumzweig said.

"Me?"

"An allegory. You see how everything fits. . . ."

"If you write letters, you shouldn't mail them," Paula said reasonably. "It got back to him you're looking for a translator."

"He doesn't need a muse, he needs a butt. Naturally it got back to him," Baumzweig said. "That witch herself told him."

"Why me?" Edelshtein said. "It could be you."

"I'm not a jealous type," Baumzweig protested. "What he has you want." He waved over the audience: just then he looked as insignificant as a little bird.

Paula said, "You both want it."

What they both wanted now began. Homage.

q. Mr. Ostrover, what would you say is the symbolic weight of this story?

a. The symbolic weight is, what you need you deserve. If you don't need to be knocked on the head you'll never deserve it.

q. Sir, I'm writing a paper on you for my English class. Can you tell me please if you believe in hell?

a. Not since I got rich.

q. How about God? Do you believe in God?

a. Exactly the way I believe in pneumonia. If you have pneumonia, you have it. If you don't, you don't.

q. Is it true your wife is a Countess? Some people say she's really only Jewish.

a. In religion she's a transvestite, and in actuality she's a Count.

q. Is there really such a language as Zwrdlish?

a. You're speaking it right now, it's the language of fools.

q. What would happen if you weren't translated into English?

A. The pygmies and the Eskimos would read me instead. Nowadays to be Ostrover is to be a worldwide industry.

Q. Then why don't you write about worldwide things like wars?

A. Because I'm afraid of loud noises.

Q. What do you think of the future of Yiddish?

A. What do you think of the future of the Doberman pinscher?

Q. People say other Yiddishists envy you.

A. No, it's I who envy them. I like a quiet life.

Q. Do you keep the Sabbath?

A. Of course, didn't you notice it's gone? —I keep it hidden.

Q. And the dietary laws? Do you observe them?

A. Because of the moral situation of the world I have to. I was heart-broken to learn that the minute an oyster enters my stomach, he becomes an anti-Semite. A bowl of shrimp once started a pogrom against my intestines.

Jokes, jokes! It looked to go on for another hour. The condition of fame, a Question Period: a man can stand up forever and dribble shallow quips and everyone admires him for it. Edelshtein threw up his seat with a squeal and sneaked up the aisle to the double doors and into the lobby. On a bench, half-asleep, he saw the lexicographer. Usually he avoided him—he was a man with a past, all pasts are boring—but when he saw Vorovsky raise his leathery eyelids he went toward him.

"What's new, Chaim?"

"Nothing. Liver pains. And you?"

"Life pains. I saw you inside."

"I walked out, I hate the young."

"You weren't young, no."

"Not like these. I never laughed. Do you realize, at the age of twelve I had already mastered calculus? I practically reinvented it on my own. You haven't read Wittgenstein, Hersheleh, you haven't read Heisenberg, what do you know about the empire of the universe?"

Edelshtein thought to deflect him: "Was it your translation he read in there?"

"Did it sound like mine?"

"I could tell."

"It was and it wasn't. Mine, improved. If you ask that ugly one, she'll say it's hers, improved. Who's really Ostrover's translator? Tell me, Hersheleh, maybe it's you. Nobody knows. It's as they say —by several hands, and all the hands are in Ostrover's pot, burning up. I would like to make a good strong b.m. on your friend Ostrover."

"*My* friend? He's not my friend."

"So why did you pay genuine money to see him? You can see him for free somewhere else, no?"

"The same applies to yourself."

"Youth, I brought youth."

A conversation with a madman: Vorovsky's *meshugas* was to cause other people to suspect him of normality. Edelshtein let himself slide to the bench — he felt his bones accordion downward. He was in the grip of a mournful fatigue. Sitting eye to eye with Vorovsky he confronted the other's hat — a great Russian-style fur monster. A nimbus of droshky-bells surrounded it, shrouds of snow. Vorovsky had a big head, with big kneaded features, except for the nose, which looked like a doll's, pink and formlessly delicate. The only sign of drunkenness was at the bulbs of the nostrils, where the cartilage was swollen, and at the tip, also swollen. Of actual madness there was, in ordinary discourse, no sign, except a tendency toward elusiveness. But it was known that Vorovsky, after compiling his dictionary, a job of seventeen years, one afternoon suddenly began to laugh, and continued laughing for six months, even in his sleep: in order to rest from laughing he had to be given sedatives, though even these could not entirely suppress his laughter. His wife died, and then his father, and he went on laughing. He lost control of his bladder, and then discovered the curative potency, for laughter, of drink. Drink cured him, but he still peed publicly, without realizing it; and even his cure was tentative and unreliable, because if he happened to hear a joke that he liked he might laugh at it for a minute or two, or, on occasion, three hours. Apparently none of Ostrover's jokes had struck home with him — he was sober and desolate-looking. Nevertheless Edelshtein noticed a large dark patch near his fly. He had wet himself, it was impossible to tell how long ago. There was no odor. Edelshtein moved his buttocks back an inch. "Youth?" he inquired.

"My niece. Twenty-three years old, my sister Ida's girl. She reads Yiddish fluently," he said proudly. "She writes."

"In Yiddish?"

"Yiddish," he spat out. "Don't be crazy, Hersheleh, who writes in Yiddish? Twenty-three years old, she should write in Yiddish? What is she, a refugee, an American girl like that? She's crazy for literature, that's all, she's like the rest in there, to her Ostrover's literature. I brought her, she wanted to be introduced."

"Introduce me," Edelshtein said craftily.

"She wants to be introduced to someone famous, where do you come in?"

"Translated I'd be famous. Listen, Chaim, a talented man like you, so many languages under your belt, why don't you give me a try? A try and a push."

"I'm no good at poetry. You should write stories if you want fame."

"I don't want fame."

"Then what are you talking about?"

"I want—" Edelshtein stopped. What did he want? "To reach," he said.

Vorovsky did not laugh. "I was educated at the University of Berlin. From Vilna to Berlin, that was 1924. Did I reach Berlin? I gave my whole life to collecting a history of the human mind, I mean expressed in mathematics. In mathematics the final and only poetry possible. Did I reach the empire of the universe? Hersheleh, if I could tell you about reaching, I would tell you this: reaching is impossible. Why? Because when you get where you wanted to reach to, that's when you realize that's not what you want to reach to.— Do you know what a bilingual German-English mathematical dictionary is good for?"

Edelshtein covered his knees with his hands. His knuckles glimmered up at him. Row of white skulls.

"Toilet paper," Vorovsky said. "Do you know what poems are good for? The same. And don't call me cynic, what I say isn't cynicism."

"Despair maybe," Edelshtein offered.

"Despair up your ass. I'm a happy man. I know something about laughter." He jumped up—next to the seated Edelshtein he was a giant. Fists gray, thumbnails like bone. The mob was pouring out of the doors of the auditorium. "Something else I'll tell you. Translation is no equation. If you're looking for an equation, better die first. There are no equations, equations don't happen. It's an idea like a two-headed animal, you follow me? The last time I saw an equation it was in a snapshot of myself. I looked in my own eyes, and what did I see there? I saw God in the shape of a murderer. What you should do with your poems is swallow your tongue. There's my niece, behind Ostrover like a tail. Hey Yankel!" he boomed.

The great man did not hear. Hands, arms, heads enclosed him like a fisherman's net. Baumzweig and Paula paddled through eddies, the lobby swirled. Edelshtein saw two little people, elderly, overweight, heavily dressed. He hid himself, he wanted to be lost. Let them go, let them go—

But Paula spotted him. "What happened? We thought you took sick."

"It was too hot in there."

"Come home with us, there's a bed. Instead of your own place alone."

"Thank you no. He signs autographs, look at that."

"Your jealousy will eat you up, Hersheleh."

"I'm not jealous!" Edelshtein shrieked; people turned see. "Where's Baumzweig?"

"Shaking hands with the pig. An editor has to keep up contacts."

"A poet has to keep down vomit."

Paula considered him. Her chin dipped into her skunk ruff. "How can you vomit, Hersheleh? Pure souls have no stomachs, only ectoplasm. Maybe Ostrover's right, you have too much ambition for your size. What if your dear friend Baumzweig didn't publish you? You wouldn't know your own name. My husband doesn't mention this to you, he's a kind man, but I'm not afraid of the truth. Without him you wouldn't exist."

"With him I don't exist," Edelshtein said. "What is existence?"

"I'm not a Question Period," Paula said.

"That's all right," Edelshtein said, "because I'm an Answer Period. The answer is period. Your husband is finished, period. Also I'm finished, period. We're already dead. Whoever uses Yiddish to keep himself alive is already dead. Either you realize this or you don't realize it. I'm one who realizes."

"I tell him all the time he shouldn't bother with you. You come and you hang around."

"Your house is a gallows, mine is a gas chamber, what's the difference?"

"Don't come any more, nobody needs you."

"My philosophy exactly. We are superfluous on the face of the earth."

"You're a scoundrel."

"Your husband's a weasel, and you're the wife of a weasel."

"Pig and devil yourself."

"Mother of puppydogs." (Paula, such a good woman, the end, he would never see her again!)

He blundered away licking his tears, hitting shoulders with his shoulder, blind with the accident of his grief. A yearning all at once shouted itself in his brain:

Edelshtein: Chaim, teach me to be a drunk!
Vorovsky: First you need to be crazy.
Edelshtein: Teach me to go crazy!
Vorovsky: First you need to fail.
Edelshtein: I've failed, I'm schooled in failure, I'm a master of failure!
Vorovsky: Go back and study some more.

One wall was a mirror. In it he saw an old man crying, dragging a striped scarf like a prayer shawl. He stood and looked at himself. He wished he had been born a Gentile. Pieces of old poems littered his nostrils, he smelled the hour of their creation, his wife in bed beside him, asleep after he had rubbed her to compensate her for bitterness. *The sky is cluttered with stars of David. . . . If everything is something else, then I am something else. . . . Am I a thing and not a bird? Does my way fork though I am one? Will God take back history? Who will let me begin again. . . .*

Ostrover: Hersheleh, I admit I insulted you, but who will know? It's only a make-believe story, a game.
Edelshtein: Literature isn't a game! Literature isn't little stories!
Ostrover: So what is it, Torah? You scream out loud like a Jew, Edelshtein. Be quiet, they'll hear you.
Edelshtein: And you, Mr. Elegance, you aren't a Jew?
Ostrover: Not at all, I'm one of *them.* You too are lured, aren't you, Hersheleh? Shakespeare is better than a shadow, Pushkin is better than a pipsqueak, hah?
Edelshtein: If you become a Gentile you don't automatically become a Shakespeare.
Ostrover: Oho! A lot you know. I'll let you in on the facts, Hersheleh, because I feel we're really brothers, I feel you straining toward the core of the world. Now listen — did you ever hear of Velvl Shikkerparev? Never. A Yiddish scribbler writing romances for the Yiddish stage in the East End, I'm speaking of London, England. He finds a translator and overnight he becomes Willie Shakespeare. . . .
Edelshtein: Jokes aside, is this what you advise?

Ostrover: I would advise my own father no less. Give it up, Hershe-
   leh, stop believing in Yiddish.
Edelshtein: But I don't believe in it!
Ostrover: You do. I see you do. It's no use talking to you, you won't
   let go. Tell me, Edelshtein, what language does Moses speak
   in the world-to-come?
Edelshtein: From babyhood I know this. Hebrew on the Sabbath,
   on weekdays Yiddish.
Ostrover: Lost soul, don't make Yiddish into the Sabbath-tongue!
   If you believe in holiness, you're finished. Holiness is for
   make-believe.
Edelshtein: I want to be a Gentile like you!
Ostrover: I'm only a make-believe Gentile. This means that I play
   at being a Jew to satisfy them. In my village when I was a boy
   they used to bring in a dancing bear for the carnival, and
   everyone said, "It's human!" — They said this because they
   knew it was a bear, though it stood on two legs and waltzed.
   But it was a bear.

Baumzweig came to him then. "Paula and her temper. Never
mind, Hersheleh, come and say hello to the big celebrity, what can
you lose?" He went docilely, shook hands with Ostrover, even complimented him on his story. Ostrover was courtly, wiped his lip, let
ooze a drop of ink from a slow pen, and continued autographing
books. Vorovsky lingered humbly at the rim of Ostrover's circle: his
head was fierce, his eyes timid; he was steering a girl by the elbow,
but the girl was mooning over an open flyleaf, where Ostrover had
written his name. Edelshtein, catching a flash of letters, was startled:
it was the Yiddish version she held.
   "Excuse me," he said.
   "My niece," Vorovsky said.
   "I see you read Yiddish," Edelshtein addressed her. "In your
generation a miracle."
   "Hannah, before you stands H. Edelshtein the poet."
   "Edelshtein?"
   "Yes."
   She recited, "*Little fathers, little uncles, you with your beards and glass
and curly hair. . . .*"
   Edelshtein shut his lids and again wept.
   "If it's the same Edelshtein?"
   "The same," he croaked.

"My grandfather used to do that one all the time. It was a book he had. *A Velt ohn Vint.* But it's not possible."

"Not possible?"

"That you're still alive."

"You're right, you're right," Edelshtein said, struck. "We're all ghosts here."

"My grandfather's dead."

"Forgive him."

"*He* used to read you! And he was an old man, he died years ago, and you're still alive — "

"I'm sorry," Edelshtein said. "Maybe I was young then, I began young."

"Why do you say ghosts? Ostrover's no ghost."

"No, no," he agreed. He was afraid to offend. "Listen, I'll say the rest for you. I'll take a minute only, I promise. Listen, if you can remember from your grandfather — "

Around him, behind him, in front of him Ostrover, Vorovsky, Baumzweig, perfumed ladies, students, the young, the young, he clawed at his wet face and declaimed, he stood like a wanton stalk in the heart of an empty field:

> *How you spring out of the ground covered with poverty!*
> *In your long coats, fingers rolling wax, tallow eyes.*
> *How can I speak to you, little fathers?*
> *You who nestled me with lyu, lyu, lyu*
> *lip-lullaby. Jabber of blue-eyed sailors,*
> *how am I fallen into a stranger's womb?*

> *Take me back with you, history has left me out.*
> *You belong to the Angel of Death,*
> *I to you.*
> *Braided wraiths, smoke,*
> *let me fall into your graves,*
> *I have no business being your future.*

He gargled, breathed, coughed, choked, tears invaded some false channel in his throat — meanwhile he swallowed up with the seizure of each bawled word this niece, this Hannah, like the rest, boots, rough full hair, a forehead made on a Jewish last, chink eyes —

> *At the edge of the village a little river.*
> *Herons tip into it pecking at their images*

when the waders pass whistling like Gentiles.
The herons hang, hammocks above the sweet summer-water.
Their skulls are full of secrets, their feathers scented.
The village is so little it fits into my nostril.
The roofs shimmer tar,
the sun licks thick as cow.
No one knows what will come.
How crowded with mushrooms the forest's dark floor.

Into his ear Paula said, "Hersheleh, I apologize, come home with us, please, please, I apologize." Edelshtein gave her a push, he intended to finish. "*Littleness*," he screamed,

I speak to you.
We are such a little huddle.
Our little hovels, our grandfathers' hard hands, how little,
our little, little words
this lullaby
sung at the lip of your grave,

he screamed.

Baumzweig said, "That's one of your old good ones, the best."

"The one on my table, in progress, is the best," Edelshtein screamed, clamor still high over his head; but he felt soft, rested, calm; he knew how patient.

Ostrover said, "That one you shouldn't throw out the window."

Vorovsky began to laugh.

"This is the dead man's poem, now you know it," Edelshtein said, looking all around, pulling at his shawl, pulling and pulling at it: this too made Vorovsky laugh.

"Hannah, better take home your uncle Chaim," Ostrover said: handsome, all white, a public genius, a feather.

Edelshtein discovered he was cheated, he had not examined the girl sufficiently.

He slept in the sons' room—bunk beds piled on each other. The top one was crowded with Paula's storage boxes. He rolled back and forth on the bottom, dreaming, jerking awake, again dreaming. Now and then, with a vomitous taste, he belched up the hot cocoa Paula had given him for reconciliation. Between the Baumzweigs and himself a private violence: lacking him, whom would they patronize? They were moralists, they needed someone to feel guilty over. Another belch. He abandoned his fine but un-innocent dream—young, he was kissing Alexei's cheeks like ripe peaches, he drew away . . . it was not Alexei, it was a girl, Vorovsky's niece. After the kiss she slowly tore the pages of a book until it snowed paper, black bits of alphabet, white bits of empty margin. Paula's snore traveled down the hall to him. He writhed out of bed and groped for a lamp. With it he lit up a decrepit table covered with ancient fragile model airplanes. Some had rubber-band propellers, some were papered over a skeleton of balsa-wood ribs. A game of Monopoly lay under a samite tissue of dust. His hand fell on two old envelopes, one already browning, and without hesitation he pulled the letters out and read them:

> Today was two special holidays in one, Camp Day and Sacco and Vanzetti Day. We had to put on white shirts and white shorts and go to the casino to hear Chaver Rosenbloom talk about Sacco and Vanzetti. They were a couple of Italians who were killed for loving the poor. Chaver Rosenbloom cried, and so did Mickey but I didn't. Mickey keeps forgetting to wipe himself in the toilet but I make him.

> Paula and Ben: thanks so much for the little knitted suit and the clown rattle. The box was a bit smashed in but the rattle came safe anyhow. Stevie will look adorable in his new blue suit when he gets big enough for it. He already seems to like the duck on the collar. It will keep him good and warm too. Josh has been working very hard these days preparing for a course in the American Novel and asks me to tell you he'll write as soon as he can. We all send love, and Stevie sends a kiss for Grandma and Pa. *P.S.* Mickey drove down in a pink Mercedes last week. We all had quite a chat and told him he should settle down!

Heroes, martyrdom, a baby. Hatred for these made his eyelids quiver. Ordinariness. Everything a routine. Whatever man touches becomes banal like man. Animals don't contaminate nature. Only man the corrupter, the anti-divinity. All other species live within the pulse of nature. He despised these ceremonies and rattles and turds and kisses. The pointlessness of their babies. Wipe one generation's ass for the sake of wiping another generation's ass: this was his whole definition of civilization. He pushed back the airplanes, cleared a front patch of table with his elbow, found his pen, wrote:

Dear Niece of Vorovsky:

It is very strange to me to feel I become a Smasher, I who was born to being humane and filled with love for our darling Human Race.

But nausea for his shadowy English, which he pursued in dread, passion, bewilderment, feebleness, overcame him. He started again in his own tongue —

Unknown Hannah:

I am a man writing you in a room of the house of another man. He and I are secret enemies, so under his roof it is difficult to write the truth. Yet I swear to you I will speak these words with my heart's whole honesty. I do not remember either your face or your body. Vaguely your angry voice. To me you are an abstraction. I ask whether the ancients had any physical representation of the Future, a goddess Futura, so to speak. Presumably she would have blank eyes, like Justice. It is an incarnation of the Future to whom this letter is addressed. Writing to the Future one does not expect an answer. The Future is an oracle for whose voice one cannot wait in inaction. One must do to be. Although a Nihilist, not by choice but by conviction, I discover in myself an unwillingness to despise survival. Often I have spat on myself for having survived the deathcamps — survived them drinking tea in New York! — but today when I heard carried on your tongue some old syllables of mine I was again wheedled into tolerance of survival. The sound of a dead language on a live girl's tongue! That baby should follow baby is God's trick on us, but surely we too can have a trick on God? If we fabricate with our syllables an immortality passed from the spines of the old to the shoulders of the young, even God cannot spite it. If the prayer-load that spilled upward from the mass graves should somehow survive! If not the thicket of lamentation itself, then the language on which it rode. Hannah, youth itself is nothing unless it keeps its promise to grow old. Grow old in Yiddish, Hannah, and carry fathers and uncles into the future with you. Do this. You, one in ten thousand maybe, who were born with the gift of Yiddish in your mouth, the alphabet of Yiddish in your palm, don't make ash of these! A little while ago there were twelve million people — not including babies — who lived inside this tongue, and now what is left? A language that never had territory except Jewish mouths, and half the Jewish mouths on earth already stopped up with German worms. The rest jabber Russian, English, Spanish, God knows what. Fifty years ago my mother lived in Russia and spoke only broken Russian, but her Yiddish was like silk. In Israel they give the language of Solomon to machinists. Rejoice — in Solomon's time what else did the mechanics speak? Yet whoever forgets Yiddish courts amnesia of history. Mourn — the forgetting has already happened. A thousand years of our travail forgotten. Here and there a word left for vaudeville jokes. Yiddish, I call on you to choose! Yiddish! Choose death or death. Which is to say death through forgetting or death through translation. Who will redeem you? What act of salvation will restore you? All you can hope for, you tattered, you withered, is translation in America! Hannah, you have a strong mouth, made to carry the future —

But he knew he lied, lied, lied. A truthful intention is not enough. Oratory and declamation. A speech. A lecture. He felt himself an obscenity. What did the dead of Jews have to do with his own troubles? His cry was ego and more ego. His own stew, foul. Whoever mourns the dead mourns himself. He wanted someone to read his poems, no one could read his poems. Filth and exploitation to throw in history. As if a dumb man should blame the ears that cannot hear him. He turned the paper over and wrote in big letters:

EDELSHTEIN GONE,

and went down the corridor with it in pursuit of Paula's snore. Taken without ridicule a pleasant riverside noise. Bird. More cow to the sight: the connubial bed, under his gaze, gnarled and lumped — in it this old male and this old female. He was surprised on such a cold night they slept with only one blanket, gauzy cotton. They lay like a pair of kingdoms in summer. Long ago they had been at war, now they were exhausted into downy truce. Hair all over Baumzweig. Even his leghairs gone white. Nightstands, a pair of them, on either side of the bed, heaped with papers, books, magazines, lampshades sticking up out of all that like figurines on a prow — the bedroom was Baumzweig's second office. Towers of back issues on the floor. On the dresser a typewriter besieged by Paula's toilet water bottles and face powder. Fragrance mixed with urinous hints. Edelshtein went on looking at the sleepers. How reduced they seemed, each breath a little demand for more, more, more, a shudder of jowls; how they heaved a knee, a thumb; the tiny blue veins all over Paula's neck. Her nightgown was stretched away and he saw that her breasts had dropped sidewise and, though still very fat, hung in pitiful creased bags of mole-dappled skin. Baumzweig wore only his underwear: his thighs were full of picked sores.

He put EDELSHTEIN GONE between their heads. Then he took it away — on the other side was his real message: secret enemies. He folded the sheet inside his coat pocket and squeezed into his shoes. Cowardly. Pity for breathing carrion. All pity is self-pity. Goethe on his deathbed: more light!

In the street he felt liberated. A voyager. Snow was still falling, though more lightly than before, a night-colored blue. A veil of snow revolved in front of him, turning him around. He stumbled into a drift, a magnificent bluish pile slanted upward. Wetness pierced his feet like a surge of cold blood. Beneath the immaculate lifted slope he struck stone — the stair of a stoop. He remembered his old home, the hill of snow behind the study-house, the smoky fire, his father swaying nearly into the black fire and chanting, one big duck, the stupid one, sliding on the ice. His mother's neck too was finely veined and secretly, sweetly, luxuriantly odorous. Deeply and gravely he wished he had worn galoshes — no one reminds a widower. His shoes were infernos of cold, his toes dead blocks. Himself the only life in the street, not even a cat. The veil moved against him, turning, and beat on his pupils. Along the curb cars squatted under humps of snow, blue-backed tortoises. Nothing moved in the road. His own house was far, Vorovsky's nearer, but he could not read the street sign. A building with a canopy. Vorovsky's hat. He made himself very small, small as a mouse, and curled himself up in the fur of it. To be very, very little and live in a hat. A little wild creature in a burrow. Inside warm, a mound of seeds nearby, licking himself for cleanliness, all sorts of weather leaping down. His glasses fell from his face and with an odd tiny crack hit the lid of a garbage can. He took off one glove and felt for them in the snow. When he found them he marveled at how the frames burned. Suppose a funeral on a night like this, how would they open the earth? His glasses were slippery as icicles when he put them on again. A crystal spectrum delighted him, but he could not see the passageway, or if there was a canopy. What he wanted from Vorovsky was Hannah.

There was no elevator. Vorovsky lived on the top floor, very high up. From his windows you could look out and see people so tiny they became patterns. It was a different building, not this one. He went down three fake-marble steps and saw a door. It was open: inside was a big black room knobby with baby carriages and tricycles. He smelled wet metal like toothpain: life! Peretz tells how on a bitter night a Jew outside the window envied peasants swigging vodka in a hovel — friends in their prime and warm before the fire. Carriages and tricycles, instruments of Diaspora. Baumzweig with his picked sores was once also a baby. In the Diaspora the birth of a Jew increases nobody's population, the death of a Jew has no meaning. Anonymous. To have died among the martyrs — solidarity at least, a passage into history, one of the marked ones, *kiddush ha-shem.* — A telephone on the wall. He pulled his glasses, all clouded over, and took out a pad with numbers in it and dialed.

"Ostrover?"

"Who is this?"

"*Yankel* Ostrover, the writer, or Pisher Ostrover the plumber?"

"What do you want?"

"To leave evidence," Edelshtein howled.

"Never mind! Make an end! Who's there?"

"The Messiah."

"Who is this? — Mendel, it's you?"

"Never."

"Gorochov?"

"That toenail? Please. Trust me."

"Fall into a hole!"

"This is how a man addresses his Redeemer?"

"It's five o'clock in the morning! What do you want? Bum! Lunatic! Cholera! Black year! Plague! Poisoner! Strangler!"

"You think you'll last longer than your shroud, Ostrover? Your sentences are an abomination, your style is like a pump, a pimp has a sweeter tongue — "

"Angel of Death!"

He dialed Vorovsky but there was no answer.

The snow had turned white as the white of an eye. He wandered toward Hannah's house, though he did not know where she lived, or what her name was, or whether he had ever seen her. On the way he rehearsed what he would say to her. But this was not satisfactory, he could lecture but not speak into a face. He bled to retrieve her face. He was in pursuit of her, she was his destination. Why? What does a man look for, what does he need? What can a man retrieve? Can the future retrieve the past? And if retrieve, how redeem? His shoes streamed. Each step was a pond. The herons in spring, red-legged. Secret eyes they have: the eyes of birds — frightening. Too open. The riddle of openness. His feet poured rivers. Cold, cold.

Little old man in the cold,
come hop up on the stove,

your wife will give you a crust with jam.
Thank you, muse, for this little psalm.

He belched. His stomach was unwell. Indigestion? A heart attack?
He wiggled the fingers of his left hand: though frozen they tingled.
Heart. Maybe only ulcer. Cancer, like Mireleh? In a narrow bed he
missed his wife. How much longer could he expect to live? An un-
marked grave. Who would know he had ever been alive? He had no
descendants, his grandchildren were imaginary. *O my unborn grand-*
son . . . Hackneyed. *Ungrandfathered ghost . . .* Too baroque. Simplicity, purity, truthfulness.

He wrote:

Dear Hannah:
   You made no impression on me. When I wrote you before
at Baumzweig's I lied. I saw you for a second in a public place,
so what? Holding a Yiddish book. A young face on top of a Yiddish book. Nothing else. For me this is worth no somersault. Ostrover's vomit! — that popularizer, vulgarian panderer to people
who have lost the memory of peoplehood. A thousand times a
pimp. Your uncle Chaim said about you: "She writes." A pity on
his judgment. Writes! Writes! Potatoes in a sack! Another one!
What do you write? When will you write? How will you write?
Either you'll become an editor of *Good Housekeeping,* or, if serious, join the gang of so-called Jewish novelists. I've sniffed them
all, I'm intimate with their smell. Satirists they call themselves.
Picking at their crotches. What do they *know,* I mean of *knowl-*
edge? To satirize you have to know something. In a so-called novel
by a so-called Jewish novelist (*"activist-existential"* — listen, I understand, I read everything!) — Elkin, Stanley, to keep to only
one example — the hero visits Williamsburg to contact a so-called
"miracle rabbi." Even the word *rabbi*! No, listen — to me, a descendant of the Vilna Gaon myself, the *guter yid* is a charlatan and
his *chasidim* are victims, never mind if willing or not. But that's
not the point. You have to KNOW SOMETHING! At least the difference between a *rav* and a *rebbeh*! At least a *pinteleh* here and
there! Otherwise where's the joke, where's the satire, where's the
mockery? American-born! An ignoramus mocks only himself.
Jewish novelists! Savages! The allrightnik's children, all they know
is to curse the allrightnik! Their Yiddish! One word here, one
word there. *Shikseh* on one page, *putz* on the other, and that's the
whole vocabulary! And when they give a try at phonetic rendition! Darling God! If they had mothers and fathers, they crawled

out of the swamps. Their grandparents were tree-squirrels if that's how they held their mouths. They know ten words for, excuse me, penis, and when it comes to a word for learning they're impotent!

Joy, joy! He felt himself on the right course at last. Daylight was coming, a yellow elephant rocked silently by in the road. A little light burned eternally on its tusk. He let it slide past, he stood up to the knees in the river at home, whirling with joy. He wrote:

TRUTH!

But this great thick word, Truth!, was too harsh, oaken; with his finger in the snow he crossed it out.

> I was saying: indifference. I'm indifferent to you and your kind. Why should I think you're another species, something better? Because you knew a shred of a thread of a poem of mine? Ha! I was seduced by my own vanity. I have a foolish tendency to make symbols out of glimpses. My poor wife, peace on her, used to ridicule me for this. Riding in the subway once I saw a beautiful child, a boy about twelve. A Puerto Rican, dusky, yet he had cheeks like pomegranates. I once knew, in Kiev, a child who looked like that. I admit to it. A portrait under the skin of my eyes. The love of a man for a boy. Why not confess it? Is it against the nature of man to rejoice in beauty? "This is to be expected with a childless man" — my wife's verdict. That what I wanted was a son. Take this as a complete explanation: if an ordinary person cannot

The end of the sentence flew like a leaf out of his mind . . . it was turning into a quarrel with Mireleh. Who quarrels with the dead? He wrote:

> Esteemed Alexei Yosifovitch:
>   You remain. You remain. An illumination. More than my own home, nearer than my mother's mouth. Nimbus. Your father slapped my father. You were never told. Because I kissed you on the green stairs. The shadow-place on the landing where I once saw the butler scratch his pants. They sent us away shamed. My father and I, into the mud.

Again a lie. Never near the child. Lying is like a vitamin, it has to fortify everything. Only through the doorway, looking, looking. The gleaming face: the face of flame. Or would test him on verb-forms: *kal, nifal, piel, pual, hifil, hofal, hispael.* On the afternoons the Latin tutor came, crouched outside the threshold, Edelshtein heard *ego, mei, mihi, me, me.* May may. Beautiful foreign nasal chant of riches. Latin! Dirty from the lips of idolators. An apostate family. Edelshtein and his father took their coffee and bread, but otherwise lived on boiled eggs: the elder Kirilov one day brought home with him the *mashgiach* from the Jewish poorhouse to testify to the purity of the servants' kitchen, but to Edelshtein's father the whole house was *treyf,* the *mashgiach* himself a hired impostor. Who would oversee the overseer? Among the Kirilovs with their lying name money was the best overseer. Money saw to everything. Though they had their particular talent. Mechanical. Alexei Y. Kirilov, engineer. Bridges, towers. Consultant to Cairo. Builder of the Aswan Dam, assistant to Pharaoh for the latest Pyramid. To set down such a fantasy about such an important Soviet brain . . . poor little Alexei, Avremeleh, I'll jeopardize your position in life, little corpse of Babi Yar.

Only focus. Hersh! Scion of the Vilna Gaon! Prince of rationality! Pay attention!

He wrote:

The gait—the prance, the hobble—of Yiddish is not the same as the gait of English. A big headache for a translator probably. In Yiddish you use more words than in English. Nobody believes it but it's true. Another big problem is form. The moderns take the old forms and fill them up with mockery, love, drama, satire, etc. Plenty of play. But STILL THE SAME OLD FORMS, conventions left over from the last century even. It doesn't matter who denies this, out of pride: it's true. Pour in symbolism, impressionism, be complex, be subtle, be daring, take risks, break your teeth— whatever you do, it still comes out Yiddish. *Mamaloshen* doesn't produce *Wastelands.* No alienation, no nihilism, no dadaism. With all the suffering no smashing! NO INCOHERENCE! Keep the latter in mind, Hannah, if you expect to make progress. Also: please remember that when a goy from Columbus, Ohio, says "Elijah the Prophet" he's not talking about *Eliohu hanovi.* Eliohu is one of us, a *folksmensh,* running around in second-hand clothes. Theirs is God knows what. The same biblical figure, with exactly the same history, once he puts on a name from King James, COMES OUT A DIFFERENT PERSON. Life, history, hope, tragedy, they don't come out even. They talk Bible Lands, with us it's *eretz yisroel*. A misfortune.

Astonished, he struck up against a kiosk. A telephone! On a street corner! He had to drag the door open, pulling a load of snow. Then he squeezed inside. His fingers were sticks. Never mind the pad, he forgot even where the pocket was. In his coat? Jacket? Pants? With one stick he dialed Vorovsky's number: from memory.

"Hello, Chaim?"

"This is Ostrover."

"Ostrover! Why Ostrover? What are you doing there? I want Vorovsky."

"Who's this?"

"Edelshtein."

"I thought so. A persecution, what is this? I could send you to jail for tricks like before — "

"Quick, give me Vorovsky."

"I'll *give* you."

"Vorovsky's not home?"

"How do I know if Vorovsky's home? It's dawn, go ask Vorovsky!"

Edelshtein grew weak: "I called the wrong number."

"Hersheleh, if you want some friendly advice you'll listen to me. I can get you jobs at fancy out-of-town country clubs, Miami Florida included, plenty of speeches your own style, only what they need is rational lecturers not lunatics. If you carry on like tonight you'll lose what you have."

"I don't have anything."

"Accept life, Edelshtein."

"Dead man, I appreciate your guidance."

"Yesterday I heard from Hollywood, they're making a movie from one of my stories. So now tell me again who's dead."

"The puppet the ventriloquist holds in his lap. A piece of log. It's somebody else's language and the dead doll sits there."

"Wit, you want them to make movies in Yiddish now?"

"In Talmud if you save a single life it's as if you saved the world. And if you save a language? Worlds maybe. Galaxies. The whole universe."

"Hersheleh, the God of the Jews made a mistake when he didn't have a son, it would be a good occupation for you."

"Instead I'll be an extra in your movie. If they shoot the *shtetl* on location in Kansas send me expense money. I'll come and be local color for you. I'll put on my *shtreiml* and walk around, the people should see a real Jew. For ten dollars more I'll even speak *mamaloshen*."

Ostrover said, "It doesn't matter what you speak, envy sounds the same in all languages."

Edelshtein said, "Once there was a ghost who thought he was still alive. You know what happened to him? He got up one morning and began to shave and he cut himself. And there was no blood. No blood at all. And he still didn't believe it, so he looked in the mirror to see. And there was no reflection, no sign of himself. He wasn't there. But he still didn't believe it, so he began to scream, but there was no sound, no sound at all — "

There was no sound from the telephone. He let it dangle and rock.

He looked for the pad. Diligently he consulted himself: pants cuffs have a way of catching necessary objects. The number had fallen out of his body. Off his skin. He needed Vorovsky because he needed Hannah. Worthwhile maybe to telephone Baumzweig for Vorovsky's number, Paula could look it up — Baumzweig's number he knew by heart, no mistake. He had singled out his need. Svengali, Pygmalion, Rasputin, Dr. (jokes aside) Frankenstein. What does it require to make a translator? A secondary occupation. Parasitic. But your own creature. Take this girl Hannah and train her. His alone. American-born but she had the advantage over him, English being no worm on her palate; also she could read his words in the original. Niece of a vanquished mind — still, genes are in reality God, and if Vorovsky had a little talent for translation why not the niece? — Or the other. Russia. The one in the Soviet Union who wrote two stanzas in Yiddish. In Yiddish! And only twenty! Born 1948, same year they made up to be the Doctors' Plot, Stalin already very busy killing Jews, Markish, Kvitko, Kushnirov, Hofshtein, Mikhoels, Susskin, Bergelson, Feffer, Gradzenski with the wooden leg. All slaughtered. How did Yiddish survive in the mouth of that girl? Nurtured in secret. Taught by an obsessed grandfather, a crazy uncle: Marranos. The poem reprinted, as they say, in the West. (The West! If a Jew says "the West," he sounds like an imbecile. In a puddle what's West, what's East?) Flowers, blue sky, she yearns for the end of winter: very nice. A zero, and received like a prodigy! An aberration! A miracle! Because composed in the lost tongue. As if some Neapolitan child suddenly begins to prattle in Latin. Not the same. Little verses merely. Death confers awe. Russian: its richness, directness. For "iron" and "weapon" the same word. A *thick* language, a world-language. He visualized himself translated into

Russian, covertly, by the Marranos' daughter. To be circulated, in typescript, underground: to be read, read!

Understand me, Hannah — that our treasure-tongue is derived from strangers means nothing. 90 per cent German roots, 10 per cent Slavic: irrelevant. The Hebrew take for granted without percentages. We are a people who have known how to forge the language of need out of the language of necessity. Our reputation among ourselves as a nation of scholars is mostly empty. In actuality we are a mob of working people, laborers, hewers of wood, believe me. Leivik, our chief poet, was a house painter. Today all pharmacists, lawyers, accountants, haberdashers, but tickle the lawyer and you'll see his grandfather sawed wood for a living. That's how it is with us. Nowadays the Jew is forgetful, everybody with a profession, every Jewish boy a professor — justice seems less urgent. Most don't realize this quiet time is only another Interim. Always, like in a terrible Wagnerian storm, we have our interludes of rest. So now. Once we were slaves, now we are free men, remember the bread of affliction. But listen. Whoever cries Justice! is a liberated slave. Whoever honors Work is a liberated slave. They accuse Yiddish literature of sentimentality in this connection. Very good, true. True, so be it! A dwarf at a sewing machine can afford a little loosening of the heart. I return to Leivik. He could hang wallpaper. I once lived in a room he papered yellow vines. Rutgers Street that was. A good job, no bubbles, no peeling. This from a poet of very morbid tendencies. Mani Leib fixed shoes. Moishe Leib Halpern was a waiter, once in a while a handyman. I could tell you the names of twenty poets of very pure expression who were operators, pressers, cutters. In addition to fixing shoes Mani Leib was also a laundryman. I beg you not to think I'm preaching Socialism. To my mind politics is dung. What I mean is something else: Work is Work, and Thought is Thought. Politics tries to mix these up, Socialism especially. The language of a hard-pressed people works under the laws of purity, dividing the Commanded from the Profane. I remember one of my old teachers. He used to take attendance every day and he gave his occupation to the taxing council as "attendance-taker" — so that he wouldn't be getting paid for teaching Torah. This with five pupils, all living in his house and fed by his wife! Call it splitting a hair if you want, but it's the hair of a head that distinguished between the necessary and the merely needed. People who believe that Yiddish is, as they like

to say, "richly intermixed," and that in Yiddishkeit the presence of the Covenant, of Godliness, inhabits humble things and
humble words, are under a delusion or a deception. The slave
knows exactly when he belongs to God and when to the oppres-
sor. The liberated slave who is not forgetful and can remember
when he himself was an artifact, knows exactly the difference between God and an artifact. A language also knows whom it is
serving at each moment. I am feeling very cold right now. Of
course you see that when I say liberated I mean self-liberated.
Moses not Lincoln, not Franz Josef. Yiddish is the language of
auto-emancipation. Theodor Herzl wrote in German but the
message spread in *mamaloshen*—my God cold. Naturally the important thing is to stick to what you learned as a slave including
language, and not to speak their language, otherwise you will
become like them, acquiring their confusion between God and
artifact and consequently their taste for making slaves, both of
themselves and others.

Slave of rhetoric! This is the trouble when you use God for a Muse.
Philosophers, thinkers—all cursed. Poets have it better: most are
Greeks and pagans, unbelievers except in natural religion, stones,
stars, body. This cube and cell. Ostrover had already sentenced him
to jail, little booth in the vale of snow; black instrument beeped
from a gallows. The white pad—something white—on the floor.
Edelshtein bent for it and struck his jaw. Through the filth of the
glass doors morning rose out of the dark. He saw what he held:

"ALL OF US ARE HUMANS TOGETHER
BUT SOME HUMANS SHOULD DROP DEAD."

DO YOU FEEL THIS?

IF SO CALL TR 5—2530 IF YOU WANT TO
KNOW WHETHER YOU WILL SURVIVE IN
CHRIST'S FIVE-DAY INEXPENSIVE
ELECT-PLAN

"AUDITORY PHRENOLOGY"
PRACTICED FREE FREE

(PLEASE NO ATHEISTS OR CRANK CALLS
WE ARE SINCERE SCIENTIFIC SOUL-SOCIOLOGISTS)

ASK FOR ROSE OR LOU
WE LOVE YOU

He was touched and curious, but withdrawn. The cold lit him unfamiliarly: his body a brilliant hollowness, emptied of organs, cleansed of debris, the inner flanks of him perfect lit glass. A clear chalice. Of small change he had only a nickel and a dime. For the dime he could CALL TR 5–2530 and take advice appropriate to his immaculateness, his transparency. Rose or Lou. He had no satire for their love. How manifold and various the human imagination. The simplicity of an ascent lured him, he was alert to the probability of levitation but disregarded it. The disciples of Reb Moshe of Kobryn also disregarded feats in opposition to nature — they had no awe for their master when he hung in air, but when he slept — the miracle of his lung, his breath, his heartbeat! He lurched from the booth into rushing daylight. The depth of snow sucked off one of his shoes. The serpent too prospers without feet, so he cast off his and weaved on. His arms, particularly his hands, particularly those partners of mind his fingers, he was sorry to lose. He knew his eyes, his tongue, his stinging loins. He was again tempted to ascend. The hillock was profound. He outwitted it by creeping through it, he drilled patiently into the snow. He wanted to stand then, but without legs could not. Indolently he permitted himself to rise. He went only high enough to see the snowy sidewalks, the mounds in gutters and against stoops, the beginning of business time. Lifted light. A doorman fled out of a building wearing earmuffs, pulling a shovel behind him like a little tin cart. Edelshtein drifted no higher than the man's shoulders. He watched the shovel pierce the snow, tunneling down, but there was no bottom, the earth was without foundation.

He came under a black wing. He thought it was the first blindness of Death but it was only a canopy.

The doorman went on digging under the canopy; under the canopy Edelshtein tasted wine and felt himself at a wedding, his own, the canopy covering his steamy gold eyeglasses made blind by Mireleh's veil. Four beings held up the poles: one his wife's cousin the postman, one his own cousin the druggist; two poets. The first poet was a beggar who lived on institutional charity — Baumzweig; the second, Silverman, sold ladies' elastic stockings, the kind for varicose veins. The postman and the druggist were still alive, only one of them retired. The poets were ghosts, Baumzweig picking at himself in bed also a ghost, Silverman long dead, more than twenty years — *lideleh-shreiber* they called him, he wrote for the popular theater: "Song to Steerage": *Steerage, steerage, I remember the crowds, the*

rags we took with us we treated like shrouds, we tossed them away when we
spied out the shore, going re-born through the Golden Door. . . . Even on
Second Avenue 1905 was already stale, but it stopped the show,
made fevers, encores, tears, yells. Golden sidewalks. America the
bride, under her fancy gown nothing. Poor Silverman, in love with
the Statue of Liberty's lifted arm, what did he do in his life besides
raise up a post at an empty wedding, no progeny?

The doorman dug out a piece of statuary, an urn with a stone
wreath.

Under the canopy Edelshtein recognized it. Sand, butts, half-
naked angel astride the wreath. Once Edelshtein saw a condom in
it. Found! Vorovsky's building. There is no God, yet who brought
him here if not the King of the Universe? Not so bad off after all,
even in a snowstorm he could find his way, an expert, he knew one
block from another in this desolation of a world.

He carried his shoe into the elevator like a baby, an orphan, a
redemption. He could kiss even a shoe.

In the corridor laughter, toilets flushing; coffee stabbed him.

He rang the bell.

From behind Vorovsky's door, laughter, laughter!

No one came.

He rang again. No one came. He banged. "Chaim, crazy man,
open up!" No one came. "A dead man from the cold knocks, you
don't come? Hurry up, open, I'm a stick of ice, you want a dead
man at your door? Mercy! Pity! Open up!"

No one came.

He listened to the laughter. It had a form; a method, rather:
some principle, closer to physics than music, of arching up and
sinking back. Inside the shape barks, howls, dogs, wolves, wilderness. After each fright a crevice to fall into. He made an anvil of his
shoe and took the doorknob for an iron hammer and thrust. He
thrust, thrust. The force of an iceberg.

Close to the knob a panel bulged and cracked. Not his fault. On
the other side someone was unused to the lock.

He heard Vorovsky but saw Hannah.

She said: "What?"

"You don't remember me? I'm the one that recited to you tonight my work from several years past, I was passing by in your
uncle's neighborhood — "

"He's sick."

"What, a fit?"

"All night. I've been here the whole night. The whole night —"

"Let me in."

"Please go away. I just told you."

"In. What's the matter with you? I'm sick myself, I'm dead from cold! Hey, Chaim! Lunatic, stop it!"

Vorovsky was on his belly on the floor, stifling his mouth with a pillow as if it were a stone, knocking his head down on it but it was no use, the laughter shook the pillow and came yelping out, not muffled but increased, darkened. He laughed and said "Hannah" and laughed.

Edelshtein took a chair and dragged it near Vorovsky and sat. The room stank, a subway latrine.

"Stop," he said.

Vorovsky laughed.

"All right, merriment, very good, be happy. You're warm, I'm cold. Have mercy, little girl — tea. Hannah. Boil it up hot. Pieces of flesh drop from me." He heard that he was speaking Yiddish, so he began again for her. "I'm sorry. Forgive me. A terrible thing to do. I was lost outside, I was looking, so now I found you, I'm sorry."

"It isn't a good time for a visit, that's all."

"Bring some tea also for your uncle."

"He can't."

"He can maybe, let him try. Someone who laughs like this is ready for a feast — *flanken, tsimmis, rosselfleysh* —" In Yiddish he said, "In the world to come people dance at parties like this, all laughter, joy. The day after the Messiah people laugh like this."

Vorovsky laughed and said "Messiah" and sucked the pillow spitting. His face was a flood: tears ran upside down into his eyes, over his forehead, saliva sprang in puddles around his ears. He was spitting, crying, burbling, he gasped, wept, spat. His eyes were bloodshot, the whites showed like slashes, wounds; he still wore his hat. He laughed, he was still laughing. His pants were wet, the fly open, now and then seeping. He dropped the pillow for tea and ventured a sip, with tongue, like an animal full of hope — vomit rolled up with the third swallow and he laughed between spasms, he was still laughing, stinking, a sewer.

Edelshtein took pleasure in the tea, it touched him to the root, more gripping on his bowel than the coffee that stung the hall. He praised himself with no meanness, no bitterness: prince of rationality! Thawing, he said, "Give him *schnapps*, he can hold *schnapps*, no question."

"He drank and he vomited."

"Chaim, little soul," Edelshtein said, "what started you off? Myself. I was there. I said it, I said graves, I said smoke. I'm the responsible one. Death. Death, I'm the one who said it. Death you laugh at, you're no coward."

"If you want to talk business with my uncle come another time."

"Death is business?"

Now he examined her. Born 1945, in the hour of the death camps. Not selected. Immune. The whole way she held herself looked immune — by this he meant American. Still, an exhausted child, straggled head, remarkable child to stay through the night with the madman. "Where's your mother?" he said. "Why doesn't she come and watch her brother? Why does it fall on you? You should be free, you have your own life."

"You don't know anything about families."

She was acute: no mother, father, wife, child, what he know about families? He was cut off, a survivor. "I know your uncle," he said, but without belief: in the first place Vorovsky had an education. "In his right mind your uncle doesn't want you to suffer."

Vorovsky, laughing, said "Suffer."

"He likes to suffer. He wants to suffer. He admires suffering. All you people want to suffer."

Pins and needles: Edelshtein's fingertips were fevering. He stroked the heat of the cup. He could feel. He said, " 'You people'?"

"You Jews."

"Aha. Chaim, you hear? Your niece Hannah — on the other side already, never mind she's acquainted with *mamaloshen*. In one generation, 'you Jews.' You don't like suffering? Maybe you respect it?"

"It's unnecessary."

"It comes from history, history is also unnecessary?"

"History's a waste."

America the empty bride. Edelshtein said, "You're right about business. I came on business. My whole business is waste."

Vorovsky laughed and said "Hersheleh Frog Frog Frog."

"I think you're making him worse," Hannah said. "Tell me what you want and I'll give him the message."

"He's not deaf."

"He doesn't remember afterward — "

"I have no message."

"Then what do you want from him?"

"Nothing. I want from you."

"Frog Frog Frog Frog Frog."

Edelshtein finished his tea and put the cup on the floor and for the first time absorbed Vorovsky's apartment: until now Vorovsky had kept him out. It was one room, sink and stove behind a plastic curtain, bookshelves leaning over not with books but journals piled flat, a sticky table, a sofa-bed, desk, six kitchen chairs, and along the walls seventy-five cardboard boxes which Edelshtein knew harbored two thousand copies of Vorovsky's dictionary. A pity on Vorovsky, he had a dispute with the publisher, who turned back half the printing to him. Vorovsky had to pay for two thousand German-English mathematical dictionaries, and now he had to sell them himself, but he did not know what to do, how to go about it. It was his fate to swallow what he first excreted. Because of a mishap in business he owned his life, he possessed what he was, a slave, but invisible. A hungry snake has to eat its tail all the way down to the head until it disappears.

Hannah said: "What could I do for you" — flat, not a question.

"Again 'you.' A distinction, a separation. What I'll ask is this: annihilate 'you,' annihilate 'me.' We'll come to an understanding, we'll get together."

She bent for his cup and he saw her boot. He was afraid of a boot. He said mildly, nicely, "Look, your uncle tells me you're one of us. By 'us' he means writer, no?"

"By 'us' you mean Jew."

"And you're not a Jew, *meydeleh*?"

"Not your kind."

"Nowadays there have to be kinds? Good, bad, old, new — "

"Old and new."

"All right! So let it be old and new, fine, a reasonable beginning. Let old work with new. Listen, I need a collaborator. Not exactly a collaborator, it's not even complicated like that. What I need is a translator."

"My uncle the translator is indisposed."

At that moment Edelshtein discovered he hated irony. He yelled, "Not your uncle. You! You!"

Howling, Vorovsky crawled to a tower of cartons and beat on them with his bare heels. There was an alteration in his laughter, something not theatrical but of the theater — he was amused, entertained, clowns paraded between his legs.

"You'll save Yiddish," Edelshtein said, "you'll be like a Messiah to a whole generation, a whole literature, naturally you'll have to work at it, practice, it takes knowledge, it takes a gift, a genius, a born poet — "

Hannah walked in her boots with his dirty teacup. From behind the plastic he heard the faucet. She opened the curtain and came out and said: "You old men."

"Ostrover's pages you kiss!"

"You jealous old men from the ghetto," she said.

"And Ostrover's young, a young prince? Listen! You don't see, you don't follow — translate me, lift me out of the ghetto, it's my life that's hanging on you!"

Her voice was a whip. "Bloodsuckers," she said. "It isn't a translator you're after, it's someone's soul. Too much history's drained your blood, you want someone to take you over, a dybbuk — "

"Dybbuk! Ostrover's language. All right, I need a dybbuk, I'll become a golem, I don't care, it doesn't matter! Breathe in me! Animate me! Without you I'm a clay pot!" Bereaved, he yelled, "Translate me!"

The clowns ran over Vorovsky's charmed belly.

Hannah said: "You think I have to read Ostrover in translation? You think translation has anything to do with what Ostrover is?"

Edelshtein accused her, "Who taught you to read Yiddish? — A girl like that, to know the letters worthy of life and to be ignorant! 'You Jews,' 'you people,' you you you!"

"I learned, my grandfather taught me, I'm not responsible for it, I didn't go looking for it, I was smart, a golden head, same as now. But I have my own life, you said it yourself, I don't have to throw it out. So pay attention, Mr. Vampire: even in Yiddish Ostrover's not in the ghetto. Even in Yiddish he's not like you people."

"He's not in the ghetto? Which ghetto, what ghetto? So where is he? In the sky? In the clouds? With the angels? Where?"

She meditated, she was all intelligence. "In the world," she answered him.

"In the marketplace. A fishwife, a *kochleffel*, everything's his business, you he'll autograph, me he'll get jobs, he listens to everybody."

"Whereas you people listen only to yourselves."

In the room something was absent.

Edelshtein, pushing into his snow-damp shoe, said into the absence, "So? You're not interested?"

"Only in the mainstream. Not in your little puddles."

"Again the ghetto. Your uncle stinks from the ghetto? Graduated, 1924, the University of Berlin, Vorovsky stinks from the ghetto? Myself, four God-given books not one living human being knows, I stink from the ghetto? God, four thousand years since Abraham hanging out with Jews, God also stinks from the ghetto?"

"Rhetoric," Hannah said. "Yiddish literary rhetoric. That's the style."

"Only Ostrover doesn't stink from the ghetto."

"A question of vision."

"Better say visions. He doesn't know real things."

"He knows a reality beyond realism."

"American literary babies! And in your language you don't have a rhetoric?" Edelshtein burst out. "Very good, he's achieved it, Ostrover's the world. A pantheist, a pagan, a goy."

"That's it. You've nailed it. A Freudian, a Jungian, a sensibility. No little love stories. A contemporary. He speaks for everybody."

"Aha. Sounds familiar already. For humanity he speaks? Humanity?"

"Humanity," she said.

"And to speak for Jews isn't to speak for humanity? We're not human? We're not present on the face of the earth? We don't suffer? In Russia they let us live? In Egypt they don't want to murder us?"

"Suffer suffer," she said. "I like devils best. They don't think only about themselves and they don't suffer."

Immediately, looking at Hannah—my God, an old man, he was looking at her little waist, underneath it where the little apple of her womb was hidden away—immediately, all at once, instantaneously, he fell into a chaos, a trance, of truth, of actuality: was it possible? He saw everything in miraculous reversal, blessed—everything plain, distinct, understandable, true. What he understood was this: that the ghetto was the real world, and the outside world only a ghetto. Because in actuality who was shut off? Who then was really buried, removed, inhabited by darkness? To whom, in what little space, did God offer Sinai? Who kept Terach and who followed Abraham? Talmud explains that when the Jews went into Exile, God went into Exile also. Babi Yar is maybe the real world, and Kiev with its German toys, New York with all its terrible intelligence, all fictions, fantasies. Unreality.

An infatuation! He was the same, all his life the same as this poisonous wild girl, he coveted mythologies, specters, animals, voices.

Western Civilization his secret guilt, he was ashamed of the small tremor of his self-love, degraded by being ingrown. Alexei with his skin a furnace of desire, his trucks and trains! He longed to be Alexei. Alexei with his German toys and his Latin! Alexei whose destiny was to grow up into the world-at-large, to slip from the ghetto, to break out into engineering for Western Civilization! Alexei, I abandon you! I'm at home only in a prison, history is my prison, the ravine my house, only listen — suppose it turns out that the destiny of the Jews is vast, open, eternal, and that Western Civilization is meant to dwindle, shrivel, shrink into the ghetto of the world — what of history, then? Kings, Parliaments, like insects, Presidents like vermin, their religion a row of little dolls, their art a cave smudge, their poetry a lust — Avremeleh, when you fell from the ledge over the ravine into your grave, for the first time you fell into reality.

To Hannah he said: "I didn't ask to be born into Yiddish. It came on me."

He meant he was blessed.

"So keep it," she said, "and don't complain."

With the whole ferocity of his delight in it he hit her mouth. The madman again struck up his laugh. Only now was it possible to notice that something had stopped it before. A missing harp. The absence filled with bloody laughter, bits of what looked like red pimento hung in the vomit on Vorovsky's chin, the clowns fled, Vorovsky's hat with its pinnacle of fur dangled on his chest — he was spent, he was beginning to fall into the quake of sleep, he slept, he dozed, roars burst from him, hiccuped, woke, laughed, an enormous grief settled in him, he went on napping and laughing, grief had him in its teeth.

Edelshtein's hand, the cushiony underside of it, blazed from giving the blow. "You," he said, "you have no ideas, what are you?" A shred of learning flaked from him, what the sages said of Job ripped from his tongue like a peeling of the tongue itself, *he never was, he never existed.* "You were never born, you were never created!" he yelled. "Let me tell you, a dead man tells you this, at least I had a life, at least I understood something!"

"Die," she told him. "Die now, all you old men, what are you waiting for? Hanging on my neck, him and now you, the whole bunch of you, parasites, hurry up and die."

His palm burned, it was the first time he had ever slapped a child. He felt like a father. Her mouth lay back naked on her face.

Out of spite, against instinct, she kept her hands from the bruise — he could see the shape of her teeth, turned a little one on the other, imperfect, again vulnerable. From fury her nose streamed. He had put a bulge in her lip.

"Forget Yiddish!" he screamed at her. "Wipe it out of your brain! Extirpate it! Go get a memory operation! You have no right to it, you have no right to an uncle, a grandfather! No one ever came before you, you were never born! A vacuum!"

"You old atheists," she called after him. "You dead old socialists. Boring! You bore me to death. You hate magic, you hate imagination, you talk God and you hate God, you despise, you bore, you envy, you eat people up with your disgusting old age — cannibals, all you care about is your own youth, you're finished, give somebody else a turn!"

This held him. He leaned on the door frame. "A turn at what? I didn't offer you a turn? An opportunity of a lifetime? To be published now, in youth, in babyhood, early in life? Translated I'd be famous, this you don't understand. Hannah, listen," he said, kindly, ingratiatingly, reasoning with her like a father, "you don't have to like my poems, do I ask you to *like* them? I don't ask you to like them, I don't ask you to respect them, I don't ask you to love them. A man my age, do I want a lover or a translator? Am I asking a favor? No. Look," he said, "one thing I forgot to tell you. A business deal. That's all. Business, plain and simple. I'll pay you. You didn't think I wouldn't pay, God forbid?"

Now she covered her mouth. He wondered at his need to weep; he was ashamed.

"Hannah, please, how much? I'll pay, you'll see. Whatever you like. You'll buy anything you want. Dresses, shoes — " *Gottenyu*, what could such a wild beast want? "You'll buy more boots, all kinds of boots, whatever you want, books, everything — " He said relentlessly, "You'll have from me money."

"No," she said, "no."

"Please. What will happen to me? What's wrong? My ideas aren't good enough? Who asks you to believe in my beliefs? I'm an old man, used up, I have nothing to say any more, anything I ever said was all imitation. Walt Whitman I used to like. Also John Donne. Poets, masters. We, what have we got? A Yiddish Keats? Never — " He was ashamed, so he wiped his cheeks with both sleeves. "Business. I'll pay you," he said.

"No."

"Because I laid a hand on you? Forgive me, I apologize. I'm crazier than he is, I should be locked up for it—"

"Not because of that."

"Then why not? *Meydeleh*, why not? What harm would it do you? Help out an old man."

She said desolately, "You don't interest me. I would have to be interested."

"I see. Naturally." He looked at Vorovsky. "Goodbye, Chaim, regards from Aristotle. What distinguishes men from the beasts is the power of ha-ha-ha. So good morning, ladies and gentlemen. Be well. Chaim, live until a hundred and twenty. The main thing is health."

In the street it was full day, and he was warm from the tea. The road glistened, the sidewalks. Paths crisscrossed in unexpected places, sleds clanged, people ran. A drugstore was open and he went in to telephone Baumzweig: he dialed, but on the way he skipped a number, heard an iron noise like a weapon, and had to dial again. "Paula," he practiced, "I'll come back for a while, all right? For breakfast maybe," but instead he changed his mind and decided to CALL TR 5–2530. At the other end of the wire it was either Rose or Lou. Edelshtein told the eunuch's voice, "I believe with you about some should drop dead. Pharaoh, Queen Isabella, Haman, that pogromchik King Louis they call in history Saint, Hitler, Stalin, Nasser—" The voice said, "You're a Jew?" It sounded Southern but somehow not Negro—maybe because schooled, polished: "Accept Jesus as your Saviour and you shall have Jerusalem restored." "We already got it," Edelshtein said. *Meshiachseiten!* "The terrestrial Jerusalem has no significance. Earth is dust. The Kingdom of God is within. Christ released man from Judaic exclusivism." "Who's excluding who?" Edelshtein said. "Christianity is Judaism universalized. Jesus is Moses publicized for ready availability. Our God is the God of Love, your God is the God of Wrath. Look how He abandoned you in Auschwitz." "It wasn't only God who didn't notice." "You people are cowards, you never even tried to defend yourselves. You got a wide streak of yellow, you don't know how to hold a gun." "Tell it to the Egyptians," Edelshtein said. "Everyone you come into contact with turns into your enemy. When you were in Europe every nation despised you. When you moved to take over the Middle East the Arab Nation, spic faces like your own, your very own blood-kin, began to hate you. You are a bone in the throat of all mankind." "Who gnaws at bones? Dogs and rats only."

"Even your food habits are abnormal, against the grain of quotidian delight. You refuse to seethe a lamb in the milk of its mother. You will not eat a fertilized egg because it has a spot of blood on it. When you wash your hands you chant. You pray in a debased jargon, not in the beautiful sacramental English of our Holy Bible." Edelshtein said, "That's right, Jesus spoke the King's English." "Even now, after the good Lord knows how many years in America, you talk with a kike accent. You kike, you yid."

Edelshtein shouted into the telephone, "Amalekite! Titus! Nazi! The whole world is infected by you anti-Semites! On account of you children become corrupted! On account of you I lost everything, my whole life! On account of you I have no translator!"

Ghost Stories

E. M. BRONER

E. M. Broner (1930–): *Esther Masserman Broner was born in Detroit, the daughter of gifted parents; her father was a noted journalist and Jewish historian, and her mother had acted on the Yiddish stage in Poland. She was educated at Wayne State University and Union Graduate School. With her husband, the artist Robert Broner, she has lived in a number of places around the country, mostly in New York City and Detroit. Her books include the plays* Colonel Higginson, The Body Parts of Margaret Fuller, *and* Summer in a Foreign Land *(the last written in verse); novels* Her Mothers *and* A Weave of Women; *and two collections of short fiction,* Journal/Nocturne *and* Seven Stories *and* Ghost Stories. *E. M. Broner has received fellowships from the National Endowment for the Arts and the MacDowell Colony; her short fiction has won an O. Henry Prize. She has taught creative writing and women's literature at Wayne State and has taught and lectured extensively in Israel, particularly at the University of Haifa.*

1. MY MOTHER IN THE MIRROR

Superimposed upon my face in the mirror is my mother's. I am about to comb my hair, but here she is, brushing hers, her thick, wavy, white hair.

We quarrelled about hair.

"Don't wear your hair so short and flat, Mom," I said. "It's too mannish."

"Don't wear yours so wild and woolly," she would reply. "It's too girlish."

In the mirror, our arms go up and down in unison.

"Monkey See/Monkey Do," says Mom.

She pulls the hair forward from under her ears and forms spit curls.

"The return of the Nineteen Thirties," I say.

Actually, her hair looked very nice the last time I saw her.

"What dress is that?" I asked my brother. "I don't recognize it."

"He didn't like the one I brought," said my brother, "and said he had an extra."

"An extra?" I ask.

"Somebody must have brought two to choose from," says my brother.

"Gives her color," I say.

There she is, eyes closed, her glasses resting on her nose.

The glasses will rest there forever.

She's in somebody else's dress, with her hair brushed away from her forehead, high and fluffy.

"It's becoming that way, Mom," I say. "Keep that style."

Now, in the mirror, she brushes, parts her hair on the side, her two hands making a wave.

"I liked it better the other time," I tell her crankily.

I find hair in my comb.

"My hair's falling out," I tell my mother.

"My hair was always strong," she says. "Like my teeth."

"Do you like this length?" I ask her. "I just went to Barney's to have it cut."

"Barney's!" she says. "How can you afford Barney's?"

I flinch. I can never, ever, now or hereafter, tell my mother how much it costs at Barney's.

"I go to the barber in the neighborhood," she says.

We are in her bedroom. I'm cleaning out closet and dresser.

"Where's my face moisturizer?" she asks.

"I took it, Mother," I say.

"What else did you take?"

"The costume jewelry," I say.

"You gave it to me for Mother's Day," she says, "and — so fast — it's gone."

"I took hankies and scarves also," I tell her, looking in the pile I made for myself.

She sees a black plastic garbage bag.

"You threw out my stockings!" she exclaims. "Perfectly good, no-run stockings. And my panties, my bras."

"No one wants used underwear," I tell her.

"Plenty of people, believe me, would have appreciated stockings without runs, underwear laundered and folded," she says.

Could she be right? And about the girdle? Do people wear girdles?

She looks through the mirror at the dresser-top.

"You didn't take my Rose Petal cologne," she says.

"I don't like the scent," I say.

"You're the only one in the land that criticizes roses."

"I like something more subtle."

Suddenly, she reaches out, lifts the cologne, presses the nozzle and sprays me.

"Don't! Don't!" I raise my arms.

"Now," says Mother, "you smell just like me."

My mother is putting on her lipstick, a bright-red. She colors the top lip and presses her lips together. Then she takes a dab from her lips for her cheeks.

I take out my tube and outline my lips.

"I don't like that shade on you," says Mother. "You look like a ghost."

"Mother," I say, "how's this?"

I wrap her pretty scarf around my neck. I fasten her earrings on my lobes. I push her bracelet onto my hand. I take a new pair of her stockings, still in the package, and roll them up my legs.

"Try my powder," she says.

"I don't wear powder," I tell her.

"I can't see you too clear," says my mother. "I've left my glasses."

"I'm going now, Mother," I say and lift my package of her belongings.

"Wait," she says. "It's getting cold. Take that warm coat."

"Whose coat is that?" I ask, about the old-fashioned dark wool with red fur collar, hanging in the garment bag.

"Your aunty's," says Mother. "I hate things to go to waste. When she left, I went right over to the house and took her coat out of the closet. 'I'll wear it for you, my sister,' I said. Give a look in the pockets."

I put my hands into the pockets. Black leather gloves.

"Stay warm," says my mother.

The mirror is clear.

2. MOTHER VISIT

I used to speak long distance, coast-to-coast, to my mother at her retirement village and, later, nursing home. Now we sit side-by-side every Friday night and Saturday morning.

I brush the crimson velvet cushion next to me, to clear it of coats, prayer books, announcements.

"Do you have enough room, Mama?" I ask.

"Plenty," she says.

Sometimes she comments briefly on the service.

"Wonderful singing. On the other hand, the sermon's too long."

People will try to sit in my pew.

"This seat is taken," I always say.

She used to speak at greater length. She's grown terser, less patient.

As we begin preparing for the Mourner's Prayer, she's already pushing me out of my seat.

"Don't be the last to rise!" she says. "It makes a bad impression."

Sometimes I have to repeat a question.

"What will I do with the kid?" I ask. "The kid's in bad shape. Tell me, Mother."

"You can't ask me any more," she says. "You have to handle it by yourself."

"That's mean!" I say.

"That's where I am," says Mother.

In the autumn, I was expecting her favorite nephew, Daniel, good to her, bad to me.

"There's no stability to them," their grandmother said. "Just one, show me the one who's stable."

My job is to defend my offspring.

"The girl is very stable," I say. "She makes friends, loves her brother, designs clothes."

Their grandmother is thinking and frowning.

"Daniel's coming for a visit," I say.

"Tell him hello for me," says Mother.

"I'll kill him," I inform her.

"Don't kill Daniel! " she pleads.

After the visit with Daniel, Mother and I meet at our regular time and place.

"I didn't kill Daniel," I tell her. "I was nice to him."

"That's my good girl," she says.

She's happiest when it's a crowded Sabbath: a *Rosh Hodesh*, a new moon, plus a baby naming, plus the calling of a bridal couple to the altar, ending with a Bar or Bat Mitzvah.

"Today I got my money's worth," says Mama.

Soon it will be winter. She and I will come to the close of our mourning. I will have to relinquish her space to other congregants.

But, if I am her good girl and refrain from killing cousin Daniel, will I hear whispered blessings ruffling my hair, my life?

I continue. "The boy, he just loves children. He teaches in a play-ground, is kind to women and is lovable.."

"Too lovable," their grandmother says. "A girl on each arm."

Apology is a part of motherhood. You apologize for a recent birthday present that went unacknowledged. If you go all the way back, you apologize to other mothers at the sandbox for the hitting with the shovel, the taking of the metal pail with the picture of a duck wearing a polka dot dress. You apologize for inattentiveness in grade school, being held back in Physical Education.

"Tell me something else good about them," says their grand-mother.

"They like each other," I say. "They like the world."

"It's just not good enough," she says. "Someone has to make a living. Someone has to start a life. Someone has to choose which girl is on his arm."

We had never worried about stability.

At the table they tried to make one another laugh with outra-geous puns and the drama of their daily lives.

I acknowledge their secret vices: in-group jokes, encapsulating themselves against the world of would-be friends, having the best vocabulary so everyone else would sound monosyllabic.

Another vice: scaring. The house prepared for Halloween with strange flashing creatures, projecting out onto the lawn, with a sound track they recorded themselves of hideous cackles and chains dragging. Little beggars were scared away.

Exploding fireworks, rockets, a rain of color from chemicals, all dangerous. The neighborhood children wanted to pour into the yard for the display but their parents tried to hold them back from such explosive children.

Despite their costumes at Halloween, I knew them behind their masks.

And, in the taped recording of Death's Castle, I knew each voice distinct. I have always recognized them: their baby voices, their ado-lescent changing ones. I know them sobbing, moaning and clang-ing at holiday time.

"They can't go on this way," their grandmother said.

But they did seem to be able to go on.

"The youngest isn't so young anymore," says the grandmother. "The oldest is even older. They don't go backwards and they don't go forwards."

"They're fine, just fine," I say.

"Go visit them," says the grandmother, "and put your foot down. Tell them, 'Things cannot go on this way.' Tell them, 'There must be stability.'"

I write down her words and visit them.

But they pun, joke, enlarge their vocabulary from a daily word calendar. They use words like *maleficent, malediction, vituperation, indefeasible, plaudit, imputation.* I cannot use their grandmother's old words on them.

Abruptly, in the midst of giving me advice, she dies, not knowing the end of things.

"It's not their fault," I say over her coffin. "I won't apologize."

It is evening. My children are in their rent-controlled apartments, eating produce from the wholesale market. Despite a roof over the head and vegetables on the table and becoming cultured, standing up at book stalls, they are in danger.

The earth has split under them.

I cannot reach them. Power lines are down. In the morning my phone rings. It's my family.

"Is every one safe?"

"We," they sing, "are on a holiday."

"Where? Where?"

"We're safe, Mom. Cool out," says the son.

"I was worried," I tell them.

"*We* were worried!" say her children.

They describe a surrealistic landscape, a city without lights, a walk without people. Neighbors of moon and stars.

"It's faulty here," says her punster son.

"Unstable," his sister continues the joke.

"We hunted each other out," says the boy, "all over the area."

"And there we were, right where we were supposed to be," says his sister.

I pause.

"Just you guys?" I ask.

"No loves," says her son. "I need my arms free to balance myself."

"Anybody have a job?" I ask.

"Mother!" they say.

They have jobs. The kind you have today in the city: half-time, part-time, adjunct-time, night-time.

"We didn't want you to worry," they chorus.

Behind them she hears the wail of fire engines. On the line she feels a trembling.

"What's that rumbling?" she asks.

"My stomach," says the joker.

"It's OK now," the sister says, "and the after-shocks aren't very big at all. We're going to stay together for a while. Nobody's going out to work."

Nobody's going to work?

"You'll need some money," I say.

"We'll pay you as soon as we get paid," says the girl.

"In the blink of an eye," says her son, "the snap of fingers."

"The cluck of the tongue," adds her merry daughter.

I hang up and, in a manner of speaking, dial their grandmother.

"Is this stable or is this stable?" I ask her.

Among the Witnesses

STANLEY ELKIN

Stanley Elkin (1930–1995): *Born in New York, Stanley Elkin moved to Chicago as a young boy and was educated in the public schools there, and at the University of Illinois at Champaign–Urbana. As a literary stylist throughout his long career, Stanley Elkin resembled no one but himself— though it's not surprising to learn that his Ph.D. dissertation at Illinois was on William Faulkner. Elkin was the author of seventeen books, including* novels (Boswell, The Dick Gibson Show, The Franchiser, George Mills, The Magic Kingdom, The Rabbi of Lud, The MacGuffin, *and* Mrs. Ted Bliss) *and collections of novellas (*Searches and Seizures, The Living End, *and* Van Gogh's Room at Arles), *short stories (*Criers and Kibbitzers, Kibbitzers and Criers), *and essays (*Pieces of Soap). *One of the great serious comic writers of our time, Stanley Elkin won two National Book Critics Circle Awards and was a three-time finalist for the National Book Award. For the last thirty-five years of his life, Elkin lived with his wife, painter Joan Elkin, and their children in St. Louis, where he taught creative writing and literature at Washington University.*

The hotel breakfast bell had not awakened him. The hotel social director had. The man had a gift. Wherever he went buzzers buzzed, bells rang, whistles blew. He's a fire drill, Preminger thought.

Preminger focused his eyes on the silver whistle dangling from the neck of the man leaning over him, a gleaming, tooting symbol of authority, suspended from a well-made, did-it-himself, plastic lanyard. "Camp Cuyhoga?" he asked.

"What's that?" the man said.

"Did you go to Camp Cuyhoga? Your lanyard looks like Cuyhoga '41. Purple and green against a field of white plastic."

"Come on, boy, wake up a minute," the man said.

"I'm awake."

"Well," he began, "you probably think it's funny, the social director coming into the room of a guest like this."

"We're all Americans," Preminger muttered.

"But the fact is," he went on, "I wanted to talk to you about something. Now first of all I want you to understand that Bieberman doesn't know I'm here. He didn't put me up to it. As a matter of fact he'd probably fire me if he knew what I was going to say, but, well, Jesus, Richard, this is a family hotel, if you know what I mean." Preminger heard him say "well, Jesus, Richard," like a T-shirted YMCA professional conscious and sparing of his oaths. "That thing yesterday, to be frank, a thing like that could murder a small hotel like this. In a big place, some place like Grossinger's, it wouldn't mean a thing. It would be swallowed up in a minute, am I right? Now you might say this is none of my business, but Bieberman has been good to me and I don't want to see him get hurt. He took me off club dates in Jersey to bring me up here. I mean, I ain't knocking my trade but let's face it, a guy could get old and never get no higher in the show business than the Hudson Theater. He caught me once and liked my material, said if I came up with him maybe I could work up some of the better stuff into a musical, like. He's been true to his word. Free rein. Carte blanche. Absolutely blanche, Richard. Well, you know yourself, you've heard some of the patter songs. It's good stuff, am I telling a lie? You don't expect to hear that kind of stuff in the mountains. Sure, it's dirty, but it's clever, am I right? That crazy Estelle can't sing, she's got no class, we both know that, but the material's there, right? It's there."

People were always recruiting him, he thought. "So?" he asked carefully.

"Well," the social director said, embarrassed, "I'll get out of here and let you get dressed. But I just wanted to say, you know, how I feel about this guy, and warn you that there might be some talk. Mrs. Frankel and that crowd. If you hear anything, squash it, you know? Explain to them." He turned and went toward the door.

Preminger started to ask, "Explain what?" but it was too late. The social director had already gone out. He could hear him in the hall knocking at the room next to his own. He heard a rustling and a moment later someone padding toward the door. He listened to the clumsy rattle of knobs and hinges, the inward sigh of wood as the door swung open, and the introductory murmurs of the social director, hesitant, explanatory, apologetic. Trying to make out the words, he heard the social director's voice shift, take on a loud assurance, and finally settle into the cheap conspiracy that was his lingua franca. "Between us," he would be saying now, winking slyly, perhaps even touching his listener's chest with his finger.

Preminger leaned back against his pillow, forgetting the social director. In a few minutes he heard the long loud ring of the second breakfast bell. It was Bieberman's final warning, and there was in it again the urgency of a fire alarm. He had once told Norma that if the hotel *were* to catch fire and they sounded that alarm, the guests would go by conditioned response into the dining hall. Well, he would not be with them at any rate. Richard Preminger, he thought, hotel hold-out. They moved and played and ate in a ferocious togetherness, eying with suspicion and real fear those who stood back, who apologized and excused themselves. They even went to town to the movies in groups of a dozen. He had seen them stuff themselves into each other's station wagons, and in the theater had looked on as they passed candy bars, bags of peanuts, sticks of gum to each other down the wide row of seats. With Norma he had watched them afterward in the ice cream parlor, like guests of honor at a wedding banquet, at the tables they had made the waiter push together. If they could have worked it out they would have all made love in the same big bed, sighing between climaxes, "Isn't this nice? Everybody, isn't this nice?"

He decided, enjoying the small extravagance, to ignore the bell's warning and forfeit breakfast. He was conscious of a familiar feeling, one he had had for several mornings now, and he was a little afraid of dissipating it. It was a feeling of deep, real pleasure, like waking up and not having to go to the bathroom. At first he had regarded it suspiciously, like some suddenly recurring symptom from an old illness. But then he was able to place it. It was a sensation from childhood; it was the way boys woke, instantly, completely, aware of some new fact in their lives. He was — it reduced to this — excited.

Now he began his morning inventory of himself. It was his way of keeping up with his geography. He first tried to locate the source of his new feeling, but except for the obvious fact that he was no longer in the army and had had returned to him what others would have called his freedom, he didn't really understand it. But he knew that it was not simply a matter of freedom, or at any rate of that kind of freedom. It was certainly not his prospects. He had none. But thinking this, he began to see a possible reason for his contentment. His plans for himself were vague, but he was young and healthy. (At the hotel old men offered, only half jokingly, to trade places with him.) He had only to let something happen to himself, to let something turn up. Uncommitted, he could simply drift until he came upon his fate as a lucky victim of a shipwreck might come upon a vagrant spar. It was like being once again on one of those trips he used to take to strange cities. He had never admired nature. He would bear a mountain range if there was a city on the other side, water if it became a port. In cities he would march out into the older sections, into slums, factory districts, past railroad yards, into bleak neighborhoods where the poor stared forlornly out of windows. He would enter their dingy hallways and study their names on their mailboxes. Once, as he wandered at dusk through a skid row, meeting the eyes of bums who gazed listlessly at him from doorways, he had felt a hand grab his arm. He turned and saw an old man, a bum, who stared at him with dangerous eyes. "Give me money," the man wheezed from a broken throat. He hesitated and saw the man's fist grope slowly, threateningly, toward him. He thought he would be hit but he stood, motionless, waiting to see what the man would do. Inches from his face, the hand opened, turned, became a palm. "Money," the old man said. "God bless you, sir. Help a poor old man. Help me. Help me." He remembered looking into the palm. It was soft, incredibly flabby — the hand, weirdly, of a rich man. The bum began to sob some story of a wasted life, of chances missed, things lost, mistakes made. He listened, spell-bound, looking steadily into the palm, which remained throughout just inches from his body. Finally it shook, reached still closer to him, and at last, closing on itself, dropped helplessly to the old man's side. Preminger was fascinated.

The talking in the other room had momentarily stopped. Then someone summed things up and a pleased voice agreed. A pact had been made. A door opened and the social director walked out, whistling, into the corridor.

In a little while he heard others in the corridor. Those would be the guests going to breakfast. He felt again a joy in his extravagance, and smiled at the idea of trying to be extravagant at Bieberman's (he thought of the shuffleboard court and the crack in the cement that snaked like a wayward S past the barely legible numbers where the paint had faded, of the frayed seams on the tennis nets and the rust on the chains that supported them, of the stucco main building that must always have looked obsolete, out of place in those green, rich mountains). It was a little like trying to be extravagant at Coney

Island. Some places, he knew, commanded high prices for shabbiness; here you expected a discount.

He had seen the expressions on the guests' faces as they descended from the hotel station wagon. They came, traitors to their causes, doubtful, suspicious of their chances, their hearts split by some hope for change, some unlooked-for shift of fortune. Later they joked about it. What could you expect, they asked, from a mountain that had no Bronx, no Brooklyn on top of it? As for himself, he knew why he had come. He had heard the stories — comfortably illicit — of bored, hot mamas, people's eager aunts, office girls in virginity's extremis.

In the army he had known a boy named Phil, an amateur confidence man itching to turn pro, who, like a mystic, looked to the mountains. He remembered a conversation they'd had, sitting in the PX one night during basic training, solacing themselves with near-beer. Phil asked what he was going to do when he got out. He had to tell him he didn't know, and Phil looked doubtful for a moment. He could not understand how something so important had not been prepared for. Preminger asked him the same question, expecting to hear some pathetic little tale about night school, but Phil surprised him, reciting an elaborate plan he had worked out. All he needed was a Cadillac.

"A Cadillac?" he said. "Where would you get the money?"

"Listen to him. What do you think, I was always in the army?"

"What did you do before?"

"What did I do? I was a bellboy. In the mountains. In the mountains a bellboy is good for fifteen, sixteen hundred a season. If he makes book, add another five."

"You made book?"

"Not my own. I was an agent, sort of, for a guy. I was Bellboy five seasons. I was saving for the car, you understand. Well, now I've got enough. I've got enough for a wardrobe too. When you have a white Caddy convertible with black upholstery and gold fittings, you don't drive it in blue jeans. I must have about a thousand bucks just for the wardrobe part. When I get out I pick up my car and go back to the mountains. There must be a hundred hotels up there. All I do is just drive around until I see some girl who looks like she might be good for a couple of bucks. I'll pick her up. I'll make a big thing of it, do you follow me? Well drive around with the top down to all the nice hotels, Grossinger's and the Concord, where all the bellboys know me, and we'll eat a nice lunch, and we make a date for the evening. Then when I pick her up that night we go out to the hotels again — they've got all this free entertainment in the mountains — but the whole time I'm with her I'm hanging back like, quiet, very sad. She's got to ask what's up, right? Well, I'll brush it off, but all the time I'll be getting more miserable, and she'll be all over me with questions about what's wrong, is it something she did, something she said — So finally I'll say, 'Look, dear, I didn't want to ruin your evening, but I see I'll have to tell you. It's the Cadillac. I've got just one payment to make on it and it's ours. Well, I'm broke this month. I lent money to a guy and I dropped a couple hundred on a nag last week. I missed the payment. They called me up today, they're going to repossess if they don't get the payment tomorrow. Hell, I wouldn't care, honey, but I like you and I know what a kick it gives you to ride in it.' Now you know yourself, a girl on vacation, she's got to have a few bucks in the suitcase, am I right? Sooner or later she's got to say, 'Maybe I could lend you some money toward it. How much do you need?' I tell her that it's crazy, she doesn't even know me, and anyway that I'd need about sixty bucks. Well, don't you see, she's so relieved it's not more she knocks herself out to get the dough to me. She's thinking I'm in to her for sixty bucks, we're practically engaged or something. The thing is, to close the deal, I've got to be able to make her. That's my insurance she won't try to find me later on. These girls make a big thing out of their reputation, and I could ruin her. It's easy. That's the whole setup. The next day I go to a new hotel. If I'm lucky it's good for the whole season. And then, in the winter, there's Miami."

Preminger smiled, recalling Phil's passion. It was a hell of an idea, and he would have to keep his eyes open for a white Cadillac convertible. But what was important was that somewhere in the outrageous plan there was sound, conservative thinking, the thinking of a man who knew his geography, who saw his symbols in the true white lights of a Cadillac's headlamps. The plan could work. It was, in its monstrous way, feasible, and he cheered Phil on. And while he had not himself come for the money, of course, he hoped to shake down a little glory from the skies. He wanted, in short, to get laid in Jewish, to get laid and laid, to abandon himself. Abandon was a new thing in his life, however, and he was not as yet very good at it. All he could be sure of was that he approved of it.

Well, anyway, he thought, playing his pleasant morning game, I'm in a new place, and there's Norma, at least.

Thinking of Norma, he felt some misgivings. It was too easy to make fun of her desperation. She was, after all, something like the last of her race — vacationing secretary, overripe vestal, the only girl in the whole damned family who had not walked down some flower-strewn aisle in The Bronx, amidst a glory going at four dollars a plate, toward the ultimate luck, a canopy of flowers, to plight what she might call her troth. Beauty is troth and troth beauty, that is all ye know on earth and all ye need to know. And Norma, he thought, on the edge of age, having tried all the other ways, having gone alone to the dances in the gymnasium of the Hebrew school, having read and mastered the *Journal of the American Medical Association* for April so that she might hold intelligent conversation with the nephew of her mother's friend, a perspiring intern at Bellevue, and having ceased to shave her underarms because of the pain, had abandoned herself to Bieberman's and to him.

He stretched in bed. Under the sheet he moved his toes and watched the lumps, like suddenly shifting mountain ranges, change shape. The sun lay in strips across his chest. He got out of the sun-warmed bed, and slices of light from the Venetian blinds climbed up and across his body.

He began to dress but saw that his ground-level window was open. He moved up to it cautiously and started to pull the string on the Venetian blinds to slant the sunlight downward. Seeing some of the guests standing in a large group beside the empty swimming pool, he paused. He remembered the cryptic warnings of the social director and shivered lightly, recalling against his will the confused and angry scene which yesterday had sickened them all. Was that the new excitement he had awakened with, he wondered.

He had even known the child slightly; she and her mother had sat at the table next to his in the dining hall. He had once commented to Norma that she was a pretty little girl. Her death and her mother's screams (the cupped hands rocking back and forth in front of her, incongruously like a gambler's shaking dice) had frightened him. He had come up from the tennis court with his racket in his hand. In front of him were the sun-blistered backs of the guests. He pushed through, using his racket to make a place for himself. He stood at the inner edge of the circle, but seeing the girl's blue face ringed by the wet yellow hair sticking to it, he backed off, thrusting his racket before his face, defending his eyes. The people pushing behind him would not let him through and helplessly he had to turn back, forced to watch as Mrs. Goldstone, the girl's mother, asked each of them why it had happened, and then begged, and then accused, and then turned silently back to the girl to bend over her again and slap her. He heard her insanely calm voice scolding the dead girl: "Wake up. Wake up. Wake up." He watched the mother, squatting on her heels over the girl, obscene as someone defecating in the woods. She struggled hopelessly with the firemen who came to remove the girl, and after they had borne her off, her body jouncing grotesquely on the stretcher, he saw the mother try to hug the wet traces of the child's body on the cement. When the others put out their hands and arms to comfort her, crowding about her, determined to make her recognize their sympathy, he looked away.

Now he stood back from the window. Several of the people from yesterday were there again. My God, he thought, they're acting it out.

He recognized Mrs. Frankel among them. She was wearing her city clothes and looked hot and uncomfortable standing beside Bieberman's empty pool. She seemed to be arguing ferociously, in her excitement unconscious of the big purse that followed weirdly the angry arcs of her arms. The sun caught the faces of some stones on her heavy bracelet and threw glints of light into Preminger's eyes as she pointed in the direction of the pool. He did not know what she was saying, but he could imagine it easily enough. He had heard her bullying before. She was like a spokesman for some political party forever in opposition.

In a moment he noticed something else. Beyond the excited crowd gathered about Mrs. Frankel, he saw Bieberman, who stood, hanging back, his head cocked to one side, his expression one of troubled concentration. He looked like a defendant forced to listen in a foreign court to witnesses whose language he can not understand. Beside him was the social director, scowling like an impatient advocate.

He turned and began again to dress.

When he approached the main building the others had finished their breakfasts and were already in the positions that would carry them through until lunch. On the long shaded porch in front of Bieberman's main building people sat in heavy wicker rockers playing cards. They talked low in wet thick voices. Occasionally the quiet murmur was broken by someone's strident bidding. Preminger could feel already the syrupy thickness of the long summer day. He climbed the steps and was about to go inside to get some coffee when he saw Mrs. Frankel. She was talking to a woman who listened gravely. He tried to slip by without having to speak to her, but she had already seen him. She looked into his eyes and would not turn away. He nodded. She allowed her head to sway forward once slowly as though she and Preminger were conspirators in some grand mystery. "Good morning, Mrs. Frankel," he said.

She greeted him solemnly. "It won't be long now, will it, Mr. Preminger?"

"What won't?"

She waved her hand about her, taking in all of Bieberman's in a vague gesture of accusation. "Didn't they tell you I was leaving?" she asked slowly.

He was amazed at the woman's egotism. "Vacation over, Mrs. Frankel?" he asked, smiling.

"Some vacation," she said. "Do you think I'd stay with that murderer another day? I should say not! Listen, I could say plenty. You don't have to be a Philadelphia lawyer to see what's happening. Some vacation. Who needs it? Don't you think when my son heard, he didn't say, 'Mama, I'll be up to get you whenever you want?' The man's a fine lawyer, he could make plenty of trouble if he wanted."

For a moment as the woman spoke he felt the shadow of a familiar panic. He recognized the gestures, the voice that would take him into the conspiracy, that insisted he was never out of it. Mrs. Frankel could go to hell, he thought. He'd better not say that; it would be a gesture of his own. He would not go through life using his hands.

Mrs. Frankel still spoke in the same outraged tones Preminger did not quite trust. "The nerve," she said. "Well, believe me, he shouldn't be allowed to get away with it."

Bieberman suddenly appeared at the window behind Mrs. Frankel's chair. His huge head seemed to fill the whole window. His face was angry but when he spoke his voice was soft. "Please, Mrs. Frankel. Please," he said placatingly. Preminger continued toward the dining room.

Inside, the bus boys were still clearing the tables. He went up to one of the boys and asked for some coffee and sat down at one of the cleared tables. The boy nodded politely and went through the large brown swinging doors into the kitchen. He pushed the doors back forcefully and Preminger saw for a moment the interior of the bright kitchen. He looked hard at the old woman, Bieberman's cook, sitting on a high stool, a cigarette in her mouth, shelling peas. The doors came quickly together, but in a second their momentum had swung them outward again and he caught another glimpse of her. She had turned her head to watch the bus boy. Quickly the doors came together again, like stiff theatrical curtains.

He turned and saw Norma across the dining hall. She was holding a cigarette and drinking coffee, watching him. He went over to her. "Good morning," he said, sitting down. "A lot of excitement around here this morning."

"Hello," she said.

He leaned across to kiss her. She moved her head and he was able only to graze her cheek. In the instant of his fumbling movement he saw himself half out of his chair, leaning over the cluttered table, like a clumsy, bad-postured diver on a diving board. He sat back abruptly, surprised. He shrugged. He broke open a roll and pulled the dough from its center. "Mrs. Frankel's leaving," he said after a while.

"Yes," she said. "I know."

"The Catskillian Minute Man," he said, smiling.

"What's so funny about Mrs. Frankel?"

Preminger looked at her. "Nothing," he said. "You're right. One of these days, after this Linda Goldstone affair had blown over, she would have gotten around to us."

"She couldn't say anything about us."

"No," he said. "I guess not."

"'Goldstone affair,'" she said. "The little girl is dead."

"Yes," he said.

"Affair," she said. "Some affair."

He looked at her carefully. Her face was without expression. What did she want from him — a *statement?*

"All right," he said. "Okay. The Goldstone affair — excuse me, the Goldstone tragedy — was just the Goldstone drowning. Norma, it was an accident. Everyone around here carries on as though it has implications. Even you. I suppose the thing I feel worst about — well, the parents, of course — is Bieberman. He's the only one who still has anything to lose. It could hurt him in the pocketbook and to a man like him that must be a mortal wound."

Norma looked as if he had slapped her. It was a dodge, her shock; it was a dodge, he thought. Always, fragility makes its demands on bystanders. The dago peddler whose apples have been spilled, the rolled drunk, the beat-up queer, the new widow shrieking at an open window — their helplessness strident, their despair a prop. What did they want? They were like children rushing to their toys, the trucks, the tin armies, manipulating them, making sounds of battle in their throats, percussing danger and emergency.

He was in his bathing trunks. On his feet were the "low-quarters" he had been discharged in. He had not had time, so anxious was he to get away, to buy other shoes, not even the sneakers appropriate for afternoon climbs like this one on the high hill behind Bieberman's.

He had lost interest in the hike. He turned his back on the sandy, rock-strewn path that continued on up the hill and into the woods he had promised himself to explore, and he looked down to see where he had come from. Below him was the resort. He had never seen the place from this vantage point, and its arrangement in the flat green valley struck him as comic. It looked rather like a giant fun house in an amusement park. He had the impression that if he were to return to his room he would find, bracketed in heavy yellow frames, mirrors that gave back distorted images. In the trick rooms, constructed to defy gravity, he would have to hang onto the furniture to keep from falling. He looked at the fantastic spires that swirled like scoops of custard in cups too small for them, and he pictured Bieberman climbing at sunset to the top of these minarets to bellow like a clownish muezzin to the wayward guests. He saw the beach umbrellas, bright as lollipops, on the hotel lawn. They were like flowers grown grossly out of proportion in a garden.

He grinned, shifting his gaze from the hotel grounds and letting it fall on his own body. It rested there a moment without any recognition and then, gradually conscious of himself, he stared, embarrassed, at his thighs, which exposure to the sun had failed to tan deeply. He traced his legs down past bony kneecaps and hairless shins and mocked in silence their abrupt disappearance into the formal shoes. Why, he was like someone come upon in the toilet. The fat thighs, the shiny pallor of the too-smooth legs, like the glaucous sheen on fruit, betrayed him. He seemed to himself clumsy and a little helpless, like old, fat women in camp chairs on the beach, their feet swollen in the men's shoes they have to leave untied, the loose strings like the fingers they lace protectively across their busts.

Just what was he really doing at Bieberman's, he wondered. He could write off his disappointment as an experience of travelers who, having left the airport in their hired cars, and spoken to clerks about reservations, and made arrangements for the delivery of bags, at last find themselves alone in strange cities, bored, depressed, sleepless in their rented beds, searching aimlessly for familiar names in the telephone directory. But what, finally, was he doing there at all? He thought of the other people who had come to the hotel and had to remind himself that they did not live there always, had not been hired by the hotel as a kind of folksy background, a monumental shill for his benefit. They were there, he supposed, for the access it gave them to the tennis court, the pool, the six-hole golf course, the floor show "nitely," the card tables, the dining room, each other. And he, fat-thighed lover, abandon bent, was there to lay them. Fat chance, Fat Thigh, he thought.

He wondered whether to start up the path once more, and turned to estimate the distance he had yet to travel. He looked again below him. He saw the drained pool. A little water, like a stain on the smooth white tile, still remained at the bottom. Some reflected light flashed against his eyes and he turned, instinctively shielding them with one cupped palm.

"I didn't think you'd see me," someone said.

Preminger stepped back. He hadn't seen anyone, but assumed that the boy who was now coming from within the trees that bordered the path had mistaken his gesture as a wave and had responded to it.

"If you're trying to hide," Preminger said, "you shouldn't wear white duck trousers. Law of the jungle." The bare-chested boy, whom he recognized as the lifeguard, came cautiously onto the path where Preminger stood. Preminger thought he seemed rather shamefaced, and looked into the green recess from which the boy had come, to see if perhaps one of the girls from the hotel was there.

"I wasn't hiding," the boy said defensively. "I come up here often when I'm not on duty. I've seen you down there."

"I've seen you too. You're the lifeguard." The boy looked down. They were standing in a circle of sunlight that seemed, in the woodsy arena, to ring them like contenders for a title of little note. He noticed uncomfortably that the boy was looking at his shoes. Preminger shuffled self-consciously. The boy looked up and Preminger saw that his eyes were red.

"Have they been talking about me?" the boy asked.

"Has who been talking about you?"

The boy nodded in the direction of the hotel.

"No," he said. "Why?" He asked without meaning to.

"Mr. Bieberman said I shouldn't hang around today. I didn't know anywhere to come until I remembered this place. I was going all the way to the top when I heard you. I thought Mr. Bieberman might have sent you up to look for me."

Preminger shook his head.

The boy seemed disappointed. "Look," he said suddenly, "I want to come down. I'm not used to this. How long do they expect me to stay up here?" For all the petulance, there was real urgency in his voice. He added this to the boy's abjectness, to his guilt at being found, and to the terror he could not keep to himself. It wasn't fair to let the boy continue to reveal himself in the mistaken belief that everything had already been found out about him. He didn't want to hear more, but already the boy was talking again. "I'm not used to this," he said. "I told Mr. Bieberman at the beginning of the summer about my age. He knew I was sixteen. That's why I only get two hundred. It was okay then."

"Two hundred?"

The boy stopped talking and looked him over carefully. He might have been evaluating their relative strengths. As though he had discovered Preminger's weakness and was determined to seize upon it for his own advantage, he looked down at Preminger's knees. Preminger felt his gaze keenly.

"Does anyone else know?" Preminger asked abruptly.

"Mrs. Frankel, I think," he said, still not looking up.

Preminger shifted his position, moving slightly to one side. "She'll be going home today," he said. "I saw her this morning. She didn't say anything." He did not enjoy the cryptic turn in the conversation. It reminded him vaguely of the comical communication between gangsters in not very good films. A man leans against a building. Someone walks past. The man nods to a loitering confederate. The confederate lowers his eyes and moves on.

He made up his mind to continue the walk. "Look," he said to the boy, "I'm going to go on up the path." Having said this, he immediately began to move down toward Bieberman's. He realized his mistake but felt the boy staring at him. He wondered if he should make some feint with his body, perhaps appear to have come down a few steps to get a better look at some nonexistent activity below them and then turn to continue back up the path. The hell with it, he thought wearily. He could hear the boy following him.

Some pebbles that the boy dislodged struck Preminger's ankles. He watched them roll down the hill. The boy caught up with him.

"I'm going down too," he said, as though Preminger had made a decision for both of them. The path narrowed and Preminger took advantage of the fact to move ahead of the boy. He moved down quickly, concentrating on the steep angle of the descent. Just behind him the boy continued to chatter. "He needed someone for the season. It was the Fourth of July and he didn't have anyone. I got a cousin who works in the kitchen. He told me. Mr. Bieberman knew about my age. I told him myself. He said, 'What's age got to do with it? Nobody drowns.' I had to practice the holds in my room." The path widened and the boy came abreast of him. He timed his pace to match Preminger's and they came to the bottom of the hill together.

He began to jog ahead of the boy but, soon tiring, he stopped and resumed walking. Though the boy had not run after him, Preminger knew he was not far behind and that he was still following him. He went deliberately toward one of the tables on Bieberman's lawn, thinking that when he reached it he would turn to the boy and ask him to bring him a drink. He did not notice until too late that it was Mrs. Frankel's table he was heading for. The wide, high-domed beach umbrella that stood over it had hidden her from him. He saw that the only way to take himself out of her range was to veer sharply, but remembering the boy behind him and the mistake he had made on the hill, he decided that he could not risk another dopey movement. What if the kid turned with him, he thought. They would wind up alone together on the golf course. He would never get away from him. He considered between Frankel and the kid and chose Frankel because she didn't need advice.

Mrs. Frankel, in her hot, thick city clothing, looked to him like a woman whose picture has just been taken for the Sunday supplements. ("Mrs. Frankel, seated here beneath a two-hundred-pound mushroom she raised herself, has announced . . .") But when he came closer he saw that she would not do for the supplements at all. Her legs, thrown out in front of her, gave her the appearance of an incredibly weary shopper whose trip downtown has failed. Her expression was disconsolate and brooding. It was an unusual attitude for Mrs. Frankel and he stood beside her for a moment. She stared straight ahead toward the useless pool.

"It's funny," she said, turning to him. "A little girl." He had never heard her talk so softly. "Did you see her? Like she was just some piece of cardboard that had been painted like a child. It's too

terrible," she said. "To happen here? In the mountains? Just playing like that? All right, so a child is sick, it's awful, but a little child
gets sick and sometimes there's nothing you can do and the child
dies." He was not sure she was talking to him. "But here, in the
mountains where you come for fun, for it to happen here? It's awful—terrible. A thing like that." She looked directly at Preminger
but he could not be certain that she saw him. "Did you see the
mother? Did you see the fright in the woman's eyes? Like, 'No, it
couldn't be.' I was there. The child wanted an ice cream and the
mother told her that her lips were blue, she should come out. She
looked around for a second, for a *second*, and when she turned
around again . . ." Mrs. Frankel shrugged. "How long could she
have been under—five seconds, *ten*? Is the pool an ocean, they
had to search for her? No, it's more important the lifeguard should
be talking to his girl friends so when he hears the screaming he
should look up and holler 'What? What? Where? Where?' Who's
to blame?" she asked him. "God? We're not savages. Let's fix the
blame a little close to home."

He shifted under her direct stare. She had recovered her sten-
torian coloratura and for this he was grateful. She was running true
to form again and her elegy or whatever it had been was only a kind
of interlude, as though the woman caught her breath not by ceasing
to talk but by lowering her voice. However, her question still hung
in the air. He didn't want to answer it but that didn't seem to make
any difference to these people. At least, then, he could give his testimony on the side he believed in.

"All right, Mrs. Frankel," he said. "What is it? All morning you've
been hinting at some dark secret. Is it that the lifeguard wasn't old
enough?" His voice sounded louder than he had intended. He
heard it as though he were listening to a recording he could not
remember having made. "Is that what's bothering you? Is that the
little secret you're determined to let everyone in on? Well, relax, it's
no secret. Everybody knows about it. It's too bad, but even if the kid
had been eighteen instead of sixteen the little girl would still have
drowned."

"The lifeguard was only sixteen?" the woman asked. It was impossible that she didn't know. She must have guessed, must have
suspected it. That had to be the reason for her outrage.

"The lifeguard was only sixteen?" she repeated. It was too much;
he couldn't be the one she learned it from. "Only *sixteen*?" she
insisted.

"I don't know how old he is," he said, reneging. "That's not the point. It was an accident. What difference does it make how old he is?" Only now was he conscious that the boy had not left them. He was standing about twenty feet away, listening. Preminger remembered seeing Bieberman stand in the same attitude just that morning, his head bowed low under the weight of his embarrassment, buffered from his enemies by the social director. He was waiting for Preminger to go on with the defense.

Blithely, however, he changed the subject. For no apparent reason he began to tell Mrs. Frankel of the walk he had just taken, of his vague plans for the future. She listened politely and even nodded in agreement once or twice to things he said. He remained with her in this way for about ten minutes, but when he started to leave he caught for a moment Mrs. Frankel's angry stare. "It's better we should all get out," she said.

He lay beside Norma beyond the closed-in tennis court. He watched the moon's chalk-silver disintegrate and drift icily to the lawn. They had not spoken for a quarter of an hour. He did not know whether she was asleep. The ground was damp. He could feel, beneath the blanket, the evening's distillation like a kind of skin. He raised himself on one elbow and looked at Norma's face. Her eyes were closed and he lay back down again and watched the sky.

The lawn was deserted; the exodus of late that afternoon had ended; the last cars from the city had gone back. He thought of Bieberman, alone beside the pool, and could still see the old man's awful face as he waved at the departing guests, pretending it was only the natural end of their vacation that took them back.

He pulled a blade of grass from beside the blanket.

"The slob," he said.

Norma stirred, made a small sound.

Preminger only half heard her. "He stood in the driveway and waved at them. He shook their hands and said he'd save their rooms. He even told the bellboy where to put everything." He tore the grass in half and threw one piece away. "The slob. I was ashamed for him."

He rolled the grass between his fingers. Feeling its sticky juice, he threw it away in disgust. "Even the social director. Did you hear him? 'I'm sorry, Bieberman, but I've got to have people. I've got to have people, right?' And Bieberman told him, 'You're a fine actor.

You give a professional performance.' It made me sick. And Mrs. Frankel didn't say a word. She didn't have to. He gave himself away."

"The poor thing," Norma said. Her voice was low and cool, not sleepy at all. He turned to her and smiled.

"*Bieberman?*"

"I meant the little girl," she said. Her voice was flat. He studied her pale face and the skin, which looked cooler and softer than he remembered ever having seen it. She seemed smaller somehow, and, in a way he did not mind, older. It's the moon, he thought.

He touched her cheek with his fingers. "You would have gone with them, wouldn't you?" he asked softly. "You would have gone with them if I hadn't asked you to stay." She didn't answer. She turned her head and his hand dropped to the blanket. "You've done that twice today," he said.

"Have I?"

He looked at her body. She lay straight back, her arms at her sides. He rolled toward her quickly and his arm fell across her breast. She tried to move away from him, but he grabbed her arms and pinned them to her sides and kissed her on the mouth. In a few minutes, he thought, my vacation begins. A nice abandoned Jewish girl in a nice abandoned Jewish hotel. She shook her head ferociously. His face fell on top of hers and he forced it with his weight toward the blanket. He felt her body stiffen, her arms go rigid. Then her arms shook in a rage against him and he was help-less to hold them at her sides. She was very strong, and with a sud-den convulsive movement she threw him off. She sprang up quickly and stood looking down at him. She seemed unsure of herself.

"Get away from me," he said.

"Richard . . ."

"Get away from me."

"Richard, I didn't want to go back."

"Get away."

"All right," she said quietly. She turned and started away.

"There she goes," he called after her. "Don't touch her, she's in mourning." His anger rose in him. "Hey, come back, I've got an idea. We'll have a lynching. We'll string the kid up to the diving board and hang Bieberman from a beach umbrella."

She was moving from him quickly, back to the hotel. He got up and ran after her. He put out his hand to stop her but she eluded him and he saw himself stumble forward, his empty hand reaching toward her. He recovered his balance and walked along a little behind her, talking to her. He felt like a peddler haggling, but he couldn't help himself. "The drowning loused things up, didn't it? It killed a stranger, but nobody around here knows from strangers." She broke into a run. From the way she ran he could tell she was crying. He ran after her, hearing her sobbing. "Let's blame someone. The lifeguard. Bieberman. *Me.* You want to know what to blame? Blame cramps and lousy Australian crawl." As he approached the hotel Preminger halted. Norma walked into the hotel and Preminger slumped on the steps. He clapped his palms together nervously in ragged applause. That kid, that lousy kid, he thought. He thought of his tantrum as of a disease which recurs despite its cure.

When the world had quieted again he knew that he was not alone. He realized that he had been aware of someone on the porch when he turned from Norma and let her go inside. He looked around and saw in the shadows about twenty feet away the silhouette of a man propped against the side of the porch. In the dark he could not make out his face.

"Bieberman?"

The man came toward him from the dark recesses of the porch. He walked slowly, perhaps uncertainly, and when he passed in front of the hotel entrance he was caught in the light slanting down from the interior like a gangplank secured to the building.

"Ah, Preminger." The voice was deep and mocking.

"Mr. Bieberman," he said softly.

The man stayed within the light. Preminger rose and joined him there nervously. "It's about time for bed," he said. "I was just going up."

"Sure," Bieberman said. "So this will be your last night with us, hah, Preminger?"

Preminger looked at him, feeling himself, as they stood together within the close quarters of the light, somehow under attack. "I hadn't planned for it to be."

"*Planned?*" The old man laughed. "The girl will be going in the morning. What will there be to keep you? The food?" He laughed again. "You'll leave tomorrow. But I thank you for staying the extra day. It will make me a rich man, and I can go myself to a hotel." He noticed the bottle in Bieberman's hand. The old man followed his glance and looked up, smiling broadly. "Schnapps," he said, holding up the bottle. "A little schnapps. I've been sitting here on my porch and I'm on a deck chair on the *Queen Mary*, which in honor of my first voyage over is keeping a kosher kitchen. The only thing wrong is that once in a while someone falls overboard and it upsets me. If we weren't three days out, I would call my wife she should swim up from the city and we would go back."

Preminger smiled and Bieberman offered him the bottle. He took it and, unconsciously wiping off the neck, began to drink.

"I guess I will be going," he said.

"I guess you will."

"I shouldn't be here," Preminger said. "It was supposed to be a lark. I didn't come slumming, don't think that. But it didn't work out. I guess I just wanted to fool around."

"Yeah," Bieberman said. "I know you guys. You've got a suitcase filled with contraceptives. Fooey."

"I just wanted to fool around," Preminger repeated.

"Nobody fools. Never," Bieberman said.

"You said it," Preminger said.

Bieberman went back into the dark wing of the porch. Preminger followed him. "I don't want you to think I'm leaving for the same reason as the others. *I* don't blame you." The old man didn't answer. "I really don't," he said.

Preminger almost lost him in the shadows. "A boy who likes to fool around doesn't blame me," the old man said.

Preminger paused. "Well," he said lamely, "good night." He went toward the door.

"Preminger, tell me, you're an educated person," Bieberman said suddenly. "Do you really think they could sue me?"

He turned back to Bieberman. "I don't see how," he said.

"But the lifeguard — the boy. If I knew he was a boy? If I knew he was sixteen? If they could prove that, couldn't they sue?"

"How could they find that out?" Preminger said uncomfortably.

"Well, I wouldn't tell them. I wouldn't run an ad in the *Times*, but if they knew it, could they sue me?"

"I suppose they could try, I don't know. I'm no lawyer. I don't see how they could find you responsible."

"My guests did."

"They'll forget."

"Ah," the old man said.

"Next year your place will be full again."

"Yes, I suppose so," he said sadly.

"Wait a minute, it *wasn't* your fault."

"It made them sick." Bieberman said so softly Preminger thought he was talking to himself. "All they could do was get away. Some of the women couldn't even look at me. Sure, that's why the Catskills and Miami Beach and Las Vegas and all those places are so important. That's why a man named Bieberman can have his name written across a hotel, and on towels." Preminger couldn't follow him. "I mean, what the hell," he said, suddenly talking to Preminger again. "Does Spinoza get his name written on towels?"

"Why don't you come inside?" Preminger said, offering him his arm.

"When a little girl drowns in such a place where nobody must drown, where you pay good money just to keep everybody on top of the water, it's a terrible thing. I understand that. You're not safe anywhere," Bieberman said. "Not anywhere. You go to a football game and all of a sudden the man on the loudspeaker calls for a doctor it's an emergency. Not during a holiday, you think. You think so? You think not during a holiday? You think so? In a forest even, by yourself, one day you notice how the deer are diseased or how the rivers are dried up — something."

"Come on inside, Mr. Bieberman," he said.

"Preminger, listen to me. Do me a favor, yeah? Tomorrow when you get back to the city, maybe you could call up those people and tell them what the lifeguard told you. You're the only one who knew about it."

The old man lighted a cigarette. He could see the glowing tip pulsating softly as Bieberman spoke. He tried to see his face but it was too dark.

"You're crazy," Preminger said finally.

"I'm responsible," he said sadly. "I just don't have the nerve."

"Well, I'm not responsible," Preminger said.

"You are, Preminger."

Preminger got up quickly. He walked across the darkened wing of the porch and came abruptly into the slanting yellow light. Bieberman called him and he turned around. "Preminger," he said. "I mean it, tell them you heard me brag once how I saved a couple hundred bucks." Preminger shook his head and started carefully down the steps, afraid he would stumble in the dark. "Preminger, I mean it," Bieberman called.

He took the rest of the steps quickly, forgetting the danger. He discovered, surprised, he was going toward the empty pool. So many times now, after he had already made them, he had discovered the pointlessness of his gestures, his un-willed movements. Ah,

I *am* abandoned, he thought, surrendering. He turned around. A light was on in Norma's room. He could still hear Bieberman calling his name. He stood among the beach umbrellas on the wide dark lawn and listened to the old man's desperate voice. "Preminger, Preminger." It was as if he were hiding and the old man had been sent out to look for him. "Preminger, I mean it."

All right, he thought, all right, damn it, all right. He would wait until the morning and then he would go to Norma's room and apologize and they would go back to the city together and he might investigate some jobs and they might continue to see each other and, after a while, perhaps, he might ask her to marry him.

When You're Excused, You're Excused

BRUCE JAY FRIEDMAN

Bruce Jay Friedman (1930–): *Bruce Jay Friedman was born and raised in the Bronx and educated in the public schools there and at the University of Missouri, where he received a degree in journalism. For some years he supported himself and his family as an editor of men's magazines, working on his fiction on the side. His first novel,* Stern, *gained widespread critical and popular approval and established his reputation as a writer of mordantly funny fiction. (The term "black humor," often used to describe Friedman's work, is a label he coined himself.) Other novels followed:* A Mother's Kisses, The Dick, About Harry Towns, Tokyo Woes, The Current Climate, *and* A Father's Kisses. *But Friedman is more than a novelist: his short stories, collected in* Far from the City of Class, Black Angels, *and* Let's Hear It for a Beautiful Guy, *have found a wide audience, and his plays,* Scuba Duba *and* Steambath, *have been produced on Broadway. He is also the author of* The Lonely Guy's Book of Life *and has written several screenplays as well. Currently he lives on Long Island with his wife.*

Having a gallstone removed at the age of thirty-seven almost frightened Mr. Kessler to death, and after he was healed up, he vowed he would get into the best shape of his life. He joined a local sports club called Vic Tanny's, and for six months took workouts every other night of the week, missing only three sessions for Asian flu. When one of his workouts came due on the eve of Yom Kippur, holiest day of the Jewish year, Mr. Kessler, who usually observed important religious holidays, said to his wife, "I've come to need these workouts and my body craves them like drugs. It's medicine and when I miss one I get edgy and feel awful. It doesn't make any difference that this is the most important holiday of all. I've got to go tonight. It's part of the religion that if you're sick you're excused from synagogue. It's in one of the psalms."

Mrs. Kessler was a woman of deep religious conviction but slender formal training. Her husband, as a result, was able to bully her around with references to obscure religious documents. Once he mentioned the psalms, rebuttal was out of the question, and she could only say, "All right, as long as it's in there."

Mr. Kessler did a great deal of aimless walking through the house for the rest of the day. His four-year-old son asked him, "Are any pirates good?" and Mr. Kessler said, "I don't feel like talking pirates." When the dark came and it was time for the gym, Mr. Kessler said to his wife, "All right, it isn't in the psalms, but it's in the religion somewhere, and it doesn't make any difference that it's such an important holiday. If you're excused, you're excused. That goes for Columbus Day and Washington's Birthday and if the Japs attack Pearl Harbor again, you're excused on that day, too. In fact, as a matter of principle, you're *especially* excused on Yom Kippur."

Mr. Kessler got his gym bundle together and his wife walked him to the driveway. "It seems dark and religious out here," she said.

"Nonsense," said Mr. Kessler.

He opened the door of his car and then said, "All right, I admit I'm not confident. I started to imagine there was a squadron of old rabbis prowling the streets taking down the names of Jews who were going off to gyms. When the railroad whistle sounded, I thought it was a ram's horn, and the wind tonight is like the wail of a thousand dying ghetto holdouts. But I've got to go there even if I just take a quick workout and skip my steambath. It's too bad it's Yom Kippur and I admit that's throwing me a little, but if you're excused, you're excused. On Yom Kippur or *double* Yom Kippur."

Mr. Kessler got behind the wheel and his young son hollered down from an open window, "Can a giant find you if you hide?"

"No giants when important things are going on," said Mr. Kessler, swinging out of the driveway and driving into the night.

Fifteen minutes later, he parked his car outside the gym and swept inside. He walked past the blonde receptionist who called out, "Where's your wife?" and Mr. Kessler said, "She only came that once, and you know damned well her hips are past help. Why do you have to ask me that every time I come in here?"

He undressed in the locker room and gave his street clothing to Rico, the tiny attendant, who blew his nose and said, "I've got a cold, but I'm glad. It's good to have one. Guys come in here to lose colds and I'm glad to have one all year round. When you have a cold, you're always taking care of yourself and that's good."

Mr. Kessler said, "I never said anything to you before because I know you're supposed to be a charming old character, but you're an idiot. It's not good to have a cold. It's better not to have a cold. Any time. I just want to take a fast workout and go home and be in the house. I don't want to kid around."

Upstairs, in the workout room, a man with a thin body was lying on the floor in an awkward position, lifting a barbell in an unnatural movement. "Do you want to know this one?" the man asked. "It's the best exercise in the gym, getting a muscle no one else bothers with. It's right in the center of the arm and you can't see it. Its function is to push out all the other muscles. You don't have very much of a build while you're getting it started, but once she's going, all the other muscles shoot out and you look like an ape."

"I don't have time for any new exercises tonight," said Mr. Kessler. "I just want to get in and get out. Besides, I don't like the kind of body you have."

Mr. Kessler did a few warm-up exercises and then picked up a pair of light dumbbells to work his biceps. A handsome and heavily perspired young man with large shoulders came over and said, "Whew, it certainly is rough work. But when I was sixteen, I only weighed 110 and I said to myself, 'I'm going to look like something.' So each night, after working in Dad's filling station, I began to lift stuff in the family garage, getting to the point where I really had a nice build and then, in later years, joining up here. I vowed I would never again look like nothing."

"What makes you think that's such an exciting story?" said Mr. Kessler. "I've heard it a thousand times. I think *you* told it to me once and I don't want to hear it again as long as I live."

"What's eating you?" asked the handsome man.

"I just want to get in and get out and not hear any dull stories," said Mr. Kessler. He went over to a rowing machine, but a sparse-haired man who was doing vigorous waist-twisting Alpine calisthenics blocked his way. "Why don't you do those at home?" said Mr. Kessler. "You're in my way. I've seen you in here and you never use any of the equipment. You only do calisthenics and you're crazy to come here to do them. What are you, showing off?"

"I just like to do them here," said the man and let Mr. Kessler get at the rowing machine. Looking up at the clock, Mr. Kessler did half a dozen rows and then leaped up and caught the high bar, swinging back and forth a few times. A police sergeant who took clandestine workouts during duty hours came by and said, "Your lats are really coming out beautifully."

"Oh, really?" said Mr. Kessler. "Can you see the delts from back there?"

"Beauties," said the sergeant. "Both beauties."

"Thank you for saying that," said Mr. Kessler, swinging easily on the bar. "I can really feel them coming out now. I don't know why, but you saying they're coming out beautifully made me feel good for the first time tonight. I was rushing through my workout because we have this big holiday tonight and I felt guilty, but now I'm going to stay up here awhile. Six months ago I was sick with a bad gallstone and told everyone that if you're sick your only obligation is to yourself. Ahead of kids, your wife and the synagogue. Now I feel good up here and I'm not rushing. This is where I should be. I don't care if it's Yom Kippur or if the mayor's been killed by a bird turd."

"I don't say I follow all your arguments," said the sergeant, "but your lats are really coming up. I'll tell that to any man here in the gym, straight to his face."

"Thank you for feeling that way," said Mr. Kessler, dropping from the bar now and taking his place on a bench for some leg-raises. Sharing the bench with him was a tiny, dark-haired man with powerful forearms.

"It pays to work your forearms," said the little man. "You get them pumped up real good and even the big bastards will run."

"I'm one of the big bastards," said Mr. Kessler. "You can't tell because I'm sitting down."

"I couldn't see that," said the little man.

"It's all right," said Mr. Kessler. "It's just that maybe you ought to tell that story to a little bastard."

"I'm not telling it to anyone," said the little man.

Mr. Kessler did his legs and then went over to the board for some sit-ups. A man with a large head came over and said, "You look awfully familiar. From a long time ago."

"Public school," said Mr. Kessler, rising to shake hands with the man. "Your name is Block and your father was an attorney."

"Accountant," said the man. "But you're right about Block."

"You lived in the rooming house and there was something else about you. How come you're not in synagogue tonight?"

"I don't observe," said the man. "We never did. This is my first workout here."

"I do observe, but I was sick and I figure I'm excused. A long time ago I remember an old man in the temple didn't have to fast because his stomach was out of whack. That was orthodox and I figure if he was excused, I'm certainly excused. I was feeling bad for a while but not any more. If you're sick it doesn't matter if it's Yom Kippur or even if they make up a day holier than Yom Kippur. If you're excused, you're excused. What the hell *was* it about you?"

"I'd like to take off a little around the waist and pack some on the shoulders."

"I know," said Mr. Kessler. "*Blockhead*. They used to call you *Blockhead*. That's it, isn't it?"

"I don't like it now any more than I did then," said the man with the big head.

"Yes, but I just wanted to get it straight," said Mr. Kessler. "A thing like that can nag you."

Mr. Kessler did ten sets of sit-ups, and when he had worked up a good sweat, he went downstairs and showered. The massage room was empty and Mr. Kessler said to the attendant, "I want a massage. It doesn't matter that I've never had one before and that I associate it with luxury and extravagance. I want one. When I came in here I was going to get right out, but there's a principle involved. We have this big holiday, very big, but you're either excused from it or you're not. And I am. I was pretty sick."

"If I had the towel concession, I'd have it made," said the masseur, oiling up Mr. Kessler's body. "You can't make it on rubs alone. You've got to have rubs and rags."

"It's crazy that they're all sitting out there bent over in prayer and I'm in here, but when you're proving a point, sometimes things look ridiculous.

"If you have any influence at all," said the masseur, "try to get me towels. I can't make it on rubs alone."

Music poured into the gym now, and Mr. Kessler hummed along to several early Jerome Kern tunes. His massage at an end, he got up from the table, showered, and then, as he dressed, told Rico, the locker room attendant, "I'm all tingling. I knew this was the right thing to do. Next year I'll be in the temple all bent over like they are, but I did the right thing tonight."

"All you need is a cold," said Rico.

"You know how I feel about that remark," said Mr. Kessler.

Upstairs, Mr. Kessler smiled at the blonde receptionist who grabbed him and began to lead him in a cha-cha across the front office. "I don't do this with girls," said Mr. Kessler, falling into step, "and I'm going right home. You have a ponytail and it's making me crazy."

"Where's your wife?" asked the girl, going off into a complicated cha-cha break that flustered Mr. Kessler.

"You ask me that all the time," said Mr. Kessler, picking up the beat again and doing primitive arm motions. "Look, it doesn't matter about her hips. Don't you understand a man can be in love with a woman with any size hips? Where's my wife, you ask? What do we need her for?"

"Do you want to go dancing?" asked the girl.

"I told you I don't do things with girls," said Mr. Kessler. "I shouldn't even be carrying on here in the lobby. What's your name?"

"Irish," said the girl.

"Irish?" said Mr. Kessler. "Do you have to be named the most gentile name there is? They're all out there wailing and beating their breasts for atonement and I'm with an Irish. But I've got to ask myself if it would be better if you were an Inge. I'm not doing anything wrong and even if I am it doesn't make any difference that I'm doing it tonight. I'm either excused or I'm not excused. I'm finished early and I'll go for about twenty minutes."

The girl put on a sweater and walked ahead of Mr. Kessler to his car. He started the motor and she said, "I don't want to dance just yet. I'd rather that you park somewhere and make love to me."

"I can't stand it when the girl says a thing like that," said Mr. Kessler. "That drives me out of my mind. Look, it was all right in there in the gym, but I'm feeling a little funny out here in the night air. As though I'm wandering around somewhere in the god-damned Sinai. But that's just the kind of thing I've got to fight. I don't think there'll be anyone behind the Chinese restaurant now. All we're going to do is fool around a little, though."

The lights in the Chinese restaurant's parking field were dark when they got there and Mr. Kessler stopped the car and put his head into the receptionist's blonde hair and bit her ear. "You smell young. About that ear bite, though. I just feel that as long as I'm being so honest about Yom Kippur I can't do anything dishonest at all. The ear bite isn't mine. That is, it's just something I do. A long time ago, before my wife got big-hipped, we took a Caribbean cruise and she danced on deck with a Puerto Rican public relations man named Rodriguez. She acted funny after that and finally told me it was because he'd aroused her. I got it out of her that it was because he'd bitten her ear. I can't use an ear bite on her, of course, but I've been anxious to try one out and that's why I worked it in."

"Really make love to me," the receptionist whispered, putting herself against Mr. Kessler.

"There'll only be some light fooling around," said Mr. Kessler. "Do you know what the hell night this is? Uh oh. The voice you have heard was that of the world's worst hypocrite. Am I proving anything if I just do some elaborate kissing about the neck and shoulders? A man is either excused or he's not excused. Oh, Jesus, you're wearing boyish-type underwear. You would be wearing something along those lines. That did it," he said, and fell upon her.

After a while, she said, "Now that you've had me, I want us to dance slowly knowing that you've had me."

"You're suggesting crazy things," said Mr. Kessler. "I'm calling my wife before I do any more of them."

They drove to a filling station and Mr. Kessler dialed his number and said, "I thought I'd get in and get out, but the car's broken. It's in the differential."

"You know I don't know what that is," said Mrs. Kessler. "It's like telling me something is in the psalms."

"The garage has to run out and get some parts," he said.

"Do you feel funny about what you did?" asked Mrs. Kessler.

"I didn't do anything," he said. "Everybody forgets how sick I was. When you're sick, the religion understands."

Mr. Kessler hung up and the receptionist showed him the way to a dancing place. It was a cellar called Tiger Sam's, catering to Negroes and whites and specializing in barbecued ham hocks. They danced awhile and the receptionist said she was hungry. "I am, too," said Mr. Kessler. "It's going to be tough getting down that first bite because I know the fast isn't over until sundown tomorrow night, but it's about time I stopped thinking that way. I forget how sick I was."

The receptionist said she wanted the ham hocks, and Mr. Kessler said, "I confess I've had the urge to try them, but they're probably the most unkosher things in the world. I'm starting in again. Wouldn't I be the most spineless man in America if I ordered eggs and told them to hold the hocks? I'll have the hocks."

When he had finished eating, Mr. Kessler began drinking double shots of bourbon until he slid off his stool and fell into the sawdust.

"I've gone past that point where I should have stopped. I only hope I don't get sentimental and run off into a synagogue. It's here where my heart starts breaking for every Jew who ever walked with a stoop and cried into a prayer book. That's just the kind of thing I've got to watch, though. It would be the best medicine in the world for me if an old Jewish refugee woman just happened to stumble in here by accident. Just so I could fail to hug and kiss her and apologize to her for all the world's crimes. And that would be that and I'd have proven that number one I was sick and number two when you're sick you're excused and number three when you're excused you're really excused."

A young Negro with a dancer's grace in his body came over, bowed to Mr. Kessler in the sawdust and said, "I'm Ben and should like to try the merengue with your lovely blonde companion. With your permission."

Mr. Kessler said it was all right and stayed in the sawdust while the two danced closely and primitively to a Haitian rhythm. Two Negro musicians sat on stools above Mr. Kessler. One handed another double bourbon down to him and said, "Like happy Yom Kippur, babe."

"I can't get to my feet," said Mr. Kessler. "You think that's funny and sort of like a jazz musician's joke, but it so happens I am Jewish. I ought to belt you one, but the point is even jokes shouldn't bother me if I'm excused from the holiday. If I got upset and belted you, it would show I really haven't excused myself."

One of the musicians dangled a toilet bowl deodorizer in front of Mr. Kessler's nose while the other howled.

"I don't know where this fits into anything," said Mr. Kessler, "but I'm not going to get upset or start feeling sentimental."

The Negro named Ben came back now with his arm around the receptionist's waist and said, "I wonder if you two would join me at my apartment. I'm having a do there and am sure you'll love Benny's decor."

The two musicians carried Mr. Kessler out to a Sunbeam convertible and put him on the floor of the rear seat, slipping in above him. The receptionist got in alongside Ben, who drove to Harlem. The two musicians kept the deodorizer in Mr. Kessler's face. "I suppose you've got a reason for that," he said from the floor, as they howled in the night air and kept pushing it against his nose.

When the car stopped, Mr. Kessler said, "I can walk now," and stumbled along behind the four as they mounted the steps of a brownstone. Ben knocked on the door, two light raps and a hard one, and a powerful pale-skinned man in leotards opened the door quickly to a huge single room, divided by a purple curtain. It was done in the style of a cave and there were bits of African sculpture on shelves, along with campaign pictures of New York's Governor Harriman. A film flashed on one wall, demonstrating Martha Graham ballet techniques, and some forty or fifty Negro-white couples in leotards stood watching it in the haze of the room, some assuming ballet poses along with the dancers. Ben got leotards for the new arrivals and led them behind the purple curtain so they could change. There, a man in a silk dressing gown sat reading *Popular Mechanics* on a divan shaped like a giant English muffin. Ben introduced him to Mr. Kessler and the receptionist as "Tor," his roommate, a noted anthropologist. "Why do I have to get into leotards?" asked Mr. Kessler as the receptionist and the Negro musicians began to slip into theirs and the anthropologist looked on. "I'll bet my new Vic Tanny's body won't look bad in them, though." After he had changed, there was a scuffle outside the curtain. The film had stopped suddenly, fixing Martha Graham on the screen with one leg on the practice bar. Several couples were screaming. A police officer was on the floor, and Ben said to Mr. Kessler, "Get his legs. He came up here and got stuck and we've got to get him out."

"I've never committed a crime," said Mr. Kessler, smoothing his leotards and taking the policeman's legs. Something wine-colored and wet was on the officer's breast pocket. "What do you mean he got stuck? I don't want to be carrying him if he got stuck."

They stumbled down the stairs with him and then walked several blocks in the blackness, finally propping the officer's body against an ash can.

"I don't know about leaving him against an ash can," said Mr. Kessler. "This is one thing I'm sorry I had to do tonight. Not because it's tonight especially, but because I wouldn't want to do it any night. But if I had to do it at all, I suppose I'm glad it was tonight. Why should I worry about doing this on Yom Kippur? I can see worrying about it in general, but not because it's tonight. Not if I'm supposed to be excused."

They went back to the party. The film was off now and couples were dancing wildly in the murk to a three-man combo, each of whom was beating a bongo. They were hollering out a song in which the only lyrics were, "We're a bongo combo," repeated many times. One of the Negro musicians put a slim cigarette in Mr. Kessler's mouth and lit it. "Hey, wait a minute," said Mr. Kessler. "I know what kind of cigarette this is. I may have always had a yen to just try a puff of one, but that's one thing I'm absolutely not doing tonight. Not because it's tonight. I'd resist even more if it were just an ordinary night. In fact, the reason I haven't spit it out already is I want to show I'm not afraid of Yom Kippur. It's working already." Mr. Kessler sat down peacefully in the middle of perfumed, dancing, frenzied feet. "My senses are sharpened. I read that's what's supposed to happen." He saw the curtain part momentarily. Holding the anthropologist's purple dressing gown toreador style, the blonde receptionist, nude now, stood atop the English muffin. The noted Swede charged forward, making bull-like passes at her, one finger against each ear. A Negro girl with full lips leaned down and caught Mr. Kessler's head to her pistol-like bosoms, holding him there, senses sharpened, for what seemed like a season, and then Ben came whirling by in a series of *West Side Story* leaps, chucking him flirtatiously under the chin and then kissing him wetly in the ear. Mr. Kessler got to his knees and screamed, "J'ACCUSE. That isn't what I mean. What I mean is I'M EXCUSED, I'M EXCUSED," but no one heard him and he fell unconscious.

When he awakened, Ben and the two Negro musicians were helping him behind the wheel of his own car. Ben tapped the blonde receptionist on the behind and she slid in beside Mr. Kessler.

"We enjoyed your company terribly much," said Ben, and the two musicians howled. "Hope you enjoyed the decor and the Ivy League entertainment."

"What time is it?" Mr. Kessler asked the girl when the Negroes had driven off.

"Almost morning," said the receptionist.

"Well, at least they're out," said Mr. Kessler.

"Who's out of where?" she asked.

"The Jews are out of synagogue," said Mr. Kessler.

"I want you to meet my brothers," she said. "Maybe we can have a few beers before the sun comes up."

"The holiday is still on, but the important part is over," said Mr. Kessler. "Then tonight it's all over."

The receptionist showed Mr. Kessler the way to her white frame house. "I was divorced two years ago," she said. "Now I live with my two brothers. They're a hell of a lot of fun and I was lucky to have them."

The night was breaking when they got to the house. The receptionist introduced Mr. Kessler to the two brothers, both of whom were tall and freckled. The older brother served cans of beer for all, and when they had finished the beers, began to open a crate of grapefruits. "Our sales manager sent these back from the South," he said. "Aren't they honeys?" He picked up one of the grapefruits and rolled it to his younger brother, who fielded it like a baseball and threw it back. "You grabbed that one like Tommy Henrich," said the older brother, rolling it back. The younger brother picked it up, made a little skipping motion and flung it back again. "Hey, just like Johnny Logan," said the older one. He rolled it once again and when he got it back, said, "That was Marty Marion."

"Or 'Phumblin' Phil' Weintraub," said Mr. Kessler.

The brothers stopped a second and then the older brother rolled the grapefruit again. "George Stirnweiss," he hollered when his brother pegged it to him. He rolled it. He got it back. "Just like Bobby Richardson," he said.

"Or 'Phumblin' Phil' Weintraub," said Mr. Kessler.

"Who's that?" asked the older brother.

"That's it," said Mr. Kessler. He got to his feet with fists clenched and walked toward the older brother.

"You never should have said that," said Mr. Kessler.

"I didn't say anything," said the boy.

"Oh yes you did," said Mr. Kessler, through clenched teeth. "Maybe I went to Vic Tanny's and shacked up with a girl named Irish and got drunk and ate barbecued ham hocks. Maybe I hid a dead cop and smoked marijuana and went to a crazy party and got kissed by a Negro homosexual ballet dancer. But I'm not letting you get away with something like that."

He flew at the older brother now, knocked him down and began to tear at his ear. "He was all-hit-no-field and he played four years for the Giants in the early forties and faded when the regular players got out of service AND NO SON OF A BITCH IS GOING TO SAY ANYTHING ABOUT POOR 'PHUMBLIN' PHIL' WEINTRAUB ON YOM KIPPUR!"

The younger brother and the girl tugged at him with fury and finally dislodged him, but not before a little piece of the ear had come off. Then Mr. Kessler smoothed his leotards and went sobbing out the door.

"I may have been excused," they heard him call back in the early morning, "but I wasn't that excused."

On the Air

PHILIP ROTH

Philip Roth (1933–): *Born in Newark, New Jersey, and educated at Buck-
nell University and the University of Chicago, Philip Roth has spent a career
writing fiction that both amuses and enrages the American Jewish community. When he won the National Book Award at the age of twenty-six for his
first book,* Goodbye, Columbus, *a novella plus stories, some observers of
the literary scene no doubt wondered if Roth could sustain the dazzling talent he'd shown in that first outing. Over the next few years that question
was put to rest, and now, nearly forty years later, it's clear that* Goodbye,
Columbus *was just the first sample of what would prove to be one of the
most brilliant careers in contemporary American literature. Philip Roth has
produced a body of work—darkly comic, often outrageous, always impres-
sively intelligent—unsurpassed by anyone of his generation. Among his
output are novels, including* Letting Go, Portnoy's Complaint, The
Ghost Writer, The Anatomy Lesson, My Life as a Man, The Professor of Desire, The Counterlife, Operation Shylock, Sabbath's Theater, *and* American Pastoral; *memoirs and autobiography,* The Facts
and Patrimony; *and a volume of literary essays,* Reading Myself and
Others. *He has won the National Book Award, the Pulitzer Prize, the* PEN/
Faulkner Award, *and many other prizes. For many years he has lived in
Connecticut.*

THE ANSWER MAN

The Answer Man! Some schmuck from Fort Wayne, Indiana,
with a deep voice who next year will be selling soap flakes
on Helen Trent! This is somebody to look up to? I spit on
him! Schmuck, with your answers, you don't begin to know the first
thing about *anything*. You want the Answer Man? I'll give you The
Answer Man, the kind of no-talent schmuckhead *goy he* is!

"And now—the Answer Man!"

"Good evening. First question, puh-lease."

"A lady from Modess, Nebraska, writes: 'Can whales actually
whistle whole songs? I say yes, but my husband, who is a sanitary

engineer, maintains that this is just a superstition prevalent in Modess. Which of us is right?'"

The Answer Man, the know-it-all *goy* with a voice like a cannon: "Interestingly enough, you're both correct." (Yeah, you *and* the plumber!). "Many young whales are born whistling, while others must be trained over a period of four to six weeks by their mothers. The whale, contrary to popular belief, is not a fish but a mammal. Next question, puh-lease."

"A priest from Mackerel Snap, Michigan, writes in to ask blah blah blah after dark, or is it the other way around?"

Answer Man: "The Mesopotamians believed that it was up to the individual. And this still holds true, interestingly enough, in many parts of that backward country today. Thank you, Father, for writing in."

"A Boy Scout, Answer Man, writes from Alaska, where he is lost, to ask whether the blah blah blah blah blah blah in the temperate zone, and when, and why?"

Answer Man: "Yes. But only in those months most suitable. Pasteur himself died at the age of sixty-three, and was buried of course at that time, so I'm afraid your friend is wrong about that. This is believed to have no connection with Arbor Day, so there *you're* wrong. Whether billions or millions, however, depends entirely upon the depth at which the coal is located; but the amount of heat generated would be sufficient to sharpen enough pencils to furnish a battalion of Chinese soldiers with sufficient rice to produce in twelve point ten seconds the old Olympic record, set in Helsinki during the reign of Queen Victoria of England, an explosion equal to four times the annual import duty of TNT by the first President of Peru, who did indeed write the lyrics to that and many another 'song of the prairie.'"

"Thank you, Answer Man!"

Yeah, thanks a lot for that load of *goyische* bullshit! Who couldn't know anyway with a staff of probably thousands feeding you the answers! I doubt that you personally can spell your own name! And what the hell *is* your name? What is this "Answer Man" shit? To impress people, that's what! You are just another sure-of-himself *goy*, and the truth is that you are a fake, just like the rest of your religion! Your name is probably John Johnson and you don't know dick! It kills me to think the influence you are having on little unformed minds! Someday, you son of a bitch, there will be a program with a Jew on it giving out the answers! We already have got the best comedians of all time on the radio—Jack Benny! Eddie Cantor! George Burns! Georgie Jessel! Henny Youngman! We have Mrs. Nussbaum on Fred Allen, on Benny we have Shlepperman and Phil Harris and Mr. Kitzel—we have, in straight drama, "The Goldbergs," and on Sunday we got "The Eternal Light" and "The Barry Sisters" both! And who's the funniest on "Can You Top This?" Not that *goy* Senator Ford! To tell you the truth, he puts me to sleep with those so-called jokes about morons and idiots. Dopey Dildock—he thinks the *name* is a joke because it's got "dopey" in it. Big *goy* joke. No, the best is Harry Hirschfield, and second to him is Peter Donald! Two Jews. And in singers who do you have to top, for an all-around beautiful voice, who do you have better than Tony Martin? I'm talking about a real voice, someone who when he puts on a dinner jacket and opens that mouth gives a person gooseflesh. The *Answer* Man! To a bunch of crap, that's what *you* got the answers to! A bunch of piddling *goyische* crap, that who needs to know such nonsense in the first place!

Dear Mr. Einstein:

I am writing you with a wonderful suggestion that I know would bring about gigantic changes in the world and improve the lot of Jews everywhere. Mr. Einstein, I am a fellow Jew, and proud of it. Your name is sacred to me as to people of our faith around the globe. That the Nazis chased you from Germany is our gain and their loss a million times over, if they even know what a loss is, and I only hope and pray that you are happy here in "the land of the free."

Here is my suggestion. Why don't you go on the radio every week with your own show? If you would agree I would like to manage you, so that your famous mind would not have to be cluttered up with business and so on. I am ashamed to say this in the same breath with your name, but probably you are aware of "The Answer Man" program which is on every night from seven to seven-fifteen. If you're not, just listen for a minute some night. Children all over America think this fake is "an Einstein" probably, when the real Einstein is something they would faint to hear in person. I would like them to know that THE GENIUS OF ALL TIME IS A JEW! This is something the world must know, and soon.

Respectfully yours,
M. Lippman,
Talent Agent

P.S. You will probably want to know what right I have even to suggest myself as a manager to the great Einstein. And all I can say is that if I had a list of the greatest names in the entertainment industry as my clientele, I would be as ashamed of my credentials as I am right now where you are concerned, The Great Albert Einstein. I feel it is even a sin to write out your whole name, that it is too holy for me to utter. But if I didn't write it out, how would you even get this letter? So forgive me. Until now, I have to tell you, I have not had a famous list of acts. Mostly I represent colored. I probably have most of the best tap dancing talent in the state under contract to me at this very moment, and am helping some of these young men — for instance, the famous Famous Brothers (Buck and Wing) — to raise themselves into a respectable life. With my new talent discoveries since Buck and Wing, I am changing their old names to the names of famous American presidents, only backwards. This way I think they still sound colored, which they should as tap dancers, and yet have a little class. Also I attend an average of two to three *bar mitzvah* parties of a single Saturday, in my endless search for young Jewish talent in singing, bandleading, etcetera.

I hope I will be hearing from you soon, and favorably, about "The Albert Einstein Show."

Again respectfully,
M. Lippman

Dear Mr. Einstein:

I can understand how busy you must be thinking, and appreciate that you did not answer my letter suggesting that I try to get you on a radio program that would make "The Answer Man" look like the joke it is. Will you reconsider, if the silence means no? I realize that one of the reasons you don't wear a tie or even bother to comb your hair is because you are as busy as you are, thinking new things. Well, don't think that you would have to change your ways once you became a radio personality. Your hair is a great gimmick, and I wouldn't change it for a second. It's a great trademark. Without disrespect, it sticks in your mind the way Harpo Marx's does. Which is excellent. (Now I wonder if you even have the time to know who The Marx Brothers are? They are four zany Jewish brothers, and you happen to look a little like one of them. You might get a kick out of catching one of their movies. Probably they don't even show movies in Princeton, but maybe you could get somebody to drive you out of town. You can get the entire plot in about a minute, but the resemblance between you and Harpo, and his hair and yours, might reassure you that you are a fine personality in terms of show business just as you are.

The kind of program I have in mind is something I would certainly have to talk with you about before embarking upon making the right contacts. For instance, should we follow "The Answer Man" format with questions sent in? Should we have a theme song? Would you object to another personality asking the questions? Something strikes me right about the idea of you being interviewed by Tony Martin, the singer. He has a beautiful speaking voice and makes a wonderful impression in a dinner jacket, and is also (contrary to the belief that he is of Italian extraction) a Jewish boy with whom you would feel completely at home. Easygoing is his whole style, *but with respect*. Whether I can get him is another story. I don't want to make promises I can't deliver so as to entice the famous Einstein. I wouldn't dare. But what I'm saying is that the sky is the limit once I get an okay from you. I am tempted to spell that with a capital letter. You. But in the middle of the sentence.

Perhaps I should have told You that my fee is ten percent. But truly and honestly I am not in this business for money. I want to help people. I have taken colored off the streets, shoeshine kit and all, and turned them into headline tap dancers at roadhouses and nightclubs overnight. And my satisfaction comes not from the money, which in all honesty is not so much, but in seeing those boys getting dressed up in dinner jackets and learning to face an audience of people out for a nice time. Dignity far more than money is my business.

With you, Mr. Einstein, I think I could really break through into something of worldwide importance in terms of doing good. Who better than you knows the persecution the Jews have taken around the globe? It will only stop when they look up to us and recognize that when it comes to smart, we are the tops. It will only stop when our own little Jewish boys and girls realize that there is an Einstein in the world who is a Jew just like them, and is a million times smarter than some *goy* radio announcer with a stuffy voice who they also give the answers to anyway. Do we want our children to grow up admiring such fakes? I have a little boy of my own, and I know what it would mean to me if I could sit with him at night once a week and listen to the Famous Albert Einstein talking around a fireside with someone of the caliber of a Tony Martin.

If you are too busy to write and discuss these matters, how about if I came to see you some Sunday? It would be a thrill if I could bring my son along.

Respectfully yours,
M. Lippman, Agent to
The Famous Brothers,
Roosevelt Franklin,
Jefferson Thomas,
Cleveland Grover, &
Monroe James

Dear *Dr.* Einstein:

No word, but I understand. I hope and pray you were not offended that I have been addressing you all along as Mister. I cannot express all my admiration for you, and it breaks my heart if you think any disrespect was intended. I am not an educated person, though I try to make up in hard work and quick thinking what I don't know from books. Every day, and this is no exaggeration, I have a hundred wonderful ideas that could improve the world. My idea to encourage you to go on the air on a regular basis is only one, Doctor.

I am sure that you are naturally nervous about me and the millions of others who probably write to you looking for "an easy buck." I have to assure you, *the money is secondary.* Uppermost is getting you on the radio and showing those *goyim* what smart really means. Why hide under a barrel something that could change the life of *every Jew alive and their children to come*? This is how strongly I believe in the power of radio. I think sometimes that the Bible stories of God talking from above to the people down below is just what they had in those days instead of radio. People, whether then or now, like to hear "the real thing." Hearing is believing! (Maybe that could be our motto for the show — if you approve. For a theme song I have been thinking along robust lines, but still meaningful — something like "The Whole World is Singing My Song.") Today we don't *hear* God as they did in the Bible — and what is the result? It is impossible for some people to believe He is there. There. The same holds true with you, Doctor Einstein, I'm sorry to say. To the general public, who is Einstein? A name who doesn't comb his hair (not that I have any objection) and is *supposed* to be the smartest person alive. A lot of good that does the Jews, if you understand what I'm saying. At this stage of the game, I'm afraid that if an election were held tonight between you and The Answer Man, more people would vote for him than for you. I have to be honest with you.

Here is my proposal. I will drive to Princeton next Sunday, arriving around two P.M. If you are not home, fine. If you are, and you happen to be at the window, and you happen to feel only like waving and that's all, well let me tell you, that would be a wonderful experience in itself. But if you want to ask a question or two about my suggestion, even through the window if that's all you have the time for, fine with me, I'll do that too, from the lawn. I will leave my wife and child in the car so that they don't bother you, though if you should want to wave at the boy, I would be most appreciative. And he of course would remember it for life.

To make a joke, don't put on a tie for my account, Doctor.

> Your fellow Jew and humble admirer,
> M. Lippman

DUFFY'S TAVERN

They were not very far from Princeton (Lippman had leaped from the car and jumped to the running board only minutes earlier, claiming he could see in the distance the beautiful towers of the famous college — he had pulled his child from his mother's lap and, balancing him on his head, cried out, "Where Einstein lives! This you'll remember forever!"), they were that close to Princeton, then, when Lippman saw yet another sight to excite his excitable nature: a sign reading ICE CREAM EVERY FLAVOR KNOWN TO MAN A REAL ICE CREAM ADVENTURE. The highway was passing through the town of Scully — so said a second sign. And a third: OBEY THE TRAFFIC LAWS. YOU MAY BE GIVING ORDERS YOURSELF SOME DAY. — SCULLY POLICE. *And then again you may not*, was written in crayon beneath the police department message — clearly, from the scrawl, the work of a child. "Ha!" shouted Lippman. It was just his delight coming out. "So how about it? Who wants any flavor known to man? Who wants a real ice cream adventure, and maybe a rest stop — before the great Albert Einstein!"

These remarks were directed, of course, to the little boy. Lippman was big on broadening experiences these days, but especially around this child, who seemed to have inherited from his mother's side all of that family's timidity. Unless he had inherited from Lippman whatever it was that had kept him a lowly shoe-dog for so long. Whichever, the more daring Lippman became with his own life, the less he could bear to see his own likeness turning into a snail. "Always raise your hand first!" These were his last words to the little boy upon delivering him to his school in September. To Lippman's disappointment, the morning of his first day of school the child had tried to get out of going by pretending to be a hopeless cripple. So convincing was he that he had even fooled his mother, sent her screaming into the bathroom where Lippman was shaving — "He can't walk!" she cried. "He hobbles suddenly! Our son hobbles!" Of course our son hobbles. What the clever little so-and-so had done was to tie his two shoelaces one to the other so that he would appear, overnight, to have become too handicapped to enter the world of the normal kindergarten student. "If the teacher says, 'Who can do it?' you jump up and say 'I can!'" "But what if I can't?" "By the time she finds out, you'll have learned! This is the clue to success in life, this is what I did not know and only discovered just in time." So said the father to his five-year-old, trembling on the doorstep to the big strange school. "You have got to sell yourself! Who can do it? I can! Little Lippman can! And don't pull that shoelace crap ever again — it's smart, but the wrong way."

Success. On Top. Somebody. Being Boss with a capital B. "Hello, this is Albert Einstein's agent calling . . ."

"Ice cream?" the mother asked. "At eleven o'clock A.M.?"

"Today's a celebration!" announced Lippman. "Today is the beginning of the next step forward!"

"But," his wife told him — and not for the first time since he had awakened her and the child to start off on this journey — "he didn't even answer one letter. How can you just barge in on such a person? How can you annoy him, one letter after another, and then because he doesn't so much as give a single reply — drop in! On Einstein!"

She shut up finally when he gave her his look of disgust and impatience. If and when he ever became famous, it would not be for his patience.

The ice cream parlor turned out to be a saloon.

The genteel Mrs. Lippman, a mannerly and pretty dark-haired young woman, with little experience of the greater world her husband had come to inhabit, reached with one hand for the back of his coat at the first whiff of beer. With the other hand she made a little cup, a little gas mask, over her child's nostrils. "*Goyim*," she whispered.

"So what?" snapped Lippman — for the child's sake. Yet even he, who by now was used to the dark places where Christians found happiness pouring whiskey into their mouths and passing it on out of their putzes (what fun! to make yourself into a piece of plumbing! to turn yourself from a human person into a length of pipe! what brains that takes, to drink something that is brown and turn it into something that is yellow! what a way to use your time!), even Lippman sensed a certain strangeness beyond the ordinary strangeness of these people.

For instance: the head of some antlered animal, stone blind, hung above the bar; not so unusual, except that the head was no larger than his fist, the eyes as big and as black as his little son's. The animal could have been no more than a baby when the head was severed from the body. Then there was the door beside the bar: in the center hung a round target, a photograph of the prizefight champion Joe Louis where the bull's-eye should be. Dangling from the target, aside from the regulation darts, were half a dozen ice picks, some Indian arrows, and a bayonet from some bygone era, rusty and heavy, hanging at a precipitous angle.

A strongly built young man, with magnificent biceps and a blond Heinie haircut, wearing white bell-bottomed trousers and an armless white undershirt, stood behind the bar — loomed *above* the bar. What a physical specimen! He was hurling wooden beer kegs through a trapdoor, raising them above his head and then, with a burst of swearwords, firing them in a downward trajectory. When Lippman (fearless, again for the sake of his child) approached the bar, he observed that the man down below, receiving the empty kegs, was a Negro, dressed like Joe Louis in satin boxing shorts, but wearing the thick cotton gloves of a garbage man.

Imagining things? Hallucinating? Lippman might have thought so in an earlier period of his life, but the lesson he had learned as a talent scout was that what you could imagine could also be so. What was not could become! Look at The Famous Brothers. Who were Buck and Wing when he found them? They were not famous, and to be frank, they were not brothers. They were two dumb nigger kids giving ten-cent shines outside his shoe store. Making funny patter and singing songs, *and* giving a shine, all for one dime. "What if — " Lippman had thought, and that was how the whole thing began. He had cleaned the lice out of their hair and made them stars.

And it had begun only as *an idea in his head* . . . When *exactly* he could not say. Seeing "The Diving Horse" in the show at The Steel Pier in Atlantic City had something to do with it, but largely it was just boredom and disgust with kneeling on his knees selling shoes — the few he sold! — that had led him one rainy afternoon to invite those two chatterbox kids, with legs on them like herons, legs right up to the armpit, to put on a special show for him. And watching them dance away, sitting there watching the four of their legs flying, and meanwhile whacking the shoe measure idly up against the side of his head, it came to him, the possibility. "A whack on the head," his wife moaned later, "was what did it. I should have known." "Whatever did it, it should only do it again!" said Lippman. For here was what he had realized: if somebody once thought up the idea to have a big white horse jump from fifty feet in the air into a tank of water — if that, why not this? When that other fellow came home to his wife in Atlantic City and said, "Honey, I am going to buy a horse and teach him to jump from a diving board with a girl in a bathing suit on his back," would anyone ever have thought that one day people would start out on vacation trips from all over the country to drive to New Jersey to pay to see such a thing? To applaud and applaud and then go home and talk about it for the rest of their lives? No. Oh, no! By comparison to that guy with The Diving Horse, Lippman was a very small-time genius, so far. All he had set out to do was to take two little jigaboos who could already tap-dance better than they could walk, and teach them to do it without saying "shee-yit" every other word out of their mouths. And to get the lice off them. Which was not nothing, he now knew — shee-yit this and shee-yit that! What it had taken him in blood and sweat just to get them to say "Good evening, ladies and gentlemen," without fifty shee-yits in between! But still, it was not so very much compared to teaching a brewery horse to take a dive, a leap, into the blue!

Oh, Jesus — the things you could make in this world! The things that were already *made*! The acts they were just *giving* away! For nothing! Gratis! Step right up, ladies and gentlemen, and pay *nothing*! Of which ten percent, Lippman's commission, was of course nothing too. Hitler, for instance — that little nut over in Germany thundering and howling at those millions of German people, and them saluting and cheering him back, goose-stepping for him all night long from one end of the country to the other, and all the time all this goose-stepping and *sieg-heil*ing is going on, all the time the torches are burning and the millions are on their feet roaring, all the time in the middle of that face *there is this little moustache*! Hitler! What an *idea*! Or that Mussolini character—with a neck on him like Two-Ton Tony Galento, with a collar on him made of his own thick flesh, and *he* is in charge of all of Italy! With that neck! Oh, just think about the big headliners and you could (in a way, in a way) die not to be handling them! "The Adolf Hitler Show." "The Benito Mussolini Comedy Hour." And how about that skinny Pope with the glasses: catch this—he raises that pale little hand of his and says some mumbo jumbo, and grown men, truck drivers, athletes, financial wizards, smack their foreheads down onto the pavement in awe. Imagine it—a man in a dress is in charge! A man wearing *a dress.* Because what else is that if it ain't a dress, an evening gown? And telling them, "Dominoes chess checkers bingo you're going to live forever Jesus Christ." And they swallow it—whole! Now, if that is no hallucination, then what is? Only it is *not*! Think of our own dear and beloved and wonderful F.D.R. There he is with that big cigarette holder and his Mandrake the Magician cape, President of the United States of America, and he has legs on him like twigs! And what about his wife, that voice of hers? And those teeth! You want to *laugh* when you look at her, you want to fall off your chair from that voice, how *incredible* it is—and yet, behind those teeth is this wonderful person! What a character, what a radio personality she could become. Bigger than Baby Snooks. And how about that little Scottie dog running around the White House and probably pee-peeing on the floors where earth-shaking decisions are made every hour of the day! Now why didn't I think that up, thought Lipp-man. Think of the laughs. Hey! Wouldn't it be something, when he is done being President, to get them to do a show like George Burns and Gracie Allen, or Fibber McGee and Molly! "Franklin and Eleanor, and their little dog Fala—and their special guest star this week, all the way from the House of Parliament, with his cigar and his English accent, Big Ben's own—Winston Churchill!" The funny things that could happen at the White House—jokes about her buck teeth (if she has the sense of humor for it, that would be up to her)—Fala leaking on Churchill's spats! Ah, what a world—Eleanor Roosevelt's teeth, Hitler's little moustache, Mussolini's thick wop neck, the skinny Pope going shopping for his dresses—"Oh, that's you, Pope, that dress is definitely *you*"—oh he could *plotz* from the acts that they were giving away *for nothing.* Ah, but Einstein, Einstein would be his—Einstein with that great hair on the outside and that brain on the inside! Who is Einstein? I'll tell you who — he is the Marx Brother who quit the act and went to medical school! . . . But if I tell *him*, will he laugh? Will he see the humor? Oh, if he can see the humor, we're in business! Because that's what people love the most in life — that is the truest thing there is, a good laugh! Imagine — if he could get the famous Einstein to crack a few jokes, *and still be a genius!* Oh, there was fame and power in store for Lippman, with a head full of ideas like his! And pleasure too. Happiness. Fulfillment. Joy. Riches. If he could only get that first nationwide break. Then he could load the airways with The Most Impressive Array of Talent The World Has Ever Known. Because every place you looked today (every place Lippman looked) there was entertainment material galore. Acts, acts, and more acts! He didn't pick up a newspaper that he didn't see another headliner passing himself off as a politician! "Some guys look at horses and see Johnny Weissmullers in disguise — I see the laugh in things! What strikes the funnybone! What's so wrong with that?" "Because," his wife said, "some things are not funny, not by any stretch of the imagination. And that goes for Hitler! And that goes for President Roosevelt! A great man who has to walk with canes and has Secret Service men to hold him up by the elbows, and you expect people to laugh. You should be ashamed, Milton, just to think such thoughts."

"But I am not ashamed! I will not be ashamed! I am a talent scout! I have to have an eye for the gimmick, for the strange! People don't notice the unusual things that happen in life until somebody that does comes along and points them out. And that is all I do, and is nothing I will 'be ashamed of.' A talent scout is only a person who happens to see what the other person doesn't — he doesn't make these things happen, *he only points them out!*"

"And if a Catholic heard you laugh at the Pope? Would you like him to laugh at our rabbi?"

Her rabbi, but he let that pass. "Ah, you don't understand."

"We have to respect one another's religion. Otherwise there is only hate in the world."

"There is only hate in the world anyway."

"Shhhhh! Not within hearing distance of the c-h-i-l-d."

"Ah," said Lippman, "forget it."

She didn't understand. It wasn't as though *he* had put the Pope in a dress. It wasn't as though *he* had given Mrs. Roosevelt those teeth. Lippman was only pointing them out, that they were *there*.

"God," he announced to his wife, "God is the Greatest Talent Scout of Us All!"

"Oh, Milton, suppose he should repeat a thing like that when he visits his little friends. Suppose he should tell the teacher something foolish like that in s-c-h-o-o-l."

"But why *shouldn't* he? Maybe it's t-r-u-e!"

"Milton," she pleaded, "God — is Almighty *God!*"

"But what if the world is some kind of — of *show!* Don't you understand me? What *if*, is all I'm saying! What if we are all only talent assembled by The Great Talent Scout Up Above. The Great Show of Life! Starring Everybody! Suppose entertainment is the Purpose of Life!" Lippman prided himself on the magnitude and daring of these thoughts; afterwards, of course, he always regretted expressing them to his wife. She made him feel like a freak because of some of the things he came up with — took objection, for instance, when he did nothing more than bring Buck and Wing home one hot summer night, stuffed each of them into a rented dinner jacket, and proceeded to teach them to eat a piece of watermelon with a knife and a fork. She lay awake in one room and her little child in the other, while in the kitchen the fanatical Lippman (fanatical in her eyes) worked over those boys until two in the morning — all night long, "those two poor colored boys" screaming and cursing with frustration, while her insane husband roared at them, "No hands, do you hear me? You cannot go on Major Bowes if you are going to pick up your food with your hands!" "Shee-yit, Mistah Lippman, why you torturing us like this! Why you gotta start us off with watermelon anyway — why can't we start off with a hot dog, something easy like that!" "Because a hot dog you're *supposed* to eat by hand — you know that as well as I do! I am teaching you dignity! I am teaching you class!" "But I'se *torturing* to death here with these pits all slipping and sliding — " "Listen to me, you two, I can go down to darkest Georgia tonight and get myself seven thousand little black boys to pick up a piece of watermelon in their *hands!* Who in his right mind is going to pay to see that?" "But they payin' to see us tap-dance, Mistah Lippman. Shee-*yit!* They payin' to see us dance, not to *eat* somethin'! Ain't that so, Melvyn?" "His name ain't Melvyn — it's Wing! And yours is Buck! And stop saying 'shit' once and for all!" "Hell, I sayin' *shee-*yit!" "Well then, pronounce it right — and then knock it off! It does not go with the dinner jacket!"

. . . Scully's Tavern. Along the walls of the barroom were long benches, occupied not by men — there were no men, other than the bartender and himself — but by women in flowered dresses and white hats, largish women with fatty creases in the wrists, the elbows, and at the ankle. And where, thought Lippman, are the husbands? Where are those drunkards? And what are they up to in their bare feet, those savages . . . Little children, in Sunday finery, clutching to themselves little black books with gold crosses embossed on the covers, rested at the feet of the women, their little flushed faces shiny and their dark clothing flecked with the sawdust that was sprinkled across the barroom floor. The women, Lippman noted (he would, in his business), had styled their hair and their clothing after the famous fat radio singer, Kate Smith. Now *there* was nothing. He put Kate Smith in a category with Senator Ford. There should be one whole network given over to people like that, he thought — Senator Ford, Kate Smith, Kay Kyser and Ishkabibble, Hobby Lobby, and that schmuckhead Answer Man. Yeah, the *Goyische* Network. Put the *goyim* on one network, give the Jews all the rest! Hey, what an *idea!*

Hey! "Duffy's Tavern!" The bartender — staring now at Lippman, holding a beer keg above his head *and* Lippman's — the bartender made him think of the radio program, "Duffy's Tavern." Sure! Suppose a Jew were to walk into a tavern by mistake — as Lippman and his family had just done. They are out looking for an ice cream for their little boy, they are on their way to meet the famous Albert Einstein, and walk into a real dumb *goy* tavern instead. A perfect situation comedy! Perfect for his Jewish network!

So Lippman — trembling with inspiration — went to work. "You'll pardon me," he said, adopting the funny accent of Mr. Kitzel from the Benny Show, "but this is a place you get an ice cream maybe?"

The bartender's muscles began to quiver beneath the weight of the beer keg. "This is a what where you get a *which*?"

Said Lippman, "Is a sign outside, every flavor ever known to man."

"What?" cried the bartender. "Every what known to *who*? *When*?"

"Menkind."

All fury, the bartender dispatched the beer keg through the trapdoor. "Take it *easy*, boss," sang the prizefighter in garbageman's gloves. "Take it easy, willya, boss?"

Mrs. Lippman whispered, "Milton!"

The bartender had now turned to the row of silent massive women, some of whom were cleansing the gulleys in their fat-ringed wrists with little cotton swabs. "It must be a what from a *where*?" the bartender screamed at them. "It must be a who from a how? What in hell is he even *saying*?"

Oh, now this does beat "Duffy's Tavern" a thousand times. This guy is rich! A real dumb muscle-bound *goy*! A stupid *shagetz par excellence*! And what about those women, cleaning sawdust out from between the folds of their flesh. Priceless. Perfect. How about a program starring this whole lot—call it "The *Goyim*"! And use that garbageman, too. Sure! A colored singing group, like the Ink Spots or the Mills Brothers. Wait a minute! "Joe Louis—and The Garbagemen!" What if he could get the champ to carry a tune! Dear Joe Louis, Champion of the World, My name is Milton Lippman, agent to Albert Einstein—

"Hey!" the bartender was screaming, now through a serving window that looked onto what must be the kitchen. Lippman heard meat sizzling away in a pan back there—sniffing, he smelled grease warming up. Phooey. They eat grease too, on top of everything else. "Can any of you guys make head or tail out of what this clown is trying to say?"

Here (and get this) the wrinkled faces of two old wispy-bearded Chinamen appear in the serving window.

"Maybe you two can understand this joker!" And then to Lippman, or the little greenhorn he took him for, the bartender cried, "Speak *English*, damn it! This is Sunday! This is a taproom, a saloon, a bar, a roadhouse—do you understand my meaning, Abie? This is a house of refreshment—and is to be respected as such!"

"Leefleshment!" said one of the Chinamen to the other, and the two fell straight backwards, disappeared in a roar of hysterical Oriental laughter. Lippman thought: Oh, this puts little "Duffy's Tavern" to shame! This puts "Duffy's Tavern" right off the air! This is the real thing! That *nobody* could make up!

"English?" asked Lippman, in his Kitzel voice. "English is already how I'm speaking, pardon me."

"What? You're speaking *what*?" The blood vessels had so expanded in the bartender's neck and arms that he suddenly looked to Lippman like some drawing of the human body in which they show what is going on beneath the skin. And Lippman's heart suddenly expanded in terror, filled his chest, his throat, finally his mouth. He imagined the *goy* going *goy*-mad. Imagined the *goy* taking their three heads and smashing them together until they were just mush and blood and splinters of bone!

Because this wasn't "Duffy's Tavern" with the familiar ding-a-ling start of each show, the phone ringing and Archie The Manager picking it off the hook and giving out with the famous first line — "Duffy's Tavern, where the elite meet to eat, Archie The Manager speaking, Duffy ain't here — oh hello, Duffy." No, this was no bull-shit about good-natured *goyim* running a sweet and cozy little saloon. This was no bullshit tavern from the radio, *this was the real thing* — only more so! The dead decapitated baby deer! Ice picks in the dart board! And a World War One bayonet! And those women — swollen, brainless, beer-inflated zeppelins! And those little children, pounds of lard (from *eating* lard) in little dark suits and white dresses, clutching to their little sleeping faces the Sunday School books tell-ing them how the Jews killed their Jesus Christ! And the men — where were *those* drunken bastards?

And here he heard the noises of their violence. So did his wife. "Milton!" My God! Cannons were firing. Shells and bullets zinging through the air no more than fifty feet away. So it sounded!

"*Guns*, Milton! *Explosions!*"

"Somebody," screamed the bartender, "somebody help me *out* with this guy, will you? Before I wind up in the hospital all *over* again! One more operation — that's all I really need! One more knife in the God damn eardrum! No — the only knife I need is the knife to cut that accent with!"

From the kitchen, one of the Chinese cooks called, "One Knife to Cut Accent With! Coming true, Chollie!"

"Coming *up*," the bartender shouted back into the kitchen. "Coming *through* is for when you're carrying something *hot!*"

And for this information he was rewarded again with their Chi-nese laughter, which in turn caused him to begin pounding out his rage — one fist after the other — upon the bar.

By now Lippman's child had taken sanctuary under his mother's dress, so that she looked to have two sets of legs, hers and a little pair in short pants and two-tone brown and white shoes.

Lippman whispered, "Let's go, okay, no ice cream here — "

Whereupon the bartender vaulted the bar beautifully — "One! Two! Hah!" the women chanted — and took Lippman by his shirt. "Ah, so you *can* make yourself understood after all! Oh you people — understand every God damn word, pretending all the time that all you know how to do is shrug your shoulders! — or is that your friends the Italians? Well, you're all the same anyway with your God damn Pig Latin! And how do *you* know we don't have ice cream? Have you even *asked*? Have you seen a God damn *menu*? No!

Because *you* can tell beforehand. All we care about is guzzling beer, right? *Right?*" he said, shaking Lippman till the talent scout's brain rattled in its cup. "The possibility that we might send *out* for ice cream just didn't even enter your head, did it? Because you know *everything*! Jee-zuz! You need a genius translator from the League of Nations to understand what language he's talking to begin with — even a slant-eyed Chink covered with tattoos speaks clearer than he does — except for those God damn l's! Oh, those l's of theirs! If I have to hear light and long for right and wrong *one more time* —! I mean, how the hell can you get to first base in a discussion on ethics with somebody who pronounces it 'light and long'! 'Light and long, Chollie!' Or how about Leno for Reno — which just happens to be some people's home town! Not to mention an important city in Nevada! Over and over again, from early morning to late at night, you'd think it's the only city they ever heard of 'Leno, Chollie, Leno!' Or are they saying 'lean over' — I don't know! I mean, this is the kind of stuff that put me in the hospital with that God damn mastoiditis to begin with! See those scars behind my ears? Mastoiditis!" Here he turned his head so that Lippman could see the flesh back of either ear, flesh bulbous, red, melted-looking, like the wattle of a turkey. How hideously disfigured this perfect specimen was! "From years of trying to understand whatever it is those two smart-ass sons of bitches are saying behind my back, that's how I got like this! How the hell was I supposed to know that all the time they were saying 'low' they really meant 'row' and were actually wanting to know where they could rent a God damn canoe! And how do you think it feels to be an ex-merchant seaman — and proud of it, for all that the Navy and Coast Guard get all the God damn glory! — and hear those two yellow bastards back there practicing their English on 'longitude and latitude'! Of all the God damn phrases in the English language to practice on, they have to pick practically my favorite two words in the entire language! And this goes on from early morning to late at night, year in and year out! I try to include them in my conversations, I try to be nice and get them interested in something educational — and what I get for my troubles is *incurable mastoiditis*! Is it any wonder I've had to spend half my life in hospitals getting my ears fixed? Seven operations. *Seven!* Do you realize the strain a bartender is under trying to understand and make happy every yellow bastard dishwasher and cook who wanders into this place for a job? Is it any wonder I'm at the end of my patience? And then *you* come along! Damn it, between you and those chinkheads, I'll be back in bandages before the weekend's over! Oh, sometimes I actually wish I *were* deaf! What good is it to have ears in this country anymore! God damn Chinks—you give them the shirt off your back, *literally*, and that's their gratitude!"

"Glatitude!" came the triumphant cry from the kitchen. "Glatitude, Chollie, coming true!"

Here eight of the seated women rose to their feet, having first deposited the cotton swabs into their little handbags and placed upon the bench the shoes each had been holding in her lap. Like little children, they linked hands. Then they looked over to the bartender. Sweetly. "See those girls?" said the bartender. "I thank my lucky stars for the existence of those girls!" And saying this, he even released his stranglehold on Lippman's shirtfront, so moved was he by the sight of those eight fat women holding hands.

The bartender reached into his bell-bottomed trousers and removed from his watch pocket a small pitch pipe—the very sight of which caused the eight women to begin to clear their throats, one after the other. "There," said the bartender, motioning toward the women, "there," he said softly, "is the only reason I don't have the doctor tie off my eustachian tubes and free me forever from this rack of earache and infection."

He blew the pitch pipe. The eight women hummed in unison. The bartender said, "A-one, a-two, a-three," and they began to sing "When The Moon Comes Over The Mountain," Kate Smith's theme song.

Little Lippman now came out from under his mother's dress to listen. And the door beside the bar swung open. The bayonet dropped out of the target onto the floor. The man who had opened the door mouthed "sorry" when the bartender turned to glare at him. A black tumor hung from the end of his hand! Not until he moved from the shadows of the doorway did Lippman recognize the bowling ball for what it was. Before the bowler moved again, obscuring Lippman's view, the talent scout was able to catch a glimpse through the door—the light was bad, the angle worse, and he had but a second to look, but he could have sworn afterwards that the room from which the bowler had emerged was a radio studio: rows of people, an audience sitting in silence, looking toward a stage . . . or were they only looking toward the bowling alleys? Was some sort of bowling match underway back there? Yes, what he had taken earlier for Gentile rifle or artillery fire must be the sound of the bowling balls banging on the alleyways and then rolling down the length of the hard polished floors toward the pins — the "explosions" were caused by the wooden pins flying into the air from the impact of the black balls. And now he realized that the women, each with a pair of workaday shoes in her lap, were the wives of the members of the bowling team. Everything was explained, more or less.

The bowler smiled at Lippman and waved to his little boy. "How do?" he mouthed to Mrs. Lippman. Then, raising the hand to which the ball was attached, he said to Lippman, "Sorry, no non-bowlers allowed." But those syllables too, he only mouthed, so as not to interfere with the singing of the eight fat women.

HOWARD JOHNSON'S

. . . Merry little children, licking ice cream cones, skipping out the open door, their smiling and healthy-looking parents on either side of them.

"Why must we stop? Why can't we go straight through to Einstein?" his wife asked. "Or turn around and go home where we belong." She was cuddling and rocking the little boy in her arms; Ira was slow getting over all he had witnessed in that saloon.

"I said I would buy him an ice cream, and that's what I'm going to do! What should be so hard about that? This is the place the sign was about in the first place!"

"But he's *afraid,*" his wife whispered.

"Of what? Stop coddling him!" shouted Lippman. "Your father," he said to the child, "is here to protect you. Why should you be afraid of an ice cream cone? The first place wasn't what I thought it was, that's all. I've never been here myself either. Anybody can make a mistake — it was time you learned that anyway."

Inside the ice cream parlor, Lippman said, "Ah *hah!*" at the sight of the long glistening white marble counter and the names of the hundreds of delicious flavors painted in colorful letters on the walls and ceiling of the big bright room. "Well, this is the real thing, after all, isn't it?" he said to the little boy. "This is really going to be ice cream that is ice cream, isn't it?" and he tried to unfasten the boy from his mother's dress and draw him to his side. "Just look at the roll call of great flavors!" But his enthusiasm was not communicated to the child . . . And all around him, Lippman noticed, the families who had been seated in the booths along the big front windows were quickly taking their leave of the ice cream parlor, abandoning upon the tables barely eaten sundaes and dishes of pie à la mode.

The young baby-faced soda jerk who came smartly and smilingly up to serve them had a thick thatch of strawlike hair across his forehead, and he stood smiling — *bubbling* — before them, pushing the hair back from his innocent eyes with an arm that did not have a real hand at its end, but a shiny aluminum device in the shape of an ice cream scoop. "Hi! I'm Billy Smith, but my Aunt Kate, the singer, calls me 'Scoop.' I only have one hand, but fortunately I've been fitted with this ice cream scoop so that I can be of value to society despite my handicap."

Lippman: *What?* What did he say? Kate Smith *again?* And look at that hand on him! Where is he hiding the real one? And where is my kid? Oh Jesus, not again. "Get him out of there," he said to his wife, once more showing four legs rather than two. "Come on out of there, you — or you're not getting the ice cream."

"I don't want one," said the little faceless round head draped beneath his mother's dress.

"Maybe I can do the job, sir!" said Scoop. "Little boy," he said, addressing himself down toward Mrs. Lippman's thighs, "can you hear me, little boy? This is Scoop, the soda jerk! There's no need to be afraid of me — or to feel sorry for me, either! I sure don't go around all day feeling sorry for myself, I'll tell you that much! I mean, just think about it — how many other people in the world have an ice cream scoop instead of a right hand? How many do you think, little boy?"

"Someone's talking to you," said Lippman. "How many do you think have a hand like him? You had numbers in kindergarten."

"I don't know," came the little voice from under the dress.

"Then take a guess," said Lippman sharply.

"Six."

"Wrong!" cried Scoop. "The correct answer is none! I am the only person like me in the world! Now, isn't that something? A lot of people come in here and say, 'Oh, look, that poor handicapped youngster with an ice cream scoop instead of a hand,' and I just have to laugh and say, 'I wouldn't trade it for the world.' People leave this place absolutely amazed by my cheery disposition. A lot of them chalk it up to stupidity, I know that — but if being stupid keeps me from boo-hooing about myself, that's fine with me! Hey, little boy — just you think about all the wonderful things I can do with my scoop, and all the fun I can have that's denied ordinary ten-fingered kids. Why I can serve punch without its leaking through my fingers — and I don't have to cut my nails, at least not on that hand!"

Here a long thin stalk of a man with a sharply chiseled face and wearing a green eyeshade — as well as elastic arm bands and suspenders — appeared at the far end of the counter. "Where the hell is everybody? Where's my Sunday ice cream trade? Has the influenza struck again? Is the fridge on the fritz? Is Sea Biscuit dead and the country in mourning? Where are all the happy Christian families, eating their ice cream?"

"Gee, Pop Scully," answered Scoop, "I didn't even notice. Oh, old duncehead me! I was so busy talking to these nice folks!"

Scully lowered his forehead to the cash register. "Good Christ, what do *they* want! Who let *them* in! And what's that supposed to be — some kind of Yid papoose?"

Resisting every impulse but the one that had brought him through the door, Lippman replied, "We want ice cream. That's my little boy under there — who is shy and only five. We're here because we understand that you have every flavor known to man — that's quite an accomplishment."

The proprietor, drawing himself up to his full six and a half feet, said, "Every flavor except *matzohs*, Moses."

Lippman, in a split-second shuffling through fifty retorts, came up with this one — because he who would soon be Einstein's agent, would not be toppled again! "Well, what else," he asked graciously, "might you have under *m*?" That's it, don't even hear the insult. Outsmart the *goy* bastard. Einstein him, but *good*! "What's your repertoire under that particular letter . . . ?" Schmuck, of course, implied.

Scoop answered enthusiastically. "Gee whiz sir, you just name it! We've got marshmallow, marmalade, and marzipan. Or if you feel in the mood for something hyphenated, we can give you myrtle-chip, mango-fudge, melba-supreme — why, we've got mixo-mixo too (that's our own special tutti-frutti), as well as macadamia-nut and milk-chocolate — and we have even got minnow ice cream, for those who like something just a little fishy," said Scoop, finishing up with a cute and endearing wink.

Scully, outsmarted indeed by a gloating Lippman, snapped at his soda jerk, "Go rest your hook, boy. Your hook looks tired, get me? Take a big box of Brillo, why don't you, all the Brillo you want for being such a good boy, and go off and work on your hook. You wouldn't want me to call up your Aunt Kate and tell her you've been serving the customers with a rusty hook, would you?"

"Oh, no, no, sir," replied the soda jerk, pushing his hair from his eyes, which were furtive suddenly and full of shame.

"We wouldn't want to tell her—" and here he whispered something into the boy's ear that prompted Scoop to take a package of steel wool from beneath the counter and depart for a back room. "I expect to see a clean and scoured hook, lad!" Scully called after him, encouragingly.

"It isn't his fault, you see," said Scully to Lippman, after the soda jerk was gone. "It's just that a lot of people, seeing how the boy is handicapped, think they can get him to do anything with that prosthetic device for a lousy nickel or dime. They just plain exploit him using what was clearly designed solely as an ice cream scoop for just about every kind of—well, act they can think of."

Lippman could not understand why, but Scully had turned civil suddenly. So he asked about what interested him most. "Is he really related to the singer Kate Smith?"

"Are you kidding? This boy is a mental reject, a ninety per cent defective, and not just in the hand, either. You know how some of them think they're Napoleon? Well, he thinks his aunt is Kate Smith. No, no, I'm afraid there's even less to this boy than meets the eye." And then, before Lippman could ask his next question ("Has he ever thought of going on the stage? Has he ever thought of The Steel Pier—or maybe the World's Fair? Or maybe we could send him to hospitals to cheer up people who are missing things—"), before Lippman could even begin, Scully had run his thumbs the length of his braces, yanked them with a snap away from his chest, and broken into an entirely new and unexpected voice. "Yessireebob!" he exploded, a Yankee farmer—a backwoodsman! "So you good folks want yourselves some of this here dee-licious ice cream! Hee-hee-hee!" he cackled. "Well, you come to the right place, hope you know that! Just about every flavor ever known to man—and then some! Betcha got some ice cream here such as this shy little devil of yours—hear me in there, you shy little devil? hee-hee!— such as he never dreamed of! Yessireebob! I'll bet he sure is something to look at—if you ever get a chance to look at him! I'm mighty glad I got me this here eyeshade, for when that handsome little devil comes glistening out into the sunshine! Hee-hee-hee! So how's about it, youngster? Which would you like to begin with? How's about some wool? A nice double-dip wool ice cream cone!"

Mrs. Lippman cried out—"Wool? Woolen *ice cream*?"

"You betchum! And hund-erd percent too! Got wool, got tape, got shoes, erasers, chalk—"

"But he doesn't *eat* chalk, he doesn't eat *anything* that you mentioned! Milton!"

"Right you are, Madam! So *far* he hasn't. But don't you kid yourself, we know our little boys and girls—we know what goes on inside those cute little heads of theirs! Ever read in the newspapers about some poor little fella who swallows a penny and is rushed to the hospital? Well, his folks didn't think he liked to eat money either, you know, till he done it. And then, you know, it's just *too* late, that is for anybody but the undertaker. And that's how come we started off to begin with—with penny ice cream. Ever heard tell of that? Penny ice cream cone? Well, that's what it originally meant, you know—not how much it cost but what it tasted like. Then, you see, we just sort of expanded out, till today we got ink, for instance, as well as Quink—we got wood, we got glass, we got shoe polish, candles—"

"Do you have paper?" The child had spoken. Through the dress.

"Darling!" cried the mother.

But Lippman said, "Let him talk for himself." He winked at Scully, a sign to proceed with the sales pitch. This was more like it—why, he would even let the boy stay in hiding, if it gave him the courage to be a little more adventurous in the end. "He wants to know," said Lippman proudly, "if you have paper."

"News, wax, or carbon?" snapped Scully.

No word now from the child. The mother was covering with five fingers what must be his mouth.

"The man is asking you something," the father said, unpeeling his wife's hand from her dress. "Newspaper, wax paper, or carbon paper—*which*?"

"Newspaper . . ."

"Well, good for you!" said Scully, and quickly, to the mother, added, "Here, here, Madam, don't you fret none, you hear? Why, you have just made an important discovery about this here young feller of yours that may save you years of agony in the future. You should be *overjoyed*, for heaven's sake! Why, left to himself one day he might just, for all you know, have set himself down at the table while you was out and devoured an entire issue of the Sunday *Gazette*. Who knows how long he has had this here craving in his cute and clever little head? Why you might just have come home one night and found your little boy in convulsions on the floor from a chaw out of the comic section of the *Evening Globe*—who knows when this affliction might have struck him down!"

"*What* affliction? He *has* no affliction. Milton—!"

But Lippman, in anger, said to her, "For God's sake, it's a gimmick! A publicity stunt for kids! Stop scaring somebody who you are going if you keep this up to turn into a first class sissy! Give the boy the ice cream, Mr. Scully. One double-dip of newspaper ice cream!"

"Just call me 'Pop,' you hear?" And Scully handed across the counter a sugar cone topped with two blobs of gray ice cream. "One Wall Street Edition! Want jimmies too?"

"Ira, come out and get your ice cream treat! Get out here, son, where you belong in the first place."

"Got your newspaper cone for you, Ira," said Pop Scully gently.

And so the child emerged, like a little boy ducking out from underneath the flap of a circus tent.

"Well," said Scully, "there's the little scalliwag, no worse for the wear. Sure is a *dark* little scalliwag, ain't he," and handed the boy his ice cream.

"Go ahead!" said Lippman. "Lick it just like you lick an ordinary ice cream."

The child obeyed.

"Well," said Pop Scully, "how's the taste, youngster? Like a newspaper? Tell your proud Mom and Dad! Taste like the *Evening Globe*, or more like the *Daily Star*?"

The child shrugged.

"Kee-rect! Just as advertised!" Scully announced, at the very moment that the child turned gray—even the whites of his eyes turned gray—and fell to the floor of the ice cream parlor, as though drugged.

GANGBUSTERS

"The Chief" arrived, a man in a blue delivery jacket and a gun belt, both worn over a pair of rumpled pajamas. On the back of the jacket white felt letters spelling OLDE CORNE; in the cartridge belt, instead of bullets, a dozen or so miniatures of OLDE CORNE whiskey bottles. Yet the gun itself, the tip of whose barrel was suddenly thrust up against Lippman's teeth, felt real. "One more word," said The Chief, "and I'll blow your incisors down your throat! I'll blast your molars into Kingdom Come! I'll turn this perjuring mouth into a volcano spewing blood. Is my meaning clear?"

"But my little boy—"

Here The Chief plunged the revolver directly into Lippman's mouth and thus forced him backwards through the door that Pop Scully held ajar. On the floor of the ice cream parlor, in a puddle of gray ice cream, Mrs. Lippman now lay faint across the fallen body of the child. Her garters could be seen where the dark dress had ridden up her legs. Lippman cried a noise into the barrel of the revolver.

"Oh damn it," said The Chief, extracting the gun and wiping it beneath his arm. "Don't start spitting into the barrel, will you? This is a precision weapon, and you're not supposed to *wet* it."

"My child," gasped Lippman, "has been *poisoned*, Officer—"

Scully, his old self suddenly, said, "See? That's just what I'm talking about, Chief."

The Chief sighed. "Reckless Accusation, eh? Reckless Accusation Against Christians. The age-old crime, right here in our little town . . ." But then he turned back to the gun. "Boy, you really know how to ruin a revolver, don't you?" he said to Lippman. "I mean, the cardinal rule about any weapon is *to keep the thing dry*. A *child* knows that much," he said petulantly, and raised his eyebrows— like a homo! "*Really!*"

"Can it," cautioned Scully, speaking out of the side of his mouth.

"Well, look, Scull," said The Chief, "I really am angry about this gun. If it were mine it would be one thing, but *it happens* to be *borrowed. It* just *happens* to be Roger's!"

"Can it!" said Scully.

"Please—" demanded Lippman, "my child—my wife . . ."

"Oh, you people and your children—and your wives!" roared The Chief, no homo now! What then? A Chief of Police—with a borrowed gun? Hey—wasn't this the bartender from that saloon? But if so, where were those scars? "You and your little Abies and Jakeys! You know something? I have seven kids of my own at home—*and* a wife—and you know what I do when they give me their back talk— take my pistol out and stick it up against their little brains! Teach them respect! But you, can you even fire a God damn pistol? Can you—I'm talking to you, Mister!" However Lippman's attention— his bewilderment, rather—was directed toward the corner of the vast storeroom, where the young soda jerk, Scoop, was sitting on the floor, twisting a ball of steel wool in the bowl of his scooper. The walls of the room were packed to the ceiling with cartons labeled "Crispy Scully Sugar Cones," the boxes arranged, like the shoes in

Lippman's old store, according to size: kiddie, regular, super, super-duper. Each box displayed on its side a picture of the traditional dunce-cap ice cream cone.

"Here!" The Chief said. "*Here*—!" and thrust his pistol into Lippman's hand. "If you're so sure you committed no crime, if it seems to you that Reckless Accusation Against Christians is some sort of trumped-up charge, go ahead then, blow my brains out and be done with it!"

Scully, speaking softly, said, "And mine too. And the brains, such as they are, of that poor helpless mental defective over in the corner, while you're at it. Kill us all, my Jewish friend, if we are such *monsters.*"

Here The Chief—yes, it *was* the bartender!—grabbed Lippman's hand and pointed the pistol at his own temple. "Look, would you like me also to pull the trigger for you? Or is it that you prefer lions? Maybe you'd like to throw us to the lions instead. Too bad I didn't think to bring my lion with me," he said, for Scully's amusement. Then he roared—"*Pull the trigger!*"—but then in the pansy voice, "Only for God's sake, when you're finished, don't drop it on the floor and break it. *Hand* it back."

Which Lippman did, then and there. Because this was a joke! And a bad joke! *Obviously* it was a pistol full of blanks! *Obviously* this "Chief" was the bartender—and obviously those scars back of the ear had been so much makeup, that mastoiditis so much malarkey! And the ice cream—had they given Ira a "Mickey Finn," or had the boy simply succumbed to his panic? But—if this Chief was such a joke, and this gun such a little toy, why was Lippman allowing it all to happen? What about his wife! his child! and Einstein! What if Einstein was getting up a lunch for them this very moment? *That* could be too!

"Oh, you Chosen People," said The Chief, "or do you pronounce it like in Chanukah, with a *choff*? Not so dumb, after all, am I? Aahh, who doesn't understand your God damn alphabet? You think we don't know the secrets you write on the outside of those salamis? You think we don't know the messages you send each other right on the butcher's window? 'Aleph, bays, gimmel, daled—chess tess, kiss mine ess!' Aahh, you Chosen People make me sick, if you want the truth! You stick your balls up over a pawnshop, and that's the last you ever see of them!"

"Nice turn of phrase," said Scully wryly.

"I'm not turning phrases, Scully! I'm speaking from experience!

I have been frisking people all my life. I have had my hand down in
the crotches of some of the worst criminals this country has ever
known. I have frisked niggers whose black you-know-whats are so
long they have to wear them twined around their legs and tucked
down into their socks, so that they don't trip and fall over them
and crack the roadways open with those big black hammerheads of
theirs! I probably know as much about balls as any law enforcement
officer in America — and I can tell you this, that for sheer weight,
the average Christian male — yes, the average '*shagetz*,' the old gray
shagetz who ain't what he used to be my friend — has got balls on
him that run one-point-eight times larger than the balls on the average Jew."

To this madness, to this idiocy, what could Lippman reply?

"Scully," said The Chief, "I do believe that our Doubting Tomashevsky here thinks I am speaking gibberish. He thinks he is listening to nothing but a dumb Christian cop, if you get my meaning.
How can we know anything you see, surrounded by cones instead
of Cohens, eh, Tomashevsky? Well, we'll just see about that. Scully,
my scale."

"The scale!" called Scully, and Scoop was there, carrying a bathroom scale beneath his normal human arm.

The Chief ran his boot across the floor. "Surface even enough
for you?" he asked Lippman, and set the scale down. Quickly then
he removed his OLDE CORNE jacket, the gun belt, and his pajamas,
and but for his cap and his boots was naked. "How's your aunt,
by the way?" he asked Scoop. "Tell her she just knocked us dead
last week with her rendition of 'There'll Be Moonbeams Over The
White Cliffs of Dover.' Anything she sings with 'moon' in it, and you
know it's destined for The Hit Parade. Wait'll she does 'Racing With
The Moon.' I pity poor Vaughn Monroe."

Then, as though to a squad of invisible subordinates, The Chief
called out, "All *ready* then," and placing a hand on either knee,
assumed a semi-squatting position directly over the center of the
scale. "By the numbers: one! two! three! ho!" And in three swift
graceful maneuvers he had brought himself to a point where his
scrotum was resting smartly on the scale. To Lippman he said,
"Look, this is no guess-my-weight contest, Tomashevsky. Get down
here and read for yourself what it says!"

Reluctantly, Lippman beheld The Chief's member. A sausage-
like object, without a head. He told himself, "I am sleeping. It is just
a matter of waking up, and then off to the office, to audition that

blind xylophonist. Yes, I am in a trance, that's all. Somebody has hypnotized me — by mistake. Maybe I went to some show where they called for a person to come up out of the audience and I was the one who let himself get hypnotized. No wonder I don't get what is happening. Probably I am walking around up on a stage somewhere, crowing like a rooster. I am under a spell — "

"Kneel!" ordered The Chief.

"Look, please," cried Lippman. "No disrespect meant — but I am on my way to an important meeting. I am not in a trance and won't be! I'm on my way to Albert Einstein! To be his talent scout! 'Can You Stump Einstein?' That will be the name of the program — you'll soon be hearing it over the radio, and that'll be because of me, and I'll send you free tickets, I promise — so let me go, what do you say, because he is waiting for me *right now* — don't you understand, Albert Einstein the world-famous genius is waiting for me *right this minute!*"

But when The Chief, having listened with hooded eyes to this plea, called to Scoop for his pistol, Lippman fell to the floor. Because what if the blanks weren't blanks after all? *What if!* "One pound," he said, gagging, "and four ounces."

"Correct! A one-pound-four-ounce pair of balls — and nothing else is resting on the scale. See for yourself. Take a good long look. Just *pure* balls."

"Yes — yes — "

"Righto then. By the numbers!" snapped The Chief, and in three movements brought himself back up to attention. "All right," he said to Lippman, "your turn."

"Oh, please — my wife! my child!"

"Boo-hoo," said Scully, "his wife, his child."

"Listen, you," said The Chief, "perhaps I ought to remind you that I am a police officer. I don't happen to go around taking my clothes off in front of people for no good reason. I thought this might have occurred to you by now."

"But neither do *I* — !"

"And I don't intend," continued The Chief, "for you to go out into the street, Big Mouth, and start *telling* everyone that I do, either. I warn you, either you remove your own clothes now, or you will find yourself under arrest not only for Reckless Accusation Against Christians, but for Peeping-Tomism, a crime that does not go down very well with the citizens of this community. Undress, like a man! Look at me, in a hat and shoes, and am I complaining? Am

I watering the flowers with my tears? Oh damn it, point that God damn pistol at him, Scoop — and when you just can't take any more, fire — okay? I really leave it up to you; I've had it with this son of a bitch."

Scoop said, "Gee," and lifted the pistol out of the holster. "This is really a lot of responsibility for me, isn't it?"

Lippman began to disrobe.

"Appears to be happening, after all," muttered Scully, removing his eyeshade and rubbing his tired eyes with his hands. "Doesn't it?"

Meanwhile The Chief, momentarily relieved of the burdens of his office, did a dozen quick deep knee bends and took a fast turn around the room, dancing nimbly on his feet and smashing out with his fists at an imaginary punching bag. As he shadowboxed past Scoop, he found a moment to help him aim the gun — "Sight through here, see" — and then asked, "By the way, how's Ted Collins, Scooper?"

"Oh, Aunt Kate says he sends his best to you, Chief."

"Good — send them my love, will you? Best God damned announcer in radio, Ted Collins. I'm telling you, Scoop, there isn't a person in this country that doesn't owe your Aunt a deep debt of gratitude for having a fellow as fine as Ted Collins as her announcer. 'And here's Kate Smith singing "God Bless America."' Christ, I get the God damn chills when he says that!"

"Well, gee, I'll tell them, Chief."

"And just fire away whenever you please, Scoop. You be the judge, all right? Since apparently in his eyes I'm too stupid or too brutish or too prejudiced to be the local law enforcement officer. Well let's see how he likes it now, with a mentally defective soda jerk in charge!"

"Boy," said Scoop, "between my scoop and this gun, I really am something — I really am just about as unique as you can get at my age!" and in his excitement fired into the floor. Out of the pistol came a bullet! "Oh gee, Mr. Scully," he said, "I'll pay for that from my salary, sir. Gee, I thought they were blanks!"

So did *I*! thought Lippman, now naked. But no — a real bullet, powder on the inside, metal on the outside, penetrated the floor only inches from his toes. A hole that could have been in him! He might just have been murdered — by a soda jerk! Yes, himself murdered, his child poisoned, his wife attacked, beaten, mutilated . . . Why? *But why not?*

And down he went onto the scale.

"Fault!" called Scully—and turned to Scoop, who was sighting the pistol. "He gets two faults, you idiot—*two!*"

Scoop reddened, looking shamefully at the hole he had made in the floor. "I'm just so darn mentally defective, I can't remember anything, it seems. Two faults. Right. Two faults—and these aren't blanks. Okay—I think I'm ready now."

Scully had now taken Lippman's shoulders between his hands and moved him slightly to his left. "You have to be centered," he said, in a surprisingly gentle voice, "or you're going to do your own cause an injustice. You just are not going to get a true reading otherwise—and I really wouldn't want to see you subjected to this kind of humiliation a second time."

Lippman's ears pointed—had he heard right?

Scully whispered, "It's your fear that arouses his fury."

"What's that?" demanded The Chief.

"I was just informing him of his constitutional rights, Chief."

"Sure you weren't impugning my honor in some disgusting way, Scully? Casting doubt upon my manliness, *peut-être?*" asked The Chief, wiggling up to Scully and flexing his pectoral muscles. "You Yankee Doodle Dandy! You vixen! You fake!"

"Can it," said Scully.

"I'll can *you*, Scull! I'll tell Roger on you, and we'll *both* can you! But good, *Mr. International Ice Cream Cartel!* You want scenes, Dolly Madison, I'll give you a scene! I'll give you what you bargained for, you Yankee vixen—and *then* some!"

Scoop had by now fallen to the floor from laughter—and gone into some kind of fit.

Scully said to Lippman, "Every time The Chief does his female impersonation, the lad gets his epilepsy. I happen to love the routine myself, but I really don't think it's fair to the boy. The Chief worked his way through maritime school, you know, as a female impersonator. And the truth is that when he dresses up in high heels and rouge, I'm telling you, you could scream. When he sits down at the bar at the Elks club, opens his handbag and lights up a cigarette—well, you actually have to gasp, when you remember that he still holds the record for yards gained rushing at the Maritime Academy."

"And pass interceptions in a single game," said The Chief, looking up from the floor, where, matter-of-factly, he had pinned the thrashing body of the soda jerk beneath his knees and stuffed the boy's ice cream scoop into his mouth to prevent him from swallowing his tongue. "Come on around now, Scooper," said The Chief. When finally the boy's pupils rolled back into view, The Chief said, "The Chief is sorry, sweetheart," and removed the scoop from the soda jerk's mouth.

"It's . . . it's . . . it's when you say 'Roger,'" drooled the depleted boy, "that I really go wild. I mean, I get epileptic over nothing, so imagine how I feel about you."

"Oh, come on, Scoop, that's just a line from a popular song, you know that as well as I do. Sometimes," he said, turning up to Scully, "I think it is the 'jerk' in soda jerk that has caused him to be what he is, and not the other way around; and isn't it true that even before his unfortunate birth he had been tentatively named Scoop by his parents, in the expectation that he would turn out the way he did?"

"Utshay, upshay, amitday," said Scully angrily. "The idyay."

"The Id yay, the Ego nay, eh Scull?" said The Chief sardonically, and turned back to the boy beneath him. "Scoop, Roger doesn't event exist, so how can he cause your epilepsy? How can nothing be the cause of something? Roger, as you well know, is an invention, an imaginary character to whom I make reference in the course of my impersonation. He's just part of the game, part of the general fun, the horsing around that makes existence tolerable."

"No," said Scoop, beginning to cry. "Roger is *real*!"

"Scooper, you listen to the Edgar Bergen show with us on Sunday nights, you know the score, boy. Is Mortimer Snerd 'real'? Is Charlie McCarthy 'real'?"

"Sure!"

"No, you fucking defective! They're dummies! They're Edgar Bergen's dummies! Don't you even know that? Their heads are wood — like yours!"

"Can it!" shouted Scully.

"Well, I am not taking the rap for his epilepsy! Suppose he someday swallows his tongue and his scoop and all that God damn tapioca pudding that he has instead of a brain, and chokes to death and dies when I say 'Roger' — am I going to get hauled off to jail and charged with murder? Would you call that 'justice'? Because of *his* narrow literalism, I should be punished? I will not be held responsible for the inability of some mental nitwit to open himself out to the simplest God damn playfulness. He has absolutely no feeling for ambiguity whatsoever — and as for a genuine work of art, he wouldn't know one if he fell over it! He thinks Irony is an industrial town in Pennsylvania. He thinks Frivolity is some guinney seaside resort! Look," he said, turning once again to Scoop, "Roger is a man's name, but it is *also* a word used as a response to a radio communication, meaning that the message sent has been received or understood. Now, if you can't fathom that—which," he said, shooting a glance up to Scully, "doesn't require that much fathoming—but if you're unable to respond appropriately to something so simple as that, how are you going to begin to enjoy the times we live in, which just happen to be the richest comic era since the Ice Age—since the glaciers themselves!"

"And so," said Scoop, sniveling, "I suppose that means I'm not my Aunt Kate's nephew either, according to you."

Here The Chief completely lost control. "Kate Smith! Kate Smith! I'm about up to here with Kate Smith, Scully!"

Scully said, "Scoop, get up from the floor. You're over there, with the pistol."

"But I am too Kate Smith's nephew! Her *favorite* nephew!"

"Oh," said The Chief, "shut your literal ass and point the gun."

"Then you didn't mean at all what you said before about Ted Collins," wept Scoop. "You were just teasing me again. Teasing a mental defective!"

"Oh shit," cried The Chief. "You're Kate Smith's favorite nephew—all right? And so is every fat-assed housewife in this town her sister. What a place—every woman over two hundred pounds singing 'When The Moon Comes Over The Mountain' out the window, morning, noon, and night!"

Here Scoop jumped to his feet and challenged The Chief. "And what harm may I ask is done to you as a consequence? You are an artiste! You are a privileged person! But consider for a moment the fat and the stupid, objects of ridicule in this life, and no more. Consider Scoop. How would you like to be a mental defective with some ridiculous metal contraption on the end of your arm instead of a five-fingered hand? Really, how can a man of your stature be so lacking in compassion?"

"Can it," whispered Scully to the soda jerk.

"Yes," said Scoop derisively. "Can it. Of course, Mr. Scully. We must can it. And can it and can it." He began to weep.

To Lippman, Scully said, "These glimpses we occasionally get of the sensitive, poetic youth he might have been had his seed come fully to fruition in his mother's womb—"

"I was ultimately ripped," said Scoop, his eyes gleaming with tears.

"Untimely," said Scully, gently correcting the boy. Then to Lippman, "See, he gets it wrong, because he's a defective. This lucidity lasts perhaps a moment or two, and then he slides back into being a defective again. Indeed, the particular poignancy of his condition arises as much from these flashes of lucidity, as from the hopeless imbecility itself. Which is why," he said, turning back to The Chief, "I trust you'll reassure him as to his family identity, so that we can then proceed."

"Kate Smith's nephew, Scooper," The Chief said. "That's who you are, kid — okay?"

Whereupon Scoop smiled with delight. "See, I'm unique after all!" and raising the pistol, pointed it between Lippman's eyes.

SPECIAL BULLETIN

We interrupt "Lippman the Talent Scout" to bring you an important news bulletin. Berchtesgaden, Germany. In the early hours of the morning throngs of cheering Germans carrying torches filled streets and squares from the Rhine to the Oder as radios blared forth the news that Chancellor Adolf Hitler has decided not to shave off his moustache. We repeat this special bulletin. Chancellor Adolf Hitler of Germany has announced to the German people that he has decided not to shave off his little moustache. Lights are reported to have burned all night long behind the starched white curtains of "The Eagle's Nest," Hitler's charming and spotless underground bunker, while the decision was being reached by the Fuehrer and his mistress, Eva Braun. It was learned that a decision as to whether Hermann Goering should go on a diet has been postponed. The announcement, speculated upon in the capitals of Europe for days, came to a frenzied nation at four-eighteen this morning. The Fuehrer is scheduled to make a major address to the German people tonight all about his moustache.

In the meantime, barbers known to have mentioned to customers that they thought Hitler might look nicer clean-shaven have been rounded up, blinded, branded and gelded, their shops confiscated, and their families are presently being tortured in ways that could make your hair curl. This last, the government reports, is part of a larger scientific experiment being conducted by the cosmetics industry of The Thousand-Year Reich to determine just what it is that does make hair curl. According to government spokesmen, if experiments continue to proceed successfully, old-fashioned "permanent wave" techniques will soon be a thing of the past.

We return you now to our regularly scheduled pogrom.

—Did his testicles come to rest than the three threw themselves flat upon the floor, chins resting up on the edge of the scale. They breathed on him in turn, first the icy breath of Scully, then the hot damp breathing of The Chief, and then the warm little puffs of excitement that came from the one-armed soda jerk. Scully said, "I don't want to call another genital fault, Chief, what with Trigger-Happy here, but it appears to me as though the Jewish contestant is now attempting to tip the scales with his penis—such," he added wryly, "as it is."

"Well," replied The Chief, "pecker and all (and cheat as they will), it is still six ounces under a pound, avoirdupois."

"Hey," said Scoop, "what in the world is the matter with his wee-wee maker? *See?*"

Lippman screamed when the cold metal touched his member.

"Good God," moaned The Chief, "it's only an ice cream scoop."

"I thought," said Lippman, "—the gun—"

"Come now, enough self-dramatization, what do you say, pal?"

"Bring on the Wailing Wall," said Scully, shaking his head. "Some kid brushes up against him with an *ice cream* scoop, and *he* starts screaming bloody murder. Bro*ther!*"

"As if the kid isn't self-conscious enough about the God damn thing, he has to draw even more attention to it!"

"Oh, well, their well-known charity toward Christians . . . Now, your question, lad?"

"His wee-wee maker," said Scoop, "it's all—blaaaah. Funnylike. Look."

And again Lippman cried out—this time it *was* the gun.

The Chief had had it. "You coward! You crybaby Yid coward!" and with a mighty swing of his boot, kicked the scale out from under Lippman's testicles. "Scooper!" he cried, and in the next instant had not only disarmed the soda jerk—two bullets being discharged in the process, one entering the floor, the other The Chief's shoulder—but with a swiftness that was awe-inspiring, jiujit-sued the young soda jerk—pinned Scoop's shoulders beneath his knees, grabbed hold simultaneously of his forearm, and in one savage rising and falling motion, sent the ice cream scoop straight up his own rectum. A quiver, a spasm, passed through the muscles of his body; a look of pain rose in his eyes excruciating to behold. Blood from The Chief began to flow down Scoop's forearm, blood a violet color. It coursed steadily out of him, whereas in his shoulder there was as yet only a button of bright red made by the bullet.

Even Scully was shaken, could only mutter, "Can . . . can . . ."

To which The Chief replied — "And just what do you call this, Scull! You want literal, all right, I'll give you literal! You want life instead of art, all right, you Yankee son of a bitch, HERE IT IS! I'm 'canning it,' you bastard — me and the Scooper are *canning it*! Scoop," he cried to the boy, "work that lever, you defective son of a bitch, and Scully, get a banana split plate and a spoon — you heard me, *get it!* Because I have had just about enough of this fellow's Jewish shit! Now he is going to eat some of mine! And with a spoon, as the saying used to go. Work that lever, Scooper — and work it so I *feel* it!"

"I'm trying, sir — "

"Pull it out of me, boy! Get it from up — oww! — oww! — where it's really the shitty shit! We'll teach this mocky to make a mockery of the human prick! See, the prick the Good Lord gave everybody else in the world, that isn't good enough for them — no, they have to make a little *improvement* on it! They have to make a little improvement on *everything*! Oh, they are very high and mighty know-it-alls, they are — " and The Chief swooned, the effect of the steady loss of his blood. When he resumed his speech it was difficult to follow the logic of what he was saying.

And it appeared that the boy's artificial limb *had* gone out of commission. The Chief pleaded for Billy to extract "two hot dips" but nothing was forthcoming. "I'm stuck," he said shamefully.

"Kill the metaphor!" The Chief screamed in his delirium. "Slaughter the simile! Fuck the fable! Piss on the parable once and for all! I'm being driven literal, Scully — I'm going stark raving literal — at last!"

"Mr. Scully, sir, I'm afraid I really am stuck, sir — "

Scully had drawn back from the blood seeping toward his shoes; he was holding in his hand a banana split plate but ceased shining it upon his apron when he heard the news that Billy's prosthesis had become immobilized. "Jesus, go find a substitute soda jerk on a Sunday!" And so he waded in, and from a position behind The Chief pushed up with his shoulder on The Chiefs buttock, in an attempt to free him from the scoop.

"Well," he said to Lippman, "what are you going to do, stand there gaping? This man has gone berserk and is losing blood, for Christ's sake! Look, this is no time for petty religious differences. This is serious! Either you're an American or you aren't! Put your God damn Jewish shoulder to the wheel!"

But Lippman was feverishly pulling on his underwear and scurrying about after the rest of his clothing, some of which was already wet with The Chief's blood. Then he saw the pistol. Scoop had dropped it. There it was. A deadly weapon. No joke. His for the taking. Why didn't he pick it up and blow their fucking brains out, once and for all?

CONTEST ANNOUNCEMENT

Is it even remotely possible that Einstein is a missing Marx Brother? If not, why did a man with a profile like Roosevelt's marry such an ugly woman? Why are ugly people put on earth, if not to make us laugh? But then why don't the Germans fall down in the streets laughing at that raving maniac instead of saluting him? Ask your friends what they think, get the whole gang talking about it. Are the glaciers really the funniest thing that ever happened? Or is Hitler? Or are the Jews? What is the funniest thing that *has* ever happened? (1) To you. (2) To any member of your family. Or (3) to mankind. Describe the incident in five hundred words or less and send it on in with the head off your neighborhood grocer. Tear at the neck, stuff in a cereal box, and send to this station along with your description of "The Funniest Thing That Ever Happened." Before you begin you might want to ask yourself these questions: Was the incident funny at the time, or only in retrospect? Do you want us to laugh "with" the people involved, or "at" them? Is the humorous aspect of the incident in good taste? (Contest hint: There is nothing funny about a person slipping on a banana peel — *unless he breaks his neck*. If he gets up and walks away, it is neither here nor there. But if he cracks his head open and is paralyzed in every limb for life, and also loses the powers of speech, sight, and hearing [and let's throw in taste and touch, just to make a point], and is then sued in the courts for cracking the concrete walk with his teeth [which he swallows, of course, and has then to be pumped out], and all of this as a result of slipping on a banana peel — *that's funny*.) At this stage of thinking about your subject, why not jot down on a piece of paper every idea that occurs to you, whether you intend to use it or not. One idea often suggests another and better one. After a reasonable amount of reflection (have your Mom time you), you will probably have more than enough material to enter our contest. Don't forget, your entry *and* the head postmarked no later than midnight! Judges' decision will be final!

—Chasing him, what blood he still had in him trickling from his rectum, and dragging behind the imprisoned soda jerk, as though he were some one-armed appendage growing from The Chief's body, as though he were some refined extension of The Chief's innards. Howling with pain, The Chief nonetheless took careful aim with the pistol. The bullet he fired struck Lippman right-between-the-eyes. But of course, right-between-the-eyes is the wrong place to shoot a Jew because that is where his nose begins. It is like shooting a Christian in his Bible or his Crucifix. We all know the stories of the Christian soldier in his foxhole whose life is saved because the enemy bullet aimed for his heart strikes instead against the religious keepsake given him by his mother or his minister before going off to war — and is thus deflected from its target. Well, the same with a Jew's nose. The bullet ricocheted off the bridge of Lippman's nose and flew in a direct line backward to its source. There it struck the bullet already lodged in The Chief's shoulder (remember?) and drove it down into his heart, killing the Gentile bastard on the spot. Thus the expression "Jewed down."

What next? Bewildered momentarily by the impact of a .38-caliber bullet on what was, in certain ways, only a nose, Lippman did not at first realize that he was still missing a wife and a child. What had become of those two while he was being held prisoner by Scully, The Chief, and Scooper? And who is this "Scully" anyway? Why is he one thing one moment and something else the next? Why is anybody, for that matter? What did The Chief mean when he called Scully "Mr. International Ice Cream Cartel"? Anything whatsoever? And what use will Lippman's nose be to him now that he knows it is bullet-proof? Will it prove beneficial in his search for his wife and his child? Will it be good for business? What humiliations have Mrs. Lippman and the child been forced to submit to? Or could it be that they are safely in hiding somewhere — could it be, in fact, that the clever child was only *pretending* to be poisoned by the ice cream, and has taken the occasion to elope, as it were, with his beloved mother? And what of Einstein? Will "Can You Stump Einstein?" forever remain no more than a program in Lippman's imagination? How can he proceed to Princeton, where the famous scientist may well be awaiting his visit, while his child is at large with his wife? And then too, there is the small matter of a ritual murder rap. What of that crowd gathering around The Chief's dead body, those angry citizens of Scully muttering amongst themselves, "Yep, Jewed him right down — in cold blood!" For the startling conclusion to this latest adventure in the life of Milton Lippman, Talent Scout! tune in to this same wavelength tomor-row — till then, to all those out there "Beyond the Pale," good night, brethren, and sweet dreams!

Electricity

FRANCINE PROSE

Francine Prose (1947–): *Francine Prose was born and raised in Brooklyn and educated at Harvard. She is the author of nine novels, including* Judah the Pious *(winner of the Jewish Book Council Award),* Household Saints, Bigfoot Dreams, Primitive People, *and* Hunters and Gatherers; *two collections of short stories,* Women and Children First *and* The Peaceable Kingdom; *and a volume of novellas,* Guided Tours of Hell. *She has taught at the University of Arizona, Harvard, Sarah Lawrence, the Iowa Writers' Workshop, Johns Hopkins, and the Bread Loaf and Sewanee Writers' Conferences. Francine Prose has received many grants and awards, including a Guggenheim fellowship and a Fulbright. Her essays, reviews, and stories have been published widely, in the* New Yorker, *the* New York Times, *and the* Yale Review, *among other places, and her fiction has been reprinted in* Best American Short Stories. *After living for many years in upstate New York, she now lives in New York City with her husband, artist Howie Michels, and their sons.*

Anita sails the baby over her head. "Earth to Spaceship Bertie," she says. "Earth to Spaceship Bertie. Can you read me?"

The baby's laugh sounds forced, like Johnny Carson's when he's blown a joke. Last week she caught Bertie practicing smiles in the mirror over his crib, phony social smiles for the old ladies who goo-goo him in the street, noticeably different from his real smile. It occurs to her that the baby is embarrassed for her. Lately she's often embarrassed for herself. This feeling takes her back fifteen years to her early teens, when she and her parents and her younger sister Lynne used to go places—Jones Beach, Prospect Park—and she'd see groups of kids her own age. At the time she had felt that being with her family made her horribly conspicuous; now she realizes that it probably made her invisible.

The house is quiet. Now since she's back is the first time Anita can remember being in her parents' home without the television going. She thinks of the years her father spent trailing her and

Lynne from room to room, switching lights off behind them, asking who they thought was paying the electric bills. Yet he never turned the TV off; he'd fall asleep to the *Late Show*. Now the TV is dark, the house is lit up like a birthday cake, and her father is down in the finished basement, silenced by the acoustical ceiling as he claps his hands, leaps into the air, and sings hymns in praise of God and the Baal Shem Tov.

In the morning, when Anita's father goes off to the *bet hamidrash,* the house of study, Anita and her mother and the baby watch *Donahue*. Today the panel is made up of parents whose children have run away and joined cults. The week Anita came home, there was a show about grown children moving back in with their parents. It reminds Anita of how in high school, and later when she used to take acid, the radio always seemed to play oddly appropriate songs. Hearing the Miracles sing "What's So Good about Goodbye?" when she was breaking up with a boyfriend had made her feel connected with lovers breaking up everywhere. But now she hates to think that her life is one of those stories that make Donahue go all dewy-eyed with concern.

The twice-divorced mother of a Moonie is blaming everything on broken homes. "Don't you ever become a Moonie," Anita whispers, pressing her lips against the back of the baby's neck. Another mother is describing how her daughter calls herself Prem Ananda, wears only orange clothes, has married a boy the guru's chosen for her, and, with her doctorate in philosophy, works decorating cakes in the ashram bakery.

"Cakes?" says Anita's mother. "That's nothing. Only my Sam waits till he's fifty-seven to join a cult. After thirty-three years of marriage, he'll only make love through a hole in the sheet."

"A hole in the sheet?" Repeating this, Anita imagines Donahue repeating it, then realizes: incredibly, she and her mother have never talked about sex. Not ever. Imagining her mother on Donahue, Anita sees only close-ups, because if the camera pulled back, it would see up her mother's housedress to where the pale veined thighs dimple over the tops of her support hose.

Anita goes over and hugs her mother so hard that Bertie, squeezed between them, squawks like one of his bath toys. The baby starts to cry, her mother starts to cry, and Anita, not knowing what else to do, presses Bertie against her mother and pats and rubs them as if trying to burp both of them at once.

Anita takes nothing for granted. When she lifts her foot to take a step, she no longer trusts the ground to be there when she puts it down. She used to say that you could never really tell about people; now she knows it's true. She never once doubted that Jamie loved her, that he wanted the baby. When he came to visit her and Bertie in the hospital and began crying, she was so sure it was from happiness that she literally did not hear him say he'd fallen in love with somebody else.

She'd made him repeat it till he was almost shouting and she remembered who this Lizzie was: another lawyer in his office. At a garden party that summer Lizzie had asked to touch Anita's belly.

Just as Jamie was offering to move out of the house they had rented for its view, for their vision of children standing at the Victorian Bay window watching boats slip up the Hudson, a nurse wheeled the baby in, in a futuristic clear plastic cart.

"Spaceship Bertie," said Jamie.

Anita's sister Lynne says that men do this all the time: Jamie's acting out his ambivalence about fatherhood, his jealousy of the mother-infant bond. This sounds to Anita like something from *Family Circle* or *Ladies' Home Journal*. Lynne has read those magazines all her life, but now that she's going for her master's in women's studies, she refers to it as "keeping up." Lynne can't believe that Anita never had the tiniest suspicion. A year ago, Anita would have said the same thing, but now she knows it's possible. Whenever she thinks about last summer, she feels like a Kennedy-assassination buff examining the Zapruder film. But no matter how many times she rewinds it, frame by frame, she can't see the smoking gun, the face at the warehouse window. All she sees is that suddenly, everyone in the car starts moving very strangely.

Anita's mother believes her. Overnight, *her* husband turned into a born-again Hasid. Perhaps that's why she hardly sounded surprised when on the day she and Anita's father were supposed to drive up to Nyack to see the baby, Anita called to say that she and Bertie were coming to Brooklyn. Over the phone, her mother had warned her to expect changes. Daddy wasn't himself. No, he wasn't sick. Working too hard as usual, but otherwise fine. Her tone had suggested something shameful. Had he, too, fallen in love with somebody else?

Pulling into her parents' driveway, Anita thought: He looks the same. He opened the door for her and waited while she unstrapped Bertie from his car seat, then sidestepped her embrace. He'd never been a comfortable hugger, but now she missed his pat-pat-pat. She held Bertie out to him; he shook his head.

"Bertie, this is your grandpa," she said. "Grandpa, this is Bertie."

"Has he been circumcised?" asked her father.

"Of course," said Anita. "Are you kidding? My doctor did it in the hospital."

"Then we'll have to have it done again," said her father. "By a *mohel.*"

"Again!" yelled Anita. "Are you out of your mind?"

Attracted by the noise, her mother came flying out of the house. "Sam!" She grabbed the baby from Anita. "Can't you see she's upset?"

The commotion had comforted Anita. Everything was familiar — their voices, the pressure of her mother's plump shoulder pushing her into the house, the way she said, "Coffee?" before they'd even sat down.

"I'll get it," said Anita. "You hold the baby." But her mother headed her off at the kitchen door.

"It's arranged a little different now," she explained. "Those dishes over there by the fridge are for meat. These here by the stove are for milk."

That night they couldn't eat till her father had blessed the half grapefruits, the maraschino cherries, the boiled flank steak, the potatoes and carrots, the horseradish, the unopened jar of applesauce, the kosher orange gelatin with sliced bananas. During the meal, Bertie began to fuss, and Anita guided his head up under her shirt.

"Is it all right if the baby drinks milk while I eat meat?" she asked. Her mother laughed.

"Edna," said her father, "don't encourage her."

Bertie cried when Anita tried to set him down, so she was left alone with her father while her mother did the dishes.

"What *is* this?" she asked him. "You never went to *shul* in your life. Aunt Phyllis and Uncle Ron didn't speak to us for a year because on the Saturday of Cousin Simon's bar mitzvah, you *forgot* — you said — and took us all to Rip Van Winkle's Storybook Village."

"I did forget." Her father laughed. "Anyhow, we didn't miss anything. Simon was bar-mitzvahed in the Reform temple. The church."

"The church," repeated Anita. "Dad, what's the story?"

"The story, Anita?" Her father took a deep breath. Then he said:

"Once upon a time, a jeweler was taking the subway home to East Flatbush from his shop on Forty-sixth Street. At Nostrand, he finally got a seat and opened his *Post* when he heard loud voices at the far end of the car. Looking up, he saw three Puerto Rican kids in sneakers, jeans, and hot pink silk jackets which said 'Men Working' on the fronts, backs, and sleeves. When he realized that the jackets had been stitched together from the flags Con Ed put up near excavations, he found this so interesting that it took him a while to notice that the kids had knives and were working their way through the car, taking money and jewelry from the passengers and dropping them into a bowling bag. Then he thought: Only in New York do thieves wear clothes which glow in the dark. The boys didn't seem to be hurting anyone, but it still didn't make the jeweler comfortable. He thought: Is this how it happens? One night you pick the wrong subway car, and bingo! you're an item in the morning paper.

"Halfway down the car, they reached an old lady who started to scream. Then suddenly, the lights began to flash on and off in a definite pattern: three long blinks, three short blinks, three long blinks. By the fourth sos the muggers had their noses pressed against the door, and when it opened at the station, they ran. 'Thank God, it's a miracle!' cried the old lady.

"Meanwhile the jeweler had his head between his knees. He was trying to breathe, thinking he must have been more scared than he'd known. Then he looked up and saw a young Hasidic man watching him from across the aisle.

" 'It wasn't a miracle,' said the Hasid. 'I did it. Follow me out at the next stop.'

"Normally, this jeweler wasn't the type to follow a Hasid out onto the Eastern Parkway station. But all he could think of was, had his wallet been stolen, he'd have had to spend all the next day at the Motor Vehicles Bureau replacing his license and registration. He felt that he owed somebody something, and if this Hasid was taking credit, keeping him company was the least he could do.

"On the platform, the Hasid pointed to a bare light bulb and said, 'Look,' The light blinked on and off. Then he waved at a buzzing fluorescent light. It blinked too. 'I lied before,' said the Hasid. 'It wasn't my doing. Everything is the rebbe's. . . .' "

Anita's father stopped when her mother came in, drying her hands. "Bertie!" Anita's mother cried, picking the baby up and waltzing him into the kitchen. "Don't listen to this nonsense! A whole life ruined for one blinky light bulb!"

"It wasn't the light," said Anita's father.

Anita wanted to ask if his story really happened or if he'd made it up as a metaphor for what happened. She thought: *Something must have happened.* In the old days, her father didn't make up stories. But she forgot her questions when she heard her mother in the kitchen singing "Music, Music, Music" to Bertie, singing "Put another nickel in, in the nickelodeon," sounding just like Teresa Brewer.

Now, five months later, watching the parents of cult members on *Donahue*, Anita decides that her father's story left out all the important parts. Such as: why he really joined. There's no overlooking the obvious reasons: old age, sickness, death. If they'd been Protestant and he'd converted to Catholicism, no one would have wondered why.

She remembers a weekend this past summer when Jamie was away on business—with Lizzie, she thinks now—and her parents came up to see her. Her father drove her to the supermarket to shop for their visit and for Jamie's return. At the checkout stand, the kid who packed their order insisted, over her father's protests, on wheeling the cart out and loading the bags into their—the old man's, the pregnant woman's—car. Like her father, Anita was angry at the kid. Couldn't he see that her father could have done it? Not for nothing did he swim fifteen laps at the JCC pool every Sunday morning. But the crazy thing was, for the whole way home, Anita was mad at her father.

Her father is still in shape. And despite all the rushing to *shul* every morning and from there to work, he seems pretty relaxed. What's hurting her family, Anita decides, is the unpredictability, the shaky sense that everyone is finally unreliable. What's bothering her mother is that the man she's shared her bed with for thirty-three years has suddenly and without warning rolled to the opposite side. She must wonder if the sheet with the hole in it has been there all along.

Anita wants to tell her mother that there's no guarantee; you can't know anything about anyone. She wants to ask: What's so strange about a man wanting to sing and dance his way into heaven? But if they've never even talked about sex, how can they talk about this?

Anita bundles Bertie up in so many layers that he does look like a spaceman, and takes him to the library. On the subway, she notices that the lights flash on and off. The train is almost empty and she thinks about muggers in hot pink Con Ed jackets, but feels that Bertie is a kind of protection. Babies are unpredictable, like crazy people; she's heard you can sometimes scare muggers away by pretending to be crazy.

The librarians in the Judaica section eye Bertie so suspiciously that he exhausts himself trying to charm them and falls asleep in Anita's arms. Juggling baby and purse, she pulls out some reference books on Hasidism and sits down.

She's surprised at how much she already knows, what she has picked up from growing up in New York, from college, reading, and sheer osmosis. She starts Martin Buber's *Tales of the Hasidim*, then decides she must have read it or else heard the stories somewhere. She thinks of Jamie's friend Ira who'd visited once a year from his Orthodox commune in Cambridge, bringing his own food in an Empire Kosher Poultry shopping bag. She can't remember him telling stories.

For information about her father's sect, she's directed to the microfilm section. The librarian hands her a flat box, then seeing that it's impossible for her to thread the machine while holding Bertie, gives her a sour smile and does it for her.

For some reason, they've microfilmed whole editions of the city papers. Anita likes flipping back through the pages; it's like reading a story when you already know the end, only eerier. Meanwhile she learns that fifteen years ago, her father's group came from Hungary via Israel to their present home in Brooklyn. In the centerfold of the *Daily News*, there's a photo of the rebbe walking from Kennedy airport to Brooklyn because his plane from Jerusalem had landed on the Sabbath, when he wasn't allowed to ride. Taken at night, the picture is blurred, hard to read. The rebbe is all white hair and white beard, Mr. Natural in a beaver hat. On the next page is an ad for leather boots from Best and Co. — thirty dollars, fifteen years ago, an outrageously low price.

Ironically, the reason Anita can't concentrate is that she's being distracted by the noise from the Mitzvahmobile parked on Forty-second Street, blaring military-sounding music from its loudspeakers. She pictures the Hasidim darting from one pedestrian to another, asking, "Excuse me, are you Jewish?"

One afternoon, not long after she and Jamie first fell in love, they were approached by the Mitzvahmobilers, and Jamie said yes, he was Jewish. They dragged him — literally dragged him — into the trailer. The weather was nice, and nothing in those days seemed like an imposition, so Anita had waited on the library steps till Jamie emerged, looking pale.

Apparently, the Hasidim had tried to teach him how to lay *tefillin*, but he just couldn't get the hang of it. He froze, his hands wouldn't work. Finally they gave up. They put the phylacteries in his hands, then covered his hands with theirs and just held them, one on his forehead, and one on his arm near his heart.

On Friday nights, Anita's father sleeps at the *bet hamidrash* so he won't have to travel on the Sabbath, and her sister Lynne comes for dinner.

As children, Anita and Lynne fought, as their mother says, tooth and nail. Now it's simpler: they love one another — so Anita feels disloyal for thinking that Lynne is just like Valerie Harper playing Rhoda. But it's true, and it's not just the curly hair, the tinted glasses, the running shoes, and the tight designer jeans. It's Lynne's master's thesis, "The Changing Role of Women as Reflected in Women's Magazines, 1930–1960." It's her job as a social worker in a family-planning clinic and her boyfriend Arnie, who's almost got his degree as a therapist and is already practicing on the Upper West Side.

Lynne and Anita kiss hello. Then Lynne puts her arms around their mother, who's stirring something at the stove, and hugs her for so long that Anita starts feeling uncomfortable. Finally she zeroes in on Bertie, ensconced in his yellow plastic recliner chair on the kitchen table.

"Look how he holds his head up!" says Lynne.

Bertie's been holding his head up since he was two weeks old, and Lynne's seen it, but Anita refrains from pointing this out. Together they set the table, then Lynne pulls her into a corner and asks what she hears from Jamie.

"Oh, he's coming to see Bertie tomorrow."

Lynne stares at Anita, trying to ascertain if this "means" anything. Then she gets her purse and starts rummaging around. She takes out a tortoiseshell case, brushes tobacco dust off it, and gives it to Anita, who knows what it is before she opens it: eye shadow, a palette of different colors.

"Thanks," says Anita. The gift moves her and reminds her of

what she's always known: her sister is less of a feminist or a Rhoda than a real magazine reader, a girl who believes in her heart that eye shadow can change your luck.

For Lynne, their mother has cooked the same company dinner she made when Anita first came home. But without their father's blessing, the meat tastes greasy, the potatoes lukewarm; the gelatin has a rubbery skin. His absence should free them, thinks Anita, but he's all they talk about, in voices so low he might as well be downstairs.

With Lynne's coaching, their mother talks, and Anita sees she's been wrong: her mother's unhappiness isn't philosophical, it's practical. Imagine being forced to start keeping a kosher home at the age of fifty-three! Two sets of dishes! The doctor says salting the meat is bad for her heart. The smallest details of life now have rules which Sam won't let her break; she has to take the train to Essex Street to buy special soap for him.

If it gets much worse, Lynne suggests, she might consider a trial separation.

"Who would it help?" their mother asks. "Would it make me happier? Would it make Daddy happier?"

"I doubt it," says Anita.

"What would make me happy," their mother says, "is for Daddy to turn back into his normal self."

Anita wonders what would make *her* happy. Lately she's not sure. Bertie makes her happy, but it seems important to remember: he'll grow up and leave her. If you can count on anything, she thinks, it's that.

She senses that Lynne is talking less about happiness than about punishment. Lynne feels that their father is responsible for their mother's troubles, just as Jamie is for hers. Anita thinks that no one's to blame for her parents' situation; and in her own case, she's partly at fault.

Her first mistake was to gain so much weight when she was pregnant. Why should Jamie have faith she'd lose it when her own doctor didn't? Now she has, but, clearly, it's too late.

Her second mistake was to quit her job, even if it was the lowest editorial job in the world, the slush pile at *Reader's Digest*. Most of the submissions were for "The Most Unforgettable Character I've Ever Met," and most of these had never done one unforgettable thing except die slowly of some horrible cancer. Jamie liked hearing about them; he said they made him feel better about *his* day. And after she quit and took to reading long novels — anything, so long as it went on for more than four hundred pages — it wasn't the same. She'd try to tell Jamie about the Baron Charlus or Garp's mother, and he'd be staring past her. Once, to test him, she said, "My doctor said it's going to be triplets," and he just kept gazing beyond her out the dark kitchen window at the lights moving slowly up the Hudson.

Which reminds her of her third mistake: they never argued. Lynne, who fights with Arnie over every little thing, has told her that she and Jamie were afraid of their anger. Maybe so. Even when Jamie told her he was leaving, Bertie was there, listening to what for him was their first conversation. How could they have fought?

Anita wonders what happened to that part of her that used to fight tooth and nail with Lynne. She imagines Jamie and Lizzie litigating over every avocado in the supermarket. It's the only way she can stand thinking of him in the supermarket with somebody else.

Once, visiting friends in Berkeley, Anita and Jamie went to an all-night supermarket for orange juice. They took a joint for the ride and got so stoned that, when they got there, they couldn't move. They just stood near the vegetable bins, talking, laughing, marveling over the vegetables, those California vegetables!

Once more, Anita feels like she's watching the Zapruder film. She's the only assassination buff who can't even handle a magnifying glass, who wouldn't know a smoking gun if she saw one.

Anita's wasted the morning trying to imagine her conversation with Jamie. She's afraid she'll have nothing interesting to say. She blames this on living in her parents' house, where nothing interesting ever happens. She feels that living there marks her as a boring person with no interesting friends she could have stayed with. But that's not true. She and Bertie would have been welcome in the editing room of Irene's SoHo loft, on the couch in Jeanie's Park Slope floor-through. But being home is easier, she doesn't have to be a good guest. If Bertie cries at night, her mother comes in and offers to sing him Teresa Brewer.

One thing she could tell Jamie is what she's noticed at the Pathmark: more and more people seem to be buying huge quantities of specialty items, whole shopping carts full of apricot yogurt, frozen tacos, Sprite in liter plastic jugs. She's heard that American families hardly ever sit down to dinner together. So who knows, maybe there are millions of people out there, each eating only one thing. She could tell him how she took Bertie to the park to see some other babies. He slept the whole time, leaving her with the other mothers, none of whom even smiled at her. At one point, a little boy threw sand at a little girl. The girl's mother ran over, grabbed the boy's ankles, and turned him upside down. Anita expected coins to rain out of his pockets like in the movies, but none did. After a while, the boy's mother came over, and, instead of yelling at the woman who was shaking her upside-down son, said, "I'm glad it's you and not me." Anita felt as if she'd stumbled in on a game already in progress, like polo or a new kind of poker with complicated rules which no one would stop to explain.

But the last thing she wants is to sound like some pitiful housewife drifting back and forth between the supermarket and the playground. She wonders what sort of lawyer Lizzie is. Corporate taxes, she hopes, but fears it's probably the most interesting cases: mad bombings, ax murders, billion-dollar swindles.

She's tempted to tell Jamie about her father, how for a week or so last month he'd been instructed by his rebbe: instead of saying grace, he should clap his hands whenever the spirit of thanksgiving moved him. In the hour and a half it took to eat—with her father dropping his silverware, clapping, shutting his eyes as if smelling something sweet—Anita tried to predict these outbursts, but couldn't; she thought of the retarded people one heard sometimes in movie theaters, shouting out randomly, for no reason. She could tell Jamie how her father came home in a green velvet Tyrolean hat with a feather; apparently, the rebbe had given out dozens of hats to illustrate his sermon: the righteous man must climb this world like a mountain.

But she knows that telling Jamie would only make her angry at him for not being around tomorrow when she'll need to tell him the next installment. Nor does it make her happy right now to think that Jamie knows her father well enough to know that in the old days, he wouldn't have been caught dead in a Tyrolean hat.

The obvious subject is Bertie. Everything he does interests her; she thinks he's a genius. Why can't she tell Jamie about his practiced smiles, about his picking up his own Cheerios? Why? Because what could be more pitiful than thinking that anyone cares if your five-month-old can pick up his own Cheerios?

Bertie's victory over Cheerios should be their victory. Instead, she can hardly talk about Bertie; it's as if she's accusing Jamie. Bertie should be the mortar cementing them; as it is, he's part of the wall.

When Jamie rings the doorbell, Anita half hopes that Bertie, who hasn't seen his father for two weeks, will not recognize him and scream. Bertie looks at Jamie, then at Anita, then at Jamie, then smiles a smile which anyone could tell is his real one.

Anita's mother says, "Jamie! There's apple cake in the fridge if you kids get hungry." Then she backs out of the room. It's so uncomfortable they could be high-schoolers dating—except for the presence of Bertie and the fact that Anita and Jamie didn't know each other in high school.

"Can we go for a walk somewhere?" Jamie is staring to the side of Anita's head, at Bertie. Anita feels as if he's asking Bertie out and is one of those guys who's scared to be alone with his date. She's the friend he drags along, the chaperone.

"Sure," says Anita. Bertie's wriggling so hard his feet jam halfway down the legs of his snowsuit and Anita has to thread them through. She knows she's making herself look incompetent, making the process of dressing Bertie look harder than it is.

On the way to the park she can't think of anything to say. She doesn't want to discuss specialty items at the Pathmark or the upside-down boy. Of course she's done this before, rehearsed whole conversations that turned out to be inappropriate. But never with Jamie.

The playground is chilly, almost deserted. In one corner, two five-year-old boys are playing soccer while their parents—all four of them in ponytails—hunker on the ground, passing a joint. There's a dressed-up Orthodox family sitting in a row on a bench. By the swings, a young mother says to her daughter, "Okay, ten more pushes and we're going home." And finally there are some boys— ten, eleven, twelve—playing very hard and punishingly on the jungle gym and slide, as if it's the playground equipment's fault that they've grown too big for it.

"When is Bertie going to be old enough for the slide?" asks Jamie.

"Tomorrow," says Anita.

The mother by the swings counts to ten, and when the little girl says "Ten more!" grabs her daughter's hand and pulls her out of the park. Jamie sits down on one of the swings and stretches his arms out for Bertie. Holding the baby on his lap, Jamie pushes off. Anita can't look till she reassures herself: she trusts Jamie that much—not to drop Bertie. She sits on the other swing and watches

Bertie, who is leaning forward to see where they're going before they get there.

"Look how he holds his head up," says Jamie. "That's my boy."

"He's been doing that for four months," says Anita.

Jamie trails his long legs in the sand and stops with a bump. "Anita," he says, "just what am I supposed to do? What do you want?"

Anita wonders what she does want. She's not sure she wants to be back with Jamie. Bertie or no Bertie, it's too late. Something's happened that can't be fixed. Basically, she wants what her mother wants: for everything to be the way it was before everything changed.

"I want to know one thing," she says. "Remember that garden party at Mel's?"

"What about it?" says Jamie.

Anita remembers a buffet of elegant, salty things — sun-dried tomatoes, smoked salmon — which by then she wasn't allowed to eat. "I want to know if you and Lizzie were already . . ." She thinks: If a woman could walk clear across a party to feel her lover's wife's belly, her lover's unborn child inside it, well then, you really can't know anything about people.

Jamie says, "Of course not," but in a tone that makes Anita suspect it began at that party, or thereabouts. She wonders: Did their fingers brush accidentally over a Lebanese olive? A long look near the pesto and sour-cream dip?

"It wasn't Lizzie." Jamie's swinging again, distractedly. "It wasn't you."

"Who was it?" she says. "Don't blame Bertie, he wasn't born yet."

"It wasn't the baby. It was me. Listen — " Jamie stops himself by grabbing the chain on her swing together with his. The seats tilt together crazily. "When I was in the seventh grade, there was a kid in my class named Mitchell Pearlman. One day we got to talking about our dads, and Mitchell said that his was a photographer. He'd been everywhere, done everything. Had he fought with the Mau Maus? Sure. Sipped tea with Queen Elizabeth? Of course. Lived with the Eskimos, crossed the Sahara on a camel? You bet.

"Naturally we thought he was lying till we went to his house for his birthday. The minute we met Mitchell Pearlman's father — mustache, jeans, big silver belt buckle — we began to think Mitchell was telling the truth. After the cake and ice cream, his father brought out the pictures of himself in front of the igloo, the camel, arm in arm with Jomo Kenyatta, dandling the baby Prince Charles on his knee. And for months after that, for years, I hated my own father. I wouldn't speak to him."

"So?" says Anita. "I don't get it."

"So, when Bertie was born, I suddenly thought: In a couple of years, he'll be me in the seventh grade. And I'll be my father. And he'll go out and find his own Mitchell Pearlman's father. And he'll hate me. I thought: We've made a terrible mistake! We should have waited to have Bertie till I was Mitchell Pearlman's father! Does this make any sense?" There are tears in Jamie's eyes.

Anita thinks: Not much. For one thing, the chronology's wrong. Jamie fell in love *before* Bertie was born. For another, Bertie isn't Jamie and Jamie isn't his father. Jamie's father owns a dry cleaners, while Jamie is a labor lawyer with interesting cases. She wants to shout at him that exchanging long looks with a lady lawyer over the pesto is nothing — nothing at all — like fighting with the Mau Maus. But she doesn't. She's beginning to see that her sister's right: this *is* something some men do. Jamie himself doesn't understand, any more than Mitchell Pearlman's father understood why he found it so easy to leave the wife and kids and take off across the Sahara.

She imagines Jamie ten years hence, taking Bertie out for the afternoon. He's one of those weekend fathers she never really noticed till she was pregnant, and then she saw them everywhere. She could always tell how uneasy it made them to take their kids places whole families went. Recently she read in the *Times*: there's a health club in Manhattan which, on Saturdays and Sundays, caters exclusively to single fathers and their children. Ten years from now, there will be hundreds of these places.

She imagines men and children lolling in a steamy pool, pumping exercycles, straining on Nautilus machines. There are no women in her vision, it's as if all the mothers have died of some plague. She hears the cries of the children, sees the shoulders of the fathers rounded as if from the weight of the children tugging their arms.

The only thing she can't picture is how Bertie will look in ten years' time.

For weeks, her father has been asking her to come to a service in his *shul*. "The worst that'll happen is that you'll have fun," he says. It's made Anita a little nervous, like having a Moonie ask her to go away for the weekend. But the day after Jamie's visit, she agrees. There's nothing but football on TV.

"Can me and Bertie sit in the same section?" she asks.

"Don't be smart," says her father.

When she comes downstairs in a turtleneck and good brown corduroy jeans, she sees him really suffering with embarrassment. She goes and changes into a long skirt from the back of her closet, Indian print from the sixties.

On the drive down Eastern Parkway, Anita and her father don't talk. Again she has the peculiar feeling of being on a date. There's not much traffic on this Sunday, and everything seems so slowed down that she's slow to notice: her father's whole driving style has changed. He used to zip around like a cabbie, teeth grinding, swerving, cursing. Now he keeps to his lane, he's got all the time in the world. His elbow is out the side window, and cold air is rushing into the car.

"Can you shut that?" says Anita. "The baby."

"Sure," says her father. "Sorry."

"What kind of service are we going to?"

"A wedding."

"Turn the car around," says Anita.

"Don't be stupid," says her father. "Would you have preferred a funeral? All right—next time, a funeral."

"What next time?" says Anita.

"You'll be interested," says her father. "The ceremony is outside, under the stars."

"Stars you can see from Crown Heights?" says Anita. "I'll be interested."

In the old days, her father used to start looking for parking places miles in advance. She remembers hours of accelerating, then falling forward as the brakes squealed in the search for a spot in Chinatown. Now as they pull up to the block in which hundreds of Hasidim are milling around, her father cruises smoothly into an empty space.

The short winter afternoon is darkening. The street lights come on. The air is crisp and clear. The men wear nearly identical black coats, the women's are of various subdued hues. Most of the women are in high, good leather boots which remind Anita of the ad on the microfilm. It's easy to spot the converts like her father in his fur-collared car coat, the young men in denim and down; it annoys her that several young women wear paisley skirts much like hers.

The crowd spills off the sidewalk, blocking the northbound lane, but the two cops parked in their squad car ignore it. Leaning on other cars, Puerto Rican kids in sweatshirts and down vests idly hump their girlfriends as they watch the Hasidim assemble. The wedding canopy is already up, held by four men who keep switching the pole from hand to hand so they can warm the free hand in their pockets.

Suddenly everyone's buzzing like bees. Anita's father leans forward and says, "The rebbe."

Anita stands on tiptoe. But from a quarter block away, the rebbe looks pretty much like the photo: Mr. Natural. That's another reason she could never join this sect: being female, she'd never get closer to the rebbe than this. She turns to say this to her father, but he's gone — drawn, she imagines, toward his rebbe.

The crowd buzzes again when the bride and groom appear. The bride's leaning on some women, the groom on some men. They both look ready to drop. When Anita gets a good look at the groom — gangly, skin the color of skim milk — she understands why the bride can hardly walk. How could anyone marry *that?*

Nearly rigid in his quilted snowsuit, Bertie's getting heavy. Anita holds him up though she knows he's too young to focus on the center of attention, too young to know there is a center. To Bertie, everything's the center: the scarf of the woman in front of him, his own inaccessible fist.

Anita thinks: the bride must be freezing. Maybe that's why she's so hunched over as the women lead her in circles around the groom. Under the veil, she could be anything — old, ugly, sick, some covered-up temple idol. No wonder the groom is so panicky!

Even with all the Hebrew prayers, the ceremony is over in no time. They always are, thinks Anita, except when people write their own. Real religions and even the state seem to know: if it drags on too long, somebody *will* faint. Anita and Jamie got married impulsively in a small town on the California-Nevada border. What she mostly remembers is sitting in a diner in Truckee, writing postcards to all their friends saying that she'd just been married in the Donner Pass by a one-armed justice of the peace.

Her thoughts are interrupted by cheers; the groom has broken the glass. Then bride and groom and wedding canopy disappear in the crowd bearing them — and Anita and Bertie — into the hall.

Just inside the door, the men and women peel off in opposite directions. Anita follows the women into a large room with a wooden dance floor surrounded by round tables, set with centerpieces of pink carnations in squat crystal vases and groupings of ginger ale and seltzer bottles.

No one's saving places or jockeying to be near friends. The ladies just sit. Anita stands for a minute or so, then sees two women beckoning and patting the chair between them, so she goes and sits down. She soon understands why the women have found places so quickly: it doesn't matter where they sit, no one stays put for more than two seconds. They kiss and gab, then get up, sit next to a friend at another table, kiss and gab some more. Meanwhile the waiters are weaving through with bowls of hot soup, shouting to the women to get out of their way. But no one's paying attention.

The woman to Anita's right is middle-aged and kind of pretty. She's Mrs. Lesser. When the waiter brings Anita's soup, Mrs. Lesser pushes it away so Anita won't spill it in her struggle with Bertie's zipper.

"Your first baby?" asks Mrs. Lesser.

"Yes," says Anita.

"I had my first when I was sixteen. Can you believe I'm a grandmother?"

Anita might not have thought it, but she can believe it; she doesn't know quite what to say.

"Can you believe it?" Mrs. Lesser puts her big face near Bertie's little one, and Bertie rewards her with his most radiant, sweetest, and most inauthentic social smile.

"Look at this baby smile!" Mrs. Lesser says to the whole table. "Look at this sweetheart!" It's Anita's introduction to the room at large, and all at once it's open season on Bertie. Mrs. Lesser gets up and someone else sits down and starts stroking Bertie's cheek.

These women have children and grandchildren of their own, thinks Anita. Why are they so interested? But they are, they're full of questions. How old is he? What's his name? Does he sleep through the night? Is he always so good?

Anita feels like Bertie's ventriloquist. She has to make an effort to speak in her normal voice as she says, "His name's Bertie. He's five months old. He can pick up his own Cheerios."

"Cheerios?" cry the women. "At five months? He's a genius!"

The partition separating the men's and women's sections stops a few feet from the ceiling. Anita's facing it when suddenly she sees three furry brown things fly up, then plummet, then fly again. Just as she figures out someone's juggling hats, she hears applause from the other side of the plywood.

With each course, a different woman is making Bertie smile and nibbling from whatever plate the waiter has put down. First comes stuffed derma, then a platter of thick roast beef, little round potatoes, canned peas. Anita picks up a forkful of peas. She isn't very hungry, it isn't very good. No one's eating much; even the fleshiest ladies are just tasting. But every woman who sits down offers to hold Bertie for Anita, or to cut her roast beef. They say to Bertie, "Too bad you can't eat roast beef, pussycat," and "Next year at this time you'll be munching little brown potatoes."

Slowly at first, the men begin dancing. Anita feels it through the floor before she hears it. Stamp, stamp. Soon the silverware is rattling, the peas are jumping on her plate. The stamping gets faster, there are shouts. Anita wonders if her father is dancing. Probably he is. The door between the two sections is open, children are running back and forth. No one would stop her from looking. But she doesn't, she just doesn't.

Singing, clapping, the men make their own music. The women have help. Two men come in with an accordion and a mandolin. The women dance sweetly in couples, a dance that seems part waltz, part foxtrot, part polka. Mrs. Lesser reappears, and when a sprightly gray-haired lady to the far side of her makes swaying motions with her arms, Mrs. Lesser says, "If you're asking, I'm dancing," and away they go. A tiny old woman approaches Anita and says, "Would the baby care to dance?"

All the women want to dance with Bertie. Young and old, they keep cutting in, passing him around. Anita catches glimpses of him, first with this one, then with that, sailing, swaying to the music, resting his cheek on their billowy breasts. When Mrs. Lesser sits back down, she asks where the baby is.

"Dancing," says Anita.

Mrs. Lesser cranes her neck. "He's smiling," she says. "He's the belle of the ball!"

Suddenly there's a whoop from the other room, and Anita sees the groom's head and shoulders over the partition. From the angle of his head, the stricken expression, she knows that this is the part where the men hoist the groom up in a chair and dance. Then the women gather and raise the bride's chair. The music gets louder, and the women begin circling the bride, dancing with such intensity that Anita goes and finds Bertie and takes him back.

At last the bride's head is nearly touching the ceiling. Above the partition, she and the groom look at each other. Anita wants to study this look. She thinks it's something she should pay close attention to. But she's only half-watching. Mostly she's concentrating on not dropping Bertie, whom she's holding up above her head.

"Look, sweetheart," she's saying. "Look at the lady in the chair!"

Bertie sings when he nurses, a sweet satisfied gulping and humming high in his nose. That night, after the wedding, Anita falls asleep while he's nursing, and his song turns into the song in her dream.

In her dream, Bertie's singing "Music, Music, Music" just like Teresa Brewer. He's still baby Bertie, but he's up on stage, smiling one of his phony smiles, making big stagey gestures like Shirley Temple or those awful children in *Annie*. One of these gestures is the "okay" sign, thumb and forefinger joined. The circle his fingers make reminds her of the Buddha. It reminds her of a Cheerio.

Anita wakes up laughing, wondering how a little baby could know words like "nickelodeon." She gets up, and without detaching Bertie from her breast, slips a bathrobe over both of them and goes downstairs. Except for her parents' bedroom, where earlier she heard her mother preparing for sleep, every room is lit up. In the kitchen, light is shining from around the edges of the cellar door. Anita and Bertie go down.

Opening the door to the family room, she sees her father sitting cross-legged on the cork-tiled floor. His eyes are shut and tears are shining on his cheeks. But he's not so out of it that he doesn't hear her come in. Looking up, he seems frail and embarrassed, an old man caught doing something he's not supposed to do.

Anita wants to apologize and leave. Then it dawns on her that she's not down there to bother him. There's something she wants to ask, but she's not sure what it is. She wants to ask why all the lights in the house are always on. She wants to ask who he thinks is paying the electric bills.

Anita's father stands up and dries his eyes with his palm. Then he says, "Hold up your hand."

Anita holds up her hand and he lifts his, palm facing hers, a few inches away. He asks if she feels anything.

She feels something. A pressure.

She remembers how when she was in labor with Bertie, she held Jamie's hand. Just before the nurses let her start pushing, she turned to Jamie and said, "I don't think I can do this." "Sure you can," he said, and squeezed her hand so hard she'd thought it was broken. By the time it stopped hurting, the contraction was over and she knew she could go on. Now she sees that Jamie didn't mean to hurt her. He was scared too.

Her father's hand is still a few inches away, but its grip feels as tight as Jamie's. She can almost feel electrons jumping over the space between them, electricity drawing them as close as she is to Bertie, who just at that moment lets go of her breast and sits up, watching them.

The Tale of a Kite

STEVE STERN

Steve Stern (1947–): *Steve Stern has written of himself that "his head . . . is an east Broadway shmoozerie populated with the denizens of a long vanished Yiddish bohemia." Born in Memphis, Tennessee, Stern was educated at Rhodes College and the University of Arkansas. His books include the novels* The Moon and Ruben Shein *and* Harry Kaplan's Adventures Underground; *story collections* Isaac and the Undertaker's Daughter, Lazar Malkin Enters Heaven *(which won the Edward Lewis Wallant Award), and* The Wedding Jester; *a collection of novellas,* A Plague of Dreamers; *and children's books* Mickey and the Golem *and* Hershel and the Beast. *His stories have appeared in* DoubleTake, The Quarterly, Tikkun, *and* Prairie Schooner. *Over the past thirty years Steve Stern has lived in London, in New Orleans, in Madison, Wisconsin, and on a rural commune in Arkansas. He now lives in Saratoga Springs, New York, where he teaches creative writing at Skidmore College.*

It's safe to say that we Jews of North Main Street are a progressive people. I don't mean to suggest we have any patience with freethinkers, like that crowd down at Thompson's Cafe; tolerant within limits, we're quick to let subversive elements know where they stand. Observant (within reason), we keep the Sabbath after our fashion, though the Saturday competition won't allow us to close our stores. We keep the holidays faithfully and are regular in attending our modest little synagogue on Market Square. But we're foremost an enterprising bunch, proud of our contribution to the local economy. Even our second-hand shops contain up-to-date inventories, such as stylish automobile capes for the ladies, astrakhan overcoats for gentlemen — and our jewelers, tailors, and watchmakers are famous all over town. Boss Crump and his heelers, who gave us a dispensation to stay open on Sundays, have declared more than once in our presence, "Our sheenies are good sheenies!" So you can imagine how it unsettles us to hear that Rabbi Shmelke, head of that gang of fanatics over on Auction Street, has begun to fly.

We see him strolling by the river, if you can call it strolling. Because the old man, brittle as a dead leaf, doesn't so much walk as permit himself to be dragged by disciples at either elbow. A mournful soul on a stick, that's Rabbi Shmelke; comes a big wind and his bones will be scattered to powder. His eyes above his foggy pincenez are a rheumy residue in an otherwise parchment face, his beard (Ostrow calls it his "lunatic fringe") an ashen broom gnawed by mice. Living mostly on air and the strained generosity of in-laws, his followers are not much more presentable. Recently transplanted from Shpink, some godforsaken Old World backwater that no doubt sent them packing, Shmelke and his band of crackpots are a royal embarrassment to our community.

Like I say, we citizens of Hebrew extraction set great store by our friendly relations with our Gentile neighbors. One thing we don't need is religious zealots poisoning the peaceable atmosphere. They're an eyesore and a liability, Shmelke's crew, a threat to our good name, seizing every least excuse to make a spectacle. They pray conspicuously in questionable attire, dance with their holy books in the street, their doddering leader, if he speaks at all, talking in riddles. No wonder we judge him to be frankly insane.

It's my own son Ziggy, the kaddish, who first brings me word of Shmelke's alleged levitation. Then it's a measure of his excitement that, in reporting what he's seen, he also reveals he's skipped Hebrew school to see it. This fact is as troubling to me as his claims for the Shpinker's airborne faculty, which I naturally discount. He's always been a good boy, Ziggy, quiet and obedient, if a little withdrawn, and it's unheard of that he should play truant from his Talmud Torah class. Not yet bar mitzvah'd, the kid has already begun to make himself useful around the store, and I look forward to the day he comes into the business as my partner. (I've got a sign made up in anticipation of the event: J. Zipper & Son, Spirits and Fine Wines.) So his conduct is distressing on several counts, not the least of which is how it shows the fanatics' adverse influence on our youth.

"Papa!" exclaims Ziggy, bursting through the door from the street—since when does Ziggy burst? "Papa, Rabbi Shmelke can fly!"

"Shah!" I bark. "Can't you see I'm with a customer?" This is my friend and colleague Larry Nussbaum, proprietor of Memphis Bridge Cigars, whose factory supports better than fifteen employees and is located right here on North Main. Peeling bills from a bank-roll as thick as a bible, Nussbaum's in the process of purchasing a case of Passover wine. (From this don't conclude that I'm some exclusively kosher concern; I carry also your vintage clarets and sparkling burgundies, blended whiskies and sour mash for the yokels, brandies, cordials, brut champagnes — you name it.)

Nussbaum winces, clamping horsey teeth around an unlit cigar: "Shomething ought to be done about thosh people," he mutters, and I heartily concur. As respected men of commerce, we both belong to the executive board of the North Main Street Improvement Committee, which some say is like an Old Country kahal. We chafe at the association, regarding ourselves rather as boosters, watchdogs for the welfare of our district. It's a responsibility we don't take lightly.

When Nussbaum leaves, I turn to Ziggy, his jaw still agape, eyes bugging from his outsize head. Not from my side of the family does he get such a head, bobbling in his turtleneck like a pumpkin in an eggcup. You'd think it was stuffed full of wishes and big ideas, Ziggy's head, though to my knowledge it remains largely vacant.

"You ought to be ashamed of yourself."

"But, Papa, I seen it." Breathless, he twists his academy cap in his hands. "We was on the roof and we peeped through the skylight: First he starts to pray, then all of a sudden his feet don't touch the floor . . ."

"I said, enough!"

Then right away I'm sorry I raised my voice. I should be sorry? But like I say, Ziggy has always been a pliant kid, kind of an amiable mediocrity. He's never needed much in the way of discipline, since he's seldom guilty of worse than picking his nose. Not what you'd call fanciful — where others dream, Ziggy merely sleeps — I'm puzzled he should wait till his twelfth year to carry such tales. I fear he's fallen in with a bad crowd.

Still, it bothers me that I've made him sulk. Between my son and me there have never been secrets — what's to keep secret? — and I don't like how my temper has stung him into furtiveness. But lest he should think I've relented, I'm quick to add, "And never let me hear you played hooky from Hebrew school again."

And that, for the time being, is that.

But at our weekly meeting of the Improvement Committee — to whose board I'm automatically appointed on account of my merchant's credentials — the issue comes up again. It seems that others of our children have conceived a fascination for the Shpinker screwballs, and as a consequence are becoming wayward in their habits. Even our chairman, Irving Ostrow of Ostrow's Men's Furnishings, in the tasteful showroom of which we are assembled — even his own son Hershel, known as an exemplary scholar, has lately been delinquent in his studies.

"He hangs around that Auction Street shtibl," says an incredulous Ostrow, referring to the Chasids' sanctuary above Klotwog's feed store. "I ask him why, and he tells me, like the mountains should tremble" — Ostrow pauses to sip his laxative tea — "'Papa,' he says, 'the Shpinker rebbe can fly.' 'Rebbe' he calls him, like an alter kocker!"

"Godhelpus!" we groan in one voice — Nussbaum, myself, Benny Rosen of Rosen's Delicatessen — having heard this particular rumor once too often. We're all of a single mind in our distaste for such fictions — all save old Kaminsky, the synagogue beadle ("Come-insky" we call him for his greetings at the door to the shul), who keeps the minutes of our councils.

"Maybe the Shmelke, he puts on the children a spell," he suggests out of turn, which is the sort of hokum you'd expect from a beadle.

At length we resolve to nip the thing in the bud. We pass along our apprehensions to the courtly Rabbi Fein, who runs the religious school in the synagogue basement. At our urging he lets it be known from the pulpit that fraternizing with Chasids, who are after all no better than heretics, can be hazardous to the soul. He hints at physical consequences as well, such as warts and blindness. After that nothing is heard for a while about the goings on in the little hall above the feed store.

What does persist, however, is a certain (what you might call) bohemianism that's begun to manifest itself among even the best of our young. Take for instance the owlish Hershel Ostrow: in what he no doubt supposes is a subtle affectation — though who does he think he's fooling? — he's taken to wearing his father's worn-out homburg; and Mindy Dreyfus, the jeweler's son, has assumed the Prince Albert coat his papa has kept in mothballs since his greenhorn days. A few of the older boys sport incipient beards like the characters who conspire to make bombs at Thompson's Cafe, where in my opinion they'd better off. Even my Ziggy, whom we trust to get his own haircut, he talks Plott the barber into leaving the locks at his temples. He tries to hide them under his cap, which he's begun to wear in the house, though they spiral out like untended runners.

But it's not so much their outward signs of eccentricity as our children's increasing remoteness that gets under our skin. Even when they're present at meals or their after-school jobs, their minds seem to be elsewhere. This goes as well for Ziggy, never much of a noise to begin with, whose silence these days smacks more of wistful longing than merely having nothing to say.

"Mama," I frown at my wife Ethel, who's shuffling about the kitchen of our apartment over the liquor store. I'm enjoying her superb golden broth, afloat with eyes of fat that gleam beneath the gas lamp like a peacock's tail; but I nevertheless force a frown. "Mama, give a look on your son."

A good-natured, capable woman, my Ethel, with a figure like a brick mikveh, as they say, she seldom sits down at meals. She prefers to eat on the run, sampling critical spoonfuls as she scoots back and forth between the table and the coal-burning range. At my sugges- tion, however, she pauses, pretending to have just noticed Ziggy, who's toying absently with his food.

"My son? You mean this one with the confetti over his ears?" She bends to tease his sidelocks, then straightens, shaking her head. "This one ain't mine. Mine the fairies must of carried him off and left this in his place." She ladles more soup into the bowl he's scarcely touched. "Hey, stranger, eat your knaidel."

Still his mother's boy, Ziggy is cajoled from his meditations into a grudging grin, which I fight hard against finding infectious. Sur- rendering, I sigh, "Mama, I think the ship you came over on is called the Ess Ess Mein Kind." Then I'm pleased enough with my joke that I repeat it, reaching across the table to help Ziggy bring the spoon to his mouth: "Eat, eat, my child!"

Comes the auspicious day of Mr. Crump's visit to North Main Street. This is the political boss's bimonthly progress, when he collects his thankyous (usually in the form of merchandise) from a grateful Jewish constituency. We have good reason to be grateful, since in exchange for votes and assorted spoils, the Red Snapper, as he's called, has waived the blue laws for our district. He also looks the other way with respect to child labor and the dry law that would have put yours truly out of business. Ordinarily Boss Crump and his entourage, including his hand-picked mayor du jour, like to tour the individual shops, receiving the tributes his shwartze valet shleps out to a waiting limousine. But today, tradition notwithstanding, we're drawn out of doors by the mild April weather, where we've put together a more formal welcome.

When the chrome-plated Belgian Minerva pulls to the curb, we're assembled in front of Ridblatt's Bakery on the corner of Jackson Avenue and North Main. Irving Ostrow is offering a brace of suits from his emporium, as solemnly as a fireman presenting a rescued child, while Benny Rosen appears to be wrestling a string of salamis. Harry Nussbaum renders up a bale of cigars, myself a case of schnapps, and Rabbi Fein a ready blessing along with his perennial bread and salt. Puffed and officious in his dual capacity as self-appointed ward heeler and committee chair, Ostrow has also prepared an address:

"We citizens of North Main Street pledge to be a feather in the fedora of Mayor Huey, I mean Blunt . . ." (because who can keep straight Mr. Crump's succession of puppet mayors?)

Behind us under the bakery awning, Mickey Panitz is ready to strike up his klezmer orchestra; igniting his flash powder, a photographer from *The Commercial Appeal* ducks beneath a black hood. Everyone (with the exception, of course, of the Shpinker zealots, who lack all civic pride) has turned out for the event, lending North Main Street a holiday feel. We bask in Boss Crump's approval, who salutes us with a touch to the rim of his rakish straw skimmer, his smile scattering a galaxy of freckles. This is why what happens next, behind the backs of our visitors, seems doubly shameful, violating as it does such a banner afternoon.

At first we tell ourselves we don't see what we see; we think, maybe a plume of smoke. But looks askance at one another confirm that, not only do we share the same hallucination, but that the hallucination gives every evidence of being real. Even from such a distance, it's hard to deny it: around the corner of the next block, something is emerging from the roof of the railroad tenement that houses the Shpinker shtibl. It's a wispy black-and-gray something that rises out of a propped-open skylight like vapor from an uncorked bottle. Escaping, it climbs into the cloudless sky and hovers over North Main Street, beard and belted caftan aflutter. There's a fur hat resembling the rotary brush of a chimney sweep, a pair of dun-stockinged ankles (to one of which a rope is attached) as spindly as the handles on a scroll. Then it's clear that, risen above the telephone wires and trolley lines, above the water tanks, Rabbi Shmelke floats in a doleful ecstasy.

We begin talking anxiously and at cross-purposes about mutual understanding through public sanitation, and so forth. We crank hands left and right, while Mickey Panitz leads his band in a dirge-like rendition of "Dixie." In this way we keep our notables distracted until we can pack them off (photographer and all) in their sable limousine. Then, without once looking up again, we repair to Ostrow's Men's Furnishings and convene an extraordinary meeting of the Improvement Committee.

Shooting his sleeves to show flashy cufflinks, Ostrow submits a resolution: "I hereby resolve we dispatch to the Shpinkers a delegate, with the ultimatum they should stop making a nuisance, which it's degrading already to decent citizens, or face a forceable outkicking from the neighborhood. All in agreement say oy."

The only dissenting voice is the one with no vote.

"Your honors know best" — this from Kaminsky, a greenhorn till his dying day — "but ain't it what you call a miracle, this flying rebbe?"

For such irrelevance we decide it also wouldn't hurt to find a new secretary.

En route across the road to the shtibl, in the company of my fellows, I give thanks for small blessings: at least my Ziggy was telling the truth about Shmelke. Though I'm thinking that, with truths like this, it's maybe better he should learn to lie.

We trudge up narrow stairs from the street, pound on a flimsy door, and are admitted by one of Shmelke's unwashed. The dim room lists slightly like the deck of a ship, tilted toward windows that glow from a half-light filtering through the lowered shades. There's a film of dust in the air that lends the graininess of a photogravure to the bearded men seated at the long table, swaying over God only knows what back-numbered lore. By the wall there's an ark stuffed with scrolls, a shelf of moldering books, spice boxes, tarnished candelabra, amulets against the evil eye.

It's all here, I think, all the blind superstition of our ancestors preserved in amber. But how did it manage to follow us over an ocean to such a far-flung outpost as Tennessee? Let the goyim see a room like this, with a ram's horn in place of a clock on the wall, with the shnorrers wrapped in their paraphernalia, mumbling hocus-pocus instead of being gainfully employed, and right away the rumors start. The yids are poisoning the water, pishing on communion wafers, murdering Christian children for their blood. Right away somebody's quoting the *Protocols of Zion*. A room like this, give or take one flying rebbe, can upset the delicate balance of the entire American enterprise.

Returned at least in body from the clouds, old Shmelke sits at the head of the table, dispensing his shopworn wisdom. An unlikely source of authority, he appears little more substantial than the lemon shaft pouring over him from the open skylight.

"It is permitted to consult with the guardian spirits of oil and eggs . . . ," he intones, pausing between syllables to suck on a piece of halvah; an "Ahhh" goes up from disciples who lean forward to catch any crumbs. "But sometimes the spirits give false answers." Another sadder but wiser "Ahhh."

When our eyes adjust to the murk, we notice that the ranks of the Shpinkers (who until now have scarcely numbered enough for a minyan) have swelled. They've been joined this afternoon, during Hebrew school hours no less, by a contingent of the sons of North Main Street, my own included. He's standing in his cockeyed academy cap, scrunched between nodding Chasids on the rebbe's left side. To my horror, Ziggy, who's shown little enough aptitude for the things of this world, never mind the other, is also nodding to beat the band.

"Home!" I shout, finding myself in four-part harmony with the other committee members. Our outrage since entering having been compounded with interest, we won't be ignored anymore. But while some of the boys do indeed leave their places and make reluctantly for the door, others stand their ground. Among them is Ostrow's brainy son Hershel and my nebbish, that never before disobeyed.

Having turned toward us as one, the disciples look back to their tsadik, who God forbid should interrupt his discourse on our account. Then Hershel steps forth to confront us, a pince-nez identical to Shmelke's perched on his nose. "You see," he explains in hushed tones, though nobody asked him, "figuratively speaking, the rebbe is climbing Jacob's Ladder. Each rung corresponds to a letter of Tetragrammaton, which in turn corresponds to a level of the soul . . ." And bubkes-bobkes, spouting the gibberish they must've brainwashed him into repeating. I look at Ostrow who's reaching for his heart pills.

Then who should pipe up but the pipsqueak himself, come around to tug at my sleeve. "Papa," like he can't decide whether he should plead or insist, "if they don't hold him down by the rope, Rabbi Shmelke can fly away to paradise."

I can hardly believe this is my son. What did I do wrong that he should chase after moth-eaten yiddishe swamis? Did he ever want for anything? Didn't I take him on high holidays to a sensible synagogue, where I showed him how to mouth the prayers nobody remembers the meaning of? That is, if they ever knew. Haven't I guaranteed him the life the good Lord intends him for?

Not ordinarily combative, when the occasion calls for it I can speak my mind. To the papery old man whom I hold personally accountable, I ask point-blank, "What have you done to my child?"

Diverted at last from his table talk, Rabbi Shmelke cocks his tallowy head; he seems aware for perhaps the first time of the presence among his faithful of uninvited hangers-on.

"Gay avek!" he croaks at the remaining boys. "Go away." When nobody budges, he lifts a shaggy brow, shrugs his helplessness. Then he resumes in a voice like a violin strung with cobweb, "Allow me to tell you a story . . ."

"A story, a story!" The disciples wag their heads, all of then clearly idiots.

The rebbe commences some foolishness about how the patriarch Isaac's soul went on vacation while his body remained under his father's knife. Along with the others I find myself unable to stop listening, until I feel another tug at my sleeve.

"Papa," Ziggy is whispering, Adam's apple bobbing like a golf ball in a fountain, "they have to let him out the roof or he bumps his head on the ceiling."

"Do I know you?" I say, shaking him off. Then I abruptly turn on my heel and exit, swearing vengeance. I'm down the stairs and already crossing Auction Street, when I realize that my colleagues have joined me in my mortification. I suggest that drastic measures are in order, and as my anger has lent me an unaccustomed cachet, all say aye.

They agree there's not a minute to lose, since every day we become more estranged from our sons. (Or should I say sons and daughters, because you can't exclude old Kaminsky's orphaned granddaughter Ida, a wild girl with an unhealthy passion for books.)

But days pass and Rabbi Fein complains that even with the threat of his ruler, not to mention his assistant Nachum (whom the boys call Knock 'em), he can't keep his pupils in Hebrew class. Beyond our command now, our children are turning their backs on opportunity in favor of emulating certifiable cranks. They grow bolder, more and more of them exhibiting a freakish behavior they no longer make any pretense to conceal. For them rebellion is a costume party. They revel in the anomalous touch, some adopting muskrat caps (out of season) to approximate the Chasid's fur shtreimel. Milton Rosen wears a mackintosh that doubles for a caftan, the dumb Herman Wolf uses alphabet blocks for phylacteries. My own Ziggy has taken to picking his shirttails into ritual tassels.

He still turns up periodically for meals, silent affairs at which even Ethel is powerless to humor us. For his own good I lock him in his bedroom after dinner, but he climbs out the window, the little pisher, and scrambles down the fire escape. "Not from my side of the family does he get such a streak of defiance," I tell Ethel, who seems curiously resigned. "I think maybe comes the fairies to take him back again," she says, but am I worried? All right, so I'm worried, but I'm confident that, once the Shpinkers have been summarily dealt with, my son will return to the fold, tail between legs.

Still the problem remains: what precisely should we do? Time passes and the Shpinkers give no indication of developing a civic conscience; neither do they show any discretion when it comes to aiding their blithering rebbe to fly. (If you want to dignify what he does as flying; because in midair he's as bent and deflated as he is on earth, so wilted you have to wonder if he even knows he's left the ground.) In response to their antics, those of us with any self-respect have stopped looking up.

Of course we have our spies, like Old Man Kaminsky who has nothing better to do than ogle the skies. He tells us that three times a day, morning, noon, and evening, rain or shine, and sometimes nonstop on Shabbos, Shmelke hovers above the chimneys. He marks us from a distance like some wizened dirigible, a sign designating our community as the haven of screwballs and extremists. We're told that instead of studying (a harmless enough endeavor in itself), the shiftless Shpinkers now spend their time testing various grades of rope. From the clothesline purchased at Hekkie's Hardware on Commerce Street, they've graduated to hawser obtained from steamboat chandlers down at the levee. They've taken to braiding lengths of rope, to splicing and paying them out through the skylight, so that Shmelke can float ever higher. Occasionally they might maneuver their rebbe in fishtails and cunning loop-the-loops, causing him to soar and dive; they might send him into electrical storms from which he returns with fluorescent bones. Sometimes, diminished to a mote, the old man disappears in the clouds, only to be reeled back carrying gifts — snuff boxes and kiddush cups made of alloys never seen on this planet before.

Or so says Old Man Kaminsky, whom we dismiss as having also fallen under Shmelke's mind control. We're thankful, in any case, that the Shpinkers now fly their tsadik high enough that he's ceased to be a serious distraction. (At first the yokels, come to town for the Saturday market, had mistaken him for an advertising ploy, their sons taking potshots with peashooters.) But out of sight isn't necessarily to say that the rebbe is out of mind, though we've gotten used to keeping our noses to the ground. We've begun to forget about him, to forget the problems with our young. What problems? Given the fundamental impossibility of the whole situation, we start to embrace the conviction that Shmelke's flights are pure fantasy.

Then Ziggy breaks his trancelike silence to drop a bombshell. "I'm studying for bar mitzvah with Rabbi Shmelke," he announces, as Ethel spoons more calf's foot jelly onto my plate. But while his voice issues the challenge, Ziggy's face, in the shadow of his academy cap, shows he's still testing the water.

Ethel's brisket, tender and savory as it is, sticks in my gorge. I want to tell him the tsadik's a figment of his imagination and let that be an end to it, but Ziggy's earnestness suggests the tactic won't work.

"What's wrong," I ask, clearing my throat with what emerges as a seismic roar, "ahemmm . . . what's wrong with Rabbi Fein?"

"He ain't as holy."

Directly the heartburn sets in. "And what's holy got to do with it?"

Ziggy looks at me as if my question is hardly deserving of an answer. Condescending to explain, however, he finds it necessary to dismount his high horse, cuffing his cap to scratch his bulbous head. "Holy means, you know, like scare . . . I mean sacred."

"Unh-hnh," I say, folding my arms and biting my tongue. Now I'm the soul of patience, which makes him nervous.

"You know, *sacred*," he reasserts, the emphasis for his own sake rather than mine.

"Ahhh," I nod in benign understanding, enjoying how his resolve begins to crack.

"That's right," pursues Ziggy, and tries again to fly in the face of my infernal tolerance, lacking wings, "like magic."

I'm still nodding, so he repeats himself in case I didn't hear.

"Oh sure, ma-a-agic," I reply, with the good humor of a parent introduced to his child's imaginary friend.

Flustered to the point of fighting back tears, Ziggy nevertheless refuses to surrender, retreating instead behind a wall of hostility. "You wouldn't know magic if it dumped a load on your head!"

You have to hand it to the kid, the way he persists in his folly; I never would have thought him capable of such high mishegoss. But when the admiration passes, I'm fit to be tied; I'm on my feet, jerking him by the scrawny shoulders, his head whipping back and forth until I think I'm maybe shaking it clear of humbug.

"I'll magic you!" I shout. "Who's your father anyway, that feeble-minded old scarecrow or me? Remember me, Jacob Zipper, that works like a dog so his son can be a person?" Then I see how he's staring daggers; you could puncture your conscience on such daggers, and so I pipe down.

I turn to Ethel cooling her backside against the hardwood icebox, an oven mitten pressed to her cheek. "So whose side are you on?" I appeal.

She gives me a look. "This is a contest already?"

But tempted as I am to make peace, I feel they've forced my hand; I cuff the boy's ear for good measure and tell my wife, "I don't know him anymore, he's not my son!"

Understand, it's a tense time; the news from the Old Country is bad. In Kiev they've got a Jew on trial for blood libel, and over here folks are grumbling about swarms of Hebrews washing onto our shores. Some even blame the wreck of the *Titanic* on the fact that there were Guggenheims on board, and right next door in Georgia comes the lynching of Leo Frank. It's a climate created by ignorance, which will surely pass with the coming enlightened age — when our sons will have proved how indispensable we are. But in the meantime we must keep order in our own house.

At the next meeting of the North Main Street Improvement Committee I propose that the time is ripe to act.

Ostrow and the others stir peevishly, their hibernation disturbed. "Act? What act?" It seems they never heard of fanatics in our bosom or the corruption of our youth.

"Wake up!" I exhort them. "We got a problem!"

Slowly, scratching protuberant bellies and unshaven jaws, they begin to snap out of it; they swill sarsparilla, light cigars, overcoming a collective amnesia to ask me what we should do.

"Am I the chairman?" I protest. "Ostrow's the chairman." But it's clear that my robust agitation has prompted them to look to me for leadership, and I'm damned if I don't feel equal to the test.

"Cut off the head from the body," I'm suddenly inspired to say, "and your monster is kaput."

At sundown the following evening the executive board of the Improvement Committee rounds the corner into Auction Street. There's a softness in the air, the stench of the river temporarily overwhelmed by the smell of potted chicken wafting from the windows over the shops. It's a pleasant evening for a stroll, but not for us, who must stay fixed on the critical business at hand. We're all of one mind, I tell myself, though yours truly has been elected to carry the hedge shears — donated for the deed by Hekkie Schatz of Hekkie's Hardware. Ostrow our titular chair, Nussbaum the treasurer, Benny Rosen the whatsit, all have deferred the honor to me, by virtue of what is perceived as my greater indignation.

This time we don't knock but burst into the dusty shtibl. As it turns out our timing is perfect: a knot of disciples — it appears that several are needed to function as anchors — are uncoiling the rope beneath the open skylight. Rising into the lemon shaft (now turning primrose), his feet in their felt slippers arched like fins, Rabbi Shmelke chants the Amidah prayer:

"Baruch atoh Adonoy, blessed art Thou, our God and God of our Fathers . . ."

The Shpinkers start at our headlong entrance. Then gauging our intentions by the sharp implement I make no attempt to hide, they begin to reel their rebbe back in. My colleagues urge me to do something quick, but I'm frozen to the spot; though Shmelke's descending, I'm still struck with the wonder of having seen him rise. "Decease!" cries Ostrow, to no effect whatsoever; then he and the others shove me forward.

Still I dig in my heels. Disoriented, I have the sensation that the room is topsy-turvy; above is below and vice versa. Standing on the ceiling as the rebbe is hauled up from the depths, we're in danger of coming unglued, of tumbling headfirst through the skylight. I worry for our delinquent sons, who now outnumber the Shpinkers, and in their fantastic getups are almost indistinguishable from the original bunch. Among them, of course, is Ziggy, elflocks curling like bedsprings from under his cap, perched on a chair for the better view.

Then the room rights itself. Holding the handles of the hedge shears, I could say that I'm gripping the wings of a predatory bird, its mind independent of my own. I could say I only hang on for dear life, while it's the shears themselves that swoop forth to bite the rope in two. But the truth is, I do it of my own free will. And when the rope goes slack — think of a serpent when the swami stops playing his pipe — I thrill at the gasps that are exhaled ("Ahhh") all around. After which: quiet, as old Shmelke, still chanting, floats leisurely upward again, into the primrose light which is deepening to plum.

When he's out of sight, my Ziggy is the first to take the initiative — because that's the type of person we Zippers are. The pistol, he bolts for the open window followed by a frantic mob. I too am swept into the general exodus, finding myself somehow impelled over the sill out onto the fire escape. With the others I rush up the clattering stairs behind (incidentally) Ida Kaminsky, who's been hiding there to watch the proceedings. I reach the roof just in time to see my son, never an athletic boy — nor an impulsive or a head-strong or a rebellious one, never to my knowledge any of these — I see him swarm up the slippery pane of the inclined skylight (which slams shut after) and leap for the rope. Whether he means to drag the old man down or hitch a ride, I can't say, but latched on to the dangling cord, he begins, with legs still cycling, to rise along with the crackpot saint.

Then uttering some complicated mystical war cry, Hershel Ostrow, holding onto his homburg, follows Ziggy's lead. With his free hand Hershel grabs my boy's kicking right foot, and I thank God when I see them losing altitude, but this is only a temporary reversal. Because it seems that Rabbi Shmelke, handicaps notwithstanding, has only to warble louder, adjusting the pitch of his prayer to gain height. I console myself that if he continues ascending, the fragile old man will come apart in the sky; the boys will plummet beneath his disembodied leg. Or Ziggy, whose leap I don't believe in the first place, unable to endure the burden of his companion, will let go. I assure myself that none of this is happening.

From beside me the wild Ida Kaminsky has flung herself onto Hershel's ankle, her skirt flaring to show off bloomers — which make a nice ribbon for the tail of a human kite. But even with her the concatenation doesn't end: the shambling Sanford Nussbaum and Mindy Dreyfus, the halfwit Herman Wolf, Rabbi Fein's own pious Abie in his prayer shawl, Milton Rosen in his mackintosh, all take their turn. Eventually every bad seed of North Main Street is fastened to the chain of renegade children trailing in the wake of old Shmelke's ecstasy.

One of the rebbe's zealots, having mounted a chimney pot, makes a leap at the flying parade, but for him they're already out of reach. Then another tries and also fails. Is it because, in wanting to pull their tsadik back to earth, his followers are heavy with a ballast of desire? This seems perfectly logical to me, sharing as I do the Chasids' despair.

Which is why I shout "Ziggy, come back! All is forgiven!" and make to jump into the air. In that instant I imagine I grab hold and am carried aloft with the kids. The tin roofs, the trolley lines, the brand new electric streetlights in their five-globed lamps, swiftly recede, their incandescence humbled by the torched western sky. Across the river the sunset is more radiant than a red flare over a herring barrel, dripping sparks—all the brighter as it's soon to be extinguished by dark clouds swollen with history rolling in from the east. Then just as we're about to sail beyond those clouds, I come back to myself, a stout man and no match for gravity.

The Library of Moloch

MELVIN JULES BUKIET

Melvin Jules Bukiet (1953–): *The son of Holocaust survivors, Melvin Bukiet has written extensively about the experience of the Holocaust, as well as the world of Polish Jews before the war. He was born in New York and was educated at Sarah Lawrence and Columbia. Bukiet's stories have appeared in* The Paris Review *and* Antaeus, *and his essays and reviews have been published in the* New York Times *and the* Washington Post. *He has published three novels:* Sandman's Dust, After, *and the forthcoming* Signs and Wonders. *He has also published two collections of stories:* Stories of an Imaginary Childhood, *which won the Edward Lewis Wallant Award for Jewish fiction, and* While the Messiah Tarries. *A former fiction editor of* Tikkun, *Melvin Bukiet now teaches in the Creative Writing Program at Sarah Lawrence and lives in New York with his wife and family.*

T hree hundred faces stared, blinked, squinted, and otherwise engaged the camera while recounting the most awful moments of the century.

"Smoke, that is the first thing I remember, that and the body of my little sister."

"Yes, they hung the village elders by their beards."

"Oh, the experiments. I had forgotten. Of course, the experiments. What was it you wanted to know? What was it *they* wanted to know?"

The library was a four-room suite of offices in the base of a gothic dormitory in which aspiring lawyers lived, ignorant of the stories that the folks with branded arms told underneath them.

One room of the suite contained a receptionist's desk, a couch, and coffee table where academic journals gathered dust. The second room was a dustless repository of videotape disks set upon rows of sleek metal shelving, along with two monitors for viewing them. Never had both monitors been used at the same time, but the initial grants to establish the library were generous.

Then there was the director's office, and the testimony room where they actually produced the videotapes. This room had the air of a dental chamber where the patient reclined in a large padded chair, the videotape machine directed at the face like an X-ray tube, aiming to penetrate the skin to the soul. There was always a cool young technician fiddling with the dials on an imposing black console with blinking red lights and fluctuating meters. These interns from the university's School of Communication Arts were more interested in the quality of sound reproduction than the meanings of the sounds reproduced. Attending the meaning, however, was a doctor, whose gentle probing elicited the words, although here it was a doctor of letters who conducted the procedure. Delicate as he was, there was also the occasional wince and cry of pain.

Other libraries have taken lesser tasks upon themselves, to contain and construe the physical properties of nature or the intellectual produce of man. The Library of Moloch sought no less than a moral explication of the universe.

Fortunately it had excellent source material. All that remains from the Crusades, for example, are a few moldy documents. Likewise, the other episodes of vast and imponderable iniquity, the Reign of Terror or the Conquest of Mexico, have faded from human memory, and hence perished in all but legend. There may be articles about Tamerlane or Gilles de Rais in the yellowing journals on the coffee table, but their ravages no longer have the pulse of life. The contemporary library has one invaluable resource that researchers into the more distant past do not, the victims. That was its avowed purpose, to find the victims of Moloch, to record them, to preserve their suffering, to remit immortality in return for the chronicle of their woe.

They had three hundred faces on file, nearly a thousand hours, tens of thousands of deaths described in ferocious detail. The library was a mausoleum; its librarians gravediggers. As for the individuals whose lives and memories were condensed onto half-inch tape, wound onto spools, stacked onto shelves — the hell with them.

Dr. Arthur Ricardo, English born, American bred, headed the project. He was a highly civilized gentleman, with many diverse interests. He enjoyed chamber music, Oriental rugs, and nineteenth-century economic theory. The latter was a family hobby, because he was a nonlinear descendant of David Ricardo, the eminent mercantile essayist and apostate. In addition to his rarified pursuits, Dr. Ricardo was an avid moviegoer who regaled his intellectual friends with tawdry tales of Hollywood excess. How he found his life's calling in the Library of Moloch is a tale in itself. His specialty was medieval literature, but he realized that his students were more interested in iron maidens and auto-da-fés than they were the quest for the grail. Only if the grail was hidden within an iron maiden had they any chance of finding it.

At the moment when he was wrestling with his charges' gruesome misreadings of Ariosto, there was a scandal at his institution, the academy that housed the library. An elderly professor who was respected by all in his field (thermodynamics) was determined to have been a wartime collaborator. Nobody accused him of any personal wrongdoing, but he had signed a loyalty oath and he withheld knowledge of this when he sought to enter America. Clearly the man needed to be punished. Equally clearly, he had lived an honorable life since his youthful indiscretions. He was, in fact, a leader of the physicians for nuclear responsibility movement. Ricardo's sympathies were with the professor, but a squat little man appeared unbidden at the provost's inquiry. He demanded to be heard. "I worked at the mountain," he said, meaning the underground silos where the rockets the venerable professor had designed fifty years ago were produced, where scientists labored in isolation while slaves died to prove the learned men's theories.

Ricardo was not present when the man spoke, but a video recording of the speech circulated, at first covertly and then, by mass demand, at public screenings. The tape exerted a bizarre fascination. The professor was hounded into retirement.

"Imagine," Ricardo said to his class, "what we could do with the personal testimonies of the prisoners of the Inquisition, what that would tell us about the nature of faith in that era."

But one student said, "Can't we extrapolate backward from this witness? Does human nature change?"

At first, Ricardo wanted to dismiss the query. The first tenet of his life was progress, implying the perfectability of man. But the question bothered him. He had to admit that if human nature did change, it most certainly did so for the worse to just the degree that his generation's atrocities superseded those of the Middle Ages. Compared to the artifacts of the twentieth century, iron maidens were couture and racks no more than chiropractic devices. The stories of that one man who "worked at the mountain" were sufficient proof.

And there were many more stories. The man who gave evidence

was the tip of the iceberg. There were others who worked the mines and others who stoked the fires. Who knew how many of these refugees from the land of brimstone were walking the streets, and each time one clutched his heart and collapsed to the pavement another storehouse of history died with him. Ricardo spoke to the videotaper, and together they conceived of the library. The university was eager to balance the scales of public opinion that had been tipped by the scandal. A board of prestigious names lined up to support the project. Grants were expedited, space allocated. Funding flowed.

Ricardo placed advertisements in ethnic newspapers, and contacted organizations that aided survivors. They tended to stick together. It was difficult to overcome their distrust of strangers at first, but their very cohesiveness made further testimonies easier. One by one, the men and women who lived through the war came to him. And he listened.

"Fire, a column of fire into the sky. It was night. The column must have been a hundred feet high. Maybe two hundred. I don't know. I'm no Galileo."

"Food, the lack of food. Hunger so great we would eat anything, grass, poison ivy, we would suck the juices from pieces of wormy wood. And you know what, Junior's cheesecake never tasted so good."

"The diseases, the scabs, the sores. We used to urinate on our wounds to anesthetize them. No, that's the wrong word. Anesthesia is what you do to the brain. My nephew's an anesthesiologist in Boston. Antibiotic? Antihistamine? Anti-something."

The more he heard, the more Ricardo needed. He grew insatiable. As the killers were driven to kill more and more, he wished to hear more and more of those they had been unable to kill. There were fifty thousand some of them, many more if one included those who hid in the woods, escaped eastward, or merely toiled away the war years in the brutal and often deadly labor camps scattered throughout the continent. Oh, he would tape them too, but it was the fifty thousand who had inhabited the capitols of death that he hunted, begged, cajoled, and, if necessary, bribed into telling their stories. He was like a collector who must attain not merely one of each species, but each and every one of the particular species he collects. To miss just one would mean an elemental loss.

"We arrived, and these men were beating us as soon as we arrived. With bayonets or gun barrels, screaming *Heraus! Heraus!* That means 'Move quickly!' There were dogs, tearing at people, and everyone was filing past this desk and most everyone was going to the left except for a few big guys who were going to the right. So I shouted, 'Healthy. Twenty. Carpenter,' and I started to the right. I was puny, sixteen, and a student, but I started to the right, and a soldier knocked me down. I got up, and started that way again, and he knocked me down again. Well, I got up and started that way again, and the soldier started after me when the officer in charge said, 'Let him be. He'll die anyway.'" The man looked into the camera and snorted, "Hah!"

It was interesting, despite their experience they were optimistic. Or was it because of their past that they were optimists, because they were able to conquer adversity, because ultimately they had triumphed. They had homes now, and businesses and children, and were able to follow the course of their lives like ordinary human beings, yet those who listened to them were devastated and came to believe in the inevitable doom of a species capable of such enormity.

Dr. Ricardo in particular suffered since his work at the library commenced. Yet the more he suffered, the greater his passion for his self-appointed mission. He ignored his students as he expanded his collection. One hundred, two hundred, three hundred tapes on the wall, a thousand hours of horror, and he knew them all by heart. His wife was eager to have children, but he would not breed. The tapes were his children.

Ricardo's eyes widened at the stories of misery, at the rivers of blood which ran from the tongues of the witnesses, at the mountains of ashes heaped up beneath the videotape camera, mountains to obscure the eye of the camera, to bury the Library of Moloch.

Most witnesses told their stories voluntarily. These stories were equivalent to their souls yet they were willing to donate them to the Library of Moloch because they believed that to tell was to verify a past that had become dreamlike even to themselves. And after all, they were people of the book. Of course, the form was strange, but they had faith that this "tape" was a newfangled kind of a book, and they were willing to move with the times.

Yet some were suspicious. They had been convinced to go to the library by their children or coaxed by Dr. Ricardo, who had obtained their home phone numbers.

One old lady arrived wearing a large rhinestone brooch on a

highly textured brocade dress. Her hair was cut short in a golden helmet. She could have been a dentist's receptionist, or a dentist's mother. When the tape started to roll, and Ricardo began by asking her to tell him "a little about yourself," she said, "Pardon me, but why do you wish to know?"

"Isn't that self-explanatory?"

"I never did understand the obvious. It usually hurt too much."

Ricardo was taken aback; he was forced to define the library's purpose. "To prevent such a thing from ever happening again."

"Ah, so you believe that my warning will keep armies from crossing borders, railroads from chugging down the tracks, fires from burning. I was not aware that I had such power."

"Well, not just your warning."

"Everybody's. Mine and Max Adelstein's and Dora Schwartz's. Poor Dora. What a responsibility. And her with pleurisy."

"Well, don't you think it is important" — and he called up a phrase from the survivors' own organizations, a deliberate redundancy that struck them as biblical in its admonition — "to remember. Never to forget."

"Ah," she nodded understandingly. "Never to forget, you say. To remember, you say. Did you ever think that we might prefer to forget?"

"But as a survivor, you have an obligation to — "

"You know, I never liked the word, 'survivor,' it suggests too much personal ability. There was no ability. There was luck. We are not survivors, but merely remainders, or the remains. And you are jackals, feasting on the last tasty flesh that sticks to our bones. Tell me, is it good?"

"That is terribly unfair. I am sympathetic."

"Leeches. Vampires. You cannot get more blood from our loved ones, so you're sinking your teeth into us. I do not think you are unsympathetic. I think you are jealous, Herr Doktor Professor."

Ricardo said, "I wish you would not call me that," his clipped words emphasizing the last of the British accent he had shed as a child.

"And what charmed world do you inhabit where wishes are granted, Herr Doktor Professor?"

"Enough! I will not be insulted. If you insist, we will stop this session."

"Oh, so you will judge the validity of my story on whether I have the proper respect for you, Herr Doktor Professor?" The tiny lady squirmed delicately in her comfortable chair, her grandmother's eyes gleaming as she removed her glasses and rubbed them on her sleeve.

Ricardo surrendered. "You are right. We cannot judge. We are not here to judge."

The old lady made a gesture, a hand floating horizontally across an empty channel. It was the rod of the shepherd who winnows his flock by determining which pass beneath it and which do not. In the Yom Kippur prayer, the U-nisaneh Tokef, that image is a symbol of God's judgment for the upcoming year, who shall live and who shall die. It was also used as a deliberate parody in the land of evil, only instead of a gnarled shepherd's rod, a sleek leather riding crop was used, and the little ones, too little to reach that glistening leather while standing on their toes so as to make their topmost curls quiver, never had the chance to be whipped with it. Their slaughter was immediate.

"So, what occurred after you were deported?"

She answered this and the other questions he posed with brisk efficiency. But then, after she described the American soldier who "liberated" the eighty pounds that were left of her, she said, "And where were you during the war, Herr Dok —"

"I was young."

"So was I," she said. "I was young and in love and in Europe."

"Bala Cynwyd."

"What?"

"It's a suburb of Philadelphia."

"A suburb. Of Philadelphia." Her voice was so skeptically inflected that she might as well have said, "A cathedral. In Vatican City."

He bowed his head. "They call it the Main Line."

"How nice."

Her tone angered him. "It was. It was very nice. And I feel fortunate, but I do not feel ashamed. All right?"

"Fine by me." She lifted both her palms.

He said, "I don't have a gun."

"You don't need one. You have a camera."

"And what is that supposed to mean?"

"Nothing. Ignore me."

He wished he could. He had gotten what he wanted, another tape on the shelf, another cache of horror. The interview was over, but he could not leave it alone. "Jealous of what? Jealous of suffering? Jealous of death?" He tried to imitate the scornful laugh of one of his previous subjects. "Hah."

For the first time, Ricardo entered onto the record as more than an interlocutor from behind the camera, and the operator looked at the old lady as if for instruction or authorization to swivel the camera to view the professor's distress. She merely gazed into the lens with complete equanimity. Then she said, "There are two separate, inviolate realms. One is memory."

Ricardo answered as if in a trance, "And the other?"

She didn't answer, and it drove the doctor crazy. What was it that she wasn't telling him? What was it that none of them had told him? What was missing from his library? He mentally reviewed the names on the shelves. They were arranged alphabetically although they were also cross-categorized by age, sex, the nature of the torture endured, and the kind of response — from sorrow to anger to hatred to mystical contemplativeness. Yet something was missing.

And then it struck him. What bound and limited the library was that all of its subjects were victims. Where were their victimizers?

Amidst all of the workings of the man-made Hades, its transportation and extermination systems, recounted in detail for the librarians who spurred the informants to unearth even the tiniest additional tidbit concerning the kingdom of darkness, there was plenty about, but nothing from the lords of the infernal regions.

Of course, there was the legitimate desire to deny these men or their female counterparts credence. We do not want to hear their stories; we may find out how similar to ourselves they are. Besides which, the evildoers were hardly forthcoming. Though they pursued their crimes with vigor and pleasure, they were nonetheless aware that their actions were heinous. One arch-villain even said that theirs was an episode which would remain hidden. But he was wrong. The library was intent on proving that. Maybe society had failed the victims. And politicians had failed them. The clergy had failed them. But the librarians would not.

Dr. Ricardo was sure that his register of martyrs hallowed them, and that his recordings of their lives saved them. Unfortunately, the beneficiary of his largesse was not convinced. The old lady not only refused to recognize his charity, she dared to question his role. "Watch out," she said. "There is only one sentence for those who tamper with forbidden mysteries."

"Do not threaten me."

"That's not a threat. It's a prophecy."

"Well, like it or not, we are in the archival era. This library does not exist in order to examine experience. Here experience exists in order to be examined."

The old lady stood as he ranted, and tottered away on the heels that brought her height to five feet shy, but the man who held the technological rod that measured her value in the new world did not notice.

When he was finished, Dr. Ricardo was alone with his roomful of gray cylinders. The camera was off, and the lady was gone. He sat in her chair, still warm, and stared at the empty lens of the videotape machine. Looking down, he noticed that the arm of the chair had been scratched clear through to the stuffing, a mixture of straw and compressed fibers. Obviously one of the interviewees had been so tormented, his or her fingernails punctured the supple leather surface.

The library had money enough to repair the damage or replace the chair. But Dr. Ricardo was curious whose memories evoked such a reaction. He supposed he would never know. The cameras focused on the subjects' faces while he focused on the words.

He reached into his breast pocket and removed the pack of cigarettes he had purchased earlier in the day. He had smoked for years, stopped for years, and recommenced when he started his series of interviews.

"The fences were electrified. This was a blessing. One could always kill oneself when the pain grew too tremendous. Many people availed themselves of the facility."

Dr. Ricardo lit a cigarette and inhaled. The very process was soporific. So he fell asleep, and twisted in the soft contours of the chair, his head filled with images of his parents' home in Bala Cynwyd, outside of Philadelphia, ringed with barbed wire, on fire. Ashes from his cigarette dropped to the exposed stuffing.

Soon Dr. Ricardo wore a crown of flames, yet still he slept.

The flames spread. They rode across the seam of the carpeting on the floor and caught at the papers on his desk.

The fire passed into the storage room, and climbed the shelves. There the cylinders buckled under the heat, and they popped open, the tapes writhing like snakes in a burning cave, and the words of the witnesses escaped, and the pictures created by their words escaped. The guard towers, the barbed wire, the fires blackening the sky, escaped into the air along with the smoke.

Throughout the dormitory, the young law students woke with shrieks of terror. Their dreams were tainted; their beds turned to pyres. They staggered outside in their pajamas, clutching their seared case books.

Finally, Dr. Ricardo also woke, coughing up burned gray phlegm, sputtering. His precious tapes, the wall of evil that he wished to preserve, was being consumed before his eyes. He tamped out what he could, but he could not extinguish the blaze.

The librarian might have been able to save himself, but there was one more question he had yet to ask. He grabbed at the last tape on the shelf, the one that served as a bookend because the secretary had not had time to file it. His fingers blistered from the touch, but he jammed the cassette into the monitor whose cord was a glowing copper filament. Nevertheless, the machine worked.

The lady appeared on television against a background of flames. "Pardon me," she said, "but why do you wish to know?"

He punched the device's fast-forward mechanism. There was a blur, and when he lifted his finger, the lady seemed to smile as she said, "I do not think you are unsympathetic. I think you are jealous, Herr Dok — "

He hit the button again, and left his finger there for what seemed like an eternity. He lifted it to see her silence and hear his own voice from off-screen, "Jealous of what? Jealous of suffering? Jealous of death?" But where he expected to hear himself give a last, resounding, "Hah!" there was only continued silence. The machine may have been damaged by the flames, which rose up the curtains. He could hear sirens.

Suddenly the lady answered, "Yes, jealous."

"What?"

"Jealous of the Holocaust."

In his delirium, he wondered if fire was the fate of all libraries. First there was the Library of Alexandria with the wisdom of the ancient world, and now, the Library of Moloch containing what its keeper truly believed was the wisdom of the modern world. Perhaps, he thought crazily amid the mounting flames, this fate was not inappropriate, for Moloch was the fire god to whom children were routinely sacrificed. Moloch, the Lord of Gehenna, lived outside of Jerusalem in what was truly the valley of the damned, forever exiled in sight of the heavenly city.

He started to answer the flickering screen, but she would not allow him an opening.

"Jealous of having a reason to hate. Jealous of tragedy, because your life is no Charleston. Jealous of a people who refuse to submit to the impurities that surround them. Jealous of those who adhere to a broken covenant. Jealous of the sacred. So here you have it, Herr Doktor, so enjoy!"

"I do not understand."

"My poor professor. You know, the killers never understood us either. 'How' they asked themselves, 'can these people meet our eyes? How can they persevere no matter the punishment we inflict?' Mind you, they were sophisticated; they knew that it was not merely the scourging of the body of the community, but the anguish of being compelled to acknowledge that animals like them shared the same cruel flesh we did, breathed the same vile air. But that was the part that made it easy. We knew we were looking at God."

"How could you tell?"

"Because God is made in the image of man. We met Him a long time ago, in Spain and Rome and Egypt, and more genteel spots. We saw Him in a topcoat and derby ducking into Whitehall. And we saw Him in Washington, too. The truth is, He is everywhere, but only we can recognize Him, because we are old friends. We know His story."

"Can . . ."

"Of course I can introduce Him to you. And now, my good fellow, prepare to meet your maker, for those who enter the Holy of Holies are condemned to burn. I told you. I told you, there are two inviolate realms."

That was it, that was what he had turned the videotape on in order to hear. That was the lesson for which he risked his own immolation in order to learn. "What are they?" he screamed at the tape, as the flames kissed his feet, and cracked his knees that were as immovable as if they were lashed to a stake.

Although the screen itself had begun to melt with the intensity of the heat, the image was calm. "I told you. One is memory."

"And the other — the other, please! The other!"

The lady answered, "Theology."

History (with Dreams)

LEV RAPHAEL

Lev Raphael (1954–): *Lev Raphael, the child of survivors of the Holocaust, was born and raised in New York. He received a B.A. from Fordham, an M.F.A. in creative writing from the University of Massachusetts—Amherst, and a Ph.D. from Michigan State University, and taught at all three of these institutions. His published work includes a novel,* Winter Eyes; *a collection of short stories,* Dancing on Tisha B'Av, *which won a 1990 Lambda Literary Award; a full-length work of literary scholarship,* Edith Wharton's Prisoners of Shame; *a volume of memoirs and essays,* Journeys and Arrivals; *plus three mysteries and four coauthored books on psychology. His stories have appeared in* Redbook, Commentary, The Faber Book of Short Gay Fiction, *and* American Identities. *Lev Raphael lives in Michigan with his partner, Gersh Kaufman, and writes full-time.*

History is as light as individual life, unbearably light,
light as a feather, as dust swirling in the air, as whatever
will no longer exist tomorrow.— MILAN KUNDERA

One Sunday in the Metropolitan Museum of Art near the top of the wide main staircase, my best friend Sandy gasped at the Canova Perseus: "That's *him*."
I knew he meant my brother Paul. It was more than the rich cold marble body, it was the cool contempt with which Perseus, on his pedestal, twice, three times our size, held Medusa's head away from himself: that was all of us, thrust at arm's length, hanging.

Paul was four years older than me, tall, gray-eyed, large and strong, far handsomer than me or our parents. The three of us were small and kind of squat. Paul seemed the son of old-fashioned TV parents, the kind he wanted: those chirpy couples drifting in their large houses, worried about their children's parking tickets and bake sales. Paul was ashamed of Mom and Dad, of the way they could suddenly fling Yiddish curses at each other in a department store when they disagreed about a toaster or a rug; ashamed of how they criticized what we wore, fussing, tugging, yanking. They were triumphantly foreign. Dad with his one after-dinner cigarette, slicing an apple for his dessert, Mom with her quick little laugh that sounded learned from a language tape.

Paul was also ashamed of the past they couldn't share. There was so little — reminiscences of their school days, summer vacations, family dinners almost always brought them to the War, to their bitter losses. They wanted to forget.

My father loved nothing more than lying in the hammock in our little overplanted back yard in Forest Hills, with the high wooden fence between him and the world. He lay in the shade, eyes closed, singing to himself in Russian, a gypsy song, one of those on the fat 78's he occasionally removed from their brown paper sleeves and dusted with amused reverence before playing. But somehow Dad's relaxation annoyed Paul, as if he expected Dad to be busy around the house when not at work — sanding, staining, hammering, nails projected from his lips, as if Dad had no right to such indolence, because he was only a jeweler in another man's store.

One Saturday afternoon while I sat out on a lawn chair breathing in the chaotic mix of scents produced by our scrap of garden, Dad had said, "I just wanted, in the mud, something green, something mine. A tree."

In the silence I felt as if all the cars, lawnmowers, bikes, air conditioners for miles around were frozen, expectant.

"Where?" I asked. "Where?"

"Stalingrad."

And what I knew of that murderous siege and battle in which three of my cousins had died, choked me.

But Paul wouldn't listen. It wasn't France, Italy, or the Pacific, it was another, uglier, less acceptable war to him. And my father hadn't been a hero, just a Jewish slave laborer for the Hungarians.

And Mom, with her unsteady little eyes, quick jumpy walk like a sparrow snatching at a worm, Mom was not acceptable to Paul either. She wasn't slim and silent enough, but could sometimes talk as if she were a slot machine spilling noisy bright coins. She even talked to herself when cooking, or back to the radio announcer or as she read. Mom loved to shop for food, to eye and handle and sort and squeeze. It took her hours, from which she'd emerge red-faced, ecstatic.

I think the neon-lit plenty was a dream for her after the flight from

Poland deep into the Soviet Union, the years of near-starvation, the cities in flame.

Mom and Dad's history of madness was so different from the waves of death back home — ghettos, concentration camps — but no easier to understand. They were survivors, and so were all of their friends, as if relating to someone without a similar past were inconceivable to them. They had a minimal social life. They took walks with their friends, played cards sometimes, the passive pursuits of inmates at a rest home, as if these moments together were merely episodes in a convalescence that would never end. Survivors. It had always seemed an ugly jagged term to me — people ripped from a larger, richer life, isolated, drowning in their loss.

I could not, as Paul did, loathe Mom and Dad, even when they drove me crazy. Dad would pass me on the phone in the kitchen, and drop, "Hang up — someone might call." Mom would lurk at the door of my room and wonder, "How many shirts do you need on the floor?" or "What did that book do to you, you treat it like garbage?" These quirks usually made me laugh — at least when I'd tell Sandy afterwards.

I couldn't feel Paul's contempt for them, but I *could* see them as Paul did. Mom lost in coupons, labels, sales, Dad selling watches and clocks, chains and rings. Dad was too harsh to Paul, suddenly cornering him and shouting, "You treat us like dirt!" when Paul was younger and refused to do his homework or his chores. Paul simply looked off to one side, blank, lifeless, even when Dad would lunge at him, force him down into a corner, grabbing at his shoulders, striking, kicking. Paul could have fought back, could have hurt Dad or at least kept him off, but he did nothing.

Later Dad would drag himself around the house, mournful, heavy-eyed, his silence a naked castigation I hated as much as his rage. Paul said nothing when he was beaten, but I yelped and begged so much Dad would laugh at me and stop: "Coward!" I'd nod eagerly, smiling, anything was fine for me.

"Just say you're sorry," I told Paul when we were both little. "Say sorry, it's just a *word*." But he wouldn't.

Mom often recalled overhearing me give Paul that advice, the story sounding like some ancient legend whose figures were metaphors of experience, not her living sons. She made so much of Dad's "sick stomach" after the beatings, proudly telling us how bad he felt, how awful, especially with what he'd been through.

In the War, I added to myself.

The lesson of it all? We shouldn't hurt them.

There were many mysteries in our home, not least of which was wondering who Mom and Dad had been before the War. They spoke so little about their families, how could we tell what in them had changed, what been intensified, what crushed? Reading memoirs of the Holocaust and histories, as I did endlessly, didn't offer a clue. But the War was everywhere, and leaked out especially when something unexpected and terrible happened. Mom would usually just go quiet and grim, seeming to disappear into grief so large it robbed her not only of words but of her very self. And Dad raged around the house, throwing things, cursing in Polish or Russian, *Sook in sin, pja krev* — curses that seemed so much tamer in English: sonofabitch, dog's blood — but sounded grisly dropped from a face all red and dark with rage. Disasters, even small ones, triggered the darkness of their past, which seemed as large and unknowable as a howling sea in which we were just a tiny craft struggling to keep on course.

Sandy and I stepped closer to the Perseus now. "Amazing," he said.

I nodded.

Sandy and I circled the statue, a little breathless. Sandy grinned and murmured so that only I could hear, "Even his *buns*. Nice and tight."

I had to agree. I'd been getting a good look lately. Paul had been working out much more heavily than usual, and had taken to drifting around nude from his room to the bathroom and back (when our parents weren't around), as if after the months of crippling bench presses at the Y and all the rest of it he had recreated himself as Arnold Schwarzenegger. I had seen him at the gym performing each repetition in a set with grunting violent heroism, like Samson bringing down the temple.

Sandy and I moved on, but I couldn't help turning back to glance at the Perseus, which was more beautiful now that I had to leave it behind. We were only fifteen, but I hoped that while staring at it before, we might have been mistaken for those art students with sketch pads who appeared never to see a work itself, but rather the problem it represented or solved. I did not want us to look hungry or exposed.

Once I asked Paul if he thought our parents' experiences in the War had influenced us.

He said no and didn't even bother changing the subject, just stared at me until I left the room.

Paul did not look *inside*. He looked ahead, wildly, spouting visions to me of wealth, of yachts and summer homes, travel around the world. He was going to be rich, he claimed, and for many years I listened with the credulity of a child whose friend asserts, "I saw a ghost." He was so blind, so sure — how could he be wrong?

For someone so relentlessly macho, I was a little surprised that Paul's vision of freedom and wealth was fired by late-night Thirties reruns. Over and over he watched TV movies on Channel 2 like "Midnight," "Holiday," "Bringing Up Baby," movies of wit and style, the elegance sharpened by the grey, black and white screen. I'm sure he saw himself smoking a cigarette in a Rolls, or crossing a lavishly statued marble hall, or sipping brandy in a barn-wide library, flirting on a veranda under a private moon. I couldn't enjoy the movies he had memorized. The world of villas and repartee seemed too cold and unreal; the Thirties were ugly years, the glamor Paul clutched at, a lie.

Even the girls he dated seemed plucked from those movies, but not the stars, the minor actresses sitting at nightclub tables or getting into limos, sleek and blonde, alien, remote. His girlfriends looked alike and had some of the vacant intensity of those young dancers surging in pigeon-toed waves around Lincoln Center, those blank silent girls with anchored-back hair and gleaming foreheads.

"They don't seem Jewish," Mom said once in our small wallpapered kitchen nook where she, Sandy and I feasted on fresh marble cake and coffee. I'd watched before with greed as she had poured the two batters together, anxiously licking the corner of her mouth as if she were handling plutonium. Sandy was always over at my house, and Mom liked him so much she hardly spoke to him.

"I mean the Jewish ones," my mother explained.

"Well, they're American," I said.

"American Jews just don't make it," Sandy said seriously, as he had to me many times before. "They don't know things."

"Like what?"

"We have too much — we're too lucky."

"Am I American?"

While my mother's back was turned, Sandy mouthed to me: "You're cute."

Sometimes, when Sandy tickled my chest or the hair coming in on my toes and called me "Hobbit," I felt cute. He, on the other hand, was indisputably much more than cute, always sought after by the girls for his looks and his attentive respectful silence, admired by the boys for his skill at baseball. We'd been schoolmates since kindergarten, and Sandy's popularity had been a constant.

My mother nodded and said to Sandy, "You're right about Americans." She had said this before, that because Americans had been spared centuries of murder and lunatic pride as national boundaries sliced across Europe like a strangler's wire, they did not, could not, know how lucky they were, how free.

Now she burst out, "Okay, your father's a boy in Ohio. Did he have to run away to Michigan because bandits from Pennsylvania burned his village and chopped up his family? There were armies ready to crush his people? What did his family die from? Sickness, drowning, accidents, tornadoes. In Poland—hah!—we had human tornadoes. Russians, Ukrainians, Poles, *zol zey brennen in fire*, they should burn up!"

Sandy and I nodded, a little scared by her intensity.

Later, over at Sandy's apartment a few blocks away in Rego Park, he said, "Your parents are so real. I think about that a lot."

I looked around the living room, a lavishly curtained little box with bowls of grinning fake fruit and lamps all in the form of buxom gold goddesses lost in swirling robes. Crystal pendants gleamed from unexpected corners.

"For us being Jewish is like someone else's buffet—a little this, a little that." Sandy leaned back on the streaky gold tufted velvet sofa and spoke as if to history: "It's not that important."

"What d'you mean?"

He shrugged and I reached to stroke his neck. He stopped my hand, gripped now by what he was thinking and trying to say.

"Why's it bother you?" I asked.

"When I'm with your parents, it's like, they know so much I'll never know."

Well that was true for both of us, but we couldn't talk about it then because Sandy's parents would be back from Alexander's, and we only had an hour in his room. We left the door open, and a Monopoly game set up, so that we wouldn't be surprised when they returned, and they would surely think we were flushed with the excitement of the game.

Walking back home later, I thought about what he'd said.

Sandy's family was fitfully Jewish, some years deciding to keep ko-sher and kashering the kitchen, some years ignoring all the holi-days, and dropping or changing Jewish magazine subscriptions, changing congregations, flailing for some consistent way to make a Jewish life. Both Sandy's parents taught at Queens College, and so they had a lot to say. Their Jewish discussions were long and exhausting. My father privately dismissed both Sandy's parents as yentahs.

But Dad liked Sandy very much, because he was so respectful, because he was an ardent Zionist. Dad and Sandy would talk politics and agree with delight on most issues. It could be very peaceful, the four of us sitting out in the back yard on a late spring or summer weekend, eating seedless grapes very slowly, savoring each cool little globe before crunching it open, drinking iced tea, with Mom idling through a newspaper, occasionally reading aloud to us in a comic high-pitched lecturing voice. She'd read fragments of articles with-out introduction or explanation and those darts of news would whiz from her chair.

Sometimes I'd think: They may have suffered, but they have *this*, and I'd feel grateful that I was not, had never been a disappoint-ment. I made few waves, had no rowdy friends, did consistently above average at school (Paul was the real brain) and had discov-ered great talent in French, which entered me like a magic potion the first year of junior high. I'd won our school's French award and my teachers pressed me to consider taking a summer study pro-gram in France when I got to high school, or even a year abroad. My parents were very proud and agreed it would be good for me.

Paul *was* a disappointment. He was inaccessible, sneering, more aloof as he became a remarkably handsome man. Girls were always leaving messages for him and after Mom took them she told Dad it wasn't dignified, though what she said in Yiddish was *nisht shayn*, not nice or decent.

Sandy didn't like my brother, but the most he'd say against him was that the two of them were "very different." Sandy tried not to malign people; he was on guard against *lashan harah* — Hebrew for evil talk. "It's so easy for things to just pop out, and then you're stuck."

"What if it's true?"

"Doesn't matter."

Sandy seemed to watch Paul as if waiting for trouble, and he was right.

The time when Paul and I were friendly, when we enjoyed each other's company, when he tied my little shoes and taught me games seemed prehistoric to me in Junior High. What followed was years of snarling and insults, as we drifted further apart. Paul's flood of girlfriends made him insolent, as did his weightlifting. I would find him constantly posing in front of the bathroom mirror, body oiled and shiny, wearing a tiny swim suit, making his muscles bulge and dance. His strong hairless body was like a holy relic borne in a procession in some huge dark canvas, shining its own light. I'm sure he wanted me to admire his strength, his masculinity, but I couldn't, because it seemed inhuman.

So did Angela, when I first met her. I thought, "Yes, she's the one." Not a girlfriend for Paul so much as a consort.

Angela went to Fordham at Lincoln Center, the Catholic college Paul had chosen, I think, not for its small size or midtown location, but because he'd encounter few Jews there, unlike City College, NYU, or Columbia, which had all accepted him.

Paul brought Angela by one afternoon of his sophomore year. She was tall, bleary-eyed, blonde, with the slack-shouldered elegance of someone like Jean Harlow. Despite myself, I saw her trailing one of those silky Thirties gowns with feeble straps, diamonds bragging in her hair. I was alone at home and Angela just sat in our plant-crazy living room as if she wished she were a hovercraft and could float her designer jeans above the couch that suddenly looked a little shabby to me.

They pretended an interest in me for a bit before I left for Sandy's and had dinner there, trying not to feel angry. Paul and Angela were both so disdainful and aloof I wondered at first how they could converse or even touch each other. They seemed like two exquisite parallel lines, drawn on to their glorious and separate futures.

Angela lived in Queens too, but in Kew Gardens, in a Tudor frenzy surrounded by reverential big trees with a low stone wall cutting along the edge of a half-block plot. I didn't like the house when Sandy and I walked by it a week after Angela's first visit. People who don't know New York are often surprised there can be these lovely tree-swathed neighborhoods with magazine houses, but I felt embarrassed to see Paul was dating that house and that street.

"It's so corny," I told Sandy. He didn't ask what I meant.

"Angela," Dad said. "Italian?"

"I don't think so. Her last name's White."

"And what else?"

I hesitated. Dad looked up from his basement worktable seething with bits of metal and tiny nonsense stones. Around us were drills, buffers, a small kiln and piles that would eventually give birth to jewelry or junk. He looked up, but not at me.

Mom had more to say. "Why doesn't he bring her to meet us?" she wondered at dinner. "He's ashamed she's a goy? I won't like her because of that? Believe me, I can find something else if I have to!"

But Angela was not a goy, not exactly. Her mother was the daughter of Russian Jews who'd fled after a pogrom. They had slipped their Jewishness like an anonymous corpse over the rails of their ship into the hungry Atlantic and raised Angela's mother American — that is, dreaming ready-made dreams, yearning for what she might never have. She died when Angela was three, before her husband's real estate career brought him the Tudor home, the Caribbean condo, the BMWs. Angela's father was a Unitarian, from Maine.

"What is that?" Mom asked me. "Unitarian."

"They believe in units."

She laughed, "America!" In their international shorthand in which Germans were killers, Poles thugs, the English anti-Semitic snobs, Americans were crazy. And even after thirty years that craziness was to Mom and Dad a perpetual delight — the way parents marvel at their infant's eyelashes, smiles. And a source of sorrow. The infant will grow into something unpredictable.

Paul's stream of girlfriends, his perplexing (and goyish) fascination with his own beautiful body, made some sense to them, fit into their larger understanding of America. But their steady reference to the broadest context sometimes struck me as restricted, draining away the day into history. I remember a wave of grave desecrations in Jewish cemeteries on Long Island and how I fantasized forcing the black spray paint cans down the mouth of whoever thought swastikas were funny. Dad reminded me, calmly, that anti-Semitism sparked in bad times.

"Yes," Mom nodded, oddly secure. "It's the recession."

And I, I felt cheated of my rage. Likewise with Watergate. They had long predicted that Nixon was dishonest and so couldn't raise their voices about the scandal. Sometimes, though, the historical perspective was funny. Like when in fifth grade Paul was rude to his teacher before Parents' Night and she demanded Mom and Dad punish him as *she* had done. Mom said that — as she understood it —

the Constitution barred being punished twice for the same crime. This became a minor family legend, told with ceremony as if it grounded us in the past and explained our present.

I don't think they were threatened by Angela. They seemed to pass her off as the vision of escape many Jews yearn for, the soft-haired Lorelei, seductive on her rock.

And I was glad Paul spent so much more of his time away from home, at parties, movies, whatever.

The first time Angela came over for dinner, Paul told a news story of some honeymoon wife falling naked from a Midtown hotel window to a fatal street. Angela grinned and topped him with someone burning to death sliding down a plastic emergency chute off an airplane that didn't explode. They were united in contempt for the unfortunate.

That first dinner was alternately very noisy and painfully quiet, and I drank five glasses of wine despite Dad's heavy glances. Sandy tapped my foot under the table now and then, but whether to slow my drinking or just connect, I don't know.

Overdressed and wearing too much perfume, Angela had loudly proclaimed how cozy our dinette was, as if she were a media-conscious monarch posing gracefully in a hovel. She signaled Mom's garnet ring for her attention, admiring it so loudly I felt a billboard had smashed into the dining room, smearing us with letters too large to read.

But Mom beamed. "My husband made it."

Angela nodded, eyes sweeping the dish-heavy table. "How long have you been a jeweler, Mr. Levy?"

"Since before the War."

Angela frowned away the ugliness of that reference and turned to me.

"What does your father do?" Mom asked warmly as if eager to discover hidden qualities in Angela.

"He owns things."

That's when I poured my fifth glass.

All through dinner, Angela took such mingy portions of salad, roast, potatoes and corn you would've thought her determined to make a show of delicacy. When I found myself silently counting the kernels on her plate, I knew I was drunk.

"She didn't like our food," Dad muttered in the kitchen when Paul took her home.

"How could she tell?" Mom shot. "She had, what, three bites?" Then they switched to Yiddish and moved to Russian. Sandy and I listened to the heavy cadences of the language that always sounded dark and sad to me, even in marching songs. From the kitchen, I heard a snarled "*Amerikanski*" a few times.

Sandy and I sat in the living room for a while before he went home.

"She's a lot like Paul," he finally said, with my parents' conversation drifting out to us, tantalizing, unknowable.

Oh yes, I thought, she was like Paul: cold, beautiful, critical. She'd glanced around our home as if every picture were crooked, cheap and vile, all the furniture needed dusting but she would overlook it. Watching Angela, I'd thought of the Greek and Roman sculpture galleries of the Metropolitan — those high rooms of tender light and silence. I never understood the raving about "classical beauty." Those private faces perched above tunics, cloaks, vague draperies seemed too removed from life to be beautiful. Now Sandy, *he* was beautiful, dark and romantic-looking.

"God, I'm lucky," I said to Sandy, who flushed with pleasure, understanding I meant him.

In bed, later, reading *Paris Match*, the room around me blurred, tenuous, I found myself wishing for things. Wishing I'd learned Russian as a child and taken Yiddish more seriously so that I could know my parents in a deeper way, think with them in languages they had not learned so much as lived. Paul was not alone in hungering for another life.

I longed for escape in my own way — what else was my dream of France, of barges on the Loire? Of wandering through Vaux-le-Vicomte and Chambord? Of exploring the bastide towns in the Dordogne? It was all a delightful patchwork for me: vermouth cassis, de Maupassant, Monet. My France was untouched by Dreyfus, Vichy, transit camps or De Gaulle's anti-Zionism, it was *La Belle France*, Europe's jewel, civilizing the world, the fantasy land that had infused each ringing high "*Bon*jour!" of my first French teacher. I imagined myself biking home with my baguette, writing letters in a Boul' Mich' cafe, smoking a Gitane on a train snaking down to the Mediterranean. It was a strange sort of return across the Atlantic, a retreat in time, wiping out history and death.

I adored my name pronounced in French; Robert became Rowbear with that wonderful rolled "R." But I shared these fantasies and visions with no one, especially at school where I covered my facility at translations, my mastery of the subjunctive with adolescent *je m'en fichisme*. Sandy disliked the French, so I couldn't imagine him my *copin*: "Everyone says they're nasty. My folks went there and hated it."

Sandy's dream was Israel, but not as a tourist (which he'd done) matching life to film scenes or photographs, not as a pretend kibbutznik for a few months. Sandy wanted to live there, work, travel, study Torah in Jerusalem.

"When I'm ready," he said, which meant after college. "Life is important there, you know why. You have to — it's a choice."

Maybe all dreams are a choice, a way of plunging reality, like a piece of sizzling, forge-worked metal into a barrel of water to cool its form.

Sandy was always bringing back loads of books from the library, reading Buber, Wiesel, collections of Yiddish stories in translation, essays on religion, the Sabbath, anything, everything, as if preparing himself for a long and hazardous voyage. He talked about his Jewish reading, and I listened in admiration, with a little distance.

Like Paul, I had lost my interest in being visibly Jewish after an undistinguished bar mitzvah, so Sandy's appeals for me to join him at synagogue, sometimes, *any* synagogue, were annoying. I could still follow a service but it led nowhere, the words heaped around me with each turned page until I felt stifled, trapped. Luckily our Seders at home were brief and every other holiday, including Rosh Hashanah and Yom Kippur, was less celebrated than talked about, passed around in conversation like a strange carving that gathers speculation with the heat of each hand. If I'd lived outside of New York I might have done more — but who needed to be Jewish in Queens when someone else could do it for you? I wanted to be French, to feel the dusty red medieval walls of Carcassonne as mine. I had no desire to grow old in Queens or Israel.

"You think because you're not like Paul," Sandy snapped one evening, "that anything's all right."

"What did I do?"

"Nothing — that's the point." Sandy wanted me to join a Jewish youth group, march for Soviet Jews, sign petitions, to do something more than dream of going abroad. He claimed I'd never really come back from France, or wouldn't want to. "It's the same thing. You'd forget about me! And Paul's going to marry Angela!"

I knew Paul wanted to, after graduating. He'd been strutting around nude a week before, scratching at his heavy rich chest and bragging about how Angela was his "slave," how she'd do "anything" for him.

"And she loves this." He flicked at his crotch.

"You're gross."

"That's right. Big." He gave it a shake.

After a pause, I said, "You want her money."

He smiled. "I'm not gonna be like Dad and his lousy little yard. Look at him, he's nothing."

"What about the War?"

"Plenty of people made it after the War."

Bastard, I thought in English, then in French: *espèce de salaud*.

"And I sure won't be like you," Paul went on, leaning on his door frame. "You'll never get to France, that's bullshit. You'll stay here jerking off with your little Golda Meir."

I froze.

He laughed. "You think I couldn't figure it out? What a little homo!" He turned and slammed his door.

I fled to the bathroom, ripped off my clothes and stood under the violent shower while I heard Mom come upstairs from the basement to ask about the noise.

They knew Paul and I didn't get along, but Mom kept trying. There was the abstract approach: "It's nice for children to get along." The apocalyptic approach: "He's all you'll have when we're gone." And even the ethnic approach: "It's a shame for the goyim to see brothers not friendly." To which I'd reply, respectively, "Yes it is" — "I hope not" — "They don't have to look."

Right about that time, Paul was bragging about an MG he'd bought from a friend at school with money saved from summer jobs. I, who spent all my earnings on movies and books and hanging out places with Sandy, had jealous visions of Paul in an accident or arrested for drunk driving, with Angela running from the scene or just sobbing her shame and fear in a greasy station house. I couldn't believe how jealous I was!

One May afternoon of my senior year of high school, and Paul's at Fordham, I came home with Sandy and heard Mom weeping in the kitchen. I had never heard her cry like this, with hysterical heavy gasping sobs that seemed wounded, alive. We stood inside the front door as if trying to fight the energy of that grief, but it pulled us through the house to the kitchen, where she sat in a chair pushed against the wall, head back, legs together, arms and hands dead on her thighs like one of those serene Egyptian tomb effigies.

"Your brother," she moaned. "Your brother and his *dripkeh* are junkies!"

I dragged a chair to her, sat close.

"Junkies!"

I didn't understand. Wouldn't I have seen the tracks?

Dad, she said, was upstairs. The doctor had been to give him a sedative. I made tea for her, brought a dishtowel soaked in cold water for her abused eyes and Sandy and I sat at the empty table while Mom told the story.

A professor at Fordharn had discovered Paul in a basement bathroom handing an envelope to another student who tried to duck out the door. It was cocaine. Angela and Paul apparently had a little business going (the money for his car, I thought). But no one was arrested, they were just expelled. The school wanted to protect its good Catholic name and the Chancellor made calls to keep the story out of the news. I knew that was possible; the same thing had happened with a suicide at Fordham the year before.

"A junkie!" Mom said again. "And don't defend him!"

I didn't try.

Angela's father, a large handsome man with glamorous white teeth and hair, came over that night, but there were no voices raised. Together, they sat hushed and defeated by their own ignorance, drinking vodka in the living room, like the victims of a flash flood marveling at their enormous unexpected loss.

Paul moved out. Angela was shipped to relatives in California. Dad abandoned his workroom, and even in his hammock strung from two big trees that were his vision of security and peace, he looked miserable. Mom took to chain reading mysteries, walling herself in with shiny paperbacks.

"We lived so long like dogs," she said to me and Sandy. "I only wanted for my sons to be happy."

I knew then that I could never tell her who I was.

Auslander

MICHELLE HERMAN

Michelle Herman (1955–): *Michelle Herman was born in Brooklyn and attended Brooklyn College and the Iowa Writers' Workshop, where she was a James Michener Fellow. Her stories have appeared in such magazines as* North American Review *and* Story Quarterly *and in the anthology* Twenty under Thirty. *"Auslander" appears in her new collection,* A New and Glorious Life. *Her novel,* Missing, *received the Harold Ribalow Award for Jewish fiction and was named one of the twenty best books of 1990 by the* Voice Literary Supplement. *She has won fellowships from the National Endowment for the Arts and the Ohio Arts Council. Currently Michelle Herman teaches in the M.F.A. program at Ohio State University, where she is associate professor of English. She lives in Columbus with her husband and daughter.*

T he translator, Auslander, was at first flattered. She listened, astonished, for a full minute before the caller — Rumanian, she had guessed after his initial words of praise — paused for a breath, allowing her the opportunity to thank him.

"No, no," he said. "It is I who should thank you, and furthermore apologize for disturbing you at your home. Naturally I am aware that this was most presumptuous. I admit I hesitated a long while before I placed the call. Still, it was difficult to resist. When I read the contributors' notes and discovered that you 'lived and worked in New York City,' I felt it was a great stroke of luck. I must tell you I was surprised that your telephone number was so easily obtained from Directory Assistance."

Auslander laughed. "I've never found it necessary to keep the number a secret. I'm not exactly in the position of getting besieged with calls from admiring readers."

"You are far too modest," the Rumanian said. He spoke hoarsely but with a certain delicacy, as if he were whispering. "Your essay was truly quite something. Such insight! Your understanding of the process of translating poetry is complete, total."

"It's kind of you to say so," Auslander said. She had begun to shiver. The telephone call had caught her just as she was preparing to lower herself into the bathtub, and she wished she had thought to grab a towel when she'd rushed to answer the phone.

"I assure you I am not being kind," he said. "Your work impressed me greatly. It is so difficult to write of such matters with cleverness and charm as well as intelligence. I imagine you are a poet yourself?"

"No, not actually," Auslander said. Her teeth were chattering now. "Could you possibly hold on for just a second?" She set the receiver down and clambered over the bed to shut the window. Across the small courtyard a man sat at his kitchen table laying out a hand of solitaire. He looked up at Auslander and she stared back for an instant before she remembered that she was naked. As she yanked down the bamboo shade, the man raised his hand in slow expressionless salute.

"Oh, I fear I *have* interrupted you," the Rumanian said when she returned to the phone.

"Not at all." Auslander cradled the receiver on her shoulder as she dug through a heap of clothes on the floor. She extracted a flannel shirt and shrugged her arms into it. "Really, it was very good of you to call."

"Good of me? No, no, not in the least." He was nearly breathless. "Your essay was *outstanding*. Brilliant, I should say."

"My goodness," Auslander said. She sat down on the bed and buried her feet in the tangle of shirts and jeans and sweaters.

"Marvelous work. Profound. I do not exaggerate."

She was beginning to feel embarrassed. "You're much too kind," she murmured, and quickly, before he could protest again, she said, "Tell me, how did you happen to come across the essay?"

"Oh" — he laughed, a taut, high-pitched sound — "I read everything, everything. I haunt the periodical room of the library. Nothing is obscure to me. The quarterlies, the academic journals, they all fascinate me, utterly. And I admit also that I have a particular interest in translation."

"A university library, it must be?"

"Ah, my God! How rude of me!" There was a soft thump, and Auslander imagined him smacking his fist to his forehead. "I am so sorry. I have not properly introduced myself. My name is Petru Viorescu. I am a student — a graduate student — at Columbia University."

Auslander smiled into the phone. A Rumanian: she had been right. "Well, Mr. Viorescu, I'm grateful for your compliments. It was very thoughtful of you to call."

This was greeted with silence. Auslander waited; he remained mute. She was just starting to become uneasy when he cleared his throat, and lowering his hushed voice still further said, "Miss Auslander, I do not want to appear in any way aggressive. Yet I wondered if it might be possible for us to meet."

"To meet?"

"Yes. You see, what I want to propose is a working meeting. Or, rather, a meeting to discuss the possibility . . . the possibility of working." He spoke quickly, with a nervous edge to his voice. "In your essay you write of the problems of translating some of the more diffuse, associative poetry in the Romance languages — of the light, respectful touch necessary for such work."

"Yes," she said. Cautious now.

"You have this touch, of course."

"I hope so," Auslander said.

"You even mentioned, specifically mentioned, a number of modern Rumanian poets. This was a great surprise and pleasure to me. I should add that I myself am Rumanian."

"Yes."

"Your biographical note included the information that you are fluent in nine languages. I assume, on the basis of your remarks in the second section of the essay, that my own is one."

"Your assumption is correct."

"And you are familiar with a great deal of Rumanian poetry."

" 'A great deal,' I don't know about, Mr. Viorescu."

"You are feeling a little bit impatient with me now, yes?" He coughed out his odd laugh again. "Bear with me, please, for another moment. Have you in fact done any translation from the Rumanian as yet?"

Of course, Auslander thought. She struck her own forehead lightly with her palm. *A poet.* "Some," she said. A *student* poet yet. More than likely a very bad one. Unpublished, it went without saying. She sighed. Vanity! Only this had prevented her from assessing the matter sooner.

"I thought so. I would be most grateful if you would consider meeting with me to discuss a project I have in mind."

"I'm afraid I'm quite busy," Auslander said.

"I assure you I would not take up very much of your time. A half hour perhaps, no more."

"Yes, well, I'm afraid I can't spare even that."

"Please," he said. "It might be that ten or fifteen minutes would be sufficient."

Irritated, she said, "You realize, of course, that you haven't described the nature of this project."

"Oh, that is not possible at the moment." It occurred to her then that he actually *was* whispering. Always such drama with poets! "I do not mean to be secretive, believe me," he said. "It is only that I am unable to speak freely. But if you could spare a few minutes to see me. . . ."

"I'm sorry," she said.

"Please."

It was not desperation — not exactly that — that she heard in this invocation. But surely, she thought, it was something akin to it. Urgency. Despair? Oh, nonsense, she told herself. She was being fanciful; she had proofread too many romance novels lately. With this thought she felt a pang of self-pity. She had lied when she'd said she was busy. She had not had any real work since early fall; she had been getting by with freelance proofreading — drudgery, fools' work: romances and science fiction, houseplant care and rock star biographies. But that was beside the point, of course. Busy or not, she had every right to say no. She had refused such requests before, plenty of times. Those letters, so pathetic, forwarded to her by the journal or publisher to which they had been sent, asking her to translate a manuscript "on speculation" — they wrote letters that were like listings in *Writers' Market*, these young poets! — she had never had the slightest difficulty answering. But naturally it was easier to write a brief apologetic note than to disengage oneself politely on the phone. Still, it was only a matter of saying no, and saying it firmly so it would be clear the discussion was at an end.

Viorescu had fallen silent again. A manipulation, Auslander thought grimly. He was attempting to stir up guilt. And for what should she feel guilty? As if her sympathy were in the public domain! What did he think, did he imagine that publishing a scholarly essay in *Metaphrasis* meant she was a celebrity, someone with charity to spare?

"I'm assuming that your intent is to try to convince me to undertake the translation of a manuscript," she said. "First I must tell you that my services are quite expensive. Furthermore, you have read only a single essay which concerns approaches to translation and which tells you nothing whatsoever about my abilities as a translator."

"On the contrary," he said. "I have read two volumes of your translations, one from the Italian, one from the Portuguese, and a most remarkable group of poems in a quarterly, translated from the German. I apologize for not mentioning this earlier; I excuse myself by telling you I feared you would question my motives, the sincerity of my praise. So much flattery, you see. But I assure you I am entirely sincere. I have not been as thorough as I might have been in my research — my time is limited, you understand, by my own studies — but I am certain I have seen enough of your work to know that it is of the highest caliber. I am well aware that the finest poem can lose all of its beauty in the hands of a clumsy translator. The work I read was without exception excellent."

Speechless, Auslander picked angrily at the frayed cuff of her shirt.

"And, naturally, I would expect to pay you whatever fee you are accustomed to receiving. I am hardly a wealthy man — as I say, I am a student. 'Independently poor' is how I might describe my financial status" — that curious little laugh again — "but this of course is important, it is not a luxury."

Auslander could not think of a word to say. She looked around at the disorder in her bedroom, a tiny perfect square littered with clothes and papers and precarious towers of books, and through the doorway, into the kitchen, where the tub stood full on its stubby clawed legs. The water was probably cold as a stone by now.

"All right," she said finally. "I'll meet with you. But only for half an hour, no more. Is that understood?" Even as she spoke these cautionary words she felt foolish, ashamed of herself.

But he was not offended. "That's fine," he said. "That's fine." She had been prepared for a crow of triumph. Yet he sounded neither triumphant nor relieved. Instead he had turned distracted; his tone was distant. Auslander had a sudden clear vision of him thinking: All right, now this is settled. On to the other.

They set a time and place, and Auslander — herself relieved that the conversation was over — hung up the phone and went into the kitchen. The bathwater had indeed turned quite cold. As she drained some of it and watched the tap steam out a rush of fresh hot water, she resolved to put the Rumanian out of her mind. The tenor of the conversation had left her feeling vaguely anxious, but there was nothing to be done for it. She would know soon enough what she had gotten herself into. She would undoubtedly be sorry, that much was already clear. It seemed to her that she was always getting herself into something about which she would be certain to be sorry later.

In truth, Auslander at thirty-four had no serious regrets about her life. For all her small miscalculations, all the momentary lapses in judgment that only proved to her that she'd do better to attend to her instincts, in the end there was nothing that really upset the steady balance she had attained. She had lived in the same small Greenwich Village apartment for a dozen years; she had a few friends she trusted and who did not make especially great demands on her time or spirit; her work was work she liked and excelled in. The work in particular was a real source of pleasure to her; and yet it was not the work she had set out to do. She had begun as a poet, and she had not, she thought, been a very bad one. Still, she had known by her freshman year at college that she would never be a very good one. She had been able to tell the difference even then between true poets and those who were only playing at it for their own amusement. Poetry as self-examination or catharsis was not for her — not enough for her — and knowing she would never be one of the few real poets, she gave it up without too much sorrow.

The decision to make her way as a translator of other, better, poets' work was one that hardly needed to be made: she found she had been moving toward it steadily for years, as if by intent. As early as the fifth grade she had discovered that languages came easily to her: the Hebrew lessons her father had insisted on were a snap, a pleasure; Yiddish, which was spoken at home, she taught herself to read and write. In junior high school she learned French, swallowing up long lists of words as if she'd been hungering for them all her young life. At that age she took this as a matter of course; it was only later that she came to understand that facility with languages was considered a talent, a special gift. By her sixteenth birthday she was fully fluent in French, Hebrew, Yiddish, and Spanish. By eighteen she had added German and Italian, and by the time she had completed her undergraduate education she had mastered Portuguese, Rumanian, and Russian as well. Her choice to become a translator, she knew, was a kind of compromise between aspirations and ability; but it was a compromise that satisfied her.

She knew her limits. This, Auslander believed, was her best trait.

She did not deceive herself and thus could not disappoint herself. She always knew where she stood. She was aware, for example, that she was not a beauty. She was content with her looks, however, for they were certainly good enough ("for my purposes," she had told a former lover, a painter who had wondered aloud if she were ever sad about not being "a more conventionally pretty type"). When she troubled to make even a half-hearted effort she was quite attractive — neatly if eccentrically dressed, solid looking, "an indomitable gypsy," in the words of the painter. Her unruly black hair and eyebrows, her wide forehead and prominent nose, her fine posture — about which her father had been insistent along with the Hebrew classes — all of this made an impression. Her figure, another ex-lover had told her, was that of a Russian peasant — he meant her strong legs and broad shoulders and hips. The notion amused her (though the man, finally, did not; he was a biochemist with little in the way of real imagination — his stolidness, which she had at first interpreted as a charming imperturbability, depressed her after several months). She knew she was the kind of woman of whom other women said, "She's really very striking, don't you think?" to men who shrugged and agreed, without actually looking at her, in order to keep the peace. And yet there was a particular sort of man who appreciated her brand of attractiveness — men by and large a decade or so older than herself, intelligent and good-natured men who had a tendency to brood, even to be sullen, and whose wit was mocked by self-criticism. In any case, she was not "on the market." She had no call to compete with the slim, lively blondes or the dramatic dark young beauties who weaved like lovely ribbons through the city, brilliantly pretty and perpetually bored and lonely. Auslander watched them at publication parties and post-reading parties, in Village cafés and restaurants and bars, and she eavesdropped on their talk with mild interest: there was a hunt on in the city; there was always talk — she heard it everywhere — about the lack of available, desirable men. Auslander herself was not lonely, never bored. She liked having a man in her life, and frequently she did, but she was most at ease alone, and she grew uncomfortable when a man tried to force himself too far into her affairs. It made her nervous to have a man — no matter how much she cared for him — poking about in her things, clattering through cabinets and riffling through her books, cooking pasta in her kitchen, sitting casually in her desk chair.

Auslander's boyfriends — a ridiculous word, she thought, when the men she knew were over forty (though the men themselves seemed to like it) — always started off admiring her "independence" and "self-sufficiency." Later, they would accuse her of "fear of commitment," "obsessive self-reliance." Her most recent affair, with a poet named Farrell — a very good poet, whose work she admired greatly, and the first, and only, poet with whom she had ever been involved in this way — had dissolved after nearly a year into a series of nasty arguments: he called her inflexible and cold; she pronounced him infantile, morbidly dependent. In the end she slept with a young novelist she met at the Ninety-Second Street Y, and carelessly let Farrell discover it. He drank himself into a rage and howled at her, pounding the refrigerator and the bathtub with his fists, and hurled a bottle of shampoo across the room; the plastic split and pale orange globs spattered the walls. She watched in mute amazement, breathless with fear, as he flung himself around her kitchen in a fury, bellowing like an animal. Finally she slammed out of the apartment without a word, and when she returned an hour and a half later he was asleep on her bedroom floor, curled like a shell among her clothes. She spent the night sitting wide awake and shivering at her desk, and in the morning when he rose he only nodded at her and said, "Well, all right, then," and left.

She had not seen him since — it had been five weeks now — and she had found that she missed him. This itself was disturbing. If he was gone, she wanted him gone: done with. She yearned for clarity; ambivalence unnerved her. They had been a bad match, she told herself. Farrell was so demanding, and what did he want from her, after all? To be a different sort of person than she was? He needed constant attention and she couldn't give it to him. But there was no getting around the fact that she liked him. More than liked him. She was fonder of him than she had been of anyone in years — perhaps ever in her life. She wasn't even entirely sure why she had slept with the young writer except that she had felt suffocated. She'd needed to poke her way out, shake things up. But still she had taken a good deal of pleasure in Farrell's company before their battling had begun.

This had happened again and again, this cycle of pleasure and discontent. Auslander could not help but wonder sometimes if she was simply picking the wrong men. To hear other women talk, most men were afraid of involvement. Her friend Delia, a playwright, had confessed to her that the man she'd been seeing for the last two years complained constantly about feeling trapped. "He says he wants to be close," she told Auslander, "but then he admits that the whole notion of togetherness terrifies him." Why then was it that the men Auslander knew seemed only too eager to cast in their lots with her? Delia laughed. She said, "Oh, sure. You ought to try taking one of them up on it sometime. He'd be out the door so fast you wouldn't know what hit you. Take Farrell, for instance. Do you think he'd know what to do with you if he had you? He'd be scared to death."

Auslander wasn't so sure. Not that it mattered anymore. Farrell, she felt certain, was out of the picture for good. They had spoken on the phone a couple of times, but he was still angry with her, and the last time they'd talked—he had telephoned her, drunk, in the dead middle of the night—he had called her a "cold ungiving bitch."

It was of Farrell that Auslander was thinking as she readied herself for her appointment with Petru Viorescu. It wasn't that she was imagining a romance with the Rumanian. She expected that she would read a few of his poems, gently tell him she could not translate them, and they would never meet again. No, it was only that this was the first time in more than a month that she had dressed and tidied herself knowing that she was going to meet with a man. She had been keeping to herself since the explosion with Farrell, seeing only the occasional woman friend—Delia or Margot or Kathleen, all of whom lived nearby—for lunch or coffee. She had not even attended a reading or seen a play or a movie since that night. It struck her now that it was as if she had been in hiding. Hiding from what? she wondered, surprised at herself. Afraid that Farrell would sneak up behind her on the street or in a theater? And if he did? What did it matter?

Displeased, she shook off the thought and took a few steps back from the full-length mirror behind her bedroom door, considering herself. She grimaced. What a specter! Brushing and tugging and straightening, turning this way and that. There was something demeaning, Auslander thought, about thinking of one's appearance. Still, it was unavoidable. She tipped her head, squinting at herself. She looked all right. She had decided it would be wise to appear a trifle stern, and in gray corduroy slacks and a black sweater, boots, no jewelry, no scarves, her hair in a single long braid, she was satisfied that she had achieved the appropriate effect. Nodding to herself, she swept out of the room, snatched up her long coat and her gloves, and was off, even looking forward to the meeting now as a kind of mild diversion.

In the Peacock Café she had no trouble spotting him. He had the hollow, unhealthy look of a youngish poet — mid-thirties, she guessed, somewhat older than she had expected — and wore the uniform of a graduate student: shirt and tie, corduroy jacket and blue jeans. He was very slight. As she took him in with a glance from the doorway, she calculated that he was about her own height, certainly no taller than five-six at most. He sat smoking a cigarette and tapping a teaspoon against a coffee mug at one of the small round tables in the front of the café.

Auslander went in flourishing her coat and smacking her gloves together, her braid flapping behind her, and moved straight to his table and extended her hand. "Mr. Viorescu?"

He started, and half-stood so abruptly the mug clattered against the sugar bowl. "Ah, Miss Auslander?"

Auslander nodded and sat down across from him. There was an alert, tensely intelligent look about him, she thought — almost an animal-like keenness.

"You are younger than I had imagined," he said. His presence of mind seemed to have returned to him. He was assessing her quite coolly.

She thought of saying: You are older and shorter. But she only nodded.

"I don't know why I should have expected that you would be older — perhaps fifty." He grinned and tilted back his chair, folding his arms across his chest. His smile made her uncomfortable and reminded her that the meeting was not likely to be a pleasant one for her. "Would you like a cappuccino? Or an espresso perhaps?"

"American coffee, thank you." She decided not to remove her coat; she would make it clear that she meant to stick by her half-hour time limit. Viorescu continued to grin at her, and she was relieved when the waitress finally idled by to take her order. They sat in silence until she returned with the coffee. Then the Rumanian leaned forward and placed his hands flat on the table. "I know you are busy, so I shall come to the point immediately. Would you be interested in undertaking the translation of the work of a poet who is, I assure you, quite brilliant, a magnificent talent, and who has never been published in English?"

Auslander raised her eyebrows. "I see you are not of the opinion that modesty is a virtue."

"Modesty?" Momentarily he was confused. Then, at once, he began to laugh. "Oh, yes, that is very good, very good."

Auslander, herself confused, did not know what to say.

"I am so sorry — I should have realized. You of course imagined that I was the poet. Yes, I would have drawn the same conclusion." He chuckled softly. "Ah, but my God, imagine me a poet! A fond wish, as it happens, but without even the smallest glimmer of hope." He shook his head. "No, no, look here. It is my wife of whom I am speaking. The poet Teodora Viorescu."

"You're not a poet?"

"Not in the slightest." He lifted his hands from the table and turned them palms up. "As it happens, I have no ability in this area at all. In fact, I have thought to try to translate a number of my wife's poems. I believed I might manage it. But I find it takes a poet to do such work, or — you said you were not yourself a poet — a rather exceptional talent which I do not possess. It was a hopeless task, hopeless. The results were . . . earthbound. Do you know what I mean by this? The poetry was lost."

Auslander sipped her coffee as she mulled this over. Finally she said, "Your wife . . . I take it she is unable to translate her own work?"

"Ah, well, you see, this is the problem. She has not the command of English I have. She has had some . . . some reluctance to learn the language as fully as she might. Oh, she is able to express herself perfectly well in spoken English. As for writing . . . that is another matter altogether."

"Yes." Auslander nodded. "This is often the case."

"I had hoped you might recognize her name, though it is understandable if you do not. Her reputation was only beginning to become established in our country when we left. She was thought of then as one of the most promising young poets in Rumania. She was very young, you understand — nineteen — but still she had published a small book and her work was included in two quite prestigious anthologies."

"Viorescu," Auslander murmured. "She has always published under this name?"

"Yes. We married when she was seventeen."

"Seventeen!"

He shrugged. "We have known each other since we were children. I was the best friend of her eldest brother."

"I see," Auslander said politely.

"And in any case, over the last eight years you most certainly would not have heard of her. Since we came to the United States there has been nothing to hear."

"Is she writing at all?"

"Oh, she is writing, she is writing all the time. But she writes only in Rumanian. None of the work has been published."

"How is it that she has never before had any interest in having her poems translated?"

"Well, it is somewhat more complicated than that." He shifted in his seat. "You see, even now she insists she has no interest."

"But then. . . ." Auslander narrowed her eyes. "You're discussing this with me without her permission?"

He poked at his pack of cigarettes with his index finger, pushing it around in a small circle. His eyes followed its path.

"You must realize that I could not possibly consider the translation of a writer's work against her wishes."

He did not raise his eyes. "Well, here is the problem," he said. "I am very . . . I am very concerned about her. I fear. . . . She is not—how can I say this correctly? She is not adjusting. She is languishing here. A poet needs a certain amount of attention to thrive. Teo is not thriving. I fear for her."

"Still it doesn't seem—"

"*We* are not thriving," he said. Now he looked at Auslander. "She sits awake at night and writes; the poems she puts in a drawer in the bedroom. She will not discuss them. She refuses to consider the possibility of their translation. She is angry—all the time she seems angry. Often she will not even speak to me."

"Well, this is a personal matter," Auslander said, "between the two of you only."

He continued as if she had not spoken. "Teo is rather frail, you see. She has headaches, she does not sleep well. Frequently she is depressed. I feel strongly that she cannot continue this way. She has no life outside her part-time job at the university. She has no friends, no one to talk with. She says I am her only friend. And it was I who took her away from her family and a promising career."

"She is sorry she left Rumania?"

"Not quite sorry, no. The situation there was untenable, impossible. Worse for her than for me. She is a Jew—only nominally, of course; it is virtually impossible to practice Judaism in our country. But this in itself made life difficult for her. No, we were completely in agreement about leaving. But here . . . she is always unhappy.

Her poetry, her most recent work—it makes me weep to read it, it is so full of sorrow. The poems are spectacular: violent and beautiful. But it is as if she is speaking only to herself."

"Perhaps this is the way she wants it."

Again he ignored her. "I have thought for a long time about finding a translator for her. I believe that if she were able to hold in her hand a translation of one of her poems, if it were precisely the right translation—she would change her mind. But how to find the person capable of this! It was daunting to me; it seemed beyond my abilities. When I read your essay in *Metaphrasis*, however, I was certain I had found Teo's translator. I have no doubt of this, still. I feel it, I feel it in my heart. As I read that essay, it was like a sign: I knew you were the one. With absolute clarity I knew also that you would be sympathetic to the problem . . . the unusual situation."

"Naturally, I'm sympathetic. But what can I do? Without her approval I could not translate a word of her writing. Surely you understand that. What you're asking of me is not only unethical, it's unfeasible. Without the participation of your wife. . . ." She shook her head. "I'm sorry. It's impossible."

Viorescu's expression was impassive as he tapped a cigarette from his pack and placed it between his lips. As he lit it, he breathed out, in rapid succession, two dark streams of smoke.

"But I would still like to see some of her poems," Auslander said. She did not know herself if she were being merely polite or if he had indeed called upon her curiosity. In any case it seemed to her absolutely necessary to make this offer; she could not refuse to read his wife's work after all he had said.

Viorescu took the cigarette from his mouth and looked at it. Then he waved it at Auslander. "Ah, yes, but are you quite sure that itself would not be 'unethical'?"

His petulance, she decided, was excusable under the circumstances. He was disappointed; this was understandable. Calmly, she said, "I see no reason why it should be." She kept her eyes on his cigarette as she spoke. "Unless, of course, you would simply prefer that I not read them."

He smiled, though faintly. "No, no. I had hoped that in any event you would want to read them." From a satchel hung on the back of his chair he produced a manilla envelope. He laid it on the table between them. It was quite thick. The sight of it moved her, and this came as a surprise. Viorescu folded his hands and set them atop the envelope. "I have chosen mostly those poems written in the last year or so, but also there is a quantity of her earlier work, some of it dating from our first few years in this country. I have also included a copy of her book, which I thought you would be interested in seeing."

"Yes," Auslander said. "I would, thank you."

"It is, I believe, a fair sample of Teo's work. It should give you a true sense of what she is about. See for yourself that I have not been overly generous in my praise."

"You're very proud of her."

"Yes, naturally." He spoke brusquely enough so that Auslander wondered if she had offended him. "Perhaps this is hard for you to understand. Teo is . . . she is not only my wife, she is like my sister. I have known her since she was six years old and I was twelve. We were family to each other long before our marriage."

A dim alarm went off in Auslander's mind—a warning that confidences were ahead. This was her cue to change the subject, no question about it. But she remained silent. Altogether despite herself she was touched.

"Ah, you find this poignant," Viorescu said, startling her.

Embarrassed, she nodded.

"Yes, well, perhaps it is. That we have been so close for so much of our lives is itself touching, I suppose. But we are not. . . . She is. . . . Ah, well." He shrugged and smiled, vaguely.

Auslander cautioned herself: This is none of your business; you want no part of this. But she felt drawn in; she couldn't help asking, "What were you about to say?" And yet as she spoke she groaned inwardly.

"Oh—only that something has been lost. This is maybe not so unusual after so many years, I think." He closed his eyes for an instant. "Something lost," he murmured. "Yes, it may be that she is lost to me already. Well, it is my own fault. I have not been a help to her. I have done a great deal of damage."

At once Auslander realized she did not want to hear any of this. Not another word, she thought, and she imagined herself rising immediately, bidding him good-bye and taking off—she did not even have to take the package of poems. What was the point of it? Did she honestly think there was a chance she might discover a hidden genius? Who was she kidding?

"It is very bad, very bad," he muttered.

A mistake, Auslander thought. Sitting here listening, offering to read the poetry of his wife—all a mistake. She could feel her chest

tightening against what she suddenly felt was certain to be a perilous intrusion into her life. For it would get worse with every moment: confessions led to further confessions. *No more.* She wanted
no more of Viorescu and his poet wife.

He pushed the envelope toward her. "Here, I can see you are
impatient. I did not mean to keep you so long."

She picked up the envelope. "It's true, I should be going." She
half-rose, awkwardly, and drew the envelope to her chest. "Ah —
shall I phone you after I've read these?"

"I will phone you." He smiled at her, broadly this time. "I should
like to thank you in advance for your time. I am very grateful."

Auslander felt uneasy. "I hope I've made it completely clear that
I'm not going to be able to take Teodora on."

"After you have read the poems," he said, "perhaps you will
change your mind."

"I'm afraid not."

"You have agreed to read them, after all."

"I am always interested in good poetry," Auslander said stiffly.
"If your wife's work is as you say, I would be doing myself a disservice
by not reading it."

"Indeed," he said, and now he laughed — his telephone laugh,
that short curious bark. "I will phone you next week."

She could feel his eyes on her back as she retreated, the envelope of poems under her arm. For his sake — and for the sake of
the unknown, unhappy Teodora — she hoped the poems were not
dreadful. She did not have much confidence in this hope, however;
the excitement that had begun to stir in her only moments ago had
already left her entirely.

By the time she had passed through the café's door and emerged
onto the street, she was convinced the work would turn out to be
inept. As she crossed Greenwich Avenue, her coat whipping about
her legs, her head bowed against the wind, she was imagining her
next conversation with Viorescu. She would be gentle; there would
be no need to tell him the truth about his wife's work. If he deceived
himself, he deceived himself. It was not her responsibility.

As it turned out, Viorescu had neither lied to her nor deceived himself. Teodora Viorescu's poems were extraordinary. Auslander, after
reading the first of them, which she had idly extracted from the
envelope and glanced at as she sat down to her dinner, had in her
astonishment risen from the table, dropping her fork to her plate

with a clatter, and reached for the envelope to shake out the re-
mainder of its contents. A batch of poems in hand, she ate her
broiled chicken and rice without the slightest awareness of so doing. She could hardly believe her eyes. The poems jumped on the
pages, full of terror, queer dangerous images of tiny pointed animal
faces, blood raining through the knotted black branches of trees,
fierce woods that concealed small ferocious creatures. And the language! The language was luminous, electrifying. What a haunted
creature the poet herself must be! Auslander thought as she at last
collapsed against her pillows at half-past twelve. She had been reading for five hours, had moved from table to desk to bed, and she
had not yet read all the poems Viorescu had given her; but she
intended to, tonight. She needed however to rest for a moment.
She was exhausted; her eyes burned.

For ten minutes she lay listening to the dim apartment sounds of
night: refrigerator, plumbing, upstairs creaks and groans, downstairs murmurs. Then she sat up again, stacked her pillows neatly
behind her, and set again to reading. When she had read all of the
poems once she began to reread; after a while she got up and
fetched a legal pad. For some time she reread and made notes on
the pad, resisting with difficulty the urge to go to her desk for a
batch of the five-by-seven cards she used to make notes on work
she was translating. Finally she gave in, telling herself it was simply
easier to use the index cards, their feel was more familiar, and with
a supply of the cards beside her she worked until dawn in something of a feverish state, feeling like one of the poet's own strange
night creatures as she sat wild-haired and naked in her bed, chewing on her fingers and the end of her pen, furiously scratching out
notes as the gray-bluish light rose around her.

For days, anxiously, she awaited Viorescu's call. On the fifth day
she checked the telephone directory and was half-relieved to find
no listing; she knew she should not phone him. But she felt foolish, waiting. Dimly she was reminded of her adolescence — hateful
time — as she stared at the phone, willing it to ring. After each of
her ventures out of the apartment — her few forays to the supermarket and the library, her one trip uptown to return the galleys of
a gothic romance — she hastened to her answering machine. The
playback yielded up several invitations to functions that didn't interest her, a number of calls from friends, one from her mother,
one from Farrell.

"Do you miss me, Harriet my love? Are you lonely?" Auslander breathed impatiently, fists against her thighs. Farrell's message was intended of course to make her angry. He never called her "Harriet" except to taunt her. Well, let him, she thought. She would not allow him to upset her. She had been less preoccupied lately with missing him; she had other things on her mind (and she'd like the chance to tell him that, she thought) — though the sound of his voice on the tape, it was true, sent a shiver of sorrow and loneliness through her. "Has it hit you yet that you're all alone? Are you enjoying it, as anticipated? Or are you sorry? Or are you not alone — have you already found someone else to resist loving?" There was a pause, then, harsher: "Don't call me back. I've changed my mind; I don't want to talk to you after all."

Eight days passed; then nine. On the tenth day — once again as she was about to take a bath, one leg over the side of the tub — the phone rang and she knew instantly it was the poet's husband.

He was cheerful. "So? What do you make of my Teodora?"

Auslander felt it would be wise to be guarded. "Well, she's something, all right. An original, no question."

"You enjoyed her work, then?"

She could not remain cautious; she was too relieved to hear from him. "'Enjoyed?' Ha! She's a terror, your wife. The real thing, astonishing stuff."

Viorescu was cackling. "Yes, yes, it's true, absolutely true. She is one of a kind, a wonder, a gem!"

Auslander stood beside the bed coiling and uncoiling the telephone cord about her wrist as they went on to talk about the poems. She excused herself to get her notes, and then she was able to quote directly from them; Viorescu was delighted. She had just launched into some observations about one of the most recent poems when she happened to glance up and saw that the man across the way was standing at his window staring blankly at her. Good lord, she thought, he would begin to imagine she strolled around naked for his benefit. She sat down on the bed, her back to the window, and pulled the blanket up around her.

"Listen, Petru," she said, "I've been thinking. I really ought to meet Teodora."

He clicked his tongue. "Well, as you know, this is not such a simple matter. I am not sure it is possible at all right now."

"It may be difficult," she said, "but surely we can manage it."

"Tell me, have you given any further thought to the question of translating her work?"

"I've already told you I would not consider it without her full cooperation."

"But you are interested! Well, this is good news indeed. Of course you must meet her. Let me think. . . . Why don't you come to dinner? Let us say, next Friday night?"

"Are you sure?"

"Yes, of course. But it would be best not to let her know immediately that you are a translator."

Auslander was discomfited. "Are you sure this is necessary?" she said. "If I'm not to be a translator, who am I? How did we meet?"

"Oh, I shall say I met you at an academic function. Teo never attends department functions with me."

"An academic function," Auslander echoed. She recalled then that she had never asked him what his area of study was. "What department is it that I am to be associated with?"

"Philosophy," he said with a short laugh. "That is my department. My specialization is Nietzsche."

"Wonderful," Auslander said. "You can tell Teo I'm a renowned Nietzsche scholar and I'll remain silent all evening."

"I can tell her that you are Hannah Arendt and she would not know the difference," Viorescu said dryly.

"Are you sure all this intrigue is necessary? Maybe you ought to simply tell her the truth."

"No. She would suspect a plot."

"Has she such a suspicious nature?"

"It does not take much," he said, "to arouse suspicious thoughts. Why take such a chance? We can tell her the truth after an hour, two hours perhaps, once she is comfortable in your presence."

For the second time, Auslander hung up the phone after talking to the Rumanian and found herself wondering what she was letting herself in for. Gloomily she paced around her bedroom — the man across the way, she noted as she went to the window to pull down the shade, was no longer looking out — and tried to convince herself that she was in no danger of becoming personally involved with the Viorescus. They needed a translator, she told herself; it was not necessary to be their friend. Still, she didn't like the circumstances; they did not lend themselves to a smooth working relationship. Even assuming that all went well — that Teodora was willing, that she could be reasoned with — the project was likely to be full of difficulties and strains, starting out the way it was. Already she had agreed to this preposterous masquerade! It was clear enough that

between Viorescu and his wife there were problems, serious problems. Auslander hated the thought of these complications.

But the poetry! Auslander shook her head, tugged at her hair as
she circled the room. *Oh, the poetry!*

She would have recognized Teodora Viorescu at once, Auslander
felt. Had she passed her on Sixth Avenue a day or two ago, she was
certain she would have thought: Might this not be the poet? Small
and pale, with hair like a slick black cap cut so short her ears stuck
out pointedly from beneath it, she felt her way through the room
toward Auslander like a swimmer.

"I'm very pleased to meet you," Auslander said. "Petru has told
me a great deal about you." She took the poet's small hand in hers.
It was very cold.

"So you are Miss Auslander."

"Just Auslander is fine."

"Ah, yes, so my husband told me." She smiled. Her face was perfectly round, her eyes also — oddly — round. How white her skin
was! As if she truly never saw daylight. And how grave she looked,
even as she smiled. It was in the eyes, Auslander thought. Her eyes
were the eyes of one of her own imaginary creatures: liquid-black
with floating pinpoints of light, emitting a steady watchful beam.

During dinner there was small talk. The food was Rumanian, traditional, Viorescu explained. He seemed very nervous and spoke
at length about ingredients and methods of cooking. Auslander
avoided meeting his eyes; she was sure it was plain to Teodora that
something was up. Teodora herself kept her eyes downcast and
picked at her food; between the Viorescus barely a word passed.

Auslander helped Viorescu move the table back into the kitchen
and pile the dishes in the sink; he tried to whisper to her but she
waved him away impatiently. Enough of this, she thought. She returned to the living room to find the poet sitting on the windowseat,
gazing out upon Riverside Drive. Auslander seated herself on the
end of the couch nearest the window and said, "Please, Teodora,
won't you tell me about your work? Your husband informs me that
you are a fine poet."

"There is nothing to tell." She turned slowly toward Auslander.
Her tone and facial expression were remote. Auslander recalled
what Farrell had told her when she'd described a famous poet she'd
met as "terribly cool and remote." "Wrong again, Auslander," he
had said. "Not *remote*. Only massively depressed and riddled with
anxiety — like me."

Auslander tried again. "Petru tells me you published a book in Rumania."

"Yes."

"And have you any interest in publishing your work in the United States?"

Teodora glanced over at her husband, who had entered the room silently and positioned himself by the bookshelves opposite the couch where Auslander sat, and spoke quietly to him in Rumanian. Auslander heard only snatches of what she said. "Unfair" — she heard this word several times — and "You should have told me." Once, clearly, she heard the poet say "unforgivable," and then — her heart sank — she heard unmistakably the Rumanian for "translator." Viorescu did not speak. Finally Teodora turned again to Auslander. "I am sorry if we have put you to any trouble. I do not wish for my work to be translated into English." Abruptly she stood and left the room.

Auslander started to rise, but Viorescu said, "Please, Auslander. There is nothing we can do."

"What do you mean 'nothing we can do'?" She was astounded. "I thought you were so eager to convince her."

"I believed she might be convinced. Apparently I was wrong."

"But you didn't even *try*."

"It would be pointless. She is very angry at having been deceived."

"Why didn't you just tell her what I was here for in the first place?"

"You must realize that it would not have mattered either way. She is obviously beyond — "

"You're giving up. I can't believe it. You do this whole. . . ." She sank back into the couch and looked up at him in amazement. "And giving up so easily!"

"Easily!" He laughed hoarsely. "I have been trying for years to talk her into having her work translated. I am giving up now *finally*." He shook his head. "There is a story — do you know it? — about a famous philosopher who decided, after long consideration, to become a vegetarian. For many years he lived as a vegetarian. He spoke and wrote of it, of course, since under the circumstances such a decision could not be a private matter only. He spoke brilliantly, in fact, and movingly, on the moral logic of his choice. Then one day he sat down to his table and began to eat a steak. His students, as you would imagine, were quite agitated when they saw this.

Why the change? they cried. What had happened? And the famous philosopher said, 'Ah, well, it was time to give it a rest.'"

"There is no relevance to this story, Petru," Auslander said wearily.

"Oh, I quite disagree, Auslander, my friend. But in any event don't you find it a charming story?"

"I have other things on my mind," she said. "Tell me. Why *doesn't* Teo want her work translated? What does she say when you ask her?"

"She says, 'Because I say so.'"

"But that's a child's logic."

"No. It's a parent's logic, rather. The child asks, 'Why not?' The parent says, 'Only because I say not.'"

"Well, then." Auslander shrugged and stood up. She was angrier and more disappointed than she could have predicted. "I guess that's it. Shall I mail the poems back to you?"

"Are you in a rush to be rid of them?" He smiled at her. "No, my friend. Let us not altogether give up. May I telephone you tomorrow?"

"What's the point?"

"Oh, I shall talk to her tonight. Perhaps it would be wise to tell her you've already read her work, extend your compliments. It will depend on her spirits."

"But I thought. . . ." Auslander stopped herself. There was no sense trying to follow him. "All right, fine. Call me."

"Tell me something," he said as he walked with her to the door and helped her into her coat. "Are you absolutely certain that if her work were translated it would be publishable here?"

"Oh, without question," Auslander said. Then a thought came to her. "Why? Do you think it will help if Teo knows this? Because if you like, I can make a few calls tomorrow, ask around, get a feel for it." Instantly she regretted this offer. Who on earth could she call to discuss the work of an untranslated Rumanian poet? Without work to show, what could she expect an editor to say? It was nonsense, absurd.

"That would be very kind."

"I should go now," Auslander said, her hand on the doorknob. As she went down the hall to the elevator, she reflected that it was a miracle that she had escaped without having made any further promises.

On the IRT heading back to the Village, she removed from her

Danish schoolbag the envelope containing Teodora's poems. She was not sure why she hadn't told Viorescu she had the poems with her — evidently she wasn't ready yet to part with them. She flipped through the pages until she found the one she wanted. From the front pocket of her bag she took out a pen and the packet of index cards she had begun to keep on Teodora's work, and she sifted through the cards, stopping at the one headed "In the Cold Field, In the Troubled Light." She ran her eyes quickly down the card; besides the title, she had already, automatically, cast a number of lines into English as she made her notes. She sighed and turned to the poem itself. Then, pen in hand, using the canvas bag as a lapdesk, she began the translation.

He did not even bother to say hello. "She wants no part of it," Viorescu announced. "She will not discuss it."

"What did you tell her? Did you explain — "

"I pleaded, I made promises, I was a madman." He laughed miserably. "She made me sleep on the couch."

"That's none of my affair," Auslander said sharply.

"I want to apologize for all the trouble you have taken."

"Yes, well, here's a surprise for you," she said. She took a deep breath and then told him about the poems she had translated last night, working until four o'clock, until she couldn't see clearly anymore.

"My God, that's. . . . Is this really true? How marvelous! Please, will you read them to me?"

For half an hour she read Viorescu his wife's poems. She had rough versions — very rough in some cases — of eight poems already; one or two were quite polished, almost perfect.

"But this is wonderful! Incredible! Oh, we must convince her. Do you think . . . what if we did as I had thought to begin with. . . ."

"I don't know. If you were to simply show her these translations she might get very angry. She might — quite justifiably — feel invaded."

"She might feel complimented."

"She might. You would know better than I."

Auslander was not altogether sure of this, however. His track record did not seem to be the best.

Several days passed. Auslander continued to translate the poems. There was no logic in it, she knew; she had almost no hope by now that Teodora would agree to have this done. She was translating the poems because she wanted to; there was no other reason. She was working at it late on Saturday afternoon when there was a knock on her door. Surprised, her first thought was of Farrell. Nobody ever dropped by without calling. Farrell himself had done so only once, and he would surely only do it now if he were drunk. Cautiously she went to the door and stood listening.

"Auslander, are you there?"

It was Petru Viorescu. She snapped away the police lock and swung the door open. He looked terrible.

"Petru! What on earth's the matter?"

"May I come in?" He brushed past her and heaved himself into her desk chair. He looked around. "What is this room? Bathroom, study, kitchen?"

Auslander closed and locked the door. "What's going on? You look like hell."

"I want to tell you something. I need to discuss this with some-one. I am going to lose my mind."

"Is it about Teodora?" she asked anxiously. "Has something happened?"

"Oh, something has happened, yes, but not what you imagine. You think she is so fragile! You are afraid that she has tried to com-mit suicide, that she has had a 'nervous breakdown.' No," he said. "She is made of iron, my wife." He laughed, but then after a sec-ond he placed his head in his hands and began to weep. Auslander stood back, uncertain what was expected of her. Finally he stopped crying; he looked up at her and very calmly told his story: He had met a young woman, someone in his department. He was in love; there was nothing to be done for it.

"I don't understand," Auslander said. "When did this happen? Just this week?"

"Months ago," he said. "Months."

"But I don't understand," she repeated. "Have you . . . ?"

"I have not slept with her, if that is your question."

"But then. . . . Have you told Teo about this?"

"Of course." He seemed offended at the implication that he might not have.

"But why? You haven't done anything. What is there to tell? You are . . . you have a crush, Petru, only that."

"No, no. It is not a crush. I am in love."

Auslander was at a loss. "Well, what do you want to do?" Then immediately she said, "Never mind. I don't want to know."

He began to weep again. Auslander wanted to scream. Suddenly a suspicion came to her. "Tell me something," she said. "How much does this business with the other woman — "

"Ana," Viorescu said.

"I don't want to know her name! How much does it have to do with Teo's refusal to have the poems translated?"

"How much does anything have to do with anything?"

"Don't speak to me that way, I won't stand for it," she snapped at him. "Answer me truthfully." She began to pace around the kitchen. "What's going on here? What is this all about? When did you tell Teo about this woman?"

"Months ago," he said. "As soon as I knew. I could not keep my feelings secret from her. We tell each other everything, we always have; we are brother and sister, inseparable."

"But you fancy yourself in love with someone else," she said sarcastically.

"One has nothing to do with the other. You must yourself know that."

"You're not planning to leave Teo?"

"No, I am not going to leave her. The question is whether she will leave me."

"But why has it come to this now, if she's known all these months? What's changed?" At once Auslander had the answer. "Petru," she said, "did the idea of having her poems translated somehow backfire on you?"

He shrugged.

"Did you come up with the notion of getting me to do this in the first place as a way of . . . of placating her? Giving her something of her own? Did you think that having me translate her poems might make things all right between the two of you?"

"This is partly true, yes."

"You could have just bought her flowers," Auslander said bitterly. "It would have saved a lot of trouble."

"I have bought her flowers," he said. "And in any case the trouble, it seems to me, was worth it. No? You don't agree? You understand that this was not the only reason I wanted to have the work translated, do you not? I have been discussing the matter with her for years, years. Long before I knew Ana, long before I met you. Years!" he said angrily. "She will not listen to reason. And what is a poet without readers? I have been her only reader for too long."

Auslander continued to stalk the kitchen, twisting her hands together as she paced. For a long time she did not speak. Finally she sighed and said, "Well, now there are two of us."

"Yes," Viorescu said. "Yes, exactly. Now there are two of us."

The call from Teodora the following night woke her.

"I am sorry to be disturbing you at so late an hour," the poet said. "But I will not be long. I wanted only to say one thing. I understand that Petru has been troubling you with problems of a personal nature."

Auslander was too startled to respond.

"I apologize for this." Teodora said. "I want you to know that I have asked him not to trouble you any further."

"Oh, really, it hasn't been all that much trouble," Auslander said.

"In all events he will not be calling you again."

"Oh, that isn't — " Auslander began. But it was too late; the poet had already hung up.

Auslander did not for a moment seriously consider the possibility that she would not hear from Viorescu. Thus she was not in the least surprised when three days later he called. There was a note of hysteria in his voice, however, which alarmed her.

"What is it, Petru? What's wrong now?"

"She wants to leave me! She says she has had enough, she is fed up. Auslander, please, I need your help. Will you call her? Explain to her? Please?"

"Explain what?" Auslander said. "I don't understand it myself."

"Please. She is at home now. I am in the library. You could call her right now and she could talk to you freely, she is alone."

"I'm sorry, I can't."

"But she wants to leave me!"

"Petru, I can't help you with this. It should be plain by now that I can't. There's nothing I can do."

"Yes, there is. But you refuse! You refuse to help!"

Auslander could not think of what else to do, so she hung up the phone. She stood staring at it. It began to ring again instantly.

She lifted the receiver. "Please don't do this," she said.

"Jesus, Auslander, you're right on top of it tonight, aren't you. I haven't even started doing anything yet."

"Oh, Farrell. I thought you were someone else."

"I wish I were."

"Please," she said, "not tonight. Look, I don't mean to be rude, but are you calling to give me the business? Because if you are, I don't think I'm up to it."

"No, actually I thought I'd take my business elsewhere." He sighed. "You're not laughing, love. What's the matter? Is something really wrong?"

"No, Farrell," she said flatly, "nothing's really wrong."

"Well, shall I tell you why I called? See, I've got this idea. What if I gave up drinking? How would that be?"

"How would it be how?"

"Come on, Auslander. You've always complained about my drinking. What if I stopped?"

"I don't know." Suddenly she felt like crying.

"Hey, what's going on with you? Are you really all right? You sound awful."

"I'm all right," she said. Then, after a second, "No, I'm not. I guess I'm not. I don't know."

"Is there anything I can do?"

She shook her head before she remembered that he couldn't see her. "No," she said. "Not a thing."

"Well, what do you think? Do you think it would make a difference? In our relationship, I mean. Do you think it would help?"

"Look, Farrell," she said, "if you want to quit drinking, then quit drinking. You know perfectly well that I think you ought to. I've said it enough times. But if you're going to do it, do it for yourself, not for me. I don't want to be responsible for the decision."

"Oh, sure, that's right. How could I have forgotten? You don't want to be responsible for anything or anyone, do you."

"Farrell, please."

"Please what? I am making a perfectly reasonable gesture toward straightening things out between us, and you're just tossing it right back in my face."

"That's not what I mean to do."

"No? What do you mean to do, then? Tell me."

"I don't know."

"You don't, do you."

"No." She realized she was gripping the phone so hard her fingers ached. "I don't."

"Tell me something, will you? *Do* you miss me? Ever? Do you even think about me?"

"Of course I think about you. I think about you a lot. I wonder about how your work is going. I wonder how life's treating you."

He laughed softly. "Oh, Auslander, my love, you should know. Life's not treating me at all—I'm paying my own way."

Into bed with her that night she took the envelope of Teodora's poems and all of Farrell's poetry that she had in the apartment— all the poems of his that she had in typescript, all the magazines that had his poems in them, his four chapbooks, even some stray handwritten lines on pages torn from legal pads, which he'd left scattered about the apartment on nights he couldn't sleep. She read all of it, every line, Teodora's and Farrell's both, read until she felt stunned and overburdened, and fell into a sleep that was a kind of stupor. Under the blanket of poems, dreaming, she turned and tossed in her sleep; poems crackled and fluttered, flew off the bed, alighted on the floor.

It was months before she heard from Viorescu again. He called to tell her that Teodora had killed herself. He had returned from the library late at night and found her. There was no note. "She left nothing," he said. He spoke of the funeral and of Teodora's family. Several times he wept, but very quietly. Auslander listened without saying anything. When he had said all he had to say, she waited, expecting to hear herself tell him that she was sorry, but she remained silent.

For a moment they were both silent. Finally Viorescu said, "There is something else I must tell you. Teodora destroyed all of her work—all the poems she wrote from the time we left Rumania. I have searched the apartment; she was very thorough. Every copy of every poem is gone."

Now Auslander was about to make herself speak. "I'm sorry," she said.

"You are not surprised, I imagine."

"That she destroyed her poems? No, I suppose I'm not."

He hesitated. "You understand that you now have the only copy of her work."

"Yes."

Again they were silent.

"You want the poems translated," Auslander said.

"This is not the time to discuss this, of course," he said. "But after a reasonable amount of time has passed, yes."

"Yes, I see," she said.

"And in the meantime you will be careful, will you not?"

"With the poems? Of course."

"Well, then. . . . We will speak."

"Yes."

As she went to her desk and removed the envelope from the center drawer, where it had remained undisturbed for months, Auslander thought briefly of Farrell's poems, which that same morning months ago she had set on the top shelf of her bedroom closet. She saw them in her mind — the bundle of poems secured by a rubber band, surrounded by the accumulated clutter of years: stacks of letters; shoeboxes full of photographs, postcards, cancelled checks; spiral-bound notebooks dating back to graduate school. Then the image vanished and she sat down at her desk; she flipped open the oak box in which her index cards were filed and removed the cards on Teodora — the notes and the dozen translations she had done. One at a time she laid the cards on her desk, as slowly and precisely as a storefront fortune teller, spreading them out carefully in a fan, one corner of each card touching the next. When she had come to the end of the cards, she shook the poems themselves out of the envelope. Now the desktop was littered with poetry. For a time she sat looking at all that she had spilled out there. Then she scooped up everything and stood, hugging the papers and cards tightly to her chest. She crossed the kitchen and with some difficulty unhooked the police lock. In the hallway she hesitated for an instant only; then she moved quickly. With one arm she held the poet's work; with her free hand she pulled open the door to the incinerator chute. It was a matter of seconds; then it was done.

The 19th Jew

ROBIN HEMLEY

Robin Hemley (1958–): *Robin Hemley was born into a distinguished literary family: his father, Cecil Hemley, was a poet, novelist, and one of the founders of Noonday Press; his mother, Elaine Gottlieb, has published fiction; and both of his parents worked as translators of Isaac Bashevis Singer's novels and stories. Originally from New York, Hemley has lived all over the United States: in Tennessee, Chicago, Indiana, Iowa, Ohio, North Carolina, and most recently in Washington state. He was educated at the University of Indiana and the Iowa Writers' Workshop. His books include three collections of stories,* The Mouse Town, All You Can Eat, *and* The Big Ear, *plus a novel,* The Last Studebaker, *and a guide for short story writers,* Turning Life into Fiction. *His work has been published in a number of magazines, including* Manoa, Ploughshares, North American Review, *and* Prairie Schooner, *and has been reprinted in* The Pushcart Prize *and* Best American Humor *anthologies, as well as featured on National Public Radio. He is the winner of numerous awards, including fellowships from the Illinois and North Carolina Arts Councils and a Nelson Algren Prize. Hemley has taught at the University of North Carolina–Charlotte and Western Washington University, where he currently edits* The Bellingham Review. *He lives in Bellingham with his wife and daughters.*

At her meeting with the associate dean, Edith Margareten asked the administrator, a woman in her mid-40s, about the climate for Jews at Notre Dame. "Oh, it's fine," she said. "I'm Methodist myself."

"Ah," Edith said, tilting her head ironically.

The woman flipped through the pages of a scrapbook-sized volume. Edith looked down at her lap and smoothed out her wool skirt, which she had bought specifically for the interview. It was gray with little flecks of brown, and itchy. The dress looked Catholic on the rack, but she regretted buying it now. She placed her hands on her knees and regarded the associate dean while the woman flipped. Edith could hardly keep her eyes open. The woman bored her and she'd slept terribly the night before. The Morris Inn on campus had the skinniest beds, as hard as pallets, designed so that no one could possibly sleep — nor consider sinning in them. Over every door in her suite, where normally one might expect to see a smoke detector, a cross hung or a swooning Jesus, or a proud Mary. Edith had unpacked, humming, "Left a good job in the city, working for the man every night and day." But no smoke detectors.

"Yes, we have 17 Jews on campus," the woman announced, pointing at a page somewhere towards the middle of this mysterious book.

"What's one more?" Edith said.

"Exactly," the woman said, lifting her hand, palm up, and giving Edith a wide open expression devoid of irony.

"You really keep track?" Edith asked, but it wasn't meant to be a question. "In a book."

This seemed to catch the associate dean by surprise. She sat up straight in her chair and locked her eyes on Edith. Edith wondered if this woman had ever read one of her books, if she even read books anymore, if she knew who Edith was. Going into the interview, she had asked the English department chair, a Milton scholar named Dan Massey, what an associate dean was. The real dean had been off-campus, and so they'd come up with this low-cal Methodist version. He'd leaned over conspiratorially and whispered, "A mouse studying to become a rat."

"There might be more," the woman said.

"These are the ones you know of," Edith said.

The woman closed her scrapbook. "This is a Catholic institution, and part of our mission is to provide an exceptional education within a Catholic framework. But Notre Dame is known for its ecumenical atmosphere. The Catholic faculty hovers around 51 percent."

Edith smiled. "They hover, too." There was no possibility, she decided, of ever working for such a place. They probably wanted to hold the line, in any case, at 17 Jews.

The job she had applied for — they had approached her actually — was hardly a job at all, more like a sinecure: The Leo L. Ward Chair in Creative Writing. Edith, if she was offered the job and took it, would be its first recipient, and she was made to understand she could keep the job as long as she wanted. Father Ward had been head of the English department in the '40s at Notre Dame, and had died in the early '50s — a volume of short stories, *Men in the Field*, was published posthumously with the Notre Dame Press. Edith had run across the book by chance at Gotham Book Mart, bought the copy, and read through it before her interview. But when she mentioned her find to the chair of the English department at a party in her honor, he cut her off. "Oh please," he squealed. "Don't embarrass me. *Men in the Field*. What, there were no women around?" Dan Massey made a gibbon-like face at her — all chin and eyes — pathetic, needy and curious, and then he gave her a wide smile.

"I found some of the stories touching," she said. "But they're vignettes really. I wouldn't call them stories."

Dan Massey began to sputter and then broke into a kind of braying. Edith stood back and regarded him with a glass of white wine in her hand. No one at Notre Dame, she assumed, had even read Father Ward's stories in decades. They simply needed his name, the tradition he supposedly represented.

"Have you read them?" she asked.

"Oh please," he said with a wave. "*Men in the Field*."

Dan Massey bent towards her and said, "Edith, we're *lantsmen*. I'm one-sixteenth Jewish. My great-grandfather." He bobbed in her direction — she couldn't say whether he was purposefully making fun of a religious Jew benching, or if it was merely an effect of the wine. And he brayed as though this was an impressive revelation and not an insult as Edith saw it.

"One-sixteenth," she said. "Coelum non animam mutant qui trans mare currant."

He smiled broadly at her.

"It's Horace," she said. "It means, 'Those who cross the sea, change the sky above them but not their souls.'"

"That's true," he said. "I know this sounds silly," and he bent close to her again with his gibbon expression, "but sometimes I feel my soul is Jewish. Especially when I read Singer."

She took a sip of wine and scratched her leg where the wool of her skirt had irritated it. The sea he had crossed was the shallowest body of water, and one hardly needed a ship, merely hip waders. Dan Massey was a fool. She was partial to fools. She wrote about them. She had married and divorced one. But this kind of fool, the academic variety, was not to her liking — his calibrations were slightly off.

She kept her demeanor cool but pleasant in a superior way, though the interview was over for her. Dan Massey was yet another reason she would never come to work for Notre Dame.

A week later, Massey called. He asked how much it would take to bring her. She didn't want to go, and she assumed that would be the end of it when she named an outrageous sum. The chair paused and said, "Edith, you charmed everyone who met you."

Years later she still wondered on occasion what had charmed them so. In her circle of friends and enemies she was considered many things: pathologically self-obsessed, pedantic, and paranoid — not qualities one normally associated with charm. She had been ready to flatly refuse Massey's offer, despite the salary, but this revelation that they'd found her charming surprised her, weakened her resolve, lulled her into a kind of curious stupor that made her willing to suspend her natural suspicion of others.

"Really?" she said.

"Everyone's been talking about you. The graduate students, the members of the department. I've never seen such overwhelming support."

The week after the interview she'd spent denigrating the place to her friends and her relatives, so when she changed her mind, many were shocked. One friend said, "You can't leave New York. You'll die," as though New York were a rare blood type. Another asked if she'd have trouble finding fresh coffee. One friend placed South Bend in Wisconsin rather than Indiana and when Edith corrected him, he said, "I'm never going there." But the only reaction that truly angered her was her Aunt Judy's, a bitter and opinionated woman who had never approved of a decision of anybody's in her life. "Five years from now you'll have lost your voice," she said, "You'll be writing Willa Cather novels."

"My values are my values," Edith said.

"But you told me — they have Jesus on the side of the library."

Yes, he loomed over campus like a benevolent version of Godzilla over Tokyo, but even that didn't change her mind. She was ready for a change. And getting used to something like a hundred foot Christ, being adaptable — that was part of living.

Seven years later, Edith was still settling in to the place, but settling in comfortably. Edith's job made few demands on her — she lived in Chicago and commuted twice a week on the South Shore railroad to South Bend, took a cab to campus, and kept an office hour. Usually, she had no interruptions and wrote during this hour — students didn't bother her because she didn't post her office hour or tell the departmental secretaries when it was. She didn't feel obligated to speak with any students who lacked the perseverance to track her down. Twice a year she taught a class to twelve hand-picked graduate students. Rather than discuss their work, she thought it more beneficial for them to hear about her own creative process — sometimes she asked them to write in class, and she took this opportunity to write as well. Sometimes she allowed them to read what they had composed.

Mostly, people left her alone. The associate dean had been right, after all, about the climate.

Before coming to Notre Dame, Edith had been spoken of as someone on the Nobel committee's short list, and the list seemed to be getting shorter every year. She had been compared to everyone, and so believed, or hoped at least, that she really must be like no one: 24 reviewers had, over the course of her career, compared her to Paley, 16 to Singer (for whom, they dutifully noted, she had translated), 14 to Elkin, 7 to Kafka, 11 to Malamud, 3 to Ozick, 2 to Bellow, and 1 lost soul had compared her to all seven. Most often, she was lumped with other Jewish writers, but sometimes Catholics, too. She dealt with moral issues in her work, with hypocrisy and comeuppance at the forefront — she often gave her characters Old Testament-type tests. They made mistakes, made the wrong decisions, like Jonah or Abraham, and that's why the Catholics liked her, she decided. They too, were always making the wrong decisions, the Inquisition, their treatment of native peoples in the New World, St. Dominic's eradication of the Albigensians on the orders of Pope Innocent III.

There was a man in her stories who almost always appeared, a fool named Brennerman, neither a Singer fool, nor a Sholom Aleichem fool, a blessed know-nothing — nor a Shakespearean fool, wise but sad, a teaser. More of a trickster. Sometimes Brennerman knew a lot, sometimes he knew nothing. Sometimes he taunted her main character, Edith's alter-ego, Francine Riemer. Brennerman liked to sit on Francine's shoulder like a conscience. Brennerman appeared in Francine's dreams, and Edith's, too, told her to stop taking herself so seriously, that the world could live without her. Brennerman existed for Edith and Francine both in the world of their imagination and in the real world. He was based on a man Edith had once seen painting directional arrows in the lanes of the parking lot of the Green Acres shopping mall in Valley Stream, Long Island. She was there shopping with her mother, who lived in

#300   03-03-2010 3:43PM
Item(s) checked out to p10343131.

TITLE: American Jewish fiction : a centu
BARCODE: 33019004580438
DUE DATE: 03-24-10

TITLE: A theft
BARCODE: 33019002335645
DUE DATE: 03-24-10

TITLE: The anatomy lesson
BARCODE: 33019001920504
DUE DATE: 03-24-10

Portland Community College Library
(503) 977-4935   www.pcc.edu/library

nearby Woodmere. The man's fellow workers were standing around smoking and talking while he was doing all the work. The lane which he painted was blocked off with orange cones. In the other lanes, all with freshly painted arrows, none of the cars paid any attention to the new directions. The man ignored the chaos around him just as the world ignored him. She decided this man's name was Brennerman. She never saw him again, but Edith's character, Francine, saw him all the time:

> *The names of God, Francine Riemer suspected, were legion, more than the combined last names of all of humanity, but how many more? How many last names could there be in the world? Had anyone counted, done a study, because she kept hearing new ones — Sloyer, Ege, Cashio, Paykue, Spawr. Francine wanted to know. She collected last names, from personal encounters, from far-off reports and news dispatches. She was a smart woman and knew, of course, that collecting names was an odd pursuit. She held out no hope for monetary gain. Her names had none of the intrinsic value of her mother's autograph collection — a Fred Astaire, a Tyrone Power, a Franchot Tone — nor her cousin Sophie's collection of Italian leather decanters.*
>
> *Francine's mother said this was an unhealthy occupation.*
>
> *"Preoccupation, Mother."*
>
> *"Aren't you happy with your name?"*
>
> *"I'm happy with my name."*
>
> *"Because if you're not happy, you should change it."*
>
> *"I like my name, Ma."*
>
> *"A name like Smith, perhaps. Or Jones. Or Arnold. That has a nice ring. Benedict Arnold."*
>
> *"Ma!"*
>
> *"Eh, what does a pig know about noodles?"*
>
> *That was her mother's favorite saying. She used it all the time, but always, Francine thought, slightly out of context, and so Francine never really felt she understood what the saying meant.*
>
> *Francine didn't feel unhealthy. Her dedication to names didn't interfere with her personal life (she had none), nor her work at the food co-op. But lately, she couldn't pass a man, a woman, a child on the street without desiring to discover who they were — at least as much as one can discover through the porthole of a last name.*
>
> *In fact, when Francine and her mother were having this discussion, the one recorded nearly verbatim above, they were walking through the parking lot of a nearly-famous suburban shopping mall, on a mission to*

*buy a hat for Francine's mother, a belated—as always—birthday gift
from Francine—when Francine and her mother walked by a man working in one of the lanes of the parking lot. The man, a young lanky fellow
in overalls, a yarmulke perched on his head, was intently painting an
arrow in the middle of the lane while three other workers stood above him,
smoking and spitting and laughing, but not lending a hand at all.*

*The man's last name pierced Francine's foot like a shard of glass and
made its way through her intestines to her heart. The name rose in her
like a complaint. "Brennerman!" she shouted.*

*The men stopped laughing. Francine's mother stood still. The man
painting the arrows looked up at her and smiled, an extraordinary smile,
his top bicuspids missing, as though he'd actually given his eyeteeth, as
the saying goes, but for what, Francine couldn't guess.*

That was how the world was introduced to Brennerman and Francine Riemer. Brennerman had been gold to her. She owed him her
entire writing career. But sometimes she still wondered, despite her
success, where the source was of that internal voice, the one that
made her stories possible. Sometimes she worried that she might
be falling into a pernicious pattern, a diction that wasn't naturally
hers, but wholly derivative. She worried even about Brennerman,
her beloved fool, whether he was truly hers or not, whether she
could rightfully claim him. She worried that what she presented to
the world might not be true enough, but merely a caricature of
Jewish literature. She despised the current crop of Southern writers for this reason—they often sounded so similar, she wondered
whether they simply passed around a pad of paper to be continued
where the last one left off. Perhaps the Nobel committee discerned
this same affliction in her own writing.

She did not want to be an imitator—discernible yes, within a
tradition, but original enough so that she could not be typed or
ethnically patronized. The comparisons people made between her
and other Jewish writers bothered her less because she knew such
comparisons were ultimately meaningless. Not only had she been
compared to other Jewish writers, but often she was compared to
gentiles—Catholics: Flannery O'Connor, Graham Greene. Latin
Americans—Cortazar, Marquez, Fuentes, Borges. Once, when
she'd written a book from a teenager's perspective, she'd been compared to Salinger and Harper Lee both. People needed to believe
in such a great Literary Chain of Being, and that's why they made
such comparisons.

Singer, perhaps, was to blame for her insecurities. He had fed them, been quite cruel to her. She had known Singer well, had translated some of his early stories when she had worked at Noonday Press and later at Farrar Straus as a young woman in the '50s and '60s. In later years, she lost touch with him, partly because of Singer's secretary, Joanne, who treated him like a windup toy. The world treated him much the same, a little Yiddish gnome, reduced, catalogued, purchased. All of his well-cultivated eccentricities, the parakeets in his home that perched on his head, his vegetarianism, the requisite copy of the *Daily Forward* under his arm, were part of the package, accessories one might purchase for a Barbie doll.

She had been deceived by that version of the man when she first met him, but saw another side once when she had dinner at his apartment. They had been working on a translation of one of his stories, although to call her work translating was a misnomer. Her knowledge of Yiddish was limited to a few curses her Uncle Al had taught her. Singer did the rough translations himself, and his translators polished his prose. They had been working on one of the stories from *Gimpel the Fool* all day, when Singer suggested she stay for dinner. When his wife walked in the door after work — she worked in the women's sportswear department at Saks — he ordered her to prepare dinner for them both, and then all through the meal he ignored her. Edith and Singer had been discussing the Suez Canal, and when his wife offered her opinion, he paid no attention, except to tell Edith pointedly that it was nice, for once, to have an intelligent conversation with an intelligent woman.

Edith had a hard time forgiving herself for being so young and stupid. She had showed him a story, but only because he had asked to see it. This was after they slept together one afternoon not long after the dinner with his wife. That night, she had a nightmare that Singer told her she was completely without talent, and when she woke up she was glad it was only a dream, but it turned out worse. He told her that he was astounded how poor her writing was. He had assumed she was good because Roger Straus had recommended her, but he wasn't even sure she had the ear now to help him with the polishing of his own roughs.

"Do you want me to leave, Mr. Singer?" she had asked.

"What does your mother do?" he asked her.

"My mother?" she said, wondering whether he wanted her mother to translate, to sleep with him, too. "My mother sells hats."

"That's a good occupation. You should sell hats, too. Forget writing. It's a tough business."

Sometimes, in her dreams, she still heard herself asking meekly, in her craven voice, "Do you want me to leave, Mr. Singer? — and waiting for his reply. He just looked at her with that impish smile. "Hats. I'll say it again. Sell hats."

Edith was asked to serve on a committee — an unusual occurrence, the first, actually, of its kind. She was not expected under normal circumstances to serve on committees, nor attend department meetings — though she had on occasion been prevailed upon to serve on the thesis committee of a particularly promising graduate student or two. But this committee was different. It was a university-wide committee established to decide on an award, a kind of junior version of her post, the Ernest Hoover Fellowship, named in honor of another beloved former professor and writer from the English department. The award would be given annually to a young writer in early to mid-career, and provide a stipend for the writer to finish a project of exceptional merit.

Dan Massey, who was no longer the chair of English, but the new associate dean, assured her that her presence on the committee was crucial, that she was the only one on campus who had the knowledge, experience and prestige to make such an important decision. "Anyway," he said, "you can't leave me alone. I'll be the only Jewish person on the committee."

"You're not a Jew, Dan," she said.

"Why don't you ever humor me, Edith? Hey, maybe you can make me an honorary Jew."

"That's a tall order."

"Who am I, trying to fool you?" he said and laughed.

She hated the man, but he seemed to think they were best friends. She knew he was right. They needed her on this committee, not because she was Jewish, of course, but because no one else could be trusted.

Edith spent much more time at the task of sorting through the applications than she had originally anticipated. Most of the writers who applied were clearly not competitive. To say that they were beginning writers would be to assume that they even knew where GO was. A beginning predicted an end, but with most of the applicants, the only end Edith could envision was her own premature death, a kind of literary aneurysm. Other applicants were clearly unworthy because they were too far along in their careers. One such writer was one of those who had initially expressed such horror at the thought of her accepting the job at Notre Dame, at venturing outside of 200 miles from New York. Now, he warmly addressed his application directly to Edith and ended his letter by writing, "I hear reports that you're getting along famously in Indiana, so it must be bearable. But I always thought you'd moved to Wisconsin!! What's the difference, right?" She gave him a handwritten reply.

> *Dear Bruce,*
>
> *When I told you I was leaving New York for the Midwest, you said that it didn't matter where South Bend was because you were never going there. You were right.*

After a month, she came across an application she liked, from a Hispanic poet with the single name Mi. The poet was barely in her 30s and had already won every fellowship in the known universe and hardly needed another: the Hodder Fellowship, the Stegner, a Whiting, a Guggenheim, an NEA. But it was difficult to deny the power of her poems. Mi had been an addict and prostitute in Houston, and she wrote persona poems from the points of view of other hookers and addicts, gang members, white businessmen, cops. While those poems were good, there was one *amazing* sequence of poems that threaded through Mi's manuscript, a fanciful but searing series of prose poems in which the world's past revolutionary leaders all visited Mi, and while she tried to talk politics with them, all they wanted to do was to satisfy their personal sexual urges. In one poem, she masturbated Mao. In another, she had oral sex with Ho Chi Minh. She whipped Lenin. She had straight sex with Che, while Fidel watched. All of them, in their turn, made excuses for not paying her. The title poem of the manuscript, called, "The Long March," detailed a night in jail, trying to keep her head from exploding, Mao, in the form of a fly buzzing her, berating her for being caught, for having it easy, for betraying the others who hid in caves and evaded planes, machine guns, torture, and bombs of the Japanese and Kuomintang. The poem was an incredible meshing of Chinese history against the backdrop of mini-mart America, and ended in a gorgeous and surprising stanza in which the poet revealed she was writing the poem from the Bellagio Center for the Arts in Italy, and that the fly lay dead on her windowsill.

Such a presence would knock their frocks off at Notre Dame.

At the next meeting of the committee, Edith suggested Mi for the fellowship. There were six members from various departments and disciplines, chaired by Dean Smoot, the former associate dean and sometime Methodist (who had since converted) who had interviewed Edith and allowed that one more Jew would not tarnish Notre Dame's Golden Dome. There was a moment of silence while the members passed around the folder, glanced at it to refresh their memories, and then looked at their laps, all except for Stan White-Watson, who agreed with Edith that Mi should be awarded the fellowship.

No one in the English department, or anywhere, as far as Edith could tell, cared for him. But unlike her colleagues, Edith did not pretend to like him. His name was Stanford White-Watson, and as he was fond of telling people within three minutes of meeting them, he had been named after the famous architect, Stanford White. Stan was an opportunist, a loudmouth, and a bully: one of those people who throws back his head and laughs after saying something terribly vituperative, but his jolliness counteracted his meanness, and so people rarely knew how to respond to him, except to laugh along in a kind of forced self-deprecation. When people spoke of powers within the university, Stan White-Watson was always among the first names mentioned. As far as Edith could tell, the source of Stan's power as well as his pretend popularity was his complete readiness and willingness to give a cocktail party at a moment's notice. When a candidate needed to be entertained or a visiting dignitary feted, Stan was the man with the wine and cheese and the full liquor cabinet.

The reason Stan and Edith did not get along had to do with a party given in Stan's honor. A couple of years earlier, Stan had left his wife of 19 years and his two children, and had moved in with David Kitto from political science. Although Edith had not known Stan's wife, Clarise, well at all (nor anyone else at Notre Dame), the rest of the department had been friends with her — the response by a number of them to the breakup of Stan's marriage was to hold a party for Stan to celebrate his coming-out. None of this interested Edith in the least, and she had refused to go to the party, not because of his sexual orientation, but because she saw the breakup of his family as a tragedy, not a cause for celebration. She had told him as much when he asked her in the hall one day why she hadn't been there.

"Too bad I didn't know," Stan said. "Clarise was holding a con-current party for self-righteous homophobes," and he threw his head back and started to shake with laughter.

"I think that what you did was selfish," she said. "But private nonetheless. It's the poor taste of your friends, nothing more, that kept me away from this party."

Edith had had enemies before — a natural result of her own hon-esty and unwillingness to compromise her values, but none seemed as contemptible and bilious as Stanford White-Watson. Now she found herself in an uncomfortable alliance with him.

"We would like to have a Hispanic," the dean finally told them, "but not this Hispanic."

"What do you mean, you'd *like* to have a Hispanic?" said Stan.

"I have to agree with the dean," said Jack Ormsby from engi-neering. "Her poems seem pushy."

The dean looked at Edith and smiled.

Another member of the committee, Millicent Kent from copy duplicating services, mentioned that she had just noticed that the ad for the position had a comma splice in it that no one had caught.

"My God," said Massey, grabbing the ad and peering at it closely. "I can't believe that got by us."

He passed the piece of paper glumly to Dean Smoot. "Too late now," she said. "We'll have to watch that in the future. That does not reflect well on us."

"I want to talk about Mi," said Edith.

The committee members looked across the table at her. Stan White-Watson tapped the edge of the table with a pencil. "Do you always have to be the center of attention, Edith?"

"The poet," Edith said. "The Hispanic poet who, for some rea-son, threatens this committee."

"I'm surprised she doesn't threaten you, too," Stan White-Watson said in a nasty tone and laughed again, but Edith ig-nored him.

"What exactly about her makes you so uncomfortable?" she asked the others.

"She's vulgar," said Millicent Kent.

"Tasteless," said the dean.

"We just don't like her work," said Ormsby.

"I don't think you're judging her work," Edith said. "You're judging who you think she is. Judge the work."

"It's vulgar," said Millicent Kent.

"I don't get it," said Ormsby.

"This is making me ill," said Edith.

"Me, too," said Stan. "We should at least bring her to campus."

"We're not authorized to bring anyone to campus," said the dean. "We make our decision and that's who wins the fellowship."

"Aren't we allowed to simply not like her work, to think she's not very good?" asked Millicent Kent.

"No," said Edith. "You're not." She stood up and pointed a finger at the woman, who shrank a bit in her seat. "What do you think, Dan?" she asked Massey.

Massey simply gave her a befuddled smile like the fool he was. But in the end, Edith and Stan prevailed, with the pliable support of Dan Massey.

There was a connection between this young poet's work and her own, Edith felt. They shared other things in common as well, such as a fear of flying. Mi currently had a Bunting Fellowship at Radcliffe, and so took the train from Boston to New York to Chicago. The committee didn't even have to ask Edith to pick her up at Union Station. Edith volunteered. She didn't want anyone getting to the young poet before she did, and possibly saying something off-putting.

On the cab ride from her Lake Shore Drive apartment to Union Station, Edith imagined a conversation between herself and Mi. Edith was always composing, talking to herself, imagining outcomes. This was what made her such a fine writer, her deep interior life, the almost spiritual plane on which she hovered.

> *"It's an injustice that you have not won," says Mi.*
>
> *"I'm sure you'll win someday," says Edith. "You've won everything else."*
>
> *"I'd tell them that they should have given it to you, just as Hemingway said that Isak Dinesen should have won—though she was a colonialist, hardly a better choice."*
>
> *"Out of Africa, indeed," says Edith.*
>
> *"Perhaps you threaten them," says Mi. "You must. But I would take that as a compliment."*
>
> *"I do, child," says Edith.*

Edith, absorbed in her dialogue with Mi, didn't notice until the cab stopped that the cabby had taken her to the Northwestern Station rather than Union Station. By the time she arrived at Union Station, she was 20 minutes late and was sure that for once a train had probably arrived on time.

In the huge waiting hall of Union Station, the indistinct echoes and cries like exotic birds bounced off the stone walls. The place sounded almost haunted. Noise permeated the waiting area, a wall of sound created by a thousand travelers. Edith sat on a bench and scanned the crowd for the poet. A chubby black girl sat beside Edith, patting out some insistent tune on her thighs, looking in every direction at once, chatting manically with her mother and sister. Edith looked at the girl's thighs, then directly at the girl, who seemed not even to notice Edith. Twenty years ago, Edith would have pretended to be color blind, would have perhaps started up a conversation with the girl to prove to herself and anyone within earshot that she was colorblind. But she thought now, if I cast this girl in a story, would I mention she was black? Yes, this was the first thing she noticed about the girl. The second thing she noticed was the girl's weight, both corporeal considerations. Why mention them? But what stood out for Edith in this hall of sound was that drumming the girl did on her thighs. Would Edith have noticed a thin white girl drumming on her thighs? She hoped so. It was the sound that annoyed her, only the sound, insistent and harsh.

Edith noticed a dark-skinned-but-not-black woman standing by a bank of phones, who seemed to be waiting for someone. The woman was tall and had an aquiline nose and a dancer's posture. Edith fled the thigh-pounding black girl and approached the young woman by the phones with a warm smile and extended hand.

"Are you Mi?" she asked the woman

The woman looked briefly with alarm into Edith's eyes. "What?"

"You're not Mi, are you?" Edith said.

The woman seemed to notice something far above her and then off to the left.

Edith backed away. "Mi. It's her name. Mi. Mimi."

But the woman seemed not to be listening. She was frozen with a grim expression, almost fearful.

"Does she look like Mi?" a voice boomed behind her.

Edith turned and saw Mi. No one Edith had ever seen looked like Mi. Her hair was reddish-blond, not brown as in the picture Edith had seen, but as she drew close, Edith could see this was a wig. Mi's most striking aspect was not her reddish-blond wig, but the full-length black fur coat the poet wore, worth thousands of dollars,

Edith was certain, but not the most appropriate fashion statement these days.

"She is not Mi. I am Mi."

"Edith Margareten," said Edith clearly and firmly to let Mi know just whom she had snapped at so imperiously. Edith held out her hand. The woman brushed her fingers to Edith's and drew them back as though Edith's fingers were sticky. She looked impassively at Edith, who panicked and thought, *She doesn't like my work. She thinks I'm bourgeois, pretentious. She'd better like my work.*

Mi hardly spoke a word to Edith until they got into the cab to go to the Inter-Continental on Michigan Avenue where Mi was to spend her first night. She turned to Edith. "So, are you a writer?" Mi asked Edith the same way Edith asked teenagers at book signings who obviously wanted to be.

Edith suddenly felt tired, and could barely keep her eyes open. She wondered if Mi had been sent by a vengeful God to mock her, to humble her. She was Mi. Mi was she. It was a dirty trick, and she wouldn't succumb, not even to God.

"Books," Edith said. "Many books."

"Tell me their titles. I want to read them." But she did not sound convincing and Edith could barely find the energy to talk.

"*My Antonia . . . Death Comes for the Archbishop,*" she whispered.

"What? Speak louder."

"My books are unimportant," Edith said.

Mi nodded. "There are so few books of true importance."

And then Mi started telling her about a trip she'd taken to the former Soviet Union a number of years back in which she gave a reading with Yevtushenko and Bob Dylan. "At the end of the reading, they gave me the flowers — they only give flowers to one person. The Russians love me." Then she launched into a tirade against the Academy of American Poets. "They continue obstinately to ignore me."

Edith nodded but she wasn't listening. She was thinking of a new story, and while she didn't know exactly what this one was going to be about, she saw the last image quite clearly. She saw Brennerman as a thief in this story, breaking into Francine's apartment and painting arrows on the walls of her kitchen. "What are you doing to my beautiful apartment?" she'd have Francine scream at Brennerman. "I thought this is what you wanted. Isn't this what you always wanted?" Brennerman would ask, and that would be the end of the story. Now she only needed a story to fit that ending.

The next day there was no one to meet Mi at her hotel to bring her to South Bend. Mi did not make it to Notre Dame, perhaps not even out of Chicago. Edith never found out what happened to Mi. No one told her, and she did not ask. The other committee members were wise enough not to mention the word "Mi" in Edith's presence, except as a personal pronoun. At the next meeting of the committee, Edith hardly said a word, and half-listened to their recommendations — until Massey brought up the name of William Cradle Flower.

"I don't remember William Cradle Flower," Edith said.

"We were holding it back from you," said Ormsby, the buffoon from engineering, staring into his coffee cup, which had a replica of the mosaic Jesus on the side of the library. "We didn't want to excite you and Stanford too much."

The faculty received two free tickets to every Notre Dame football game, and ever since the committee had formed, she'd given her tickets to Ormsby. But no more. She'd go back to tossing them in the trash, maybe ripping them up with great ceremony and scattering them in the hallway. The only time she'd ever been near a Notre Dame football game was once when she went to observe the strange men who prayed at the grotto and lit candles before every home game. Ormsby was probably their head priest, their oracle.

"He's just kidding," Massey said. He smiled at Edith warmly, and for the first time, she felt a nickel of warmth for him, too. Maybe he wasn't hopeless.

Ormsby blew on his coffee. "The application came in late, past the deadline."

"Who cares?" said Edith. "Is he good?

"He's written a novel," said Massey, "that takes place . . ."

"If you like that kind of thing," said Ormsby. "But it didn't go anywhere."

"It didn't have a car chase?" White-Watson asked.

"I think it's a beautiful novel," said Millicent Kent. "It's mythic."

Edith looked down at her notes, pursed her lips, and waited a few seconds. Then she looked up at the woman from copy duplicating services and said, "The term 'myth' implies an irreality that native people do not feel. For them, there is no border between the empirical world and the world of dreams or myth. Ultimately, it's a patronizing term."

"Oh . . . well . . . what I meant was . . ." said Millicent Kent, and she put on a long face. "I didn't mean to patronize . . ."

"Are we allowed to ask his tribal affiliation?" Massey asked the dean.

"Cradle Flower," said the dean, picking at something on the sleeve of her jacket. "Cradle Flower. I can't stop saying it."

Edith took the novel home with her to Chicago, read half of it on the train, and finished it that night at her kitchen table while sipping tea. She finished it by 2 but didn't get to sleep until dawn — a combination of the tea and the excitement of discovering such a talent kept her from sleeping. The novel was titled *Incurable Hearts*, and that was the main character's name. Incurable Heart was a Crow who, by day, worked as a park ranger at the Little Bighorn National Monument and by night worked as a blackjack dealer at the Little Bighorn Casino just outside of the battlefield. Incurable Heart felt conflicted about the past of his tribe because the Crow had scouted for Custer against the Sioux, their enemies, and had been rewarded with one of the largest reservations of all the tribes by the federal government. He hardly ever slept and had visions of a coyote spirit, a trickster who was always confusing him. Sleepless and befuddled, he sometimes dealt blackjack to the RV tourists at the monument who wanted to hear about what a hero Custer was, and who still referred to the battlefield as the Custer National Memorial. And sometimes Incurable Heart gave lectures on Benteen and why he wasn't able to come to Custer's aid, but he delivered these lectures at the casino while dealing to the same tourists who had visited the battlefield earlier in the day, the tourists who now wanted only to drink beer, sing karaoke in the lounge, and get rich. Eventually, he was fired for incompetence and set off on a kind of inverted Candide-like adventure, accompanied by Coyote, who like Pangloss in *Candide*, had his own reductive and impossibly buoyant outlook, despite the many deprivations and injustices they encountered on the road. Finally, they wound up in Los Angeles at the La Brea tar pits, where Coyote fell in and was trapped forever among the mastodons, despite Incurable Heart's best efforts to save him by making a lifeline out of his 501 Levis. The novel ended with Incurable Heart spending the night in the drunk tank, arrested for vagrancy, public intoxication, and indecent exposure, trying to convince anyone who would listen that it wasn't too late to save his friend, that Coyote could hold his breath for an impossibly long time.

This was the new voice of a generation. Elements in his work reminded her of Marquez and Calvino, Kundera and Rushdie, Donald Barthelme and Delillo, Erdrich and Morrison, Malcolm Lowry. But of all the people he could be compared to, William Cradle Flower's work felt most like her own vision. She gleaned in his work a brilliance that she rarely saw in any of the younger writers. And best of all, unlike Mi, William Cradle Flower had not been discovered by anyone else.

The host of the welcome party for William Cradle Flower was Stan White-Watson. No surprise there. He lived in a sprawling house on Riverside Drive built in the Knute Rockne days. It wasn't much of a river. Not the Hudson, but the St. Joseph. And not New Jersey on the other side but . . . the other side. After all these years, she still missed New York, and secretly felt sometimes that she'd made the wrong decision to come to the Midwest. Her reputation, while still solid, seemed to be stagnating, and she worried that people back East had forgotten her. Here, a party was only a party. People were supposed to have fun — they could do no more. Not that she missed the people, but the parties she used to attend back East were more than gatherings of people, but gatherings of reputations. The people took up only part of the space — their reputations filled the gaps.

William Cradle Flower, who was being escorted by Dan Massey, had not yet arrived when Edith showed, but half of Notre Dame seemed to be there, including many from her own department whom she had never met or whose names she'd forgotten. She burrowed through them, found her way to the dining room, and poured a glass of wine from the many bottles on the table. Retreating to a corner, she stood there with her coat still on and sipped, glancing away when anyone looked in her direction.

"It's the Phantom," Stan said, reaching out his arm toward her in mock horror.

The people gathered around him turned and smiled meekly at her. "Edith," said Howard Salinas, the new chair of the department, waving her over, obviously trying to counter Stan's rudeness. Stan, Edith knew, acquired his personality via his liquor stock, and most of it was pretty cheap — so she rarely was offended anymore by his barbs.

"Stan was just telling us about something called 'Soul Retrieval.'"

"At a place called the College of Shamanistic Healing in Santa

Fe," said Tess Narokin, Howard Salinas' wife, who taught Russian and French.

"Make fun of it if you like," said Stan, "but I found it healing. We all need to be healed. All of us."

He looked at Edith, but she said nothing and simply took a sip of her wine. She felt as though they were setting her up — Stan, especially, seemed on edge, already drunk.

"I, for one, prefer not to be healed," she said finally.

"What do you mean?" asked Tess.

"I mean that I'm a kind of Christian Scientist of the spirit. I acknowledge the sickness in my soul, but refuse all known treatment, especially from doctors of divinity."

"I knew she'd make fun of me," said Stan.

"I'm serious," she said. "My refusal to be treated makes me a better writer."

The front door opened, and Dan Massey appeared accompanied by a wisp of a man dressed in jeans, a sports jacket, a blood-red shirt, and a little rope tie. He stood there for a second looking as though he'd entered the wrong bathroom and wanted to turn around, but Dan Massey ushered him in and closed the door. Stan, of course, was the first to greet William Cradle Flower. "Stanford White-Watson," he said solemnly, grasping William Cradle Flower's hand, and leading him into the living room. "One of those three-barreled names like yours," he said, but Edith cut him off before he could launch into the extended history of his name. She could almost hear his teeth grinding. If there was one way to torture Stan White-Watson, it was to cut him off, either speechwise or liquorwise. Like so many of these academics, he had a compulsion to hear himself speak.

"Edith Margareten," she said, extending her hand. "Your novel was superb. Welcome."

William Cradle Flower looked at her with wide little-boy eyes. But he wasn't a little boy. His hair was thinning and he had deep smile lines around his mouth. His eyes were blue and his hair was sandy blond, what Edith's mother had always called dirty blond.

"Can I get you anything to drink?" Stan asked.

"A rum and Coke," said William Cradle Flower.

"Rum and Coke?" said Stan. "How old *are* you?" and he gave one of his trademark laughs and left.

Massey, standing in between Edith and William Cradle Flower, glowed like he was marrying them.

"We had dinner at the Lasalle Grill," Massey told Edith. "Bill was telling me that he admires your work more than almost anyone alive." Massey was speaking loudly, distinctly, and a little more slowly than normal.

"Do you like to be called 'William' or 'Bill?'" Edith asked, wishing she could protect this frail and quiet young man from the buffoons around them.

He seemed not to hear her. He brought a finger up to his mouth and started gnawing at a fingernail.

"Here's your rum and Coke," Stan said, handing the drink to Cradle Flower. "So, as I was saying, my father was a frustrated architect, and he named me after Stanford White. I suppose he would have preferred that I become an architect, too, but all I build are castles in the air. My last name is Watson, like Sherlock Holmes' assistant. But I'm not a doctor, though I have a doctorate, and the detective I assist is not Mr. Sherlock Holmes, but Mr. Jacques Derrida. The crimes we investigate are crimes of hermeneutics."

William Cradle Flower looked up as though a smoke alarm had gone off. His eyes brightened, glowed almost mischievously, and he said, "My father was a frustrated rabbi."

"He wanted to be a rabbi?" Edith asked.

"He was a rabbi . . . he was frustrated," said Cradle Flower. "For a while, I wanted to be a rabbi, too. But I have always felt, even as a little boy, like an Indian."

Edith's stomach turned over. She rooted in her coat for a hard candy. She was down to her last one. The little candy sat snugly in its roll, a long snake of wrapping trailing around it.

The novel was good, she thought, but not that good. If she hadn't been so tired when she read it, she would have discerned how derivative it truly was.

"We have met before," said Cradle Flower to Edith.

"Oh boy," she said. "When was that?"

"Twenty-three hundred years ago, when I was a Levite. That was before the Temple was destroyed." He pointed to Massey. "You made music." He pointed to Stan. "You made the fire."

"What did she do?" Stan asked, indicating Edith.

"You made the sacrifice." Cradle Flower said, turning to her.

For a second, Edith could see herself with the knife in her hand, poised over the animal's throat.

"But those other people no longer exist. We have all changed our names. I had my name changed to fit my true nature. I am a Miami warrior. I was here in South Bend when La Salle came through. I sat under the Council Oak and exchanged gifts with him."

Cradle Flower gulped down his rum and Coke and sat beside Edith on the Victorian loveseat she occupied. He smiled shyly at Edith and said in an almost-normal voice, "I'm so happy you liked my writing."

Edith popped up and the candy went down her throat undissolved.

"What was your name before you changed it?" she asked. She wondered what the dean would put in her scrapbook under Cradle Flower's name. "In this lifetime."

"As ego fades, we return to the elements that surround us," Cradle Flower said.

"Your name," she said again. "Your real . . . name."

"Ha ha ha," Cradle Flower sang in a sing-song. "Who's afraid? Ha ha ha. Who's afraid?" and he rocked back and forth in the loveseat, his eyes fixed on Edith.

"This man is insane," said Edith to Massey. "We can't award him anything."

Massey fluttered his hand. "Legally, I don't know." he said. "It's done, Edith. And it's only for a year."

"But, our reputations," Edith said weakly. She saw herself in a cemetery, dressed in mourning. She saw herself rending her garments. She saw Mr. Singer. "I told you," he said. "Hats . . . are your true calling."

She bent down and pulled one of the large buttons off Cradle Flower's red shirt like an officer stripping a subordinate of rank. "We paid for an Indian."

"Edith," said Massey.

"I always knew she was a bigot," Stan said, and gave one sharp laugh. "A hell of a nom de plume," he said to Cradle Flower. "You had us fooled. Oh well." Stan looked at Massey and said, "You need your drink freshened?"

Cradle Flower stood up and stopped his sing-song. He stood stiffly at attention, his eyes on some invisible point like a national flag that only he could see, but which claimed his undying loyalty. "My name," he shouted, "My undying name . . ."

The room quieted and they waited for the man who called himself Cradle Flower to speak. Even Edith waited, as though an eternal mystery was about to be solved.

"My one true name is Crevecoeur," he said.

"Heartbreak," yelled Tess Narokin with the intensity of a jackpot winner. "That means heartbreak in French."

"Or Willow," said Cradle Flower. "Or Otter . . . Mackinaw Island . . . Space Needle . . . Or the wind. Or Grandfather. Or The Spirit That Resides in All Things, or Bebe Rebozo, Jack Lord."

"You never know," said Stan, draining his glass.

"It's still a hell of a novel," said Massey.

"Or Dream Pillow," Cradle Flower said. "Skunk Medicine. Or the Owl. The Pussycat. At sea in a pea-green boat. We are living in the time of the Seventh Fire. We have no need for names."

Edith wanted to cry, wanted to jump into the St. Joseph. Arrows. Everywhere, she saw arrows. In their hands, instead of drinks, through their hearts, on the walls. On the floor. Like a goofy joke, she imagined an arrow poking through her head. This is what she looked like, what she'd been carrying around for so many years, the source of her pain, her voice, everything rich and bankrupt, ridiculous and blessed.

"What a fool," she said to no one in particular, patting the side of her head. She looked around the room and saw her *lantsmen*, her people. She was almost ready to embrace them.

"Brennerman," she said, a name she detested now.

"Or Brennerman," the man said, nodding, his eyes no longer lucid.

The Revisionist

HELEN SCHULMAN

Helen Schulman (1961–): *Helen Schulman is a native New Yorker, educated at Cornell and Columbia. She has taught at Emory, New York University, Bard College, and the Bread Loaf Writers' Conference. She lives in New York and teaches in the Graduate Writing Program at Columbia. Her* stories have appeared in The Paris Review, GQ, Ploughshares, *and* The Antioch Review. *Schulman has published a novel,* Out of Time, *and a collection of short stories,* Not a Free Show. *She has written several screenplays and has edited an anthology of essays titled* Wanting a Child. *Her second novel, tentatively titled* The Revisionist *and related to the story reprinted in this book, will be published soon. She lives in New York with her family.*

I t had been a hundred years since Hershleder had taken in a late afternoon movie, a hundred years since he had gone to the movies by himself. It was 5:45. There was a 6:15 train Hershleder could still make. But why give in, why not not do something as inevitable as being home on time for dinner? At heart he was a rebel. Hershleder walked up the avenue to Kips Bay. There, there was a movie house. He could enter the theater in daylight. When was the last time he had done that — gone from a dazzling summer afternoon, when the air was visible and everything looked like it was in a comic book, only magnified, broken down into a sea of shimmering dots — into the dark, cool mouth of a movie theater? It was a dry July day. It was hot out. Who cared what was playing? Porno. Action. Comedy. All Hershleder wanted was to give himself over to something.

He was drawn to the box office as if the gum-chewing bored girl behind the counter was dispensing pharmaceutical cocaine and he was still a young and reckless intern — the kind he had always planned on being, the kind Hershleder was only in his dreams. She had big hair. Brown hair, sprayed and teased into wings. She had a dark mole beneath her pink lips on the left-hand side of her face. It looked like the period that marks a dotted quarter in musical notation. She was a beautiful girl in an interesting way. Which means if the light were right (which it wasn't quite then), if she held her chin at a particular angle (which she didn't, her chin was in a constant seesaw on account of the gum) when she laughed or when she forgot about pulling her lips over her teeth (which were long and fine and, at the most reductive — canine) she was a lovely, cubist vision.

Hershleder bought two tickets from this young girl. He bought two tickets out of force of habit. He entered the building, passed the two tickets toward the ticket taker and realized that he was alone.

Back at the box office, the girl wouldn't grant Hershleder a refund. She said: "It's a done deal, doll." But she smiled at him.

Hershleder gave the extra ticket to a bag lady who sat under the marquee where the sidewalk was slightly more shaded than the street, where the open and close of the glass doors to the air-conditioned theater provided the nearest thing to an ocean breeze that she would feel on this, her final face.

Hershleder the blind, Hershleder the dumb — oblivious to the thrill of a beautiful big-haired girl's lyrical smile, a smile a musician could sight-read and play. Blind and stuck with an extra ticket, Hershleder gave it away to the old lady. He wasn't a bad guy, really. Hadn't the old woman once been somebody's baby? Wasn't it possible, also, that she was still somebody's mother? Were there ever two more exalted roles in this human theater? This woman had risen to the pinnacle of her being; and she'd fallen. She suffered from La Tourrette. Hershleder held the glass door open for her; he'd been well raised by his own mother, a woman with a deep residing respect for the elderly.

"Bastard," said the old lady, smiling shyly. "Cocksucker."

Hershleder smiled back at her. Here was someone who spoke his language. Hadn't he seen a thousand and one patients like her before?

"Fucking Nazi prick," the woman said, her voice trailing low as she struggled to gain control of herself. Her face screwed up in concentration; she wrestled with her inner, truer self. "Faggot," she said through clenched teeth; she bowed her head now, trying to direct her voice back into her chest. The next word came out like an exhalation of smoke, in a puff, a whisper: "Motherfucker."

The old lady looked up at Hershleder from beneath hooded

lids—in her eyes was a lifetime of expressions unfortunately not held back, of words unleashed, epithets unfettered—there was a locker room of vile language in her head, but her face seemed apologetic. When Hershleder met her gaze, she fluttered her lashes, morse-coding like the quadriplegic on Ward A, then turned and shuffled away from him.

It was delicious inside the theater. Cold enough for Hershleder to take off his jacket and lay it flat like a blanket across his chest. His hand wandered across his crotch, stroked his belly. In the flirtation of film light, Hershleder felt himself up under the curtain of his jacket. There were a couple of teenagers in the back of the house who talked throughout the movie, but what did Hershleder care? It was dark, there was music. Stray popcorn crunched beneath his feet. A side door opened, and he got high off the smell of marijuana wafting on a cross breeze. An old man dozed in an end seat across the aisle. A beautiful girl on screen displayed a beautiful private birthmark. A bare-chested man rolled on top of her, drowning Hershleder's view. Above war planes flew, bombs dropped, the girl moaned, fire fire fire. Something was burning. On screen? Off screen? The exit sign was the reddest thing he'd ever seen. It glowed on the outskirts of his peripheral vision. Time passed in a solid leap, as in sleep, as in coma. When the lights came up, Hershleder was drowsily aware that much had happened to him— but what? Couldn't the real world have jumped forward at the rate of onscreen time in quantum leaps of event and tragedy and years? The movies. Like rockets hurtling a guy through space.

It was a way to make the hours pass, that's for sure, thought Hershleder. For a moment he had no clue as to what day it was.

Grand Central Station.

Hershleder waited for information. On the south wall was a huge photo essay, Kodak's, presenting the glories of India. A half-naked child, his brown outstretched hand, an empty bowl, his smile radiant. A bony cow. A swirl of sari, a lovely face, a red dot like a jewel amidst the light filigree of a happy forehead. A blown-up piece of poori: a bread cloud. The Taj Mahal . . . *In All Its Splendor.*

The lobby of Bellevue looked something like this. The women in their saris, the homeless beggars, the drug addicts that punctuated the station like restless exclamation marks. Inge, his chief lab technician, had told him that at the hospital, in the ground floor women's bathrooms, mothers bathed their babies in the sinks. Hershleder could believe this. There, like here, was a place to come in out of the cold, the rain, the heat.

The signboard fluttered its black lids, each train announcement inched its way up another slot. Hershleder's would depart from Track 11. There was time for half a dozen oysters at the Oyster Bar. He headed out past Zaro's Bakery, the bagels and the brioche, the pies of mile-high lemon frosting. Cholesterol — how it could slather the arteries with silken ecstasy! (Hershleder had to watch himself. Oysters would do the trick — in more ways than one. What was that old joke . . . the rules of turning forty: never waste an erection, never trust a fart.) He hung a left, down the curved, close passageway — the tunnel that felt like an inner tube, an underground track without the track, an alimentary canal, a cool stone vagina. Vagrants sagged against the walls, sprawled beneath the archways. There was a souvenir stand. A book store. A florist! Daisies, bright white for Itty, beckoned from earthenware vases. This was a must-stop on his future trek to Track 11. The passageway smelled like a pet store. The horrible inevitable decay of everything biological, the waste, the waste! Hershleder did a little shocked pas de bourrée over a pretzel of human shit, three toe-steps, as lacy as a dancer's.

They slid down easy, those Wellfleets, Blue Points. Hershleder leaned against the polished wood and ordered another half dozen. Not liquid, not solid — a fixed transitional state. A second beer. So what if he missed his train? There would always be another. Death and taxes. Conrail and the Erie Lackawanna. The fact that oysters made him horny.

They slid down cold and wet. Peppery. Hershleder wasn't one to skimp on hot sauce. The shell against his upper lip was blue and smooth, his lower lip touched lichen or was it coral? Pinstripes made up his panorama. The other slurpers were all like him. Commuters. Men who traveled to and from their wives, their children, "the Office." Men with secret lives in a foreign land: the city. Men who got off on eating oysters, who delayed going home by having yet another round of drinks. They all stood in a row at the bar the way they would stand at a row of urinals. Each in his private world. "Aaach," said Hershleder, and tipped another briny shell to his lips. His mouth was flooded by ocean.

Delays, delays. A lifetime full of delays. Hershleder the procrastinator, the putter-offer. Hershleder of the term papers started the night before, the grant proposals typed once into the computer, the postmarks fudged by the hospital's friendly postmaster. He was the kind of man to leave things to the last minute, to torture himself every moment that he did not attend to what needed attending to, his tasks, but also the type always to get them done. While in his heart he lusted after irresponsibility, he was never bad enough. Chicken-shit. A loser.

Hershleder's neighbor at the bar was reading *The New York Times*.

"Hey, Mister," said Hershleder, sounding like he was seven. "Would you mind letting me look at the C section?" Now he spoke like a gynecologist.

The neighbor slid the paper over without even glancing up.

Hershleder turned to the book review.

David Josephson. His old pal from college. A picture of the sucker. A picture; why a picture? Hershleder thought. It wasn't even Josephson's book. He was just a translator, that schlep was.

Josephson had not fared well over time, although to be fair, the reproduction was kind of grainy. A hook nose. A high forehead. He still looked brainy. That forehead hung over his eyes like an awning at a fancy club. Hershleder read the article for himself.

A 1,032-page study of the Nazi gas chambers has been published. . . . The study is by Jacques LeClerc, a chemist who began his work doubting that the Holocaust even took place. . . . The book, written in French, (translated by that bald rat Josephson!) . . . presents as proof, based entirely on technical analysis of the camps, that the Holocaust was every bit as monstrous and sweeping as survivors have said. . . . It is also a personal story of a scientific discovery during which, as Mr. LeClerc writes in a postscript, he was converted from "revisionist" to "exterminationist."

Exterminationist. What a hell of an appellative. Hershleder shook his head, in public, at the Oyster Bar, at no one in particular. Exterminationist. Is that what he himself was ? His beloved mother, Adela Hershleder, just a child, along with her sister and her mother, her father recently dead of typhus, smuggled out of Germany on Kristallnacht. His mother's mother lost six brothers and sisters in Hitler's crematoria. And the friends, the extended family, even the neighbors they didn't like — all gone, gone. Hershleder's grandfather Chaim and his grandfather's brother, Abe, came to this country from Austria as refugees after World War I, the sole survivors of the sweeping tragedies of Europe that did away with their entire extended family.

And *heerre* . . . was Hershleder, the beneficiary of all that compounded survival; Hershleder the educated, the privileged, the beloved, the doctor! Hershleder the first generation New York Jew, Hershleder the bar mitzvahed, the assimilated, Hershleder with the shiksa wife, the children raised on Christmas, bacon in their breakfast, mayonnaise spread across their Wonder Bread, the daughter who once asked him if calling a person a Jew was really just another way to insult him.

He was lucky; his ancestors were not. What could you do? Isn't this the crux of it all (the history of civilization): those of us who are lucky juxtaposed against those of us who are not?

Mindy and Lori, his sisters, married with children, each active in her own temple, one out on Long Island, one on the Upper West Side. Irv, his father, retired now, remarried now, donating his time to the Jewish Home for the Blind. Were they any more Jewish than he was? Wasn't it true, what his own mother had told him, that what mattered in life was not religion per se, but that one strived to be a good person? Wasn't he, Hershleder — the researcher and, on Tuesdays and Thursdays, the healer (albeit a reluctant one), the father, the husband, the lawn mower, the moviegoer (he did show that bag lady a good time), the friend to Josephson (at least in theory) — a good person?

My God, thought Hershleder, just imagine being this chemist, this LeClerc, having the courage to disprove the very tenets upon which you've built your life. But Hershleder knew this kind, he had seen them before: LeClerc's accomplishments were probably less about bravery than they were about obsessive compulsion: LeClerc was probably a man who practiced a strict adherence to facts, to science. After all, Hershleder had spent much of his adult life doing research. You let the data make the decisions for you. You record what you observe. You synthesize, yes, you interpret; but you don't theorize, create out of your own imagination needs and desires. He knew him, LeClerc, LeClerc the compulsive, the truth-teller. They were alike these two men, rational, exact, methodical. Science was their true religion. Not the ephemeral mumbo jumbo of politicians, philosophers, poets.

Hershleder and LeClerc: they told the truth, when they were able, when it stared them in the face.

Hershleder folded up the paper and left it on the counter, its owner, his neighbor, having vanished in the direction of the New Haven Line some time ago. Paid up and exited the comforts of the Oyster Bar and headed out into the festering subterranean world. He stopped at the florist to pick up those daisies, two dozen, a field of them, a free-floating urban meadow. He held the bouquet like a cheerleader's pom-pom in his hands.

"Daisies are wildflowers," said the florist when he wrapped them up, those hothouse posies, in a crinkly paper cone. What did he think, that Hershleder was a poster child? He'd been to summer camp, away to college. Didn't he live in the suburbs and have a wife who cultivated daisies of her own? Daisies smell awful, but their faces are so sunny and bright, so fresh, so clean, petals as white as laundry detergent.

As he made his way to Track 11, Hershleder had a musical association: "Daisy, Daisy, give me your answer true." He had a poetic association: "She loves me, she loves me not." He had a visual association: the daisy stickers on the leaded glass windows that faced his yard, the plastic daisy treads that his mother had stuck to the bottom of his bathtub so that he, Hershleder, her precious boy-child, the third born and most prized, wouldn't slip, hit his head and drown. The big bright patent-leather daisies that dressed the thongs of his own daughter's dress-up sandals. The golden yolk, the pinky white of Itty's eyes when she'd been crying.

Hershleder walked through the vaulted, starred, amphitheater of Grand Central Station with a sensual garden, his human history, flowering bitterly in his hands.

"Smoke," hissed a young man in a black concert T-shirt. "Thai stick, dust, coke." The young man stood outside Track 11. Hershleder saw this dealer there, this corrupter of the young and not so young, this drug pusher, almost every day for months and months. Hershleder nodded at him, started down the ramp to the main tracks, then stopped. He had been a good boy. At Bronx Science he had smoked pot, at Cornell he'd done magic mushrooms once in awhile at a Dead show — then usually spent the rest of the night in the bathroom throwing up. For the most part, he'd played it safe; a little blow on a prom night or some graduation, but no acid, no ups, no downs, (well, that wasn't true, there were bennies in med school, valiums after), no needles in the arm, no track marks. No long velvety nights of swirling hazy rock songs. Drugwise, he was practically a virgin. Hadn't this gone on long enough?

Hershleder backtracked up the ramp.

"How much?" asked Hershleder.

"For what?" said Mr. Black Concert T-shirt.

For what? For what?

"Heroin?" asked Hershleder, with hope.

Mr. Black Concert T-shirt looked away in disgust.

"Pot?" asked Hershleder, humbly, in his place.

"Smoke," hissed the young man, "Thai stick, dust, coke."

"Thai stick," said Hershleder. Decisively. "Thai fucking stick," said Hershleder the reckless, the bon vivant.

And then, even though he was in danger of missing his train (again) Hershleder went back into the lobby of the station and officially bought cigarettes. He bought Merit Ultra Lights, thought better of it, backtracked to the kiosk and traded in the Merits for a pack of Salems.

The john was small enough that if you were to sit your knees would be in your armpits and your elbows in your ears. Hershleder and his daisies floated in a cloud of smoke, mentholated, asiatic (the Thai stick). The chemical smell of toilets on trains and airplanes permeated all that steam. The resultant odor was strong enough to etherize an elephant, but Hershleder the rebel was nose-blind to it. He was wasted.

The MetroNorth rumbled through the tunnel. Outside the scenery was so familiar Hershleder had it memorized. First the rude surprise of 125th Street, all those broken windows, empty eye holes, the flash of graffiti, of murals, loud paint. The decals of curtains and cozy cats curled up on cheery sills pasted to crumbling bricked-up tenements, the urban renewal. Then onward, the Bronx, Riverdale, Spuyten Duyvil. The scramble of weedy green, the lumber yards, factories, houses that line the train tracks in the suburbs. At night, all of this would be in shadow; what he'd see would be the advertisements for *Cats*, for Big Mac attacks, for Newport cigarettes: usually of a man gleefully dumping a bucket of something over an equally gleeful woman's head. The lonely maid still in uniform waiting for the train to carry her home two towns away. A couple of emasculated teenagers without driver's licenses. A spaced-out commuter who had stumbled off at the wrong station. Hershleder knew this route by heart.

In the train car itself, there was always the risk of running into one of his neighbors, or worse yet the aging parents of a chum from college. Better to hang out in that safe smoky toilet pondering the meaning of life, his humble existence. He was stoned for the first time in years. Drunken synapse fired awkwardly to drunken synapse. His edges were rounded, his reflexes dulled. The ghosts that lived inside him spiraled around in concentric circles. Hershleder's interior buzzed. His head hung heavy off his neck, rested in the field of daises. A petal went up his nose, pollen dusted his mouth. He couldn't really think at all — he was full to the brim with nothing.

It was perfect.

"Laaarchmont," cried the lock-jawed conductor. "Laaarchmont," ruining everything.

Hershleder lit up a cigarette and coughed up a chunk of lung. Larchmont. The Station. A mile and a half from Casa Hershleder, a mile and a half from Itty and the kids, a mile and a half from his home and future heart failures. His eyes roved the Park and Ride. Had he driven his car this morning or had Itty dropped him off at the train? Had he called for a cab, hitched a ride with a neighbor? Where was that beat-up Mazda? His most recent history dissolved like a photograph in water, a dream upon awakening, a computer screen when the power suddenly shuts down. It receded from his inner vision. Must have been the weed . . . It really knocked him out.

Good shit, thought Hershleder.

He decided to walk. What was a mile and a half? He was in the prime of his life. Besides, Hershleder couldn't arrive home like this, stoned, in front of his innocent children, his loving wife. A long stroll would surely be enought to sober him; it would be a head-clearing, emotional cup of coffee.

Larchmont. Westchester, New York. One curvy road segueing into another. A dearth of street lights. The Tudor houses loomed like haunted mansions. They sat so large on their tiny lots, they swelled over their property lines the way a stout man's waist swells above his belt. A yuppie dog, a dalmatian, nosed its way across a lawn and accompanied Hershleder's shuffling gait. Hershleder would have reached down to pat its spotty head if he could have, but his arms were too full of daisies. He made a mental note to give in to Itty; she'd been begging him to agree to get a pup for the kids. There had been dogs when Hershleder was a child. Three of them.

At different times. He had had a mother who couldn't say no to anything. He had had a mother who was completely overwhelmed. The longest a dog had lasted in their home had been about a year; Mrs. Hershleder kept giving those dogs away. Three dogs, three children. Was there some wish fulfillment involved in her casting them aside? His favorite one had been called Snoopy. A beagle. His sister Mindy, that original thinker, had been the one to name her.

Hershleder remembered coming home from camp one summer to find that Snoopy was missing. His mother had sworn up and down that she had given the dog to a farm, a farm in western Pennsylvania. Much better for the dog, said Mrs. Hershleder, than being cooped up in some tiny apartment. Better for the dog, thought Hershleder now, some twenty-eight years later, better for the dog! What about me, a dogless boy cooped up in some tiny apartment! But his mother was dead, she was dead; there was no use in raging at a dead mother. Hershleder the motherless, the dogless, walked the streets of Larchmont. His buzz was beginning to wear off.

Why neurology? Mrs. Hershleder had asked. How about a little pediatrics? Gynecology? Family practice? Dovidil, don't make the same mistakes I made, a life devoted to half-lives, a life frozen in motion. But Hershleder had been drawn to the chronic ward. Paralysis, coma. He could not stand to watch a patient suffer, the kick and sweat, the scream of life battling stupidly for continuation. If he had to deal with people — and wasn't that what a doctor does, a doctor deals with people — he preferred people in a vegetative state, he preferred them non-cognizant. What had attracted him in the first place had been the literature, the questions: what was death? What was life, after all? Did the answers to these lie, as Hershleder believed, not in the heart but in the brain? He liked to deal in inquiries; he didn't like to deal in statements. It was natural then that he'd be turned on by research. Books and libraries, the heady smell of ink on paper. He'd been the kind of boy who had always volunteered in school to run off things for the teacher. He'd stand close to the Rexograph machine, getting giddy, greedily inhaling those toxic vapors. He'd walk back slowly to his classroom, his nose buried deep in a pile of freshly printed pages.

Hershleder was not taken with the delivering of babies, the spreading of legs, the searching speculum, the bloody afterbirth like a display of raw ground meat. But the brain, the brain, that fluted, folded mushroom, that lovely intricate web of thought and

tissue and talent and dysfunction, of arteries and order. The delicate weave of neurons, that thrilling spinal cord. All that communication, all those nerves sending and receiving orders. A regular
switchboard. Music for his mind.

A jogger passed him on the right, his gait strong and steady.
Hershleder's dalmatian abandoned him for the runner.

Hershleder turned down Fairweather Drive. He stepped over a
discarded red tricycle. He noticed that the Fishmans had a blue Jag
in their carport. The Fishman boy was his own boy's nemesis. Charlie Fishman could run faster, hit harder. No matter that Hershleder's own boy could speak in numbers — a = 1 b = 2, for example,
when Hershleder arrived home at night the kid said: "8-9 4-1-4"
(translation: Hi Dad!) — the kid was practically a savant, a genius!
So what, the Fishman boy could kick harder, draw blood faster in a
fight. Could Charlie Fishman bring tears to his own father's eyes by
saying, "9 12-15-22-5 25-15-21" when Fishman's father tucked him
in at night? (Even though it had taken Hershleder seven minutes
and a pad and pencil to decode the obvious.) Charlie Fishman had
just beaten out Hershleder's Jonathan for the lead in the second-
grade play. The Fishman father was a famous nephrologist. He
commuted to New Haven every morning on the highway, shooting
like a star in that blue Jag out of the neighborhood, against the
traffic, in the opposite direction. Hershleder admired the Jag from
afar. It was a blue blue. It glowed royally against the darkness.

The jogger passed him again, on the right. The dalmatian loped
after the runner, his spotted tongue hanging from his mouth. The
jogger must have circled around the long circuitous block in record time. A powerful mother-fucker. Bearded. And young. Younger
than Hershleder. The jogger had a ponytail. It sailed in the current
of his own making. His legs were strong and bare. Ropy, tendoned.
From where he stood, Hershleder admired them. Then he moved
himself up the block to his own stone Tudor.

Casa Hershleder. It was written in fake Spanish tile on the front
walk, a gift from his sisters. Hershleder walked up the slate steps
and hesitated on his own front porch. Sometimes it felt like only
an act of courage could get him to turn the knob and go inside.
So much tumult awaited. Various children: on their marks, getting
set, ready to run, to hurl themselves into his arms. Itty, in this
weather all soft and steamed and plumped — dressed in an undula-
tion of circling Indian shmatas — hungry for connection, attention,
the conversation of a living, breathing adult. Itty, with tiny clumps

of clay still lodged like bird eggs in the curly red nest of her hair. Itty with the silt on her arms, the gray slip-like slippers on her bare feet. Itty, his wife, the potter.

By this point, the daisies were half-dead. They'd wilted in the heat. Hershleder lay them in a pile on his front shrub then lowered himself onto a slate step seat. If he angled his vision past the O'Keefe's mock turret, he would surely see some stars.

The steam of summer nights, the sticky breath of the trees and their exhalation of oxygen, the buzz of the mosquitos and the cicadas, the sweaty breeze, the rubbing of his suit legs against his thighs. The moon above the O'Keefe's turret was high, high, high.

The jogger came around again. Angled right and headed up the Hershleder walk. His face was flushed with all that good clean high-octane blood that is the result of honest American exertion. He looked young — far younger than Hershleder, but hadn't Hershleder noted this before? Must be wanting to know the time, or in need of a glass of water, a bathroom, a phone Hershleder thought. The jogger was jogging right towards him.

In a leap of blind and indiscriminate affection the dalmatian bounded past the runner and collided with Hershleder's head, his body, his lap. David was stunned for a second, then revived by the wet slap of the dog's tongue. He was showered with love and saliva. "Hey," said Hershleder. "Hey there, Buster. Watch it." Hershleder fended off the beast by petting him, by bowing under to all that animal emotion. The dalmatian wagged the bottom half of his spinal column like a dissected worm would, it had a life all its own. His tail beat the air like a wire whisk. His tongue was as soft and moist as an internal organ. "Hey, Buster, down." Hershleder's arms were full of dog.

The jogger jogged right past them. He wiped his feet on Hershleder's welcome mat. He opened Hershleder's door and entered Hershleder's house. He closed Hershleder's door behind him. There was the click of the lock Hershleder had installed himself. That old bolt sliding into that old socket.

What was going on? What was going on around here?

Buster was in love. He took to Hershleder like a bitch in heat, this same fancy mutt that had abandoned him earlier for the runner. A fickle fellow, thought Hershleder, a familiar fickle fellow.

"Hey," said Hershleder. "Hey," he called out. But it was too late. The runner had already disappeared inside his house.

The night was blue. The lawns deep blue-green, the asphalt blue-black, the trees almost purple. Jaundiced yellow light, like flames on an electric menorah, glowed from the Teretsky's leaded windows. At the Coen's, from the second floor family room, a T.V. flickered like a weak pulse. Most of the neighborhood was dark. Dark, hot, blue and yellow. Throbbing like a bruise.

A car backfired in the distance. Buster took off like a shot.

Hershleder sat on his front step feeling used. He was like a college girl left in the middle of a one-night stand. The dog's breath was still hot upon his face. His clothes were damp and wrinkled. The smell of faded passion clung to him. His hair—what was left of it—felt matted. He'd been discarded. Thrown-over. What could he do?

Stand up, storm into the house, demand: What's the meaning of this intrusion? Call the cops? Were Itty and the kids safe inside, locked up with that handsome, half-crazed stranger? Was it a local boy, home on vacation from college, an art student perhaps, hanging around to glean some of his wife's infinite and irresistible knowledge? The possibilities were endless. Hershleder contemplated the endless possibilities for a while.

Surely, he should right himself, climb his own steps, turn his key in his lock, at least ring his own bell, as it were. Surely, Hershleder should do something to claim what was his: "If I am not for me, who will be for me? If I am not for mine, who will be for mine?" Surely, he should stop quoting, stop questioning, and get on with the messy thrill of homeownership. After all, his wife, his children were inside.

The jogger was inside.

Hershleder and LeClerc, they told the truth when it stared them in the face. In the face! Which was almost enough but wasn't enough, right then at that exact and awful moment to stop him, the truth wasn't, not from taking his old key out of his pocket and jamming it again and again at a lock it could not possibly ever fit. Which wasn't enough, this unyielding frustration, to stop him from ringing the bell, again and again, waking his children, disturbing his neighbors. Which wasn't enough to stop him, the confusion, the shouting that ensued, that led Itty *his wife* to say: "Please, Sweetheart," to the jogger (Please, Sweetheart!) and usher him aside, that pony-tailed bearded athlete who was far, far younger than Hershleder had ever been, younger than was biologically possible.

She sat on the slate steps, Itty, her knees spread, the Indian shmata pulled discreetly down between them. She ran her silt-stained hands through her dusty strawberry cloud of hair. There were dark, dirty half-moons beneath her broken fingernails. She was golden eyed and frustrated and terribly pained. She was beautiful, Itty, at her best really when she was most perplexed, her expression forming and reforming like a kaleidoscope of puzzled and passionate emotion, when she patiently and for the thousandth time explained to him, Dr. David Hershleder, M.D., that this was no longer his home, that the locks had been changed for this very reason. He had to stop coming around here, upsetting her, upsetting the children, that it was time, it was time, Dave, to take a good look at himself; when all Hershleder was capable of looking at was her, was Itty, dusty, plump and sweaty, sexy-sexy Itty, his wife, his wife, sitting with him on the stoop of his house in his neighborhood, while his children cowered inside.

Until finally, exhausted, (Hershleder had exhausted her) Itty threatened to call the police if he did not move, and it was her tiredness, her sheer collapsibility that forced Hershleder to his feet — for wasn't being tired one thing Itty went on and on about that Hershleder could finally relate to — that pushed him to see the truth, to assess the available data and to head out alone and ashamed and apologetic to his suburban slip of a sidewalk, down the mile and a half back to the station to catch the commuter rail that would take him to the city and to the medical student housing he'd wrangled out of the hospital, away from everything he'd built, everything he knew and could count on, out into everything unknown, unreliable and yet to be invented.

Sarah

ALLEGRA GOODMAN

Allegra Goodman (1967–): *Born and raised in Hawaii in a traditional Jewish household, Allegra Goodman published the first of her amazingly mature, complex short stories in* Commentary *when she was a freshman at Harvard. Her stories continued to appear in* Commentary *and the* New Yorker *throughout her undergraduate years, culminating in the publication of her first collection,* Total Immersion, *when she was twenty-one. ("All the muse-fairies were present at her birth," Cynthia Ozick announced.) While pursuing her Ph.D. in literature at Stanford, Goodman continued to publish stories, most of them appearing in the* New Yorker. *Her second book, a novel-in-stories titled* The Family Moskowitz, *was published in 1996 and garnered superb critical resonse. As was the case with her first collection, this book combines clear, precise language with a satirist's eye for small, absurd details. Goodman's stories are often wickedly funny but never mean-spirited. Her subject matter has centered largely on the conflict between orthodoxy (religious and intellectual) and the liberalizing forces of modern society. Allegra Goodman lives and writes in Massachusetts.*

Sarah parks at the Jewish Community Center of Greater Washington, her large purse on the seat next to her, along with a bunch of marked assignments. She has written copiously on each one, making her comments in green because the students find red threatening. Sarah took a series of pedagogy workshops years ago, and she scrupulously applies the techniques she learned. Her students, all adults, always comment on her warmth and motherliness. They don't realize that these are aspects of Sarah's professionalism. They do not see the teacher within, by turns despairing and chortling.

She takes out her compact and applies fresh lipstick, gathers all the papers and her purse, and strides into the building. She walks quickly, with a firm step; she has short gray hair, and eyes that had been blue when she was younger but are now hazel flecked with gold. The class is called Creative Midrash, and it combines creative writing with Bible study. Like the commentators in the compendium the Midrash, the students write their own interpretations, variations, and fantasies on Biblical themes. Sarah developed the concept herself, and she is happy with it because it solves so many problems at once. It forces the students to allude to subjects other than themselves, while at the same time they find it serves their need for therapy—because they quickly see in Scripture archetypes of their own problems. Above all, Creative Midrash forces the students to read, so they realize they aren't the first to feel, think, or write anything down, for God's sake. She always begins on the first day by playing a tape of Vaughan Williams's *Fantasia on a Theme by Thomas Tallis.*

It is five-thirty in the afternoon, and they are waiting for her, all ready to go, their notebooks out and turned to a fresh page, their pens poised. They love pens: fountain pens and three-color ballpoints, even elaborate, hollow pens that store twelve different ink cartridges inside. "Fifteen minutes of free writing," Sarah says, and they begin, covering their white notebook pages. She watches them. They range in age from thirty to somewhere near sixty, three women and one man. They are, in their own words, a mom, a retired homemaker, an actress, and a landscape-maintenance specialist. Sarah watches them all and thinks about dinner. She has a chicken thawed and the leftover sweet potatoes, but they need a vegetable. She'll have to stop and pick up something on the way home. She has to get something else, too. They are out of something, but she can't remember what. Something small, perishable. "All right," she says. "Why don't you finish up your thought." She waits. "Then let's begin. Debbie." She turns to the actress. Debbie has long hair and pale-blue eyes. You could call her nose large. It is a strong nose, beautifully straight. Everyone, including Sarah, takes out a copy of the poem Debbie wrote last week, and Debbie shakes back her hair and intones:

Eve

flesh of your flesh
bone of your bone
wo man
womb an
I am Eve
you are my day and night
I am Eve the twilight

in between
sweet soft neither dark nor bright
and how did I feel when
I was born from your dream?
no one was interested

Tomatoes! The thought comes to Sarah unbidden. That's what she has to pick up, because the ones in the fridge spoiled.

from my birth I belonged to you
you had named the beasts
already you had named me
you are the sun and I the moon
you burn
but I pull the waters after me
I slip from your garden to consort
with the enemy
because I would rather be wild
than beget your patriarchy
I would rather cover you with shame
you can have the cattle the foul of the air
and all the beasts of the field
the night will glow with the eyes of my cats

"Comments?" Sarah asks. No one says a word, so she begins. "Debbie, that was very strong. I like the way it flows and builds momentum. There was almost a rhythmic expression in your tide image. Were you playing with the word *foul* intentionally?"

"Where?" asks Debbie.

"Where you wrote 'foul of the air.'"

"Oh, that wasn't on purpose," Debbie says.

"You might want to change it, then," Sarah suggests. "Other comments?"

Michelle, who is the mom, says, "I noticed you didn't use any capital letters, except for 'I' and 'Eve.'"

"Yeah, I did that because I feel that capital letters and punctuation interrupt the flow of the poem and I associate them with male discourse and hierarchy, sort of dichotomous and either-or oriented, night-day, yes-no, and I see Eve as more of a mediator figure. But I didn't want to use a lower-case *i* or write *eve* without a capital, because I feel that in a way E. E. Cummings appropriated that idea, and what I was trying to do was take back the *I* for the female voice."

"It's about subversion," says Brian, the landscaper, once a gradu-ate student, then sidelined for ten years by drugs, but now making up for lost time. He is an unnaturally thin man, sunburned, with a scant beard.

"Yeah, and it's very close to what I'm going through right now," Debbie says. "I'm having a conflict with my boyfriend about my cats right now."

Then Brian begins to read his "Dialogue Between Jacob and the Angels on the Ladder."

> *Scene: Desert at midnight, countless stars shining. On the rungs of Jacob's ladder, the spirits of* THOREAU *and* WALT WHITMAN, *sitting with* JACOB.
> WHITMAN (to Jacob, with a look of ecstasy): *You*
> *shall be as many as the stars in the sky*
> *You will multiply into millions*
> *and every last one of your children will be million*
> *heirs because this is the night of your birth*
> *this is your birth-night*
> *and every grass blade, every insect and tiniest being*
> *in the world knows it*
> *every animal, bird, fish, and locomotive knows it*
> THOREAU: *Given a choice, I think any man would rather sit by a warm fire than become a nation.*

"Wait, wait," Debbie says. "You're talking about grass blades? I thought this was supposed to be a desert."

"Maybe you should say grains of sand," Michelle suggests.

"Well, I think that's already in the Bible." Ida, the retired home-maker, is wearing her reading glasses and flipping through Genesis.

"There's nothing wrong with using images that are already in the Bible," Sarah says.

Ida pulls off her reading glasses and looks over at her. She has snowy-white hair. "Then I want to change mine," she says. "Can I change mine?"

"All right," Sarah says. "Brian, what do you think about using grains of sand?"

"But I was trying to sort of allude to *Leaves of Grass*."

"I don't know, this is really heavy. Really—abstract." Debbie is staring at the play. "Have you thought about getting some more action into it? I mean, I don't think you want to end up with just all these talking heads!"

Brian looks dismayed.

"I see it more as a Platonic dialogue," Sarah says.

This seems to cheer Brian. "I want it to be like *Under Milk Wood*," he confides to the class. "That's my dream."

Sarah picks up the groceries and then the dry cleaning on her way home. "Four shirt, two dress, one skirt, pleated, one blouse. This could not come out," the cashier tells her. She looks around wearily as the cashier rings everything up. As always, hanging in the window is a wedding dress, freshly cleaned, in clear plastic, the dry cleaner's tour de force.

When Sarah gets home, Ed comes out of the house to help her carry everything, so they are both outside when the phone rings, and Ed runs up the steps in front of her with his keys jingling in his pocket and his shirt coming untucked. "Who is it? Your mother?" Sarah calls out as she comes in.

He waves his hand at her impatiently. "Ma? What is it? What? You're in the hospital? What happened?"

Sarah picks up the phone in the kitchen and hears her eighty-seven-year-old mother-in-law crying. "Yes, yes, I'm in the hospital," Rose sobs from California. "They took me here. I didn't even know what was happening to me. I was unconscious. I could have been dead."

"Mother, wait, slow down. Start from the beginning. What happened?"

"What hospital are you in?" Sarah breaks in.

"St. Elysius? Or Egregious?"

"No, no, that can't be it. That's a TV show. Try to think, Ma."

"Maybe St. Elizabeth's," Rose says. "How should I know? I was unconscious."

"Ed, I think we should talk to Dr. Klein," Sarah says.

"Sarah, I'm trying to hear what happened. Start from the beginning, Ma."

"I told Klein I needed a new prescription. My refills ran out. I went to three different pharmacies, and they wouldn't fill the prescription for my pills. I went to Longs, Rexall, and Pay Less, and they all said I needed a new prescription from my doctor. But when I told Klein I needed him to write a new one he wouldn't do it, and so I told him that if he didn't write me one I would tell the state medical board he drugged Gladys and Eileen when they passed away, and he just said he didn't know what I was talking about. I said,

'You damn well know what I'm talking about. You killed them with morphine.' Then he just walked out and left me alone in his office. So I had to go all the way home, on the bus, by myself. I was exhausted, I was ill. I went straight to bed. I put on my videotape of *Pride and Prejudice*, and I took some of the pills I had saved, because I felt so ill. Then, when I woke up, I was in a hospital bed in a hospital gown."

"Oh, Christ," Ed groans. "Ma, now I want you to give me the telephone number by your bed. I'm going to call the doctor."

This is not the first time Rose has overdosed and collapsed, but that doesn't make it any easier. Sarah remembers Rose's second husband, Maury, who passed away in 1980. He was a cheerful man ten years older than Rose, and as the years went by he only seemed to become more jovial. He whistled happily, walking with his cane through the increasingly grim streets of Washington Heights. He became ever smaller and more spry, his clothes hung on him, and his face was shrunken behind his black-framed glasses; he had almost turned into Jiminy Cricket, but every day he and Rose went out to lunch at the deli, and every week he brought home stacks of large-print books from the library. The two of them traveled, and he used to collapse in dramatic places. On the observation deck of the World Trade Center. In the botanical gardens in Montreal. In Hollywood, on Hollywood Boulevard. He would sit in the hospital and talk about the service in different cities. Sarah had always marveled at him because he was such an extraordinarily cheerful man. When he died, she found out that he had been taking Percodan, among other things. It wasn't just good nature. He'd got Rose started on pills. After the funeral, they also found out that he hadn't paid taxes for years, and that he had squirreled away his money in small sums in over a hundred different bank accounts around the country. It was then that Rose drafted her amazing handwritten will, a document she never tires of showing the family. Ed was the one who took care of all Maury's deferred aggravations. He closed up the Washington Heights apartment, collected the money from all the accounts, and moved Rose to Venice, California, where she could be near her other son, Henry, who was managing a gallery there. But Henry left for England — years ago — to start one of his new lives, and taking care of Rose is again Ed's responsibility.

Ed is pacing in the living room with the phone, talking to Dr. Klein, and Sarah picks up her extension in time to hear Klein say,

"Well, it seems that she was stashing the pills away. She wasn't taking the prescribed dose. Unfortunately, she took them for her moods."

"Well, why didn't you check on her before?" Ed says.

"Well, Ed, I cannot control everything that she does in the privacy of her own apartment. I cannot take total responsibility for her actions. Of course, I asked her whether she was complying with the prescription, but I'm afraid she didn't tell me the truth."

"No, no, I'm sorry, my mother is not a liar."

"She has a severe dependency on her medication and — "

"Well, that's the point. I thought that was what we were trying to work on, to wean her away with the limited doses."

"Yes, that is what we were trying to do, Ed," Klein says. "But it wasn't working. I think we've had this discussion before. It's really a question of patient management. Now, Rose has decided to enter a residential treatment program at Santa Rosa."

"Why weren't we consulted about this?"

"It was her decision."

"No, I think it was *your* decision," Ed snaps. "You told her she had to do this."

"I advised her to do it, because she has got to start understanding her dependency. She has to find other ways to deal with her boredom and loneliness."

"Oh, so this is really all my fault," Ed says. "Because I'm trying to take care of her long distance. It all comes down to me. I should be there twenty-four hours a day. It's not your fault and it's not her fault, so it's got to be my fault."

Sarah is up half the night because Ed is so upset. He lies on his left side and then rolls over, punching his pillow with his fist. He kicks at the blankets, then flops onto his back. Sarah lies on her stomach and thinks about Rose. Boredom and loneliness. It's a real question: Can an elderly woman subsist on *Masterpiece Theatre* alone? Rose is, as Sarah's student Ida calls it, a retired homemaker — except that she was never so professional about being a homemaker, or about being retired. What she really wants, Sarah thinks, is to return to the houses of her childhood. She is nostalgic for them; they are still the backdrops of the romance she has developed about her life. Her parents' house in Bukovina, her foster parents' grand house in England, where she was sent during the First World War — a place with servants and vast drawing rooms. Rose did not suffer in the wars directly, but she imagines she did, and in her mind's eye sees them sweeping away the world she loved. She has often told Sarah that *Gone with the Wind* is the most beautiful novel ever written, and urged her to try to write one like it, threatened to write it herself, although she says she has never had the strength. But it is hard to sustain a life with memories, especially when the best memories come from novels.

"I call these Identity Haiku," Michelle tells the Creative Midrash class the following week. She pauses, then adds, "I was going to do traditional haiku, but it was really cramping what I wanted to say, so I didn't do the syllable thing."

1.
generations
stars in sky
yellow stars
holocaust

    2.
    sun rise
    moon rise
    tower
    sun down
    moon down
    babel

        3.
        cut
        cry
        covenant

"These are really beautiful," Debbie says.

"Why didn't you use titles?" asks Ida.

"Um, I just thought it would be overkill. I felt like it would be almost stating the obvious if, say, I titled Number 3 'Circumcision.'"

"I love the way you stripped down your images to the essentials," Sarah says. "Tell us more about why you called them Identity Haiku." As she learned in her pedagogy class, Sarah shows with her body language that she is listening to Michelle. She leans forward and nods her head, but she is thinking about Rose, who has been calling each night. The residential treatment center is a prison! It's Sing Sing. Auschwitz. No one can leave. What do they do there? They sit in a circle; they have to talk about their past with a facilitator. She can't bear it. To listen to them talk. This one was raped when she was seven years old! That one was assaulted by her own father and brother. This one was a prostitute! "Such horrible things! Things we would *never* talk about. Now they put all of it on TV, but I would never watch!" Sarah can only imagine Rose sitting in that circle of chairs with these other patients, some the age of Rose's children, some the age of her grandchildren. And then Rose herself, half dead from shock, asked to tell about her own abuse. And even to begin, to talk about her childhood after what she has heard! To speak of her own treasured past, the elegant life that she has always treated as something to fold and fold again in tissue paper. No one listening to her, no one interested except the facilitator, probing with long needles, trying to draw blood. Naturally, she wants to go home, but she cannot just check out. "This is a clinic," the doctor told her, "not a hotel." Ed took a flight out to L.A. last night to talk to the doctors or straighten out the Medicare insurance claims or save Rose, depending on how you want to look at it.

It is Ida's turn to read. She is a beautiful woman. A woman who goes to the hairdresser every week and comes to class with her white hair curled and shaped. And she dresses up for the class. She comes in suits and gold jewelry—quite a contrast to Debbie in her rumpled shirts or Brian, who sometimes forgets to take off his bike helmet. She is the oldest in the group, just as Rose is. Her voice is tense as she reads; it chokes up on her and she is embarrassed.

Naomi and Ruth

My daughter and I are like Ruth and Naomi, but with a twist. When my husband passed away, may he rest in peace, and we went on the way, as it says in the Bible, I said to Ellen, "Don't stay with me, go on and live your life."

"I want to stay with you and take care of you," she said.

"No, you need to live your own life," I said.

"Okay," she said. So she went back to New York where she was attending NYU film school.

I stayed here alone in the house. She wants to make films, and if that is what she wants, so be it, but I tell her, "Ellen, I wish you would meet someone. You are almost thirty."

She tells me, "Mother, I have met someone, and we have been living together for five years." But this is something that is breaking my heart. This man, a broker, is eleven years older than Ellen and not Jewish.

This is what I want to ask her—"How do you think you can live in New York like a Ruth gleaning in the alien corn? How do you think you can come to him and lie at his feet in the night so that one morning he will marry you? How can you go on like this living in his apartment for five years? If I had known this would happen when we went on the way, I would not have told you to go. I would have said, 'Stay.'"

Something about this pricks at Sarah. Tears start in her eyes.

Debbie rakes back her long hair and says to Ida, "Well, she's got to make her own choices."

"I have a question about the genre of this," Michelle says. "Is this like an essay or a short story?"

"Ida," Sarah says, "this is — " She wants to say that it moved her, but she cannot. The words would sound cheap in the context of the class with its formalized intimacy. "It's very simple and beautiful," she says.

Debbie is looking over her copy, pondering Ida's work. "I guess it's an age thing," she says.

Sarah's desk stands at the window of her bedroom. She has always wanted a study, and she and Ed are hoping to redo one of the other bedrooms in the next few years. The kids are away at college — one at medical school — so they don't have the money to do anything with the house. Sarah and Ed went to a local one-woman performance of "A Room of One's Own," and it occurred to Sarah as she left the theater that Virginia Woolf never had any children. Her own desk is piled with papers, some hers, some Ed's, also bank statements she has not yet filed, bills marked paid, issues of *Writer's Digest* and *Poets & Writers Magazine*, and copy for the Shaarei Tzedek newsletter, which she edits. Sarah is the Washington stringer for several national Jewish periodicals, and she writes frequent book reviews. She sits at her desk and thinks about what insufficient time she has for her own work. She has written one novel, published in 1979 by Three Penny Opera, a book about a woman — a painter — growing up in Brooklyn and Long Island, but she didn't move fast enough after that publication, didn't follow it quickly enough with a second novel, and she regrets this, the loss of momentum. She writes poetry as well, poetry that is perhaps too old-fashioned for a contemporary audience. With its wordplay and complicated rhymes it is closer to the seventeenth century than to John Ashbery. It has been difficult for her as a poet, to be influenced by Donne, Marvell, and Herbert, but to write about giving birth, a son's bar mitzvah, Yom Kippur. Several years ago she sent a collection of her poems to her brother-in-law, Henry, who runs a small press of his own in Oxford. But Henry felt that Sarah's work, while "extraordinary," was not moving in quite the direction that Equinox was trying to move in with its current series. She still finds it strange that even Henry, who loves Victorian furniture, eighteenth-century books and bindings, antique china, and plush novels—he who, as a person, is almost baroque—nevertheless admires poems that are sleek, smooth, minimalist, functioning like state-of-the-art appliances. As she boots up her computer, the phone rings.

"Sarah?" Ed says. "Hi. Listen, we've got a mess here. She's already racked up twenty thousand dollars for hospitalization. That and the treatment program are covered, but there is another sixteen hundred for consultations with Klein, which they aren't covering."

"What do you mean?"

"They say they aren't covering it. We're disputing the bill, so—"

"How is she?" Sarah asks.

"Not so hot. Disoriented, exhausted. She's lost weight." He sighs. "Sarah, I got here and I realized this is it. We can't kid ourselves about this any longer—she can't stay out here alone. We've got to bring her home."

"You mean bring her here?"

"Yeah, we've got to bring her back to Washington."

She thinks for a moment. "I can cancel my Thursday class," she says. "I'll try to get a flight out tomorrow."

Sarah and Ed sit in a pair of chairs in Dr. Stephen Klein's office. For Sarah, the scene is vaguely reminiscent of certain meetings with the assistant principal of Woodrow Wilson Junior High School concerning their son, Ben, and his academic progress.

"Well, I have spent at least an hour with her in private consultations each day of her stay here," Klein is telling them.

"And these were the sessions where you . . . ? What did you do exactly?"

"I listened to her. I talked to her about dependency, addictive behavior—"

Ed interrupts. "All I know is that my mother looks terrible, she's lost weight, you've run her ragged."

Dr. Klein shakes his head. "Remember, you haven't seen her for at least six months. And she is recovering from a massive overdose."

"Massive overdose!" Ed's face reddens. "Is that the way you like to dramatize it to your patients? Look, my mother is eighty-seven years old. Spare her the shock therapy. You've got her out at Santa Rosa in a program with a bunch of teenage junkies. I thought this was the age of multiculturalism, mutual respect, universal access, emancipation of the elderly. You're sitting here rubber-stamping an elderly woman, putting her onto the therapeutic conveyor belt with no regard to her age, her cultural background — "

"Can I show you something?" Klein asks. He puts a videotape in the VCR and turns on the television. "Rose?" a woman's voice asks. "May we have your permission to videotape this conversation for you and/or your family to look at later?"

"All right," Rose replies. She is sitting up in a hospital bed looking small and gray, an I.V. in her arm.

"Now, Rose, tell me, how are you feeling — on a scale of one to ten, with one being the worst and ten the best."

"I feel lousy," Rose says.

"But on a scale of ten, how do you feel?"

"One is the best?"

"One is the worst, ten is the best."

"Ten is the best?"

"That's right."

"And what's the worst?"

"One. Rose?"

"I have a one."

Sarah smiles in spite of herself, but Ed bursts out, "Can — can you turn that off?"

"Why?" Klein asks.

"Because we are having a conversation here!"

"I understand that, Ed, but I thought the tape was relevant."

"It may be relevant. However, I am not going to watch my mother being interrogated, okay? It's ugly."

"Addiction is ugly. It's also complicated, and really I think this is something you should consider — not now, when you're upset, but later on. I think counseling as a family would be very valuable for Rose — and for you."

"Oh, my God," Ed snaps.

"I see a lot of anger here," Klein points out gently.

"Damn right."

"No, I don't mean the anger at me. The conflict is between you and your mother. This isn't about me at all."

"Oh, yes it is," Ed fires back. "This is all about you and your

indiscriminate diagnoses, your mismanagement of an elderly patient's prescriptions, and the fact that you railroaded her into entering a totally inappropriate treatment program."

"That's — that's a serious charge," Klein says. "I repeat that it was
her decision to enter the program. I have her signature on all the
paperwork."

"You can give me the paperwork, because you are no longer her
doctor," Ed snaps.

"I'll be happy to release the records to you as soon as her account is clear. I know that you're worried, I see that you're upset,
but I can assure you I have given Rose the best treatment I knew
how to give, and I have been generous with my time. I'm not even
charging you for our session here today."

At this, Ed stands up, turns on his heel, and strides out of Klein's
office through the reception area and out the door.

Sarah turns and walks out after him, but she stops at the desk of
Klein's receptionist. "Do you take Visa?" she asks.

For the next three days, Ed and Sarah pack up Rose's apartment in
Venice. They phone Goodwill and several of the Jewish agencies to
try to give away the washer, the dryer, and some of the big furniture.
"You know, it's telling," Ed says to Sarah. "Now you have to pay a
collection fee to give things away."

"Well, sure," Sarah says. "They have to come with a truck. They
have to sort the stuff." She imagines the warehouses with piles
for everything that comes in: REHABILITATE, SCRAP, SMITHSON-
IAN. A triage system, something like the Santa Rosa treatment center? Now that Rose is home, she looks much better. She is
frail, of course — thin — but her color is back, her eyes bright. The
apartment is bustling. She is going home with her dear son and
daughter-in-law, and she will not be alone anymore. She is supervis-
ing the movers as they pack up her china and her little cut-crystal
liqueur glasses. She is being swept away to a new place, beginning a
new chapter, and this is something she enjoys. But Ed and Sarah
look terrible. Disheveled, exhausted from packing, paperwork, and
schlepping. Each night they drag themselves back to the Sea Breeze
Motel and collapse with muscles aching. The motel has bars on the
windows and, in the bathroom, tiny white towels that seem to have
been put there mostly for symbolic value. They picked the place
because of its location near Rose, and it turns out to have one other
advantage. For fifty cents they can get the bed to vibrate, and this

soothes their aching backs. At the end of the day they try to un-
wind, lying on their backs, feeding quarters to the bed, and watching c-span on television.

On the third night, they are lying there on their backs watching
the *Prime Minister's Question Time*, the bed vibrating beneath them,
and Ed is talking on the phone to his brother, Henry. "Well, of
course we're giving away the secretary," Ed says. "We're giving all
the big furniture to Hadassah. That's what Ma wants. What? What?"
He turns toward Sarah. "He says he wants the secretary."

"So let him ship it to England," Sarah says.

"It's a very fine piece? No, okay. No, I would call it a — nice piece,
not a very fine piece . . . You want to ship it to England, you go
ahead . . . What — are you crazy? Where are we going to put it in
D.C.?" He looks over at Sarah.

"If he really wants it, he can ship it to England," Sarah says.

"What? I can't hear you," Ed talks over her into the phone. He
turns to Sarah again. "Henry says Ma will want the secretary in
Washington. She may not want it now, but she will later. And she'll
want the lamps with the silk-shantung lampshades."

"He may be right," Sarah says. "She'll want them later."

"Henry, have you *seen* those lampshades in the last five years?"

"Ed, maybe we should get a container and ship everything
to D.C."

"What did you say?" Ed asks her. She repeats what she said. "All
right, fine." He hands her the telephone. "You and Henry work it
out, I'm getting an Excedrin." He takes another couple of quarters
off the Formica nightstand and feeds them expertly into the meter
on the headboard.

Henry is still talking, unaware that the phone has changed
hands. "Now, the carpets are simply not worth shipping. They aren't
really Chinese carpets, you know. We could very well give those
away, but the lamps could be considered antiques in a few years,
and silk-shantung lampshades are almost impossible to find anymore. They just don't make — "

Sarah teaches the first class after her return home in a haze of jet
lag. She had given the students an assignment to do while she was
gone: "Write a midrash about the crossing of the Red Sea in a genre
you have not yet used in this course." Now, as she listens to the
students, she finds that the results are mixed. Michelle has written

a short story about a young Jewish girl who is in love with an Egyptian and has to watch her lover fall with his horse and chariot into the sea. Naturally, she refuses to join Miriam and the other women as they sing and dance in triumph after they have crossed to safety. Instead, she writes her own song to sing by herself to the desert air. Brian has written an essay of questions, hypotheses, and test cases in true Midrashic fashion. It begins:

> It is a mystery why it says in the Torah that after all Moses' pleas, God hardened Pharaoh's heart. Why would God want to make it harder for the Israelites if he was on their side? Was it a test? Or is this some kind of mystical metaphor? I, being of philosophical inclination, take it as such. I think these phrases in the ancient scriptures are invitations to us to ask questions about the nature of human agency and its interactions (reactions?) to God as a historical agent in the world.

After hearing only seven pages of this, Debbie looks at Sarah and asks, in her blunt way, "Is this creative writing?"

Sarah is annoyed. "Let's let Brian finish," she says.

"Sorry," Debbie mutters.

When it's Ida's turn, she shakes her head. "I apologize," she says. "I wasn't able to complete the assignment. I'm still waiting for an idea."

"Don't censor yourself," Michelle advises her.

"Yeah, I used to be really bad about that," Debbie says. "Do you ever try brainstorming?" For her part, Debbie has written an autobiography of Pharaoh's sacred cat:

> I with my green eyes have seen three hundred generations. My dam was the Upper Nile and my father the Lower Nile; my older sister the Great Sphinx, who taught me the riddles of man.

When Debbie finishes, Sarah nods her head. "That's very — strange and compelling," she says. She hates it. Rose is staying in their daughter Miriam's old room. Sarah has been taking her to look at residences. Every day she drives her out to see them, and every day Rose insists she could not possibly live in one, and that the only times she was ever happy were when she was in the midst of the family.

"I was wondering," Michelle says to Sarah, "would it be possible for us to do an assignment that isn't a midrash? Because, for me, it's hard to connect my feelings to the Bible all the time."

"It's *really* hard," Debbie agrees.

"Could we just try to write a story set in modern times?" Michelle asks.

Ida adds to this, "I'd like it if you would bring in a midrash of your own that we could look at."

"Have you ever written one?" Brian asks.

"Yes, I think I did one years ago," Sarah says. "I could look for it. But I want to remind all of you that creating art is hard work, and that the artist sees restrictions as opportunities. Now, for your next project, your first restriction is that you cannot use the word *I*."

"Oh, jeez," Debbie groans.

"What about using *me*?" Michelle asks.

"But we can use all the other pronouns?" Brian asks.

Sarah makes hamburgers that night, and the three of them sit down for dinner—Sarah, Ed, and Rose, who eats her burger plain on her plate with a knife and fork. "I heard you didn't like the Helena," Ed says to his mother.

"The facilities were gorgeous," Sarah says.

"Were they gorgeous, Ma?" Ed asks.

"Cold," Rose says.

"What? You said the air-conditioning was wonderful!" Sarah says.

"I mean the atmosphere was cold. It was institutional."

"Well, it's an institution," Ed says.

"Yes, it was no home for me."

"They had a lovely swimming pool."

"I don't swim," Rose points out.

"And they have buses to the Kennedy Center for all the performances."

"You could go to the symphony and the ballet, Ma. And the theater."

"I didn't like it," Rose says.

"What's not to like?" Ed demands.

"The people." Rose taps her head. "Not all there."

Sarah shakes her head. "They were lovely people. Cultured people!"

"You see what you want to see," Rose tells her.

Ed takes another burger under Sarah's disapproving eyes. "Your furniture is coming, Ma. We have to settle you in."

"You know, they have chamber music there every week," Sarah tells Ed.

"Look, I'll tell you what, Ma," he says. "Sarah and I are going to move to the Helena, and you can stay here. How would that be?"

Sarah sits down at her desk after dinner. She tries to work on one of her overdue book reviews, but her heart isn't in it. She is too tired, her mind full of too many other things: the knowledge that in order to get any work done, she and Ed need to settle Rose in a residence. They hate pushing her into it, but Rose is not going to leave their house happily. They are going to have a fight about it. Ed will be miserable. The knowledge that her class is not going well. These particular students do not work well together as a group. Discussion is fractured. All sniping and defensiveness. The chemistry is wrong. She told them today she once wrote a midrash of her own, but she does not know where it is. It was a little piece about the Biblical Sarah and about her own feelings about becoming a mother. She picks up the King James Bible that she had assigned as a class text along with Robert Alter's *The Art of Biblical Poetry*, and Peter Elbow's *Writing Without Teachers*, and she turns to Genesis 21. She reads: "And the Lord visited Sarah as he had said, and the Lord did unto Sarah as he had spoken. For Sarah conceived, and bare Abraham a son in his old age." And her eye skips down to where it says that Sarah said the child's name is Isaac because "God hath made me to laugh, so that all that hear will laugh with me." As she looks at these verses, she sees them differently now from the way she saw them in the past. She is fifty-six years old, and she has four grown children, and it occurs to her that she is not much like the Biblical Sarah in that respect. She did not have a child in her old age. She has certainly never had any problems with fertility. She has pined, but not for children. She has pined to have a literary career, to have her work discovered by the world. This has been her dream since her school days, when she discovered John Donne and felt suddenly and secretly clever, as if, like a safecracker, she could find the puns and hidden springs in his poetry. And when she wrote her essays in college about this image and that metaphor, what she was really wondering was how to become like Shakespeare — without seeming to imitate him, of course. When would she be called into that shining multitude of poets and playwrights, mainly Elizabethan, who rose in shimmering waves before her at Queens College? She wrote her M.A. thesis in English Literature about Emma Lazarus — not about the poem on the Statue of Liberty but about her major and forgotten works, the verse plays and poems.

But she did not have enough time to be poetic. She had her small children, and she had Ed's career to think about. Her professors warned her of the time and the sacrifices she would have to make if she pursued a Ph.D. One old codger had even suggested that if she got a Ph.D. and an academic position, she would be blocking the career of some talented man with a family to support. Of course, that idea never went far with her. But she did have the idea that a Ph.D. would be hard to get. And a job harder. She decided against it. The truth is, it was easier for her to worry about Ed's career. She did not have to face the possibility of failure.

She had wanted fame, not classes at the Jewish Community Center; she had wanted to write dazzling poems, not just for her friends and relatives, but for the world. She was thirteen when she lay in bed in her parents' house, read *Hamlet*, and wanted to be as good as Shakespeare. And now that she is over fifty, if the Lord came to her in a dream and said, "You will achieve what you desired," she would laugh, certainly. If an angel or an agent came down from New York and said, "You, Sarah, will write a great novel, a best-seller. Not a pulp romance, but a good book, wise and luminous, with a future movie bursting from its pages," then she would laugh for all to hear — although she would take down the phone number of the agent just in case. In the meantime, she has her book reviews, her class, her children, her mother-in-law. She gets up from her desk. She has written none of this down, and so she will have no model for her students when she comes in to the next class. She can tell them that she looked in her files and couldn't find the midrash she wrote. Or she could tell them she thinks it is important for them to find their own voice, and that she doesn't want them to look at her work, because it might cramp their style.

"Knock, knock," Rose says at the door.

"Yes. Come in," Sarah calls back.

Rose opens the door. She is wearing a pink quilted robe and matching slippers. "Sarah, dear, do you have any books? They packed all my books, and I can't find any."

"Oh. Of course we have books. Downstairs." Sarah adds absent-mindedly, "What kind of book do you want?"

Rose considers the question. "I like trilogies," she says.

"You know, I think the only trilogy in the house is Ed's *Gulag Archipelago*."

"Nonfiction?"

"I'm afraid so."

"Ed never read fiction. Do you have a novel? I like any kind of novel, not too sad. About a family—with some romance. But well written. It must be well written."

On a whim, Sarah opens the closet and hunts around on the floor for the box where she keeps copies of her own novel. "Here, Rose, why don't you read this?"

"*Irises, Irises.*" Rose ponders. "Oh, that's your book. Sarah Markowitz. I've read that already. Of course. Years ago. Do you have a sequel?"

"No, I don't."

"You must write a sequel."

"Well, I have to come up with an idea."

"The next generation," Rose says immediately.

"Well, maybe you could reread it and give me some advice."

Rose takes the book, and the two of them walk down the hall to Miriam's old room. Sarah mentions that there is a literary discussion group at the Helena.

Rose shakes her head. "I could never live there."

"But all your things are going to arrive, you know. We couldn't fit the secretary in here."

Rose looks around the little bedroom, considering the problem. "It could fit," she says. "But it wouldn't look very elegant, one thing on top of another."

Sarah hardly expected this. She feels a rush of hope. Her house to herself, and Rose at the Helena. Of course, she doesn't know that in the next three weeks she will be looking for new silk-shantung lampshades and spending hours at House of Foam, out near the airport, as workmen pump new, high-density stuffing into Rose's sofa. For a moment, she sees free evenings unfolding before her, the empty rooms expanding. What are wistful literary dreams compared to that?

Acknowledgments

Many people helped me in my work as I put together the stories for this anthology. The anonymous outside readers for the University of Nebraska Press offered many suggestions along the way and helped point me in useful directions. Sanford Pinsker, Hilda Raz, Steve Stern, and Melvin Bukiet also gave me guidance at crucial moments. Marta Boswell and Pam Weiner helped me with careful, painstaking technical support.

This anthology would not have been completed without the presence and support of the Norman and Bernice Harris Center for Judaic Studies at the University of Nebraska–Lincoln. Special thanks go to Professor Alan Steinweis, director of the Harris Center, who provided me with generous financial support to help procure the rights to the stories included in this volume. I'm grateful to the Harris Center—to Norman and Bernice Harris, all the other donors and my colleagues in Judaic Studies—for their support of my efforts.

I owe a debt of thanks to the Research Council at the University of Nebraska–Lincoln, which also contributed vital funds to make it possible to obtain publication rights to stories for this book. My thanks to Linda Pratt and David Stanley-Samuelson for reading my Research Council proposal and suggesting revisions. My gratitude goes to my colleagues in the Department of English, as well; they've given me the time to work on this anthology and have encouraged me in every way, at every turn.

I'd like to thank my parents for giving me books—for giving me, in fact, a house full of books, a life full of books—and for their continual efforts, throughout my childhood, to instill in me a love of all things Jewish. And most important, I want to thank my wife, Judy, for her steadfast support and wise counsel over the two years I've spent compiling the contents of this book.

"A Ghetto Wedding" is reprinted from *Yekl and the Imported Bridegroom and Other Stories* by Abraham Cahan, published by Houghton-Mifflin and Co. in 1898. Reprinted by Dover Publications, 1970. Copyright © 1970 by Dover Publications.